9 Romances
Marriage Partne
Out of N

THE
Convenient
BRIDE
COLLECTION

Erica Vetsch

Amanda Barratt, Andrea Boeshaar, Mona Hodgson,
Melissa Jagears, Maureen Lang, Gabrielle Meyer,
Jennifer Uhlarik, Renee Yancy

BARBOUR BOOKS
An Imprint of Barbour Publishing, Inc.

The Substitute Wife © 2015 by Amanda Barratt
One Way to the Altar © 2015 by Andrea Boeshaar with Christina Linstrot Miller
Keeper of My Heart © 2015 by Mona Hodgson
Blinded by Love © 2015 by Melissa Jagears
Bonnets and Bees © 2015 by Maureen Lang
A Groom for Josette © 2015 by Gabrielle Meyer
Wedded to Honor © 2015 by Jennifer Uhlarik
A Bride for Bear © 2015 by Erica Vetsch
Have Cash, Will Marry © 2015 by Renee Yancy

Print ISBN 978-1-63409-097-1

eBook Editions:
Adobe Digital Edition (.epub) 978-1-63409-533-4
Kindle and MobiPocket Edition (.prc) 978-1-63409-534-1

All scripture quotations are taken from the King James Version of the Bible.
This book is a work of fiction. Names, characters, places, and incidents are either products of the author's imagination or used fictitiously. Any similarity to actual people, organizations, and/or events is purely coincidental.

Published by Barbour Books, an imprint of Barbour Publishing, Inc., P.O. Box 719, Uhrichsville, Ohio 44683, www.barbourbooks.com

Our mission is to publish and distribute inspirational products offering exceptional value and biblical encouragement to the masses.

Member of the
Evangelical Christian
Publishers Association

Printed in Canada.

Contents

THE SUBSTITUTE WIFE
Amanda Barratt

Dedication

To my sister, Sara.
For all the laughter, late-night conversations, and
loving my characters almost as much as I do.
You are a blessing and a treasure.

Chapter 1

Bristol, Connecticut
June, 1883

I
f men were mosquitoes, Grace Whittaker would be surrounded by every eligible gentleman in Bristol.

Instead she knelt outside in the family garden, not a man in sight. Unless one counted old Timothy Taylor watering his orchids next door. Audrey, on the other hand, sat in the blissfully cool parlor, her fiancé beside her. Giggling like a schoolgirl of sixteen instead of a bride-to-be, while Dr. Raymond McNair attempted serious conversation.

He failed miserably. What with Audrey rattling on about her dress, her bridesmaids, and the traveling theater company currently in town, the poor fellow barely got a word in edgewise.

Grace stood, rubbing the small of her back. At least she had a basket of roses to show for her labors. Something fragrant and summery to decorate the parlor with.

So much left to do. Including making sure Dr. McNair left at a reasonable hour. It wouldn't do for the groom to see the bride the night before the wedding.

A sigh found its way to her lips. Tomorrow her sister forsook her girlhood forever, leaving Grace the only Whittaker child still at home. Of course, she would never dream of going anywhere.

Not that there was any place to go.

Grace crossed the porch and pushed open the door. Sunlight streamed through the tall front windows and cascaded over the honey-wood floor, now polished to a gloss. With the help of their cook, Mrs. Ackerman, she'd spent most of the morning waxing it. That is, when she hadn't been occupied with packing Audrey's trunk, shining the silver, and laying out the family's best china. And a million other things.

More laughter streamed from the parlor, mingling with the muted melody of a Beethoven sonata. Audrey did love to perform. Especially when she had a rapt audience.

She entered the room quietly, so as not to interrupt. Audrey perched on the piano bench, her pink lawn skirts spread around her, a neat ribbon holding back her thick cinnamon-colored hair. Her face wasn't reddened by the sun, nor her hands cracked and chapped. *She* was a lady. No wonder Dr. McNair was enraptured.

Out of the corner of her eye, Grace chanced a look at the man on the settee. A gray pin-striped suit encased his broad shoulders, and his mahogany brown hair had been slicked back with some sort of pomade. He flashed her a smile, his eyes crinkling, before riveting his gaze on Audrey. Fixated. Entranced. Just like every man, after her sister laid on the charm.

With Dr. McNair she slathered it a mile thick.

Audrey finished the piece with a flourish and spun around.

"Well? What do you think?"

"Very nice, darlin'. Very nice." He crossed the room and rested his hand on Audrey's shoulder, in the possessive way of a husband-to-be.

Her green eyes narrowed. "Nice? Is that all you can think to say? I wonder if you even heard a note I played."

"Why, darlin', of course I did. I heard every bit of it. And 'twas fine indeed, sure it was." He chuckled, though it rang false.

Grace pressed her hands behind her back. Audrey wasn't about to have one of her tantrums, surely? Not with all the work that still needed to be done. Not in front of Dr. McNair, the night before their nuptials.

"Sure it was! Humph! I doubt you comprehended half of the emotion, the pathos of the piece. How could you, when you spend your days stitching people up?" Her cranberry lips screwed into a pout.

"Ah, darlin'. You know I love your music better than any sound in all the world." He bent and kissed the top of her head. "You're just edgy, 'tis all. Fretting about tomorrow." Grace could easily imagine him in his role as doctor, soothing an irritable patient with that voice of his. It slid over her ears, rich music, punctuated with the lilts and slurs of his native Ireland. Like hot and creamy chocolate steaming in a mug.

Audrey smiled, obviously mollified. "Oh, get on with you, you silver-tongued charmer. I've got lots of things to do before tomorrow."

"As m'lady commands." He kissed the nape of her neck, his arms around her waist.

Grace looked away. She shouldn't be here, witnessing this tender moment between an almost married couple. Yet no one ever seemed to notice her, continuing on with their lives whether she was present or not.

As inconspicuous as the wallpaper.

A strange ache pinched her heart. Perhaps if she were pretty and lively like Audrey, a man might notice her. Look at her with love and longing, the way Dr. McNair did.

No. Audrey was satin slippers; she a pair of work boots. Practical. Dependable. Well worn.

And the sad truth remained. Men as handsome and distinguished as Raymond McNair wanted satin slippers.

Never boots.

Today, he'd gain his treasure.

Audrey Whittaker would become his beautiful bride. He, her adoring and adored husband. At last, he'd have a family to call his own.

Raymond rubbed a brush across the front of his new frockcoat, purchased especially for the occasion. He'd spent a pretty penny on his clothes, even more on the ring and the special gift he'd bought Audrey for their wedding night. But for her, it was worth it. He'd give her the moon if she asked him.

There. He stepped back and surveyed the array spread across the bed. Everything in readiness. Too bad he had over five hours to wait before going to the church.

He crossed to the window, gazing out at the street. A horse and buggy rattled past— the Taylor rig. Up early to make their weekly trip north to visit their children, as they did

every Saturday morning. He waved, then leaned against the sill.

Lord, I pray Your blessing upon our marriage. May we love richly and give generously. And I pray, that if it be Your will, we would soon have a child to call our own. Amen.

He couldn't wait another minute. Of course there'd be no seeing Audrey, but surely Grace wouldn't mind if he dropped by the Whittaker house. Sat in the kitchen drinking coffee and eating one of Mrs. Ackerman's featherlight strawberry muffins. Just to be near the woman he loved, even for half an hour.

It didn't take long to dress quickly, not in his wedding finery, but in a simple everyday suit. Then he went out of the small apartment at the top of his medical practice. It always amazed him—the practicality of living above his office. If a patient arrived at one in the morning, or nine at night, he'd be only a few steps away.

Sadly, Audrey didn't share his view. She wanted a proper house. But what woman wouldn't? Though his apartment boasted four rooms, it wasn't what a girl like her deserved. Once he added a wee bit more to his savings, he'd buy her the home she desired.

At length, he arrived at the Whittaker residence, a spacious brick house in the heart of town. His marriage to the eldest daughter of Mr. Bromley Whittaker, owner of the finest dry goods store in Bristol, was a step in the right direction. Of course, even if she'd been a pauper, it wouldn't have made a whit of difference. Not when he cared for her so.

He stepped onto the porch and gave a brisk rap. A moment later the door opened.

Grace stood just inside, an apron around her waist, her light brown hair twisted in a serviceable knot. She smiled, her pale gray eyes lighting.

"And a fine morning to you, Miss Grace." He tipped his hat. "Might I beg a cup of coffee from Mrs. Ackerman?"

"You're not supposed to be here." She placed her hand on the door frame as if to bar him entrance. Although if he'd wanted to get in, it would be an easy task. Wouldn't take much more than a stiff wind to plow the petite lass over.

"Aw, come now, Miss Grace." He gave her his most charming grin. "I'm marrying your sister in just a few hours. I just want to be near her, 'tis all."

She stepped aside, reluctance crimping her brow. "Very well. But if Audrey comes down, you'll have to hide."

"Agreed." He moved past her, catching the scent of lemons. She looked tired, poor thing, dark circles under her eyes, a pale cast to her skin. No doubt the past weeks had been exhausting, assisting her sister with the planning and all. Strange. Audrey never showed fatigue, her features always as bright and cloudless as a summer day.

The warmth of the kitchen greeted him. Tantalizing scents of meat sizzling and coffee brewing made his mouth water. The Whittaker's robust cook stood at the counter, putting finishing touches on an enormous three-tiered cake.

"What do you think you're doing here, young man?" Mrs. Ackerman turned, brandishing her spoon like a weapon. "Today of all days! When I have so much work to do too."

He hid a smile. "Why, Mrs. Ackerman, where did you get that absolutely divine cake? Did some fine restaurant from the city come and prepare it?" He gestured wildly. "Just look at the intricacies of the icing. The elegance of the. . .the. . ." How else could one describe a cake?

She beamed. "I made it myself, Dr. McNair, as you well know. You handsome devil, you. Now sit yourself down and I'll get you some coffee and one of my strawberry muffins."

He settled himself in a chair and drank in the peace that always swept over him at the Whittaker house. A home well run and properly managed. Soon, he would have such a place for himself. So very, very soon.

"Dr. McNair?"

He turned. Grace stood by the table, her face pale as bleached muslin. Her hands. . .were they shaking?

"Whatever is the matter?" Fire and thunder, the lass looked ready to collapse. His medical instincts sprang into action. Get her a chair so she didn't fall on the floor. Some water. Salts volatile.

Her words stopped him short. "It's Audrey." Her breath came out in a shudder.

His heart kicked against his ribs. "What about Audrey?"

"She's. . .she's. . ."

He stood and grasped her shoulders, forcing her to look into his eyes.

Grace swallowed hard. "She's gone."

Chapter 2

Her next words would tear this man's world apart. Unravel it completely, link by link, strand by strand. Grace couldn't bear to think of it. But she had to tell him. She'd already revealed the worst. The rest was just detail.

Her father chose that exact moment to lumber into the kitchen, glasses perched on his nose, paper beneath his arm. Like so many other mornings, he wore his faded velvet dressing gown over his vest and trousers. Unlike so many mornings, his carefully laid plans were about to change.

"More coffee in the dining room, if you please, Mrs. Ackerman." Then his gaze landed on Dr. McNair. "What are you doing here, my boy? You should be at home. Not here where my daughter could come in and see you."

"Father." Grace did her best to steady her tone and speak with authority. "Audrey isn't here."

"What do you mean she isn't here?" Her father's brow knit until it seemed as if the two salt-and-pepper caterpillars under his forehead would plow into each other.

"She ran away. I found this." Grace pulled the letter from her apron pocket. Audrey had left it in her chamber. Next to her wedding gown.

The contents had already stamped themselves indelibly on her brain, but she forced herself to listen as her father read aloud.

> *To my family,*
>
> *Once you have received this letter, you will have already discovered my absence. I hope it shall not come as much of a surprise to you. Please do not take the trouble to search me out, as I have no desire for anyone to do so. I have grasped my future with both hands and have no intention of letting it go. Perhaps you may guess with whom I have thrown in my lot.*
>
> *Please give Ray my sincerest apologies, and my dearest hopes for his health and happiness. Although he is not the man I love, I wish him only the best.*
> *Love to all,*
> *Audrey*

The letter fluttered to the ground. Her father's face reddened. Grace glanced from him to Dr. McNair. He stared into space, jaw clenched. Emotions battled in his formerly warm eyes, now cold as iron.

"Ungrateful little hussy. I know just where she's gone. That traveling theater manager she's talked so much about. Well, I hope she's wretched indeed. Bringing this disgrace upon the family. The very day of her wedding to a decent, honest man." Her father paced the room, arms swinging wildly. Mrs. Ackerman stood motionless by the cake, icing dripping off her spoon and pooling onto the floor.

Dr. McNair sank into his seat. He leaned his arms on the table, his strong, broad shoulders now crumpled in defeat. Grace's own eyes filled with tears. Only moments ago, there had been so much happiness, such anticipation. Now it lay in a heap at their feet, a cold, dead pile of ashes.

Audrey was flighty, of course. Had flirted and flitted from beau to beau for years. It had been a relief to them all when she'd at last settled upon the new town doctor. She seemed so happy with him. No one would have ever dreamed she would do such a thing.

Except Grace. She'd seen the signs. The blushes whenever Mr. Ransom was mentioned. The excuses to stop by the theater company's encampment whenever they passed that way. She should've known. Warned someone. Perhaps if she had, this never would have happened.

Her heart squeezed. Now this good, upright man had to pay the price. She was used to picking up the pieces after Audrey scattered them around. Dr. McNair wasn't. How would he endure the shame and humiliation of being left at the altar? Would his medical practice suffer? Would the townspeople still look at him with the respect he had received so far?

No. Plain and simple. No.

Dr. McNair straightened his stance, as if drawing from deep within an ounce of courage. "I'm sorry about this, Mr. Whittaker, sure I am. Please let me know what I can do to assist you through this difficult time. I'll go to the church and tell Reverend Hansen there will be no wedding."

"Not so fast, young man." Her father wheeled around. The same determination that had taken a simple country store and turned it into the best establishment in town now lined his features. "Why shouldn't there still be a wedding?"

"But, sir." Dr. McNair shifted in his seat, raw pain in his face. "How can there be? I have no bride."

"Why not?" Her father strode across the room and stopped directly in front of her. Grace swallowed hard. "You forget, my boy. I have more than one daughter."

The air choked from her lungs. Father couldn't mean. . .? He couldn't be suggesting. . .? He couldn't actually be offering. . .?

Herself as Audrey's replacement.

"Sir?" Dr. McNair stiffened. "I haven't the pleasure of quite understanding you. What can you be meaning?"

"I mean that since my eldest daughter is ungrateful enough to reject your suit, my youngest will take her place."

The world she'd known crashed down again. She, wed Dr. McNair? Little, unremarkable Grace? Had her father lost his mind? As a replacement for Audrey, she was laughable. Dr. McNair would never agree. Nor would she. Would she?

"You wish to give me Miss Grace's hand in marriage?" Dr. McNair looked ready to bolt out of the room. She didn't blame him. Right now, she wanted nothing more than to crawl back under the covers and forget this terrible morning ever happened.

"Why not? Grace is all of nineteen years of age. Although she may not be as. . . well. . .as noticeable, she is just as capable as Audrey in running a house. The man who weds her will be most fortunate. And after all the trouble and expense I've been put to, it seems shameful for it all to go to waste."

Noticeable? *Just say it, Father. Audrey is ten times more likely to capture a man's attentions than I.* The words burned deep within her throat.

"Do you not care to ask the lass if she be willing?" Dr. McNair's gaze sought hers.

A tingle spiraled down her spine. His chocolate-brown eyes. His chiseled features. Strength and masculinity. He couldn't actually be considering. . .her?

"Why, of course she's willing. What better offer could there be for her?"

The words stung, more because of their truth than anything else. Father was right. She would get no other offers. Except perhaps from some desperate widower who simply wanted a housekeeper.

But of course, she would never be anything more to Dr. McNair. He'd chosen her sister.

"I want to hear what she has to say." The doctor looked down at her. Nothing resembling ardor filled his gaze. Only deep, heartrending sorrow.

"I would do anything to make amends for what my sister has done." Tears swam in her eyes. For this man who her sister had so carelessly wounded. He'd given her his heart. She'd tossed it in the rubbish heap.

"There you have it. Now, Dr. McNair. What do you say? Shall you take my Grace in her sister's place?" Her father laid a hand on her shoulder. She looked up at him. Instead of the usual censure in his eyes, something else lingered. As if he might, for a moment, think her special. Something valuable.

"Well? Will there be a wedding today or not?"

If only one could reel in events as easily as fishing line. Raymond would reel it all back, starting with yesterday evening. If he'd known of Audrey's plans, surely he could have convinced her to stay, work things out. Somehow. Then he'd take back the events of the morning from the moment Grace had stepped into the kitchen. The letter. Mr. Whittaker's anger. His substitute arrangement.

Had Mr. Whittaker taken leave of his senses? Women weren't horses. You couldn't simply exchange one for another. Audrey was the woman he'd fallen in love with. Not Grace. How could he, in good conscience, marry a girl he didn't love? He couldn't. Could he?

Still, he needed a wife. Every respectable doctor did. Someone to run the house and assist in the practice. That, along with his attraction to her, was the reason he'd decided to tie the knot with Audrey. Now she'd jilted him for some slick theater manager. No doubt he'd have her in his act soon enough. She'd like that. Audrey did enjoy putting on a show. Apparently including one that, up until yesterday, had cast her in the role of a devoted bride-to-be.

He chanced a glance at Grace. She studied him, her large gray eyes troubled. He'd always thought her a sweet lass. Quiet and mousey, but sweet. But to make her his wife?

Yet, he must have a wife. He'd thought to have one of his choosing, someone he loved and who loved him in return. Now love was no longer a consideration. After his

heart had been tossed in the dirt and trod upon, how could it be? If he married Grace, he would gain a respectable wife. One with whom he could form a successful partnership. Omitting romance, he would still get exactly what he wanted.

"Come now, my boy. We're waiting." For a man whose daughter had committed such a transgression, Mr. Whittaker's tone was a wee bit over-impatient.

Raymond swallowed, the roof of his mouth dry and gritty as plaster. "No. . .yes." Yes? Where had that come from? As if some force outside of himself had taken hold of his tongue and spoken the words for him.

"You're agreed then?"

Every ounce of good sense he possessed begged him to retract the words. He glanced at Grace. A shy gleam lit her eyes, like the hesitant flicker of a candle.

He'd chosen Audrey. But she wasn't here. He still needed a wife. Though he didn't love Grace, perhaps they could make things work. A convenient arrangement of sorts.

"If Grace is willing, then yes. I'm agreed." He tried to sound firmer than he felt.

"It's all settled. I'll go down and speak to the minster. He should have no objections. Since your sister is unworthy of the honor, Grace, you, instead of her, may wear your mother's wedding gown. I know she'd be proud to see you in it, if the Lord in His Providence hadn't taken her from us." His eyes took on a faraway look for a brief moment. "You'd better go and finish your preparations, my boy." Mr. Whittaker clapped his hands together and hurried from the room.

Raymond cleared his throat. Grace clasped her hands behind her back, seeming at a loss for words. Something her sister never had difficulty with.

"I'll do my level best to be a kind husband for you, lass." He offered her a smile. "Though we haven't had time to get properly acquainted, we can be friends at least, can we not?"

"I'd like that." She returned his smile tentatively. So timid. Like a little sparrow afraid to venture far from home. Contrast that with Audrey's butterfly brightness. He should have known better than to trust a butterfly. Too many others were attracted to her color and beauty.

He nodded. "Later then?"

Her only answer was another smile, before she ducked her head and flitted from the room.

Fire and thunder be on your head, Audrey Whittaker. Faithless, faithless lass!

The Holy Word demanded he forgive her. He'd promised to obey God as a young lad and wouldn't stop now. Sometimes though, when one's heart had been trod upon and smashed to bits, fighting back seemed so much more satisfactory than turning the other cheek. For a hot-blooded man like himself, anyway.

He made his way out into the mocking sunlight. Why should it shine when inside his heart blew a cold drizzle of rain?

Chapter 3

Grace adjusted the lace veil with trembling fingers. It fell to her waist in thick folds, hiding her unremarkable brown hair. Though the gown had been altered for Audrey's taller, less petite frame, she'd made do with a few pins. And she had to admit that bedecked in the cream-colored silk, a flush to her cheeks, she did look somewhat like a bride. Albeit a plain one.

It still seemed surreal that Dr. McNair had actually agreed to the wedding. Her heart thudded beneath the fine gown. Perhaps he was so much in shock he hadn't quite realized what he promised to do. Then he would arrive at the church and realize there'd been a terrible mistake. Could she endure the embarrassment if that happened?

She had to. This was her chance to have a home and a husband. Even if they were Audrey's castoffs. Kindness had lingered in his coffee-brown eyes as he asked if they could be friends. Maybe they could try. She wasn't fascinating or beautiful like Audrey, but she'd try to make him happy. Someday he might grow to care for her. Be glad they had married.

Lord, guide me. Help me to be a good wife to Dr. McNair. I know I'm not Audrey, but help me to try. And to be brave whatever happens this afternoon.

She smoothed the front of her dress one last time then picked up the flowers waiting on the dressing table. With her veil down, perhaps no one would notice who the bride was. At least during the ceremony. But afterward, there would be curious stares. And many questions. The town gossips would want all the details and were never shy about getting them. Oh, how she hated it when people stared. Especially at her.

She wouldn't be alone, though. Dr. McNair would be with her. They could be stared at together.

Her father waited at the foot of the stairs, looking every inch the successful store-owner in his dark suit and tie. He'd brushed his thinning hair back, and his gold watch gleamed bright. Her pulse sped up. Since she'd been a child, she'd spent countless hours dreaming of her wedding day. Wearing her mother's wedding dress, her father walking her down the aisle. The love in her groom's eyes.

She'd have the first two at least. She could make do without the third.

"Thank you, Grace." Her father smiled. "At least I have one daughter worthy of the Whittaker family name. Your mother would be so proud."

"Thank you, Father." Tears gathered in her eyes. She'd always longed to please him, to be a daughter he could be glad of. Now, in a strange twist of fate, she'd accomplished just that.

The carriage waited outside, and in a matter of minutes they arrived at the church.

The gray stone building with its tall steeple, a cross at the tip, always filled her with a sense of reverent awe. Today, even more so. Within these walls she would be transformed from Grace Whittaker into Grace McNair. A different person. One who could perhaps be something other than plain and unimportant.

Within the church, people laughed and talked, the strains of a piano intermingling. Clutching her skirt with one hand and her father's arm with the other, Grace climbed the steps.

Another melody swelled from the piano, banged out by Mrs. Morgan's knobby fingers. Mendelssohn's "Wedding March." She sucked in a breath. In mere moments she would pass the point of no return. There'd be no taking back this hasty decision.

Her hand delicately placed atop her father's arm, Grace took the first step. The long aisle stretched before her, a sea of faces endlessly ahead. At the end stood Dr. McNair. So very handsome in a gray, double-breasted suit, his sun-bronzed face pale. She faltered as around her, people gasped, no doubt realizing the switch in brides. Still, she made herself keep going. One foot in front of the other.

At the altar, the minister waited, the small black book solemnly in his hands. Dr. McNair moved to take her arm. Her throat tightened as she gazed up at that firm, resolute face. No sign of love, only determination. She should expect nothing less, of course, but. . .

His large hand all but swallowed hers, and as moisture slicked her palm, her grip began to slip. She tightened her fingers around his and looked up at the minister.

"Dearly beloved. . ."

The ceremony passed in a blur as she pledged herself to a stranger. To love and cherish him till death did they part. Such lofty promises. Could she keep them? Would he keep his and care for her in sickness and in health? Forsake all others and keep only unto her as long as they both should live?

Had they both made a terrible mistake, entering into a contract so binding? Perhaps she should never have agreed. But the deed was done. She was in for a penny and in for a pound.

"By the power vested in me, I now pronounce you husband and wife."

He gave her a slight smile as he lifted her veil, throwing back the lace to reveal her identity to the entire assembly. More gasps and piercing stares. The piano burst into another piece. If she'd been Audrey, he would've kissed her in celebration. Instead, he simply took her hand.

Into the sunlight they went, racing down the steps as showers of rice streamed in their direction like hundreds of tiny good wishes.

If the first few moments of their marriage were any indication of how the rest would be, they'd certainly need them.

They'd survived the gauntlet of stares and questions and emerged basically unscathed. Thank goodness it was over. Raymond couldn't imagine a worse three hours than those spent at the Whittaker home during the reception. Though few had actually asked outright, the hints and innuendos had been more numerous than he could count.

A dull ache pounded in his temples as the carriage stopped at the door of his practice. He jumped down and offered his hand to Grace. In silence, they climbed the steps. He

opened the door. He'd always imagined carrying his new bride over the threshold before giving her a long and lingering kiss. For over a year, he'd dreamed it would be Audrey. Now, a small and silent girl stood in her place, so he simply opened the door and stepped back to let her inside.

The waiting room was deserted, of course, the books and periodicals stacked neatly on a small table, the clock ticking away above the frame that held his medical degree. That scrap of paper he'd slaved so hard for during four long years, an Irish kid from the coal mines who shouldn't have amounted to a darn thing. He'd been determined to succeed in his career. With God's help he'd succeed in marriage as well.

He climbed the stairs and unlocked the door. Twilight flickered across the carpet, the walls he'd so painstakingly re-papered, the sofa and easy chair he'd purchased. A vase of flowers sat on the kitchen table. Audrey's favorite orchids. All of it done for her, only her, and she'd thrown it in his face!

An intense wish for an ax and a pile of wood to demolish came over him. Something to burn the anger and frustration hovering in the corners of his mind. Beasts rattling their chains of self-restraint, begging to be unleashed. His gaze landed on Grace, wavering by the door like a little sparrow who would take flight at the slightest threat. He had to put her at ease. Irish men were gentlemen, no matter the circumstances.

"This is the parlor." He lit the lamp atop the fireplace mantle to give the room some light. "And sort of the dining room as well." He opened the kitchen door. "Through here is the kitchen. I had a pump installed so you don't have to go outside to get water. Audrey. . .your sister said your house had one. Then, across the hall is your room." His, actually. But there was only one bedroom, and he wouldn't have her sleeping on the sofa. It would do just fine for him.

She crossed the room in silence and opened the chamber door. A fist closed around his throat. He'd even bought new linens to replace the old sheets he'd been using, and covered them with a new quilt that the wife of one of his patients had made.

Raymond brushed past her, into the room. "Give me a moment to collect some things and then I'll be out of your way." He opened the closet and pulled his few suit jackets and trousers off their hooks.

"I'm sorry. . .to put you out of your room." Her voice came out thin as a reed.

He grabbed his shaving kit and comb and added them to the top of the pile. "I'm fine." One last sweep of the room. Only the things in the drawers remained. Those he would retrieve tomorrow. Good. He could get out of here now. "There's leftover stew in the kitchen if you're hungry."

"Thank you." She perched on the edge of the bed. "You've been very kind."

He shifted the pile of stuff in his arms. "If there's nothing else you'll be wanting, then I'd best go see to the horses." He all but ran from the room. The door clicked behind him.

Once in the parlor, he deposited his pile on the sofa then escaped down the stairs. The comforting scents of his clinic wafted over him. The spice of herbal remedies. The pungent antiseptic he cleaned with. The starch of the clean linens atop his examining table. After the events of the day, this at least remained unchanged. Something to throw himself into. A surefire way to forget the woman upstairs who now shared his name.

Lord, I need Your strength. In Your Word, it promises You never leave nor forsake us. Never

am I more glad of that than now. Be with us in the days to come. And somehow, help us to make this work.

He ran his fingers through his hair. Enough. Despite his problems, Blarney and King still needed to be fed and stabled.

Thank heaven for work.

Chapter 4

Why couldn't she be beautiful like Audrey? Why did her features have to be so small and unremarkable, her straight hair such a muddy shade of brown? Not blessed with effortless curls like Audrey's, her tresses hung to her waist like a sheet. Leaving no practical way to style it, save in a knot at the nape of her neck.

She jammed in pins, smoothed her fingers over the chignon, then hurried from her room. No use looking in the mirror again. She'd only dislike what she saw.

Morning light streamed through the parlor windows. Grace stifled a yawn. She'd scarcely slept last night, overwrought by her change in surroundings and the nearness of the man in the next room. She opened the kitchen door. Deserted save for a table, two chairs, a stove, icebox, and dishpan. Where was Dr. McNair?

No matter. She smoothed the front of her apron. She'd simply have breakfast waiting for him. She opened the icebox and peered inside. A jug of milk, a bowl of eggs, and a rasher of bacon. Plus, the leftover stew he'd spoken of.

Either he ate breakfast food at every meal, or this man just plain starved. Perhaps there'd be some flour in one of the cupboards. She opened one and found it empty. The other held a set of china dishes and a few pots and pans. Thankfully, the last contained a bag of flour, some sugar, and salt. Perfect. Pancakes and eggs for breakfast.

Standing on her tiptoes, she managed to grab the jars of flour and sugar and set them on the counter then added the bowl of eggs and jug of milk. Now for mixing it all together. She'd seen Mrs. Ackerman make pancakes hundreds of times, surely doing it oneself couldn't be that difficult. Could it?

She took down a bowl and scooped a couple handfuls of flour inside. There. Looked like enough. Now what? Oh, yes, three eggs ought to do it. She cracked each into the bowl and chucked the shells in the dishpan. One pinch of salt or two? Hmm. Perhaps she'd better use just one. Milk? She unscrewed the lid and dumped some in. A bit of sugar and she'd be all done. Cooking was easy. She'd be a gourmet in no time.

Wherever Dr. McNair was, he'd at least lit the stove. She placed the frying pan on it and poured in some of the batter. Now she could work on the eggs. And coffee. Men liked coffee.

How many eggs should she cook? Four perhaps. That made two for each of them. She cracked them into a pan and added the shells to her pile in the dishpan. Now coffee. But how in the world did one go about making that?

Grace found a box marked coffee in one of the cupboards and scooped a couple handfuls of the beans into the pot along with a cup of water. Then she placed the kettle on the back of the stove. She could set the table, and everything would be ready the moment

19

Dr. McNair came inside.

Something smelled like. . . Oh, no! The pancakes. She grabbed a spoon and scraped them onto a plate. Not golden like Mrs. Ackerman's, but burnt and black. Her nose crinkled. Doubtful even a dog would eat these.

With a sigh she added more batter to the pan. This time she'd be sure to watch them. She checked the eggs. Cooking nicely, thank goodness. Now she could set the table.

She carefully placed two plates on the table and added silverware and cups. If only he had a tablecloth somewhere. Then she could make it truly elegant.

A hissing sound emitted from the stove. She turned. A scream caught in her throat. The coffee bubbled over, overflowing its pot. Grace ran to the stove and grabbed it. As hot metal burned her skin, the kettle crashed to the floor. Water and coffee beans doused the kitchen and soaked her skirts. She snatched a towel and knelt to wipe up the mess.

Lord, whatever happens, I beg You not to let Dr. McNair come in just now.

Once the floor had been sufficiently dried, she returned to the stove and checked the eggs. Burned, along with the pancakes. She dumped the pots into the dishpan and sank into a chair, covering her face with her hands. Tears stung her eyes, and she let them fall. She wanted so much for breakfast to be a success, but instead flopped every last bit of it. Why hadn't she ever asked Mrs. Ackerman for cooking lessons? Because she'd been too busy working at the store, that's why. She'd never had a moment to spare, what with Father always asking her to balance the books or wait on customers.

Well, there was plenty of time now. She straightened her shoulders and dried her eyes.

Action was far preferable to crying. She'd learn how to cook, if it was the last thing she did.

❧

Shadows darkened the house by the time Raymond arrived home. Ten house calls in one day and over twenty miles of travel. Thank goodness for dependable King. Without his faithful horse, these calls would be impossible.

Softly, he climbed the stairs and opened the door. His stomach growled at the thought of something to eat. His hastily packed sandwich and apple hadn't been nearly enough. Sure and certain, he'd have a decent meal. Now he had a wife. One who, no doubt, had dinner waiting on the stove.

He opened the kitchen door and squinted in the darkness. Grace sat at the table, her head pillowed on her arms. He moved closer. Beside her sat an untouched plate of food. Stone cold.

He studied her in the twilight. Her hair had escaped its usual prim pinnings and cascaded over her shoulders and down her back. Soft, even breaths rose and fell from her chest.

Should he wake her? The poor thing looked exhausted. Best to let her sleep. Gently, he lifted her from the seat and carried her from the room. She sighed softly, nestling against his chest. Gossamer in his arms. The scent of lemons filled his senses. Wispy, delicate, like the young woman herself.

He kicked open the door and placed her gently on the bed. She barely stirred. For a long moment he stood over her, his heart twisting. In slumber, her features looked even younger, more innocent. She'd been entrusted to his care, and he would take care of her.

As a gentleman, he could do no less.

Silently, he left the room and returned to the kitchen, lit a lamp, and surveyed the plate of food. Potatoes, gravy congealing in a lump. Some kind of meat, chicken perhaps. He picked up the biscuit and bit into it, wincing as he nearly broke a tooth.

Obviously cooking wasn't among his wife's finer skills. But how could it be? From what Audrey had told him, their mother died when the girls were but children. Mrs. Ackerman had consequently been hired to care for the house and do the cooking. Audrey also said that from the day Grace had graduated from school, she'd spent six days a week at the store, from the time the sun went up, to day's end. No doubt it was cheaper for Mr. Whittaker to make use of his child than hire another employee. Audrey, on the other hand, had rarely worked at Whittaker Dry Goods. In fact, now that he thought of it, she never worked at all. Whenever he came to call, he'd always found her practicing the piano, reading a book, or writing a letter. Thus, no doubt, a great deal of housework also fell upon Grace.

He hadn't given it very much thought at the time, he was so blinded by Audrey's beauty. Perhaps too blinded.

Tomorrow he wouldn't leave before Grace awoke. They'd have breakfast together, share conversation. He'd do his best to become acquainted with this wife of his, and perhaps she'd stop being so timid.

It would at least be a start.

Chapter 5

D r. McNair cooked breakfast the next morning.
 A flush heated Grace's cheeks as she sat down to a table that seemed effort-
lessly prepared. Pancakes as golden as Mrs. Ackerman's. Sizzling bacon that
made her mouth water. Apple slices elegantly arranged in a bowl. He, a man, had done it
all. Which only further compounded her failures.

He pulled back his chair and sat down, tucking a napkin into his shirt. She folded
hers and laid it across her skirt.

"Everything looks delicious." She managed a smile.

"It's not very hard, and I've had years of practice." He returned her smile.

Not very hard? Easy for him to say. She supposed he could also make biscuits fluffy
as air and gravy creamy as pudding.

Dr. McNair asked the blessing before getting up from his chair and pouring coffee.
Grace played with the edges of her napkin as steam swirled upward from her mug. She
should be the one pouring while he sat and ate breakfast. Not the other way around.

"I'm going to be in my clinic most of the day." He lifted a forkful of pancakes to his
mouth.

She nodded and took a tiny nibble of bacon.

"If you need anything for the house or kitchen, don't hesitate to go shopping. Just
add it to my account. I pay the bills at the end of the month. Of course, in my profession,
people often pay in trade, rather than in money. So things like eggs and milk I usually get
in exchange for services."

She nodded again.

"If you'd care to, you can come down to the clinic later and I'll show you round."

"Very well. After I do the dishes." Though her empty stomach protested, she could
scarcely eat a bite. What with him sitting across from her, able to observe her every
move. They'd shared many meals together at the Whittaker home, but he'd always been
Audrey's betrothed. Not Grace's husband.

"Fine. Fine. If you like, we could take a walk this evening, go visit your father. I'm
sure he'd appreciate it. And if there's anything you'd like to get from the house, you could
do so."

Like cookbooks? The old alarm clock? She hated being the last awake in the morning.
And a new set of brains.

"I'd like that." She took a sip of her coffee.

He pushed back his chair. "Well, that's settled then. We'll walk over after dinner."
He tossed his napkin on the table beside his empty plate. "I'd best be getting downstairs."

She nodded.

"Later, then." He made a bow as politely as if they passed each other on the street.

As quickly and efficiently as she could, Grace did the dishes. Thank goodness, she at least had experience in that regard. After making sure the kitchen was in proper order, she untied her apron and went downstairs, stopping at the waiting-room door. This was his domain. Did she dare enter? Well, why not? He'd invited her, after all.

She pushed open the door. No patients sat in the waiting room, so she gave a rap on the closed examining room. She'd scarcely drawn her hand away before it swung open.

"Oh, thank the saints above you're here, Grace. I need your help." Dr. McNair dashed back inside. She followed him in.

And screeched to a halt.

A man sat on the exam table. Coughs and gasps emitted from his large form as he deposited the contents of his stomach into a basin Dr. McNair held. Vomit covered the floor, the man's clothes, and the table. Grace pressed a hand to her mouth and took a step back.

"Don't just stand there, Grace. Get that pitcher of water and a towel and help me clean this up!" Dr. McNair's tone could have belonged to the captain of a warship. "Now, Mr. Cooper, I need you to take some of this. It will absorb whatever it is that's upsetting your system."

Dizziness swooshed over her. She gingerly crossed the floor and grasped the pitcher and a towel with shaking hands. Water splashed onto the floor. The man's hacks and heaves rang in her ears. The rancid odor of bile sent nausea rising up in her throat. She looked helplessly at the mess on the floor then back at Dr. McNair. Spots danced before her eyes.

She couldn't do this. Not wasting another second, she ran from the room and out the door. Kept going until she left the clinic and stood on the steps, gulping in fresh air, leaning against the edge of the building to steady herself.

Awful. It had been just awful. And he'd expected her to help with such a thing? How could she have summoned the nerves for it? She sucked in a deep breath, letting the warmth of the sun soak into her. She should go back in and assist. But how? Nausea threatened just thinking about it.

Tears needled her eyes. She was a failure. Not at all fit to be a doctor's wife. She couldn't cook, and she sure couldn't handle medical matters. The only things she did well were run a first-rate dry goods store and keep a house tidy. The second might prove useful but never the first.

A strand of hair blew in her eyes. She swiped it away.

Lord, why am I so useless? Why can't I be beautiful, brave, and an amazing cook? Why do I run whenever something upsets me?

She stared up at the cloudless sky. Obviously the Almighty didn't know, either.

Then she'd just have to conquer it herself. Starting with going back inside and seeing if there was anything she could do to help.

This time, no matter what she faced, she wouldn't run.

❧

Now that he'd cleaned up the mess and had Mr. Cooper comfortably settled with some charcoal water to drink, a wave of guilt assailed Raymond. Who did he think Grace was?

A Johns Hopkins intern? Her first introduction to his practice and he'd asked her to do something that made even him a wee bit queasy. She'd never want to come downstairs again. He'd acted without thinking, caught in the urgency of the moment, and she'd fled quicker than a frightened rabbit.

He needed to apologize and ought to do it quickly before she decided to pack her bags and go back to Whittaker Dry Goods indefinitely.

The door to the exam room opened. He turned. Grace stood outside. He followed her and closed the door, leaving Mr. Cooper resting within.

"You must think me a weak-kneed ninny." She met his gaze, apology in her eyes. A strand of hair dangled near her ear, brushing her creamy skin. He nearly reached out and ran it between his fingers but drew his hand back before he could attempt it. Crazy thoughts like that shouldn't be entering his head.

"On the contrary. I think you're brave for staying as long as you did. Most first-time assistants would've lasted sixty seconds. You managed a full one hundred and twenty." A grin tugged at his lips. "But in all seriousness, it is I who should apologize. I should have never asked you to help. Forgive me?"

Her smile warmed, reaching her eyes and turning them bright. She nodded. "How is Mr. Cooper now?"

"Resting comfortably at present. I'll send him home in half an hour. You'll be happy to know you're not the only female who gets queasy. His wife left right after she brought him in, and I haven't seen her since. Of course, she has the excuse of being in a delicate condition."

"I'd still like you to show me around, if you want to." She surveyed the waiting room. "Perhaps after your patient leaves?"

So the sparrow of a woman wasn't quite as breakable as she first appeared. He had suspected there was more than first met the eye when it came to her. What other layers lay beneath the delicate tissue paper of her exterior? Would he ever know?

"I'd be glad to," he answered. He needed to look away, avert his gaze from her smile and that distracting curl that brushed her cheek. Gazing at her wasn't part of their convenient arrangement.

"I'd better go upstairs and make lunch. Will you have time to eat?"

"I'll be up just as soon as Mr. Cooper leaves."

She hurried away, and he returned to his patient. Yet, as he pushed open the windows to let in fresh air, a thought sprang to his mind and made him grin.

Audrey wouldn't have lasted anywhere near a hundred and twenty seconds.

Chapter 6

She hadn't expected him to be so gracious. Didn't deserve it even. Still, he seemed to forget about the incident as he showed her around the clinic and later, as they had dinner with her father.

While the men discussed politics, Grace slipped from the room and went upstairs. She opened the second door down the hall and stepped into her room. Everything remained unchanged. Her girlish patchwork quilt lay across the bed, and the worn rag rug covered the polished wood floor. She moved toward her armoire and pulled the remaining dresses off their hangers. Taking a carpetbag from the depths of the closet, she packed the dresses neatly inside and closed the clasp, breathing in the lemon peel sachets she kept among her frocks.

A barely discernible knock sounded. Grace spun around.

"Come in," she called softly.

The door opened and Mrs. Ackerman entered. She still wore her grease-splattered apron from dinner and kept her hands behind her back.

"Can I help you with something?" Grace faced the woman. A nervous furrow knit the cook's brow, and her gaze darted to and fro.

"This came for you in today's mail. I didn't show it to your father." Mrs. Ackerman held out an envelope. One glance at the script sucked the breath from Grace's lungs, bringing with it a gust of doubts and fears. Audrey's handwriting.

With an unsteady hand, she opened the seal.

Grace,

Word has reached me of your marriage to the gentleman that was to have been mine. Knowing you, I suspect you did it out of your elevated sense of duty and responsibility. Be that as it may, I thought it only fair to warn you that though you may share his name, you will never have his heart. That still belongs to me. And though my own affections lay with another, his shall always remain fixed on me alone. You with your few or, may I say, no advantages whatsoever could never hope to win the heart of such a man. I write this not to discourage you, but to deter you from wasting your time try-ing. Be his housekeeper, sister mine, but don't attempt to be his wife.

Your Most Devoted Sister,
Audrey

Grace lowered the letter, her entire body shaking. She closed her eyes and drew in a sharp breath. Leave it to Audrey to write such words. Her, with her cadre of men. Would she not rest until every one of their hearts belonged to her? How had she found out? Why couldn't she simply wish them well?

"Does she say where she is?" Mrs. Ackerman's words caught her ear.

"No." Grace sank down on the bed.

"Does she say she's coming back?" Mrs. Ackerman twisted her hands in her apron.

"No." Grace balled the letter and threw it into the cold hearth. "I don't care if I ever see her again." The vehemence of her own words shook her. She had no reason to care. Audrey had never considered her. Never loved her. Thought of her only as a commodity to be used for her own purposes. Like one of those newfangled vending machines that dispensed notepaper whenever one put in a coin. It should be different between sisters. Yet it had gone on for too long to hope for anything else.

"Why, you don't mean that, Miss Grace. Surely not." Mrs. Ackerman's eyes widened.

Grace stood and picked up the carpetbag. "I hate to admit it, but I do. And if she had been your sister, you might agree with me."

"Well, I can understand you not wanting her back now that you're wed to her beau. As a matter of interest, how are things between you two?"

Best to dodge that and keep things within Mrs. Ackerman's province. "They'd be a sight better if I knew my way around a kitchen. Do you have any cookbooks I might borrow?" Despite Audrey's words, she wouldn't stop trying. Not so soon anyway. It wouldn't be fair to herself or Dr. McNair. And for once in her life, she wanted to prove her sister wrong.

"Why didn't you say so in the first place? Cookbooks? Bah! I can do one better than that. If you come over tomorrow morning first thing, I can teach you to cook a roast sure to win any man's heart. Lots of other things, too. Everyone knows my pies are the finest in all of Bristol. And it was only just last year I won a blue ribbon for my blackberry jam."

Grace smiled. "Oh, would you really? I'd be so grateful."

"Pshaw. You don't even have to ask. If cooking a fine meal is all that stands between you and wedded bliss, there I can help you."

A sigh found its way to her lips. "If only that were all, Mrs. Ackerman. If only that were all."

Though her cooking had improved in the past two weeks, everything else in their marriage had stayed much the same. Near silence at every meal. Late nights coming home to find dinner on the stove, and his wife already asleep. Sitting across from her at breakfast as she wore a plain dress, her hair in a severe knot that did nothing to accentuate her quietly pretty features.

Suffice it to say, Grace wasn't Audrey. And Raymond was no closer to finding out who she truly was. He'd tried. But the most he got out of her was a few sentences. He'd never been partial to chattering females. Except Audrey, of course. Still, sometimes he wished she'd take a lesson or two from the typical woman and just talk. He didn't care about what, any subject would do. Just as long as she said *something*.

He dried his hands and hung the towel neatly on its peg. Tonight, there was no way he'd sit in the parlor feeling like a trapped animal, watching her mend or read. He simply

couldn't do it. After a long day at the clinic and on house calls, a bit of relaxation for him and his wife was well deserved. What to do? Oh, yes. Why didn't he think of it before? A picnic dinner on Lake Compton. They could go and watch the sun setting over the lake, enjoy the fresh air. He'd taken Audrey before, and she loved it—

He needed to forget about her. She wasn't in his life anymore. Grace was.

He opened the door. Grace sat on the sofa, head bent over a piece of mending. Was that one of his shirts? It sure looked like it.

He sat down beside her. "What are you working on?"

"Oh!" She glanced up with a start. "One of your shirts. I was doing laundry and I noticed it had a hole in it. I hope you don't mind."

"Mind? Of course not. Thanks very much. I can't sew worth a darn." He grinned.

She smiled her usual soft smile.

"What have you done today?" He stretched his legs out and rested his arm on the back of the sofa.

"I visited Father at the store and helped him with the books. I hope you don't mind. I made certain all the housework was done beforehand." That frightened sparrow look again. Like a child cowering under blows. What did she think he'd do? Beat her because she hadn't stayed home all day?

"Why would you think I'd mind? You're my wife, Gracie, not a prisoner." Gracie? Where had that come from? Yet somehow, it fit her better than Grace.

"Oh." Her eyes widened as if the knowledge was news to her.

"I had a plan for tonight—"

Banging. On the door. "Doc McNair! Doc McNair!"

Blast it all. He stood and strode across the room, opened the door. Mr. Cooper stood outside, bent over, round cheeks puffing from exertion.

"It's Muriel. It's her time! You'd better come quick." Mr. Cooper looked at him like a drowning man clinging to a rope, his eyes two huge fear-filled disks.

"I'm right behind you." He turned. Grace sat on the sofa, motionless. For saints' sake, couldn't Mrs. Cooper have picked another evening to have her babe? Why had she chosen the very night he hoped to spend time with his wife? Not that the expectant mother had much choice in the matter. Yet why did crises always come at the worst times?

"I don't know when I'll be home," he called over his shoulder, following Mr. Cooper down the stairs, half running to keep up with the man's loping strides.

He grabbed his bag and supplies then jumped into the empty seat in Mr. Cooper's wagon. The man whipped his horses into a gallop, and Raymond gripped the seat. Was it wise to drive this ancient conveyance at madcap speed? He didn't exactly relish being thrown from his perch and into a ditch.

"Hurry, boys! Hurry, Star! We've got to get back to Muriel!" Mr. Cooper snapped the reins. Wind whooshed past them, the chill evening air seeping into Raymond's bones. Mr. Cooper glanced at him.

"Will she be all right? Her and the baby?" His large farmer's hands white-knuckled the reins.

"She'll be fine. Childbirth is a perfectly normal and natural experience. Women have babies every day." Raymond put on his best bedside manner voice.

"But you don't understand, Doc. This ain't just any woman. This is Muriel, my wife. Boy, do I love that little gal." A smile split Mr. Cooper's work-worn face. "She's. . .she's

like the sugar to my spice, the bread to my butter, the Jill to my Jack. My one and only. Honestly, I can't imagine my little old life without her. And if something were to happen, I'd just die inside. Am I making any sense?"

Raymond nodded slowly. Mr. and Mrs. Cooper shared a once in a lifetime love. What he'd known with Audrey had been infatuation, that he now realized. With Grace? He couldn't describe the complicated mix of emotions that went through his brain when he thought of her.

But one thing he did know.

More than anything else, he wanted a once in a lifetime love. Someone to share hopes and dreams with, coffee in the morning and their bed at night. Someone he couldn't imagine existing without.

Wanting was one thing. Having quite another.

Chapter 7

She couldn't stay here another day. She was choking, drowning to death each and every moment. Drowning in the mistake she'd made a month ago, marrying a man who could never love her and whom she could never make happy. She couldn't do it anymore. Their marriage had been a sorry mistake, and wasn't it better to face up to it now than to live with more regrets? Audrey was right. Grace was a failure. Totally unworthy and incapable of ever winning the heart of a man like Dr. McNair. She just couldn't bring herself to relax, let her guard down, even though he encouraged her to do so. No one had ever encouraged her like that before. The very process was unnatural. And she was tired of trying to be someone she wasn't.

She wouldn't go back to her father's house. That would only bring further disgrace upon everyone. She'd set off by herself, perhaps find a job as a teacher or store clerk somewhere far away. Anything would be better than staying here and continuing to live this lie.

Tears stung Grace's eyes as she packed her belongings in a carpetbag. She'd married Dr. McNair hoping they could make things work. None of it had come to be. She was a jinx, a failure, and it was wrong to force her presence upon him any longer.

She clasped the bag shut and ran her gaze once more over the room. The one he had prepared for Audrey. Ever since she stepped through that door, she'd been an intruder. An interloper. And she was through playing second fiddle to a memory. Of being the substitute wife.

She smoothed the lacy coverlet then opened the door. All yesterday, she'd scrubbed every inch of the house. It was the least she could do, leave his home in better order than when she arrived. She picked up her hat from its peg and placed it atop her head.

The front door burst open. Dr. McNair raced in. His hair stuck up at all angles, and real fear emanated from his gaze. An apron swathed his waist, streaks of red marring the white. She gasped.

"I know I have no right to ask this, Gracie, but I need your help." His breath came out in short gasps. "There was a hunting accident and a man got shot in the back. I need to perform emergency surgery. If you say yes, you'll have to promise to stay with me throughout the entire operation. Can you?"

He truly needed her. She sensed it from the pleading in his eyes, the urgency stretching his every muscle.

She could do this. One final task before she left forever.

But if she could be of use to him. . .could she really leave at all?

"I'll help you." She took off her jacket and followed him down the stairs, snatching

up her skirts and taking the treads two at a time. At the examining room door, he paused.

"There's a lot of blood. Are you ready?"

Lord, give me strength. Help me to assist Dr. McNair in saving this man's life.

She nodded. "I'm ready."

The moment she entered the room, the metallic scent of blood assailed her like a weapon, trying to disarm her resolve. Red. Everywhere. On the table, the floor, caking the sheets wrapped around the man's lower back. So much red.

Dizziness unsteadied her, but she shoved it back and moved forward. Dr. McNair rolled up his sleeves and washed his hands in the pitcher and basin. He dried them and faced her.

"First, we're going to clean the wound so I can assess how much damage has been done. I need you to go upstairs and heat some water. Don't make it too hot." He hurried to the table and began to unravel the bandages. She dashed from the room with as much speed as the first time she entered his clinic. But unlike last time, she would be strong. She would show Dr. McNair he could rely upon her.

It seemed to take an eternity for the water to heat, but it finally warmed to a sufficient temperature and she carried it back downstairs. By now, Dr. McNair had removed the bandages, exposing the man's bare back, blood oozing from a small but lethal hole. She shivered.

Quickly but carefully he cleaned the wound. By the time he finished, the water was crimson. He handed her the basin, and she placed it on the floor.

"Thank God it doesn't appear to have hit any vital organs." He surveyed the hole. "Still, removing the bullet will be tough. I'm going to have you administer the chloroform. Just soak that cloth in the liquid in that bottle and hold it over his mouth and nose. All right? Once he's out, you can help me."

Grace unscrewed the bottle and poured some of the contents on the cloth. A sickly, sweet fragrance filled the air. She pressed it tight against the man's face, and soon his groans and shudders subsided.

"Hand me the scalpel on that tray. I'm going to have to cut around the hole so I can remove the bullet."

Grace handed him the tool. Forced back the nausea at the sound of knife breaking flesh.

Lord, give Dr. McNair strength. And, please, keep me from fainting.

"Have you found it yet?" She tried to keep her voice steady.

"Not yet. It's deeper than I thought." More cutting. "There. I see the tip of the bullet." He glanced at her. Blood covered his hands, his forearms. Could this patient live after undergoing such a procedure?

A furrow knit his brow.

"What's the matter?" Her words trembled a bit.

"It's too near the renal artery. Go ahead. Wash up."

"Wash up for what?" Grace bit her lip.

"So you can apply pressure to the artery while I remove the bullet. If we don't, there's a very good chance he will bleed to death."

Her heart slammed against her ribs. No. It wasn't possible. Assist, she could do, but put her hand into that mess of blood and tissue? She wasn't that brave.

"Not by might, nor by power, but by my Spirit." The verse came unbidden to mind. God

would give her strength. And Dr. McNair would help her.

Trembling, she washed her hands and made her way to stand beside him.

"Do you see it?"

She nodded. Up close, the tang of blood was even more overpowering, the hole angrier. The top of her head brushed the firmness of his chest, the warmth of him so close.

"You can do this, Gracie. Just be brave, lass." He pressed a piece of gauze near the wound, holding it open.

She took a deep breath. Her legs wobbled.

A life depended on her. She could do this.

She reached inside, her fingers pressing against the artery. Perspiration dripped down her back, the heat of the room strangling.

Beside her, Dr. McNair worked with his instruments, his face a study in concentration. Her fingers slipped. She pressed harder.

"You're doing fine, lass." The gentle lull of his tone unwound some of her anxiety. She took another breath.

Please, God, let this be over soon.

Suddenly, he held the bullet in his palm. They'd done it. Her legs nearly buckled under the relief.

With careful precision, Dr. McNair cleaned the wound then threaded the needle and began to close the hole. Grace focused on the intensity of his face, the chiseled lines of his jaw as he worked. A dull ache throbbed between her shoulder blades, but she kept her post beside him. The worst was over.

At last, he made the final stitch and, after washing his hands, bandaged the wound with fresh linen strips. She handed him the final bandage then collapsed to the floor. The enormity of what she'd just done struck her afresh, and she leaned her head against her knees, trying to still her thundering heart. Right now, bursting into tears sounded like the most refreshing thing in the world.

She sensed him beside her and looked up.

"You were wonderful, Gracie." His eyes warmed, turning their brown depths to milky coffee. "I've never been prouder of any assistant. I couldn't have done it without you."

Tears misted her eyes. She'd helped him. Perhaps that would make up for the mistakes she'd so far made. For the first time in her life, as she looked into his eyes, one word came, like a song to her hungry heart.

Valued.

Truly, honest-to-goodness valued.

In a million years, he would never have believed that his shy little sparrow could put her fingers into a man's flesh with a cooler head and steadier hands than a third-year medical student. Sure, she'd been nervous, but she'd managed in spite of it, and rather than fainting on the floor afterward, assisted with the remainder of the operation.

She intrigued him. A mystery. So guarded and hesitant. What thoughts ran through that mind? What hopes and dreams did she cherish?

He wanted to know everything about her. Her likes, dislikes, thoughts, and aspirations. The things that made her laugh and those that made her cry.

And sure as Ireland was green, he wasn't going to accomplish any of it unless things

changed. Though they'd been married over a month, he knew less about her than he did about Audrey after only one church social.

So he'd court his wife. Lay on the charm until her eggshell exterior cracked, revealing the softer parts within. To start with: their long delayed picnic on Lake Compton.

He opened the door to his examining room. Grace sat in a chair beside their patient's bedside, head tilted back, eyes closed in slumber. Their patient also appeared to be sleeping, thank goodness. Like the professional doctor he was, Raymond went first to the patient and checked pulse and respiration. All good. The man would live. Not only that, but he would enjoy a full and active life for many years to come. He could have attributed it to his own skills, but truly he couldn't have done it without Grace. Nor the strength of the Lord he served.

He knelt beside the chair and studied her. His breath faltered. In sleep, her features relaxed, long lashes fanning over her rose-tinted skin, no one in their right mind would describe her as plain. Nor gorgeous, either. She had the sort of beauty that grew on a man, drew him closer. Like layers of the finest silk, making him want to go deeper, understand more.

She stirred, her eyelids fluttering open. "You should be in bed sleeping." She blinked, her hair falling down around her shoulders.

"And just where should you be, lass?" Teasing sternness lilted his tone.

"Where every good doctor's wife is. Caring for the patient." She smiled, sweet and shy.

Doctor's wife. His wife. The words struck him anew in their poignancy. This wasn't just any woman he intended to court. He'd already married her. She was, in the legal sense anyway, his.

Yet he wanted more than a marriage license that pronounced them man and wife. They'd accomplished the legalities. Could their hearts join as well?

"Time for bed, Mrs. Doc." He fought the sudden desire to pick her up and carry her upstairs, her arms around his neck, her slight frame so close. . . "I'll sit with the patient. I want you to get your rest."

"Why?" She attempted to subdue the tangles of her hair.

He offered his hand and helped her to her feet. "Because tomorrow we're going on a picnic. And I don't want my wife yawning over the sandwiches."

Chapter 8

Monet himself couldn't have painted a prettier landscape for their day. Sun glittered over the lake like hundreds of tiny diamonds carelessly tossed upon a blue carpet. The air smelled of fresh-cut grass and flowers, of summer and promise. Grace tipped her head back and inhaled a long breath.

Their buggy rolled to a halt near the lake, and Raymond tied the horses to a hitching post. He looked different out of his professional attire, in a shirt and vest, a straw hat atop his head. Younger. Less serious. Terribly handsome.

He walked to the buggy where she sat. "May I?"

She nodded. He placed his hands around her waist and lifted her down. The warmth of his fingers pressed against the thin material of her dress. A shiver curled up her spine. Why did this man's touch have the power to do such absurd things to her? Turning her from a calm, collected person to a blushing schoolgirl.

"There's a nice spot near the lake." He grabbed the picnic basket and blanket. She followed. It was nice having someone else to do the carrying. Why, she felt like a fine lady of leisure walking alongside him, with nothing for her hands to do but fold primly at her waist.

They made their way toward the lake, and he spread the blanket near the water's edge. She settled herself atop it, adjusting her skirts, then opened the picnic basket. He'd insisted on procuring everything himself, not allowing her to cook a thing. Not that she minded. Although her kitchen skills had improved, her liking of the task had not.

She gasped. A slab of thickly cut ham. A loaf of crusty bread. Sliced cheese. And a large bowl of strawberries. Her mouth watered at the sight of the plump fruit. Her favorite.

"Where did you get all of this?"

He seated himself on the blanket, leaning against a shady oak tree, his hat beside him. The wind toyed with his dark hair, rebellious strands falling over his forehead. "I went shopping, lass. What do you think? The fairies brought it?"

"Everything looks perfect." She busied herself with preparing plates for both of them. "Thank you for getting it all."

"My pleasure. It's not every day I take such a lovely lady for an excursion. One who not only mends and cooks but assists in operations as well. I wonder what other talents she has?" A grin played on his lips.

A lovely lady? She almost looked around to see whom he referred to. He couldn't mean her. She wasn't lovely, but plain and practical. Boots, not satin slippers.

"Th–thank you," she stammered. As quickly as she could, she handed him his plate. If

he kept on with these compliments, she'd be liable to drop his lunch all over the blanket.

He took the plate. "It was a compliment, Gracie. Not a million dollars. Hasn't anyone ever given you a compliment before?"

She fiddled with the edges of her napkin. "I don't really remember. I'm sure someone must have, but I can't recall."

"Then there's a great deal of back payments to be made. I hope you're ready for the onslaught." He grinned, so much charm in it, she smiled back.

"I'll accept only truth." A flush warmed her cheeks, and she focused her attention on the lake.

"Since there are so many wonderful things to be said about you, there will only be truth. Now, let's get to work on this fine meal, so we can go play in the lake."

"Play in the lake?" Her eyes widened. What was he suggesting? That they swim in their underthings like a couple of adolescent boys? Although she'd visited Lake Compton many a time, she'd never so much as gotten her feet wet.

"Right you are, lass." His eyes sparked with amusement.

After their meal, he insisted on putting everything away himself, while she sat and rested. What had come over him? He was giving her the sort of attention he'd paid to Audrey, only somehow it seemed different. A girl could become drunk on such kindness and compliments.

"Ready to play in the lake?" He latched the lid of the picnic hamper.

"Perhaps you should tell me what you mean by 'play.'"

"We'll just get our feet wet. Nothing too drastic. Haven't you ever been wading before?"

She shook her head.

"Then it is high time you did." He helped her up, and they made their way to the water's edge. "You haven't really lived until you've felt the sand beneath your feet and the water around your ankles. Take a doctor's word for it."

"I've been *living* just fine, thank you." She kept her tone prim.

"You won't think so after you do this." He bent and unlaced his shoes then pulled off his socks. Every ounce of ladylike decorum commanded her to turn away. She ignored it, staring at his feet and legs. Tanned and corded with muscles, dusted with dark hair. She drew in a breath. If it weren't for the cool breeze, a fire would have started in her cheeks.

He crossed the sand, stepped into the water, and stood there, the gentle waves lapping around him. The wind was doing crazy things to his hair.

His hair was doing crazy things to her heart.

"Now it's your turn." He held out his hand.

She hesitated only momentarily. Then bent and untied her shoes. Unrolled her stockings and placed them inside. The sand tickled her toes, and she tunneled her feet deep into the pearl-white grains, lifting her skirts a bit.

"Come here." He held out his hand.

She placed her hand in his, let herself be drawn along by his strength. The first step in the water stole her breath, as icy pinpricks rushed over her skin. Yet as she went farther, moved to stand beside him, the chill lessened and she concentrated on the waves frolicking around her. The solidity of his fingers mingling with hers.

He was right. There was freedom in this. In risks and improprieties. In stepping out of the mold placed around oneself.

"Like it?" He studied her.

"It's glorious." The sand squished between her toes, water spraying her hem. Her heart pounded, but surely it was because of the adventure rather than his nearness, the gentle pressure of his arms as he wrapped them around her waist. A tingle of heat spread over her. She pushed it aside and concentrated on the view stretched out before them, a canvas of beauty.

He whispered something she couldn't catch. She wondered what he said, but didn't ask. Words weren't needed. Somehow, it felt right without them.

She could have stood there for an eternity. Nothing plagued them here, no household cares or family pressures. It was just her and the waves. And. . .him.

"We should go now," he said at last. "You're probably freezing."

She nodded, placed her hand in his again, and they went up the shoreline, back to hard reality. Back from what had, for a few short moments, been something like their own secret world. Secret world? With him? Had she gone mad?

When they returned to the buggy, she turned to him and shyly took both of his hands in hers. "Thank you for taking me."

"You're welcome, luv," he answered, reaching out and brushing back a windblown strand of hair from her cheek.

She gasped at the feel of his fingers against her skin, tried to still her racing heart. *Love?* She wasn't his love. Could things become more confusing than they already were?

"I'm cold," she murmured. "Ought we not to go back?"

The moment shattered and was gone.

Since their lakeside picnic, things changed between them. Conversation filled what had formerly been silent mealtimes. They talked of the day's activities, mutual acquaintances, the latest headlines in the paper. Anything but their relationship. It was easier that way. He let himself enjoy the companionable moments. Having someone to come home to at day's end, to share dinner and laughter with. . .perfect. The home he'd never had.

After hours of studying her, he learned things. The furrow in her brows when she was deep in thought. Her hesitant smiles. Sometimes, even her laughter. Her favorite color was pink, she found organization relaxing, and had a weakness for Shakespeare and strawberries.

He wanted, no needed, to go deeper. Friendship was all well and good, but it wasn't enough. Nor would it ever be.

Together, they cleared the table, and he helped with dishes. Thank goodness, no one needed medical assistance tonight.

"Raymond." The sound of his name on her lips wreaked havoc with his good sense.

"Yes." He dried a plate and placed it in the cupboard.

"I was cleaning out the closet today and found this." She crossed the room and held up an instrument case, hidden behind the table. "What is it?"

"My old guitar." He closed the cupboard and went to where she stood. She handed him the case. "Haven't seen the thing in ages. Must have been buried behind all my old fishing gear." He ran his hand across the case, dusting it off.

"Can you play it?" Interest flickered in her eyes.

"Sure as shamrocks are Irish, I can." He grinned at her and opened the case. The

polished wood and smooth strings hadn't changed since he'd last played it several years ago for a friend's wedding. He picked it up and strummed a few notes. A wee bit off but nothing some tuning wouldn't fix.

"Would you like me to play something for you?" He finished the tuning.

Her smile answered for her.

He strummed a few notes, the sound taking him back to his boyhood when he'd take his guitar to Lake Compton and play for hours, sitting on the sand, the gentle waves his only audience.

He launched into the first verse and began to sing softly:

> *"The pale moon was rising above the green mountain,*
> *The sun was declining beneath the blue sea;*
> *When I strayed with my love to the pure crystal fountain,*
> *That stands in the beautiful Vale of Tralee.*
> *She was lovely and fair as the rose of the summer,*
> *Yet 'twas not her beauty alone that won me;*
> *Oh no, 'twas the truth in her eyes ever dawning,*
> *That made me love Mary, the Rose of Tralee."*

She propped her chin in her hands, eyes wide. He studied her, the curve of her throat, her delicate fingers. How could he have overlooked her before? Perhaps it was true, the saying that love went beyond beauty. Not that Grace lacked loveliness, but it deepened with her. The sweetness and purity of her heart, her kindness, all of it shone through. Far more attractive than mere superficial prettiness that faded like a piece of calico with time and wear.

Grace would be beautiful fifty years from now, because her spirit would still be beautiful. Untarnished by time.

> *"The cool shades of evening their mantle were spreading,*
> *And Mary all smiling was listening to me;*
> *The moon through the valley her pale rays was shedding,*
> *When I won the heart of the Rose of Tralee.*
> *Though lovely and fair as the Rose of the summer,*
> *Yet 'twas not her beauty alone that won me;*
> *Oh no, 'twas the truth in her eyes ever dawning,*
> *That made me love. . .Gracie, the Rose of Tralee."*

He winked at her. She smiled, a rosy blush flushing her cheeks. He hadn't meant the song to be a declaration of his feelings, merely something to make her smile. Still, the words rang through his mind. Had she won him? Become his Rose of Tralee? Lovely and fair with truth in her eyes?

He strummed the last notes. He couldn't consider the answer. Too dangerous. For both their hearts. When he'd wed Grace, his motive had been simple. To marry a wife for the sake of respectability. Could he risk having more with the sister of the woman who'd

jilted him? He wanted to, but. . .

She clapped, her eyes sparkling. "That was beautiful. You sing so well."

"Thank you, thank you." He gave a mock bow then launched into the next song. Why did all Irish songs have to be about love or death? Singing about the latter was too depressing, the former too close to his own emotions. Too bad he'd never bothered to learn any of the American ones.

"Fancy brings a thought to me
Of a flower that's bright and fair
It's grace and beauty both combine
To make the thought more rare."

The jaunty music released the tension knotting through him. Grace clapped her hands to the music, her feet tapping under the table.

A lass who so loved music deserved to be danced with. Didn't she?

He set aside his guitar and held out his hands to her. She laughed and took them, all traces of the shy sparrow vanishing like mist over a sunlit meadow. He twirled her in and out, her skirt swirling, while he kept singing. Then waltzed her around the kitchen, bypassing the table and stove. Although she faltered at first, she soon followed his lead easily and with surprising elegance. His gaze traveled the length of her, the wisps of light brown hair haloing her forehead, the fullness of her lips, the soft curves of her figure, her small waist. . .

Her hand felt right in his. Perfectly so. He drew her closer. Closer still. She gasped but didn't pull away. The faint fragrance of lemons surrounded him like a heady perfume, uniquely her. He breathed it in. She gazed back at him with those wide eyes a man could drown in.

If only this moment could last forever. And ever.

Though his singing was the only music, and the kitchen their ballroom, the sweetness of this dance rivaled any done by Bristol high society. Perhaps because the woman in his arms was one he'd grown to care for. Much more than he'd ever intended to.

The moment it ended and he stepped away, a void yawned deep within him. He considered making up more verses just to keep holding her, but all rational thoughts had fled his mind.

"That was fun." Her voice was breathless.

"You're a grand partner, Gracie McNair." He moved to the table and placed his guitar in its case.

She moved to the kitchen and wiped the counter with a towel then crossed the room, pausing at the door.

"I best say good night then."

"Good night." He closed the lid and hefted the case under one arm.

Good? With her so near, yet so far away? Hearing her stir in the next room while he lay on his cold, solitary couch?

Anything but good.

Chapter 9

Grace scoured the pot, rubbing furiously to eliminate the final specks of grime. If only she could scour her thoughts away just as easily.

She'd barely slept last night, her mind full of their dance. The rich baritone of his voice. The pressure of his hand against her waist. No wonder some churches forbade dancing. The thoughts that it could make one think. . .highly improper.

He made her feel so much. Made her believe she was beautiful. And she drank it in, every last delicious drop. Like a wilted flower finally receiving water, she'd begun to bloom. All because of him.

Softly and slowly, she'd given him her heart. Only he didn't know it yet.

Should she confess her feelings? Tell him she wanted their marriage to be more than one of convenience? Surely he felt something for her. He'd added her name into the song, hadn't he? If he felt nothing, he wouldn't have done that.

She closed her eyes and let herself dream. Of days spent in this little house, helping him with his practice, cooking his meals. Of children with his hair and her smile. Of being treasured and adored. Finally feeling worthy.

She'd tell him. Not doing so would leave her with too much regret. She'd plan dinner by candlelight, fix his favorite dishes, and afterward she'd tell him.

Stepping to the cupboard, she pulled out a bag of flour.

"Love me, too, my darling," she whispered, pressing the bag to her chest. "Oh please, love me, too."

Three cases of hay fever, a splint removal, and a tooth extraction. All in all, a busy morning.

Humming, Raymond washed his hands at the sink and dried them with the towel. No time for lunch. Mrs. Cooper and her baby were due to come at noon for a one-month checkup. He'd have to starve now and eat later. Donning his suit jacket, he opened the examining room door and stepped into the waiting room. A lady stood at the opposite end, her back to him. Her dark green skirt brushed the ground and her feather-bedecked hat concealed her hair.

A thread of recognition wove through him. Along with a niggling sense of worry.

"Can I help you?" He ran a hand through his hair.

She turned. His world stilled.

Trouble had knocked at his door. In the form of a petite brunette too pretty for her own good.

Audrey.

"Yes, I believe you can." A smile tilted her lips. She sailed toward him, stopping a few inches away. "It's nice to see you again, Ray. I've missed you." Her lashes fluttered, deceptively sweet.

He was through with deception.

"What are you doing here?" He ground out the words.

"Just passing through and thought I'd say hello." She pulled off her gloves, one finger at a time, in a motion intended to tantalize. "Why? Aren't you glad to see me?"

"You know I'm not." At his side, his hand clenched into a fist. She'd wooed him with her charms, dumped him at the altar, and now returned weeks later, insisting he should be glad to see her. As if he were some doll that she could throw on the ground and pick up at her pleasure, still expecting to see a smile on the china face. Well, she had a surprise or two coming.

"I must confess I'm hurt." Her lip quivered. "I thought a gentleman such as yourself would at least greet me with some common courtesy. I suppose that is too much to ask."

"I, too, am surprised. That a *lady* such as yourself would make me believe up until the morning of our wedding that you cared for me. I married your sister to maintain the respectability that, apparently, you don't give two straws about." True, Grace now meant so much more to him. But at the time he'd been angry. Suddenly, all that anger came rushing back and landed on him like a ton of grapeshot.

"So your Christian charity still hasn't forgiven me?" Bitterness leeched into her words. "I'm surprised at you, Ray. Doesn't the Bible say to forgive seventy times seven? I thought you professed to be a man of God."

He sucked in a breath, the words finding their mark.

"I've done my best to forgive you for the wrong you've done me." He kept his tone even, low. "But that still doesn't mean I welcome your presence."

She laughed. "You don't understand. I'm reformed. Completely repented of my girlish folly and with full intentions of righting the wrongs I've done. Starting with the fulfillment of my promise to marry you."

"You forget one minor detail. I'm married to someone else." He folded his arms across his chest.

"Yes. I heard about that. You married my mouse of a sister. Dearest Ray, you'd be lying if you told me you were happy with Grace. I don't know how you've endured it thus far. So meek and retiring." She leaned closer, her perfume overwhelming. "A man like yourself could never be truly satisfied with her."

Hot anger boiled through his veins. If she'd been a man, he'd have struck her for those derogatory words about Grace. Knocked her down and taken satisfaction in it. But even if she were not a lady, he would remain a gentleman.

"If I were you, I would not say such things. Even my 'Christian charity' has its limits."

She laughed again, harshly. "Don't tell me you've fallen in love with her. I don't believe it. I won't believe it. No, my darling Ray. You're mine. And nothing will stand in our way. Especially my sister."

The door swung open, the jingling bell announcing the presence of Mrs. Cooper and her baby.

"I shan't disturb you any further." Audrey lowered her tone to a whisper. "But be

warned, Ray. We're not finished." She spun around and headed for the door, nearly plowing into Mrs. Cooper and her cooing baby. Raymond ran his hands down the front of his waistcoat and forced himself to smile.

We're not finished.

A frisson of fear dripped down his spine.

Chapter 10

A heavenly aroma curled under the kitchen door, like perfume seeping from a bottle. Grace inhaled the fruit of the past two hours' labor as she dusted the top of the mantle over the fireplace. Mmm. Blackberry pie and roast chicken. Hopefully it would please Raymond. Oh, how she wanted to do just that. To see his smile of appreciation as she dished out the dinner, hear his words of praise. He'd made her feel so special, what with the dancing and picnics and all. It was high time she did something for him.

She'd wear her new dress tonight, too. Made from fabric purchased on a whim, it wasn't the typical serviceable frock she usually chose. When she first tried on the rose-pink frock, she twirled in front of the mirror like a little girl playing princess. In it she felt beautiful, like a woman worthy of Raymond's hand. Perhaps there, too, she'd gain his smile of appreciation.

A tune danced on her lips as she dusted, rearranging the candlesticks and scattering the cobwebs.

"Fancy brings a thought to me..."

"So the little housewife is hard at work at her labors."

Grace spun around. The chair almost toppled. Her heart boomed in her ears.

Audrey stood in the doorway, one gloved hand draped casually on the sofa's edge. Her too-red lips curled into a smile without warmth.

Grace clambered off the chair.

"Audrey...you startled me." She approached her sister and managed a smile.

The prodigal had come home. Yet unlike the prodigal son, her sister still looked as elegant and well cared for as when she left. The gown draping her reedlike frame was new.

The look in her eyes was not.

"Sorry, little sis." Audrey responded to Grace's smile with all the enthusiasm one might show upon greeting a prickly cactus. "The door was unlocked, so I just came in." She crossed the room, looking this way and that. "Nice place. Not half as bad as I feared it would be. But perhaps you've been cleaning it." She swiped her gloved finger across the edge of the tea table, sniffed.

Grace hurried to push the chair she'd been standing on back against the wall. Why had Audrey returned? Everything in her letter suggested she planned never to do so. Oh, please no. Her sister couldn't possibly have come back for Raymond. Could she? A cold ball of dread curdled her stomach.

Audrey sank down on the sofa, her skirt billowing around her. "So tell me, little sis. Does marriage agree with you?"

Grace pressed her hand against the edge of the stone fireplace. "I am perfectly happy here."

"Of course." Audrey leaned forward, lowering her voice to a stage whisper. "You're not *truly* married, are you?"

A flush flamed Grace's face.

"I thought not. Which suits me perfectly, as I have every intention of having him back."

In a single moment Grace's gossamer dreams crumbled to powder at her feet. Their quiet dinner. Her words of love. Those brown-eyed children. All of it would never come to be. Because Audrey had come back. Audrey wanted Raymond.

And Audrey always got what she wanted.

Grace swallowed back the hard knot rising in her throat. There was no way she'd give her sister the satisfaction of seeing her cry.

"What do you mean?" She lowered herself into a chair.

"Don't look so pale, Grace. It doesn't suit your already wan complexion. You needn't be alarmed. In fact, I'm very happy with you. You've done your duty to the family and saved us from disgrace. You've been a good little housekeeper to Ray while I've been away. But I've repented of my indiscretion and don't ever intend for it to happen again. I want to go through with my promise to marry Ray, and I'm going to do it as soon as possible."

"You forget, he married me." She needed to concentrate on breathing calmly. In. Out. In. Out.

"An annulment can easily be granted, if you say what I tell you to. I've already thought it all out." Audrey propped her feet on the tea table. "Running off with Murphy was a mistake. He said he'd make me a star in his show, but all I ever did was cook, clean, and do his laundry. I hated every minute of it. So I left." She pulled something from her handbag, something long and white. Grace's eyes widened as Audrey struck a match and put the cigarette to her lips, blowing a hazy curl of smoke.

"Don't look so shocked, little sis. Ladies can smoke now. Perhaps not in public but discreetly."

"Father would lock you up for a month of Sundays if he saw you with that thing!" Grace strode to the window and pushed it open.

"Then it's a lucky thing he isn't here now, isn't it?" Audrey laughed.

Grace shivered. Her sister was wild before she went away, but wherever she'd been had turned her into a cyclone. Swirling in, bent on destruction, leaving the wreckage behind her. Now she'd come for Raymond. Would he still have her?

She studied Audrey. Her almond-shaped eyes fringed with sooty lashes. Her poise and glitter. A hothouse rose beside a roadside wildflower.

Which would Raymond chose?

Oh, if only she'd spoken earlier. If he knew of her feelings, she might still have a chance. But she'd been silent and shy, as closemouthed as an oyster. Audrey would have no trouble winning him back.

"If it's Dr. McNair you've come to see, he's not in at the moment." She raised her chin and tried for a measure of decorum.

"Attending to patients, yes. I've already spoken to him." Audrey continued to smoke.

So the decision had been made. He'd already chosen. But. . .

"What did he say?" She couldn't keep the desperation from her voice.

"My apologies, little sis." Audrey stood and moved to the window. She flung a glance laden with false sympathy over her shoulder. "Men never did flock to you."

He'd always been able to smell trouble a mile away.

The moment he entered his house it overpowered his senses like a barn full of manure. Audrey Whittaker lounged on his sofa, her hat off, her jacket unbuttoned, and a man-killer smile on her pouty lips. Grace was nowhere in sight.

The hour of reckoning had come. Not a minute sooner than he anticipated. Audrey never did waste any time.

He'd set things straight with her once and for all. In the past hours at his office he'd had sizable time to think. About his courtship with Audrey. His marriage to Grace. The two women. One, vibrant as a butterfly, but inside pure selfishness prevailed. The other, his sparrow, as timid and unassuming as they came but with a faith in God and a love for others far more precious than rubies. The one woman dazzled his senses, stirred his lust. The other won his respect and slowly, but truly. . .

His heart. His love. The overwhelming desire to turn their marriage into something more, to have her by his side every minute of every day. The realization had come upon him suddenly, like a smack in the face, yet the more he thought about it, the more he realized it had been there all along. Coming softly. Surely.

It was time Audrey had a dose of reality.

"Hard day at the office?" She stood and sidled toward him. He wrinkled his nose. Why did his usually clean parlor smell of cheap cigarettes?

"Not particularly."

She tugged at his tie with languid fingers. Gently, but firmly, he put her hands aside.

"Audrey, I want a word with you."

"You do?" She smiled. "I want to talk to you, too."

"I generally hold to 'ladies first,' but tonight I'm going to talk and you're going to listen. Understood?" He took a seat on his sofa, and she flounced beside him.

"Go ahead, Ray." She fingered the buttons on his shirt. "I'm all ears."

"Stop that, please." He placed her hands in her lap. "I want you to be serious now."

"Oh, I am." She giggled. "Utterly serious."

"Good. Because I am, too." He used the firm tone inherited from his da. "Audrey, I gave my promise to marry you several months ago. And if you had stayed, by all means, I would have kept that promise. But you left, and by your leaving released me of any obligation. So I married someone else."

"Yes, I know. My sister." She frowned. Then instantly brightened. "I admire you, Ray, for wanting to uphold the honor of my family. It was dashing of you. But now that I'm here, we can continue our plans."

"No."

"No?" She bit her lip.

He stood. Where was Grace? Hopefully out visiting her father or shopping or something like that. Perhaps he could conceal this all from her, for a time. No need for her delicate heart to be wounded by Audrey's careless hands. "No. After you left, I realized some things about you that I had been. . .rather blind to before. And although I once thought you a charming person, we would never be happy together."

"Whyever not?"

"Because we don't have the same values, you and I. We want different things out of our futures. I like the simplicity of life here, whereas you—"

"That never was a consideration before." She narrowed her eyes. "There must be something else. Don't give me these lame excuses. Tell me the real truth. It's Grace, isn't it? Honestly, Ray, you can't really be in love with my sister."

"Yes. It's Grace." He surveyed her, this sad, broken woman whom he could feel nothing but sympathy for.

She inhaled sharply. "You love her then?"

He nodded.

"And what about me?" Her tone held more vulnerability than he'd ever heard from her. But he wouldn't believe it. Audrey Whittaker cared about one thing and one alone. Herself.

"I'm sorry if I wronged you, Audrey. I should never have consented to our courtship. I know now that it is character and not outward appearances that determines a person's true worth, and I should have waited until I knew yours better. Then I would have saved both of us a great deal of disappointment."

"I hope your conscience suffers forever because of it. You have treated me ill. After all, it was your Irish charisma that captured my *simple*, trusting heart." She stood, drawing herself up. "You'll regret this, Raymond McNair. One day you'll look across the table at your mousey little wife and you'll bitterly regret this." She swished toward the door. "Don't worry about *me* though. You're not the only fish in the sea."

He stood. How could two sisters be so different? Both in looks and disposition. Both had held a place in his heart. Only one would keep it.

"Have you seen Grace?"

"As a matter of fact, I have. We had quite a nice chat. She's obviously as smitten with you as you are with her. Got all choked up when I told her of my designs upon you. She just ran out of the house. Haven't seen her since." She gave an offhand shrug. "Nice seeing you, Ray. I doubt we'll have occasion to meet again." The door clicked shut behind her.

Grace, gone? His heart started to race. He could see it now. Her startled expression upon seeing Audrey, the hurt she always tried so hard to hide. Undoubtedly, she thought he'd run straight into Audrey's waiting arms.

Would his Rose of Tralee ever realize what a treasure she was?

God help him, she would when he found her.

Chapter 11

S he should be used to this by now. Audrey, the favored sister. Beautiful, bright Audrey with the world dangling in her hand.

Once, on Grace's thirteenth birthday, her aunt had given her a beautiful cameo pin. She'd always admired the brooch and had been delighted that her aunt deemed her grown up enough to possess such finery. She dreamed of passing it along someday to her own daughter or niece. Yet the moment their aunt was out of sight, Audrey had thrown a fit. Insisted that as the eldest Whittaker daughter, the brooch belonged to her. To keep the peace, Grace relented and gave her sister the cameo. Then she'd gone to the barn, curled up in the haymow, and sobbed her heart out.

Six years later, here she was again. Crying her heart out in a haymow because of what her sister had stolen. A different, but greater loss. One that stabbed at her like a spike. Driving deeper, deeper, deeper.

Would she ever have anything of her own? Something dear to her that would never be stolen? Perhaps she wasn't worth it. Perhaps, like a pair of worn-out boots, she was only good enough for the rubbish heap. A castoff. There to clean up messes and make life smoother for those better than she.

She swallowed back a sob. All she ever wanted was to be special to someone. Anyone. She strove for it in school, with her friends, her father. Even Raymond. She'd always believed her happiness lay in the way others perceived her. When they looked favorably upon her, she looked favorably upon herself. But when they scolded or ignored her, she felt worse than the ashes in the coal scuttle.

"For thou hast possessed my reins: thou hast covered me in my mother's womb. I will praise thee; for I am fearfully and wonderfully made: marvelous are thy works; and that my soul knoweth right well. My substance was not hid from thee, when I was made in secret, and curiously wrought in the lowest parts of the earth. Thine eyes did see my substance, yet being unperfect; and in thy book all my members were written, which in continuance were fashioned, when as yet there was none of them."

Like a warm wind on a cloudy day, the verse swept through her mind. She'd always thought it applied only to babies, but suddenly it took on new meaning. She'd been fearfully and wonderfully made as an infant, and she was still. God had designed each of her days before they'd ever taken place. He loved her for who she was, not compared to those around her. He didn't play favorites. He simply cared for her. Cherished her. Valued her.

Fresh tears filled her eyes. Even if Raymond chose Audrey and she never saw him again, God would still be there. Like a careful Father watching over his little girl, He never left her. Every moment in her marriage to Raymond He'd been there. Helping her

through those first awkward days, giving her the strength to save a man's life. Beside her as Raymond won her heart. Even today as Audrey had destroyed her future.

"For I know the thoughts that I think toward you, saith the LORD, thoughts of peace, and not of evil, to give you an expected end. Then shall ye call upon me, and ye shall go and pray unto me, and I will hearken unto you. And ye shall seek me, and find me, when ye shall search for me with all your heart."

Perhaps this was why she lacked peace. Though she attended church week after week and read her Bible diligently, she'd expended her energy seeking the approval of others, instead of God's. Why had she been so foolish? Pursuing what would never last and forsaking what would never leave.

"Lord, I'm sorry. I've desired other things more than You. The approval of others, the love of a husband. When all I should have been seeking is You. Please forgive me. Make Yourself real to me. I want to be Your daughter and to live like it, not just on Sunday but on Monday through Saturday, too. Help me to trust You, whatever happens to Raymond and me. If it is Your will that we go our separate ways, help me to accept that and to trust You for whatever comes next. Amen."

Sobs shook her shoulders, and she covered her face with her hands. God might deem it best to take Raymond away forever. Perhaps she loved him too much. Whatever He decided, she would accept. Like a true daughter, she would bend to her Father's will. Trust Him for whatever came.

Raymond's face rose before her mind. His mesmerizing eyes with their magnetic twinkle. His grin. The way his arms had felt, clasped tight around her waist.

"Lord, if I can't have him, then take my feelings away, too. Because if he chooses Audrey over me, I don't know how I'll ever face the heartbreak."

Chapter 12

Warmth surrounded her like a cocoon. Hands stroked her hair. The musky scent of leather filled her senses. She never wanted to leave this dream, this sensation of being warm and loved and whole. Still, light tugged at her eyelids, urging her awake.

Grace opened her eyes. Her breath caught. Raymond lay beside her on the hay, leaning on his elbow. Watching her. No wonder she'd been having such a wonderful dream.

Bits of straw clung to her hair, her dress. She hastily brushed them off. How long had he been here? What time was it?

"Good morning, Sleeping Beauty." A lazy smile angled his face. Straw clung to his hair, and she resisted brushing it away.

"Morning?" She'd been here all night? What about him?

"Yep. I considered carrying you home, but you looked so peaceful, I didn't want to disturb you. I hope you're not too cold."

Cold? Not in the least. In fact, she couldn't remember when she'd had a better night's rest.

Then it all came crashing back. The events of yesterday. Audrey. Why was Raymond here and not with her?

"Does anyone else know we're out here?"

He shook his head. "It took a bit of doing for me to get the barn door open. I don't think the thing's been oiled in years."

"I guess I just shoved it. I was upset, and. . ." Her words trailed off. She shouldn't be telling him that.

"I know." Light from the broken window filtered over his features, illuminating his eyes, his hair, the loose lines of his linen shirt unbuttoned at the neck. "Audrey told me you'd run off."

"Where is she now?" She could scarcely trust herself to say the words.

"I'm not sure. She left. She got angry." He ran his fingers through his hair.

"Why?"

"We got into somewhat of an argument. She kept insisting she wanted our relationship to start again, and I kept telling her that was impossible. Everything is over between us." He shifted closer to her on the straw, facing her. She swallowed hard, unwilling to meet his gaze. Over between them? A heady swirl of joy started in her heart and spiraled downward to the tips of her toes. He hadn't chosen Audrey.

He hadn't chosen Audrey!

"Why?" Her voice emerged, paper thin.

"Because I told her I love you."

"What?" The words scarcely registered. "What did you say?"

"I told her I love you." He reached out and took her hands between his. "That though our marriage was one of convenience, I've grown to have feelings for you I never had for her."

She drew in a jagged breath. His hands closed around hers. Possessive. Had he just told her. . .?

I love you.

No. Her sleep-dazed mind must be playing tricks on her. She had to be hearing things. Human beings could only ask for so much happiness. Breaking off with Audrey was enough to content her for a long while. More would be too much.

"You what?"

"Gracie, Gracie." He stood up, drawing her with him. "How many times must I repeat it, lass? I *love* you. I love your smile, your laughter. How you look with flour on your face and an apron around your waist. The way you wrinkle your nose when you're mending my shirts. I love your faith in God and your kindness to others. You're precious, Gracie. And will continue to be, no matter how things go between us. But I want you to be mine."

Tears filled Grace's eyes, and before she could force them back, a burst of sobs overtook her. She hid her face with her hands in mortification. He would think her childish, losing control of her emotions. She tried to dry her eyes with her sleeve, but he stayed her hand.

"I hope those are glad tears you're crying, Gracie lass. I've not offended you by my words?"

"Offended?" A shaky laugh emerged. "Oh, Raymond."

"Let me win your heart, sweet one. Just give me a chance. That's all I ask."

Win her heart? She, who had never before had a man so much as glance in her direction was now being spoken to in such a way?

Lord, thank You for this blessing.

"It's too late, Raymond," she whispered.

"Too late?"

She smiled through a sheen of tears. "It's too late because. . .you already have."

In a sudden motion, he drew her against him and brushed his lips against hers, his kiss so gentle, so sweet. As if she, above all else, was what mattered in the world.

Time seemed to stand still, then slowly she kissed him back, letting her love and longing win. His fingers threaded through her hair, the pins falling to the ground, but she barely heeded them. She inhaled the scent of him, shaving water, soap, and a faint hint of leather. Her heart accelerated as he deepened the kiss, and she allowed herself to melt into his arms.

The arms of the man she loved.

Slowly, he stepped back, his gaze cradling hers.

"You care for me then, Gracie?" His brogue thickened. How she loved his accent. Some might think it an annoyance, but to her it was the most wonderful sound in the world.

"Not just care, Raymond." Boldness overtook her and she fingered the buttons on

the front of his shirt. "Love. So much so that I want our marriage to be more than just an arrangement."

"Truly, Gracie?"

She could have wept again, looking up into those coffee-brown eyes. For once, hers was not a devotion unrequited. At long last, she would have a life of absolutelys. Absolutely blessed. Absolutely loved.

And in answer to Raymond?

"Absolutely, yes."

"Oh, darlin'." His hand captured hers. The quiet beating of his heart reverberated through her fingertips. "My sweet one." He kissed her once. "My forever love." Twice.

"Go on." She smiled up at him.

More devotion than she'd ever dreamed possible radiated from his eyes as he folded her in his embrace. "My treasure."

Amanda Barratt has won several awards for her work and enjoys writing about eras such as Regency and Victorian England, and the Gilded Age. A member of American Christian Fiction Writers, she lives in northern Michigan with her family, where she reads way too many old books, watches period dramas to come up with new plotlines, and dreams of taking a trip to England. Amanda loves hearing from her readers on Facebook and through her website amandabarratt.net.

ONE WAY TO THE ALTAR

by Andrea Boeshaar with Christina Linstrot Miller

Chapter 1

Montana, 1902

A bath. A refreshingly cool bath. That would lift her wilted spirits after this horrid journey. *Please, Lord. . .*

Leah Hermaning whispered the prayer. Six days on the train in a hot, stuffy passenger car, three hours in a rickety stagecoach that bounced her like a child's rubber ball—and now she was finally here.

In the middle of nowhere.

The stage pulled to a bone-jarring halt, and Leah climbed out unassisted. The driver and his helper tossed down her trunk as if it didn't contain everything precious left to her. "Here ya go, lady."

Such rudeness! Uncle Robert would have had something to say about that. She glanced around. Now. . .where was he?

She searched the dusty street for a sign of him or Aunt Estelle. Horses tethered to hitching rails in front of water troughs, wagons clattering by on the dirt road—she was in another world, far from the comforts of Newport, Rhode Island. But somehow she'd adapt. . . .

Wouldn't she?

Now where could her aunt and uncle be?

Amid laughter and loud voices, a half-dozen men burst out of the freight office and headed toward her on the boardwalk, their clothing and faces as dirty as the language spewing from their mouths.

No, Leah was certainly not in her refined Newport neighborhood anymore.

She pressed herself up against the unfinished outer wall just in time to dodge the men. No doubt she'd blend into the background as usual, despite her lavender dress and leaf-green vest. God had given her brains, not beauty, and nothing could enhance her drab brown hair and the plainness of her face. And those men, who looked right through her as they passed, gave testimony to that fact.

Of course, she'd expected nothing more. Twenty-six years was time enough for Leah to accept her less-than-lovely looks, along with the fact that she would always be a spinster. But she was in a new place now, with a new teaching position waiting, and she'd make the best of her God-given days.

And she'd do that if Uncle Robert and Aunt Estelle showed up. . . .

Leah stepped into the depot office and approached the baggage clerk's window. She gave the man a smile to cover her growing uneasiness. "I'm Leah Hermaning, the new schoolteacher."

The stench of cigar met her as the long-faced clerk paused in his duties, eyeing her

with so much suspicion in his gaze, Leah feared he'd heard of the trouble in Rhode Island that had sent her to Montana. "Schoolteacher?"

"That's correct. May I leave my luggage here while I find my uncle, the Reverend Hermaning?"

"Nope. Sheriff Waite don't take a shine to unattended baggage settin' outside. He says it's a source of trouble." He glared at her as if she, not her trunk, were the source of trouble.

If she were pretty, she could bat her lashes at the man, and he'd be quick to do her bidding. As it was, that tactic wouldn't work, so she reached into her reticule and found two nickels—all she had left.

"Will this compensate for your inconvenience?"

The man swept the coins toward himself and deposited them into his vest pocket. "Be quick about it. If the sheriff comes around and gives me a fine, you're payin' it."

Grudgingly, she nodded. Chances were, the sheriff was a pudgy, power-hungry oaf, and she'd have a hard time convincing him to dismiss the fine. She'd been acquainted with his ilk in Newport. "Which way is the church?"

"Ain't no church. If yer the preacher's niece, like you say, you'd have knowed that."

No church? How could that be? "But my uncle—"

"Is a missionary. Not a parson."

"Yes, but his church—"

"Meets under that tree over yonder."

Under a tree—not in a church building? As the surprise took root, Leah dared to look. Sure enough, in the far distance, six benches angled toward the sturdy trunk. Oddly, the tree was the one beauty she'd seen in this town so far.

"But—what do they do if it rains?"

"Reckon they pray it don't."

The freight office door opened and closed. The man stepping forward filled the dim space. Strikingly handsome, in a rugged sort of way, he seemed to fit his surroundings without blending in as Leah always did. He held a battered leather hat, and his blond hair curled over the collar of his checked shirt. His well-groomed beard appeared a soft reddish-brown, and his bright blue eyes regarded her keenly.

"Miss Leah Hermaning?"

"Yes?"

A broad smile tempered his chiseled features. "We've been expecting you, ma'am."

His deep voice held a hint of a drawl—smooth and manly—and yet it sounded as sturdy and unyielding as the leather holster at his hip.

"Hope you've had an uneventful trip."

"Yes, thank you." While the man was polite, his expressive gaze told her something was amiss. Then she glimpsed the silver star affixed to his brown vest. "You're the sheriff?"

He smiled and inclined his head. "Name's Jesse Waite."

"A pleasure to make your acquaintance." Leah offered her white-gloved hand. As he held it, she took in the sight of his strong jaw. His ruggedness, contrasted with the softness of his eyes, stole her breath. But she'd learned long ago that no man this handsome would look at her in a romantic way. She pulled back her hand as she pulled back her heart.

And then she remembered her baggage. "Oh no. . ."

A frown. "Beggin' your pardon?"

"I can explain."

"You can?" He arched thick golden eyebrows.

"I had to leave my luggage outside. Of course, I can't transport it by myself. My uncle was supposed to meet me, but"—she held out her arms, indicating the empty boardwalk—"he's not here."

"I know."

"Please don't fine the baggage clerk."

"Well now, I—"

"He said I'd have to pay it if you give him a fine, and I'm afraid I've spent all my savings on my trip here from Rhode Island."

There. She'd admitted the truth. However, men, particularly the handsome ones, enjoyed making an example of her rather than extending their mercy. Like the arresting police officer at the women's suffrage demonstration in Newport and the city's haughty district attorney, not to mention the highbrowed judge in the courtroom. And, of course, there wasn't a man in the world as insensitive as Mr. Bonfield, the school superintendent who'd terminated her teaching position.

The sheriff strode toward the baggage clerk's window and stuck his hand between the bars. "I don't plan on fining Givens. In fact, I think you might've accidentally left some money with him."

The clerk fished in his vest pocket, produced two coins, and dropped them into Sheriff Waite's hand. "Now, Jesse, a man's gotta earn a living."

"Not by coercing innocent females into paying him for nothing." He rolled the nickels in his palm before offering them to Leah. "I believe these are yours."

"It wasn't a bribe," she explained quickly. "I only wanted to acquire the man's cooperation."

"I'm sure you meant no harm, Miss Hermaning." He smiled, wider this time, and his teeth appeared all the more white against his autumn-colored beard. "And you're lucky. It usually takes more than ten cents to get Warren Givens to *cooperate*."

"In that case, heaven must be smiling on me today." And not just heaven, either. If this man greeted every stagecoach, smiling like that, he could have women lined up from here to the East Coast.

Leah accepted the coins and dropped them into her reticule. She needed to turn her thoughts in another direction and pay attention to what was going on around her. The last thing she wanted was to get herself mixed up in any trouble here in One Way and cause her aunt and uncle—and herself—further shame.

"Can my baggage remain outside the freight office awhile longer? I promise to stay with it until my aunt and uncle come for me."

"Don't worry about your luggage. As for your relatives. . .they're tied up at a funeral this afternoon. They won't be back for a while, so your uncle sent me to fetch you and take you over to the boardinghouse."

"Is that where my aunt and uncle are staying?"

"Yep. And I'll rustle up a couple of men to bring your things later. I'm sure you're anxious to get settled."

"Extremely." And she wanted a bath!

He gave her another of his easy smiles. "I'll bet if I ask him real nice, Warren'll keep an eye on your things."

"Will I have to pay him more than ten cents?"

"Naw." The sheriff reached for Leah's elbow and walked her out of the depot and to a shady spot in front of the land office. "That cantankerous old owl owes me a favor or two. Stay put. I'll be right back."

"Where are you going?"

The sheriff glanced over his shoulder. "I see the window is empty, so I need to hunt down Givens and get him to watch your baggage. I promise I won't be long."

With a nod, Leah watched him saunter off. She sensed she could trust Sheriff Waite. Uncle Robert would never have commissioned a scoundrel to meet her in his absence.

How wrong she'd been in her initial assumption. Sheriff Jesse Waite was certainly not pudgy, nor was he an oaf. As for power-hungry, that remained to be seen.

Unpleasant memories of the past months resurfaced, and Leah tamped them down. Her life back East was over, and she had the chance to begin anew with Aunt Estelle and Uncle Robert. But it was a pity her future had to be here in One Way.

One Way. Even the town's name sounded like a life sentence.

She gazed down the thoroughfare at the handful of sun-blanched wooden structures lining it. Fewer than a dozen businesses and maybe fifteen houses stood along the town's only street. The general store caught her attention when a family of five exited onto the boardwalk. If she'd thought the town quiet before, she changed her opinion once the three boys broke into a gallop toward a meadow, near where the church tree stood.

Before long, she'd be corralling these same boys into the schoolhouse after recess— and, she hoped, into Sunday school, if her dream of teaching it came to pass. Their energy sparked some life into her as well. If she could meet these rambunctious three and learn their names before school began, she'd be that much ahead.

Just as she started toward them, the boys took off for the river and the lone tree. Rather than hike across the expanse of tall grass—and probably still not catch them—she turned to meet the parents.

As they approached, Leah was struck by the woman's fashionable Parisian-style dress and hat of black silk velvet—with a real ostrich plume. The man's striped cassimere suit was every bit as stylish.

The woman's smile was friendly enough to encourage Leah to introduce herself.

"Good afternoon. I'm Miss Hermaning, the new teacher. I noticed your boys and hoped to meet them before school resumes this fall."

The woman looked so taken aback, Leah felt herself pale. Wouldn't everyone in town expect her arrival? Why the look of surprise? And the gentleman—he looked even more uncomfortable. Had news of that unfortunate scandal back East somehow leaked out?

The man recovered first. "Miss Hermaning, allow me to introduce myself. I'm Reverend Bigelow, and this is my wife, Elizabeth."

"Reverend?" Apprehension prickled at the back of her neck.

"We're delighted that you're here." Mrs. Bigelow's smile was as warm as the August sunshine. "When did you arrive?"

"Minutes ago." But the real question was, when did the Bigelows arrive? And why? This town already had a preacher.

The reverend cleared his throat and looked at his wife as if trying to assess how much to say. "I take it you've not seen your uncle yet."

"That's correct. He's preaching a service for a funeral somewhere."

"Oh yes. The funeral. Mind you, I would have done the honors so your uncle could meet you, but we just arrived yesterday. My lovely wife and I are still unpacking."

"I understand." The deeper truth of her own statement startled her. She truly did understand.

One Way didn't need two preachers!

The truth gripped her. Uncle Robert and Aunt Estelle were missionaries, just as Mr. Givens had said, and as long as Leah had known them, which was all her life, they never stayed long in one spot. Once they established a church and found a pastor, they packed their clothes, their few dishes and pots, and their Bibles into what resembled a small converted delivery wagon, and moved on. "Light and efficient and unencumbered by worldly goods," Aunt Estelle always said.

Could it be they were doing just that? Would they leave her behind?

Chapter 2

"I don't want any more trouble from you, Warren." That distinctive deep voice, edged with controlled authority and just the right amount of friendliness, cut through Leah's gloomy thoughts. She gazed over at Sheriff Waite, who had just walked back outside with Mr. Givens.

Mr. Givens snorted. "After Welton wins the election next week, you won't have any more trouble from me—or anyone else."

"Well, he ain't won yet, and until the election is decided, I'm the law." The sheriff squatted down and shoved Leah's trunk through the office doorway. Filled with everything she owned, that trunk had to weigh two hundred pounds. Yet he seemed to expend no more effort to move it than he did now with her valise.

And there stood Leah, gawking at him like some silly schoolgirl.

She mustered her dignity and returned her gaze to the Bigelows.

"We should be on our way, dear." The reverend cupped his wife's elbow. "Will you excuse us, Miss Hermaning, while we collect those wildcats? We have much to do back at home."

"Of course. It was nice to make your acquaintances."

In the moments Sheriff Waite took to finish his conversation with Mr. Givens, Leah blinked back the surge of loneliness that now hit her as hard as it had the night Mother died almost three years ago.

Redirecting her thoughts, Leah peered across the way at the pretty tree, a silent Presence seeming to guide her gaze. The cloudless sky was so blue and hung so low, she was tempted to reach out and touch its vastness before the azure heavens met the earth tones of the Badlands. Even the river appeared sandy-brown as it wound its way around town. When Aunt Estelle wrote that One Way had a waterfront, Leah naively compared it to the beach at Newport. Now, however, it was painfully obvious that she'd never again hear the comforting surf that put her to sleep every night back home.

Sheriff Waite came toward her with strides as smooth and confident as his smile. She appreciated his kindness thus far.

"Warren'll keep an eye on your things for a while and deliver them over to the boardinghouse later." Smile lines lingered around his eyes, showing Leah that his charming disposition wasn't a mere act for her benefit. "I'll give you a tour of the town as we walk there. And more good news—it ain't a long tour or a far walk."

His good spirits gave her the courage to respond likewise, as a tour of the town wouldn't take much more than a full minute. She silently blessed him for lightening her mood. "Tour the whole town at one time?"

His easy laugh put her more at ease, and so did his sky-blue eyes as they flashed admiration for her retort. He pointed ahead, gazing at her with a roguish twinkle in his eye. "This here's the land office. Luther Welton is the man to see if you're looking for a good plot for ranching or homesteading."

"Hmm. Herding cattle, plowing fields—I'm not sure those jobs fit my talents."

"How about forging iron, then? We're passing the blacksmith shop."

"Not sure that will work, either, Sheriff. I'm used to holding a pencil, not a lump hammer."

They walked by a building with a huge SALOON sign at the entry, and a wicked grin crossed his face. "Guess a Bible-totin' preacher's niece wouldn't want to work there, either."

Leah had to laugh. "I wouldn't mind working to *shut it down*."

He chuckled. "Well, then, you might be interested to know that the State of Montana pays five dollars for every wolf and coyote skin." He pointed to the taxidermy shop. "You could make a good living trapping or shooting the varmints. Unless you prefer to keep them as trophies."

"This city girl has no idea how to shoot. Or trap. Perhaps I should stick to my chosen profession and just teach."

His eyes turned a shade darker, and the mood shifted somehow. "Well, Miss Hermaning, I'll admit you seem like a woman who should be surrounded by children—lots of them."

What did he mean by that? His comment was innocent enough, but it seemed to have more behind it than a mere reference to her profession of teaching. The sheriff had left behind his bantering mood.

If he wanted to discuss their professions, that was fine with Leah. "Are you the only lawman in the area?"

"I'm the only sheriff in One Way—unless folks vote someone else into the position come next Tuesday." He pointed up the dirt street. "My opponent is Luther Welton. Not only does he own the land office, but he has an invested interest in the saloon, too. He has ideas to build a hotel and gaming facility that sports dancing girls and other entertainment for the men in town."

Mr. Welton sounded like a man who would benefit from Uncle Robert's preaching.

"Sheriff's office is coming up here to the left. . .and see that rambling building with the two-story porch down there a ways?"

It wasn't much to look at, but Leah nodded all the same.

"That's the widow Rigley's boardinghouse." They walked farther down the road, passing a well-kept yard surrounded by a white picket fence. "And this"—he stopped on the boardwalk and nodded toward the clapboard house with green trim in front of them—"is my sister Nellie's house."

The lace-covered curtain fluttered in the front window. Moments later, a slim young woman hastened outside and to the street, carrying a baby on her hip. "Jesse, what a surprise!"

He grinned and reached for the baby. "Miss Leah Hermaning, this here's my sister, Mrs. Nellie Evans. And, of course, baby Henry."

Mrs. Evans stepped forward and gave Leah the warmest hug possible. "I couldn't wait for you to get here. We don't have a lot of women our age since the town's so small. I

know things aren't like you expected, but I'm sure you'll find happiness with—"

"I think she expected a bigger town." Sheriff Waite gave his sister a slight frown and an almost imperceptible shake of his head.

Mrs. Evans's eyes widened for a moment. "Oh, right. . ." She cleared her throat. "Well, while it doesn't look like much, it's a fine town. Our pa helped to settle this parcel of Montana, and he and Jesse built One Way from the ground up."

The sheriff turned to Leah. "My sister is prone to exaggeration. Wasn't just me and Pa alone. We had lots of help."

Leah looked from brother to sister and back again. "That's quite an accomplishment, Sheriff."

"Not really. Like I said, Nellie stretches the truth."

"Oh, I do not, Jesse Waite." Mrs. Evans glanced at Leah. "Pay him no mind—unless doing so lands you in jail."

Jail? The blood drained from her face. No! She'd never want to spend time behind bars again as long as she lived! "I'll heed your warning, Mrs. Evans. I wouldn't want to break the law."

Sheriff Waite didn't seem to notice anything amiss. He grinned at Henry, who tried to cut his teeth on the sheriff's star.

"I am most impressed that you're a town founder, Sheriff."

"All I did was help build a few houses and barns."

"And stores, and the bank. . . Let's see, what else?" Mrs. Evans ticked off each item on her fingers. "The livery, the mercantile. . ."

"Old history."

"Maybe to you, Jesse, but half this town thinks you're a hero."

The sheriff sighed, and Leah smiled at his chagrin.

"Jesse's got big plans for One Way," Mrs. Evans continued. "He wants the railroad to come through so we'll have an easier time getting supplies—and we'd get regular mail delivery, too. But best of all, Jesse wants to build a church and a school."

"I like his plans for One Way's future more than Mr. Welton's, that's for sure."

"We hoped you'd feel that way. Right, Jesse?"

He turned to Mrs. Evans and cleared his throat—rather loudly and with a slight frown.

"I'll say what my brother is too polite to tell you, Miss Hermaning, and that is that Luther Welton is a smooth-talking, crooked businessman. Even so, he claims to be a family man, and most folks here think that's an important quality for One Way's next sheriff."

"A family man?" She felt as though a marble had lodged in her throat.

A new preacher in town.

Aunt Estelle and Uncle Robert were traveling missionaries.

Sheriff Jesse Waite needed to win an election.

Oh, Lord, please let this apprehension merely be my imagination running away with me! Her aunt and uncle wouldn't punish her by sentencing her to an arranged marriage and a life in One Way. Would they?

"We'd best be on our way." Sheriff Waite carefully placed Henry in Mrs. Evans's outstretched arms. "Miss Hermaning hasn't yet spoken to her aunt and uncle."

A knowing gleam entered Mrs. Evans's eye. "Well, then, I mustn't keep you."

"A pleasure meeting you."

"Likewise, Miss Hermaning, but we're sure to see lots more of each other. Right, Jess?"

"I'm sure, small town and all." He shifted his weight before kicking a stone off the boardwalk.

Leah forced a smile, her nerves taut. Something was brewing. Its energy crackled in the summer air.

The sheriff's gaze met Leah's. Smile lines vanished, and a soft light entered his eyes. In that moment Leah knew her fate had been decided.

Chapter 3

Jesse sneaked a good look at Miss Hermaning as he walked her toward the boarding-house. While she wasn't the kind of woman who made men swivel in their saddles for a second glance, she wasn't unpleasant to the eye, the way Miss Estelle had described her. The words the reverend's wife used were "plain" and "uncomely," and at the time, Jesse assumed the older woman had been overly kind in describing her niece's looks, as aunties were wont to do. So he'd expected hound-dog ugly, although even hounds were loveable.

And Jesse should know: Sarge was one of those hounds.

Besides, who wanted all the other men in town leering at his wife? Not Jesse, that was for sure.

However, Miss Hermaning was lovely, in a pure yet plucky way, and Jesse felt a niggling of attraction to her. Gray eyes sparked with telltale emotion, and her smile seemed to make an already sunny day that much brighter. And she had to have figured out her uncle's scheme, at least in part, when she met the preacher minutes ago. Yet she'd shaken off her confusion or disappointment—or both—and made their walk through town downright pleasurable. A lighthearted woman who could laugh at adversity would be a blessing to any lawman.

Days ago, he'd asked God to show him if Reverend Hermaning's idea had merit—and to show him straightaway if it did. Jesse now believed marrying Leah Hermaning was, indeed, God's will, based on what he'd heard from the preacher about his niece and seen so far in Miss Hermaning.

Could a man really know so quick that he wanted to marry a woman he'd just met?

But the real question was whether Miss Hermaning would go along with her uncle's plan. Jesse wouldn't be able to bear it if she married him and was miserable the rest of her life.

But God knew that, too.

"Whoa, there, Jesse." A man hailed him from across the street. "Hold up a minute."

He turned toward the familiar voice he'd come to dread. "Luther Welton."

The heavyset man, whom some folks called handsome, jogged from the saloon and stopped when he reached the boardwalk in front of Miss Hermaning. He carried a newspaper folded under his arm.

"Now, Jesse, you ol' scoundrel, what'd you go and do, get one of them mail-order brides so you could win this election?" Welton eyed Miss Hermaning in a way that made Jesse clench his fist. "Ain't you gonna introduce me?"

"First off, I am not a mail-order bride." Miss Hermaning's gray eyes were like sparking flints.

Jesse gave her elbow a gentle squeeze. "Miss Leah Hermaning, please meet Luther Welton, owner of the land office and an investor in. . .other holdings about town."

"Charmed, I'm sure." Miss Hermaning gave Welton a dismissive glance and gazed down the street.

Welton grinned, revealing those large, white, even teeth of his that made him look like a wolf. And wouldn't Jesse like to be the one to turn in that pelt! He'd even forego the five-dollar payment. "A pleasure, Miss. . .Hermaning, is it? Any relation to Reverend Hermaning?"

"I'm his niece."

"Ah. . ." He snickered. "Well, don't worry none. I won't hold it against you."

"I beg your pardon?" Anger flashed in her eyes.

Jesse guided Miss Hermaning beside him so she no longer faced Welton. "Nice to see you, Luther. Have yourself a fine rest of the afternoon."

"Likewise, Jesse." He paused. "Miss Hermaning."

She didn't reply but gazed in the direction of the river.

Welton ambled back across the street to the saloon.

"Let's get you settled, shall we?"

She looked up. "I'd appreciate it, Sheriff Waite."

Jesse gave a nod. Admirable. She'd just met the town's most notorious resident, and she didn't seem traumatized.

Now, if she survived meeting Mrs. Rigley, all would be well. . .at least until she learned of her uncle's plans to marry her off.

"Where do you live, Sheriff?"

"Near where the Powder and Yellowstone Rivers meet. You can see my homestead from here. It's right next to that large cottonwood." He pointed off toward the southeast.

"It's a pleasant-looking house. Did you build it?"

"Sure did." He couldn't wait to show it off to her. If she became his wife, he'd want her to be happy in the house he'd built with his own hands.

"I can see you're a gifted carpenter. I'm quite impressed."

"Thank you." Strange how the back of his neck heated up more from her kind words than from the afternoon sun.

They reached the boardinghouse and Jesse ascended the porch stairs ahead of Miss Hermaning. He rapped on the front door before extending his hand to assist her up the last step.

Within moments, Mrs. Rigley appeared. "Why, Jesse, what are you doing here?"

He slid off his hat. "Afternoon, ma'am. I'm here to introduce Miss Leah Hermaning, the reverend and Miss Estelle's niece. I believe you've been expecting her."

"So I have." The older woman crossed her arms over her spindly chest. "Introduce her then."

Jesse hurled up a silent prayer that the landlady would behave. "Miss Hermaning, this is Mrs. Rigley, the proprietress of the boardinghouse and a longtime family friend."

Miss Hermaning stepped forward. "It's a pleasure to meet you, ma'am. My aunt wrote that you're a devoted servant of the Lord."

"God knows, I try my best." The older woman patted the side of her head as if securing any wayward gray hair. She gave Jesse a frown. "Well, don't just stand there. Bring the girl inside."

"Yes, ma'am." He should have known Mrs. Rigley would be as cantankerous as ever and twice as amusing.

"And wipe that silly grin off your face."

He tried, unsuccessfully.

"I've been telling him to quit smiling since he was knee-high to a deer fly, for pity's sake." Mrs. Rigley gave her newest guest a once-over glance. "I never did see a man smile so much when there's nothing out of the ordinary to smile about."

This time Jesse chuckled. He couldn't help himself. He cast a glance at Miss Hermaning and saw her battling a grin of her own.

Mrs. Rigley expelled an exasperated-sounding sigh. "Your room's up this way, missy." She pointed at the stairs. "Jesse, fetch her bags."

"Warren Givens'll be along with them shortly."

"That no-good bum?"

At Miss Hermaning's curious stare, Jesse shrugged. But on the way upstairs, he caught her arm. "Don't let Mrs. Rigley fool you," he whispered close to her ear. "She's a sweet old lady underneath that weathered exterior."

"I'll take your word for it," she whispered back.

Then she smiled real sweetlike—not a syrupy simper, but something warm and genuine. Jesse's heartbeat quickened. And suddenly it felt awfully warm in this boardinghouse.

"Well, here you go," Mrs. Rigley said when they reached the end of the hallway. "It's nothing fancy, mind you, 'cause I ain't charging the reverend for your room and board."

Miss Hermaning took a step forward then halted in her tracks. "Mrs. Rigley, there's no window. While this room is tidy, a person is liable to suffocate in here."

Jesse cast a look inside. Mrs. Rigley had to be joking. This was the space she'd always kept as a utility room. Now, emptied of buckets, mops, brooms, wood scraps, and other miscellaneous items, only a single bed fit inside it.

"There's no room for my trunk."

Mrs. Rigley sniffed. "Put it under the bed."

"Won't work." Jesse shook his head. "I moved that trunk, and I can tell you it's too tall to fit under that bed."

Mrs. Rigley settled her hands on her narrow hips and scowled until her eyebrows looked like one long, furry caterpillar. "This is the room I'm offering. Take it or leave it."

Judging by Miss Hermaning's horrified expression, she'd leave it. Her next words confirmed Jesse's suspicions.

"I believe I'll go on outside and wait for my things to arrive." She hurried past them and down the stairs.

"You do that." Mrs. Rigley had the nerve to appear insulted when she ought to be ashamed.

Jesse couldn't recall feeling more disappointed in a person. He pointed at the offensive room. "You can't put a guest—the reverend's own niece—in a closet."

"But she's from a missionary family, and missionaries are supposed to stay humble."

Jesse held back the retort on the tip of his tongue, and that only because she was his elder, a lady, and his late mother's friend. Instead, he made for the door, following Leah. He found her out front on a shaded part of the boardwalk.

"I think I'll wait to get settled until I speak with my aunt and uncle." She kept her gaze averted. "Perhaps they might have different plans for me."

Indeed they did.

"Miss Hermaning, please believe me when I say I had no idea Mrs. Rigley would behave so rudely. I know she's tightfisted with the little money she has, but I wouldn't have guessed she'd put you in a converted closet."

"A closet? Is that what that was?" Miss Hermaning blinked those big gray eyes of hers as if trying to hold back tears. "I'm grateful that Mrs. Rigley is willing to give me a place to live. But the truth is I'd rather sleep on one of the benches under the church tree."

"I think we can do better by you than that. We only arranged a room at the board-inghouse in case you—"

"In case I. . .what?"

"In case you. . .you objected to the other accommodations." At his home. As his bride. But he had to allow the reverend to explain. After all, Miss Hermaning was his niece.

"Other accommodations? Hmmm. . ." She glanced in the direction of his homestead. "I see."

Yep, she'd figured it out.

Jesse drew a deep breath and let it out slowly. "That boxy-looking wagon up ahead, coming this way, is your uncle's."

"Good. It'll be nice to see him again. We obviously have much to discuss."

They sure did.

Jesse ran his finger along the inside of his collar. He'd been in on some tense meet-ings in his life, but he'd give his pa's pearl-handled pistol if he could somehow skip out on this one. But he couldn't. Miss Hermaning would be the one to decide this matter, and he was no closer to guessing how she'd answer than he was an hour ago.

Taking a step back, Jesse waited for the gavel to fall.

Chapter 4

As the black wagon drew nearer, Leah breathed a wordless prayer, unsure what to ask God for. To leave this town with her family—the only family she had left? Yes!

She gazed toward the approaching vehicle, marveling that two adults managed to reside in such a contraption while traveling from town to town. She recalled it being a shining black, with Uncle Robert's name in gold letters painted on the sides. Now it looked worn and dusty. It creaked and clattered as the wheels hit ruts in the dirt road.

At last Uncle Robert reined in the two mules. Should she pray for her relatives to get settled somewhere and send for her?

Doubtful. Those benches by the church tree proved that tithes weren't exactly pouring in, so they'd never be able to afford to pay for her transportation. And praying to go home—that would be asking the impossible.

But all was not lost. She had her new teaching position here in One Way, and lonely as it might be, she could carve out a life for herself. As far as marrying the sheriff, should that be her uncle's wish, Leah would politely refuse. Goodness, but she didn't even know the man, although Jesse Waite would have her vote for sheriff.

"Are you ill, Miss Hermaning? You look a bit peaked."

She felt it, but nodded and smiled for the sheriff's benefit. "I'm eager to get this day over with, that's all." And climb into a cool tub of water! Was it too much to suppose her accommodations, wherever they may be, would include a bathtub?

The wagon came to a stop in a swirl of dust. The sheriff helped Aunt Estelle from the conveyance.

Her feet had no more than hit the dirt street when she engulfed Leah in her embrace. "Leah, sweetheart, you're the picture of your late mother, bless her heart."

Leah returned her hug. "Thank you. I'm glad to see you, Auntie, and you, Uncle." Her gaze rested on the stoic-looking man moving their way.

Her uncle merely tipped his hat to her, silent as usual. For a man who earned his living by talking, he certainly kept his peace when out of the pulpit. Or, in One Way, when away from the tree.

"Your uncle and I are staying at Mrs. Rigley's boardinghouse. Let's step inside the parlor. All of us need to have a nice, long talk."

All of us? Yes, Leah knew what was coming. An offer of marriage. . .either that or the sheriff wanted to place her on probation.

"You're a good girl, Leah. Always have been, aside from that demonstration incident."

"Estelle, we agreed not to mention that." Uncle Robert trailed them to the door. "Remember?"

"I'm sorry, Robbie. My memory isn't what it used to be."

Leah glanced at Sheriff Waite. Had he heard? Did he know of that "demonstration incident"?

Aunt Estelle stumbled, and Leah caught her arm. After the older woman had recovered her footing, Leah searched for a stone or weed growing up from under the porch. She saw nothing but smooth wooden planks. Nothing lay in the way that Auntie could have tripped over.

"Goodness, but it's dangerous out here. A woman needs a good, strong man just to help her into the house." Aunt Estelle fluttered her bony hand toward Jesse.

He hastened to catch up and took Aunt Estelle's other arm.

"Not me. Her!" Auntie said in a stage whisper. "Robbie will look after me."

Leah couldn't hold back a grin. So that was her sweet auntie's game. Even as silly as it was, Leah's heart warmed at the attempt. But her aunt would be disappointed when she refused to marry the kindhearted sheriff.

Jesse offered his arm to Leah.

She hesitated as he regarded her with something unreadable in his eyes. "There's no need. Unlike my dear auntie, I'm having no problems walking into the boardinghouse."

He continued to hold out his arm. "It's my pleasure, Miss Hermaning."

My, but he must want to get reelected awful badly. Was he really that desperate? However, his voice had deepened and turned husky, as if he meant every word, and the sudden tenderness in his eyes made her bite back the teasing remark she'd been about to make. She reached out tentatively, unsure why this simple gesture seemed so monumental. Hadn't dozens of men offered their arm to her in escort in her lifetime?

Yes, but always under obligation. Never for the sheer pleasure of accompanying her. And yet that was exactly what she now saw in Jesse's gentle expression.

How could that be? Jesse Waite was handsome, manly, interesting—and she was plain, dull Leah Hermaning, the old-maid schoolteacher.

Would it be a sin to enjoy his escort, just this once?

Leah thought not. And as she slid her hand into the crook of his arm, she imagined for the first time how it must feel for a lady to have a man cherish her.

Aunt Estelle chattered on about the funeral they'd just come from, the hot August weather, and heaven only knew what else. At least Auntie carried the conversation, leaving Leah free to ponder the man beside her.

"Are we in the parlor yet, Robbie?"

"Almost."

Couldn't Auntie see that they'd just entered the cramped foyer? Leah stopped short and turned to Jesse. "What's wrong with my aunt?" She spoke in a tone meant for his ears only.

"Eyesight's been failing for a while now. She's been falling, losing things. . .can't walk around town by herself anymore."

What a pity for her sweet aunt who loved so much to read her Bible. Leah had been foolish to get sentimental over a man offering his arm while her aunt struggled to see what was ahead of her.

The older couple eased onto one of the room's two settees, Aunt Estelle perched

on the edge like a little brown wren. Leah started toward a surprisingly plush-looking armchair by the empty hearth, but Uncle Robert waved her toward the second settee facing his.

"Jesse, seat yourself next to Leah there."

Removing his gun belt and holster, the sheriff followed Uncle Robert's instructions. It made for a tight fit on the settee, his arm pressed against Leah's.

Aunt Estelle sighed happily. "We think this will be a delightful arrangement. You might not immediately agree, Leah. You've got your mother's stubborn nature. But I promised her that I would make sure you were always taken care of, and I intend to keep my word. Nothing could please us more than to see you—"

"Estelle, please. . ."

The elderly woman clamped her lips tightly together and ceased her rambling.

Leah felt as though a fist had slammed into her midsection. So her suspicions were correct. But how could her aunt and uncle put her on the spot like this? And poor Sheriff Waite!

She slid her gaze to him. He'd doffed his hat at the door and now sat smoothing its brim, a slight tremor in his fingers.

"Leah, there has been a change of events since I wired you about coming to One Way." Uncle Robert's tone was the same he used to admonish his congregation. "As you're aware, I had arranged for you to become the town's first official schoolteacher."

"And you would have been, too, if Luther Welton hadn't—"

Would have been?

"Estelle, dear, allow me to finish."

"Of course, Robbie. Go ahead."

Leah squelched the urge to run. But run where?

"Unfortunately for all of us, Miss Collette Welton's fiancé broke their engagement. For that reason, Luther Welton, the superintendent of the school, replaced you with his younger cousin Collette for the teaching position. Even though Mr. Welton agreed with our decision to hire you at first, we had no recourse after he changed his mind. Mr. Welton is a powerful man here in town. Half of One Way backs his every decision."

"I have no job?" She had no school? No livelihood? And ten cents to her name—no, this couldn't be happening. . . . "There must be other employment for me."

"I'm afraid not. You see. . ." Sheriff Waite hesitated, shifting. "I know the lawmen in all the surrounding towns, and I've queried all of them. Seems there's no respectable positions available for a female." The sheriff set his hand over hers. It felt warm, comforting. "Miss Hermaning, believe me. I tried my best."

"I'm sure you did." She forced a jagged breath through her constricting chest.

"Leah, even though the ministry kept us away much of the time, we've always loved you like the daughter we never had." Uncle Robert left his seat and now stood near the wooden fireplace mantel. His voice was low and fatherly, as if he truly cared about her welfare. "And it's with deep regret I tell you that your aunt's eyes have been failing her for a while. We've heard of a doctor in Portland, Oregon, who is familiar with advanced medical techniques. He replied to our inquiry and believes he can help. We're eager to get there as soon as we can, before your aunt gets any worse."

"But Uncle Robert—"

He held up a hand.

Leah swallowed her protest. "When will you leave?"

"Tomorrow. At first light."

"But. . .I hoped we could spend some time together."

"We can't waste a moment more." Uncle Robert's voice said his mind was made up. "We need to be up in Glendive by Saturday evening. An evangelist is purchasing our wagon and mules for his ministry."

"Selling your wagon?" They had owned and operated their ministry from it for as long as Leah could remember.

"It's the only practical thing to do, although we'll receive a mere pittance for it and the animals."

"How will you get to Portland?"

"On Monday, your aunt and I will board the Northern Pacific in Glendive, and we'll reach our destination on Wednesday. Your aunt sees the doctor Thursday afternoon."

"So you see, dear," Auntie said, squinting at Leah, "we're on a very strict schedule."

"Take me with you," she begged. "I'll help you as we travel, and I'll take care of Aunt Estelle. I'll do anything you want."

"We don't have the funds. We're not getting much for our wagon and mules. But even if there was a way to take you along, your aunt and I don't believe it's God's will." A weighty pause. "Sheriff, why don't you take a turn to speak?"

Leah held her breath, not trusting herself to glance at the handsome man beside her.

He cleared his throat. "Miss Hermaning, I know this is sudden. . ." His voice wavered as his calloused palm tightened around her hand. She looked at him then, and he stared into her eyes as if—as if he sincerely meant the words to come.

But how could he?

The softness in his gaze said otherwise. "I'd be honored if you'd. . .that is, I'd like for you to. . .well. . ." He inhaled then blew out his breath. "Miss Leah Hermaning, I'd consider myself blessed if you'd become my wife."

Chapter 5

She didn't seem too surprised by his proposal, although the look on her face, which could only be described as utter dismay, did nothing to assure Jesse that she'd accept his offer. Rather than love and adoration, expressions he would have liked to see in the woman he hoped to marry, he saw disappointment and sadness. But what more could he expect, given the circumstances? No woman would jump for joy at a marriage offer like this.

But what set him back the most was the shame he sensed in her. She'd done nothing wrong. Sure, Miss Estelle had told him of the trouble Leah had gotten herself into, but, wanting the facts, Jesse learned the details for himself. He found no crime and saw no shame in what she'd done.

However, he figured Leah Hermaning was a woman who needed a man's protection, especially out here. She needed a place to call home. He needed a wife to run his homestead, a help meet, as the Bible called it. He liked her a whole lot already, and he could tell she liked him, too.

Sounded like a perfect fit to Jesse.

And then there was the upcoming election. Being a family man would undoubtedly give him a leg up, although it surprised even him that his intentions went beyond the immediate future. Even if he lost to Welton, Jesse knew that he and Miss Hermaning would have a happy future together. The peace he felt inside told him so.

Now, if only she'd see it that way.

"But, Uncle. . ." She swiped her eyes with the back of one hand. "I can't marry a man I don't know just because it's convenient." She glanced Jesse's way. "No offense intended, Sheriff."

"None taken."

"Now, Leah, in time you'll see that marrying Jesse is the best you could hope for, all things considered. He'll take care of you. And it will be good for him, too." Reverend Hermaning hesitated. "You might have heard that an election is coming up next week."

"I heard." She sounded so hurt that Jesse could have kicked himself with his own spurs for springing marriage on her this way.

But there wasn't time for courtship—not if she wanted her aunt and uncle present at the wedding.

"Miss Hermaning, believe me. The election is not the only reason I'm proposing. I need a wife. I want a family." Jesse rather enjoyed the pink blooming in her cheeks. Real sweet.

"Leah, dear, your aunt and I would have failed in One Way without Jesse. At first, we

had no success at all. Sunday after Sunday, we set up church under that tree by the river, and each week for the first three months, we sang hymns alone, and I preached only to your aunt."

"And that got old in a hurry." Miss Estelle rolled her failing eyes. "Wouldn't you agree, Jesse?"

He cleared his throat and worked the smile off his face. Since the day they'd met, he'd found Miss Estelle's childlike candidness amusing.

"We called on every home in town and a lot of them outside the town, but nobody wanted to come to church or hear our message of salvation through Jesus," the reverend continued. "We were so discouraged, we wanted to move on."

Miss Estelle sighed. "I did everything I could to get Robbie to quit this town. I didn't understand why we couldn't seem to bear fruit here. We'd been successful everywhere else we'd lived." She pulled a handkerchief from her sleeve and dabbed the sudden tears. "I thought we were out of God's will. It was a hard time for me."

It was the first time Jesse had ever seen sadness in the older woman's eyes. But when she pulled a second hanky out of the other sleeve and handed it to Leah, he realized his intended was all teared up, too—

Well, she was almost his intended.

What could he say to make her understand there was no shame in his proposal? Sure, there'd been no flowers or sweet words of love, but he could easily make that part up to her in the future. And who knew whether deep love could come from this awkward beginning?

"Miss Hermaning, I'm sorry you're taking my offer of marriage so hard, but—"

"Jesse, you're a smart man, but you don't know much about women." Miss Estelle blew noisily into her hanky. "She's upset about my hard times, not your marriage proposal."

"Oh?"

Miss Hermaning gave a bob of her head. "I had no idea you suffered so, Auntie." She sniffed.

"Dry your tears, ladies." The reverend peered at his niece, his thick dark brows pinched together. "Leah, the reason I told you this story is because I thought it'd make a difference to you. You see, one Sunday morning, Jesse showed up under that tree. After hearing the Gospel, he repented of his sins and became a Christian. Word got around, and the next week we had three families at church besides Jesse. Since that day, we've seen his faith tested and grow."

"So you see, dear, why your uncle and I are so fond of him. He's a product of our ministry—the ministry we thought was dead. However, if Jesse isn't reelected, there'll be no church building."

"Why can't the church meet in the schoolhouse?"

"We don't have one. School will meet in Luther Welton's barn. He's the man with the money in this town, and he's the only man with the space. We're still a pioneer town, and everybody besides Luther built as small as they could with high hopes to expand later." Jesse sat back on the settee. "Unfortunately, the town board has to approve all construction, and its members are waiting on the election results. Building the church will have to wait until spring—and to see who wins next week."

"What does a sheriff have to do with the town board's decision?"

"Here in One Way, Miss Hermaning, the sheriff sits on the board and has the deciding vote."

A spark of understanding lit in her gray eyes. "And let me guess—Mr. Welton is dead set against the idea of a church, but his plans for his hotel and gaming facility will be approved if he's elected sheriff."

"You hit the nail squarely on the head." Jesse grinned, pleased to see the light of concern in her gaze. Another woman might not care about anything but herself.

Miss Hermaning rubbed her temples as if combating an oncoming headache. "It's too much to think about. I'll need time to make a decision."

"I'm afraid we have no time, my dear." The reverend clasped his hands together as if the decision had been made, and Jesse's heart went out to Miss Hermaning.

Sitting forward, he took her hand and stood. "Will you come for a short stroll with me as you think about my offer?"

The Yellowstone River couldn't run as deep as Leah's feelings of humiliation. At least there was some dignity and acceptance in spinsterhood. But this sort of marriage—one arranged for a purpose and without love, without friendship even—that was a sham. She wanted no part of it!

And yet she had no viable options. No job, no money, and soon, no family to help support her.

Jesse held her hand all the way outside to the porch. There he pulled one of the ladder-back, rush-seat rockers close to the other. As they sat together, she shivered, even in the heat of summer. She should say something, at least answer his proposal, but words wouldn't come.

If only she were back in Newport, secure in her home and happy with her position—

Leah stopped that thought cold. To say she happily taught school children each day didn't accurately describe her life up until now. Certainly, she enjoyed her vocation, but being a spinster didn't make her happy. A family—a big family—now that would make her happy. Mother used to say that she prayed Leah would find happiness with a loving husband.

Was God answering Mother's prayers? Through a stranger's marriage proposal? Through Uncle Robert and Aunt Estelle?

"Miss Hermaning, may I call you Leah?"

He may as well. "Yes."

"I'm real sorry for dropping this marriage proposal on you the way I did. I'm sure that, like any young lady, you'd rather have a regular courtship. But my only chance at courting you is right now, and all I have to offer is myself and my homestead."

His humble words, spoken softly with his lazy, subtle twang, charmed her the same way his smile did.

"Is there no one else in this town for you to marry, Sheriff Waite?" It seemed preposterous that he'd have no prospects. But wasn't that what he'd said to his sister? No prospects?

"Call me Jesse. And no, there aren't many available young ladies in this town—in the county. And I can't marry just anyone. I need a woman who's heading in the same direction as I am, a woman of faith and prayer. Your aunt and uncle told me of your salvation experience, and after meeting you, I'm sure there's not another woman for me. Only you."

She should feel flattered. Instead she felt trapped.

As the sun began to turn the Yellowstone River to burnished copper, Leah's destiny became crystal clear.

"Can I pray for you, Leah? For us? Right now?"

Touched by the request, she nodded and allowed him to take her hand again. As he started his prayer, clearly confident in the Lord, his words touched a place in her heart that she hadn't known was there. A place of discontent that needed to be filled with—what?

"*Trust in the LORD with all thine heart; and lean not unto thine own understanding. In all thy ways acknowledge him, and he shall direct thy paths.*" Leah knew that passage from the Proverbs as well as her own name.

Was the Lord directing her paths even now? Surely she wasn't the first female thrust into an arranged marriage—Queen Esther came to mind. Esther's decision to follow her relative's instructions saved the Jewish people from certain destruction. Her marriage to the king fulfilled a greater purpose than her own.

"Sheriff Waite. . . I mean, Jesse, are you sure you want to marry me? Perhaps you're feeling pressured by my aunt and uncle—or the upcoming election."

"Yes, I'm sure." Another charming smile. "I've spent many sleepless nights thinking it over and committing the matter to prayer."

"But I haven't had the luxury of praying about it."

"That's why I brought you out here, to sit awhile and pray."

Leah wanted days to pray about it, not just a few minutes.

"You could always stay here at the boardinghouse." He gazed off in the distance. "Maybe respectable employment will open up somewhere. The Bigelows will welcome your help with their ministry, although I'm sure they can't pay you. They came from a large church in Billings, answered the call out here. Any money they have comes from their own savings, which they'll likely need to pay expenses in One Way until our church grows."

While an alternative, it seemed like more of a gamble. What if no employment opened up? What if Mrs. Rigley insisted on charging Leah rent? And to live in such a tiny place as that closet sounded like a death sentence.

Jesse's offer, on the other hand, had the promise of life. New life.

"*Trust in the LORD with all thine heart; and lean not unto thine own understanding. . .*"

Yes, God was here, directing her path. However, the one thing she'd gleaned from this time of prayer was that her life would never be the same—*she* would never be the same.

For Leah, there was only one way to find possible happiness. "Yes, I'll marry you, Jesse."

Chapter 6

While Leah remained outside on the porch, Jesse went back into the parlor to deliver the "good news" to Aunt Estelle and Uncle Robert. He returned several minutes later saying the older couple would meet them at Jesse's homestead, where the wedding would be held. Aunt Estelle needed to ride over in their wagon because of her poor eyesight.

He offered his arm, and Leah took it. They began walking toward a log house, a barn, and several outbuildings. Nervous flutters filled her insides. How could she live in such a place? No brick structures, churches, schools. No paved roads. . .no department stores!

"Could we stop just a moment under the church tree?" Perhaps it would calm her.

"If that's what you'd like."

When they reached the tree, Jesse picked a bunch of wild white blooms from the riverbank and presented them to her. "They're windflowers. Probably not as good as a wedding bouquet of roses, but—"

"They're lovely, Jesse. Thank you."

She glanced up into the treetop. Barely any breeze stirred the heart-shaped leaves, but they rustled and made a sighing sound—just like the one sound she missed most: the surf.

She sat on the bench nearest the trunk and closed her eyes. "How can this be? I can almost imagine I'm at the seashore."

"Well, never having heard the ocean before, I'm not one to say, but more than one traveler has told me that when the cottonwood's leaves rustle, they sound like waves."

"Will I be able to hear it from inside your house?"

"Most likely, if you listen real close. The front and bedroom windows face this way."

Thank You, God. Leah would probably never see the ocean again, but it would still lull her to sleep every night during the summer. Such a perfect wedding gift from her heavenly Father.

Standing, Leah took Jesse's arm again. She felt more ready to see her new home.

No sooner had her foot touched the first step of the wide front porch when a large black-and-white dog came running from around the house. He skidded to a halt, barking at first then wagging his tail and sidling up to Jesse.

He knelt and gave the hound a good rubbing. "Your aunt said you don't mind pets."

"Actually, I love animals."

"Glad to hear it." Jesse stood. "This is Sarge."

Leah allowed the dog to smell her hand before she gave him a scratch behind the ears. "Sarge, I hope you and I will become good friends."

But, more importantly, she hoped she and her husband would become good friends. Someday.

If that wasn't the sorriest excuse for a wedding. It was over within minutes. The marriage license had been signed, Nellie and her husband Zeb penning their names as witnesses, while close friends gathered around. But Leah deserved better than such a hasty affair. It ended so quick, he didn't get a chance to give her her special wedding gift—his mother's ring.

Worse, he didn't kiss his bride after they took their vows!

Why this fool idea of marrying Leah off practically the minute she got off the stagecoach? Maybe he should have insisted the wedding take place tomorrow. . .except he knew the reverend's intentions were honorable. The man was simply preoccupied with Miss Estelle's failing health and their journey to Portland.

Besides, Jesse could kiss his bride later.

Yes, sir, she was a treasure, and he knew it. But where did her aunt and uncle get the idea that she was so plain? Standing here, watching her fuss around the kitchen alongside his sister, Jesse felt particularly pleased with his new wife.

They'd be happy together, all right—once her shock wore off.

After enjoying the supper provided by several guests, Nellie and Zeb took baby Henry home for bed. The Bigelows, with their boys in tow, and Mrs. Rigley left next. Will and Emma Canfield, owners of the town's general store, took their leave shortly thereafter.

Finally, the reverend and Miss Estelle were the only two left.

"Good-bye, my dear," the reverend told Leah, although he made no move to give her a hug.

"Good-bye, Uncle."

Miss Estelle grabbed ahold of her and hugged her tightly. "You were the prettiest bride I've seen in a long while."

That wasn't saying much, since Miss Estelle couldn't see the next step in front of her face.

Leah didn't seem to take notice. "Thank you, Auntie. I'll miss you both. I'm sorry I won't see you tomorrow before you leave."

"At first light you'll have your own duties to fulfill," the reverend said. "We'll say our good-byes now. It's best for all of us."

Leah's features fell with obvious sadness. Jesse slipped his arm around her waist to show his support. She could lean on him if she needed to.

"You'll be fine, dear." Miss Estelle patted Leah's arm. "Robbie and I are leaving you in the hands of a good, strong, capable man."

Leah merely nodded and sniffed into her hanky.

Poor thing. He tightened his hold.

"I'll expect a letter soon, telling me of a baby on the way."

He heard, and felt, Leah's sudden intake of air, although she didn't reply.

Jesse chuckled to cover for her, unsure who was more outspoken and opinionated—Miss Estelle or Mrs. Rigley.

Leah moved to hug her aunt one last time, and Jesse released his hold on her. He

walked the aging couple to their wagon and saw Miss Estelle safely inside. "Godspeed, Reverend. Let us know when you and Miss Estelle arrive in Oregon and what the doctor says."

The older gent tugged on the rim of his hat. Then with a flick of the reins, the wagon started forward.

Back inside the house, Jesse closed the door. Leah turned into a busy hummingbird, flitting here and there.

Jesse trailed her into the bedroom—their bedroom. With that big, built-up hat of hers now on the dresser, she looked a half foot shorter—and softer, too.

"Leah. . ."

She rushed past him and back into the kitchen. She rummaged around in the cupboard, looking for who-knew-what, while he stayed out of the way.

"What can I help you find?"

"Nothing. I'm just looking around, getting familiar with the layout of things."

The layout? On their wedding night? "Can't that wait till tomorrow?"

She turned from the open drawer, her gray eyes wider than usual.

Was she frightened? Of course she would be. She didn't know him—or know that Jesse wouldn't force his husbandly rights on her. Well, he wouldn't.

"Let's sit out on the porch and relax until the mosquitoes chase us inside."

Her entire being seemed to melt with relief. "Yes, I think I'd like that."

She poured them some leftover coffee, and, tin cups in hand, they headed outside and sat down.

Night sounds filled the air, but the silence between Leah and him didn't seem natural. Jesse had to break it.

"Leah, I'm honored that you've become my wife."

That brought her gaze up from her cup. "Thank you. I'm sorry that I'm not great company. I get quiet when I'm tired."

So that was it. At least her silence didn't mean she was completely disgusted with him. "I think we should take things kind of slow. You can have your privacy in the bedroom, and I'll bunk out in the barn."

She fell silent for several agonizingly long seconds. "Thank you," she said at last.

Jesse stood and stretched. "You've had a hard day, so it might be a good idea to turn in early."

The sound of harness and horse drew his attention. Warren Givens's rig pulled up the road and stopped right outside the door. *Leah's luggage.* He'd forgotten about it in all the fuss of the wedding. Jesse stood to greet Givens, who eased himself down off the wagon bench.

"Heard you married Reverend Hermaning's niece, Jess."

"That's right, I did."

"You still can't win the election Tuesday. Getting hitched today don't make you a family man like Luther Welton."

Jesse almost laughed. Welton, a family man? No, he was a man who enjoyed exploiting women, and Jesse doubted he treated his wife with the reverence God demanded.

Taking one side of Leah's trunk, Jesse motioned for Givens to take the other. Grudgingly, he did so. They carried the weighty object into the house then set it under the open north window. Leah followed them in, carrying hatboxes and her valise.

"Appreciate you bringing her belongings over." Jesse saw the man to the door.

"Sure thing." Givens held out his hand.

Jesse dropped a few coins into it, and Givens left.

Closing the front door, Jesse turned to find Leah standing closely behind him, her expression tentative.

"I. . .I have a request."

"All right," Jesse said. "Let's hear it."

"A bath. I've been delighting in the idea of a bath for days. Will you point me in the direction of the tub?"

Jesse rubbed the back of his neck. "No tub here in the house." At her disappointed pout, he added, "But there's a nice spring-fed pond out back. It's real secluded. And the outhouse is fairly new."

"AAAEEEHH!" The sound was akin to a cougar's angry screech. Leah whirled on her heel, marched into the bedroom, and slammed the door.

Jesse put his hands on his hips. *Whoo-eee!* That woman had some fire in her veins.

He shook his head. So this was what married life was like.

Chapter 7

As the sun came up, painting burgundy and gray streaks across the eastern sky, Jesse strode to the barn. Quietly, he saddled his horse and rode into town. After tethering the sorrel outside the sheriff's office, he went inside, made coffee, and shuffled through the pile of paperwork waiting for him on his desk. But when the jailhouse clock struck eight, he hightailed it to Will Canfield's mercantile.

If Leah wanted a bathtub, he'd buy her one.

He even stayed up most of last night, drawing plans for a bathroom facing that tree she was so fond of. During the summer months, his bride could soak in her tub to her heart's content, listen to the rush of the cottonwood leaves, and pretend she was on her seashore back East.

An indoor, private bathroom. That'd make her happy. . .wouldn't it?

Jesse reached the store's entrance just as Will flipped the OPEN sign on the door.

"Well now, I didn't expect to see you so soon, Jess." Will ran a hand over his balding head. "Whatcha lookin' for?"

"One of your catalogs. My wife wants a bathtub."

"No foolin'? And you're going to get her one?"

"Yep. I want her to be happy. I mean. . .happier than she already is." He blew out a breath. He couldn't let word get out that Leah was unhappy.

"Understand."

Will set down the catalog and Jesse leafed through it, marveling at the many makes and models of tubs. Which one would Leah want?

After several minutes of turning page after page, he slapped the catalog closed and looked at Will. "Reckon I'll bring Leah in first thing Monday morning and let her pick out which one she wants."

"You're smarter than I thought."

Jesse grinned at his friend's wisecrack.

The bell above the door jingled, and Jesse glanced over to see Luther Welton swagger into the store.

"Thought I saw you walk in here, Jesse." Welton made his way over to the counter. His midsection overlapped his belt buckle, and reaching his destination, he hiked up his gray trousers. "Things must not be going well at home if you're here so early this morning."

Jesse ignored the taunt. "Things are just fine at home, Luther." He leaned sideways against the counter. "How 'bout with you? You're up and about early."

"Just so happens that I ate breakfast with Dirk Fields and Bob Boswell."

Jesse knew the men well. Fields owned the bank in town and Boswell raised cattle

on his nearby ranch. While they were supportive of Jesse, they'd been waffling with their votes for some time.

"Those fellas are real keen on my business ideas." Welton copied Jesse's stance. "Furthermore, I can negotiate with the railroad, same as you—maybe better. So if you think you'll win this election on account of marrying some traveling preacher's niece last night, you're dead wrong."

Jesse didn't rattle that easily. "The good folks of One Way will decide who's the better man for the job come Tuesday morning."

"And so they will." Welton jutted out his chin. "By the way, I heard from my sweet little cousin Collette, who heard from Mrs. Rigley, who heard from Mrs. Hermaning, that your wife is here 'cuz she got into some trouble back in Newport. That true?"

"What kind of trouble are you talking about?"

"Criminal kind of trouble."

Jesse had figured the particulars of Leah's past would surface sooner or later. He'd hoped later. But One Way was a small town, and gossip spread like the plague.

"I'm aware of a demonstration my wife was involved in, but she didn't do anything unlawful."

"We'll just see about that. Unlike you, Sheriff, I've got friends in high places all over this country."

"I'm glad for you. What man doesn't need friends?" With a nod at Will, Jesse took his leave. While irritated, Jesse didn't feel troubled in the least. He and Leah had the truth on their side.

He just prayed his new wife was up to facing it—head-on.

Leah awoke far later than she'd intended, but sleeping in a real bed, a comfortable one at that, felt heavenly. Over the past six days she'd snatched catnaps while sitting on the train, since she hadn't been able to afford a berth in the sleeping car.

Yawning, stretching, she peeled back the quilt and stood. Pulling on her wrapper, she strode to the bedroom door and opened it. The house was quiet.

"Jesse?"

No answer.

Leah padded into the front room to get a good look at Jesse's craftsmanship. The waning light of her early evening wedding hadn't given her the opportunity to appreciate the details she now saw in the stone hearth and chimney. And the oak mantle had been polished until it gleamed. Functional and beautiful with its rockers and armchairs, all the room needed was some decorations. She saw none, no artwork, no knickknacks, no photographs. Would Jesse mind if she placed her framed portrait of Mother and herself on one of the side tables?

Across the room, the solid dining table took up most of the space. On it, Leah glimpsed the windflowers in a jar of water, sitting in the middle of the table. Her wedding bouquet. How thoughtful that Jesse preserved it, although she'd rather have no reminders of that disgraceful display called her wedding ceremony.

Leah spotted Jesse's Bible. Had he been reading it before he left this morning?

She ought to be more grateful. This good man had given her a home and his name, and he'd made no demands on her on their wedding night. What's more, he'd given her

a chance to restore her dignity with a new life.

But would she find happiness here? With him?

Her gaze fell on several rough sketches. Examining them, she realized they were plans to build a room with a bathtub. She perked up. He'd do that for her? Construct an indoor bathroom? No one else had ever done anything of this magnitude for her. Never.

Now she felt even more ashamed over her temper fit last night.

Setting down the sketches, she found Jesse's note to her. He had some work to finish and had gone to the office. He'd be back in time for supper.

Leah felt put off by his abandonment, although this might be an ideal time to settle in and familiarize herself with her new surroundings after she finished her morning routine.

After visiting the outhouse, a true wilderness experience, Leah returned to the bedroom, where she washed with water from a pitcher Jesse had brought in last night. Then she dressed and pinned up her hair. Catching her reflection in the mirror, she saw that she didn't appear any different. The same tree-bark brown hair framed her oval face. However, she felt different—and her life was very, very different.

She was married now.

A knock sounded on the front door, followed by a few more raps. Jesse's hound's deep bark resounded through the house.

"Hush, Sarge." Leah gave the door's handle a yank and found a smiling young mother with wispy blond hair peering back at her. A small girl rested on her jutted-out hip. Sarge ventured out and circled the woman's wagon and mules as if inspecting them.

"Are you the new Mrs. Waite?"

Leah almost said no, but. . .yes, she was. She nodded.

"This is for you and Jesse." She held out a basket of eggs. "Just a little something to wish you both well in your life together."

"Thank you, Mrs. . . ."

"Smith. Rebecca Smith. My husband, Eden, and I have a place not too far from you. Eden was at the livery last night and heard Jesse got hisself a wife. I just had to come over and say hello." She smiled, looking somewhat bashful.

"I'm glad you did. My name is Leah. Please, won't you come in?"

"Wish I could. Maybe another time." The woman transferred the child to her other hip, her green skirt rotating slightly. "I have errands and chores to tend to. I was just passing by."

"Well, thank you again. Perhaps we can get better acquainted at church tomorrow. We meet beneath the cottonwood tree near the river. Everyone's welcome."

The woman seemed to think it over. "Maybe we'll join you. I'll check with Eden."

Leah bid Mrs. Smith farewell and watched as the young mother set the child in the back of the wagon, climbed aboard the driver's bench, and, flicking the reins, drove off.

Would Leah have to learn how to drive a wagon? Gracious, but she knew nothing about it—or the horses or mules. She was accustomed to riding in trolleys on paved streets. . .and bicycles.

As she set the eggs in the cool pantry, Leah's gaze fixed on the empty shelves. They'd need some basics. Flour, sugar. . .

Another knock on the door. A second neighbor stood on the porch, bearing fresh-baked bread. She was followed by another and another. The traffic in and out of the

house didn't stop until noon.

The sun shone high in the sky when Leah collapsed into a chair on the porch. Another wagon pulled up, and Leah grimaced. While she enjoyed meeting other ladies, young and old alike, her body ached with exhaustion and she felt overwhelmed with the task of getting her new home in order.

It's Nellie. She relaxed, watching her new sister-in-law climb down from the perch. She waved to Leah before lifting baby Henry from the makeshift crib in back of the wagon along with a small carryall.

"I'm glad to see you," Leah called. "Here, let me help you." She met Nellie at the edge of the porch and took the tapestry-covered bag.

"I came to deliver a message from Jesse. He and several other men went after some cattle rustlers. Jesse wasn't sure when he'd get home and said I ought to let you know. He and his men rode out of town at a full gallop. I'm surprised you didn't hear the commotion."

She hadn't. "Jesse went after cattle rustlers?" Leah pushed her hair off her forehead. "But that's dangerous."

"That's his job."

"Has anybody ever gotten hurt doing a job like this?"

"I can see the concern all over your face." Nellie started toward the entrance. "But no need to fret. Instead, let's go inside. Jesse mentioned something else, which prompted me to form a grand plan for the two of us."

"What is it?"

"I'll tell you, but first, do you mind if I put Henry down for his nap? He likes the back porch just fine. Jesse made the sweetest nest for him out there."

"Of course I don't mind. You're welcome here anytime."

Leah set down the soft-sided bag, her mind whirring. She should have thought earlier about the hazards of Jesse's job—possible danger every day of his life. And all she could do was pray and wait for him to come home unharmed.

"Give me just a few minutes to rock Henry to sleep."

As if understanding, the baby squawked in protest.

While Nellie rocked and sang the infant to sleep, Leah could hardly sit still in the chair next to her. Every time she tried to make a mental list of all the tasks she needed to do in her new home, her mind raced with imagined scenes of Jesse shot or injured while trying to bring in the rustlers.

"Are you ready?" Nellie held her snoozing son.

Leah hastened to her feet. Anything was better than sitting here, worrying. "I'm ready. . .I think."

"Follow me. And please bring my bag with you." Nellie led her across the back lean-to porch. She stopped by the crafted wooden crib, sheltered from the elements by an overhang, a safe haven for Henry.

The hound ran over to them, sniffed around, then plopped down nearby.

"Sarge lets me know if Henry starts crying. Between the barking and the bawling, they make such a racket that I can hear them in the barn."

Leah caught Nellie's smile. Like brother, like sister. Always smiling.

Nellie reached for her carryall and led Leah down a pathway that wound around a half-dozen fruit trees, their apples and pears nearly ready for harvest. At the path's end, a

crystal-clear body of water spread out for at least a quarter of a mile. So this was the pond Jesse mentioned last night.

"Here's your nature-made bathtub."

Leah sighed, wistfully. . .regrettably. "Nellie, I appreciate your idea. I'd like nothing better than a good soak, but I am not bathing outdoors." She glanced around. "In the open! What if another neighbor stops by?"

"Your nearest neighbor is half a mile away, and Main Street is equally as far in the other direction. It's Saturday afternoon. No one is out and about. Men are working and women are home tending to children and homes and preparing supper." Nellie unbuttoned her dress and pulled it over her head. "Now, strip down to your chemise and your drawers, and let's have ourselves a bath. I even remembered soap." She pulled a bar from the carryall and then produced several thick towels. Next she removed her corset before sitting on a nearby rock, pulling off her shoes, and rolling down her stockings.

And she expected Leah to do the same? But how could she undress in the wilds of Montana? Heavens, no!

Clad in only her underwear, Nellie jogged to the water's edge and splashed as she made her way into the wide, deep pond. Soon she floated on her back. "Come on in, Leah. The water is so refreshing."

It looked it, and on this hot August afternoon, Leah felt just as wilted and exhausted as when she climbed off the stage yesterday.

"Are you sure no one will come calling and see us?"

"Positive. Besides, everyone around here bathes in one of the nearby rivers or a pond during the summer months. I learned to bathe in my basics so I can wash them when I wash myself. Saves me time and, quite often, embarrassment."

"I imagine."

"Jesse's lucky to have a pond so protected by trees and shrubs, although he keeps them cut back. Growing up, we called this place 'Hidden Pond,' and then years ago, Jesse purchased the land and built his homestead."

Leah's confidence grew, yet she still hesitated.

"Your only other option for a bath is the boardinghouse, but then you'll have to listen to Mrs. Rigley's grousing and Collette Welton's whining."

That sounded dreadful.

"Collette has been in a huff since the day she arrived in One Way. Her cousin Luther wants to teach her some responsibility. He not only gave her your teaching position, which Collette thinks she's too good for, but he also arranged for her to live at the boardinghouse instead of with him and his family in that great big home he owns. He insisted Collette pay rent to Mrs. Rigley." Nellie's laugh seemed to rise as high as the towering pines.

"Seems odd." Leah unbuttoned her shirtwaist and shrugged out of it. "I would have expected Mr. Welton to welcome his cousin into his home."

"I thought so, too, at first. Now I believe it's about the wisest thing Luther's ever done—not giving Collette your job, but everything else. Besides, Luther values peace in his household. Collette is always up to some sort of trickery."

Leah made a mental note to stay clear of Collette Welton.

She finished undressing down to her "basics," and within moments she joined her sister-in-law in the pond. The water, at its deepest, came up to their chins, and oh! how

delightful it felt against her perspiring skin. If only she could also wash away her growing concern for Jesse's safety.

She lathered up with the mildly scented soap and washed her hair while Nellie made a quick dash up to the porch to check on Henry—just in case Sarge gave in to instinct and chased a rabbit or wild turkey. She returned with the report that the baby and hound still slept soundly.

"Did Jesse say where they thought the cattle rustlers were headed?" Leah took a turn around the pond, floating on her back, staring at the endless blue Montana sky.

"West of here, I think."

Leah scanned the western horizon as if she thought she'd see her husband there. What would she do if something happened to him? Even if he was fine today, he'd face life-threatening danger every day of his life—if he won the election.

And who'd have thought she'd care so much about his safety after only one day of marriage?

Nellie interrupted Leah's thoughts with a splash of water and a grin. "I thought a good soaking might be exactly what you'd enjoy after a long journey."

"You were right." And her heavenly Father provided it, using Nellie as His conduit. While this "bath" wasn't what Leah had planned or expected, it far exceeded all she'd asked.

"Jesse mentioned that he's buying you a tub and building a room just for it."

"Yes, I assumed so, when I saw the plans he drew up. I can't tell you how happy it made me to see them. In Newport, where I come from, everyone has a bathtub, and I'd miss it."

"My brother wants to make you happy, that's for sure."

"I hope to make him happy as well." But could she accomplish such a feat?

Of course she could. . .and would. She had plenty of time to become a good wife to Jesse. They had the rest of their lives together.

A shiver ran through her. That is, if he came home today. . .alive.

Chapter 8

After turning Patriot loose to graze in the pasture behind the barn, Jesse walked back to the house. The soft lamplight glowing from the side window told him Leah had waited up. Even so, he tiptoed through the back door in case she'd fallen asleep.

"Jesse!" She met him as he reached the kitchen. "Thank God, it's you. I thought a burglar was sneaking into the house."

He grinned at her big-city terminology. "Not too many burglars around here." But they did have their share of horse thieves, cattle rustlers, and thugs, like those who ran in Butch Cassidy's Wild Bunch gang. However, Jesse wasn't about to tell Leah that.

"You're all right?" She rushed toward him then stopped short.

Had she been about to embrace him? Jesse smiled. He'd like that. He closed the distance between them and pulled her into his arms. She didn't resist, and, slowly, her arms came up and she rested her hands at his waist. He closed his eyes. She smelled so sweet, with her silky brown hair falling down her back.

Jesse held her closer. Would she prefer he slept in the barn again tonight? He'd prefer not to.

"I was worried about your safety."

"I'm just fine," he whispered near her ear.

To his disappointment, she pulled away. "You must be hungry. I can fix you some eggs."

Jesse kneaded his whiskered jaw. He was hungry, all right—they'd ridden the range all day without stopping to eat. "Eggs will taste real good."

"Scrambled?"

"I'm not picky." But he probably smelled awfully ripe from sitting in the saddle all day beneath the hot sun. "I'll go wash up, so take your time cooking."

He strode to the closet containing linens and found it had been rearranged. Nicely rearranged. He pulled out a towel. In the bedroom that looked suddenly very lived-in, he found his clean clothes occupying one side of the wardrobe with Leah's hung and folded on the other side. It pleased him to see she was settling in.

A change of clothes and a towel tucked beneath one arm and a bar of soap in his hand, Jesse passed Leah, purposely too close and earning him an excuse to put his hand on her waist.

"Oh, pardon me, Jesse. I didn't mean to get in your way."

"You're not in my way." He would have liked to get a kiss, but what did he expect? They'd known each other for only a day.

Leah sat at the table with Jesse as he ate and told her about the hours they'd spent tracking the thieves.

"You're a good cook," he said, changing the subject.

"Scrambling eggs isn't difficult. And the sweet bread came from a neighbor who stopped by this morning."

"There's good folks in One Way."

"So I've learned." Her fingertips fell on his sketches. "I saw these this morning." She held up his plans for her bathroom.

"What do you think?"

"I think I'll be the envy of all the ladies in One Way." Maybe she already was, having married Jesse Waite. Leah was sophisticated enough to know she could have fared much worse, considering hers was a marriage of convenience.

But God had a purpose for her, just as He had a purpose for Queen Esther.

"Does it. . .make you happy?"

Leah smiled. As Nellie told her this afternoon, Jesse wanted to please her. "Yes, it makes me very happy."

"Whew!" He sat back in his chair. "That's a relief. I fretted about it all day."

"But you were hunting down cattle rustlers. I would have thought you'd fret over finding them, not worry about my bathtub and me."

"You're more important to me than finding rustlers."

Touched, she traced a scratch in the tabletop with her forefinger. "Did you find them?"

"Yes, I found several in the store's catalog. But I figured I'd let you pick out the one you want on Monday morning."

"No, Jesse, not the bathtub—the cattle rustlers." She giggled. "Did you find them?"

"Oh. . .yeah, we found them. Returned the cattle to the Abby Springs ranch, too."

"All in a day's work, eh, Sheriff?" Leah couldn't help teasing him just a bit.

"And without firing a single shot." He sent her a wink.

She grinned. Perhaps she would enjoy being married to Jesse Waite.

Rather than explore that possibility, she hastened to clear his dishes from the table. "I hope you don't mind, but I'll clean up the kitchen tomorrow before we go to church. I'm exhausted." She made for the bedroom. "Good night."

"Night, Leah." His voice sounded soft and full of tenderness. If he felt miffed by her hasty exit, it wasn't evident in his tone.

Once in the sanctity of the bedroom, she closed the door and leaned against it. Her breaths came in short bursts, as though she'd run up to the house from the pond. How could this be happening to her? She and Jesse had met only yesterday. Oh, but he was so handsome. . .and so kind.

Could it be?

She pondered the question. *Lord, could I be falling in love with my husband?*

Listening to Reverend Bigelow deliver an eloquent message beneath the whispering cottonwood, Leah decided Uncle Robert would be so proud. She hoped her aunt and uncle were safe in Glendive. Tomorrow morning they'd board the train for Portland. For all

his terseness, Uncle Robert surely loved God. And he clearly loved Auntie, too, taking that long trip, selling his wagon and possessions, seeking help for her failing eyesight—treatments that may not even work. Leah never noticed, never appreciated until now, the subtle way husbands loved their wives as Christ loved the Church.

She glanced around the small congregation and counted six children, including Reverend and Mrs. Bigelow's boys. And what a joy to see Rebecca Smith and her husband, Eden, here today with their little girl. Of course, Nellie and Zeb had come with baby Henry. Leah caught her sister-in-law's gaze, and they exchanged smiles.

And then it hit her. While Leah had said good-bye to her only living relatives yesterday, God had graciously, lovingly, given her a new family. A new beginning.

Looking at her husband sitting beside her, Leah threaded her hand around his arm. He glanced her way and gave her hand an affectionate squeeze. So far, this hadn't been punishment at all, and she truly believed that her aunt and uncle had her best interests in mind when they'd instructed her to join them in One Way after she'd gotten herself in such a mess back home.

Back home. . . No. This was her home now.

She peeked at Jesse from beneath her pompadour and decorated hat. At breakfast, he'd told her women were plain and practical out here and that she needn't fuss with her appearance, but Leah wasn't quite ready to abandon the latest fashions just yet. Her refusal to comply, however, caused her to look a bit silly this morning, although before they left the house, Jesse had said she looked lovely.

She didn't deserve such a good man, and she knew she had to tell him the truth about what happened in Newport, no matter how much shame and pain it brought her.

And tell him she would. Someday.

The service concluded with "Bringing in the Sheaves." Zeb accompanied the singing with his fiddle, although it didn't drown out Mrs. Rigley's enthusiastic and slightly off-key alto voice. When the believers dispersed, Jesse led Leah around and introduced her to some people she hadn't yet met.

"Jesse, as a businessman," Mr. Fields said, his slicked inky-black hair shining beneath the sun, "I have to admit I like the hotel idea that Welton's proposing. He has a point—a church can meet anywhere. A school, too."

"Well, Dirk, it's your vote and your prerogative."

Leah couldn't believe what she'd just heard. The statement was hardly that of a man running for public office. Jesse's character and qualifications for the job far exceeded Luther Welton's. She'd gleaned that fact as soon as she'd met Mr. Welton. Surely everyone else couldn't be so fooled.

But even if they were, why didn't Jesse do his best to convince the man he conversed with and others that he was most suited for the job? And a church and school. . .they were essentials to a town.

Leah caught something out of the corner of her eye. A woman a ways off, standing outside the boardinghouse, waving a hanky.

"Jesse?" She tugged on his arm. "Excuse me for interrupting, but who is that near Mrs. Rigley's place?"

He glanced in that direction. "That's Collette Welton." He squinted, watching her. "But what she's doing is anyone's guess."

As the last syllable rolled off his tongue, the ground beneath them began to rumble.

A thundering off in the distance rapidly drew near.

An earthquake?

Leah clung to Jesse. A collective gasp went up from the ladies. A couple of children whimpered while men murmured among themselves.

A heartbeat later, riders on horseback came into view, seven of them, all galloping at a breakneck pace past the church tree and Jesse's homestead. They stirred up a cloud of dust that wafted over the gathered believers. Leah coughed despite the hanky she held to her mouth and nose.

" 'Scuse me, Leah. . .Dirk. Seems I have work to do."

"No, Jesse. . ." Leah lurched forward as he pulled from her grasp. Despite the heat, a cold shiver shook her to the bones and rattled her mind. Those reckless, rowdy men outnumbered her husband. He could be hurt—or worse.

"Arrest those men for disturbing the peace!" Reverend Bigelow called after Jesse's retreating form.

"Throw them in jail, and toss the key in the Yellowstone!" Mrs. Rigley hollered.

"Jesse, come back!" Before Leah could go after him, Nellie stepped into her path. The expression on her sister-in-law's round face spoke volumes. Leah's shoulders sagged. "You're going to tell me he's just doing his job, aren't you?"

Nellie gave a nod but took Leah's hand. "He's a big boy. He can handle himself. Don't you worry."

But she did worry. *Lord, please, protect him!*

And in that moment, Leah got a taste of what it felt like to be a sheriff's wife. But, even more, she glimpsed what life in One Way would be like if Luther Welton became the law in this town. A renewed sense of purpose sprang up inside Leah, and she knew what she had to do.

Somehow, some way, she had to make sure Jesse was reelected on Tuesday morning.

But how?

Chapter 9

"If Welton was sheriff, we wouldn't be standing in this jailhouse right now."

"Yeah. A man can't have no fun while you're the sheriff, Jesse Waite."

He ignored the men's griping. He'd caught up with five of the miscreants involved in the horse-racing incident this morning and had just fined them for disorderly conduct, disturbing the peace, and endangering the lives of One Way's citizens.

"You were menaces to society. Folks were out and about with their young children. Someone could have been hurt. . .or killed." His words clearly did little to impress the men. They stood in front of his desk like misbehaving schoolboys.

Jesse handed each man his ticket and hefty fine, then he scheduled the court dates. "You can pay me now or wait and argue your side in front of the judge when he comes at the end of the month. If your case isn't dismissed and you don't pay your fine, I'll get the marshal involved. Understand?" Jesse returned their holsters and firearms. "Now, get out of here."

Jesse followed the rowdies outside, his gaze trailing them as they swaggered back to the saloon. He glanced at Leah, standing off to the left. She'd been waiting patiently on the boardwalk until he finished his business, looking fetching in her cream-colored dress. A straw hat decorated with feathers was pinned to her poufy hair that was supposed to be fashionable. Jesse didn't know much about that, but he knew his wife looked pretty—pretty enough to show off here in town.

He gave her a smile. "All done."

"Good." She appeared happier than Jesse had seen her yet. "How about if we go on a picnic—just the two of us—this afternoon?"

"I'd like that." He hadn't done that in years. Sounded like just what he needed after a morning like this, too. He offered his arm. "A picnic."

But it was more than that. A romantic outing was just the place to give Leah her wedding present. Who knew. . .maybe he'd get a kiss in return.

❧

Her hand in Jesse's, Leah walked beside him along the Yellowstone River. Could this day get any better? A handsome man, a basket filled with Mrs. Dinsmore's gift of fried chicken and biscuits, and a prairie stretched out before them—it seemed like the perfect Sunday afternoon to Leah.

They crossed the river on the cable-drawn ferry as the sun hit the middle of the sky. Reaching the opposite shore, they hiked into the Badlands and spread their blanket at the foot of a butte.

"How did you enjoy your first church service under a tree?" Jesse stretched out his

legs in front of him.

"I enjoyed it—until the horse race. If I were a betting woman, which I'm not, I'd say Luther Welton was in on that practical joke to disrupt our fellowship."

"You'd win." Jesse arched a brow. "If you were a betting woman."

Leah grinned and unpacked their picnic lunch as patches of long grass stirred on a gentle breeze. A hawk soared above them and landed on a high, rocky ridge. "It's barren out here and yet peaceful. . .pretty."

"At night, it's wickedly dangerous, with bears and wolves. See to it you never get stranded on this side of the river."

"I'll make sure I don't." She passed the chicken and biscuits to Jesse before making a plate for herself.

Jesse prayed over their meal, asking God to bless Mrs. Dinsmore for her kindness. Then he dug right in. "This tastes a lot like my ma's chicken."

Leah took a bite, tasting a peppery seasoning. She liked it. "I don't know much about your family. How long ago did your mother pass away?"

"Going on ten years. She developed a fever, and consumption set in. Her last days were the worst of my life. All we could do was watch her waste away. Pa took it the hardest. He was so overcome with grief, he left southeastern Montana for the silver mines out west."

"And you stayed here."

"At first, since Nellie needed looking after because Pa returned to mining. But then my baby sister insisted on some education, so I found her a boarding school in Billings and I joined the army so I could pay for it. The next year, Pa was killed in an explosion." Jesse leaned back against a tall, smooth rock, his gaze far off. "It was hard, but we made it."

He blinked, and the past vanished. A smile spread across his face. "After I served my term, I came back here, bought land, and decided to homestead. Nellie returned soon after I did. She met Zeb and got married."

Leah's life had its share of heartaches, too. "My father died when I was three, so it was just Mother and me." She didn't add that her father was an abusive drunk.

"How did you get by?"

"Mother managed to get a job teaching school, and she inspired me to earn my teaching certificate, too." A familiar sorrow cast a pall over her. She swallowed hard. The last thing she wanted was to spoil their day with her tears.

"I'm glad you're my wife, Leah." Jesse's deep voice cut through her pain. "You, me, your aunt and uncle, Nellie, Zeb, and baby Henry—we have a good start to a fine family."

She had to agree. Blinking off her pitiful background, she handed him a bottle of sarsaparilla and opened another for herself. Then she held it high. "A toast to our new life together?"

"Hear, hear." Jesse took a swig from his.

She giggled. While it was hardly a prestigious beverage, and she wasn't sipping from crystal stemware, the ritual carried the same celebratory effect.

After they finished eating, Jesse pulled a folded checkered handkerchief from his shirt pocket. "I've failed to do a lot of things since we met. But I want to make this right before any more time goes by."

His sudden solemnity claimed her breath.

"I neglected to give you a wedding ring the night we took our vows." He unwrapped

the cloth and revealed a smooth gold band. "This was Ma's. The day she died, she gave it to me to give to my bride. Will you wear it? If you'd rather, I can buy you one of your own."

His mother's ring. How precious. "Thank you, Jesse."

He slid the simple band onto her finger. "I thought long and hard about what a man's got to do for his woman about as soon as I decided I needed a wife. So I'm going to make you a promise that goes beyond the wedding vows we took." Jesse cupped her face in his strong hands. "I promise you that I'll do all I can to make you happy, to lead you in a stronger relationship with the Lord, and to provide for you the best I can."

"This ring will always remind me of those words, Jesse. It's as beautiful as your promise."

"As beautiful as my bride."

Beautiful? No one, other than Mother, had ever called her that. A shyness came over her, her face flaming.

"You're the heart of my homestead—our homestead."

Our home—for her to care for. And a man who seemed to care for her.

"And that home needs a bathtub." He released her and relaxed against the butte again, his tone lightening as he snatched another chicken leg from the basket. "Tomorrow morning, we'll head on over to the general store so you can pick out the one you want. While we're there, I'll order some lumber and the window for your new bathroom."

"Jesse, I will adapt without a tub and indoor bathroom. You don't have to go to such lengths to please me."

"I want to. Your happiness is important to me." He wiped his hands on a napkin then reached for her hand and kissed her fingers. His whiskers tickled, but the warmth of his lips ran up her arm and straight to her heart. How amazing that his kindness affected her so.

Charming, sweet, and sensitive, this man was quickly becoming the center of her world. At this moment, his happiness ranked high on her list of priorities as well. Leah appreciated such qualities in her new husband, but how long would it last? Months? Days? Weeks?

And how would he react after she told him the details about her past—a past that included an arrest and jail time?

Jesse couldn't recall a finer afternoon as he and Leah strolled back to the house—and not only because of the nice weather, either. She'd removed that frilly hat of hers and tucked it under her arm, and the sun brought out golden strands in her walnut-brown hair.

"Jesse, I've been thinking. Would you show me around the barn?"

He couldn't help his wide grin. "Didn't Nellie take you inside yesterday?"

"No, we never got to it, and I've been thinking that if this is our homestead, I need to contribute more to it. Since I'm not teaching, I'll have time on my hands, and I can help with the animals and such when you have to work late."

"Or maybe just keep me company while I do it." Arm around her waist, he gave her a squeeze. Her smile told him she didn't mind his suggestion.

In the yard now, they made for the long, low barn, and Jesse felt more encouraged with every step. Leah was already making his bare-bones house into a home. If she was interested in livestock, he'd make sure she got what she wanted. A real homestead needed a woman's touch, even outside the house and yard.

"The only animals on the place now are my horse and some barn cats. But I've been meaning to put time into this place—just needed a reason to." And a wife to be that reason. "I plan to plow up a garden spot next spring and get you a dozen hens and a rooster. Cow, too."

"What other animals could we have—that I can take care of?"

"Anything you want." He grinned, thinking back to their banter during her "tour" of the town on Leah's first day in One Way. He was going to make this woman happy if it was in his power to do it, and she seemed happiest when they were lighthearted. He opened the walk door, and they entered the barn, the scent of clean straw greeting them. "Hogs are nice."

She broke out in a tinkling little laugh. "Too much work for you. You'd have to plant dozens of rosebushes to cover the smell."

"How about mules?"

"You have enough stubborn females on this homestead."

"Ducks?"

"Even this city girl knows better—"

Mice scampered past them and Leah shrieked, flinging herself into Jesse's arms.

He was more than happy to wrap her in a protective embrace. "Well now, I'll definitely get some more mice."

"Oh, you!" She pushed away from him, giving him a good-natured shove. "I'm not afraid of mice. They just startled me."

"Whatever you say." He chuckled. He picked up her fancy hat, which she'd dropped to the straw-covered floor, blew the dust off it, and handed it back to her.

Reclaiming it, she cautiously stepped around, peeking up to the loft and the cats batting their paws at the dust motes in the air. Jesse followed close by.

"Leah, honey, stop right there."

She whirled on him. "Trying to scare me again? You're as bad as a ten-year-old schoolboy."

"No, there's a snake just a foot ahead." Jesse moved her behind him then reached for the hoe hanging on the wall. He hooked the hoe underneath the snake and carried it dangling from the tool and toward the door. Leah followed him as he dumped the creature in the grass behind the barn. "It's just a bull snake. Harmless. Probably after those mice. Sure you want to go back in?"

She squared her shoulders. "I'm sure."

Jesse admired her gumption. . .and wouldn't it figure she'd lead the way back into the barn, too?

"What else is in here that I should know about?"

"Tack room's to the left, where I keep my saddles and bridles and such. Feed room's on the other side." He replaced the hoe, then he took her hand and walked her around the barn. "This stall could be for a cow. I put my horse, Patriot, in the other one when the weather's bad."

"I like horses, but I don't know much about them. You've got a farm wagon, I see."

"Nothing fancy. Front and backseats, a long wagon bed. Comes in handy when I need lumber or supplies."

Or to transport his family as it grew. . .

"Jesse, let's go to the house. We can sit on the porch and watch the sunset."

"I prefer watching mice and snakes if it means you'll jump into my arms again."

"Jesse Waite!" She smacked him playfully with her hat. "You mind your manners and come along."

"Yes, ma'am." He grinned.

As they walked across the yard, Jesse explained some particulars to her so she'd be safe whenever she ventured outside in the future. She was an intelligent lady, and he had every confidence that she'd learn quickly. And her new interest in the homestead proved that she'd fit right into his life.

But could she learn to love him?

Only time would tell.

Chapter 10

The persistent ringing of Leah's alarm clock awakened her the next morning. She turned it off, yawned, stretched, rolled over. . .

And stared at the snoring hound in bed next to her. Not quite the face she wanted to see the minute she opened her eyes. She'd much rather stare into Jesse's handsome face.

She snuggled deeper under the quilt and thought over the lovely afternoon yesterday. She'd enjoyed it when Jesse folded her hand into his and when he held her in his arms, safe and secure from a world of hurts. And with his blue eyes twinkling and his smile shining through his reddish-blond beard, she forgot all about the cares that so easily beset her.

Then last night, as dusk fell upon the homestead—their homestead—she'd wanted him to kiss her. But something undefined, something indescribable, had held her back from letting him know her true feelings, and Jesse respectfully slept in the barn.

Sarge bounded from the bed, barking at who-knew-what outside the window, nearly scaring the liver out of her.

That dog belonged in the barn. Her husband belonged with her.

At last Leah rolled out of bed. After she dressed and pinned up her hair, she accompanied Jesse outside to watch him feed and groom Patriot. Maybe one day she would learn to ride, even have her own horse. For now, Jesse seemed pleased that she was interested in his chores, and that would have to do for today.

And Jesse made good on his promise to take her to the mercantile.

Inside the store, she leafed through the pages while Jesse and Will walked out back to the lumberyard. So many tubs to choose from. And Jesse didn't give her a price limit.

In the quiet of the early morning, a loud bell clanged, deep and resounding. It couldn't be a church or school bell—there wasn't a church or school in town. Within moments, Jesse and Will raced back into the store.

"Let's go," Jesse said, visibly shifting to his sheriff role.

"I can't imagine what happened. Folks clang the bell only when there's an urgent public announcement or an emergency," Emma explained to Leah as they left the store.

Outside on the boardwalk, the townspeople gathered around a short, narrow platform near the livery. Luther Welton stepped up. "Listen up, folks."

Jesse groaned as the din of the curious crowd dwindled to near silence.

"As you all know, the election for town sheriff is tomorrow morning."

Mutterings and nods from the townsfolk.

"But what you might not know is why I'm the best man for the job."

Leah sighed, already bored with the announcement. Selecting a bathtub seemed ever so much more exciting than listening to this nonsense. But Jesse made no move to return to his errands, so Leah stood patiently at his side as Mr. Welton listed off his inflated qualifications.

Nellie came to stand alongside Leah, bouncing baby Henry in her arms, and shortly thereafter Zeb joined them.

"So now that you know about me, let's talk about Sheriff Waite. You might think you know all there is about the man, but what you don't know is that he's a yellow-belly when it comes to crime. Why, he married a common criminal."

With his words, reality tightened its fist around Leah's hope. Eyes wide, she raised her gaze to the heavens and then dropped it to the dusty road—looking anywhere but back at that platform or her husband beside her. *No, God, please!* She'd made a mistake, and she wanted to be the one to tell Jesse, not have him hear it this way! In public. The last thing she ever wanted was to hurt him.

"Luther, this election's between you and me," Jesse called, his arms folded over his suede vest. "Leave my wife out of it."

"It's true, Jesse." Her lips trembled as she quietly confessed. She stared up at him, her knees weak. "I was arrested for demonstrating and spent a night in jail. I was going to tell you. . ."

"I know all about it." He flicked a glance her way. He was angry, she could tell, but not at her. "I've known for some time."

"You have?" She blinked and managed a shaky smile. "And you still wanted to marry me?"

A soft light entered his eyes. "Course I did. You're a fine woman. You did nothing wrong back in Newport."

Jesse's arm encircled her waist. She sagged against him.

"Good people of One Way, I did some digging." Welton lifted his hands, looking for all the world like some diabolical preacher. "I found out through an acquaintance of mine in Newport that the new Mrs. Waite is a reg'lar malefactor. She rioted in the streets for a women's rights movement, turning wives against their husbands, daughters against their fathers."

No, it wasn't true—Leah would never have done that!

"A vote for Jesse Waite tomorrow jeopardizes every household in this town!"

"That's a lie!" Her claim went unheard above the murmuring throng. She looked up at Jesse. In that moment, she knew what she had to do to help her husband win. "I'd like the chance to set the matter straight. Please, may I? Perhaps if people hear the truth from my mouth, they'll believe it."

"No, Leah. You'll only get hurt."

"No, I won't. I can face the truth." God had a purpose, even for her blemished past, and Leah sensed this was it. Now was the time. She thrust her shoulders back with a confidence she'd never experienced before. "Please, Jesse? It might help you win tomorrow."

"I don't give a whit about this election. Not if it means you'll be humiliated."

"But I won't be. We have God on our side."

Jesse pursed his lips, obviously considering the idea. "You sure you want to open yourself to the public like a book?"

"I'm sure. With God directing my paths and your support, I can do anything."

He inclined his head in silent acquiescence then led her through the crowd to the

platform. Jesse jumped onto it and helped Leah up. "Folks, you heard what Luther had to say. Now my wife would like to speak."

She glanced around, silently praying the townsfolk would listen. "In part, Mr. Welton is correct. I was arrested for demonstrating for women's rights. . .but only because men like him have oppressed women for thousands of years. But I, in no way, condone the idea of women usurping their husband's authority in the home." Leah looked at Jesse. "I'm not sorry that I stood up for women's rights, but I regret that my actions brought shame to my family, my husband. . ."

"There's no shame in what you did, Leah." Jesse stepped forward and draped his arm around her shoulders. "Folks, thirty-six women demonstrated that day in Newport. Authorities, like Luther's friend, incarcerated them, keeping them away from their homes and families overnight and violating their constitutional right to legal counsel."

"Now, wait just a minute here—"

"The charges against my wife and the others were dropped." Jesse ignored Welton's attempt to cut in. "The coordinator of the event had a permit for the assembly. But in order to make sure additional demonstrations didn't occur, bureaucrats printed the ladies' names in the local newspaper, thoroughly humiliating them."

Leah was amazed that Jesse not only knew about the incident but also its details.

"As a result, Leah suffered unnecessary consequences. Her aunt and uncle convinced her to come out here, and. . ." He smiled that smile she'd learned to love on her first day in One Way. "Well, I wasn't going to pass up the chance to make a fine lady my wife."

"Won't help you win the election, Jess," a man in the crowd hollered.

Some agreed, including Welton.

"Doesn't matter. I already won the prize when I married Leah."

His words filled her heart in a dizzying way.

"If Luther Welton becomes sheriff," Jesse warned, "you can be sure he'll make examples of whomever he pleases."

"We agree on that much, Sheriff. I won't tolerate any disturbances, especially from women!"

"Even if it violates their rights?"

"Don't put words in my mouth. Law-abiding folks have nothing to fear from me."

"Just as long as it's your law they follow." Amid more murmurings from the crowd, Jesse helped Leah off the platform. "We've said all we have to say. I hope you all search your hearts before tomorrow's election and then vote as your consciences dictate."

"I'm proud of you, boy." Mrs. Rigley rapped Jesse's arm as he passed her. "You, too, Mrs. Waite."

At least Leah had won over the older woman. Now, if only her admission helped her husband win tomorrow, all would be well in One Way.

⌘

"How can you sit there so calmly?" Leah placed her hands at her waist as she regarded Jesse, sitting on the porch, his booted feet on the railing, and leisurely reading a newspaper. "The election results will be in any moment."

"Buzzing around here like a bee in a flower garden ain't going to change the way men voted today."

"Are you saying that I *buzz*?"

He peeked over his paper. "No, just saying—"

"I've got a bee in my bonnet?"

He laughed, perhaps with a good amount of relief, realizing she teased him. "Come sit down." Leaning over, he patted the chair beside his.

And he was right, of course. She worried needlessly. God had everything under control, as always.

"Sorry I wasn't home much yesterday."

"That's all right." She'd fallen asleep before he got home, and Jesse had respectfully spent another night in the barn.

"Lots of dangerous criminals to apprehend."

"Really?" Between chores and errands today, they hadn't talked much about yesterday.

"The culprit, the Bentleys' cow, got loose and trampled Mrs. O'Connor's cabbage patch. A felony, according to Mrs. O'Connor. I ended up fixing the fence, and the Bentleys insisted on feeding me supper."

"All in a day's work, Sheriff?" Leah smiled.

"Without a shot fired."

They shared a laugh.

"Have I told you that I'm proud of you and what you did yesterday?"

"Yes." Only a dozen times.

After breakfast this morning, they'd strolled to the bank, where the voting took place. Jesse cast his ballot and then it was off to the mercantile. Leah selected her bathtub, a claw-foot white enamel and cast-iron monstrosity that any Rhode Islander would covet. But, oddly, her new bathtub paled in comparison to her new husband. He consumed nearly all her waking thoughts.

"When do you think the votes will be tabulated?" As the last syllable tumbled off her tongue, the town bell clanged.

The election results were in.

Reverend Bigelow held up his hands to silence the crowd gathering around the platform. "Everyone. . .your attention, please."

Leah gazed up at the minister, her husband at her side. Four days ago, she couldn't have cared less about the election for sheriff, but now she was deeply concerned and yet quietly confident, too.

"We've counted all the votes. The new sheriff of One Way is. . ."

Leah wove her fingers between Jesse's. He squeezed her hand affectionately.

". . .the incumbent, Jesse Waite."

A joyous weightlessness overcame Leah as cheers went up around her. Men tossed their hats in the air.

"Come on up and speak, Sheriff." The reverend waved him onto the platform.

Jesse leaped onto the narrow wooden stage and offered his hand to Leah. Stepping up, she took her place beside him. The cheers continued, and Jesse inclined his head in silent gratitude.

At last the hoopla died down.

"I want to thank everyone who voted for me. As sheriff of One Way, I vow before you today to see that justice is served and the citizens of this town are protected. I also look

forward to presenting plans to the town board for a church and school. As I've promised, I'll do my part in negotiating with the railroad so it comes through town and benefits us all." He gave a nod. "Again, thank you."

Amid the townsfolk's applause, Jesse turned to Leah. With a delighted laugh, he took her in his arms and twirled her around.

Had she ever been this happy?

"I love you, Leah." He whispered the words against her ear.

She pulled back and gazed into his sky-blue eyes. "I love you, Sheriff Jesse Waite." Amazingly, she meant each word.

Onlookers cheered all the more.

Then he kissed her, an exquisite, gentle kiss filled with hope and promise, as the town bell pealed the news across the land.

Andrea Kuhn Boeshaar and her husband, Daniel, have three sons, one daughter-in-law, and five grandchildren. Andrea writes articles and devotionals but particularly enjoys writing fiction. Her stories incorporate godly romance with reality and hope with heart-break. Find out more at: www.andreaboeshaar.com.
"LIKE" Andrea on Facebook: www.facebook.com/andrea.boeshaar
Follow her on Twitter: @AndreaBoeshaar

Christina Linstrot Miller has always lived in the past. Her passion for history began with her grandmother's stories of 1920s rural southern Indiana. Christina enjoys historical architecture, the coastal South, and early American antiques. A pastor's wife and worship leader, she lives on her family farm with her husband of twenty-seven years and Sugar, their talking dog. Find out more about Christina at: www.christinalinstrotmiller.com.

KEEPER OF MY HEART
Mona Hodgson

And ye shall know the truth,
and the truth shall make you free.
JOHN 8:32

Chapter 1

May 1866

Neelie pushed the gun belt into place at her hips. The raucous sound of a tinny piano slowed her steps on the boardwalk outside the Cottonmouth Saloon at Fort Kearney. She needed funds, and the opportunities for a woman were limited, to say the least. If she expected to make it to San Francisco for that job, she had some shooting to do.

Tugging at the bead on the straps under her chin, Neelie loosened her sombrero. She drew a red kerchief from the pocket of her trousers and wiped the sweat from the back of her neck as she stared at the swinging doors. She hated this part. But if the last two years had taught her anything, it was that what or how she felt didn't amount to a whit of difference. What she *did*, however, *could* make a difference.

Pulling herself up to her tallest and fortifying herself with a melodramatic chuckle, Nellie pushed open the double-hinged doors and stepped into the smoky darkness. The pungent mix of smoke, sweat, and liquor always carried her back to the first time Archie had made her strut into a saloon. Blinking to adjust her vision, she swallowed the bitter memories. Worn boots with jangling spurs carried her across the wooden floor to the ornate bar. The bulbous-nosed man behind the dark wood monstrosity tipped an amber bottle over a glass while staring at her, his thick eyebrows nearly knit together.

Silencing the piano with one sharp glance at the bald, stick-thin player, the man with too much nose for his pockmarked face tugged at the soiled apron tied above his ample belly. "I don't serve no drinks to females, unless they work for me." His nettling snort stiffened her spine.

"Good thing for both of us I didn't come here for a drink. Or a job." Wishing she had her brother's height, Neelie drew in a deep breath. "I'd be obliged if you've got six empty bottles you can spare."

The man scrubbed the whiskers on his double chin and, without uttering a word, turned toward a closed door at the end of the bar.

Good. She had pegged the barkeep for the curious sort. But then, most men were when they saw a lady who didn't look or act like one. She'd fallen far from that moniker—*lady*.

Soon the barkeep ambled out the side door, dangling three empty bottles from each hand. He set the bottles on the bar, still clutching them by the neck. No doubt waiting for payment of some sort.

She gave him a forced smile. "Thank you, kindly."

His face didn't soften. Nor did he loosen his grip on the bottles.

Neelie leaned forward, close enough to smell onions on his breath. "What do you say we work as partners, mister? You collect the bets, and we'll split the winnings down the middle."

Nodding, the man released his grip. "Sure hope you know what you're doin'."

Neelie gave him a sharp nod then pinched the bottle necks in her hands and started for the door. She stopped halfway and did a slow turn, meeting the gazes of a dozen men. She set three of the bottles on the corner of a table then reached up and bumped the brim on her sombrero, pushing the hat to the back of her head.

"I know what you're all thinking," she said. "You're thinking, 'What's a little lady doin' walkin' into a saloon and carryin' out empty bottles?' " Allowing for a theatrical pause, Neelie watched their heads bob. "Well, friends. . ." She raised one set of bottles as she picked up the others from the table. "Be prepared to be amazed."

With an invitational nod toward the door, Neelie resumed her stroll to the street. The sound of chairs scraping the wood flooring provided sweet music for her steps out the door and across the boardwalk.

In the center of the street, she set the bottles about ten paces apart. A gaggle of men followed her, stumbling and muttering as she led them toward the edge of town, where she'd tethered her Spanish mustang in the shade of a cottonwood tree.

She loosened the reins from the branch then pulled two lumps of sugar from her pocket and held it out to her horse. "Here we go, Whistle."

Setting her foot in the stirrup, Neelie swung up into the Mexican saddle and spurred her horse once. When Whistle broke into a gallop, Neelie flung herself into a standing position and pulled one of her cross-draw six-shooters in one swift movement. As the horse carried her past the first bottle, she shot and shattered it.

The men scattered off the street and onto the boardwalks.

When the last bottle exploded in a mist of broken glass, Neelie holstered the gun, dropped into the saddle, and pulled up on the reins. Whistle reared as he turned back toward the saloon.

Neelie lifted her hat and spun it in the air. "Tell all your friends. And be here at six o'clock tonight for the real show. I'll go up against the best shootin' man the town's got. Bring your money."

Murmurs and whistles filled the air as the men funneled back into the watering hole. "Wow, lady!"

Neelie pulled the reins around to face the piano player from the saloon.

"Sure too bad you weren't here a couple weeks ago. You missed a bunch of rubes that rolled through in wagons headed west."

Smiling, Neelie drew in a deep breath. If her guess could be trusted, she had plenty of suckers right here. But it was good to know she had something to look forward to out on the prairie.

❧

That evening, no less than fifty folks showed up on the edge of town with their supposed best shooter. The piano tickler might have been considered a real good shot if Archie and his scoundrel cronies hadn't taught her to aim and steady herself.

As the crowd dispersed, Neelie rode Whistle to the Cottonmouth. Leaving her horse standing at the railing with the reins wrapped around the pommel, she took quick steps

across the boardwalk. Time to collect her share of the wagers.

The saloon doors thumped on their hinges behind her. Cigar smoke stung her eyes, forcing her to blink hard to focus her vision.

The barkeep leaned on the counter, a grin bunching his whiskered face. "You had yourself quite a show."

She nodded. "Yes. And I expect we both had a healthy take."

"Some sizeable winnings, all right." He reached under the bar.

But instead of pulling out the cigar box he'd used to collect the bets against her, the barkeep brandished a coach gun and pointed it at her chest.

Her mouth suddenly dry, Neelie moistened her lips. "We had a deal. I cut you in, so you have no use for that thing."

His brow furrowed. This could go from bad to worse right quick if she didn't find a way to draw out the man's sense of decency. Assuming he had one.

"I hadn't considered all the extra work you had to do, given the overwhelming response we had. Fifty percent doesn't seem fair, so keep sixty percent of it, and I'll take forty."

His chest puffed out. "I was in New Mexico Territory before I came here, *Neelie Shott*."

Neelie's stomach knotted. He'd recognized her.

"The sheriff might want to talk to you." He looked out at the men bent over faro and roulette tables, watching them. "Seein' as how you were nice enough to entertain me and the fellows here, I'm goin' to consider the pot a gratuity for my silence."

Theirs weren't the only weapons in the place, and loyalties wouldn't stack in her favor. She didn't feel a need to hash the past with the sheriff. Nor did she wish to be delayed.

Backing away and barely making it out the door ahead of a half-dozen men, Neelie jumped off the boardwalk and onto her mustang. "Haw!" She spurred the horse west.

She'd be catching up to that caravan of wagons sooner rather than later.

Chapter 2

Trudging through prairie grasses and over another rise, Ian Kamden set one heavy foot in front of the other. It seemed all he'd been able to manage since Doc Le Beau climbed out of the Conestoga and told him Rhoda hadn't made it.

Angus, the eldest of their five children, had tied their horses a quarter mile back so they could hunt on foot. His son walked beside him, his shoulders slumped and his voice silent. No doubt, still wrestling with his own memories.

The sun, beginning its journey to the horizon, seemed bent on harassing Ian. He tugged down the brim on his tam cap to block the glare. If only he could yank the troublesome thoughts from his mind as readily. He scrubbed the beard he'd let go. He never should've taken Rhoda away from Saint Charles. It had been their home for five years, until he'd loaded his goods and family into two wagons and set off across the wilderness with the Boone's Lick Wagon Train Company like some kind of crazed man in search of gold.

Now Rhoda was dead. He'd walked away from the fresh mound of dirt that concealed her lifeless body in order to journey on...to where? They'd talked about Montana, Colorado, Idaho, even California, where so many of the company were headed, but they'd not made a decision. They had time, or so they thought. And Mither, well, she didn't seem to care, as long as they hurried to get there.

Ian shifted his Colt's long barrel, resting it closer to his collar. It'd be nice if even a slight breeze would lift the damp fabric from his arm and shoulder to cool him. Today the company had only traveled ten miles, stopping early, which afforded him daylight for hunting.

"Faither?"

Angus's voice cut into Ian's thoughts and halted his steps. His son sported a smattering of freckles across his nose like the ones Ian had despised on his own childhood face. And at eleven years, Angus was nearly as tall as his mother.

Had been.

Ian looked toward a stand of scraggly cottonwoods. "Did you spot something?"

"No, sir." His son's sigh lifted a lock of brown hair that draped across his forehead. "Were you thinkin' on Mither?"

"I was." Little else could gain ground to occupy his thoughts. But now that she'd been gone awhile and the initial shock was wearing off, he had his motherless children to think about.

Ian blew out a long breath and rested his hand on his son's shoulder. "It'll take us some time to—"

To what? Grow accustomed to not having a wife or mother?

Angus pointed to the trees about a mile away. "I'll climb a tree. Might be able to spot somethin' from there."

Several minutes later, Ian cupped his hands beneath his son's shoe and gave him a boost. Angus grabbed hold of a low branch and swung up into the cottonwood then crawled out onto a sturdy branch. His legs curled around the gray bark, and he peered off into the distance.

"You see anything, son?"

"Nothing at the closest watering hole." His arm hooking the branch, Angus pointed toward the north. "But I see something off that way. It's dark. Brown. And real big."

"Buffalo?"

"That's what it is, all right. Lots of buffalo." His son's voice swelled with excitement, while Ian's chest tightened.

"How close are they?"

"Looks like a couple miles away, maybe." Angus inched back toward the trunk of the tree.

Ian wouldn't mind coming across a buffalo off on its own, but he had no intention of tangling with a herd of the enormous beasts.

"So long as they don't get spooked, they won't be any bother. We'll go a little farther south with our gunfire, away from them. Better safe than sorry."

Angus dropped to the ground and fell into step with Ian.

They hadn't walked but a quarter mile, just reaching the other side of a rise, when a gunshot rang out.

Both of them froze in their tracks. No one else from camp had come this direction, and they hadn't seen any other companies in the area. But clearly they weren't alone. Whoever had fired that shot either hadn't seen the buffalo or didn't know any better.

A sudden thunderous rumble tensed Ian's shoulders. He turned around and hurried back to the rise with Angus at his heels. A brown mass in the distance kicked up a cloud of dust that threatened to block the sun.

"Stampede! Hurry, son. We've gotta get into a tree."

A lone tree stood about thirty feet away, and they both ran toward it. When they reached the sycamore, Ian lifted Angus onto a low branch. As his son scrambled higher, Ian followed, using only the sturdiest limbs for his ladder. Once he'd climbed as high as he dared, Ian laid his trusty single shot across his leg.

"Look! There, Faither." Angus pointed at a small man on foot, darting toward the tree. One gloved hand held a sombrero on the man's head, and the other gripped a limp rabbit. A pair of six-shooters bounced in cross-draw holsters. He had to be the one who set off the herd.

A few feet from the base of the tree, the man, wearing a poncho despite the heat, stopped and looked up at them. Panting, he glanced back at the growing cloud of dust then dropped the rabbit and leaped toward the lowest branch. His boy-sized boots scrambled up the trunk. Quite a feat, given that his trousers would fit a man two sizes bigger.

Ian sighed. He didn't wish anyone harm, even the lout who had gotten them into this mess. He hooked his arm on the branch then braced his rifle, leaned forward, and extended his other hand.

The fellow grabbed Ian's wrist and swung up into the tree. When he'd settled onto a branch just above Ian, he tugged the brim of his hat down, hiding his eyes. His chin was curiously smooth.

"The buffalo, they scared my horse away." A youngster's voice. "I'd gotten off him to hunt the rabbit." What was a kid doing out here alone?

Ian hoped the herd would turn before *their* horses became spooked. Or worse. He braced himself against the tree trunk and raised his rifle. Faster than he could draw a breath, the kid had the barrel of a six-shooter pointed at his chest.

Ian shook his head. "Put that thing away." Whoever this kid was, he was fast on the draw. Come to think of it, he was a good shot, too, if he had nailed that rabbit with only one bullet.

Ian fired his rifle into the air. "That should turn the herd away." He looked up at the interloper. "You always draw on a man who helps you into a tree and out of danger?"

"You could've said something." The kid slid the six-shooter into its holster and shifted, brushing his hat against the branch above him. The sombrero tumbled to the ground, revealing short, golden-brown curls.

"It's a girl!" The rise in Angus's voice expressed Ian's surprise as well.

Ian looked away and started down from the tree. He wasn't dealing with a boy. A vein in his neck throbbed as he swung to the ground. What was a female doing out here alone? Especially one with the sense of a groundhog and the skill of a marksman?

Neelie held onto the Scotsman with her fingertips. When Ian Kamden had refused to double up with his son and let her ride the pinto, she said she'd ride with the boy to the wagon camp. Mr. Kamden wouldn't hear of it. Not that she blamed him for being cautious. Given the chance, she might've taken off with the boy's horse, if for no other reason than to find Whistle. How was she to put on Wild West shows without her mustang, let alone get all the way to San Francisco?

Mr. Kamden insisted she ride behind him. The boy, Angus, carried the rabbit she'd shot, setting off a chain of events that chased off her horse and left her beholden to a stranger out in the middle of the prairie. He and his son were part of the wagon caravan she'd spotted from the hills. If only she'd been looking in the direction of the buffalo herd instead.

Neelie stared at the wall of broad shoulders in front of her. She had no horse. No supplies. With only the clothes on her back and the guns in her holsters, she had no option but to hook up with the wagon company. If she sowed her seeds right, she might be able to put on a show in exchange for a horse and supplies. If Whistle didn't find her first. The reality, though, was that she didn't know how far her mustang had run or if he'd fallen into the hands of someone on the trail.

Mr. Kamden's palomino stumbled, and Neelie tightened her grip on his striped shirt, breathing in the smell of sweat and wheel grease. A family man with a wife and at least one child.

The boy called Angus cleared his throat. "*Mem*, you have a husband?"

Neelie swallowed hard. "I did. But he died." She'd trusted Archie with her heart, and within moments of her arrival in Santa Fe, he'd crushed it. She wouldn't let that happen again. She was the keeper of her heart. And she'd locked it and tossed away the key.

"My mither died, too." The boy's words stung her spirit.

That meant Mr. Kamden was widowed. Neelie loosened her grip on the shirt in front of her and looked at the child. "I'm sorry for your loss."

"Thank you, mem. Yours, too." Angus scrubbed his freckled cheek. "She was real sick. Died on the trail."

They rode a mile or so in silence but for the sound of horse hooves and the squawk of a magpie overhead.

Angus guided his horse closer to her, his shoulders and his chin drooping. "I'm sorry about your horse, mem. I'd be real upset if Patches run off." He patted the pinto's withers.

Neelie nodded. The mustang had been her only friend the past couple of years and her right hand in her shows.

"Faither, are you sure we can't go look for Miss Neelie's horse?"

Mr. Kamden angled toward his son, his profile revealing soft crow's-feet framing his eye. "Like I already told her, we can't risk wandering aimlessly looking for a horse that could've gone anywhere, or. . ."

Been trampled. Neelie's mind finished the thought for him, her stomach knotting in its wake.

"The sun's already sinking in the sky, Angus. It's too dangerous to be wandering out on the prairie come dusk."

A frown pinched the boy's eyes. "Sorry we can't help you find your horse, Miss Neelie, but we probably have extra stuff in our wagons."

Wagons? "You have more than one wagon, Mr. Kamden? Are you the captain of the caravan?"

"That would be Mr. Garrett Cowlishaw."

Cowlishaw was the man she'd talk to about putting on a show, then.

"We have five children," Mr. Kamden continued. "That's why we have two wagons. But I'm sure we have a few supplies we can spare."

We. After Archie was killed, it took Neelie three or four months to stop saying *we*. If his wife had died on the trail, this man was likely less than two months out from the burial and caring for their five children. She didn't envy him his load.

"My mother is with us. And there is a young woman traveling with her brother and mother who helps us out during the daylight hours."

Clouds of smoke drew Neelie's attention to a valley just beyond the rise. The woodsy scent of campfires teased her senses as a semicircle of wagons came into view. They'd camped beside the Platte River at the edge of a scanty line of oaks and elms.

Neelie brushed a persnickety curl behind her ear. It would feel mighty good to wash up before setting off on her own again.

The wall of shoulders turned slightly and Mr. Kamden pointed to an encampment at the bottom of the hill. "This is it."

Cows and oxen congregated in the grasses while hobbled horses grazed. Several children darted around, apparently engaged in some sort of game. Women stirred pots at the campfires. Off to the side, three men bent over shovels. Looked like latrine duty. One man big like Mr. Kamden, only rounded. Another short and wiry, who wore a cavalry hat. Brown hair dusted the collar of the third man. A sweaty shirt clung to a torso nearly equal to the length of his legs.

Just like—

"That don't look like any wild game I ever seen, Kamden." The wiry fellow wiped his brow with a kerchief.

Mr. Kamden cleared his throat. "You best finish up there right quick, Boney. Me and Angus found a female."

The third fellow straightened and looked at her with eyes the color of cocoa. *Like Mother's.*

But he couldn't be Caleb. Caleb was dead.

Chapter 3

Neelie's heart pounded her chest. Placing her hands on the cantle, she pushed herself up and sprang backward over the horse's rump. She landed on both feet behind the palomino. "Caleb?" She blinked feverishly. "But you're dead!"

The man with a startling resemblance to her brother let his shovel fall to the ground. "Do I know you?"

The voice was unmistakable. She opened her mouth to reply but couldn't push so much as one word past the sudden lump of emotion clogging her throat.

He held out his hand. "Caleb Reger."

Her knees threatened to buckle. Her brother was alive? How was it possible? "You let us believe you were dead." She yanked the sombrero from her head.

He jerked backward as if she'd struck him. "Neelie?"

"Yes, it's me." Though she bore little resemblance to the Cornelia Rose he'd left at their parents' home in Nashville. Tears stung her eyes.

"Where's Archibald?" He studied her. "I don't understand. What are you—"

"Doing out here on someone else's horse? Wearing a sombrero and trousers? It's a long story." One she couldn't tell him. She blinked away the tears. "I have a few questions of my own. For instance, when did you come back to life?"

"I didn't die." A shadow darkened his eyes. "I was the only one in the regiment who didn't."

"But a letter came from the War Department. Said you'd been killed in an ambush at Centralia. Mama and Daddy were never the same after that. Neither was I."

"I'm so sorry." His warm breath brushed her cheek, awakening a memory of their last good-bye when she saw him off to war in one of the many regiments sent from Nashville.

Had she known she still had her brother's love, would she have remained with the new Archie and allowed him to push her into his schemes?

"I should've gone home, but I couldn't face—"

"Do they know?"

Caleb nodded. "They should by now. I wrote a letter to Mama and Pops. Mailed it at Fort Kearney." He tugged his shirtsleeves straight. "Do they know where you are?"

"No. I haven't been in touch with them since I sent the telegraph when I first arrived in—" She stopped short of saying Santa Fe. If she wasn't careful, she'd say too much.

"Caleb!" The female voice turned Neelie's head. A young woman dashed toward them, pinching her skirts at her side, and practically skidded to a stop beside Caleb.

Panting, she pressed her hand to her chest just above the eyelet neckline on her red plaid dress. "What is going on here?"

In a poor attempt to suppress a grin, Caleb captured the woman's hand. "Anna, I'd like you to meet my sister, Neelie Reger Finch."

Anna's mouth dropped open.

"It's Neelie Shott now. Fits better with my profession as a shootist."

Caleb blinked then smiled. "Neelie, this is my wife, Anna Goben Reger."

"Your sister?" Anna's chin nearly hit her chest.

"Wife? Not only are you alive and out here in the middle of the prairie, but you're married?"

Anna studied Neelie. "I thought you said your sister was a—"

"A southern belle?" Neelie regretted the sarcasm the moment it slipped out. Why would Caleb have thought anything different of her? The sister he'd parted from wore embroidered gowns, her long hair swept up and held in place with pearled combs.

"Yes, my sister." Caleb returned his attention to Neelie. "Things have obviously changed. A lot. For all of us."

"For the better." A warm smile brightened Anna's eyes. "The more family, the happier."

"Thank you, Anna." Neelie turned to her brother. "To answer your question, Archie is dead."

"I'm sorry." Caleb and Anna spoke in unison.

"Thank you." She wasn't sorry her husband was out of her life, but the way he died still kept her awake some nights.

"That explains why you're alone." Caleb ground the toe of his boot into the loamy soil. "But not why you're out here. You were with the folks in Nashville when I left for the war."

"I stayed there for a while." He didn't need to know any of the details. They would soon go their separate ways and weren't likely to cross paths again. Not if she wanted to protect her secrets.

"You're just in time for supper. My grandfather is traveling with us, and it's his night to cook." Neelie's newfound sister-in-law snatched her hand and pulled her toward a covered farm wagon.

Neelie surprised herself and allowed it. For a number of years now, no woman had bothered to give her the time of day. Unless it involved tittle-tattle whispers. To have another woman eager for her company was nice for a change.

Within thirty minutes, Neelie sat on a wood-slat chair with a tin plate balanced on her lap. Caleb and his wife shared a bench. Anna's grandfather, Otto Goben, a beanpole of a man, perched on a stool. Neelie stabbed another crusty bite of meat and lifted the fork to her mouth. "What did you say this was?"

"*Wiener Schnitzel*. It's a German favorite. We bread veal when pork isn't available."

"It's quite good. Thank you." Neelie drizzled honey on her second biscuit and bit into it. It wasn't roots or rabbit, so the meal had a leg up right there. She scooped up another forkful of the potato salad.

"My Anna said your husband died." The accent was thick, but the softness in Mr. Goben's voice matched the tenderness in his gray-blue eyes. "My grandson—Anna's

brother—died in battle." His shoulders slouching, he sighed. "The war claimed so many good men."

Nearly choking on the potato salad, Neelie reached for her coffee cup. She'd thought Archie was a good man. That was why she'd married him. Nobody needed to know how he'd really died, or why. He might not have died during the war, but it changed him. Got him killed just the same.

Chatter drew Neelie's attention to the front of the wagon as a horde of children rounded the tongue and stopped mere feet from her chair.

Angus led the pack. "I apologize for interruptin' your meal, mem, but I been telling about you. About your gun and your shootin' the rabbit with only one shot."

Not about the stampede that one shot *had caused?*

"We wanted to meet you." The comment came from a little girl no taller than the hub of a wagon wheel.

Angus rested his hand on the girl's shoulder. "This here's my baby sister, Maisie."

"I'm almost four." Maisie's hair had more twists in it than a bean vine. She clutched a fabric bunny. "Can you really shoot as good as Angus says?"

Caleb cleared his throat and rose to his feet. "Children, my sister has had a busy day. Do you think you could save the introductions for another time?"

"Sure, Preacher. Sorry." Angus turned to leave then looked over his shoulder at Neelie. "We'd surely like to see your shootin' another day, mem."

Preacher? Her brother was alive, married, and he was a preacher? "We'll see." Even if she had her own horse, putting on a show for the caravan no longer seemed appropriate with her brother—the preacher—in the mix. Doubtful he'd smile on gambling. Anyway, taking advantage of bumpkins wasn't quite as safe when your own kin were in the crowd.

"Angus. Maisie. Duff." The familiar voice drew Neelie's attention to broad shoulders and intense eyes. "It's suppertime."

Mr. Kamden's three children waved at her and rounded the Conestoga to the right, while the other children dispersed in various directions.

The Scotsman doffed his cap. "I apologize for the intrusion, Preacher. I don't have enough eyes or legs to keep track of them all." He glanced at the plate on Neelie's lap. "I best go and see about serving my rabbit stew." His mouth tipped in a grin.

"Figured it was payment for your trouble." She wasn't going to go hungry around Caleb and his family. "We're straight then?"

"We are, mem." Ian brushed the brim of his woolen cap. "Have a good evening, folks."

After he walked away, Neelie busied herself with the last bites of veal and biscuit. A brother who was alive and well. A sister-in-law who was clearly shocked by her appearance but not repulsed. A widowed stranger who helped her to safety in a tree even when she'd been the one to put his life in danger. She was grateful for all of it. Rolling out of her bedroll that morning, she never would've imagined eating supper with Caleb that night. Sitting around the campfire was the best she'd felt in years.

But she doubted Caleb and Anna would welcome her so freely if they knew the truth. Neelie swallowed hard. She had her future to think about, that job with Buckskin Joe's Wild West Show in San Francisco, and she couldn't allow the reunion with her brother and any entanglements with his new family to stand in her way.

Chapter 4

Neelie hovered on the outside end of one of the rustic benches that lined the center of camp. Caleb stood in front of the mismatched congregation with his childhood Bible open.

It hadn't been her idea to resume church attendance, but Anna wasn't the only one who had dreamed of having a sister. Neelie had, too. That must be the reason she found it so difficult to tell her sister-in-law no. While under the influence of Anna's breakfast cakes and bacon, Neelie had agreed to come to church.

Caleb cleared his throat, drawing her attention back to the service. "This morning," he said, "I'm reading from First Samuel, chapter 25.

> *"And David arose, and went down to the wilderness of Paran. And there was a man in Maon, whose possessions were in Carmel; and the man was very great, and he had three thousand sheep, and a thousand goats: and he was shearing his sheep in Carmel. Now the name of the man was Nabal; and the name of his wife Abigail: and she was a woman of good under-standing, and of a beautiful countenance: but the man was churlish and evil in his doings. . . ."*

Neelie glanced up at a lone cloud in the blue sky. He could have been talking about Archie. Her husband had without doubt turned churlish after the war.

> *"But one of the young men told Abigail, Nabal's wife, saying, Behold, David sent messengers out of the wilderness to salute our master; and he railed on them. . . ."*

Neelie bit her lip. She couldn't count how many times Archie had railed on her. On anyone in his path.

One time too many.

> *"Then Abigail made haste, and took two hundred loaves, and two bottles of wine, and five sheep ready dressed, and five measures of parched corn, and an hundred clusters of raisins, and two hundred cakes of figs, and laid them on asses. . . ."*

Anna patted Neelie's trousered knee. "I'm so thankful you're here," she whispered.

Caleb flipped a page in his Bible, crinkling the onionskin.

"And when Abigail saw David, she hasted, and lighted off the ass, and fell
before David on her face, and bowed herself to the ground. . . ."

Neelie's stomach churned. She'd done all she could to try to make Archie happy; to
make him forget the atrocities of war.

"David said to Abigail, Blessed be the Lord God of Israel, which sent thee
this day to meet me. . . ."

She wasn't like Abigail. Nothing she'd done trying to improve or spare her husband's
miserable life had made any difference.

Following the music, Caleb introduced Neelie—his wayward sister—to the entire
congregation. He hadn't called her such in so many words, but he'd described her appearance as *unexpected.* Judging by the widening of his eyes and the drop of his jaw when he'd
finally recognized her, *shocking* would've been a more apt accounting. But no matter, the
introduction was a mere formality. As soon as Mr. Kamden's palomino rode into view
and folks saw her sitting behind the recent widower, her presence among them had been
widely known.

The children may have been bolder and more direct in their inquiry of her, but Neelie
hadn't failed to notice the clusters of adults who had casually passed by Caleb's camp last
night, their steps slowing while their gazes settled on her. Being a spectacle had served
her well when her objective was to garner attention for her shooting exhibitions and
illicit wagers on her abilities, but it had been a long while since she'd tried to mingle with
churchgoing folks.

She drew in a deep breath and glanced at the front row. The wiry fellow she'd seen
digging the latrine sat with the men Anna had pointed out as the other trail hands and
the captain of the caravan. Neelie was doing her best to avoid the captain's scrutiny, just
in case he'd read Santa Fe newspapers, too.

Angus twisted around in the middle of the row in front of her. A tuft of brown hair
stuck out over his forehead. He sat beside a taller girl. The younger brother she'd seen
wearing the kerchief at his neck and another boy sat on either side of a well-dressed
woman Neelie supposed was the children's grandmother. Angus's crooked smile caused
a strange warming in her heart. She'd been surprised by how much the boy's sympathy
had meant to her.

She couldn't remember the last time she'd had any dealings with children. She did,
however, remember when she let go of the dream of having children of her own—the first
time Archie slapped her. He'd knocked her to the ground, and she'd lost her unborn baby.

Neelie offered the boy the best smile she could muster, and he turned back around.
Mr. Kamden had his arm draped across his youngest daughter's back, her curly head
leaning into his side. Maisie. What a charmer she was. The little one had the same spark
Neelie had glimpsed in the father's eyes when he asked her if she always drew a gun on
someone who was trying to help her, and again when he mentioned having to get back to
his camp to serve the rabbit stew. Despite her first impression, Ian Kamden was likable
enough.

Looking away from the Kamden family, Neelie locked gazes with that of an older woman with her nose in the air. The woman's eyelids fluttered and she jerked her head, nearly deposing her feathered hat. Her mouth moved like the flutter of a hummingbird's wings at the ear of the younger woman seated beside her.

Lifting her chin, Neelie faced her brother. Good thing she was only planning to remain with the caravan until they reached Fort Laramie.

❦

Maisie lifted her cheek from Ian's arm. Rubbing her eyes, she smiled up at him then returned her sleepy head to his side. In that moment, it felt like all was right in his world. He could almost imagine Rhoda flanking his other side. He could nearly detect the hint of lavender that followed her.

Ian heard bits and pieces of Caleb's sermon on Nabal, Abigail, and King David, but his heart seemed more intent on listening to the rhythm of Maisie's sleep breathing. And his mind was set on other things.

The extra pillow from his bed.

The haggis Rhoda used to make for him. He craved it now, although he'd never had the heart to tell her it wasn't his favorite dish.

His motherless children. They needed a woman's touch, and it all seemed too much for Mither.

His thoughts also circled the woman seated at the end of the row behind him. A woman who wore trousers and a man's shirt, both two sizes too big for her. He'd overheard bits of her conversation with Caleb and Anna, and he'd gotten the distinct impression she'd been raised as a lady in Nashville. What would sway such a woman to leave home and become a gun handler?

The devastation of war had proven to be a great stimulus for change for everyone. But hundreds of thousands of women had lived through the war and the loss of a father, brother, or husband and not totally changed their identity, the way they dressed and carried themselves.

Ian glanced to the left. On the other side of the road from camp, the Sand Hills of Nebraska rolled and peaked. The dunes paralleled much of their journeying these days, some as high as three hundred feet. Neelie was no less a phenomenon than those dunes.

Caleb strolled the aisle between the rows of benches. "Every time I read this story, I'm reminded of the truth that what we let take hold of our hearts influences what we do."

What we let take hold of our hearts influences. . . Ian had heard that part of the sermon, loud and clear. Was he letting grief take hold of his heart? The loneliness? The overwhelming task of raising his children alone?

❦

Neelie went through the motion of eating her smoked sausage and potatoes, but her mind wasn't on the Sunday supper or on the family that surrounded her. Her thoughts returned to the night before, when Ian showed up looking for his children. He had indicated he was having trouble keeping track of them, and he'd said he'd cooked the rabbit. His mother apparently couldn't cook. The poor man surely had his hands full.

She looked over at Caleb, who bit off a chunk of a crusty roll. This morning she'd seen a side of her brother that made her heart ache for what could have been. Had she known he was alive. Had she not joined Archie in New Mexico Territory and let him

suck her into his shenanigans. Caleb's topic made her wonder if he knew more about her than he'd let on, but his teaching had a peaceful quality to it. It didn't seem the war had changed him the way it did Archie.

If things were different, she'd choose to spend more time with Caleb and Anna. Maybe even join them wherever it was they planned to settle out west. But things weren't different, and her remaining with them too long wouldn't be best for any of them. No, she needed to stick with her plan to go to San Francisco and make provision for parting ways with them at the next settlement or fort.

Neelie watched as Caleb took his last bite of smoked sausage, then cleared her throat to draw his attention. "Caleb, may I speak to you for a moment?"

He nodded and stood. "You wanna go for a walk?"

"I'd like that." Although she couldn't help but wonder if her chances for a favorable answer were greater if Anna were present.

Anna took the empty tin plate from Caleb, and he walked with Neelie on a footpath toward the river. When Neelie felt they were far enough from camp, she drew in a fortifying breath and turned to face her brother.

"I have a proposal. I appreciate all you and Anna are doing for me, but I can't remain with you indefinitely."

Caleb removed his hat and raked his hair. "You know you're welcome."

"Thank you, but—"

"We still have a lot of catching up to do."

"Caleb, I can't depend on you to support me. It's not fair to you or to your wife."

"Anna loves having you around." He set his hat back on his head. "So do I."

He wasn't making it easy for her to protect him and his new family from her past. "I have a job lined up somewhere else. The buffalo spooked my horse, and everything that wasn't on my person was lost when he ran off. I'd like to put on a shooting exhibition. I'd accept a set fee to watch the show. That would give me enough to buy a horse. I'm hoping someone here might have one they can spare. I need a few supplies, too. So for those who can't come up with two bits, they can pay for the show with an extra cooking pot or spoon or something." Anna had already given her a bedroll.

"No."

"Like it or not, Caleb, shooting is what I do to make my living. And I'm real good at it."

"If you still insist on leaving when we reach Fort Laramie, I'll help you with supplies there."

"I told you." She stopped, willing herself to soften her voice before continuing. "I have a job opportunity, and I can't afford to dillydally. I need to be ready to ride when the time comes." Especially if that time came sooner rather than later, should someone recognize her and threaten to reveal her secret.

"Neelie, these women here are trying to raise their children. . .their daughters to be—"

"Something I'm not." She glanced from her gun belt to Archie's worn boots on her feet. "You're saying you can't approve my exhibition, because you're embarrassed by me. Ashamed of me because I'm not prim and proper like Anna."

His shoulders squared, and she knew she'd gone too far by mentioning Anna. "You've been here one day. You have no idea what Anna is made of." He drew in a deep breath and let it out slowly. "I'm saying no because it's not a good idea for this group, and the captain

would give you the same answer." Caleb turned back toward camp and glanced over his shoulder. "Are you coming?"

"In a while." One way or another, she had to leave them behind and make her own way. Given the choice, she'd rather do so with a horse and supplies than without. She'd just have to think of another way to get them.

Chapter 5

B y the time Ian and Caleb reached the rise after hearing the gunshot, Neelie stood surrounded by a half-dozen children. Smiling, she gripped the brim of her sombrero and waved it in a flamboyant bow.

Duff clapped. "That was grand, Miss Neelie."

"She's faster than a bolt of lightning with that gun!" Nicolas Zanzucchi punctuated his statement with a low whistle.

"Ma'am," Ian said, "I don't appreciate your disregard for common sense. You have no business showing off your shooting skills in front of the children. And on a Sunday, no less."

"Mr. Kamden, I hardly think cougars care whether it is the Lord's Day or Tuesday when their stomachs take to growling." A grin teased the corners of her mouth. "Do you?"

"A cougar?"

"Yes, Faither." Maisie stretched out her arm, pointing. "It's dead. Right there."

Ian looked in the direction Maisie pointed and saw a cougar lying lifeless in the tall grass, less than twenty feet from the children.

Angus stepped toward Ian. "Miss Neelie saved us."

Ian swallowed his frustration and returned his focus to the woman shooter, who set the sombrero atop her curls. "Thank you. They were so determined to see you shoot, that I thought—"

"We sure was." Duff hooked his thumb under the blue bandanna tied around his neck. "That's why we were following her."

Caleb placed his arm around his sister's shoulders. "I, for one, am glad she had the presence of mind as well as the skill to protect our children."

"Of course, I am, too," Ian said. "Neverthless, I'm not sure a woman shootist is the kind of influence we want for our children in this wagon train." No one on the trail needed the distraction. Least of all, him.

That night, Ian lay under a waxing full moon, chiding himself. Caleb and his sister had been reunited less than twenty-four hours before Ian had scolded her for giving a shooting exhibition on a Sunday. What right did he have to decide she didn't belong with the caravan? So what if she was different than any woman he'd known and his children were enthralled with her larger-than-life persona and skill? He sighed, looking at the myriad stars overhead. If he were being honest, he'd have to admit that Neelie's differences and his concern for his children weren't the only reasons he wanted her gone from their midst. She challenged him and intrigued him. And he found the latter especially unsettling.

Upon his announcement that he didn't appreciate her influence on the children, Neelie had shrugged out of her brother's embrace and walked away without speaking a word. The children started after her, but Caleb stopped them. He had held his tongue, but the look of disapproval he sent Ian was just as strong as the one from Angus.

Ian had gone to Caleb's camp to apologize to Neelie, but she hadn't returned. He'd made his apologies to Caleb, but Caleb hadn't been the one judged and offended. He'd seen Neelie return to camp before dark, but by now she was bedded down. His apology would have to wait until morning.

Sitting up, Ian pulled his pillow onto his lap and kneaded it like he'd watched Rhoda do with bread dough. He was finally ready to lay back and try to find sleep again when he heard twigs snap not more than thirty feet out from where he lay. What if the cougar Neelie shot wasn't the only one roaming this area? He reached for the rifle that lay alongside his pallet. Probably just a fox or a coyote minding his own business. He'd just about convinced himself of that when he saw swift movement. Not an animal, but the silhouette of a petite person wearing a sombrero.

Neelie.

Standing, Ian blinked hard to focus his vision. She carried a pack. His gut clenched. It wasn't safe for her to be out here alone. He grabbed his hat from the ground and, rifle in hand, set out after her. His steps intentionally light, he followed Neelie toward the line of elms and cottonwoods. She was headed for the river and would be hard to track in its muddy water. He couldn't let her get that far. By the time he reached the edge of the trees, he'd lost sight of her in the dim light. An owl hooted in the distance. The river meandered in near silence.

No footfalls. Had she heard him and hidden?

"Ma'am, it's Ian Kamden."

Neelie stepped from behind a tree and chuckled. "Of course it's you. Who else would it be with those clomping steps and a growling burr?"

"Fair enough." Ian hooked his thumb on his coat pocket. "I want to apologize. I was wrong about you and your reasons for shooting amid the children. I jumped to conclusions. I was wrong to judge you; wrong to think you didn't belong. You do belong on the trail with all of us. You do."

Neelie lifted a shoulder and let it fall. "I'm not so sure. But it doesn't matter. I have a job to get to. I was on my way there when I found Caleb."

"Your brother didn't object to you leaving at this hour?"

"He doesn't know."

"You left your family without saying good-bye?"

Neelie tucked a curl behind her ear. "It's for the best."

How could she say that? He'd seen the joy on her face at seeing Caleb alive.

"I'm not the sister Caleb knew in Tennessee. Time has passed. Things have happened."

Ian propped his rifle against the trunk of a tree and took a step toward her. Neelie's brown eyes glistened in the moonlight. Had she been crying? It was obvious even to him that something dreadful had happened to close her heart. Why else would she wear a man's clothes and be so secretive? "I don't know why you think you have to be so tough, and I probably have no right to even mention it, but my guess is that someone hurt you."

She looked away.

"Might have even been your husband. Rest his soul."

When Neelie took slow steps toward a couple of fallen trees, Ian followed. She sat on one and set her pack on the ground. He settled on the other, facing her.

"Your wife, she was a good woman?" Neelie asked.

"Yes. And she deserved better. I knew my wife leaned toward infirmity." Feeling the weight of his decisions, he leaned forward and rested his forearms on his thighs. "I was afraid I might lose her when she birthed Maisie. I never should have—"

"And I should never have boarded that stagecoach west to join Archie in New Mexico Territory."

She'd traveled west alone. This was a woman of incredible strength of character and determination.

"He didn't die in the war." She stood, and he did, too. "Someone killed him. Later."

"I'm sorry."

"I suppose I should be." Moonlight drew long shadows across her face.

"He mistreated you?"

Neelie blinked hard then scooped up her pack. "I shouldn't have said anything."

"Please come back to camp."

She glanced upriver.

Anyone could've knocked him over with a hummingbird feather when she started off toward the encampment. Ian followed, his mind spinning with questions he didn't have the freedom to ask. Not if he had any hope of returning her to her brother.

Chapter 6

Clutching the stem of a black-eyed Susan, Neelie set one foot in front of the other, her steps punctuated by the sound of bawling cows, clanging pots and pans, and chattering children. Fabric bunnies and dolls poked out of the pockets on Maisie and her friend Gabi's pinafores. Giggling about who-knew-what, the little girls followed a throng of boys, Lyall, Duff, and Angus among them. The wagons rolled single file, Otto Goben's, led by Anna, and then the Kamdens' wagons. Sixteen-year-old Hattie Pemberton held the lead on the farm wagon, and Blair, Ian's oldest daughter, directed the lead ox on the Conestoga. Her grandmother perched on the bench, wearing her feathered hat like a crown.

While the animals' hooves churned the dry dirt, Neelie's mind roiled over recent events. Principally, her decision to leave the camp last night then being followed by Ian Kamden. Would Archie have even noticed she'd left?

"Someone hurt you."

No matter how many times she asked herself why she'd disclosed so much to Ian, she couldn't imagine a suitable answer. She hadn't even told her brother that her husband had been killed after the war ended. No one but the gang Archie ran with knew how he'd treated her. And not one of them ever cared that he'd hurt her.

Yet a stranger out on the prairie had noticed.

Ian Kamden was as different as a buffalo from a prairie dog from the man she'd married and traipsed the west with like a vagabond. Like a common criminal. The Scotsman cared for his family. Despite his frustration with her, he'd given her a ride when she'd lost everything she owned. He didn't even know her, and he'd seen to her needs.

Neelie swatted at the swarm of no-see-ums buzzing about. First thing that morning, Caleb had apologized for being so hardheaded about her being a shootist. He even said he was thankful she had the skill to protect the children.

"I'm repeating myself, but I'm so glad you're here." Anna smiled.

Neelie looked at her sister-in-law, who didn't seem the least bit rattled by the clunking of yokes behind them, the buzzing gnats, or the sweat beaded on her forehead. "I am, too." It wasn't a lie. She was grateful Ian Kamden had stopped her last night.

Archie would say she'd gone soft for not organizing a shooting exhibition while she had a captive audience. And maybe he'd be right. But finding Caleb felt more like a second chance at family than a missed opportunity for a fleecing.

Neelie matched Anna's steady stride. "I'm assuming you and Caleb were friends in Saint Charles before the wagons rolled out."

A smirk lifted one corner of Anna's mouth and brightened her blue eyes. "We'd met all right, in a dry goods store. But, at the time, friendship seemed quite impossible. Even

during those first weeks on the road."

"But you married him. Must have been something, uh, between you."

"Antagonism, that's what there was between us." Anna giggled. "I'd backed out of marrying Boney Hughes."

"The trail hand?"

"That's the one. Caleb thought I was fickle and cruel. Didn't like me in the least, and the feeling was mutual."

"Something must have changed, because you two seem well matched. And not in the least antagonistic."

Anna blushed. "Your brother is a real good man, though he can be more than a little stubborn, at times."

"He was like that even as a boy." Neelie cocked her head. "To be fair, it runs in the family."

"I can see that." Anna's grin revealed a dimple in her cheek. "But you're both in good company. My mother was a drinker and said I have the doggedness of a long winter. I thought I could separate her from the bottle, but in the end, I couldn't save her. She got hold of some rotgut whiskey and died the other side of Fort Kearney."

"I'm sorry." Regret clutched Neelie's throat, making her wonder if her own parents were still alive. She'd been too ashamed to send them a letter since she left home two years ago. "It sounds like we've all lost a lot. Caleb, his regiment. You, your brother and your mother. Ian, his wife."

Anna glanced at the ragtag group of children flanking them. "And now," she whispered, "those dear children are without a mother."

Neelie nodded, a surprising lump forming in her throat. The four youngest ones had not hesitated to befriend her, coming to see her at her brother's camp, walking with her on the trail, and thanking her for coming to their rescue with the cougar. Blair, being the oldest, had been given responsibilities looking after the Conestoga and her grandmother. They hadn't done more than cross paths. The children needed a mother, especially on such a long journey and settling in new territory.

And she needed to keep her heart free of attachments.

"Good day, ladies." The greeting came with a Scottish flair to it.

Neelie looked over her shoulder. Sitting atop his Palamino, Ian Kamden doffed his tam cap. He had referred to her as a lady, something that hadn't happened since her first weeks in Santa Fe.

"Mr. Kamden." Neelie worried a button on her shirt, suddenly wishing she'd taken more time to freshen up that morning.

"Please, call me Ian."

"Ian, then. Good day."

Anna pressed her lips together, but that didn't hide the grin adding shine to her eyes. "You have any scuttlebutt to report?"

"I might. Boney's back from scouting with Isaac." His beard looked more red than brown in the sunlight. "He said we'll camp upriver from an Arapaho settlement tonight."

Good. Maybe she could get a proper washing in the river.

"He said they have moccasins to trade, if anyone is in need of footwear." He glanced down at Neelie's worn boots then over at the gaggle of children. "They minding their p's and q's?"

"And then some. Lyall gave me a shiny rock." She pulled the stone from her pocket then raised the flower. "Maisie brought me this black-eyed Susan."

Ian's face blanched and his lips pinched together. Had she done something wrong? Was he upset because his children liked her?

He shifted in the saddle, and his coloring improved. "Maisie used to pick wildflowers for her mother."

Neelie's stomach clenched. Nodding, she focused on the Palomino's muzzle. "You needn't worry about them. I've been keeping an eye on the children, and they're fine."

"Thank you. It's kind of you to help out."

Was that what she was doing, helping out? Or was she growing attached despite her best intentions?

Neelie walked alongside the four oxen pulling Caleb and Anna's covered farm wagon. Her new beaded moccasins peeked out from under her rolled trouser cuffs, making her smile. The Arapaho had gladly accepted a dozen of Anna's beeswax candles for them, and Anna beamed with delight when she gifted them to Neelie. Today, Neelie insisted Caleb and Anna let her help out so they could spend some time together. Watching them ride off on Caleb's Tennessee pacer and Anna's bay, bantering and giggling, made Neelie's heart ache for something more. Her brother and sister-in-law shared the kind of love she had once thought she had with Archibald. But she and Archie were never that sappy. Or even that kind to each other.

She'd been traveling with the wagon train company for eight days now. Before Caleb's Bible reading that morning, the captain announced that they had another month or so to travel before reaching Fort Laramie. The caravan was slow going. Could she afford to wait that long before striking out on her own again?

Duff Kamden scuffled toward her, tugging at the blue kerchief at his neck. Lyall, Angus, and Maisie lagged behind him. "Miss Neelie, we saw the preacher and his missus out riding. Thought maybe you could use some company."

"I'd like that. Thank you"

"There's more." Maisie raised up on her tiptoes, staring at Duff.

"Oh?"

"Yes, mem." Duff adjusted the curled rope hanging from his shoulder. "We'll be stoppin' soon for a rest, and we want you to eat with us for the midday meal."

She looked at his siblings. They smiled, their nods exaggerated. "Have you talked to your father about this?"

"He likes you now, Miss Neelie." The freckles over the bridge of Duff's nose danced when he smiled. "Miss Hattie said we're having shortbread and ham. I'll even get the extra stool out for you."

Not an easy invitation to refuse.

Within the hour, the wagons formed a semicircle. Neelie walked to the back of the Kamden's covered farm wagon. Still questioning her decision to accept the children's invitation, she viewed the scene in the shadow of the wagon.

Little Maisie sat on a quilt in the grass, with Miss Hattie bent over her bare feet. Her brother, Lyall, sat beside her, burrs and foxtails covering his trousers and stockings.

The eldest sister, Blair, stood at the back of the wagon, peering into the grub box. Duff stood off to one side, swinging a loop of rope. Several three-legged stools dotted the grass topped with various toys. Duff let the rope fly, lassoing Maisie's cloth flop-eared bunny.

"Floppy!" Maisie's screech split the air.

"Duff Kamden!" Hattie straightened abruptly, rocking the straw hat on her head. "Thanks to your tomfoolery, I like to have pushed this thorn deeper into your sister's foot."

"I'm practicing to be a cowboy."

Hattie's shoulders sagged in a deep sigh. "Practice somewhere else."

Duff stuck his tongue out at Maisie. "The stupid bunny is all right."

"Floppy's not stupid." Maisie pumped her hands, reaching for the doll. "Give her to me!"

Neelie took a step forward. "Duff, you heard your sister. Hand over the bunny."

Hattie jerked around. "Ma'am. I didn't see you there."

His eyes wide, Duff took quick steps to his sister and thrust Floppy into her arms. "I'm sorry." His apology was a bonus Neelie hadn't thought to request.

No one could be more surprised by Neelie inserting herself into a family matter than she was. Since when had she taken it upon herself to be the children's keeper?

"Miss Neelie!" Maisie looked up, her green eyes glistening with tears. "I'm glad you came to save me."

If hearts could melt, hers just had. Something about this little one—these children—seemed to bring out the best in her. They made her wish things were different. For her. And for them. One thing was certain—these children needed a mother. *Their mother.* Hattie was in over her head and no doubt anxious to spend more time with her own family.

Neelie walked to the quilt where Hattie held tweezers over Maisie's angry red foot. "What happened?"

Hattie peered up at her, a frown framing her mouth. "She decided to follow Lyall into a sticker patch."

Blair closed the lid on the grub box and walked toward Neelie, carrying two cloth-wrapped bundles pressed against her plaid pinafore. "Did you need something?"

"Me and Angus and Maisie invited her to eat with us." Duff set the coiled rope over his shoulder.

"Did you ask Faither?"

The girl's cocked head and tight lips told Neelie she didn't belong here. Ian had said so, too, even if he'd later claimed he was wrong and apologized. Clearly, his oldest daughter didn't want her here. Neelie forced herself to take a deep breath. She'd faced down criminals and shady barkeeps. Was she really going to let a girl not yet ten intimidate her?

"Where is Angus?" Neelie asked.

Blair's deep sigh pierced Neelie's heart. Maisie might be ready to pick flowers for other women, but her big sister wasn't feeling so accommodating. Something Neelie understood. She met Blair's gaze. Blue-green eyes like her father's.

"He went with my father to help Dr. Le Beau with a wagon wheel."

"If this isn't a good time for me to be here, I'll go." Neelie turned to leave.

"No. We want you to stay." Lyall spoke from the blanket. "We do, don't we, Blair?"

"Blair!" Mrs. Kamden peered out the front of the Conestoga, practically hanging on the canvas flap. "I'm feeling the vapors. I need you, dear."

Blair held the two bundles out to Neelie. "Will you help me get the food set out?"

"Gladly."

Sharpshooting might not impress Blair, but lending her a helping hand might make an impression. Neelie watched the girl take quick steps to the Conestoga. She couldn't say why she wanted Blair to like her, but she did.

At the worktable, Neelie freed a stack of shortbread pieces from one of the bundles and salted venison from the other. After slicing the venison, she pulled a stack of tin cups from the box.

A gasp caused her to look up to where Ian stood with his mouth hanging open.

Ian couldn't believe his eyes. Where Rhoda had been unassuming and constant, predictable, Neelie seemed to be none of those things.

Tin cup in hand, Neelie went to the pot boiling above the campfire. She filled the cup with coffee and held it out to him. "You'll be trapping flies in there, if you're not careful."

"Thank you." Ian closed his mouth and looked directly into her eyes. "You're here? Preparing our meal? Is something the matter?"

Hattie cleared her throat but didn't get up from the quilt where she sat with Maisie and Lyall. "Mrs. Kamden said she had a case of the vapors and needed Blair's help."

Duff walked toward him as if he'd been in a saddle all day. "We invited Miss Neelie to eat with us."

Angus joined him, carrying a stick. "Today when we were walking, and she said yes."

"Blair was upset we didn't ask you," Duff added.

"Then Nana needed Blair." Maisie clung to the fabric rabbit her mother had made.

"I told Blair I'd help." Neelie removed the lid from the mustard jar. "I hope you don't mind."

"Not at all." Ian drew in a deep breath, trying to ease the tension tightening his stomach. It felt foreign to see another woman in his camp, taking charge. Serving him. He drew in another deep breath, savoring the rich scent of the coffee, then looked her in the eye. Eyes the color of the brew with a drip of cream in it. "I'm glad you're here. Uh, sounds like we needed your help."

Neelie looked away, toward the worktable. "I think I have it all laid out."

Following Hattie's explanation of Lyall and Maisie's venture through a weed patch and Blair settling her grandmother for a rest, seven of them each grabbed shortbread and meat from the table and settled onto a stool. He sent Hattie back to her wagon to eat with her brother and mother.

Most of the conversation centered around the dry heat, chapped lips, and sticker patches. Although Neelie mentioned her love of the trees in Tennessee. Before he'd drained his second cup of coffee, Ian was fighting a sudden urge to walk among the trees with a certain sharpshooting widow.

Chapter 7

Neelie's boots sank into the damp grasses where the caravan had pastured its livestock during the midday rest. Scattered showers had chased them for most of the morning, and now the company prepared to roll out again under blue skies.

Walking beside Caleb, Neelie went to the oxen that pulled his wagon and reached for the lead ropes on two of them. One of the other women looked up from the mules she led and waved at her, and Neelie returned the greeting. Anna had been inviting various women in the group to walk with them so Neelie could get better acquainted. Mary Alice Brenner was one of three who had invited her to join them in the sewing circle Sunday afternoon.

Caleb snagged a couple of oxen leads. "Only been a couple of weeks since you joined us and you seem comfortable enough."

"You surprised?"

He pushed the derby back on his head and wiped his brow. "Didn't know what to expect."

"I'm sure not." Neelie tapped the brim of her sombrero, wondering if it might be time to replace it with one of the sunbonnets Anna had offered her. "I know I'm surprised. I didn't expect to stick around any longer than it took to get a good meal, a horse, and supplies."

"Until you saw that your dear brother was alive and you could spend time with him."

"With my sister-in-law, actually." Neelie smiled and Caleb chuckled. "Not surprising, seeing as how I enjoy Anna's company, too."

"Neelie!"

Ian took long strides toward them, one hand holding his cap in place.

Caleb cleared his throat. "You and Ian Kamden seem to be more comfortable with one another, too."

Neelie shot her brother a look that she hoped told him to keep his notions to himself.

Ian stopped in front of Neelie and her brother, his mouth suddenly dry. He'd rehearsed what he wanted to say, but now the words seemed to have vanished with the clouds.

"Ian." A grin filled Caleb's face.

Ian focused on Neelie. "Anna said you were out here."

"You wanted to speak to me?" Her eyes widened in surprise.

"Yes, I hoped for a word with you."

He and Neelie both looked at Caleb, whose eyes widened. "I take it this is meant to be a private conversation."

"If it's all right with your sister," Ian said.

Neelie handed the leads she held to Caleb. "I think the captain intends to roll out soon, but—"

"Good," Ian said. "It won't take long. I know we don't have much time."

While they walked away from Caleb and the others in the pasture Ian watched Neelie out of the corner of his eye. She wrung her hands, moistened her lips, and then pushed the sombrero from her head and let it fall to the ground behind her. Was she intentionally ridding herself of the hat, or was she too nervous to care that she'd dropped it? He'd never known a woman who wore her hair short, but it was quite becoming. On her, anyway. He stopped at the edge of the pasture and faced Neelie. She brushed at a curl that dangled at the top of her ear.

His mouth dry, Ian moistened his lips. "We don't have much time, so. . ." He looked her in the eye. "You are a capable woman, Neelie, wouldn't you say?"

"I like to think so."

"You don't seem squeamish."

"No. Not usually." A shadow darkened her brown eyes.

"My children have really taken a shine to you."

"They're good kids. Active, mind you." She giggled, something he hadn't heard her do a lot of. "But enjoyable enough."

"When Blair needed help, you jumped right in and prepared the meal."

"It's what any woman here would've done, is it not?"

"That shows strength of character."

Neelie flung her hands into the air then let them drop. "You've lost me. What is going on here, Ian? I don't recall asking you for a reference." Her eyebrows arched. "Is Hattie tired of helping out, is that it? You're looking for a nanny and wondering if I qualify?"

"Marry me." There, he'd said it.

"What?"

"Your brother is a preacher. He could marry us."

"But why?"

"We need each other. I need someone to help me with the children. And Mither. You are a widow, a woman alone out here."

"You don't even know me. We only met two weeks ago."

"After our talks the night you thought about leaving the caravan and the day you helped prepare our midday meal, I know you well enough." It wasn't how he'd felt about Rhoda when they'd married, but drastic circumstances demanded drastic measures. At least, that was what he'd grown up hearing his father say. Besides, he liked Neelie—the way she helped look after his children without having to be asked to do so. And he couldn't explain it, but he felt more lighthearted around her.

"You said we should marry because we need each other, but you must admit, your need is far greater than mine." Neelie rubbed her arms as if she'd taken a chill. "Right now, my brother is providing for me until I can get to the job awaiting me."

Ian stepped closer. "Can you say you're content with living your life alone? A life without family?"

She opened her mouth, but nothing came out.

"I've seen you with Anna. You enjoy her company. And your brother's. And the way you interact with my children." Ian squinted into the sun. "You were made for more than

entertaining strangers. Will you at least consider my proposal?"

"I'll think about it. But right now I need to help Anna." She glanced toward the wagons.

He nodded. "First, there's something else you should know."

"Besides the fact that you have five active children and a mother who struggles with the vapors?"

"Yes." Fine time for his eyelid to start jumping. "I loved Rhoda, and I still miss her. You would sleep in the farm wagon with the younger children and Mither."

"I understand." The stunned look in her eyes told him she'd already thought about his proposal and hadn't decided in his favor. Good chance he'd have his answer by the time they reached camp that evening.

Then what would he do?

Neelie wasted no time leaving Ian at the pasture. She didn't know whether to feel flattered or pitied. A proposal of marriage hadn't played a part in any of the scenarios she'd imagined when first seeing Ian Kamden perched in a cottonwood tree.

The landmark that had dominated her view of the prairie the past couple of days taunted her. In the distance, Chimney Rock's towering peak rose hundreds of feet from the earth, reminding her of hearth and home.

Her heart racing, Neelie recalled what Anna had said about her and Caleb being antagonistic toward each other when they first met. That aptly described some of her first encounters with Ian. She took quick steps toward the farm wagon at the center of the semicircle. She needed to speak to Anna privately. That was what sisters were for, wasn't it? Sisters confided in one another, or at least that was how her dreams of having a sister had unfolded.

Women packed up foodstuffs and gathered children, while men greased wagon wheels and secured harnesses. The area around her family's wagon was tidy and empty except for the four yoked oxen.

"Neelie? Is that you?" Anna's voice came from inside the wagon.

"Yes." Neelie stepped up onto the wheel spoke and pulled back the flap. Anna knelt in front of an open trunk and waved her inside.

Neelie climbed over the rim and onto the seat. She hadn't been inside the wagon yet. Trunks, barrels, and a couple pieces of furniture crowded the floor except for a narrow aisle down the middle. A hammock hung suspended between a couple of bows.

Anna closed the lid of the trunk then sat on it and looked at Neelie. "Caleb said Ian Kamden asked to speak with you."

Neelie sank onto a cask. "He did." She leaned closer to Anna, fearing someone would overhear her. "Ian suggested that we marry."

"Each other?" The second word went up an octave.

"Yes. Him. Me. Marry."

Anna pressed her hand to her eyelet collar. "What did you tell him?"

"That we don't really know one another, and that I have a job waiting for me."

"What did he say to that?"

"Basically, that I'm a very capable woman and that we could help one another. He asked me to consider it. But I'd be crazy to marry a man I hardly know, and what I do

know is that he lost his wife only a couple of months ago and has five children and a mother who requires special attention."

"That right there says why marrying you might help him, but do you think marrying him could help you?"

Neelie shifted her position on the cask. She wanted to say she didn't need help from him or from anyone else. But being here with Anna and these people was making it more and more difficult for her to lie to herself.

"There isn't much protection for a woman out on her own, even one who can shoot. Getting lost in the middle of that family would give me added protection. Hattie is doing her best to help out, but she has her own family to think of."

Anna tapped her finger against her cheek. "How does that help you?"

"I'd have the satisfaction that I'd done something good. For his children."

"Sounds to me like you're considering it."

Was she?

"Neelie?" A man's voice with a Scottish burr derailed the question. Did he expect an answer already? An impatient sort.

Neelie poked her head out of the puckered cloth at the grub box. Ian stood with arms akimbo, her sombrero atop his head.

She couldn't help but smile.

"You dropped your hat in the pasture. I thought you might miss it on the trail."

He'd noticed her hat missing and gone back for it? He wasn't impatient, just thoughtful. And surprisingly likable.

God help her, she had her answer.

Chapter 8

Ian wrung his hands. He sat on a trunk, alone in the Conestoga, wearing clean brown trousers and the yellow dress shirt Rhoda made for him before they left Saint Charles. And now, less than four months later, he was about to marry someone else. And why?

That was the question Neelie had asked when he delivered his proposal two days ago. *We need each other.* That was what he'd said, but was convenience enough?

How convenient would being married to a pistol-toting woman who looked more like a frontiersman truly be? Ian swatted at a pesky fly.

On the trail, it could be plenty convenient to have the added protection of an ace shooter following his children around. He smiled, remembering Neelie's response to his scolding about her shooting demonstration for the children. *"Mr. Kamden, I hardly think cougars care whether it is the Lord's Day or Tuesday when their stomachs take to growling. Do you?"*

Sassy but efficient. He could live with that.

In addition to the widow's ability to defend his children, she seemed to have gained their respect in a short time. Hattie had told him how Duff quickly returned the fabric bunny to Maisie in response to Neelie's prompting and even apologized to his sister. And Maisie had expressed her approval of the widow when she picked a black-eyed Susan for her.

Ian scrubbed his freshly trimmed beard. Neelie hadn't said much about her life with her husband, and she seemed to regret saying what little had spilled out. Someone had killed him. After the war. Was her tough exterior and sharpshooting meant to protect more than her grief? Her heart, as well?

He couldn't blame Neelie for wanting to leave the past behind and start over out west. He was doing the same thing.

Ian reached for the tin photograph he'd set on the salt barrel and traced the lines of Rhoda's face with a quivering finger. He doubted his ability to let go of the past with Rhoda. But, for the sake of his young ones he needed to think of the future, not the past. Tugging at his shirt collar, Ian drew in a deep breath. He was doing the right thing for his family.

"Faither?" Blair called. "The preacher asked if you're ready."

Standing, Ian ran his finger over the rough lines in Rhoda's image then slid the tin-type back into the trunk and closed the lid.

"If you're not, I can tell the captain and Mr. Caleb so."

"I'm ready." Ian stepped out over the seat.

Blair stood at the tongue of the wagon, her clasped hands bouncing against her skirt. Not yet ten, she carried the weight of his collapsed world on her narrow shoulders. If his marrying Neelie could lighten the burden for his daughter, then doing so was more than mere convenience.

It was a necessity.

Neelie wouldn't admit it, but she needed him, too, and his family. Ian climbed down from the wagon.

Blair chewed her bottom lip.

"I know this is hard for you. Me marrying again." He set a hand on her shoulder.

The strain of grief in her blue-green eyes pierced his heart. "I just wish Mither could come back to us."

"I do, too."

Blair sighed. "I know that's not going to happen."

Ian shook his head. He missed Rhoda, but the hardest part of losing her was watching his children suffer in their loss. Marrying Neelie wouldn't right everything that felt wrong, but having her around would ease some of the burden.

Ian captured his daughter's hand. "She can't replace your mother. No one can. That's not what I'm trying to do."

"I know." Blair tugged at her bodice as if it were too tight. "But she's nothing like Mither."

An understatement, if he'd ever heard one. "No. She isn't."

That was the only reason he could marry her. The fact that she wore trousers, a sombrero, and a gun belt assured him that he'd never confuse his emotions and forget Rhoda.

Neelie perched on the rim of a cask, staring at the shadow cast by a dim candle on the canvas. She still wore the green calico dress Anna had loaned her for the brief ceremony. Now that it was all said and done, she was expected to sleep in Ian's farm wagon with Maisie, Duff, Lyall, and Davonna.

The older woman fidgeted in a hammock across the back of the wagon while the three children slept curled on trunks. Neelie turned to glance out through the flap she'd tied open. The countless stars that had served as her blanket most nights reminded her of the freedoms she'd lost. Freedoms she'd given away for a different surname and a place to hide out while she made her way west.

Was it just because she felt sorry for Ian's motherless children? Or because what Ian had said rang true? She'd grown weary of a life with strangers who placed bets on her. A life without family.

"Dear."

Neelie looked at the hammock, where Davonna Kamden held the ruffle of her nightcap up above her eyes like a curtain.

"You look lost, dear."

"I suppose I am, ma'am. I've never slept in a wagon before."

"Think of it like a cabin, dear. Only smaller." Davonna looked at the canvas ceiling above her swinging bed. "And the roof and walls dance." She waved her arm, nearly upsetting the hammock. "But the sad truth is, it's nothing like home." *Home.* A job and a room at a boardinghouse in San Francisco—that was what Neelie had been working

toward the past six weeks.

"You'll get used to it." The smile in Davonna's eyes seemed genuine. "Some of it. That blowing dust, you just can't get away from it. We haven't had a real bad thunderstorm yet." She shivered. "I sure hope we don't." The older woman seemed more like a vulnerable and frightened child than a pioneer.

"I encountered one last summer in Arizona Territory."

Davonna sighed. "Well, now you have a good husband to take care of you."

A man who hadn't said ten words to her since the ceremony.

"Ne. . . What was your name, again, dear?"

"Neelie."

"I can't seem to remember that. But you look real pretty in that dress."

"Thank you."

"I could tell my son liked it, too. I was watching him."

Neelie had seen Ian's reaction, too. She doubted he thought her pretty though. Probably just struck him how different she looked. But it didn't matter whether he liked it or not. Tomorrow she'd go back to her old way of dressing. Ian had made his expectations clear, and she couldn't afford to have affection for someone who didn't care for her in that way.

Chapter 9

Shortly after sunup, Neelie pulled the wooden paddle spatula from the worktable and returned to the cooking fire between the wagons. The air smelled of coffee and griddle cakes. Ever since Mr. Isaiah, one of the trail hands, sounded the horn, the camp had buzzed with activity. Davonna was dressed and out of the wagon. So were the children. Blair set out tin cups for coffee for the adults and tea for the children, while Lyall went off with Ian to fetch the oxen. The other three had completed their respective chores and seemed bent on grating on one another's nerves. An activity she and Caleb had delighted in as children. As far as she was concerned, things were going better than expected.

Neelie couldn't say she'd adjusted to sleeping atop a trunk in a covered wagon, but in just five days, she felt pretty good about the adjustment she'd made to cooking for a big family and helping set up camp with wagons, oxen, and travel furniture. That didn't mean she wasn't overdue for some peace and quiet. Thankfully, Saturdays meant they'd settle into a spot early and camp for two nights. Tomorrow she'd see about using one of Ian's horses for a Sunday ride.

"Give it to me!" She'd heard eagles with a quieter screech than Duff's.

Neelie spun around in time to see Angus getting away with Duff's rope. She squared her shoulders. "Angus Kamden, stop where you are."

He did. Just as Davonna rose from her stool, apparently unaware of the commotion surrounding her. Angus froze in place, not one foot away from her. She jerked and tripped over the stool, tumbling with it to the ground.

"Mither!" Ian dropped the leads on the oxen near the yoke and dashed toward his mother.

Neelie let the spatula fall to the ground. "Is she all right?"

Ian glanced over his shoulder. "How could you let this happen?"

Neelie went to Davonna, muttering under her breath. "Let this happen?"

"Rhoda never would've allowed all that horseplay at the camp."

Neelie's shoulders tensed. "She isn't here."

Ian clamped his jaw shut, his right eyelid twitching.

Davonna groaned. "Just listen to you two." She rolled off the legs of the stool. "Son, you don't know what Rhoda allowed and didn't allow. You were always off tending the animals or working on somebody's wheels."

Neelie struggled to rein in her myriad emotions. Not only did Davonna have spunk, the woman had come to her defense.

"I'm sorry, Nana," Angus said, his face stricken. "I—"

Davonna waved her hand. "I'm fine, Angus Boy. I lost my balance, that's all."

"I think we should have the doctor look at you," Ian said. "Make sure nothing broke."

"If I'd broken something, you'd know it."

When Davonna reached for Neelie's hand, Neelie carefully helped her up. "Are you sure, Mrs. Kamden?"

"That's you, dear." A quiver layered the old woman's voice.

Neelie sighed and made the mistake of looking at Ian. Judging by the set of his jaw and the frustration clouding his eyes, she wouldn't be Mrs. Kamden for long.

She wasn't Rhoda. Never would be.

That evening, Neelie sat on the board floor of the wagon with Anna's writing desk on her lap. Candlelight cast a shadowy glow on the paper beneath her hand.

The Kamden's camp was quiet, free of horseplay, accusations, and awkward glances. Ian had taken Davonna and all five children to the central campfire. Neelie had declined Maisie's invitation to join them. As unsettling emotions hammered her, she could only shake her head. Neither she nor Ian knew what to say to each other. How to act around the other.

Neelie pulled the quill and ink from the box. Ever since she'd reunited with Caleb and begun traveling with the caravan, she'd been wondering what to tell Buckskin Joe at the Wild West Show. According to his reply to her telegram, he was expecting her to arrive in San Francisco the first of July.

Today, she had no doubts about her answer. She couldn't let the children or Davonna become any more attached to her than they had. Not when Ian would clearly never accept her.

She dipped the quill into the ink, tapped it on the rim, and began writing.

Chapter 10

Neelie dragged a soapy cloth over the table, her nerves as twitchy as a trigger finger in a showdown. Walking the trail today, she'd shared some of her frustrations with Anna, who said all she and Ian needed was more time alone. They'd no sooner set up camp, before Caleb and Anna took Davonna and the children to practice for the upcoming Independence Day relay races.

"If the table's not clean by now, it never will be."

Heat rushing into her face, Neelie glanced at the three-legged stool where Ian sat, whittling on a piece of wood. "I already washed it?"

He nodded, a smile teasing the corners of his mouth. "*And* all the dishes and pots."

He'd been watching her. It shouldn't matter whether he kept track of what she did. It didn't matter, really. But it felt good to know he at least cared enough to notice her.

"Without the children and your mother here, I don't know what to do with myself."

Ian pointed to an empty stool. "Come sit down and relax. Rhoda would quilt or do mend—" He stopped mid-word, a frown deepening the lines framing his mouth. "I shouldn't have mentioned her."

Neelie laid the cloth out to dry on the table. "I confess, comparisons to her do upset me. I always come up short."

Ian set his knife and carving on the ground and leaned forward, elbows on his knees. "I was wrong to blame you for my children's behavior the other day, and my mother's fall was an accident."

Neelie glanced at the cloth, wanting to scrub something. "We're not ourselves when we're grieving."

"Rhoda isn't coming back. I know that. I buried her." He walked to the other end of the table. "And I am glad you're here."

She felt her mouth drop open and quickly closed it.

"Despite my thoughtless accusations, you're good with the children. And Mither really likes you."

Of course he was glad she was here. As a nanny to his children and a companion to his mother.

"I've not seen you stitch or quilt. What do you do, just for yourself?" He glanced at the guns holstered on her hips. "You shoot things?"

"Yes. But you've made it clear that I shouldn't."

"I don't like you to shoot when it causes a stampede. I'm not comfortable in trees."

"Fair enough." Was he saying she could take time away from the family for some shooting practice?

Ian glanced at the sky. "There's plenty of daylight left and no sign of buffalo. What do you say we knock over a few targets?"

"You and me?"

"According to your brother, the preacher, we *are* married. I'm sure that would fall well within our rights." A warm smile curved his full lips.

At a loss for words, she simply nodded.

Ian didn't stand a chance against her. She liked those odds and couldn't help but smile.

Pulling the horse around, Ian guided his palomino toward the riverbank for some target shooting. They'd let the captain know they'd be shooting and from which direction. Ian carried his Colt revolving rifle in a scabbard strapped to the saddle. He couldn't say when he'd been this excited about an outing.

Neelie rode the chestnut mare, Rhoda's favorite. A sack of bottles hung, clinking, from the saddle horn, and the brim of her sombrero bounced with each clomp of the horse's hooves. The cross-draw revolvers rode high and ready at her slender waist. He'd never actually seen Neelie shoot, but she had nailed a running rabbit with one shot and done it again with a charging cougar. Chances were better than good that she was about to show him up. He'd never pitted his skill against a marksman.

Or a marks*woman*.

After seeing Neelie wearing that green dress during their wedding ceremony, without holsters, there was no denying she was a woman. A handsome one, at that. A twinge of guilt knotted his stomach. He had no business thinking on such things. She seemed to need his help, and he certainly needed hers—that was why he'd married her. While he had yet to figure out why she'd agreed, he knew it wasn't because she was expecting. . .*that* kind of marriage. Or any modicum of romance, for that matter. She'd confirmed it the very next day when she stepped out of the farm wagon wearing the men's trousers and shirt.

"Ian?"

Startled out of his thoughts, he drew in a deep breath and looked at her. "Did I miss something?"

"I asked if you're sure you want to do this."

"See you shoot? Yes. I'm sure." It was competition that had him nervous, and being alone with her wasn't helping matters.

His heart might still belong to Rhoda, but Neelie was his wife now. And she'd already done a lot to help him with the children and Mither, all while he was still mourning. Providing her with a little recreation was the least he could do.

"Well, then, I think we've found the perfect place." Neelie pointed to the embankment about fifty yards away. "We can set the bottles along the ledge about halfway up."

"Looks good to me."

When Neelie dismounted, Ian swung down from his horse and looped the reins over a low branch, grabbed his rifle and scabbard, and followed her. She stopped just before

reaching the bank wall and turned around. He'd been following closer than he'd realized and had trouble stopping in time to avoid a collision. As he looked down at her, she moistened her lips. Apparently, he wasn't the only one whose mouth had gone dry.

Neelie reached inside the sack and pulled out a couple of medicine bottles.

"I'll set some up on the other end." Ian reached into the sack. When he brushed her thumb, she looked up at him, her face flushing. He turned away.

In awkward silence, they set up a neat row of bottles on the berm and then walked out about thirty yards.

While he pulled his rifle from its scabbard, Neelie shattered the air and the smallest bottle with one shot. A smile lit her face and reached her brown eyes, now sparkling with golden flecks.

"I hope to get in at least one good shot. I do have some manly pride, you know." Ian lifted the rifle and carefully sighted on the largest of the bottles. Releasing a cloud of smoke, the .44 exploded the bottle.

Neelie's eyebrows arched as she pulled both revolvers from their holsters and shattered the two targets on the end.

He let out a low whistle. "I am on your good side now, right?"

She tipped her head and grinned. "You're getting there."

This outing was one of his better ideas. She was having fun, and so was he. He liked seeing her playful side. And her competitive side.

"No wonder shooting has been your livelihood. You're really quite good." He slid the rifle back into the scabbard. "I figure my job is to keep food on the table, and if that big bottle were a stag, I'd be dressing him out by now."

"I'm sure you would." Neelie holstered one of her revolvers. "But you never know when you may want to impress your wee ones." She spun the other revolver then offered him the grip. "Ever shoot a gun like this?"

Ian shook his head. "Never shot a revolver before. I'm a rifle man."

"Well, if you don't mind taking tips from a *woman*, I could give you a couple."

There was no comparison; Neelie was nothing like Rhoda. He swallowed hard and took the pistol from her. "Teaching this dog new tricks might be more difficult than you think."

"I'll take my chances." After a quick smile, Neelie pressed her hand to his elbow and turned him toward the embankment. Then she set one hand on his forearm and braced his hand with the other.

Suddenly feeling a little light-headed, Ian shifted his weight to his other leg.

Neelie looked up at him. "Relax. Let yourself feel the pistol as an extension of your finger pointing at the target." A curl the color of honey bounced in front of her ear, not far from her mouth.

She suddenly let go of his arm, and despite the sweat beading on his neck, he felt a chill shimmy up his spine.

He'd been staring, and she didn't like it.

"We best get back to camp." Neelie reached for her pistol and seemed almost afraid to touch him.

"Good tips."

"Thank you." She holstered her gun and retrieved the two bottles they hadn't shattered.

As they walked back to their horses in silence, Ian's light-headedness returned, along with some of Rhoda's last words. *"You will need a wife and the children will need a mother. Let yourself find someone."*

He had.

But Neelie had agreed to a marriage of convenience, and nothing more. Would that be enough?

It would have to be.

Chapter 11

J *ust as I am, though tossed about*
with many a conflict, many a doubt,
fightings and fears within, without,
O Lamb of God, I come! I come!"

A hymn hadn't occupied Neelie's mind for many years. But on this Sunday, after hearing it sung in Ian's baritone, the tune and words to the third verse of "Just As I Am" lingered in her mind. *Conflicts. Doubts. Fightings. Fears.* She had them all. God couldn't want her, just as she was.

As Neelie nudged the languid chestnut into a slightly more energetic amble, she doubted her qualifications to care for Ian's children. They needed someone more focused on homemaking and such things.

And fears. . . She feared what she'd felt Wednesday, riding side by side with Ian and the enjoyment of showing off for him. His recognition of her skill. The warmth of his arm and the tingle she'd felt in her fingers. She wasn't about to admit it to anyone, but she had a wagon full of fears.

Fightings. Even now, she fought the temptation to run from it all. She had her six-shooters and a horse. She could hunt and find enough water to make it to the next fort, where there was sure to be folks who would wager to see a woman shootist in action.

Neelie allowed her mount to return to a more sluggish pace and patted her mane. It wouldn't be easy to train her to be a show partner, but she'd be able to trade the horse for one that could be trained.

But Neelie didn't want to leave the caravan. Anna and Caleb. The children and Davonna. Or Ian.

She'd seen conflict on Ian's face when she'd asked to use a horse.

"Alone?" His eyes had widened. Ian didn't want to trust her with the horse for fear she'd leave. He'd seen her do it before.

But he did trust her.

He'd cared enough to spend time with her without the children. . .to take her out to practice with targets when he had to know she would outshoot him. That meant something.

She wasn't Rhoda, but neither was Ian, Archie.

A shade tree had just caught Neelie's attention when she heard hoofbeats not all that far behind her. She pulled back on the reins and listened. One rider, on the other side of the rise.

Had someone followed her from camp? Or worse. Her shoulders tensed. Had someone who knew of her past caught up to her? She slid from the saddle and pulled a six-shooter from its holster. No point in trying to make it to the tree. Instead, she stood her ground, facing the direction of the rider.

When the rider rose into view, Neelie recognized the Tennessee pacer and the man beneath the derby.

Her brother raised his hands. "I come in peace."

She holstered her gun. "Did Ian ask you to follow me?"

"He doesn't know I'm here." He lifted his hat and wiped beads of sweat from his brow. "Could we talk in the shade?"

Nodding, she climbed back into her saddle and followed Caleb to the lone tree. Within minutes, the horses grazed and Neelie sat with her back against the trunk of the cottonwood.

Caleb sat facing her, legs crossed. "I see myself in you, Neelie, and I'm not just talking about physical resemblances."

"Oh?"

"Before I left home, I met some fellows who hung out at the Wildhorse Saloon. I started drinking with them. Often."

She nodded. "I knew you came home drunk a time or two."

"It was all I wanted to do during the war."

"You're a preacher now. Married. You put all of that behind you."

"I told you I was the only one who survived from my regiment. I didn't tell you why." Caleb set his derby on the grass beside him, and she did the same with her sombrero. "After the war, I saw an advertisement for trail hands and went to Saint Charles to join the caravan. I wanted nothing more than to run from my past. Run from what happened that day during the war when I drew watch and drank anyway. The day I passed out. The day my regiment was ambushed and everyone perished but me."

Neelie groaned. Her brother had faced so much anguish. How was he able to live with it? And become a preacher, no less?

"I fled and clung to the shame I felt. Because I kept my grief and disgrace locked inside, I couldn't let myself care for anyone else. I couldn't allow anyone to come too close."

She had more in common with her brother than she'd imagined.

Caleb plucked a grass stem from the ground. "When I was in that state of mind and battling my failings and fears, I wanted to run."

"That's why you followed me here. You thought I was running?"

"It crossed my mind." He expelled a sigh as if it carried the weight of the world. "Yes."

"I'm married, and I have children to look after."

"Don't be surprised if that's not enough." Her brother wasn't judging her. He might not know what all had grieved and shamed her, but he was saying he understood.

"I did run. Or tried to." Neelie folded her arms then unfolded them. "That first Sunday night in camp. Ian saw me leaving and came after me."

"Is that when you began to care for him?"

Neelie wanted to say she didn't have feelings for Ian. "Probably. He apologized for misunderstanding and misjudging me when I shot the cougar. We talked some, and he asked me to return to the camp." She readjusted her position against the tree trunk. "I

thought about leaving today, but I couldn't."

"Good. We don't want you to go." Caleb shook his head. "A part of me always wanted so badly to care for Anna. To let myself feel something for her. But because of my secrets, I kept pushing her away. Then, because I couldn't be honest with her, she pushed me away."

"What changed?"

"I did." Caleb glanced up at the sky. "I had prayed and pleaded with God to forgive me. All the while, I was convinced He wouldn't pardon me. That He couldn't."

"Because what you'd done was too horrific." It wasn't a question. Neelie knew the feeling.

"Yes. And I worked hard to try to make up for the hurt I'd caused so many people, including my own family."

Tears stung Neelie's eyes. Was that why she'd married Ian? Was she trying to make up for not being able to help Archie? Was she trying to earn God's forgiveness by taking care of motherless children and their grandmother? Blinking hard against the tears, she watched a prairie dog poke its head up out of a hole, look around, and then descend into the ground again. That was what she'd been doing. Living life afraid of her own shadow.

Not anymore. She was tired of hiding.

Her brother's eyes held nothing but compassion.

"I've been hiding behind secrets, too. Behind these clothes." She tugged at the oversized trousers she wore.

"You don't have to hide anymore, Neelie. Everyone has fallen short of God's righteousness and needs His mercy and grace."

"For telling a lie. Stealing an apple. Cheating on a school exam. I was married to a man who soured in the war and became a member of an outlaw gang."

Surprise widened Caleb's eyes, and he reared his head. "Archibald?"

"Yes. He ended up in a hospital in Santa Fe. I received a telegram saying he needed me to come. I was his wife, so I boarded a stagecoach and went to him."

"Alone?"

She nodded. "Turns out he'd mouthed off in a saloon and gotten himself beaten pretty badly. When he recovered, he and his cronies taught me how to ride and shoot, then when I would put on a show, and everyone in town was gathered to watch me, Archie and the brothers cleaned out the tills in shops and telegraph offices. Whatever they could get into."

"I'm so sorry."

Neelie yanked a handful of grass out by the roots. "I knew it was wrong." She tossed the grass into the breeze. "I thought he loved me. I trusted him. And by the time I realized I couldn't trust him, I believed I had no way out of that life."

"If only I'd known." A muscle in his tight jaw twitched. That was the big brother she loved—the one who would protect her, if he could. "If you'd known I was alive, I could've—"

"Gotten yourself killed, that's what." She stood, and he did, too. "Archie was drunk and complaining about his take on a robbery when the leader shot him."

"How awful. But they let you go?"

"I managed to escape the hideout just before the posse showed up to take them all in."

"How did the posse find them?"

"I'd had enough. I found a woman at the mercantile who seemed nice enough and slipped her a note for the sheriff. I told him where to find the brothers and Archie. I didn't know they'd kill him before the sheriff had time to catch them."

Caleb blew out a long breath. "You did the right thing."

"Archie's still dead. And I'm the one who followed him down paths I'm ashamed of."

Caleb leaned forward and reached for her hand. "I know what it feels like to take paths that bury you in shame."

They had so much in common. "Anna helped you get back on the right path?"

"Yes. God used Anna, the captain, and a couple of the other trail hands. They reached out to me and helped me see the truth and trust God with my past. They reminded me that I couldn't earn His forgiveness or make things right by my actions, and that I wasn't beyond God's unexplainable grace and mercy." He looked her in the eye. "You aren't either, sis."

Neelie took several breaths, soaking in his words. Tears pooled her eyes, and she let them fall. "Though tossed about?"

"Just as you are." He pulled her into an embrace, and her tears drenched his shirt.

Angus had seen past her appearance and taken an instant liking to her. Maisie, too. Anna had treated her like a long-lost sister. And Caleb, though surprised at first and maybe even put off by her rough exterior, had provided for her and followed her today because he didn't want her to leave. Had God been using them to reach out to her?

On the ride back to camp, she'd have a long-overdue conversation with Him. But now she at least knew where to start.

Lord, I need You. Please be the keeper of my heart.

They'd ridden about a mile when the squeaks and groans of a wagon and the hoof-beats of a team lifted Neelie's gaze to the road up ahead. A covered farm wagon led by four mules was approaching. An older couple sat on the seat swaying with every turn of the wheels.

"Looks like they might have had company at camp while we were gone." As the mules drew closer, Caleb waved his hat in a greeting.

The wagon rolled to a stop in front of them and a stick-thin man waved a weathered hand. "Hello, folks. Headin' that way, you'll come across a camp of wagons. Real welcoming folks. Had some coffee for us."

"Good afternoon." Her brother set his hat back on his head. "We're part of that company, thank you. I'm Caleb Reger. This is my sister, Neelie."

Neelie gave the couple a polite nod. "Sir. Ma'am." They had her attention until a high-pitched whinny jerked her gaze to the back of the wagon. "Your horse?"

"A Spanish mustang we found a couple weeks back."

"Whistle!" Her heart pounding, Neelie practically jumped off the chestnut mare and dashed to the back of the wagon where her mustang bucked the rope, kicking up a cloud of dust. His head nearly pushing her over, she managed to untie the lead. She grabbed a hank of mane at his withers and sprang onto his back. He glided into kicks and spins— part of the countless shows they'd put on. When she finally brought Whistle to a stop, she saw that Caleb and the couple stood at the front of the wagon watching her, their mouths hanging open.

"Ma'am." The man held his felt hat to his chest. "I'd say that's your horse. He wasn't

at all keen on letting anyone near him. . .until you showed up."

"Yes, sir." Neelie patted the mustang's neck. "Whistle and I got separated in a buffalo stampede a few weeks back. I thought I'd never see him again."

"When we found him, he had a saddle on him. No rider."

No mention of saddlebags. Knowing Whistle, he'd probably wasted no time peeling those off against a tree.

The white-haired woman clapped her hands together. "My husband said. . .well, never mind that. You're alive. We said many prayers for the poor soul."

For her. They'd been praying for her? Neelie wiped her eyes and gave Whistle's ears a good rubbing.

Ian stood at the edge of camp. Again he searched the horizon in the direction he'd seen Neelie ride out more than three hours earlier. She'd asked to use the chestnut mare for a ride. Said she needed some time alone and found it easier to think on the back of a horse.

In the meantime, he'd packed all eight wheels with grease. He'd played a game of checkers with Lyle, Duff, and Angus. He'd watched Blair show Maisie how to start a sampler quilt. He'd visited with a passing couple having coffee with the captain and his wife. He'd filled the water barrel and gathered more wood for their campfire.

While watching the sun's descent, Ian mulled over the past few weeks. After he'd found Neelie leaving camp that night, he'd believed she wanted a better life than the one she'd been living—alone and afraid of her shadow. He didn't understand it, but he'd wanted to protect her. To provide that better life for her. It was what he'd tried to do for Rhoda.

When he asked Neelie to marry him, he'd admitted that he needed her. But not like this. Not when he couldn't be sure she wouldn't run if given the opportunity.

Rolling his shoulders, Ian glanced up at the clouds, which were tinted in pastels of oranges and pinks. Even if Neelie had stopped to do a little shooting, she should've been back. Daylight would soon bow to the deep purple of dusk.

During their horseback ride and target practice, he'd realized he might feel more for Neelie than he'd ever thought possible. If she'd realized how badly he'd wanted to kiss her, she might have been scared off.

"Ian." Garrett Cowlishaw tugged the brim of his white slouch hat in greeting.

"Captain."

"Sure shapin' up to be a pretty sunset, isn't it?"

Ian nodded, but what he felt had nothing to do with appreciation for colors in the sky.

The captain glanced the same direction Ian had been studying. "Guess Caleb's not back yet."

"Back?"

"Yeah. He rode off in that direction awhile back."

Caleb had gone after his sister. Her own brother didn't trust her to come back.

"If you have the time," Garrett said, "I could use your help with a cracked spoke."

"I'd be happy to." Waiting around for his wife to return certainly wasn't doing him any good. "Just give me a minute to let my mother and Blair know where I'll be." He

returned Garrett's wave and took quick steps toward his camp.

He'd been foolish to trust Neelie.

He had more than himself and his own heart to think of. Mither and the children were growing more and more attached to Neelie. Even if she did come back with Caleb, he couldn't live like this, wondering when, not if, she would leave him.

Chapter 12

Neelie watched as Caleb held up his last horseshoe. His first throw had been close enough, hooking the post and dropping just past it.

Davonna had volunteered her and Ian to participate in the Independence Day horseshoe tournament. Caleb and Anna had outscored the captain and his wife, Caroline. According to Boney Hughes, trail hand and unofficial announcer, Anna had *leaners* on both throws.

Unless Neelie and Ian could get at least one ringer, they'd lose.

Clang.

"It's a ringer!" Boney held up two fingers.

Waving his derby like a victory flag, Caleb dashed across the makeshift court and pointed at the shoe that encircled the stake. He wore the grin of a Cheshire cat.

"Show him what you're made of, Neelie."

The deep burr turned her head. Ian stood behind her, his eyes greener than Tennessee spring grasses. A smile lifted the corner of his mouth. She hadn't seen him smile since she'd taken the chestnut out for the ride last Sunday. By the time she and Caleb had returned that night with Whistle, Ian was helping the captain repair a wheel. He seemed surprised to see her and hadn't said much to her since.

"Throw good, Miss Neelie." Duff waved his coiled rope. The children's cheers spurred her on.

Boney stood beside the closest stake, holding two horseshoes out to her. As she reached for them, he bent toward her. "If I was a gamblin' man, I'd place my money on you and Ian, ma'am."

For the game? Horseshoes wasn't something southern belles in Nashville or outlaws in the Wild West engaged in, and she doubted Ian had ever thrown horseshoes. But he did have a wheelwright's arm. She couldn't help but notice that much when she had braced his arm for the shooting lesson. Just thinking about their time at the embankment warmed her neck and face.

Perhaps a friendly game of horseshoes would ease whatever was troubling him.

Horseshoes in hand, Neelie stepped up to the stake and looked down at the blue skirt Anna had given her. After Sunday's discussion with Caleb, she'd decided she was done with hiding from her past. She'd donated the oversized trousers and shirt to Caleb.

She grasped a horseshoe in her left hand then used the other one to pull the skirt tight to her side. The first shoe grazed the post but bounced off.

"One point."

"That's okay, dear." Davonna's voice rose above Boney's. "You'll do better on your next throw." Her mother-in-law's confidence in her warmed Neelie's heart.

Neelie held the second horseshoe up like she'd seen Caleb do, then swung and let it go. *Clang.* One edge of her horseshoe lay against the stake, like Caleb's first throw.

"A solid leaner! Two points." Boney turned her way. "Some mighty fine throwing."

Ian stepped up beside her. "I was sure you said this was your first time playing the game."

"It is." Neelie patted his solid chest. "Now let's see what you're made of."

He looked down at her hand. "I hope it's enough."

Neelie swallowed hard and reached for her skirt to step out of his way.

Ian took both horseshoes from Boney. He sighted his target through the first shoe and let it fly. Straight to the stake.

Clang!

"It's a ringer! And now a two-point game."

Cheers erupted, including her own. Ian looked back at Neelie and gave her a wink that weakened her knees. He turned back around and got into position with the second horseshoe.

Clang!

"Another ringer!" Boney's voice rose over the thunderous cheers. "The winners— Ian and Neelie." He reached out to shake their hands. "Congratulations! Go pick out your pie."

When they'd stepped away from the horseshoe pit, Neelie looked up at Ian. "You never said you'd played before."

"You didn't expect me to give away all my secrets, did you?"

"I suppose not." She certainly hadn't revealed all of hers, although she finally wanted to.

"The fellows down at the docks in Saint Charles had picnics and tournaments every summer."

"Well, it paid off. You gave us the win."

But she doubted he'd be able to give her what she really wanted. His heart would probably always belong to Rhoda. Neelie let out a long sigh. Wearing a dress and a bonnet instead of a sombrero wasn't going to change that.

Three hours later, after relay races and a feast fit for the founders of the nation, Neelie went to the wagon to tidy it while Ian, Davonna, and the children helped clean up after the big picnic.

She knelt in front of the small trunk Anna had given her along with some skirts, blouses, shoes, and bonnets that had belonged to her mother. She'd said she couldn't bear to see them mold in a trunk or be used as rags. Neelie pulled back the corner of a shawl and slid an envelope out from beneath it. Things had changed a lot since she'd written the letter to Buckskin Joe. She'd changed.

So had her plans.

After tucking the envelope into her waistband, Neelie climbed out of the wagon and added a buffalo chip to the campfire. A smoky fire seemed the only thing anyone could do to discourage the mosquitoes. She pulled the letter from the envelope. Only

twelve days had passed since she'd penned the words. Twelve days that had changed her life forever.

"Neelie."

She hadn't heard Ian walk up. He was alone.

"Where are the children? Your mother?" she asked.

"They're going to stargaze with Caleb and Anna." Instead of settling on a stool, he stood on the other side of the fire and removed his cap. "I wanted to talk to you."

Good. He was no longer avoiding her. She had something to say to him, too.

The dried droppings crackled under the heat, and white smoke danced between them. Ian glanced at the paper she held.

Neelie drew in a deep breath. "It's a letter I wrote to the owner of the Wild West Show I was headed to."

"Must admit, I'm curious. What did you tell him?"

"I'll read it to you." Breathing a prayer for courage, Neelie unfolded the parchment and read the message she'd written to the man who had promised her a job.

When she finished, Ian reached for the back of his neck and rubbed as if the tension had settled there. "You've been delayed. That's what you told him, not that you'd married?"

"I wrote this letter nearly two weeks ago."

"I can't live life not being able to trust you. Thinking that at any moment you could leave and never come back." The pain in Ian's eyes seared her heart. That was why he'd been avoiding her since last Sunday.

"You thought I had run and my brother brought me back, like you did?"

"I was only thinking of my family's needs. I should've known it would be too much to ask you to settle down." Ian slapped the palm of his hand with his cap. "I'll make sure you have the supplies you need. Go to that job, if that's what you want."

She didn't want that job anymore. But did she have the courage to tell Ian what she really wanted?

Neelie tossed the letter and the envelope into the fire then took slow steps toward Ian, their gazes locked on each other. "The day I wrote that letter, your mother had fallen and you were angry with me. I didn't feel like I belonged here."

His gaze lingered. "And now?"

Neelie untied the straps on her bonnet and let them hang. "Now I'm wearing skirts and bonnets. The shooting exhibitions, the job in San Francisco, the men's clothing—all of it was me hiding from past hurts. Avoiding any commitments that could lead to future disappointments. After Archie was done with me, I vowed I'd never be that stupid again. I'd trust no one." A pop drew her attention to the campfire, and she watched a spark fly up and burn out. "That was before I met you. And before I had a long talk with God on my ride back to camp the other day. That's not the life I want now, Ian."

His eyebrows arched and his mouth fell open slightly.

"Would you like to know what I want?"

Ian nodded in slow motion, never looking away from her.

Neelie pulled the bonnet off and let it fall to the ground. She looped her hands around his neck and pulled him close. She closed her eyes, kissed his mouth. And he kissed her.

"I want more than a marriage of convenience." She cupped his whiskered cheek. "I

love Maisie and Lyall and Duff and Angus and Blair. I love your mother. And I love you. I know you still—"

He pressed his finger to her lips. "That's the best news I've heard in weeks. I love you, too, Neelie Kamden." Bending, he scooped her bonnet from the ground then captured her hand. "Would you like to know what I want?"

"I would."

"I want to make you my blushing bride."

When he bent to kiss her again, she giggled and pulled him toward the Conestoga, a prayer of thanks giving her heart wings.

Mona Hodgson is the author of nearly forty books, historical novels, and children's books, including her popular Sinclair Sisters of Cripple Creek series. Visit her at www. MonaHodgson.com.

BLINDED BY LOVE

Melissa Jagears

Dedication

To those who hold onto their thoughts until they believe
they have something worthwhile to say.
Thanks for sharing

Chapter 1

California, 1888

B ooks and sewing machines made decent companions. Truly they did.

Helen would not allow herself to think of the companions she'd rather have as she sat under the churchyard oak, far from her niece's wedding party. She hitched up her shoulders and forced up the corners of her mouth in case anyone looked her way. Not that anyone would. Some might console her sister, Margaret, for having the last of her seven children leave the house. But no one would bother with the spinster aunt— even if Helen would mourn her youngest niece's departure more than her sister would.

Now that she was no longer needed to tend Margaret's brood, she'd have to be content reading and sewing in her brother-in-law's tiny attic room for the rest of her life.

With a poorly wrapped box in hand, Neil Oliver stepped into the churchyard and strode toward the gift table. Helen raised her eyebrows. Her sister surely wouldn't have invited Mr. Oliver. Margaret considered him dreadful company because he rarely discussed anything other than the sermon—and since Helen was the only one who actually enjoyed debating him, he rarely spoke to anyone else in the family.

Not that he really talked to other people, either. Though he owned a good portion of the properties and factories in town, most people left him alone—a brooding, handsome, rich bachelor was the most intimidating kind of man.

Helen sighed, dismissing the idea of getting up to get some of the cake they were cutting. She wasn't in the mood for chitchat.

Too bad the marriage ceremony was read from the *Common Book of Prayer*. Mr. Oliver certainly couldn't find anything divisive enough in that book to want to debate it with her. But with no more children's fibs to expose or mathematical gymnastics to perform to buy enough food for ten people on her brother-in-law's fluctuating salary, hopefully Neil would still spar over controversial verses. If not, she'd have no occasion to use her brain again.

Maybe she should ask him to debate her every Sunday instead of only occasionally. And every Wednesday, too. . .

Oh, who was she kidding, he wouldn't waste his carefully saved breath on her more than he already did.

And yet, the second he laid eyes on her, he set down his gift box and walked her way.

"Miss Barker?" The gray, highlighted cowlick above his right eye was mussed more than usual. He never was quite put together lately, as if he hadn't the time to look in a mirror.

"Mr. Oliver, so glad to have you come witness Lena's happy day." Had he come with a gift just to seek her out? She rolled her eyes at herself. He'd not deliberately seek her

out. Surely she'd simply overlooked him at the ceremony—he'd probably hidden in a dark corner to avoid talking to anyone.

"It's a beautiful day for a wedding." Mr. Oliver ran the tips of his fingers over his right eyebrow as if to press out a headache. "The weather is quite pleasant, don't you think?"

She opened her mouth—to ask—to respond—to. . .to what? Not once in the ten years they'd attended church together had Mr. Oliver *ever* attempted small talk. She'd always appreciated that he never bored her with prattle but rather gave her something to ponder—expected her to think. Unlike her brother-in-law, who never conversed with a woman beyond what he wanted her to put on the shopping list. "Are you feeling all right, Mr. Oliver?"

"Besides my eye troubles, I'm fine."

Eye troubles? Had she missed his prayer requests concerning his eyes? No, she'd have remembered such. He never asked for anything for himself at prayer meetings—no worries, pains, problems—he only mentioned others' needs. Maybe he felt he couldn't ask for prayer since he was better off than most. "Would you like me to mention your eye problems at Wednesday's meeting?"

His mouth twitched a bit before he pulled in a breath. "If you feel inclined."

She pursed her lips. That was likely as close to a yes as she'd get from him. "All right."

But instead of bidding her good day, he stood there looking toward the bride and groom, a puzzled expression on his face. She looked, too, but noticed nothing amiss. Lena's bright red hair accentuated the pink in her cheeks as she laughed at a well-wisher patting her new husband on the back. Margaret and Don were beaming over Lena's favorable match, since marrying off the other four girls had left the youngest without an attractive dowry.

"*That's what a pretty face gets you,*" Margaret had said when Lena had announced her engagement to the oil tycoon, callously hinting at Helen's reason for never catching a man's eye. Plain features, a tall, stocky body, and no money easily landed a woman in a relative's attic for the rest of her life.

"So what are your feelings regarding matrimony, Miss Barker? Is it better to remain single as Paul did, or to marry—whether or not one burns?"

Though she had a darker complexion than her niece, Helen's cheeks were now likely turning as bright pink as the bride's. She put a hand against her face, her cold fingers doing little to cool her skin.

Imagine going from talk of weather to. . .*burning with passion.*

She shook her head a little, but the memory of his choice of words didn't change.

Surely he'd not thought through his wording.

At least Mr. Oliver was acting as expected now—coming straight to the point of whatever bit of the sermon he'd hoped to discuss.

Though. . .had any of Paul's passage to the Corinthians been included in the recitation of wedding vows?

Mr. Oliver cleared his throat. "What do you think? Are there reasons besides love that a man or woman should cast away their gift of singleness?"

Levelheaded debate should soothe the fire in her cheeks. She let out a steady breath, imagining the heat draining with the air. "If I recall correctly, that passage is Paul's opinion, and therefore, I can only offer mine. On deciding whether or not to marry—beyond the command given by God to be equally yoked with a believer—wisdom should be

employed. I wouldn't bother to offer an opinion, however, unless I knew the circumstances of the specific parties."

"And what bit of wisdom keeps you a spinster?"

She licked her dry lips and glanced over at her sister sitting at the bride and groom's table. Today's tête-à-tête with Mr. Oliver was not turning out to be as fun as usual. "I'm afraid I never had a decision to make. Lack of opportunity explains my marital status."

"And why's that?"

She generally liked his straightforward chatter, but not so much today. However, he wouldn't appreciate her dancing around flat-out truth. There was nothing feminine about a five-foot-eleven-inch woman with large feet, square shoulders, and a face that could pass as a man's if she ever cut her hair like one. Her strong features had made her father handsome, but what she wouldn't have given for one soft feminine attribute from her mother. However, God had bequeathed all beauty to Margaret. "For someone who analyzes scripture to pieces, you have obviously not taken the time to look me over from head to toe."

She braced herself for him to raze her with a glance and find her wanting, but all he did was frown, his gaze fastened to her eyes as usual. Behind his thick glasses, his greenish-gold irises appeared smaller than they really were, but his lenses never distorted the sincerity and seriousness that always rested within his pupils. He might be brusque and reticent—which many took for rudeness—but she'd watched his eyes enough during previous conversations to know he cared about ideas and people and truth.

Though whether or not he cared much about her in particular. . .well, why should he?

"So you're not opposed to marriage if the opportunity came about?"

She let out a cynical huff. "I'm forty-seven, Mr. Oliver. I no longer entertain the slightest hope—"

"As you said, deciding upon a spouse should be undertaken using wisdom. I think we'd both agree choosing a marriage based upon appearance is reckless."

Easy for him to say. He was one of the more handsome men she'd met and likely one of the richest. He might flatter his morality by believing he'd choose an ugly woman if it was a wise decision, but he'd never have to actually do so. "I think marrying purely for attraction is rash, certainly. However, though a woman's looks are inconsequential to her character, they tend to be highly sought. Physical attraction seems to have a stronger pull than practicality when considering a match for one's self."

"That's why I choose you, Miss Barker."

She blinked. Choose her for what? Their discussions? Ah yes, no need to worry about anyone finding their talks inappropriate when no one would fathom to think him attracted to her.

He turned his head slightly to the side and squinted as if seeing was giving him great difficulty.

And now she knew firsthand how her sister felt during the awkward silences that always swathed this man.

She dipped her head, unable to look at him anymore. And for years, she'd had such warm thoughts about him, even imagined he thought of her as a friend—as much as the most reticent man on the planet could possess a friend.

"I assume you'll want more time to think about it."

She opened and closed her mouth twice—figuring out how to respond to him seemed

to be impossible today. Think about what? "Mr. Oliver, I've never before been at a loss for knowing what point you were dissecting or what Scriptural nuance you were probing, but you have puzzled me this afternoon from the moment you commented on the weather."

His forehead wrinkled as he squinted. He looked like he was having difficulty swallowing.

"Are you all right?" It was not appropriate for her to feel a grown man's head in front of the entire congregation, but Mr. Oliver needed some kind of comforting—he looked ready to keel over. Maybe illness explained this strange conversation.

She stood but kept her hand to herself. "Why don't you take my chair."

"No." The single word tore out from what sounded like a scratchy throat.

Maybe she shouldn't get too close. Whatever he was coming down with might be catching. "I think I saw Dr. Mathers over—"

"No." He grabbed her wrist.

She stared at his hand. He'd never touched her before. His hands were rougher than she'd expected for someone so scholarly.

And was he actually pulling her closer? Feeling unbalanced, she took a step toward him—but just a little step.

"I. . .I suppose, Miss Barker, since I've never asked anyone this before, that I messed up. But I meant for our Corinthians discussion to naturally lead into asking you to marry me."

❧

While he hadn't expected Helen to give him the evil glare he'd seen women give men they had no interest in, he hadn't expected the mirth lighting her eyes, either.

He'd not meant to be amusing in the least.

Her smile only grew. "No other man on earth would use Paul's opinion on favoring singleness as the opening to a marriage proposal."

The muscle in his cheek that jumped when he was nervous began to pull at his lip. Unfortunately there was no way to stop the confounded tick.

He should grow a beard to hide it.

Not that he planned to do this again.

"I'm sorry, Miss Barker, for choosing something you find amusing for what I don't find. . .amusing, exactly. I was in earnest."

"I'm sure you were. If I know anything about you, you never jest."

He scratched behind his ear. Was that true? No, he used to tease his younger sisters. But then, he'd left them over twenty years ago. Since then, had he ever been comfortable enough to tease someone—especially a female? He tried to summon a witty rejoinder to prove Miss Barker wrong.

No, he was decidedly too uncomfortable right now for lighthearted banter while his fate teetered upon her next words. He rubbed at his constricted throat. He'd spoken with her many times after services, for up to a half hour sometimes when disagreement enlivened her spirit, but he'd never felt so. . .so drained as now.

"What's your reasoning, Mr. Oliver?"

"About what?" He leaned forward, trying to see past the darkness floating in front of her face. Of all the times for his vision to blur so badly.

"The motive behind your proposal. I'm sure you have an extensive list of reasons for

160

approaching me instead of another."

Of course he did. He'd thought about this for the last twelve days, every hour spent pondering his life's next turn. "Almost two weeks ago, my doctor informed me there is an exceedingly high likelihood that my vision's rapid decline will end in blindness. Despite cutting back on my hours of reading and writing, my vision steadily worsens."

He pushed down the lump in his throat and pulled in some oxygen. He would not question God's sovereignty. But this trial. . .well, considering it all joy was not coming easy.

"But don't you care that I'm about as comely as an anvil?"

Did she think he cared about such things? "If I'd wanted a comely woman, my numerous holdings, investments, and properties would have lured one in by now, don't you think? I prefer to converse with a woman who ponders more than what color ribbon she should thread through her next bonnet."

He could just make out the slight pull of her lips to the right. She often did that when he'd backed her into an intellectual corner and she had to concede a point.

Without his vision, he'd have to start figuring out if she had any aural cues that would give her away.

If she ever bothered to debate with him again after this, that is.

"Even with your blindness, you could still lure in a woman half your age and three times as handsome as I, who also uses the brain God gave her."

That he could find such a woman was likely, she knew it as well as he. Was this her way of refusing him?

Or maybe. . .no, wait. His sisters used to do this. He closed his eyes and breathed evenly. It'd been a long time since he'd had to deduce a woman's true feelings despite the contradictory words she spouted. "Your age and appearance don't concern me, Miss Barker, but not because I will no longer see you. A mind as lithe as your own, a spirit as generous, and an innate pleasing character makes taking your appearance into account needless."

Now that look was the happy sort he'd hoped for earlier. Though he couldn't quite tell if tears rimmed her eyes or if the moisture was his own from trying so hard to see her reaction.

But now, she seemed to be frowning. . . .

His cheek muscle started ticking again. He turned the right side of his face away from her.

"So why must you have a spouse now, Mr. Oliver? What pressing need drives you to choose me?"

Did she not find ensuing blindness an urgent matter?

The thought of letting her know exactly why he needed *her* made his vision swim even more. "I need someone trustworthy to take over my business, who's teachable and would be willing. . ." He pressed his lips together in an effort to stop the tick. Futile. "Who'd be willing to care for me. . .as well."

Not that he expected a vibrant and feisty woman like Helen to truly fall for someone as socially awkward as he, but he could get through life if he had someone to rely upon when he was incapable of getting around on his own. Hopefully she'd at least come to care for him a little so he wouldn't be much of a burden to her. "Once I go blind, I'll need someone to help me get around and care for me, quite possibly around the clock."

"Why not hire someone?"

"Anyone can fill an employment position. But I figured since both of us are entering a season of life where we can no longer do what we have done for so long, we might be open to a different avenue."

Had his faith been so weak God had to put him through this? He pressed a hand against his temple in an effort to soothe the jabbing behind his eyes that was impossible to touch. He needed to stop dwelling on something he couldn't reason away. "I intend to entrust my entire estate to you, if you'll entrust me with. . ."

And what exactly did he need from Helen? "Promise me your loyalty, Miss Barker. I've seen it on display in regard to your family and faith; it's all I ask of you."

Chapter 2

Helen pinched her nose shut to keep the dust she'd just stirred from tickling up a sneeze.

"I just can't believe you'd agree to marry him in a week. It's. . .it's . . ."

Helen clamped her free hand against her forehead, hoping to smash away the headache Margaret created by her nonstop talking while pacing in front of the footboard. Why couldn't her sister fold the items on the bed waiting to be packed into Helen's two trunks instead?

"It's unseemly."

"Achoo!"

"God bless you."

Well, that was one way to get her sister to bless this marriage—probably the only way. Helen sniffled and searched for her handkerchief amid the pile of embroidered linens she'd collected. She'd placed them around the house years ago when she realized they'd never leave this house for a home of her own.

Not anymore. She smiled but then noticed the coffee stain on one of her crocheted doilies. Would Neil want her old handmade things? He could probably afford to buy all the fancy linens she desired. And they'd all be pristine.

Would he care about the stains? He wouldn't be able to see them soon anyway, and since he wasn't marrying her for love, he probably cared even less about the things she brought with her.

"In the week since Mr. Oliver proposed, he hasn't taken you for a walk, a carriage ride, or to the hotel for dinner." Margaret stood looking out the window, her hands clenching her hips. "He didn't even drop by to see you—"

"He saw me at church on Wednesday."

"That's not the same. You've let him get away with doing nothing to win you. Just because no one else has wanted you, doesn't mean you can't get something more out of him. He's got more money than all of Don's brothers combined. He could at least have taken you to see that opera singer who came through town yesterday."

Rather Margaret had hoped he'd take them all to see the opera singer yesterday.

"Whatever are you going to talk about to that man? You can't discuss the Bible every day."

Helen sniffled again, using the handkerchief to hide her smile. Talking about theology was far more interesting than last night's dinner argument over whether Don and Margaret could afford to reupholster the ottoman and the settee to match, or just one of the items, or neither. . . .

"He can't possibly love you, so how'd you capture his interest?"

And now she used the handkerchief to hide a scowl. Of course no one could actually be interested in Margaret Abernathy's ugly sister.

She'd believed that herself only just a week ago.

Of course, Neil wasn't really interested in *her*.

"He's not good enough for you, Helen."

"Come again?" Now her head *truly* ached. She'd never thought highly of her sister—just as Margaret had never thought much of her—but she must have misunderstood. "How can a poor, homely spinster be too good for a rich, handsome man?" Never mind the reason she had no money was because she'd helped Margaret raise her brood. Maybe she should've found a paying position all those years ago. Her sister and late mother might actually have thought her valuable then. But now that her youth had slipped away, finding a position would likely be difficult, if not impossible.

"Well of course he's *good* enough. But, but. . .well, he could afford to pay you quite the sum for your assistance, yet he's figured out a way to steal your services for free. *We* can't afford help, yet *he* could hire a hundred people off the street if he wanted to."

Helen crammed her winter petticoat into the trunk and pressed her lips together. *Breathe.*

"Achoo!"

All right, don't breathe too much. She snatched up her handkerchief to cover another sneeze.

"God bless you."

"That's right, Margaret, God blessed me." She moved to empty her side table's little drawer. "You'd have been happy if Mr. Oliver had asked for any of your girls' hands."

"But he's at least twenty years older than Lula, and he's way too old for any of the others."

"Yet if he'd asked for Lula's hand years ago, you would've given your blessing despite the age difference."

"Money isn't all that matters."

"I don't believe that was your sentiment when Eunice got engaged." Money was the only reason Eunice married Delbert, a man fourteen years her senior. And Margaret had been thrilled with the match.

"Well, what about Jeffrey?"

Helen placed her three journals and pen set into one of the little compartments in the tray sitting across the top of the trunk. "Marrying Neil won't change anything about that."

"But surely he'll feel you are condoning what Mr. Oliver did to him."

Neil hadn't done anything besides make a good business deal for himself. And though Don often chastised his son for not thinking things through, Margaret insisted Neil had swindled her favorite son from his property. How else could a man she found socially unacceptable make so much money if not by cheating?

Perhaps Neil hadn't told the boy he was underselling. . .and maybe he had and Jeffrey didn't care. Either way, Jeffrey was miffed after learning Mr. Oliver was making a handsome profit with the property.

And with Jeffrey just returning from another jaunt around the West Coast, would he fume over his aunt marrying Neil?

But how could she not pursue a future beyond this small attic? As much as she loved Jeffrey, he was a bit of a hothead. In a few years, he'd engage in some other business idea and would care little about his past transaction with Neil. And she'd have declined this opportunity for nothing. Besides, she couldn't change the past. . .but she could transform the future. "As Neil's wife, I'll be in a position to keep other young men from being taken. . .if that's even necessary."

"I have a bad feeling about this." Margaret frowned, evidently too busy wringing her hands to pack the two winter petticoats left to stuff into the larger trunk.

Helen snatched up the garments and crammed them in. "Here, hold this lid down." She'd not let herself react to her sister's jealousy or pettiness.

"Miss Barker?" Mrs. Wall poked her white-capped head into the room. "A driver's waiting for you downstairs."

Margaret stiffened, but at least kept her weight on the trunk lid. Her sister was always annoyed when the house staff spoke to Helen instead of her—as if no one in the household could function without her input.

Helen pulled on the leather straps until the buckles lined up with the holes then picked up the timepiece hanging from her waist. "It's not even lunchtime yet." Neil had told her they'd marry at three. She'd not expected him to send someone for her until nearer the ceremony.

"He's in the parlor."

Margaret bristled even more. Hopefully the driver wasn't touching anything when they went down to talk to him.

With one last glance around, Helen made sure everything had been packed. She'd not meant to finish early, but perhaps it was a good thing. Was Neil always ahead of schedule? Was he anxious? Had he forgotten what he'd told her?

Making her way down the narrow stairs, Margaret treading heavily behind her, Helen brushed at the dust clinging to her blue-and-cream-striped skirt. She shouldn't have donned her wedding outfit until after packing, but nothing could be done about it now.

They stepped into the dark-green-and-gray-wallpapered parlor, where the driver, a man of maybe forty years, in a jacket and trousers that'd seen better days, stood ill at ease holding on to a ledger of some sort. He tipped his hat then must have realized he was still wearing it inside, because he snagged it off. "Miss Barker, ma'am?"

"Yes."

Margaret cleared her throat, but the driver ignored her.

"Mr. Oliver wanted me to give you this." He handed Helen the thin dark green ledger—or was it a journal? "He told me to wait for your answer." Fidgeting, the man's gaze darted around at the frilly furniture.

Mrs. Wall stepped around Margaret. "Since it's lunchtime, I propose Mr. Ferguson come to the kitchen. I've got an extra meat pie."

"What answer is Mr. Oliver expecting?" Margaret eyed the notebook and the dust-covered driver.

"I don't know, ma'am. Miss Barker could answer though."

Helen crossed to the short fancy chair in the corner of the room and sat before opening the journal. She didn't need to sit, but it'd keep Margaret from looking over her shoulder. A single piece of paper lay just inside the cover.

Dear Helen,

> *I realized I hadn't said all that I meant to say Wednesday. I was surprised that you agreed so readily, and my tongue, as usual, stayed tied. I, however, want to make sure you know what kind of man you're marrying, and rather than attempt to say it and forget things again, I figured writing would give me the time to ponder all that needed to be said. I want to lay out all my foibles and perhaps what you'll consider assets before you go through with your vows. I don't take vows lightly, and from what I know of you, you won't, either. I've told no one of our engagement. If what I've written here makes you reconsider our arrangement, inform my driver, Mr. Ferguson, and he'll inform me. I promise not to react in any way detrimental to you if you change your mind. Regardless of your choice, I hope you'll still discuss the finer details of scripture with me in the future.*
> *Earnestly,*
> *Neil*

She smiled at the words on the page.

It'd be too easy to love Neil. Except their match had nothing to do with love. Mutual need and convenience was all their relationship was supposed to be. But could she keep her emotions in check? What happened if she came to love him but he stayed as aloof as ever?

Her hands started trembling. Could she remain in her sister's suffocating attic when she could help run a business and have a house of her own?

No. So she'd figure out what to do with love or the continued lack thereof later—if that ever became an issue.

And why did she have this glimmer of hope that he might come to care something for her? She was too old to believe in fairy tales. No handsome prince fell for the ugly duck paddling in his pond.

Helen laid the note down in her lap. "Mrs. Wall, if you'd escort Mr. Ferguson to the kitchen and have my lunch brought to me, I'll have him on his way shortly."

The big wooden door to the church creaked open behind Neil. He didn't feel like talking to anyone right now, so he kept his head down and continued praying. . .though his prayers hardly contained words—more an attempt to shake the uncertainty off his shoulders and onto the cross.

"Neil?"

He glanced up and over his shoulder, blinking several times against the dim interior, waiting for his eyes to adjust.

Stupid. His eyes weren't going to adjust. "Helen?" He'd spoken her Christian name aloud on Wednesday and it had felt wrong, but he had to shed the informality lest he keep barriers between them. He'd kept people at arm's length his whole life, but he couldn't do that with a wife.

"Yes."

He started at the voice only a few feet away, as if she'd come out of nowhere. He

could just make out her silhouette. The sanctuary's darkness must be more encompassing than he'd thought. Otherwise he should have seen her movement sooner—he wasn't that bad off yet—he shouldn't lose that much vision in an hour or two.

But why was she here early? He surely hadn't been praying for three hours already. "What time is it?"

"One."

The air fluffed between them when she sat, the fabric of her skirt beside his leg looked striped. Probably the blue pinstripes she often wore, the pattern giving the illusion she had more curves than she did.

He swallowed against imagining her profile too much. Of course, her shape or lack thereof was likely the only thing he'd see of her from now on. "How did you know I was here?"

"Mr. Ferguson told me."

He'd sent his driver to the Abernathys' only minutes before noon. She couldn't have read everything he'd written already. At least not with enough time to ponder all the implications.

She turned toward him. "Were you planning to sit in the dark for another two hours?"

"I didn't think praying would hurt anything."

"I don't think praying ever hurts."

"Not so sure about that." He clasped his hands in front of him, trying to see if they were trembling as hard as they felt. "David was a rather brave man. 'Search me, O God, and know my heart: try me, and know my thoughts: and see if there be any wicked way in me.' I myself haven't been brave enough to truly pray *that* very often."

"I suppose not many of us ask God to be so truthful with us, as if we could keep our faults hidden if we refuse Him permission to look."

He nodded. Were his faults why she'd come early? Had she seen the truth about him in the small notebook he'd filled over the last three nights and realized she'd been too quick to agree to marry him?

She *had* been too quick to agree. He'd been pondering this arrangement for almost two weeks, and she'd given him an answer in three days.

Was this why he'd felt such unease?

But he'd promised, and he'd decided; so he'd follow through—if she'd have him.

He sat in silence, keeping his eyes on his hands, so he might get a glimpse of her face from his peripheral vision. It was difficult to look away from what he wanted to see and rely on his eyes and brain to piece together the images from the edges of his vision. Today's darkness seemed worse than yesterday's though. Would it clear up again?

Helen remained silent beside him.

Why was she here if not to break things off? "Mr. Ferguson gave you the notebook?"

Surely after laying bare the deficiencies of his character, she couldn't be antsy to marry him.

"Yes, he did. Were you trying to talk me out of marrying you?"

"No." Not exactly.

"Good, because it didn't work."

His facial twitch started acting up. He knew it wasn't as visible as it felt, but unable to see her expression, he couldn't do anything but imagine her staring at his blasted cheek.

"Your failures are anything but. You seem to believe that giving away *only* twenty-five

percent of your income or punching a man's face hard enough to disfigure him despite the fact that he was"—she cleared her throat—"forcing his attentions onto a woman should be looked down upon. Well, you're wrong; those don't deserve to be included on your list of failures—"

"Granted those two things could be seen as something I shouldn't regret, but did you read the whole list? I also let my sister string along a man, knowing she'd likely jilt him, because I'd hoped that by some miracle she wouldn't. And then there's my pride over having acquired so much when most came through God's favor. And that time I took a drunk man's purse so he couldn't purchase any more liquor, but then justified keeping his money so I wouldn't have to go back and talk to him—"

"I read it." Her hand landed on his, and suddenly he had a nervous muscular tick near his thumb as well.

Her long, soft fingers were cool to the touch, so he wrapped his hand around them. When he realized what he'd done, he forced himself to keep hold of her. Holding the hand of the woman he was about to marry wasn't improper, but he'd not thought about how her skin would actually feel. . . .

"I trusted you before I read your letters, and after reading them, I know my trust isn't misplaced. But the real question is whether you should trust my abilities. I've never been involved in any type of business. I've done nothing much beyond household duties: clean floors, change diapers, cook meals."

"I trust *you* whether or not you have the right job qualifications." Not that he was hiring her for a job.

Please God, sometime in the future, I hope You'll help her feel something more than obligation toward me.

He squeezed her hand thrice. "I know your character, Helen."

She fidgeted. "You didn't mention your dealings with Jeffrey in your journal."

"Who?"

"My nephew, Jeffrey Abernathy. He has red curly hair and a thin mustache. He stands a little shorter than you but is skinny as a rail. He sold you property near Orchard Street."

"Oh." One of her sister's large brood. "He sold that to cover a debt, as I recall."

She said nothing more.

Surely she didn't want him to pick apart her nephew's character—she had to know he wouldn't have much good to say. Jeffrey wasn't particularly a bad kid, but there was definitely troubling aspects to the young man's personality. "Is there a reason you brought him up?"

He caught a subtle movement he assumed was the shake of her head.

She squeezed his hand tighter. "I trust you."

The ensuing silence lasted long enough that the noise of their timepieces slowly went from ticking separately to in sync. Did she intend to sit with him for two hours? "Do you want me to summon the pastor, or. . ."

"Why don't you go back to praying?" She scooted closer. "I don't hear you pray much."

He swallowed and concentrated on his hands again, except one of them held a woman's fingers, warmed by his own. Had his sisters' hands been this soft?

His mouth was too dry to form words. What had she asked him again?

"Dear Lord," Helen began, "I ask that you help both of us become the people you

want us to be—together. We've been on our own for so long, we may have difficulty learning to consider each other above ourselves. . . ."

He smiled a little as she prayed. She likely thought he'd be uncomfortable praying aloud since he had difficulty conversing, and decided to start the prayer for him. But that hadn't been the problem, her hand had been the problem. Still was a problem. He stopped running his thumb along her index finger and concentrated on her words.

After a few minutes of praying, a glimmer of light, a loud creak, and a thump occurred toward the front of the sanctuary.

Helen straightened then dropped his hand to stand. "Reverend Atlee."

"Oh, excuse me." The man's voice boomed from the front. "I didn't know you two were already here. I thought the ceremony wasn't until three."

Neil stood beside Helen. "We don't mean to be an inconvenience. We were just praying while we waited."

The reverend cleared his throat. "I'm actually glad you're here. The Wicketts were just at the parsonage. Gilda has fallen gravely ill, and they were hoping I'd visit soon, since the doctor thinks she could pass at any time, and I. . .well, might we move up the ceremony? If your witnesses could come earlier, that is."

"We were only expecting you and your wife to witness."

"Oh, well, Georgiana is just behind me. She wanted to bring in flowers."

"Did you need me?" A high, chiming voice invaded the room along with the faint smell of irises.

Neil blew out his breath, hoping to relax. "Mrs. Atlee, your husband wondered if we could wed now. We're ready whenever you are." He turned a bit toward Helen and whispered, "Right?"

"Right," she whispered back, and he let out the breath he'd held.

Helen pressed against the back of his arm just enough so he could tell she was leading him yet trying to disguise the pull, as if she were simply holding on to his arm as if they were a couple.

Well, they were a couple.

His heart raced to keep up with his stupid facial tick.

He thumped his hip against the pew's corner and stifled a groan. Maybe they should've waited for Mrs. Atlee to light a hundred candles to go along with her flowers.

He tried to move forward as if he were leading Helen like a confident groom. No, he was confident. He'd thought this all through.

"It'll be all right." Helen's lips nearly grazed his ear with her whisper, causing a quick shiver to cross his shoulders.

"All right, you stand here." Reverend Atlee clasped his shoulder and turned him to face Helen.

Her hand dropped from his arm.

"And you turn this way." Helen's warmth disappeared, and he squinted, attempting to look at her but not straight on since he couldn't see much that way. He could just make out the pinstripes, the curls. All such blurry images for this day, a day when most men probably memorized the sight of their bride's appearance to cherish in the future.

After the reverend cleared his throat, he read aloud the marriage ceremony's familiar words. Reverend Atlee hadn't been fooling; he was ready for this marriage to happen now.

Neil rubbed his hands against his slacks then grabbed Helen's hands and squeezed

them. His throat dried as he tried to follow along and not miss when he was expected to repeat, but blast it, he wanted to see his bride today. If he kept his head still and didn't move his eyes, perhaps the darkness stubbornly floating in front of him would settle enough to see more of her face than the soft curls she must have pulled out from her usually severe updo. There was some pink in her cheeks. The neckline of her dress was modestly covered in lace. But every time he thought he caught a glimpse of her eyes, he lost focus. He concentrated on relaxing so he could see the pink in her cheeks again. Her long, straight nose came into view, her lips moving to say something he should be listening to—

"You may kiss your bride."

He blinked and looked at the pastor. He was done already? Had the vows between Helen's niece and her new husband gone so fast last week?

He shouldn't have looked away. The darkness stirred as he tried to return his focus on to his bride. What rotten timing. He didn't want to embarrass Helen by kissing her nose or having to hold out his hands like an invalid needing assistance.

Her dainty fingers slid up onto his shoulder and he reached out to pull her close, but instead of moving in to kiss him, her cheek grazed his.

Her mouth was once again against his earlobe. Her breath tickled his ear. "There's no need. Kissing isn't required by the Bible, is it?"

No need? He didn't want this to be a convenient marriage forever, but how could he voice that to a woman he admired but wasn't quite comfortable with yet?

But when had he ever been comfortable laying out his feelings with words? His heart raced at the idea of talking about it. Surely things would naturally progress and he wouldn't need words.

She backed away, but he reached up to capture her jaw. Talking wouldn't work right now, but the kiss the reverend expected him to give her might... He brought up his other hand to cup the side of her face and moved his thumbs until they met the corners of her mouth.

Just because he wasn't required by biblical mandate to give her a kiss didn't mean one would be useless.

He pulled her toward him until their lips met. A bit off center, but he wandered toward the middle until he'd captured hers. After a brief second, she rocked away, probably in an effort to break the kiss, but he didn't let her. He held on to her jaw, firmly yet gently, until she quit leaning back.

Her lips actually softened against his. A throat-clearing to his left registered, but Helen's lips upon his was the most interesting sensation—

After Mrs. Atlee's throat cleared again, Helen broke away. Though he couldn't quite make out her expression, he heard her quick intake of air and heavy swallow.

"I'm sorry." He hadn't meant that to go on as long as it did.

He'd convinced himself he'd have more control over his life by marrying and staying in California than going to live with his sister in Kansas.

But maybe he'd just unwittingly surrendered what little control he'd had.

Chapter 3

Behind his desk, Neil fiddled with his pen, almost able to see its whole length clearly, when a knock interrupted. "Come in."

"Good morning, Neil."

He shifted his focus onto his wife and the scent of coffee. He'd disappeared into his study before she'd awakened—he felt more secure holed up in here. Having a woman in his house for the past week had made him feel exposed somehow. . . . Why, oh why, had God made him weak and reliant on somebody?

Over the last five days, Helen had been industrious, mainly cleaning his small house from the moment she'd arisen until she bid him good night. If he didn't know better, he'd have suspected his housekeeper had stopped cleaning thoroughly after his vision began to fade, but he knew that couldn't be the case. He only hired people with a history of integrity. Rose wouldn't shirk responsibility, even if he'd never know.

But since the wedding, Helen had turned quiet. He was happy with companionable silence, but over the last day or two, he'd begun to wonder if her silence was not as peaceful as his.

He shouldn't have kissed her after she'd suggested otherwise—maybe she wanted their marriage to remain convenient. He should have let things progress naturally, as he'd intended.

Her shadowy form still hovered in the doorway, so he beckoned her in. She needed to step away from the sun lighting her from behind so he could see her better. He pushed aside the stacks of books he'd been trying to work through. He needed his desk cleared anyway, so he could answer Professor Larson's letter asking to visit.

And he had to say yes. He'd practically begged the man to come in past letters, so he could hardly deny the professor's request now just because he'd not gotten used to Helen yet. Somehow he didn't think his mentor would approve of their relationship—the convenient aspect of it anyway.

He'd need to reserve a hotel room for the professor to hide the fact that there wasn't a bed big enough for the newly wedded couple. He'd thought to allow Helen to furnish the house to her satisfaction after the wedding but had been stymied when she'd been uninterested.

So he'd ended up on the couch. He'd never realized how uncomfortable that piece of furniture was. Never had reason to sleep on it before.

The professor was coming in a week and a half. Could he make his marriage look more conventional by then? Nine days wasn't much time to win Helen over.

Despite knowing it would be futile, he blinked repeatedly, trying to better see his

wife in the chair across from him. The slow way she'd lowered herself, and the way she now seemed to sit uncomfortably, bespoke anxiety.

But after many ticks of the clock, she still hadn't asked him for whatever had driven her into his study. Had she finally decided to order new furniture? Everything in the house might as well be changed to her liking since he'd not be seeing much of anything soon. But she claimed she felt uncomfortable with the expense.

Well, he was uncomfortable on the couch. "Have you decided how to redecorate?"

It would be a far better use of her time than rearranging. Did she not realize that moving chairs on a near-blind man would confuse him? But if that's how she made herself feel at home, he'd pray she wasn't afflicted with the same malady that caused his mother to move furniture around whenever she felt restless.

"There's no need to waste money. Your home is adequately furnished."

Hmmm, his mother would never have been happy with *adequately furnished*. This house was also much smaller than his mother would expect of a wealthy man. But then, Helen was a more practical woman. "I can afford more than adequate."

"I know."

He blinked at her but couldn't quite read her expression. Well, so be it. It wasn't like he'd be able to appreciate her decorating efforts. If she was content, he'd let her be so.

But his room did need a bigger bed. . .eventually. . .probably. He needed something.

He looked down at where he should have been able to see his feet, but his brown shoes disappeared against the wood boards. Maybe this was her way to keep him on the sofa indefinitely. Did he have room in the study for a bed?

She'd been skittish since he'd kissed her at the wedding, so outright telling her he needed to move into the bedroom would make everything more awkward. He tapped his pen again. Any other man would probably have wooed his wife by saying her eyes sparkled or something. But, of course, she'd see through such compliments, considering he couldn't see much of her at all.

If only he hadn't rushed this. He'd done well in business by pushing forward with his decision the moment he'd made a plan. But then, relationships were hardly businesses, and friendships were not his forte. Though his few friends were loyal, he didn't realize how rarely he saw them until they sought him out.

But he couldn't sleep on the sofa much longer. He was too tall—the thin wooden arms either attempted to cleave his head in two or cut the blood to his ankles where they hung over the end, and he was too big to curl up sideways. "Do you prefer pine, oak, cedar, or cherry?"

She fidgeted, the chair creaking beneath her. "Cedar, I suppose."

Good, at least she had a preference. He'd go by the furniture maker this afternoon and order a headboard, footboard, wardrobes, a chest, and a mattress as spacious as the room would allow. Something simple, since she didn't seem to want to spend money.

"I'm antsy to learn about your business before your vision makes sharing difficult."

He glanced over at her. Had he not told her his vision had improved a little since the wedding? The stress of his diagnosis and decision to marry had probably caused some of his visual problems that were now settling a bit.

But to tell someone about his aches and pains, where he was going, his hopes and fears—well, he normally shared nothing with anyone beyond the business contracts or Greek grammar he was pondering.

Was learning to be a husband at fifty-three more than he should've taken on? "I didn't want to rush you."

She'd seemed content to clean the past week, or had his vision kept him from noticing some other emotion at work in her?

"I'd like to start. With you having a cook, a maid, and secretaries. . .well, I would like to occupy my time with important things."

She didn't have to rush. Did he remember to tell her she could read his books? He hadn't once seen her in here perusing his floor-to-ceiling bookshelves. "You do know that if I don't have the sort of books you want to read, you're free to purchase as many as you'd like."

"Thank you, but you've overestimated my ability to take over your business if you don't think I need to start learning right away. I've never done anything beyond keep house. When your secretary came by yesterday, I wish I could've done more than tell him when I expected you back."

"Next time, feel free to ask him what he wants. He came to ask how I wanted to handle the sawmill supervisor who's irate over one of our supplier's behavior."

"But how would I have known what to do?"

"Well, it was more of a personal issue than a business decision. I'm sure you could've talked Mr. Yates through the situation. But if it had been something more operational, he could have explained it to you."

"So you don't intend to teach me." Her tone sounded disappointed. "You want me to learn everything through Mr. Yates?"

"No." He blew on the coffee she'd warmed up and took a sip. "We'll go through everything together. But you don't have to defer to me, even now. My workers have been informed that in my absence, you're their authority and your word holds."

"But I hardly know what you do beyond you own a sawmill, several textile mills, and you lease several buildings in town."

"I trust you, Helen. If you don't know what decision to make, I'm sure you'll ask for more information, get someone's advice, or tell them to wait if you want to discuss it with me." He placed his arms flat on the table and leaned forward. "But if you're ready, I can start showing you around my properties this afternoon."

Maybe his tongue would loosen over the business talk they'd have to do. He stared at one of the white rectangles on his desk that was likely Professor Larson's letter. Even if they talked about his properties, that wasn't close to the kind of talk a husband and wife should be doing. And yet, it had only been a week since they'd wed. Surely people who married for love courted for a much longer time before feeling comfortable together.

Hopefully Professor Larson wouldn't be interested in his marriage at all, because if he was, he would slice right through all the uneasy excuses and probe Neil's deficiencies. He'd always liked the man for not dancing around hard topics—when it came to religion. But would he still feel that way when he pointed out the trouble Neil had gotten himself into by taking on a wife, when he could barely maintain a friend?

❧

Helen shifted her weight from one foot to the other. How many hours had they walked up and down the floors of the three textile mills Neil owned? She needed to order a more comfortable pair of boots. She glanced at her timepiece as Neil patiently listened to the

woolen mill's third-floor supervisor complaining. Evidently this man was rarely satisfied with anything.

"Are you all right, Helen?" Neil's hand clutched her elbow. The portly supervisor was staring at her as if she'd purposely interrupted his harangue.

"A woman my age isn't used to so much walking."

"Come now, don't put us in the grave yet." Neil smiled at her then beckoned to Mr. Yates. "Would you see my wife home while I finish with Mr. Sackett?"

"Certainly. My own feet are begging for a reprieve." Mr. Yates's hair was prematurely gray, and the gentle laugh lines around his eyes crinkled at the slightest provocation. "And I'm not even old enough to have grandchildren."

She shrugged but couldn't muster up even a glimmer of amusement. She'd never have any grandchildren. And though she'd come to terms with that ages ago, the sting of sadness was more acute now that she'd actually married.

Not that she and Neil would have had children earlier, considering blindness was the only thing that had turned his head her way.

She should be grateful for being chosen to help him now.

And yet, if only he'd spend a little more time with her, talk to her some more.

For what purpose? She rubbed at her eyes. This discontent was ridiculous. What other person in the whole state of California had as much attention from Neil as she? He was plenty hospitable and never once made her feel ugly and old—like she was.

Yes, she should be plenty content with his genial attention.

She looked over her shoulder, but Neil had already walked off with the unhappy supervisor.

Mr. Yates led her down to the carriage and handed her inside then took a seat up with the driver.

Within minutes, they were in front of Neil's modest home, and Mr. Yates jumped down to help her out.

She'd never really thought of where Neil lived before she married him. She'd assumed he lived in a house at least the size of her sister's, since his income was enormous compared to Don's, yet this house was nothing more than a small two-bedroom cottage. And one of the bedrooms, the larger of the two, had been converted into a library and study.

She'd assumed she'd have her own bedroom. . .a choice of bedrooms, actually. But then, she should've known better. Neil wasn't the kind of man who needed a room to entertain overnight guests.

But after he'd unexpectedly kissed her at the ceremony. . .

He'd laid out his plan for marrying with such precision that she'd truly not expected to be more than his companion with legal claim to his estate. But then he'd kissed her, even after she told him she didn't expect one. And it hadn't been a simple kiss, no, he actually seemed to have put some feeling into it, as if. . .as if he actually thought she was worth—

She tripped on an uneven pavestone, and Mr. Yates's arm tightened about hers.

"Be careful, Mrs. Oliver."

"Sorry about that." She needed to get her head out of the clouds.

Though if she'd learned anything from watching Neil these past few days—meeting his business partners, looking over his books, seeing every bit of property he'd acquired, getting her name added to paperwork—the man made sure everything that needed to be

done was done, and done properly. Including sealing a marriage deal with a kiss.

She was stupid to think the kiss meant anything to him beyond what needed to be done to finalize the marriage. Maybe because she'd never been kissed before, she'd been surprised into feeling it meant something more. Maybe all kisses felt that way.

Yet, lately her mind betrayed her and dredged up the dreams of her youth where a rich, handsome man could actually love a woman like her. Drat that kiss. She'd have been better off if he'd sealed their marriage with nothing more than a handshake and his signature on the license.

Maybe after a few more weeks of companionable silence, her memory would give up the longing he'd created for something she'd never believed she was going to get.

The kiss was short, really, just a few seconds, it couldn't take that long to forget. . .if she could stop dwelling on it.

But really, how many old, unsightly women got kissed by a man so handsome?

She let out a frustrated growl. If she didn't stop thinking about that kiss, the memory of it would never go away.

"Are you all right?"

She blinked at the door in front of her and glanced up at Mr. Yates, still holding on to her arm. How could she have been so deep in her traitorous thoughts that she'd not even felt his arm around hers?

"I'm fine." She needed something to talk about—something that had nothing to do with kissing. "Some of the tenants today seemed surprised by Mr. Oliver's appearance. Does he not visit them often?"

"Not much. He completely trusts me, just like he did Mr. Cannes, who used to take care of things and report to him. He's making these rounds for you."

She took out her keys. Over the last few days, she'd pieced together that Mr. Yates had expected to take over Mr. Cannes's position, but she'd be the one to do so now. "I hope you aren't too upset that he's chosen me to oversee things when you're clearly more knowledgeable than I."

"No, ma'am. I'm flattered with the wholehearted trust Mr. Oliver has in me, and yes, I'd assumed after Mr. Cannes died that I'd take over—but the amount of time he spent doing his job is more than I care to work. My only child just left home, and I'm looking forward to spending time with my wife. I'm content with a good boss, a decent salary, and a lovely woman to go home to."

Helen swallowed at the thought of a man more focused on a woman than his business. If this man hadn't already proven himself by answering her silly business questions with the utmost patience when Neil was busy, she'd have put her trust in him right now.

Of course, Neil seemed extremely good at selecting only the most upstanding associates—who all seemed incredibly loyal to their reserved employer.

She'd always assumed she was the only person willing to debate theology with him, but over the last week, she'd seen more than one man converse with Neil. He was always polite and seemed genuinely attentive, giving advice when needed—good advice, too. His words were always few and to the point, though he somehow managed to never sound curt.

But he never started a conversation on his own. Not even with men under his employ for years like Mr. Yates.

"Why did Mr. Cannes work so many hours?" Neil seemed plenty capable of handling

the work he was showing her. Or maybe he hadn't yet shown her all of what he expected her to do.

"Mr. Oliver always chastised him for the time he spent working, but your husband, well, he's so short on words that Mr. Cannes spent a lot of time listening to the complaints his employees didn't bother Mr. Oliver with, in an effort to respect his time."

"But he seems quite willing to listen to them."

"He is, but a boss so standoffish is a bit intimidating to talk to. Sometimes it's hard to know if we're pleasing him."

Try being that man's wife.

Mr. Yates let go of her arm and cleared his throat.

She plunged the house key into the keyhole. "Can I get you lemonade or tea before you go?"

"No, thank you, ma'am. I should be heading home now." He doffed his hat and stood waiting for her to go in.

"Thank you for escorting me home, Mr. Yates."

Once the door shut behind her, she headed to the kitchen and opened the icebox. She plunked chipped ice into a pretty blue glass and pumped some water before lowering her achy body onto the sofa in the parlor.

Her feet thanked her for sitting, though they begged to be released from the pretty, but tight-toed boots she'd never had problems with before. Neil had given her permission to redecorate. Maybe she could order a slipper chair. She'd always wanted one of those low, wide chairs to take off her shoes with grace and ease, and Neil could afford it. But where would they put more furniture in this little house? She sighed and settled for extending her legs and wiggling her toes.

Her sister would be the sort of person who'd enjoy spending Neil's money and figuring out what furniture would work in his small house. But Helen wasn't about to let her sister see where Neil slept. As if she needed to hand Margaret another reason to belittle her.

Leaning her head back, Helen closed her eyes and thought over all she'd learned about Neil's work in the past week. Nothing she couldn't handle, as long as she could ask him for help when a sticky situation came up, and since his deteriorating vision wouldn't keep him from having a long life, there shouldn't be any problems.

But she didn't want to spend those long years in silence. She'd have to figure out how to draw him out—without getting her hopes up for much more than an extended friendly theological debate.

She pulled one of the books he scattered about the house closer to her. So back to debating theology she would go. And surely discussing the lofty things of God would help keep her mind from wandering back to that one kiss she'd need to be content with.

Chapter 4

The carriage swayed to a stop, and Neil pressed his fingers against the throbbing at his temple. As if trying to walk without stumbling like an oaf wasn't enough, all the conversations he'd had with his tenants, employees, and Helen today hurt his jaw—and now he had a headache.

Mr. Ferguson opened the carriage door. Bright orange highlighted the darkening sky behind him. "Here we are, Mr. Oliver. Home at last."

His driver had never sung such a cheery greeting when he'd delivered him home before. Then, of course, maybe he had at first but soon realized superfluous talk wasn't needed. Maybe he was cheery for Helen's sake.

He glanced over at his wife gathering her notebook and shawl. Why hadn't she said anything on the way home? Over the last several days, she'd asked him questions in the carriage. Perhaps she'd noticed the pain written across his face this evening.

Hmmmm, he was gritting his teeth against the throbbing. Maybe that's why his jaw ached.

Trying to relax, he followed Helen out of the carriage but nearly tumbled down the steps. Thankfully, he caught the door.

He pulled out the carved cane he'd started to use to walk. With attempted confidence, he strode toward the house despite knowing he could not see that one uneven pavestone. He needed to hire someone to fix that.

Mr. Ferguson's cologne grew stronger, and Neil looked up from his attempt to watch his feet and nodded at his approaching driver.

"If you have no more need of me, sir. . ."

"None, and tomorrow, take a holiday. I intend to stay home." If he didn't talk to anyone for twenty-four hours, he might actually get rid of his headache. How did Mr. Cannes deal with so many people every day?

"All right, sir." The movement and swish of air indicated Mr. Ferguson had doffed his beat-up felt hat as usual, then he walked past whistling.

Helen cleared her throat. "I suppose you don't want me going out on my own then?"

"I'm sorry." He'd forgotten to take Helen into account when he'd dismissed Mr. Ferguson, but surely she'd want to rest as well. "Did you want to go out? I think we deserve a respite."

"If that's what you wish."

Did he note a bit of frustration in her tone? But the doorway was now an empty rectangular hole, so he marched forward, slowing where he knew there was a step, and went in after her. The smell of garlic and rosemary made his stomach rumble. His insides

pinched with the hunger his headache had helped him ignore.

"Smells good, Mrs. Winthrop," Helen said from somewhere inside.

The robust older woman had never made a meal that disappointed, though he'd have eaten almost anything. Some days he had to wait an extra hour for dinner when she'd decided her first attempt was a failure, but she made sure he was fed only the best she could make.

Shrugging out of his coat, he followed his wife to the kitchen table, where Mrs. Winthrop hummed contentedly. For some reason, his cook seemed happier cooking for two.

"Just let me get the butter crock, and you two can eat."

He heard his chair scrape in front of him, and he grabbed the back. He could do that himself; he wasn't quite an invalid yet. Plus the scraping. . .ugh, he grit his teeth again. He took a deep breath and tried to lower himself in the chair without accidentally bumping anything on the table.

"Good night, you two." And the powdery smell of Mrs. Winthrop passed him and dissipated.

"I feel rather unnecessary."

Neil stilled his attempts to find the knife that should be beside his plate. "Come again?"

He looked across the multitude of candles between them. Why had Mrs. Winthrop started burning so many? Did she think that would help him see? Thankfully, he could afford to burn as many as she chose to light, otherwise he'd have to give up reading at night. Someday he'd have to give up reading all together, so he was determined to read as much as he could before then.

"Mrs. Winthrop does the cooking. Mrs. Giles does the cleaning. I follow you and Mr. Yates around, doing nothing but feeling like a third leg."

"Soon you'll be able to take over the weekly rounds, if you wish." Not that he'd force her to do so while he could still get around. However, whenever she felt ready to take over the talking, he'd certainly let her do that.

"I just feel wrong about not doing the things I'm actually capable of doing. Like making dinner."

"You can if you want to." He didn't relish the idea of firing Mrs. Winthrop, but if his wife wanted to cook, he hoped she was good at it.

After praying, he scooped potatoes from the roasting pan and pulled Matthew Henry's commentary closer. He felt around for the big magnifying glass he'd just received in the mail yesterday, then he pulled a few candles closer and. . .there, he could see words. Not too many at a time, but enough to read. He sighed and plopped a few potatoes into his mouth.

After a minute or two of steady clinking of silverware, Helen sighed and grumbled something.

Was the roast not to her liking? He wouldn't have minded more pepper.

"I feel like a piece of furniture."

"What?" He brought his hand up after realizing he'd talked with his mouth full. Did she say something about furniture?

"Nothing."

"All right." He went back to reading, even though his head throbbed more. After a week of frustration with his other magnifier, he'd breathed easier with yesterday's post,

thankful that reading had yet to be stolen from him. Too soon, he'd have to ask Helen to start reading to him. Maybe tonight's headache was more from long reading with his new magnifier last night than the talking he'd done today.

Maybe he should limit his reading time.

He let out a small sniff of amusement. No, he'd cram in as much reading as possible. It wasn't as if his eyesight had improved when he'd tortured himself last year by not reading for two months.

"Did you read something funny?"

He startled. "I—uh no, I was just talking to myself and realized I shouldn't bother to listen to my own advice."

"So you're over there talking silently to yourself while I'm right here?"

"Do you want me to talk to you?" He set down his glass.

"No, I want you to want to talk to me."

He straightened in his seat. Though he couldn't quite see Helen giving him a biting glare, he could feel it. Back when his sisters and mother were in a huff, he'd simply disappeared from the room and let his father deal with it.

Maybe he should've stuck around back then and paid attention to how his father diffused the situation.

"I suppose that's more than you're willing to give though." Her silverware clinked and the ice in her glass rattled.

Confound the stupid candles, he couldn't see anything but movement behind them.

More than he was willing to give? Did Helen doubt his loyalty? Hadn't she said right before the wedding she trusted him? "I vowed to you my life—as expected by God. If you want to talk—"

"Your life?"

He cocked his head. Doubt completely underlined the tone of her voice. "Yes, not that my life is worth much, seeing that I'm going blind."

"Your life is your books, Neil."

He felt the bend of paper under his palm, his fingers still near where he'd stopped reading. He pulled his hand away.

"Oh, go back to your reading. I didn't mean to intrude upon your life." She stood. "I have a headache anyway."

Had she finished eating already? How long had he been reading?

And a headache made her want to leave? So had she wanted to talk or not?

She dumped her plates into the wash bin then glided past him and shut the door to her room.

He picked up his fork and pushed around his cold dinner. His pursuit of knowledge and business had consumed his time for decades. Did she really want him to abandon reading when he'd soon be forced to anyway?

Did she truly expect him to become as talkative as the late Mr. Cannes or as congenial as Mr. Yates, when she'd known he was neither before she married him? Could people change their personality?

He'd not been lying about being prepared to lay down his life for her. Death did not scare him. But did he have to give up his studies for her?

The food he'd been chewing became suddenly difficult to swallow. Giving up his books would be far harder to do than flinging himself in front of a train.

He pulled his Bible over to find the fifth chapter of Ephesians. He'd read the verses many times while contemplating proposing to Helen. Had he missed something?

"So ought men to love their wives as their own bodies. He that loveth his wife loveth himself."

And if his wife wanted him to talk during dinner instead of read as was his habit, was that all it'd take to prove he truly did love her as he did himself?

But did he love her?

He'd assumed laying down his life was biblical love, all that was truly required. But loving a wife as he did himself seemed much more. . .involved.

He closed the leather cover of his Bible and stood to take his dishes to the sink. Scraping off soap into the water, he started washing the dishes for Helen since she refused to let them sit overnight for Mrs. Giles to clean in the morning.

With each item he washed and rinsed, with each tick of the clock that told him Helen would not return before he retired, the more he wished she'd come and spend the quiet evening hours with him.

Never before had he wished for someone to disturb his solitude. He'd always felt more energized when alone.

He'd have to lay down his books. Maybe not forever, hopefully not. But he'd have to leave behind the solitary habits he'd developed over decades of bachelorhood until he spent enough time with Helen to figure out what she really wanted from him.

He couldn't use his personality as an excuse to keep from following the Word of God.

If his attention and conversation were what she wanted, he wanted to give her that and anything else she asked for. Just as he wished to be understood by her, he also longed to understand her.

I do desire to care for my wife as much as I would care for myself.

I do love her.

So what was he going to do about it?

❧

"Oh, how I've missed your apple pie, Aunt Helen." Jeffrey rubbed his hands together as he took an exaggerated sniff of his dessert, his eyes shut tight. "When they'd told me you were moving out, I shed a tear or two."

"I haven't left the state. You can always come over to get—" Helen licked her lips. She hadn't baked anything since moving in with Neil, whose cook outshone her completely. Though she'd informed him she could cook, why would he want her to?

She scraped at a burnt piece of crust. "Well, if you want apple pie, give me notice before dropping in, since I'm not baking anymore. Mrs. Winthrop leaves us with a dessert every other day. Yesterday we had blueberry crumble."

"But you don't like blueberries." Margaret wrinkled her face as if she'd tasted something foul.

Helen rubbed a hand under her nose, masking the desire to tell her sister she never cooked with blueberries because Margaret didn't care for them, not because she herself was averse.

"If he's going to marry a woman and not expect her to cook, he should at least make sure his cook makes stuff *you* want to eat." Margaret dolloped some whipping cream onto her pie. "Don, now that we don't have Helen, I really think we need a cook. I just can't handle the stove's heat on days that aren't at least fifty degrees or colder."

Helen cut through the pie to serve herself a second piece. As if it had been pleasurable for her to cook in ninety-degree weather while seeing to her sister's children as well. "I'm surprised you haven't hired a cook already."

Margaret sniffed and glared across at her husband. "See, even she thinks we need one."

They definitely didn't need one. If they hadn't needed one with ten people in the house, then they didn't need one now. But Don not caving to her sister's whining for one? Impressive.

Had they even eaten every night? Margaret hadn't done much more than bake bread and boil tea since Helen had moved in with them.

"And a hired cook would actually listen when I say the fried chicken needs more salt." Margaret gave her a glare.

Helen kept her hands under the table where she wrung her napkin as if it were her sister's neck. Why couldn't Margaret be a smidgen grateful for all the cooking she'd done?

With Neil's perpetual silence these past few weeks, she'd forgotten how many underhanded insults she'd endured every day at her sister's house.

Why not tell Margaret right now how that'd felt? She didn't have to live here anymore. But venting would only ruffle her sister's feathers. She'd not stoop to her level just because she no longer relied on her good graces to keep clothed and fed.

Even so, she couldn't just give up on her family. Who else could help them change?

Sighing, she passed the cinnamon to Jeffrey, who'd pointed at the shaker since his mouth was too full to ask politely. Maybe she didn't deserve her sister's gratitude for helping raise her family if this was an example of her nephew's best table manners. What other childish habits had he not shed despite being five and twenty?

"Did you see this sale advertisement, Jeff?" Don smoothed out the newspaper he'd been reading and slid the paper over to his son. "Isn't this the property you sold to Mr. Oliver?"

Jeffrey leaned over the paper and read the ad. "Yes, that's the block. He's added another building though, but wait—" He pulled the paper closer. "He's asking five times what that property's worth." He glanced over at Helen for a second before shaking his head. "That's highway robbery."

Her lips twitched, like they had for decades when she worked to keep her thoughts to herself at the Abernathy table. Just because Jeffrey didn't like the price didn't mean Neil was forcing people to buy.

"Well, Helen is supposed to be Mr. Oliver's go-to now." Margaret pointed her fork at her sister. "Why don't you ask your aunt for a deal. That's all Mr. Oliver married her for."

And now her throat was dry and her face aflame, but the two men didn't even blink at the insult.

She was supposed to do business on Neil's behalf, yes, but she wasn't yet comfortable with it all. Still, what would Margaret think of her if she refused to do the one thing she'd bragged about Neil needing her for?

Though if he'd taken more time to adjust to his vision loss, he would've realized he didn't need her at all. How long until he figured out marrying her was a mistake? She forced herself to stop twisting her napkin. "I'm sure if you wanted the property, he'd sell it back to you."

"I thought you could make decisions." Margaret's broad grin irked.

"I can make decisions, but—"

"What would you want to pay for it, Jeffrey?" Don wiped the apple pie crumbs from his mustache. "You certainly know what it's worth."

The young man sighed then gazed at the ceiling as if calculating. "A third of that price would be fair. It'd cover the improvements he made since I sold it." He reached over to touch his mother's hand and smiled. "Have I told you I've decided to stay in town for good? If I can find property I'm interested in, that is."

Margaret's mouth quivered. "Oh, Jeffrey. I'm so pleased."

Helen bit her lip. How could she not help Jeffrey? He'd always been her sister's favorite.

Margaret grabbed Helen's hand. "You will help him get it, right?"

"I'm sure I can." What did it matter who bought the property? If she kept Jeffrey from buying this piece of land, her sister would never let her hear the end of it.

And with Neil as quiet as he was, could she let go of the only family she had over a deal that wouldn't hurt Neil much one way or the other?

"Well, since I sold it to him for spittle, he shouldn't be upset about going down two-thirds in price for me." Jeffrey scratched his chin and looked at his father. "If you drew up papers, then they wouldn't even have lawyer's fees to contend with."

Don leaned back and shrugged. "Sure, we could go to Mr. Oliver's secretary as soon as we've finished lunch and start the process."

"At least half, Jeffrey." Helen bit her lip. Why had she just blurted that out? Jeffrey would give her a fit now if she tried to negotiate higher. But him thinking he could just decide the price for her made her tongue stupid. "Granting that's enough to cover any debt Neil has on the place."

Jeffrey smirked and looked sideways at his father, who smiled back before folding up his newspaper, tucking it under his arm, and standing. "I'm finished eating. Why don't we head over to Oliver's office?"

The apple pie all of a sudden felt heavy in her gut. Would it be worth fighting these two? Neil wasn't in any financial distress. One sale below market value wouldn't hurt him, and he was generous with his tenants. "What do you intend to do with the property, Jeffrey? I hope you won't bet it in a card game again."

The room stilled.

"No, Aunt Helen, I've grown wiser in five years. Please don't keep me from making a good start in this town because of one mishap in my past."

How could she not offer the boy a second chance? "I'll see what I can do."

Chapter 5

I'll see you tomorrow. Is seven too early?" Neil shook the hand of the man he'd corresponded with for decades, amazed at Professor Larson's frail bones, since his strong personality had leaped out of his letters. Dusk had just crept into the sky, and the older man was flagging. They'd been conversing for over four hours.

Probably the longest Neil had ever spoken to another person in his life.

He'd used Helen as his excuse to leave the professor to rest, though he could have easily continued with their conversation had his mentor not been fighting to keep his eyes open.

Professor Larson smoothed down the long wispy white hairs that flopped in the wind instead of covering his freckled bald head. His hand trembled, but not his smile. "Seven is fine, Neil. I'm up before the sun whether I want to be or not. I can't wait to meet your wife. I do admit, that was the last reason I expected for tonight's visit to end. Why had you not told me you were courting a woman?"

Neil's cheek muscle jumped to life. Thankfully the man's eyesight seemed about as good as his, so he'd likely not notice the twitch, but would he hear it in his voice? "I didn't exactly court the woman."

"Oh?"

The silence following made his cheek jerk even more.

If it had been anyone else, he'd have ignored the questioning silence, but this man was only here for a few days, and if he trusted anyone in the world to give him advice... "You know how my eyesight's been in decline. And Helen was a woman needing a future. Since I don't have anyone to provide for, I figured I could provide for her, and she'll be a great help to me once I can't see anymore."

"And what if you never go completely blind?"

Not likely, according to the doctor. "Then she's no longer a spinster without means."

A minute of silence passed, and Neil worked hard not to jump in and defend himself. That last sentence sounded pretty cold. But what if he admitted wanting more of a relationship despite the fear of how much he'd have to change to have it? Would the professor fill his future letters with questions of how things were going between him and Helen?

What if he failed to become the kind of man Helen wanted? Could he truly transform into someone different than he'd always been?

He'd only just admitted to himself that he wanted to love her as she should be loved. He did indeed want her as happy as he was himself, even if that meant forcing himself to talk more. But what if she never wanted anything beyond a decent dinner conversation?

The professor thumped Neil on the shoulder. "You're taking the easy way out, aren't you?"

Neil shook his head. "I'm finding nothing easy about this at all."

"Reading your letters, I've pictured a man stalwart and strong in his convictions and set in his way of life. That's why you surprised me by mentioning a wife just now." Professor Larson rubbed the white stubble on his chin. "I was married for thirty-four years before Bernice passed away. You can't keep a woman under your roof with some altruistic thought of only providing for her—not if you want to remain happy. You have to open up, allow yourself to be vulnerable, and love her like Christ—that was in the vows I assume you took."

"Yes, to lay down my life for her. She mentioned the other day that my books were my life, so I'm trying to give her more time than my reading." Or he would anyway. He forced himself not to kick at the dirt. He'd not done well the last two days—only attempting theological debates with her again. But since she'd brought up her disappointment with his books at dinner two days ago, she hadn't seemed interested in discussing verses.

"Christ didn't just give up His time or His life. He gave up everything to make Himself nothing because we needed the kind of love only He could give. He *cared*. Cared enough to let mankind kill Him, despise Him, reject Him."

Neil ran his tongue around his mouth. It wasn't that he didn't care, but if he cared more. . . What if Helen didn't like what she found when he opened himself up?

A giant yawn took over the professor's face. He covered his mouth with a scrawny hand, taking a step back with the yawn's intensity. "Oh my, I think this old bird better hop in his nest before he falls off a branch."

"See you in the morning then." Neil shook the man's hand.

"You have to care, Neil, in order to change. Let it happen, though it might hurt. If you don't, no matter what you do, it won't be enough."

He'd known his mentor wouldn't be happy with his marriage of convenience.

But then, was he happy with it himself? "All right."

After climbing onto the buggy's backseat, he waved at the professor as Mr. Ferguson drove away.

As was typical, his driver wasn't concerned with pleasantries. The man had learned not to bother.

But if he were going to stretch himself and start talking to Helen, maybe he should practice with someone who wouldn't be as intimidating to impress. "Mr. Ferguson, I'm sorry to keep you out so late."

"No problem, Mr. Oliver." The man got the horses up to speed then relaxed.

The buggy swayed, tempting Neil to lean back and revisit the stimulating discussion he'd had with the professor over Hebrews chapter six. But he drew breath into his lungs and tried again. "I hope you don't have family waiting on you."

"Well, I do, but they aren't upset when you keep me late, since you pay me more."

"They? Children, I assume. How many do you have?"

"Twelve, sir."

"Twelve? How did I not know you had so many?"

"You never asked, sir." A sparkle of merriment infused Mr. Ferguson's tone. He was a rather happy chap.

But a quick calculation of how much he paid Mr. Ferguson raced through Neil's

mind. How could he be happy on his salary with fourteen at home? "How do you keep them all fed and clothed?"

"Well, two of them are out of the house. The oldest girl helps the wife with the laundry they take in from the men at the mill next door. The next oldest girl watches the little ones, and the next two oldest boys chop and deliver firewood around town."

"Are they not in school?"

Mr. Ferguson shrugged. "Can't afford to keep them in school past twelve."

Neil played with his lip. "Did any of your children wish to stay in school?" How he'd loved school as a child—still did, if he counted the studying he did. Books were wonderful escapes whenever he felt too exposed talking to others.

Exposed.

The professor told him he needed to become vulnerable with Helen. He'd have to take down his shield of books, but besides the business talk she was surely tired of by the end of the day and the theological debates they'd always engaged in, what else could they talk about?

Mr. Ferguson clicked to his team and they turned onto Eighth. "My eleven-year-old is certainly not looking forward to joining his brothers hauling firewood. He dreams of becoming some fancy word for a scientist who studies bugs. Since there can't be money in that, he'll just have to keep it as a hobby. So if you find any interesting dead moths or beetles, he'll happily take them off your hands."

"What's he do with them?"

"Well, he drowns live ones in the alcohol his mother can't believe I bought for him, and he goes around to the stores that sell cigars, hoping for more boxes for his collection. The wife puts up with all the dead bugs in the boys' room, even leaves up spiderwebs for him to watch after he's done with chores if there's a spider on it."

"What an interesting hobby." And quite the dedication. Maybe he could help the boy somehow. At least he paid Mr. Ferguson more than most, but still. Twelve children. "Sounds like you have a great wife."

"She is that." Mr. Ferguson clicked his tongue to the horses, who turned in simple obedience down the lane.

What if Mr. Ferguson could help him figure out how to woo a woman? Considering he had twelve children. . . "And how did you capture Mrs. Ferguson's heart?"

"Ice skating."

"What? Where can one ice skate in California?"

"We grew up in Michigan. A young man can capture a lot of female attention cutting patterns in the ice and zipping around everyone else on the pond." He chuckled. "Carved Lucy's name in the ice with a heart around it to propose."

The buggy halted and Neil blinked. They were home already? Darkness had descended and he didn't see any lights in the windows.

Usually he found conversation so tedious. But after his talk with the professor and now his driver. . .maybe talking wasn't so bad.

What if courting his wife wasn't as intimidating as he'd feared it to be?

Helen wiped her clammy palms against her shirtwaist as two men maneuvered several large pieces of furniture around in their small house. Neil hadn't told her there'd be a

THE Convenient BRIDE COLLECTION

shipment of things coming today. In fact, she hadn't even seen him last night. He'd spent the entire evening at the hotel with his friend.

What should she tell them to do with the bed she'd been sleeping on? The men had propped it up in the kitchen to create room to wrangle the larger frame through the bedroom door.

"Where do you want this, Mrs. Oliver?" The taller man pointed to the small slumped mattress in question. Oh, how her cheeks burned to know they knew about her and Neil's sleeping arrangements.

Which Neil must be ready to change.

And the movers knew his intentions at the same time she learned of it.

Pressing a hand against the swirl of her stomach, she desperately looked around for an answer. "Uh, why don't you leave it? My husband failed to tell me what he wanted done with it." Failed to tell her anything about the furniture he'd evidently custom ordered.

"All right, ma'am." The man pulled on the brim of his slouch hat and exited the house with the brawny youth who'd helped him lug in the bed, wardrobe, chest, and cedar trunk they'd crammed in around the other furniture in her room.

Or rather, Neil's room.

Their room.

She sagged against the door she'd shut behind the movers and let out a shaky breath. What should she do now?

The door jiggled behind her. She moved to open it. "Did you forget—"

She held her breath, seeing the bunch of daisies in Neil's hands.

"I saw the Newton boys drive away. Did the furniture come?"

Her throat refused to work, so she nodded.

"Great." He moved forward, and she couldn't help the sneeze.

"Bless you."

She wiped at her watering eyes, her nose tickling again. "Please don't bring those in."

He frowned at the flowers. "These?"

"Achoo! Yes, those."

"I'm sorry, I thought all women liked flowers."

"I think they're pretty—from far away. But you won't find me strolling through a flower garden."

He tossed the bunch toward the road then flipped a red box over and over in his hands. "I talked to Mr. Ferguson on the way home last night."

Did he think that was newsworthy? But then, he was talking about something other than the book of Hebrews, which was a nice change.

"It wasn't so bad actually. He's interesting."

She let out a silent chuckle. Did he think no one talked about anything beyond the weather? But then, her sister's family really didn't talk about anything interesting, unless one cared about the goings-on of the Abernathy household.

"We talked for the whole ride home this afternoon as well." He was beaming like a child who'd just won the spelling bee.

"I'm not sure I believe you."

He shrugged and smiled. "I need to practice. Here." He held out the little red box. "This is for you."

She took the box, trying not to sneeze again from the tickle the daisies had left in

her nose and throat. After untying the lid, she peeped in to see shards of peanut brittle. With a small smile, she nodded. "Thanks." She'd have to remember to take the box to her sister's. Jeffrey was the only one in her family who ate the candy. Fishing for her handkerchief but not finding one in her pocket, she headed into the kitchen, slipped the box onto the table, and went to retrieve a tissue from her room.

"I got that wrong, too, didn't I?"

She wiped her nose and came out of the room. "What'd you say?"

"You don't like peanut brittle."

Well, after putting it so flatly, how could she agree without hurting his feelings? It was the first gift he'd ever brought her. "You tried."

"Hmmm." He rubbed the back of his neck, looking like an awkward schoolboy wondering why a girl didn't appreciate finding his pet toad in her desk.

But then, it was sort of awkward. He didn't know her at all. Not really. There was only one thing that could've been worse. "You might want to make a note not to bring me strawberries. They give me hives."

He pulled out a kitchen chair and melted into it. "I suppose I should've talked to *you* first before I wasted money."

She smiled at his "waste." Her sister spent more on hats every week, and God and everyone knew Margaret didn't need any more of those. "My nephew loves peanut brittle—he'll enjoy it."

"Mr. Yates told me he and your brother-in-law were in my office this morning. . .wanting to finalize the details on the Orchard Street property you're selling them, but couldn't, since neither you nor I were there. I'm surprised at the price you quoted them."

Oh, why hadn't she taken a bigger whiff of those daisies so she could avoid this conversation by hiding in that massive bed with her itchy eyes? Why couldn't he have cloistered himself up in his study after walking through the door like he usually did? She had prayed her deal with Jeffrey would go through unnoticed. Neil was selling a lot of property right now to simplify his business for her, so why did Mr. Yates have to bring that one up? Her family had already rescheduled and met with Neil's secretary an hour ago.

What if, with her first foray into making a business deal—an admittedly bad one—in a vain effort to win her sister's elusive regard, she lost Neil's? "I. . .I admit I was too hasty in letting them think I could quote them a price."

"No, you've got full authority to quote a price."

"Well, you shouldn't have given me that authority."

"Why's that?" He was squinting at her as if he were measuring her expression. Could he see well enough to see how stupid she felt?

She turned her head to look out the window. Thankfully her sniffing could be blamed on the daisies. Making a mistake was a dumb reason to get teary, but she had captured so little of Neil's regard, and a man who chose only the best workers, workers who'd take a pay cut before they entered into a bad deal on their boss's behalf, couldn't be happy with her rash decision. "Because I can't be trusted. You picked the wrong business partner."

"I wouldn't have married you if I couldn't trust you. And—"

"Well, I can't be trusted to make good decisions where my family is concerned then."

"Why's that?"

She blew out a breath, not daring to look at him. "Because I stupidly think that one day I can gain their. . .their admiration. Someday they're bound to think of me as more

than an inconvenient relative." She lowered her voice to a whisper. "Not sure why I care anymore anyway."

"If they haven't realized what a help you were to them by now, then they never will. People don't change."

"I can't believe that. If so, what hope is there for me? What hope is there for. . ."

Us.

If something didn't change soon, marrying Neil would become nothing more than jumping from one household that only tolerated her to another. And if she'd ruined Neil's trust in her because of a stupid need to prove herself worthy of Margaret's esteem, then she was every bit the fool Margaret thought her to be. "Jeffrey's made mistakes in the past, but how can I believe he'll never be a better man? If no one gives him a chance to prove himself, then how can he?"

"It's not good intentions, but good character that determines the future."

"And you've never had good intentions go awry?"

That seemed to shut him up. He sighed and glanced over at the peanut brittle. "I suppose I've done that today." He crossed his arms. "But there's a difference between praying for people to change and trusting them before they do."

"Well then, you've made a bad decision with me." She blinked against the warm threatening tears, thankful that Neil's vision would keep him from seeing how ugly she could be when she tried not to cry.

"Now, Helen—"

"If Mr. Yates made the same deal with Jeffrey as I did, would you keep him on?"

Neil shrugged. "Depends on how often he'd made poor decisions. Too many times, and then the mistake becomes mine for keeping him on."

"See—"

"But he's my secretary, you're my wife."

She shrugged. "Not much difference."

"I'm afraid you're right about that."

Well, she hadn't expected him to agree so easily. Her heart sank to her knees.

"But I don't want it to stay that way."

Oh yes, the bed. She took a step back. "Maybe things should just stay as they are." How could she be that close to a man who viewed her as nothing but a helper through his infirmity? Whom she would surely disappoint many times over, though he couldn't fire her like he could Mr. Yates?

She'd never won her mother or sister's affection, so how could she have possibly thought she'd win over a man who'd never formed much of an attachment to anyone— who for the first time in his life had messed up by taking her on as a business partner?

How had she ever thought to make him happy? "I'm. . .I'm tired. I need to rest." Praying he wouldn't follow her, she slunk into her room, stared out the window, and tried not to think about how all she'd ever been was a perpetual disappointment.

Chapter 6

Oh, how he rued keeping his mouth shut yesterday when Helen declared their marriage should remain as it was and disappeared into her room for the evening. Granted, he was exhausted, and for a small space of time, he'd let himself believe his natural reticence was a good excuse for not barging into her room immediately to straighten things out.

But after a second day of talking with Professor Larson about women, relationships, and God's expectations of him, he'd come home planning to talk about something easy, like starting a new hobby together, not dealing with a woman's emotions. But he'd been wrong not doing the hard thing that needed to be done.

Why had he told her people didn't change? What a dolt he was.

Though he still didn't trust Jeffrey, he couldn't begrudge Helen wanting to give her nephew a second chance. So what he needed to do was help the young man want to change—just as he now desired to do for Helen's sake.

He drew up his shoulders as Don and Margaret Abernathy's house came into view. He was grateful Mr. Ferguson had known where his wife ran off to this morning. Why did Helen care to impress her sister's family anyway? They treated her poorly—more so than he had last night. He sighed and slumped in his seat.

"So I take it the flowers didn't work last night?"

He started at Mr. Ferguson's inquiry. Had the man ever initiated a conversation with him before? Was he so prickly no one dared? "No, unfortunately the wife is allergic."

Mr. Ferguson clicked his tongue. "Sorry for the bad advice."

"Not bad advice. You couldn't have known, but I should have."

His driver stopped the team, and Neil slid down from the buggy, careful to feel for the curb he couldn't quite see.

"Good luck," his driver called, but then all of a sudden Mr. Ferguson was at his side, grasping his elbow.

Neil sighed. "I suppose I was kidding myself to think I could do this without my cane. I don't mean to make more work for you."

"Nothing to be ashamed of, sir." Once Neil made the sidewalk, Mr. Ferguson let go. "Better to accept help with dignity than fight off a friend."

A friend? Did Mr. Ferguson consider them friends? Maybe he did, considering how many years the man had worked for him. "And if anyone needs help, it's me."

"Do you need me to escort you all the way to the door then?" Mr. Ferguson stepped nearer.

Neil chuckled. "No, I was talking about needing help with the wife."

"Don't we all?" He tipped his hat. "As I said, good luck."

Neil squeezed his driver's shoulder then made his way up the sidewalk, sliding his feet in case there were uneven cracks to trip him. At the door, the housekeeper answered and escorted him down a dark hall toward the clinking of silverware.

"Neil?" Helen's voice sounded from his left.

He turned to look, but the chairs where her voice had come from were in front of a row of windows letting in the rays of the afternoon sun.

He squinted and moved forward, hoping to catch a chair's back to aid him in walking toward her. "I hope it's not too much of an inconvenience for me to join you for lunch. I missed you."

"None, Mr. Oliver." Margaret answered from somewhere to his right, a bit of perturbance in her voice despite the answer. "Mrs. Wall can put out another place setting. We've just hired a cook. I hope she'll impress us all."

Neil nodded across the table after locating redheaded Margaret sitting in a bright green dress. "Obliged."

Helen stood up on his left and pulled out a chair. "You can sit here."

"Thanks." He reached for her hand resting on the back of the chair and squeezed it before she moved away to sit.

"Pleasure to have you with us, Mr. Oliver." The deep male voice on the far right was languid and a bit gravelly, most likely the elder Mr. Abernathy.

"Thanks for letting me barge in. I heard from my secretary, Mr. Yates, that Helen gave you a deal on the property young Mr. Abernathy sold to me years ago." Actually, Mr. Yates had told him Helen had tried to figure a way out of selling it at her verbally stated price but hadn't succeeded. "Half off is a great price."

With his eyes now adjusted to the bright room, he could tell young Jeffrey wasn't at the table as he'd hoped. "I'm hoping Jeffrey isn't intending to turn around and sell the property for the profit his aunt could have made herself. I hope he'll honor her trust in him by living up to the potential she sees."

"Well, I'd just—" Helen's wobbly voice stopped, and she cleared her throat.

Mr. Abernathy set down his paper. "I don't believe there were stipulations on what he could do with the property to get that price."

"No, but I trust no one in this family would purposely take advantage of my wife, considering I'd never have business dealings with the family or anyone associated with them again if they did so."

Silence from the end of the table was likely Helen's brother-in-law calculating how many of his clients dealt directly with businesses under the Oliver name.

"I also came to offer Jeffrey any guidance with the property he might desire. It's in much better shape now than when I bought it from him and will make him a good return if it's handled correctly."

"Then why did you sell it?" Margaret asked.

"With my failing eyesight, I thought it best to trim down my holdings. Make them easier for Helen to handle."

"I'm surprised you're giving my sister-in-law so much say." Mr. Abernathy grunted when Margaret handed him the plate of rolls.

"Why would I marry a woman I didn't trust to speak for me?"

"Yes, why would a man marry a woman he didn't trust with anything beyond pin

money?" Margaret's biting tone turned the table silent again.

Neil accepted the plate of rolls and hoped he could butter one without making a mess. But since he couldn't see any butter on the table, he'd rather live without it than embarrass himself by asking for something that was likely right in front of him. He might have to become more vulnerable for his wife's sake, but looking weak in front of the Abernathys wouldn't be wise at the moment. "Do you have enough pin money, Helen? I do hope you allocated yourself some when I asked you to talk the budget over with Mr. Yates. I forgot women had such a thing."

"I didn't bother. Mr. Yates showed me the overly generous percentage you allocated for my wardrobe and entertainment, which is essentially the same thing."

"Oh." He thanked the person who set down his plate of roasted meat and searched for his fork but couldn't find it.

Helen handed him silverware rolled up in a napkin of the same color as the tablecloth.

"So, Mr. Abernathy, I've been working on my conversational skills for my lovely wife's benefit and found out my driver used to ice skate, and his son collects bugs. Do you have any interesting hobbies to help keep our conversation from veering back to business, which will likely bore us all? And since Helen's the only one who's ever shown an interest in my love of theology, I don't want to bore you with that, either."

The heavenly smell of the pork made him want to forget dinner conversation altogether, but he'd force himself to keep up the conversation and try to mention how lucky he was to steal Helen from them as often as possible—even if his meal grew cold to do so.

Helen closed the door to her sister's house and smiled at Neil standing on the front step rubbing the sides of his head. For hours the man had not only kept up congenial conversation, but he'd praised her more throughout lunch than she'd ever heard Don praise Margaret. Last night she'd skulked off to her room thinking she'd never be more to him than a glorified assistant, but the shy smile he'd directed her way as he talked about her this afternoon made her believe he actually did feel something for her, though he likely couldn't voice it.

The poor man had a hard enough time talking about the weather, how had she believed he'd be able to talk about feelings when they were so much more intimate and complicated than sunshine and rain?

"I think I got a headache from talking too much." Neil moved his mouth back and forth as if stretching his face. "My jaw's even sore."

She rolled her eyes and took a step toward him, put her hands on each side of his stubbly jaw and gave him a kiss on both cheeks. "Better?"

"No." He looked over his shoulder to where Mr. Ferguson waited for them at the carriage, but pulled her closer anyway. "More might help though. But in the direction of my lips."

She stepped back before their driver noticed them, and threw her glance to the ground. He might not be able to talk about what went on inside him, but it seemed a kiss or two did wonders for his boldness. Could Mr. Ferguson see the blush crawling up her neck from that far away? "I don't think kissing in front of the driver is entirely appropriate behavior."

"You started it." Neil winked then waved a dismissive hand at Mr. Ferguson. "We'll walk home."

She frowned at him. "It's at least twenty blocks."

"That's all right." He held out his hand to her as their ride drove away. "You can keep me from stumbling."

She gave him her arm and watched the buggy disappear around the corner.

"And we can talk."

She turned to frown at him again. "I thought your jaw was sore."

"It is, but I don't mind making it sorer if you'll promise to try to make it feel better again when we get home. The more it hurts, the more kissing required."

The blush indeed filled her face this time. Maybe it was a good thing Mr. Ferguson had left if Neil was going to tease her over the kisses she'd impulsively given him.

She'd never heard him tease anyone before, and marveled that he'd even consider wasting words to do so.

Of course, with the look he was giving her right now, perhaps there was absolutely no teasing going on at all.

Swallowing hard, she started guiding them forward so she could look elsewhere and avoid melting into a pool of blush. "What more could you possibly want to talk about? You've already discussed the weather, the church's fall picnic, and my sister's need for new curtains in the parlor."

He put his free hand to his brow. "Ah yes, I definitely earned another kiss and maybe a neck massage for having to discuss your sister's curtains."

"You didn't have to discuss anything. You technically weren't invited." She waved at a lady from church walking on the other side of the road. "I never would have thought you'd want to dine with them anyway."

"If you're going to eat there, I want to be with you." His free hand came over to softly rub the back of her hand, dancing shivers up her arm. "Mr. Yates informed me this morning that you had tried to use me as an excuse to get out of the deal you gave Jeffrey. I don't want you to do anything to make them think I don't trust you to handle my business. Because I do trust you."

She exhaled. As much as she wanted him to think her capable, she needed to let him know she wasn't. "Did you see the newspaper I was looking at after dinner?"

"I saw you with a paper, but I wouldn't attempt to read anything without my magnifying glass."

She hadn't meant to bring up his visual problems. "Well, I found the paper Don showed Jeffrey two days ago with the advertisement for the property I sold them." She sighed. "It's a five-week-old paper."

"And that's significant because?"

Oh, if only she wasn't about to kill his trust in her completely. Trying to memorize the feeling of his arm around hers, she forced herself to keep speaking. "They pretended as if they'd just seen the paper when they brought up the property with me, but my brother-in-law reads his paper every day. He'd not bother to read an old one. They staged the whole thing." She kept her eyes forward so she wouldn't see the moment Neil realized she'd been taken. "You were right yesterday. It's not intentions, but character that decides the future. I'm afraid I sold that property to someone who's going to ruin it. And now you'll have even more reason to be disappointed in me for

practically giving that property away."

"I'm not disappointed in you, Helen. Your heart's still the same, though maybe wiser. And I was wrong about people being unable to change. Look at me. We're walking down the street talking about something other than theology after I just forced myself to discuss the most boring things for an hour already."

"You've certainly talked more this afternoon than I've ever heard." She steered him away from an uneven crack in the sidewalk.

"If I can change for you, then don't give up on Jeffrey wising up one day, and I won't, either. I meant what I said to your brother-in-law about helping your nephew. If you make me want to change to make you happy, maybe he'll want to do the same."

"You're talking more for my sake?"

"I'm trying, though I evidently need lots of practice to keep from clamming up when it gets hard. Last night I let you walk away believing I don't want to change, because the talking I did yesterday had exhausted me. And well, I'm not used to saying what's in my head. It's hard to talk about. . .feelings."

They both nodded at another couple passing them on the sidewalk.

But what did Neil feel for her exactly? Was it wise to push him to voice his emotions on a public street when he'd already talked more today than he likely had in a month? His praising her in front of Margaret and Don was enough to know he esteemed her greatly—and it seemed that being hoodwinked by her nephew hadn't changed his opinion of her, since he still caressed her arm.

Had she actually married a man who would love her despite her faults when her own family had never done so?

Maybe words weren't necessary. His attempt to produce them for her benefit was enough to prove he cared. She squeezed his hand, and he squeezed her hand back thrice.

A few steps later, he shook her hand a little. "One day, I hope you'll squeeze my hand back four times."

"Why's that?"

He stumbled a bit, but she held his arm tight. He frowned at his falter, likely unhappy that it had happened right in front of a man coming up the street, but he pressed on. "When I was little, my mother realized I had trouble expressing myself, so she'd squeeze my hand three times to tell me she loved me, and I would squeeze back four to tell her I loved her, too. I could tell her how I felt without having to push the tangled words off my tongue."

His hand still held hers tightly. He'd just squeezed it three times, hadn't he? "Are you saying you love me?"

"Yes." He squeezed her hand three times again.

"Wait, you've squeezed my hand like this before. At my sister's just now, and I remember you deliberately trying to crush my hand to death at the wedding."

He laughed. "Nerves made my grip harder than I intended, I suppose."

Her throat clogged up. "But how could you have loved me then? You hardly knew me."

"Though I hadn't talked to you much, I knew you were the finest lady in town, and I intended to love you because the Bible told me to." He stepped closer to her as they moved to the side to let a couple pass them. "You still are the finest lady I know, but I don't need the Bible anymore to make me choose to love you. I just do."

Despite her blush flaring back up again, she cleared her throat to push out the words

that'd be easier to keep inside. He couldn't see her flush anyway. "I wish you hadn't sent Mr. Ferguson ahead."

"Why's that?"

God might be allowing Neil to go blind, but He was just now opening her eyes to the gift of love He'd planned for her all along. It'd been a long wait, but now that she had this man's affections, she'd do whatever it took to return them tenfold. "What you just said deserves a couple more kisses along with the ones I already owe you, but I can't give them to you until we get home."

"If I talk the whole way there, how many will I get?" He took her hand and kissed the back of it after another couple passed them.

"We'll have to see, but there's a chance I could be persuaded to give you as many as you'd like."

He squeezed her hand three times.

And she squeezed back four.

Much to her introverted self's delight, Melissa Jagears hardly needs to leave her home to be a homeschool teacher, day-care provider, church financial secretary, and historical romance novelist. She doesn't have to leave her home to be a housekeeper either, but she's doubtful she meets the minimum qualifications to claim to be one in her official bio. Find her online at www.melissajagears.com, Facebook, Pinterest, and Goodreads, the Inspirational Historical Fiction Index website, or write her at PO Box 191, Dearing, KS 67340. To be certain to hear of Melissa's new releases, giveaways, bargains, and exclusive subscriber content, please subscribe to her email newsletter located on her webpage.

Bonnets and Bees

Maureen Lang

Chapter 1

Paul Turnbridge stared at the bee at the corner of his window. A familiar honeybee, no doubt sidetracked from his sojourn to or from the flowers Paul had ordered planted around his large farmhouse to attract little fellows just like this one.

"Yes, of course..." He spoke the words in response to something his younger brother had just said, newly arrived from Milwaukee some three hours to the east. He hadn't the faintest idea what he'd just agreed to, but knowing John it was likely a harmless request. His brother had a way of droning on that wasn't in the least bit as fascinating as the drone of a healthy bee.

"You—you will? You'll do it, then?"

Paul stepped around his brother, gently trapping the bee that was too focused on the glass to realize it had only to swoop lower to be free. Scooping the flyer inside an errant sheet of paper—a drawing of the original westward migration of the honeybee—he guided the little creature below the window's frame until it found what it had been seeking. Freedom. It then buzzed away.

Finally he turned to John, whose visit should have intrigued him if only because it was so rare. John never came asking for favors, and yet apparently he'd done just that.

"I'm sorry, little brother, but I was distracted by the bee. You see? There are several out on that honeysuckle bush. I can always count on that to draw the bees straight to me. Now, what did you say you needed?"

John was not quite a younger replica of Paul himself. His skin was fairer, although Paul had to concede his days following bees in his pursuit of study had undoubtedly darkened his skin. Bees, after all, primarily flew when the sun was high in the sky. But John had the same thick dark hair, the same blue eyes, the same nose that was straight and well defined.

"You and these bees!" John's voice had a familiar ring, learned from their mother. She'd never understood Paul's love of study, either. It had been clear since Paul's childhood that both of them thought him as dull as a doorknob.

"Yes, me and these bees." Paul stepped back around his brother, returning the drawing to its pile on the corner of his large desk that was filled with books, maps, and other drawings he loved to examine. "You'd admire them, too, John, if you let yourself get to know them. They're hardworking, industrious, a bit more social than I am—"

"A hibernating bear is more social than you are, brother mine. And that's why you're perfect for what I've just asked you to do."

"Why don't you get around to details, then? I have work to do."

"The arrangement will be in name only. Legal, of course, but completely impersonal.

She's depending on that and would be prepared to compensate you in some monetary way, but I plan to assure her you won't make any demands at all. That's the agreement: no demands either way."

"She? Who?"

John drew his lips tight. "Virginia Haversack. The woman I'd like you to marry."

Now it was Paul's turn to gape at his brother. "What? Marry? A woman?"

"Yes, that's typically how it's done. I pity a woman who would actually have to live with you, so you may consider this my contribution to any other woman you might have chosen on your own—if such a miracle had ever happened. Are you listening? You don't listen to anything but the buzz of a bee."

"Well, once you know how individual such buzzing can actually be... Now wait just a moment. You're saying you want me to marry someone? Have you come here in jest, then? You cannot be serious."

"I'm completely serious, and yes, that's exactly what I want you to do. Virginia is very dear to Sarah, and frankly, the only way out of the dilemma she faces is to find herself a husband. In name only is enough to satisfy the ridiculous demands of the will her father restricted her to."

"Slow down, John! So this...this Virginia is a friend of Sarah's?"

John nodded. "A very good friend. She owns the hat shop in the building next to my office, and lives just above. Sarah has worn her bonnets for years, and the two are like sisters."

"What are the details of this dilemma?"

"It's this blasted will her father left behind. For years now, even before her father died, Virginia has successfully run the hat shop her father built. In fact, she devoted herself to her father and to that shop and ignored any chance at marriage herself. Something her father continually scolded her for. He even tried to arrange for any number of suitable young men—"

"Yes, yes, so she's a spinster, and one her own father couldn't rid himself of. Get on with it. Now her father is dead and she's running the shop her own way. Where is the trouble?"

"The man's distant cousin will take ownership unless she weds. Her marriage is specifically stipulated in the will, or this cousin has the right to come in and own the whole kit and caboodle. Sweep it right out from under her, even though she's the one who made the business what it is today. She makes a splendid bonnet, and women like Sarah all flock to her. I suppose her father meant well enough, not wanting her to be alone for the rest of her life, but confound it, I think it was awfully unfair."

Paul barely listened once he understood the nature of the problem. So a woman needed a husband in order to inherit. A woman who must at least be a capable sort, having been successful in a business she took over from her father. A woman Sarah, whom Paul thought was too good for John anyway, liked.

And what need had Paul for a wife, other than one in name only? None whatsoever.

"Fine." He turned back to his desk. Once a decision was made, there was little point mulling it any further. "Why don't you arrange for the documents to be signed and the ceremony performed by proxy somewhere convenient to this woman, and have done with it. Send me the papers when they're ready." He eyed his brother and added somberly, "Just so long as the terms you presented are honored. No demands either way."

After receiving not only a nod from John but a raised palm as if swearing to an oath, Paul reached behind his desk for the bellpull. "I'll have Mrs. Higgins bring lunch, then you can be on your way."

Virginia Haversack tied off the royal-blue thread then snapped the needle away, holding the finished bonnet at arm's length to assess her latest creation. Fanchon style, it would stay in place with a pin rather than ribbon. Petite and feminine, it offered the perfect blend of blue and emerald green—a bonnet even a peacock might think improved its attire.

She smiled at the silly thought, sending up a silent prayer of thanks for peacocks everywhere. God was such a magnificent designer, throwing all of the most complementary colors together to please the human eye. She never had to look further for inspiration than the nature God provided, even here in Milwaukee. Although she'd never seen a real peacock, she'd seen plenty of drawings that lent her enough inspiration to keep her in hats for the rest of her life.

No sooner was the bonnet set aside, however, than a sigh escaped her lips. It was so easy to forget her troubles when she worked, which was likely why she'd finished a half-dozen bonnets in just a few days. Worry sent her searching for release, and that she could find only in creating one lovely hat after another.

It was a good thing she had so many clients waiting for her work.

Shaking away the sudden pins and needles in her fingers, she stood from her worktable. It was well past the time to go upstairs to the apartment she called home. She'd closed the shop two hours ago. Besides, she could always work upstairs.

Standing, she found herself hungry and realized she hadn't eaten since noon. She really mustn't forget to eat again. The words rang in her ears, an echo of her father's voice chiding her for being too thin. Her heart twisted at the thought of him. It had been only a month since his death; a month of far more free time since she no longer needed to see to his every need in his sickbed, but also a month of worrying about the ramifications of his will. The relief that he no longer suffered, and from the work that went with trying to ease that suffering, was only partly tainting the pure grief that came of missing him. She must see about finding a husband.

Turning down the gas lamp, she eyed the showcases of her millinery shop. In the dimming afternoon light shining through the windows displaying her wares, the contents made her sigh again. How she loved running this place, hearing the delighted gasps from her clients, knowing women came from all over Milwaukee just to ask her to design a hat for them. For tall women and short, young or old, for thin faces or round, for fancy occasions or simply for an afternoon walk in the park. . .Virginia could imagine a hat for every face and form, and one for every event. This place needed her, just as she needed it—to fill her days and dreams.

A tap at the door stopped her from going to the stairs at the back of the shop. An insistent knock, accompanied by a muffled voice calling her name. This was no ordinary customer, late for a pickup. Nearing the door, she recognized Sarah's voice immediately.

"I'm so glad I caught you before you went upstairs! I know you can't hear a thing up

there. Oh, Virginia! He'll do it! Paul will actually do it! John just got home, and I couldn't wait until tomorrow to tell you."

"Who will do what?"

"Paul! John's brother. You remember, I told you all about it yesterday after that man came to tell you your appeal to the judge to change the stipulations of the will won't do you any good."

She certainly hadn't forgotten that final word yesterday; the anticipation of it had kept her awake for two weeks, ever since having the idea to contest the will. And Sarah had mentioned some sort of plan. . . . But Virginia hadn't really paid much attention. Her worry had gotten in the way.

Virginia looked beyond Sarah to the waiting carriage. Sarah and her husband, whose office was next door, lived only a few blocks away. She'd taken the family coach, and a driver waited without even a glance their way from the curb.

"Can you come in and tell me about it, or is John expecting you back right away?"

Sarah, her blond curls bouncing beneath a pink and purple bonnet of Virginia's making, stepped past Virginia into the shop, closing the door behind them. "I can't stay too long, but certainly long enough to help you choose what to wear tomorrow."

"Whatever for?"

"For your wedding, silly goose! What else?"

Sarah was a bit shorter than Virginia, somewhat stout yet not at all round. She was petite in every way, from a small sloped nose to tiny hands and feet. But just now she could have been a giant for the gaping way Virginia knew she was staring at her friend.

Because it all came back, the plan that Virginia had certainly heard but had never considered plausible. Sarah happened to be in the shop when the man delivering the bad news about the tightness of her father's will had arrived. "*All you need*," Sarah had said after the man left, taking Virginia's breath with him, "*is a husband in name only.*"

Sarah had even suggested her bachelor brother-in-law, but Virginia had thought she'd only been talking to ease Virginia's initial shock. Just making conversation to stir more ideas about how to deal with the confines of the will. She had six months in which to find a husband. Six months to do what came as no simple feat to her: attend parties where her hats roamed freely and frequently, but places where she herself least wanted to go. In fact, other than the errand boy who regularly dropped off supplies or picked up her boxed hats for delivery, Virginia didn't even know an unmarried man, let alone one who might be remotely interested in marrying her.

When Sarah had rushed out the day before, Virginia had no idea she'd actually taken steps to make good on her suggestion.

"Are you saying. . .your brother-in-law will actually. . .marry me?"

Curls bouncing again, Sarah nodded with excitement, her brown eyes so merry that laughter bubbled out from behind her matching smile. "All of your problems are solved! And in only one day!"

Though Virginia's pulse sped at the thought of not having anything more to worry about, the idea of a marriage—a legal and binding one, if not a real one—was something she had to consider for far longer than a moment's notice, particularly to a man she didn't even know. Granted, he was John's brother and that could only mean he came from good stock, but marriage? Even if she never lived with the man, might he assume certain. . .rights?

"Now wait just a moment, Sarah! I thought you were joking yesterday. I know you mean well, and I certainly do want this problem taken care of. But I have six months, after all."

Sarah crossed her arms as a frown took the place of her smile. "Virginia. You know I love you, don't you? That you're like a sister to me?"

Virginia nodded.

"Then take this advice with all the love it's given: You're twenty-seven years old. Where in the world will you find a husband at your age, when you've never in your life given husband-hunting a thought?"

Virginia's heart sank in a twirling motion, knowing Sarah was right. But was she so desperate already to take such drastic measures? Marry a complete stranger?

"But marriage. . .I don't know, Sarah."

"Well of course it's marriage! That's what this whole situation is about." Sarah stepped closer, grabbing both of Virginia's hands and squeezing them. "I know Paul Turnbridge, Virginia. And I know you. If ever a business arrangement could work between two people, it's you two. He's. . . Well, he's a gentleman but lives a quiet life of study. He's never shown any interest in marriage, which is why he's available now. And you. . . Well, you've never shown any interest in marriage, either. See? You already have something in common. Honestly, my dear Virginia, I don't think you have a choice."

Virginia stared at her friend's earnest face, that sinking feeling confirming that Sarah was likely right.

"Besides," Sarah said, lifting one hand to pat Virginia's cheek, "what better way for us to be really sisters than this? I want my baby to have you for an aunt!"

Virginia gasped. "Baby! Oh, how wonderful! Does John know?"

"Of course. It's why he wants to have this ceremony as soon as possible. He doesn't want me traveling, even though I'm healthy as a horse. But I won't miss your wedding, since without me it wouldn't even be taking place. So tomorrow, Virginia. It's a three-hour ride, straight west. You'll be ready when John and I come for you? At ten? You'll have to close the shop for the day, but it's worth it to stay in business, isn't it?"

Awhirl with confusion, worry, gratitude, and what seemed her only hope, Virginia nodded and hugged her friend, who then scooted back outside to her waiting carriage.

Chapter 2

Paul entered his home through the kitchen, a habit he'd had since childhood. Although his father had farmed so that his heirs could be what some from the old country might call "gentleman farmers," Paul hadn't quite lived up to the man of leisure his father had provided for. Paul blamed his father that neither Paul himself nor John had ever spent a day chasing idleness, since Father himself had so well modeled working.

He hung his equipment on the pegs designed for such use, his net and jar, the veiled hat and thick gloves he wore when investigating a hive. At his feet were already the smoker and drumming sticks he used to temporarily drive bees away from the investigations he carried on in the hives themselves. Normally he would have passed through the kitchen with little more than a greeting to his cook and housekeeper, Mrs. Higgins, but she was bent over the most extraordinary cake, and he was caught not only by the care she took to add a pink dollop of frosting on the bouquet of flowers decorating its top but by the concentrated effort on her pleasantly lined face.

"And what have we here?" he asked, reaching a finger toward the base of the cake to snatch a taste of the sugary creation.

She slapped away his hand, not as gently as she might have had the cake been for him. Obviously she was serving this masterpiece for a very special occasion.

"It's your wedding cake, Mr. Paul, and I don't want it sampled before this afternoon!"

"My wedding cake," he repeated, bewildered. "Mrs. Higgins, you realize this isn't a real wedding?" John had made all of the arrangements yesterday, assuring Paul he needn't do a thing except be home at one o'clock. At least he'd known Paul wasn't likely to go to the city to do this favor! "The minister will provide the service in the garden, we'll sign a paper, and the woman will return on her way. I doubt she'll stay for cake."

Mrs. Higgins shooed him away, waving a small spatula in his face. "You leave this to me. There won't be a wedding in *my* garden without a cake. Now off you go."

"Your garden! Well, I like that. You, who complain every day that the flowers attract too many bees."

"Out! Go straight up to your room for a shave and a freshen, and wear that shirt I put the iron to. I've left it laid out on your bed."

Paul opened his mouth to protest over being treated like a child, but since Mrs. Higgins had mostly filled the role of mother even before his own mother died, he did her bidding.

He would have this favor done with, and tomorrow things would return to the peaceful, quiet routine he'd cultivated in his life.

But at least there would be cake today. While he enjoyed the honey that his industrious bees produced, he seldom thought to ask Mrs. Higgins to do any baking.

Virginia peered through the carriage window at the countryside lined with fields of grass broken by the occasional cluster of bushes or trees, and even more occasionally a field of wheat or corn or some other vegetation she couldn't name. Having been born and raised in the city, she couldn't understand why anyone would choose to live so far from others on these remote oases called farms.

She was tempted to look at her watch pin but caught herself before doing so. No sense in being teased by Sarah again. Yes, she was counting the moments until she would meet John's brother, even if it was ridiculous to spend a moment wondering what he would be like. It simply did not matter. This ceremony would take place for one reason, and that was to fulfill the demands of her father's well-meaning but obviously misguided will. After today, she would likely never see this about-to-be husband of hers.

Yet another lump formed in her throat, this one larger than the last. Swallowing nearly brought tears to her eyes. Marriage was a covenant of God, a symbol of the devotion He extended to those He'd made in His image. *A symbol to me, a promise that His love will last forever!*

Was she treating it shabbily, this rite that was clearly meant to be a holy union? God forgive her if she was—and yet, hadn't her father done the same with this absurd demand, using the one thing—her bonnets—that meant anything to her?

"Don't worry," Sarah whispered, patting Virginia's gloved hand with her own. Virginia stole a glance at John across from them, who broke away from his own perusal out the glassed window, as if surprised by Sarah's soothing tone. What had she to worry about, after all? Wasn't this ceremony meant to banish all of her worries?

"I'm just eager to have it over, I suppose. So I can get back to work."

John shook his head. "You don't know it yet, Virginia, but what you've just said has convinced me that we're absolutely right in this whole farce. If ever there were two people who deserve a marriage in name only, it's you and my brother."

"Why do you say so?"

"Because he's likely thinking the same thing you are."

Chapter 3

"He's waiting for you in the garden, Mr. Paul," said Mrs. Higgins after he opened the door of his bedroom to her gentle knock.

He intended to stride past, but Mrs. Higgins stepped in his way. "Now just a minute, little mister," she said, his old pet name slipping from her lips as it sometimes did. That he'd towered over her since he turned fifteen had little to do with it. She reached up to straighten the silk tie hanging haphazardly from his neck—an accessory he seldom wore but had dutifully donned, since she'd laid it out on the bed for him.

"And the hairbrush?" she asked.

He waited long enough for her to take a few quick brushstrokes to the back of his head, something she hadn't done for him since he better fit the term of endearment she obviously still held of him.

"All right, then," she said, stepping back to eye him with a look of satisfaction. "Go on. The minister wants a word with you before your bride arrives, and she's due here any time now."

My bride. . . What a strange sensation came with such words. But now was not the time to get sentimental, so he found his way to the garden, going through the glass-paned doors of the dining room rather than his usual route through the kitchen. He might as well play the part his father had left to him, if only for the minister's benefit, and use a proper door.

However, what caught his eye first stood at the edge of his garden: the tall glass box he'd been working with for several days now. He'd been luring bees to it with a bit of sugar here, the nectar of a flower there—smeared into the corners of the box he'd fashioned so he could see inside. So far he'd succeeded in capturing far too few specimens to be worth so much trouble—but there now! A fair swarm of them, their sweet buzzing like a symphony to his ear.

Without a word to the figure in black waiting amid the rest of the flowers in the abundant garden, Paul hurried to the kitchen door where he kept his gloves and veiled hat. Although he barely felt a sting anymore even if a bee did protest his accidental contact, today was not the day to suffer an uncomfortable stab. He emerged from the back of the house a moment later with his head and hands safely covered then walked right past the staring minister to take advantage of what nature had sent to him. All he needed to do was slip the glass top on the box, and he would have what he needed. It would only take a moment.

The bees were busy as usual, too busy to take much notice of him. Moving slowly, carefully so not to alarm them, he leaned down for the lid he'd made of glass and glue

and netting-covered air holes.

In a moment he would place the lid on top, temporarily imprisoning the bees that enjoyed what he'd provided for them. He would get this ceremony over with and then, once the bees had had their fill, he would free them to follow back to their hive. He had enough of them now to easily track their path.

But he couldn't help pausing to admire the creatures as they collected the sweet provision.

Virginia followed John after he helped first her and then Sarah from the carriage. Distracted as she was by what was about to take place, she still couldn't miss the loving care John offered to his wife. Her recently discovered pregnancy might not be the topic of polite conversation, but Virginia was fairly certain it was all both of them thought about these days. John treated her as if she were porcelain. Or perhaps a queen.

But she refused to dwell on the ripple of unexpected envy that swept through her. Sarah was so very dear to her, and Virginia celebrated that her friend had a husband who rejoiced in how precious she—and their coming child—was to him.

However, once they were both safely on solid ground, John fairly sprinted to the front door. It was barely opened by a middle-aged, salt-and-pepper-haired woman who pointed around the house before John waved them to follow through a narrow though perfectly manicured pathway amid thriving flowers surrounding the entire house.

"The minister is here," John called over his shoulder. "They're both in the back garden, my brother as well. You don't mind if I run ahead, do you? I want to make sure all is in order."

Sarah's laugh followed him, though Virginia doubted her husband could hear the words that followed. "What does he think could go wrong? Isn't this a perfectly normal occasion? A wedding?"

Virginia grabbed Sarah's hand, hoping she could absorb some of her friend's obvious peace and approval of the day. But it didn't work.

"Now don't you worry, too!" Sarah said. "I know this is meant to be. My instincts are never wrong, and I have a very definite feeling we're doing exactly the right thing. Come along. No dawdling now that we're here."

It was true, Virginia had dawdled. Now she stopped altogether. "Shouldn't I... Well, take a moment to freshen up after the journey?"

Sarah looked her over. "You look lovely! We don't want to keep the minister waiting."

"All right, but wait."

With trembling hands, Virginia reached up to unravel the delicate lacing she'd sewn into her yellow bonnet. It was black, perhaps not quite the color a bride should wear but taken from a butterfly design. The yellow and black color combination was ordained by God Himself. She knew the veil would obscure her face, but perhaps that was fitting, considering the details of the union about to take place.

Virginia couldn't help but notice the profusion of flowers that lined the wide flagstone path leading them around the two-story brick house. The city had its parks, windows had their boxes, and florists had their bouquets ready to be delivered anywhere in Milwaukee. But this place was a mix of cultivation and a wild array of color and scent. She couldn't name half of the buds that drew her eye, as the sight of such beauty

permeated the tension she'd carried with her from the city.

Rounding the corner of the house, she saw a man beside John. Both seemed to be staring in the other direction. A third man in strange garb was off at the corner of the garden, decked in a wide-brimmed tan hat with a veil even thicker than the one she wore. And his gloves were surely too cumbersome to work the ground. He was staring into some sort of glass box, and barely moving.

What sort of gardener wore such attire? Where was John's brother? And—goodness, a hint of panic assailed her—what was his name? Obviously Turnbridge, since that was John's name. But what in the world had John called him?

"There's Paul," Sarah whispered.

Ah! Paul! Her husband-to-be was named Paul. Not that she would have occasion to address him, but it was nice to know such a detail.

She followed Sarah's gaze and to her bewilderment it led her straight back to the odd fellow staring so intently at that unusual box. She watched as he moved with smooth, measured progress to place some kind of lid on the stand before him and then, some moments later, turned to see those who awaited him in the garden.

Chapter 4

Paul was used to seeing the world through the thick black veil protecting him, and he instantly noticed the three new arrivals. Skimming past his brother and his wife, his eye settled on the woman he was to marry. Instantly he noticed his was not the only veil between them, and he wasn't sure why he felt disappointed at the limited first sight of her.

She was taller than he expected, nearly as tall as John, who was only a few inches shorter than Paul himself. And though she wore a capelet over her gown, he could tell her form was pleasing. Her hair, what he could see of it behind the veil and the ribbon holding what even he could tell was an artfully designed yellow bonnet—the exact shade of a bumblebee, especially with its accompanying black—was a mix of sand and gold, darker than Sarah's hair but undeniably fetching.

None of which should matter, though he couldn't deny he wished he could see her face.

He approached, in no particular hurry as he contemplated what was about to take place. He hadn't any qualms about it while it was still just a favor for his brother and Sarah. But now, seeing there was a real live person attached, it suddenly seemed. . .important.

Reaching the little cluster of visitors, he took a place at his brother's side rather than by his bride, who stood clutching Sarah's hand as if she needed to be kept in place. That surprised him. It was for her benefit, after all, that this whole thing had been arranged.

"Reverend," Paul said, choosing to greet him first out of pure consternation over how to greet the woman whose name, at least, would forever be linked to his.

Reverend DeWeis filled the black garb of a minister to perfection. Tall, dignified, a thatch of silver hair complementing the figure he cut as a man to be trusted, respected, sought for advice. On the few occasions Paul made it to church, he was always impressed with the man's dedication to his flock.

Just now, however, rather than the traditional smile with which he normally greeted Paul on his rare visits, the man turned to him with a frown.

"Your brother came to me yesterday with the most extraordinary request to be here by one o'clock, with a marriage license I am to file, prepared to wed you to a woman this very day." Turning to include the woman in his attention, he added, "And I surmise this is the woman you are to wed."

"Yes, it's true," Paul said and would have continued but John jabbed him in the shoulder.

"Would you take off that blasted beekeeper's hat!"

Paul had nearly forgotten he wore it, but realized he likely looked silly in it now.

He pulled off the hat, then the gloves one-by-one, and tossed them to the wrought-iron bench he frequented when waiting for new visitors to his flowers.

For some unexpected reason he only managed a quick glance in his bride's direction, unaccountably wondering what she might think of the face of her husband. It was, after all, more information than he had of her. All he could tell was that her nose wasn't over-large, because the veil didn't protrude much. For all he could see she didn't have a nose at all.

Reverend DeWeis looked between Paul and his bride. Virginia. Her name floated easily to his mind, a name he suddenly found himself liking.

"Am I to understand this is an arranged marriage in every sense of the word, then?" the reverend asked.

"Yes," Paul said, "you could call it that." What more did the man need to know? He must perform weddings of all kinds; surely this wasn't the first couple he'd joined that he didn't personally know very well.

The minister eyed him suspiciously, but soon let his gaze travel farther from the garden to include the house and fields in the distance, easily spotted from their somewhat elevated height. "I understand your desire to leave a legacy, Mr. Turnbridge. You've been blessed with much and no doubt want the future of this fine estate to stay in the family. However, it's my habit to meet with the couples I marry, to interview them so to speak. There is the matter of being unequally yoked that I'd like to avoid. I'll not put my blessing on a couple the Lord does not see fit to be joined in the ministry of life."

Paul clasped his hands behind his back, wondering just how honest he was expected to be. Surely John had told the man the conditions of the agreement when he'd set up this ceremony? Why was the minister so intent on details like knowing whether or not he and his prospective wife were matched with similar faith?

"Reverend DeWeis," he said slowly, considering his words before letting each one out and purposely avoiding the gaze from his bride, "as you know I am unconventional in my faith." He lifted his hand to indicate the beauty of nature surrounding them. "I can more easily worship God from this cathedral right under His sky than I could in the far more humble building you call a church. But rest assured I submit to the authority of God in three persons, Father, Son, and Holy Ghost."

The reverend turned to the bride. "And you, young lady?"

Virginia could barely tear her gaze from the man who seemed to be purposely avoiding hers. He was like John, and yet so different. Taller, of course, which pleased her, because so many men reached her nose and not beyond. And John was certainly handsome, with his wavy dark hair and watchful eyes. But this man had something else in his eyes, a sort of soulfulness she hadn't seen in John that couldn't help but catch her attention.

None of which mattered, of course. Not even his height. This was the first and last day she would be seeing him.

Despite the truth behind their wedding ceremony, despite the sure knowledge that an heir to this lovely garden and beyond was most certainly not forthcoming from her—ever—she had no qualms about declaring the veracity of her faith.

"I am a Christian, Reverend, and strive to serve the God of the Bible because He first loved us. How could one not love a God who became man, suffered, and died, just so our

blame-filled lives could be acceptable to a just and blameless Creator?"

The reverend, not surprisingly, seemed more pleased with her answer than he had with Paul's a moment ago, but evidently both answers passed his test. Still, he did not lift the little prayer book already in his hand, which likely held the vows they were about to exchange.

"Arranged marriages are often the most fulfilling," he said, "simply because both parties come to the union with few misconceptions of the other's humanity. In other words, you won't be blinded by a veil of love, but rather come together and let life mold your teamwork more naturally. I do hope, Mr. Turnbridge, that you will be able to attend the *humbler* cathedral that is my church now that you will have a wife who will no doubt want to keep up her training in the Word of God?"

The crooked smile on Paul's face made Virginia's heart skip a beat. My, but he was handsome. Why had he never married, if only to provide that heir the minister had just proclaimed him in need of?

"I shall continue to send in my tithe, Reverend DeWeis, which I'm sure you will be happy enough to see without me. Beyond that, I will make no promises, lest any promise could be broken."

Virginia's heart, so shallow and eager to jump at the recognition of a handsome face, now skidded to a halt. He might believe in God, but how could he grow in knowledge of spiritual matters if he wasn't willing to go to church and be tutored by those who made study of the Bible their mission in life? And what of joining in worship with others, in community, to join a choir of no less than angels to sing and celebrate God's blessings?

Though the minister raised his book at last, he put a hand on Virginia's shoulder and spoke as if commissioning her to action. "Perhaps you, my dear, will have more success than I in bringing this believer under a real church roof."

Then, without delay, he began the heavenly work of binding two souls into one by the power of holy matrimony.

Chapter 5

V irginia pinned the hat in place on Mrs. Schumacher's ample hair. She was one of Virginia's best customers, the wife of the watchmaker whose business shared the same upper floor as John's law office.

The hat was blocked straw covered in mustard-colored velvet, its underbrim edged in cotton lace. The hat would sit better if a chin ribbon were allowed, but Mrs. Schumacher never liked anything to tickle her neck and so she'd opted for pins—the silver pins that Virginia ordered especially for her.

With fall already upon them, Virginia's customers loved the colors she used to reflect autumn's blaze as God transitioned earth's jewelry from lush and green to reds and golds and yellow, readying it for the whites and sparkles of snow and ice to come. On top of the velvet Virginia had added the smallest burnished red bow, with a bit of netting to keep it from flapping in the wind.

"Another lovely bonnet, Miss Haversack!" Mrs. Schumacher turned her head from side to side before the mirror to enjoy the fuller effect. "I don't know how you keep coming up with such lovely creations, but I'm glad that you do."

"Thank you, Mrs. Schumacher," Virginia said. She hadn't bothered to inform any of her customers that, legally at least, her name was now Mrs. Turnbridge. Why have people wondering what sort of marriage she'd entered when her life had not changed these past five months? No sense anyone asking after the health and well-being of a husband she hadn't seen, since agreed, since their wedding day. She'd hurried away right after the minister finished the ceremony, refusing an offer for cake. Sharing such a traditional treat would only lend credence to a ceremony she didn't want it to have. So, on the heels of the departing minister, she'd urged John to take them back to the city.

She walked Mrs. Schumacher to the shop's door but kept hold of the handle for fear of a fierce wind that had been blowing all day and might bang the door against the display window. A hot, dry wind off the prairie that even here in the city seemed to suck the last meager bit of moisture from everyplace and everyone.

With a glance at another blue sky on this fall day, she bid Mrs. Schumacher a good afternoon. "And don't forget to pray for rain!" she called as the woman stepped onto the sidewalk.

"Oh, yes, indeed. My husband says the whole of the Midwest is a veritable tinderbox!"

Instead of returning inside, Virginia pulled the key from her pocket, locked the shop door, and made her way next door. While her own upper floor offered a comfortable apartment, the two floors above the building beside hers housed only offices or other shops. A haberdashery, a candy store, John's law office that he shared with his partner, and

also a publishing office. But the largest space was taken up by the entire third floor, where a tailor employed several dozen workers every day of the week except Sunday. Virginia herself sometimes borrowed a few of the young seamstresses to help with her bonnets when she was especially busy.

As she'd done every day for the past week now that Sarah was so close to the baby's arrival, Virginia hurried up to John's office. Sticking her head around the door, she saw him bent over one of the two desks that filled the good-sized room.

"Any word yet?"

"Not yet," he said, needing no explanation. Every morning and every afternoon, sometime before John was expected to leave for the day, Virginia checked to see if the little neighbor boy assigned to fetch John had made an appearance.

"All right then," she said, starting to close the door again. John's voice stopped her.

"Everything all right with you, Virginia? Water buckets all filled? Coal fires tended?"

"It's hardly been cool enough to light the coal, even at night, don't you think?"

"I found the boy in the candy shop warming himself by their stove in the basement this morning. An empty bucket at his feet."

She frowned. "I hope you made sure he keeps that water bucket filled. Perhaps speak to Mr. Fassbinder?"

The owner of the candy shop was notoriously indulgent, proving how fit he was to sell the sweets he loved to create. Hopefully he'd cautioned his young employee about the dangers of fire, especially lately, but his everlasting smile and friendly nature weren't likely to produce any lasting impressions, at least as far as discipline was concerned.

"Remind Sarah I'll be stopping by this evening, won't you? And I'll stay the night if she needs me."

"Thank you, Virginia," John said with a grateful smile. "You're her sister in every way."

The following day, Sunday, came and went without the arrival of the newest little Turnbridge. Taking time away only to attend church services, Virginia stayed by her friend's side. John was there as well, quietly somber, ready to shout from the rooftops first for a doctor then whatever good news was sure to follow. Virginia assured Sarah she would call the footman to summon the doctor and not depend upon John's rooftop method when the doctor's services were needed.

But on Monday, with no sign of change except Sarah's growing restlessness, Virginia returned to her millinery shop for another day of bonnet making. Three days a week young Melissa Maynard came to help with sales while Virginia worked, and today when Melissa arrived her eyes were lit with worry and color highlighted her cheeks, as if she'd run all the way to the shop.

"Did you hear the news?"

The only news Virginia expected was of the baby, and she'd only just left Sarah's side a few hours ago. "But I told them to let me be the second one summoned, right after the doctor!"

Melissa tilted her head, a look of confusion on her pretty young face. "It's the fires I'm talking about! Burning to the north of us, and to the south. Up in the northern woods right here in Wisconsin. And Chicago! They say only God can save the city now, because it's been burning throughout the night."

"Oh, no! How awful for everyone."

Then Virginia hurried to the back of the shop to the boiler closet. Unlike the older building that housed John's office, her building came equipped with boiler and radiators to keep both the shop and apartment above warm. She checked the boiler regularly, as her father taught her to, making sure no pressure was building up and the temperatures were evenly set. She hadn't even lit the boiler yet this year because of the unusually warm weather, but now she unnecessarily checked to be sure everything was as it should be.

She vowed not to light the thing until the city was blessed with rain.

Paul didn't keep many hives, just a half dozen for his own honey production. He wintered them in the cellar some twenty yards behind the house, but it was certainly too early to move them yet. He'd just come from a neighboring hive that produced far more honey than his, and had heard the disturbing report that a farm just five miles to the south had lost its entire corn crop to fire.

He looked again at the sky, which for the first time in more days than he could remember was starting to gather some promising gray clouds. *Let it rain, and rain soon— before all the crops not yet harvested succumb to similar fires.*

Then he went in search of his foreman, to make sure harvesting was still at full speed.

Chapter 6

S queeze my hand harder if you must, Sarah! Let me share what you feel!"
Virginia hadn't meant to say those words, as if she herself longed to feel the
excruciating pain of childbirth that Sarah suffered, if only in her fingers. Certainly
she had never allowed herself to dream of being a mother, at least not since she was little
more than a child herself. But at the moment she would give anything to take some of the
pain from her dear friend, who grunted and pushed as no lady in society would admit, in
order to free the life that had grown inside her and allow it to join the world as its own
little person.

"Oh! Virginia!"

"I'm here, Sarah. You're doing everything right, just as you always do. Now let me feel
the next push, and with the doctor's help we'll get to meet your little darling!"

It wasn't quite with the next push, but soon enough Virginia was wiping sweat from
Sarah's brow, brushing away her mussed hair, and placing the bundled and squirming
baby boy into her friend's arms.

The miracle of life made Virginia's heart soar for Sarah. And for John. And even, a
little bit at least, for the distant uncle who would have his heir after all.

When Virginia opened a parlor window the morning after little Elijah Turnbridge was
born, it didn't take long to smell that something not far away must be amiss. She looked
outside, wondering if a nearby house had a problem with its boiler or stove.

"Fire! It's in your building, Mr. Turnbridge!"

Virginia heard the boy before she saw him, the same one commissioned to run for
the doctor last night. Now he ran with his bony arms flailing at the same time as he
rushed up the porch and banged on the door before she could reach it.

"Get Mr. Turnbridge! His building's afire!" Then the boy hurried back from where
he'd come, not bothering to wait and see if his warning made it to John.

Virginia was half tempted to run after the boy, thinking of her own building's prox-
imity. But she knew what she must do first. She went upstairs to find John.

She could barely utter the words that would be in such sharp contrast to the joy he
surely felt at Sarah's side, staring in amazement at the son they had created together with
God's help. At least she could spare Sarah from too much worry. They didn't even know
the extent of the fire yet, and it might not have touched John's office at all.

Besides that, the real importance was their family was intact. John's office and all of
its contents could certainly be replaced.

"John," she whispered, seeing Sarah was nearly asleep beside her dozing child.

He came from the bedroom, meeting Virginia in the hall.

"I think we had both better go to your office. A boy came running down the street, saying the place was afire."

"What!" He sprinted toward the staircase but stopped at the top, looking back at the door to the room where his wife and child lay. Before he could even ask, Virginia spoke.

"I'll make sure your housekeeper watches over her," she assured John. "I'll follow as soon as I can."

"Must you? Can you stay until I return?"

She wanted to, but with her own uncertainty growing, so fresh on the heels of devastating tales from Chicago, she knew her own worries would only multiply.

"I'm a little eager to be sure my own place is all right. Would you mind if I just ran over to make sure then came right back? Sarah will be all right. Surely both she and the baby will sleep awhile after the night they had changing the world."

John offered a grim smile and a slight nod. "You're right, of course. You'll let the housekeeper know, then? They're not to be left alone?"

"Yes, John, of course. Now go. I'll follow as soon as I can then hurry right back."

Everything went exactly as planned until Virginia turned the corner to the block where she worked and lived. She peered through a crowd of staring and pointing onlookers who repeated phrases like "what a blessing it didn't spread" and "God surely watched over the neighborhood with the losses so contained." Before she could decipher why the street's landscape looked so shockingly different, John appeared and took both her hands.

"I'm so sorry, Virginia. So sorry."

She stepped around him, and the crowd parted politely, silence taking the place of the sounds she'd heard just moments ago. Then she saw what everyone else had already seen, and she gagged trying to take in a breath of the sooty air.

John's three-story building was gone, leaving behind only the charred ruins of a few stubbornly standing beams in memory of the floors and walls they'd once supported.

And her own two-story shop and apartment building was nothing more than a heap of still-burning rubble.

It couldn't be simply gone. Not gone! Hadn't someone just said God had surely protected their neighborhood? How could He have done that, while allowing her home and business to burn?

Chapter 7

P aul unfolded the paper, an obviously hastily scrawled note written by his brother yesterday, though it hadn't reached Paul until this afternoon.

> *Fire devastated our business, but worse for Virginia as she has lost all.*
> *Please come to the city.*
> *Yours, John.*
> P.S. *You are an uncle.*

Frowning, Paul reread the few words that contained such a mix of horrid and joyous news. It was bad enough for John to lose the contents of his office—irreplaceable records, deeds, letters both corporate and personal—but for Virginia?

He may have given as little thought to his wife as she'd spared of him these past five months or more, but he wouldn't have wished anyone to suffer what she must be facing right now.

And yet. . . The rest of the words made an impression as well. He was an uncle. Of what, he wondered? Did he have a niece or a nephew? That alone was enough to warrant an unprecedented visit to the city he normally chose to avoid.

"Mrs. Higgins! Would you please pack a bag for me? I must leave immediately."

Virginia watched Sarah with the baby, as she talked to him gently and lovingly stroked the cheek that Virginia knew was softer than any silk she used to cover her bonnets.

How she wanted these first days of little Elijah's life to offer only the joy-filled memories that they should. She wanted to be happy for Sarah, proud that she'd done so well during childbirth, remarkably withstanding the pain. Not only that, she'd produced an amazingly healthy seven-and-a-half-pound baby boy who looked very much like his father. And uncle.

Virginia turned back to the window in Sarah's room where Sarah was recovering her strength since giving birth two nights ago. Despite the peace they'd had all day inside the closed door, John's home was no longer the untouched, quiet sanctity the baby had been born into. No one had been more surprised than John to learn the tailoring shop upstairs had not only employed but also *housed* a half-dozen young apprentices who had barely escaped the fire with their lives. One young girl had suffered a broken leg from jumping out a window, breaking the arm of the desperate friend below who'd tried catching her.

They were just as homeless as she was, and John, having invested in the building

itself, had seen fit to take several of them in. His partner, Mr. Thackery, had done so as well, and so even had the Schumachers.

Thankfully for Virginia, John was taking care of the paperwork end of things, following through with insurance claims. Because Virginia's father had taken John's advice about ample insurance, they should be able to rebuild without too much trouble once they collected on their policies.

A carriage drew her notice as it stopped in front of the house. If she'd slipped off to await dinner in the room she'd been using at the back, she'd have missed seeing the arrival of none other than her very own husband.

Paul tapped on the door. When he heard a variety of voices coming from within, he double-checked with a glance thrown over his shoulder to make sure the front yard was as familiar as he remembered it to be. It was more than odd that he would hear multiple young female voices. Laughter, even one voice raised in song. Perhaps a brood of women celebrating the arrival of his new niece or nephew?

While plausible since no life had been lost in the fire, it did seem too grim a time to be having a party.

He swallowed hard. Being in the city was distasteful enough without being subjected to a bunch of women congregated in a small room fawning over a baby. He nearly marched right back to his carriage.

But he did want to ask about Virginia, at least to see how she was doing after her great loss. So when the door opened—after a second knock—he squared his shoulders and asked to see John.

The girl who received the question was dressed in an ill-fitting cotton gown, one that was obviously meant for someone a good deal older than this person's perhaps dozen years. Nonetheless both the gown and she were clean, hair neatly brushed and gathered with a matching ribbon.

"Oh, Mr. Turnbridge hasn't come home yet. But I can tell him you visited if you like."

"I am also a Mr. Turnbridge, the brother of the owner of this home. I'll wait. Will you let Mrs. Turnbridge know that I'm here?"

"Thank you, Mossie," said a voice from the staircase that ended not three feet from the front door. "I'll let Mrs. Turnbridge know her brother-in-law has arrived."

Paul looked at the woman on the stairs with some relief, though he was surprised at the quality of her clothing. If she was a servant, she dressed extraordinarily well even for a housekeeper. She finished her descent, crossed the few steps between them, then greeted him with what he could only call a stiff smile.

"Good afternoon. . .Paul. Sarah is upstairs resting with the baby, but John should be home soon. I'm afraid there aren't many quiet places to be found around here, except perhaps John's office. I'm sure you know the way. . .don't you?"

What was this? Paul? Sarah? John? Who was this housekeeper, that she would address the family with such familiarity—even if she had said his name with a definite edge of awkwardness?

She led the way he barely remembered, not having visited his brother's house since John had purchased it shortly after his marriage to Sarah some three years ago. He passed by the archway connecting the parlor to the foyer, seeing a few girls as the fountain from

which the majority of the house noise originated.

John's office was at the back of the house, opposite the kitchen and behind the dining room. It was, as this woman had suggested, somewhat quieter here, although he could still hear the muffled voices from the parlor and a sporadically opened water pipe from the kitchen. If he wasn't mistaken, the baby was crying from somewhere above.

He was surprised when the woman closed the door with herself inside the room along with him. Looking at her for the first time, he found a touch of pleasure accompanying his surprise. While he was in no way a philandering man, he was fully human and appreciated the wide eyes, graceful movement, and full lips that blessed this woman with something not far short of absolute beauty.

Then, noticing her hair was the exact color of the woman he'd married the previous spring, he felt his heart lurch and his jaw drop. "You—you're Virginia?"

Her brows lifted, first in surprise he guessed, then with a slight dip of disappointment and perhaps even a bit of hurt. He couldn't blame her there. After all, it wasn't often that a man didn't recognize his own wife.

"As you can tell by the number of houseguests, your brother was kind enough to take in a number of us after the fire two days ago."

Reflexively he stepped closer, taking her hand in his as if it were the most natural thing in the world. And wasn't it? Shouldn't it be?

"I'm so sorry to hear of your loss, Virginia," he said softly. His heart swelled with compassion as other words he hadn't quite expected came to his tongue. "It's been quite a year for you, hasn't it? First losing your father, forced to comply with a will you obviously would have contested if possible, and now losing both your home and business. I'm sorry. Truly sorry."

When she raised her eyes, he might have been alarmed to see tears welling at the rims, but it was as if some mysterious force filled him, making him unexpectedly unvexed around this woman who was obviously about to cry. If Mrs. Higgins could see him now, as he prepared to gather up this woman for a good cry on his shoulder, she would likely accuse him of having lost the wits that usually restrained him.

Chapter 8

Virginia could hardly believe she was being held in a man's arms, a handsome man's arms—and incredibly, this man comforting her was her husband! Some weak voice in the back of her mind called out a warning, inspired no doubt from years of schooling and attempts at fitting into the social set. *You barely know him! He doesn't know you at all! How can you allow yourself to be so vulnerable when the agreement was clear?* He owed her nothing, and she owed him the same.

And yet she couldn't remember having so little control over her tears. She had cried when her parents died, first her mother then her father. They were quite a bit older than most of the parents she knew from schoolmates or other friends, and so their deaths were neither untimely nor unexpected, especially her father's. It was, she'd been told by every wise person or pastor who had spoken to her after their funerals, the natural cycle of life. Children bury their parents; it's only really difficult when it's the other way around.

But now every corner of her being was filled with grief, not just for the fire and the loss of every single belonging she'd ever owned, every finished and unfinished bonnet. More than that, it was the loss of each irreplaceable photograph she had of her parents, every trinket or letter they'd ever left to her. She found herself immersed in the grief of losing her mother and father all over again. In spite of having been taken in by Sarah, her would-be sister, and her generous husband, Virginia had never felt so utterly alone.

"I—I'm sorry," she whispered at last, forcing herself to take control of her tears if not her hidden emotions. "I suppose I wasn't expecting your sympathy, given that we barely know one another. And the circumstances are. . .well, awkward at best. Scandalous at worst."

He pulled what appeared to be a freshly cleaned and ironed handkerchief from his pocket and handed it to her, offering her his crooked smile as well. "Scandalous? That a man should comfort his wife? Technically speaking, it would only be a scandal if I didn't."

Wiping away her tears, she tried to meet his smile with one of her own. "But the nature of our marriage. I'm sure if your Reverend DeWeis knew the details, he'd have refused to let his services be so manipulated. And for purely monetary reasons."

"You make it sound much less sensible than it was," he said, leading her to the leather settee that sat along the side of the room. "As I understand it, neither greed nor selfishness had anything to do with it. That cousin of yours, though I don't know so much as his name, had no right to inherit the shop you and your father built. I suppose your father knew you would feel that way, and guessed you would accept one of no doubt many proposals you've received over the years."

As she took a seat with him on the small sofa, she nearly laughed at his words. Only

fear stopped her, fear that he might question her sanity if she went from one emotional extreme to the other. Many proposals, indeed. She was amazed he would say such a thing, particularly the way she must look now with puffy eyes and a red nose.

The quiet between them lengthened, since she had no idea what to say. Perhaps her lack of conversational prowess would speak for itself as to why those proposals hadn't been forthcoming.

"Do you know how long it will be before they start to rebuild your shop and home?" he asked, filling the silence. "I assume your insurance will cover the expense?"

She nodded, grateful to have something less personal to talk about. "John is meeting yet again with someone from the insurance company this afternoon. I'm surprised he's so late, but he did say the insurance company was quite busy these days. Evidently it's a large company, with insured clients from as far as both Chicago and Peshtigo."

Paul frowned. "Let's hope it's large enough to absorb the losses then. Or that only a small percentage of their other clients were affected by the tragedies that happened in those places, too."

She hadn't thought of that, thankful only that John had chosen a company so large it undoubtedly had many customers—and their fees—to cover both their losses.

"And now, I have a question that has plagued me since receiving John's note earlier today. He says I'm an uncle, and I can only faintly hear the occasional cry from upstairs. But what sort of child did they have? A boy or a girl?"

Paul stared at the sleeping face of the infant in Virginia's arms. A boy. Elijah Turnbridge. Not for the first time, he envied his little brother even as he rejoiced in the knowledge that the Turnbridge name wouldn't stop with them.

Virginia had eagerly agreed to retrieve the baby, even though Sarah was still confined to her recovery. He'd waited in the office with the door open, hearing her light footsteps on the stairs. He couldn't imagine carrying a baby down a flight of stairs, but evidently it didn't bother his wife. He'd gauged her continued progress down the hall by the ooohs and aaahs of the other houseguests, although who those young women were exactly he had no idea.

"Would you like to hold him?"

"Positively not," Paul said quickly. Whatever gift he'd received from above to handle her tears a moment ago now abandoned him. A baby was even further outside his realm of comfort than holding a sobbing woman in his arms. "But I'm glad to meet him."

"I promised Sarah I would bring him right back, although I'm hoping she might take the opportunity to nap. This little guy demands her attention often enough during the night, if last night was any indication."

She disappeared once again, and suddenly the quiet room felt too empty. A surge of laughter burst from the parlor, and first he hoped they hadn't awakened the sleeping infant. Then he reminded himself such an intrusion on his thoughts was exactly why he preferred the solitude found on the farm.

Something tugged at his mood with the realization that Virginia had gone to what anyone would call extreme measures to hold on to a business dependent upon city life. She must be happy here, living and working among so many people.

Likely she could never call a place like his quiet solitude home, either.

It was time to remind himself that the kindness he felt toward her could be nothing more than that, even if he had every legal—and spiritual—right to do something silly like fall in love with her. Truth was, anything but their marriage in name only would undoubtedly lead to heartache, with each of them so devoted to different parts of Wisconsin.

Instead of sitting on the settee again, Paul chose to wait on one of the chairs that rested opposite John's desk for Virginia's return. Let her have the settee alone; sitting too close might stir the temptation to touch her again, to give whatever comfort he could in case the grief she must be suffering revisited.

But it wasn't Virginia who opened the door. It was John, and his face was etched in such a deep frown that for a moment he looked older than Paul himself.

"Ah, Paul," he greeted but barely looked at him. Another sign something was amiss. He laid a file on his desk then tugged at the tie that was already loose. "I'm glad you've come."

"You look tired, young man," Paul said, watching his brother nearly fall into the chair on the other side of his desk. "Is it the baby keeping you up—congratulations, by the way—or all this mess figuring out how to reclaim the losses? Or that your home has suddenly become a hotel?"

"All of that," John said, scrubbing his face with his hands. Then he looked at Paul squarely. "And more. It's the insurance company holding our accounts. Mine, and Virginia's. The losses in Peshtigo already filed from the fire there have bankrupted them. They're out of business. Broke."

Paul leaned forward, his gaze intently settled on his brother. "I was afraid of that when Virginia told me the company had holdings there. What do you plan to do? Is there any other recourse?"

"We can try a few avenues of lawsuits, I suppose. But frankly, there isn't a thing we can do that's likely to be successful. Insurance companies are closing all over Wisconsin and Illinois, between the fire up north and in Chicago. The need for help is simply too great for many of them to handle."

"Surely there is another way to find help. The federal government, Wisconsin itself. The church?"

John leaned on his elbows, his face hanging. "I'll be all right, in time. I'll still have my clients, and by the grace of God some of my most important papers were in the safe, which melted a bit but didn't burn through. Between what I have filed here and what I can salvage, my work will be interrupted, but that's all. It's Virginia, Paul. I was the one who recommended to her father which insurance company to use."

"You couldn't have known."

"No, but that doesn't make me feel less guilty."

"She's young; she has good business sense, doesn't she? Ran her own hat shop? She'll need to rebuild, but like your business, this is only an interruption."

"An interruption? What kind of interruption?"

Paul wished he'd heard her coming, but he'd been too focused on John to register her soft, feminine footfall. He stood, going to her and leading her back to the settee. He knew he would have to tell her; John looked as though he might crack under the weight of his grief for her.

"The insurance company holding your account has gone bankrupt, Virginia."

"Bankrupt. . ." Her voice was little more than a whisper. "Well," she started, more brightly than the situation demanded, "companies do that sometimes, don't they? And then sometimes. . .start again? Is that the kind of interruption you were talking about when I came in? The insurance company's service will be interrupted, but it'll start again, won't it? Just as mine will start again, too."

Paul started to nod slowly, though he couldn't force a hopeful glint to his eye, no matter how hard he tried. Then he stopped his insincere nodding and shook his head. "No, Virginia. The insurance company has no money left, and they'll likely face a long line of suing creditors. I doubt you'll see a penny of what you were expecting."

"But—but they can't do that!" She looked at John at last. "Can they? I've paid my premiums. Faithfully, every last one. They signed a contract. Surely they can do. . .something?"

Like Paul himself, John only shook his head.

If she was going to cry again, Paul was fully prepared to take her back into his arms, even in front of John—who likely wouldn't expect such a gesture coming from his hermit of a brother. Although one tear did glisten at the corner of Virginia's eye, it did not dare to fall. The look on her face was too grim for that.

"This is more than just my livelihood. It's my whole life."

Paul took both of her hands in his.

"And you'll have it again. I will pay for the rebuilding myself."

Chapter 9

If Virginia hadn't just fought a second wave of tears, perhaps she might have won this third battle. But she felt a few tears roll, hot and wet, all the way down what felt like fever-ridden cheeks. "I cannot accept such an offer, Paul. Not when I already owe you so much."

"What do you owe me?"

"A favor, at the very least. And at most, that I still own the business—or did until the fire."

"Then we're agreed I have a vested interest in the matter. Let me do this."

Her heart pounded so hard she was afraid it might burst, or crack through the thin casing of her body. As much as she wanted to throw her arms around Paul and offer her eternal gratitude and loyalty, she knew she could not. She'd stretched God's laws already when it came to this man, and now that she knew him to be both kind and generous, she couldn't imagine letting him do so much for her.

"The only way I would consider such a thing is if it's done as a loan." Her gaze shot to John. "Legally. Papers and all. I will borrow the money, but Paul must agree to fair terms of repayment."

Paul and John exchanged what looked like perplexed glances. "Virginia," John said, "have you forgotten? Paul is your legal husband. His money is already yours. I can't draw up papers between a man and wife. It's simply not done, at least not in my office."

Virginia stood, going to John's desk. "A blank piece of paper then, please?"

With a lifted shoulder and look of interested capitulation, John glanced first at Paul then handed to her what she'd asked. She reached for the pen, dipped it in the inkwell, and wrote hurriedly yet with determination. Then she handed both the paper and the pen to John.

"If you'll sign this as witness?"

He read what she'd written. Although her penmanship might be a bit uneven because even now her hands trembled, she knew the meaning was clear enough. Simply stated, it was a declaration of repayment of a yet-to-be-determined amount of money, on loan from Paul Turnbridge and to be reimbursed with no less than 7 percent interest by Virginia Haversack.

To her consternation, John handed it back. "That's no longer your legal name, Virginia. You can call yourself—and expect others to call you—whatever you like. But Haversack hasn't been your name for more than five months now."

Exasperated over such a minor point, she took back the paper, scratched out one name and replaced it with the other. When John received it this second time, he winked.

"Welcome to the family."

Then he tore the paper into pieces.

Paul came up behind his brother, patting him on the back. "Well done, John. Now, is it too late to get things started? Had you a builder in mind once the insurance funds came through?"

John nodded, telling him about a Mr. O'Shea who came with good references. Although he and John chatted about details concerning the reconstruction of not only Virginia's building but also John's, Paul was never more aware of Virginia as she looked on with what he could only guess was a mix of frustration and—it had to be—relief.

And that brought more satisfaction to him than he would have imagined possible. Perhaps not all people outside the family were as much of a bother as he'd always believed the general population to be. But then, smiling inwardly, he reminded himself she wasn't outside the family, after all.

Dinner was served soon, an affair that nearly obliterated whatever feelings of peace, even good cheer, Paul had harbored since realizing his visit to the city had done some good, for John and especially for Virginia. Confronted by a table filled with young women all asking a lot of questions, he was ready before dessert to fetch his carriage and go home.

But there was cake, and so he stayed.

"Are you married, Mr. Turnbridge?"

The question came during a lull in conversation, from the same girl who had answered the door earlier.

With a glance at Virginia, who sat directly across from him, on John's other side at the head of the table, Paul nodded. But he left it at that. He'd barely said a word during the entire meal, so Mossie took his response for what it was: an answer but not compliance with conversation.

It was after dark by the time the dining room emptied, and it occurred to him if he had intended to return home tonight he ought to have started out before dinner. Country roads in the dark were dangerous for both man and beast. But, eyeing those who filed back into the parlor, he realized that was preferable to staying here.

"I'll be going then, John," he said as his brother paused in the hallway, as if uncertain where to lead his variety of guests. Evidently he wasn't the only one not looking to take a place among the girls in the parlor.

"Going? So late in the day? It'll be midnight before you're home."

"Yes, well, it can't really be helped, can it?"

From the corner of his eye he saw Virginia watching him, and he wondered if she might be concerned. If for nothing else, since he conceded they were still strangers after all, she might worry about losing her financier. That was something, anyway, and he was glad yet again to have made the offer. It was satisfying, this feeling of helping her. So much more personal than just handing over a check to the church to help nameless and faceless unfortunates as the church saw fit to bless.

"But you haven't even seen the baby yet!" John protested.

"Ah, yes, I have," Paul said. "Did you hear me say I'm happy for you? My little brother, a father."

"Listen, Paul," John said, his voice lowered, "I'd like you to stay. You can sleep in my office. It's about the only place left that isn't occupied if you don't count the kitchen. The settee isn't any good for sleeping, but if you put the two leather chairs together it's bearable."

Paul sent him a teasing smirk. "Sarah sends you to the office to sleep on occasion, does she?"

"Not yet, but if Elijah continues to be our bunkmate I may resort to such a thing. It's just this. There is something I wanted to propose, and it can't be decided quickly."

"I thought we had it all settled? I'll take care of Virginia's building, and you've already arranged your own funds, between your investments and that of the others who shared your building."

"Yes, yes," John said, keeping his voice lower than Paul's. He glanced first at Virginia, then at the parlor behind them, then back at Virginia. "It's something else."

"Well, what is it?" Paul wasn't keen on mystery, and the way his brother acted had all the flavor of one. "I'll be honest, John. That chair arrangement doesn't hold much more appeal than a bumpy ride on dark roads, considering my own bed is at the end of the journey."

"All right. At least come back to the office for a word, will you?"

Paul stepped in line behind his brother, but Virginia started in the other direction. Paul stopped. He didn't want to miss saying good-bye to her, and it looked as if she might retire for the evening.

But John, seeing neither of them was following him, stopped as well. "Virginia, this concerns you, too. Actually, perhaps especially you."

"Oh? Is it anything to be worried about?"

"No, but it's a matter Sarah and I have discussed in some detail. I would include her in this, but I'm not sure she'd forgive me for holding family business in our bedroom, and her in her nightclothes and the baby to disturb."

Now Paul exchanged a curious glance with Virginia. What more family business was there? They'd settled everything that mattered.

They went to the office, where John went behind his desk but didn't take a seat. Perhaps this wouldn't take long.

"Sit," he said, motioning to the chairs and settee.

Paul let Virginia choose where to sit, and when she took the settee, he decided to occupy the place right next to her. Just in case more tears were on the way. Who knew, the way John was acting?

Stirring a vague sense of alarm in Paul, his brother did not sit after them. In fact, his face looked every bit as somber as it had when delivering the news about the bankrupt insurer. Then, instead of addressing whatever problem he'd asked them in to discuss, John leaned over his desk, bent his head, and appeared to be. . .praying!

It shouldn't have come as quite a shock to Paul that his brother would do such a thing. At least privately, Paul himself often sent up more than just greetings to the Creator who'd given them so many gifts in nature. But this prayer business being shared between others, or in front of others, well, that was another matter altogether.

He was about to demand John get to the point when at last his brother straightened, looked at Virginia then directly at Paul, where his gaze lingered a moment longer.

"Sarah and I have been praying over something that seems to have come to the

forefront of both our minds since the fire. Somehow it's highlighted our part in your nuptials."

Paul nearly breathed a sigh of relief. "Whatever pang of conscience you're suffering, John, you can put it aside. It's all done, and in fact it hasn't inconvenienced me in the least, and I don't think Virginia will complain about how it's worked out, either."

"Not at all!" she said. "I'm the one who has benefited, and if anyone deserves the blame for manipulating holy matrimony, it's me."

John's brows rose, and he wagged a finger like a teacher whose pupil had just shown a dawn of learning. "That's just it! That's exactly how I've felt, though I kept it to myself until all this fire business changed everyone's life. You do see it, then, Virginia? The wrong we've all done?"

If she had a response, Paul didn't intend to let her utter it. He didn't want some obscure reason for guilt to change a situation he was happy to let continue. "What's wrong with it? It served a purpose, and no harm was done."

"No, not exactly," said John. "Not monetarily. But spiritually?"

Paul shook his head, standing in the hope of ending this ridiculous conversation. "As I said, no one has been inconvenienced or harmed, therefore there is no reason to end such an arrangement."

Virginia popped to her feet. "End?"

"Who is suggesting an end?" John asked. "No, brother, what I'm suggesting is just the opposite."

Chapter 10

Nearly overcome with confusion, Virginia almost fell back to her seat. Sheer will not to be seen as any weaker than she'd already displayed earlier kept her standing. She had no idea what sort of proposal John was prepared to make, but she knew one thing: she would not see this marriage ended. Even if it hadn't nor ever would be consummated, the dissolution of marriage must be just as great a sin as starting one for the wrong purpose. She would have no part of that.

John rounded his desk to stand in front of both of them. "What I'm thinking is so obvious I cannot believe God impressed this upon only me. Even Sarah agrees, wholeheartedly. Don't either of you see what must happen?"

Virginia looked at Paul to see if he was more enlightened than she, but he appeared every bit as confused as she felt.

"Virginia, you must go to the farm with Paul. You're his wife, you no longer have a home here in the city, and you owe it to the sacrament of marriage to see this as an opportunity to at least investigate the possibility of honoring the vows you both took."

"We *are* honoring them!" Paul said, taking the words right out of Virginia's mouth. "At least in the sense of support. And have you forgotten that once her home is rebuilt here she will want to return to the life she was happy with?"

"Yes, John," Virginia added. "I agree the terms of this union are unusual, but as your brother has already said, he hasn't been inconvenienced. I don't see anything *but* inconvenience for him were I to invade his life as you suggest."

John's face went rigid. "I must insist on this, I'm afraid. In fact, tonight's dinner reminded me of how many people's lives have been inconvenienced by this fire. Inconvenience is common. I'm already working on finding other employment, at least temporary, for the girls we took in. Soon enough they'll be out of here, too, living lives of their choosing. They don't want to be boarders any more than I want my house over-occupied, especially now that we have Elijah to consider."

Virginia wrung her hands. Perhaps Paul hadn't found their marriage an inconvenience—yet—but John, and perhaps Sarah as well, did find so many houseguests an inconvenience. "I thought. . .I could be of some help with the baby," she whispered.

"Virginia," John said softly, "I'm sure I bungled how I've said all of this, because we do consider you family. It's just that both Sarah and I have wondered if this fire didn't provide an opportunity for you and Paul to see if this marriage was ordained by God not just for financial security but something more."

She turned away, refusing to fight another battle with tears. It was obvious from Paul's reaction that he didn't want her to come to the farm, and yet it seemed just as obvious she couldn't stay here for as long as it would take to rebuild the shop. Where

could she go? She had a little money in the bank but not enough to live on for very long. Still, she would manage. She must.

"I'll go, John. I hadn't considered how hard this must be for you and Sarah, with your new little family needing peace and quiet." She stole a glance Paul's way, not surprised to see outright shock on his face. Surely he was dismayed at the thought she was actually considering going to the farm, intruding on the reclusive life he was used to. She hurried to put him out of his misery. "But not to the farm. I'm too grateful for the help you've been to me, Paul, to make myself a burden to your home life."

His brows drew together. "I have no intention of forcing a decision from you one way or the other, Virginia. But where could you possibly go? I assume if you had a choice you'd already have gone elsewhere, with this place so crowded."

She squared her shoulders. "I can get a little room, I don't need much. And I can work, can't I? I thank God every day I wasn't at home when that fire broke out, or I might have died in it. As it is, I'm fully capable of making the same bonnets—popular bonnets, if I do say so myself—and selling them door-to-door if I must. My regular clients have always been loyal, and the only way I see that loyalty endangered is if anyone knew I'd married for so selfish a reason. They'd likely see me as a fortune hunter willing to misuse one of society's most respected unions, marriage. All sympathy would be in your corner." She had to add, "As it should rightly be."

He frowned. "You're certainly no fortune hunter, and just so you are fully informed, the funds for the rebuilding will come from a mortgage on my land, not some inexhaustible bank account that some might mistake as a fortune if they had an inkling of this situation, misinformed or not."

"A—A mortgage! Oh, Paul, I cannot make you go into debt for me."

"It isn't debt, it's an investment. I happen to have seen your bonnets, at least the ones Sarah has no doubt worn, and I'm convinced your business is sound."

Something lifted from Virginia's shoulders then, with his statement of confidence in her. She could do this. And she would.

"But if we each have a vote," Paul went on, his voice barely above a whisper, "then I have no objection to your coming to the farm while you wait for your shop and home to be rebuilt. You won't have much of a market for your bonnets there, I'm afraid, but you'll have plenty of room to produce them."

Until the words were out, Paul wasn't sure he'd have had the courage to issue that invitation. It was obvious Virginia floundered after John's ill-chosen words. It was as if his little brother had kicked her out! And valiant as she might be to try supporting herself, Paul had no intention of letting her think that was her only choice.

The possibility of her refusing his offer was what he feared. She already knew just how far his farm was from the city, or from any town. She had no idea how long the winters were out there, and that interminable season was right around the corner.

"Paul," she said, her eyes downcast so he couldn't read whatever he might find if she'd looked at him. He drew in a breath, prepared for her refusal. Isn't that what people did who were about to disappoint someone? Hide their eyes? "When you agreed to the terms of this marriage, it was with the understanding that your life wouldn't change. I cannot impose myself upon you without feeling I'm the worst burden. I won't have you paying

so dearly for all of my troubles."

She hadn't outright refused; in fact, her response convinced him she was persuadable. Just why he was so intent on offering that persuasion, he wouldn't ponder. But it was the right thing to do, even if John was being a bit too high-minded about the whole situation.

"If I promise to lock you in one room, far, far from my own, and have Mrs. Higgins deliver a crust of bread to you now and then just to keep you alive for your bonnets and my investment, will you then agree? I'll hardly know you're there."

Thankfully, she already knew him well enough to burst into laughter.

Chapter 11

Virginia was quiet when they set out for the farm the following afternoon. She'd spoken at length with Sarah, who was evidently furious enough with John over his handling of the situation to make Virginia wonder if he'd be taking Paul's place on the office chairs tonight. Sarah didn't want Virginia to leave, though she did admit in the end that she understood John's guilt over having participated in the whole fake marriage to begin with. But she didn't hide a mischievous smile at the prospect of Virginia spending time with her lawfully wedded husband, revealing she still held little or no doubt regarding her own instincts about their marriage being right no matter the foundation.

It was that very notion that had Virginia so quiet now. The farm was indeed far from everything she knew. And setting out alone with Paul reminded her how little she really knew about him. He didn't even go to church! He'd professed faith at their wedding, but how could she know his faith was real if he didn't act on it?

Besides that, she was still mourning the loss of her work. She was grateful that Paul had waited the entire morning while she hurriedly visited the material and supply shops she dealt with so she could take an entire trunk load of bonnet goods with her. Perhaps he was kidding when he'd said he wanted her to work while she was at his farm, but with that she was happy to comply. She had every intention of staying out of his way, no matter how lonely that farm became.

The prospect of a three-hour journey was the first challenge. How could she make it clear to him she wouldn't be a bother? She'd seen last night at the dinner table how he'd resisted all attempts to make light conversation, and she was determined not to prod him into offering companionship he preferred not to give.

For nearly an hour, neither said a word. The awkwardness was like a veil between them, an impenetrable barrier that prevented any idea of how to make herself pleasant yet undemanding company. How did one provide company if the other person preferred being alone?

So she waited for him to speak.

But he didn't.

※

Paul slowed the horses for the plank bridge ahead. It was a rickety thing over this particular gully, but it saved a good deal of time going the long way around to a smoother crossing. He ought to have one of his farmhands come out here and fix it, since no one else seemed interested in maintaining it.

But they were still another hour and a half from his farm, and on a public road, so he was neither responsible nor obligated for such repair. Until today, it had never bothered him. The idea that he might be going back and forth between the city more than once

every three years, however, made him wonder how one went about having such a thing improved if he didn't oversee it himself.

He might have voiced his thoughts, now that he had the unprecedented company of someone else in his buggy, but wasn't at all sure she wanted to hear such mundane musings. He couldn't figure out why Virginia was so quiet. Perhaps leaving the city behind was harder than she expected. She'd cried when Sarah, who had come downstairs fully dressed and looking more like her old self than he'd expected, saw them off. They'd clung to each other as if they'd never see each other again.

Perhaps that was how Virginia really felt, this drastic change to her life.

"So you're facing yet another loss," he said aloud, before he could catch the words back.

"Pardon?"

He couldn't very well ignore the fact that he'd spoken, so he might as well repeat himself. At least he wasn't about to broach such a dull topic as road conditions.

"You. Another loss. The loss of the city around you, at least for a while, and all of its conveniences. I'm sorry my solution to the crisis of your homelessness is so remote."

"I'm very grateful for all you've done," she said.

How could he tell her he didn't care about gratitude? That the notion of someone feeling indebted to him made him uncomfortable? Perhaps in some communities this was acceptable, even desired if there was hope of some give-and-take. But the society he knew best was that of the bees, the one where every member did their work, knew their place, and was rewarded—or not, and often with startling consequences for a society that outwardly worked so well. Nature, human or otherwise, could be cruel. Which was why he'd always sought to remove himself from human society.

A cloud passed overhead, drawing his eye when it blocked out the sun for some time. "Bees don't like rain," he said, once again surprised to hear his own voice.

"No?"

"No."

He slid a sideways glance at her. He didn't need to talk to pass the time; there were days on end when the only other person he spoke to was Mrs. Higgins, and some when he didn't even speak to her. The farm ran itself, his overseers knew their places and their jobs, just as dedicated as worker bees. Far be it from him to know if any woman, this one included, liked conversing. But that was what he always believed of females, if he could judge from the way Mrs. Higgins always talked to the others in his employ. He'd given Virginia two opportunities to hold a conversation—blast it all, to give this thing called holy matrimony a tiny, if timid, step forward. But she simply didn't seem interested.

It was just as well. She'd be going back to the city just as soon as her shop was rebuilt.

Chapter 12

Mrs. Higgins dropped the basket of apples she'd been holding when she caught sight of Virginia sitting beside Paul in his buggy. Virginia watched as the red fruit rolled every which way, and both she and Paul hurried to help pick them up after they emerged from his buggy in front of Paul's home.

"Well, well, this is quite a surprise you've brought home, Mr. Paul," she said as they filled the basket. "Mrs. Turnbridge, welcome home!"

Now it was Virginia's turn to gape, as Mrs. Higgins had upon sight of her. Paul hadn't even recognized her the first time he'd seen her since the wedding, yet this woman did, who'd only greeted her a moment before the ceremony?

"Thank you for remembering me, Mrs. Higgins," she said, glad Paul had mentioned the woman's name so she could somewhat return the familiarity.

"How could I forget you, ma'am? I've thought of you often since that day, wondering when the good Lord would bring you back. And here you are!"

"Have you, Mrs. Higgins?" she asked. "You weren't offended by the whole thing?"

"Now, what right have I to judge anyone else? Come inside, both of you, before the rain comes. We'll be like bees to the hive, isn't that right, Mr. Paul?"

Virginia recalled the protective gear Paul had worn just before the ceremony, guessing it likely had something to do with his obvious interest in bees. She had been sorely tempted to ask him further about such things when he'd briefly commented about rain earlier, but had refrained.

It wasn't easy trying to be invisible.

She was more than relieved by Mrs. Higgins's welcome. At least with her she could be herself. Inside, she felt welcomed all the more. If Paul liked being a hermit, at least he was a comfortable one. The door opened to a large room with plush furniture: a long sofa, two overstuffed chairs in front of a wide fireplace. A table held an oil lamp, a neatly stocked bookshelf boasted countless hours of reading nearby, and beyond that room appeared to be a small dining room and an open door to what she guessed must be the kitchen. A stairway tucked to the side at the end of a corridor likely led to bedrooms upstairs.

Someone else had joined them outside, but no one had introduced him until he brought in Virginia's two trunks. One was filled with several items of new clothes, from sleepwear to day dresses. The advantage of having a half-dozen apprentice seamstresses nearby was the incredible speed they had been able to create everything she needed. The other trunk was her bonnet-making goods.

"This is Tim," Mrs. Higgins said, "who is everything from footman to handyman. My nephew."

Virginia reached out her hand, which seemed to surprise him since he wiped his palm on his trousers as if he hadn't prepared himself for human contact. "Nice to meet you, ma'am."

"Now I suppose you're hungry after that long trip from the city, so I'll just take these to the kitchen"—she held up the basket of apples—"then see about dinner. How does roasted chicken sound to you?"

"Lovely! I'm famished."

"Mrs. Higgins won't disappoint," said Paul, having just come in from outside. Virginia had last seen him checking on the horse after his long job of hauling them so far. "You wouldn't happen to be using those apples for a pie, would you?"

Mrs. Higgins laughed, already on her way from the room. "What else would I be doing with them?"

Tim stepped closer to the door to make his exit, but Virginia detained him. "I suppose I should have asked your aunt," she said, "but is there a pump where I can get some water to freshen with? I'm afraid the road was a little dusty." She looked past him, out the open door. "Although I suppose I could just stand outside in that rain!"

"I'll fill a pitcher for you, ma'am. And bring it right upstairs to—" He stopped abruptly and looked at Paul. "Aunt Leah said you got married awhile back, Mr. Paul. I expect this is the woman who came out here for the nuptials. Should I bring the water to your room for her, then?"

Virginia's heart leaped right to her throat, and she eyed Paul, who seemed every bit as uncomfortable with Tim's assumption. "No, Tim. To the guest room, although I suppose I should go up there and see if it's dusty. It hasn't been used since John and Sarah's last visit, and that's years ago now."

"My aunt don't allow dust, Mr. Paul, in a room used or not."

Judging by the gleaming surfaces around them, Virginia had no reason to doubt him. Likely Paul knew that as well and had been hoping for an opportunity to flee upstairs as an excuse to free himself of her company.

"Could you take her trunks up there, then? I'm sure you're right about the dust."

When Tim left with his first trip carrying one of her trunks, Virginia wandered to the bookshelf rather than stand in awkward silence, alone with Paul. She hoped he didn't think her nosy, but she'd regretted not bringing any reading material from the city. She'd simply forgotten, in the haste of the decision, to purchase anything to replace what she'd lost in the fire.

Since he didn't protest, she assumed she was free to investigate. Many of the thicker volumes were natural science books, which might prove interesting considering there was so much more room out here for nature than in the city. But it was the second shelf that interested her most. He owned nearly every Dickens book she'd ever heard of!

"Oh!" she said with delight. "Do you mind if I borrow some of your Charles Dickens books on occasion? I do love his way of telling a story."

"Help yourself. They were my mother's."

"Well, then," she said as she pulled off her gloves, "you might have Mrs. Higgins toss a book into my room now and then, along with that crust of bread."

His returning smile warmed her heart. Perhaps her concentrated silence had been worth it to build his trust, after all.

Paul couldn't have been more relieved that Virginia seemed to be more herself since they'd arrived. But if it wasn't dejection over leaving the city that had her so quiet all day, what could it have been?

He decided not to worry about it overmuch. As long as she looked as content as she did just now, he would be content as well.

And all it had taken was the promise of a Dickens novel.

Chapter 13

For the next two weeks, Virginia kept to herself, hiding away in a bedroom that was far more comfortable than the one that had burned to the ground. She'd always lived in the same room she'd grown up in, never having taken over the larger quarters her parents had occupied. Her room had offered a narrow bed with a lumpy straw mattress, supporting ropes that were forever loosening, a small stand with pitcher and basin, and a worktable she used when she wasn't working in the back of the shop. In the winter, her small upstairs apartment was warmer and so she often worked there by gaslight. Even on sunny days it was a little dark, but the warmth contained inside the thick walls compensated for its lack of light.

She must tell Mr. O'Shea, the builder John had hired, to make sure the new rooms upstairs had bigger windows and a way to keep the space warm even on the coldest days.

But this bedroom had a generously wide double window graced with lacy curtains, a feather bed larger even than her parents' bed had been, fluffy pillows, down-filled blankets, two bright lamps, an ample armoire for all her clothing, and a writing desk she could easily use to hold material for each bonnet she made. It was both homey and safe, under a solid roof that resisted even the prairie wind that came after that first day of her arrival.

The first bonnet she'd created in her room had been for Mrs. Higgins. It didn't take long to guess the woman favored blue, since both her work dresses and apron carried the shade. She'd been delighted, and so, she hoped, was Paul when he saw how happy the woman was to receive it. She'd given her the hat just before dinner one night, the only time of day she was bound to see Paul. The only time she left her room was when she spied him from her bedroom window, carrying some sort of equipment, including his veiled hat, off into the woods that weren't far from the end of their garden.

She'd asked Mrs. Higgins where he'd gone, and the housekeeper had been a wealth of information. He studied bees, she'd been told, and sent his observations to a university in New York, a service for which they paid him on a regular basis. Mrs. Higgins sang his praises whenever she had the opportunity, telling her the name Paul Turnbridge would live in history as prominently as Mr. Huber's and his bee observations.

In the two weeks since her arrival, Virginia had learned a great deal about Paul. About his mother, who had been sickly and so Mrs. Higgins had been both housekeeper and nanny to Paul and John. About his father, whose sole enjoyment had been to work the farm and hire others who would expand his efforts so they could all share the spoils and sell the surplus. He'd set the farm on a firm foundation, so that it practically ran itself.

And mostly about how Paul had stayed in the same routine he'd established long ago: wake up, study nature, send in reports to the school he'd attended, if only for a short time, back East. He hadn't liked the school because it was in a city, and far preferred nature as his tutor. The school agreed, eventually finding his chronicles so valuable they paid him as if he were on staff. The best part, at least for him, was that he never had to interact with humans.

"*Nature,*" Mrs. Higgins had told Virginia, "*is how Paul communicates with God.*"

That statement, coming from the person who undoubtedly knew Paul best, had been more than just a relief to Virginia. It had been the beginning of a new struggle for her, not to think of him day and night.

Mrs. Higgins offered little help to dispel Virginia's thoughts of Paul. She was convinced he didn't realize his life was going by. "*A man can't really go by himself all the way through, now can he?*"

And yet, Virginia had to admit, Paul seemed intent on doing just that. She was here in his house, even his legal wife if one wanted to be technical about it, and yet he never sought her out. Dinners were amiable enough, but quiet.

Perhaps tonight she would ask him about his bee work. Would that be too much of an imposition?

❧

Paul shut the front door, thanking Tim for retrieving the mail. It was more than an hour trip back and forth to the nearest town, one Paul rarely made but which either Tim, Mrs. Higgins, or both made twice a week, at least while the weather was fine. And this fall continued to be fair, even this far into October.

There were two letters from Milwaukee, besides his usual communication. And one of them was for Virginia. He smiled, tucking it into his pocket along with the one that had come for him. She would be coming downstairs for dinner soon, and they could read their letters from John and Sarah together. Perhaps that might be a way for her to stay in his company a little longer, rather than hurrying back up to her room as she normally did. She must have enough finished bonnets up there to fill a warehouse.

Not that he didn't know she spent some of those hours reading, too. She'd happened to take the Dickens novel he'd been reading himself a few days ago, and wondered how long it would be before she returned it to the shelf for another.

Dinner, Mrs. Higgins informed him, would be delicious, with stuffed eggplant from the garden, escalloped tomatoes, and even a pastry puff to end the meal the way it ought: with a sweet.

All thought to the meal passed when he saw Virginia coming down the stairs. She really was lovely. He reminded himself yet again her presence was only temporary, but if he was honest with himself he would admit he liked having her here. More than that. He wished, somehow, he could get her to stay. But that wasn't very likely, since she was at her most quiet when in his company.

He'd heard her laugh and chat with Mrs. Higgins, even with Tim. But with him? If she didn't hurry away, she rarely initiated any conversation and shortened whatever feeble attempt he made to extend her presence with him.

He knew he had a lot to learn about charm, but something in him, some long-lost memory of his father doing the same for his mother, made him hold out an arm in the

hope of escorting her properly to the dinner table. To his delight, she smiled and took his arm just the way he'd hoped.

"I have a surprise for you," he said before he seated her. Then he slipped the letter from his pocket. "From Sarah." He held up the other. "And I have one from John. I thought we might read them together."

"Oh! How wonderful!" She snatched up the letter but stilled suddenly, watching him take his seat on the opposite end of the table. "And how wonderful of you to want to share this with me. I'm glad you waited, Paul."

His heartbeat ticked a bit faster. She certainly didn't seem eager to flee his company at the moment, even if it was truly due to letters from those they both loved. He might as well take advantage of it. "It's my pleasure. Shall we?"

With a smile and a nod, they took up their knives and sliced into the envelopes.

Chapter 14

Virginia read Sarah's letter eagerly, fully intending to share every word with Paul if he gave her the chance. And why wouldn't he? Mrs. Higgins was only now delivering their meal, and they each continued to read in silence until she disappeared back into the kitchen.

But he did set aside his letter long enough to say a traditional prayer of thanks for the meal, something she noticed he'd begun doing only a few days after the first meal they'd taken together. It was possible, though she hadn't the courage to ask, that he'd noticed her silently pray before each meal then took the initiative himself to say one aloud for them both.

She recalled the Pastor's words last spring, his hope that she might be the influence needed to bring Paul to church. But Paul's prayers before meals, brief though they were, had quickly convinced her his faith was as real as Mrs. Higgins had claimed it to be.

"Is your letter as filled as mine with boasting about the baby?" he asked as he began eating.

She hadn't quite finished her letter, which was considerably longer than what looked like a single sheet of paper John had sent to Paul.

"Oh, yes! How much he's growing already, how he's changing every day. That Sarah is feeling much stronger now, and that the girls will soon be moving out now that they have jobs elsewhere. I hope the tailor shop will have enough workers once the building is finished!"

"Did Sarah mention the progress they're making? John made it a point to tell me they're concentrating all work on your building first and may even have the roof on before the end of November."

Was it her imagination, or had his voice grown more serious at the mention of such unexpectedly swift advancement of the rebuilding plans? She had a hard time swallowing Mrs. Higgins's excellent meal; something was in the way that had nothing to do with its taste.

"Yes, she did mention it. I'm glad, but I did have a few improvements in mind that I wanted to mention. Perhaps we could send a note to John about it?"

"What sort of improvements?"

"Nothing too major. A larger window in the rooms upstairs. Perhaps some improvement to the heating. And more room behind the shop instead of the front. Bonnets don't take up much display space, really. I occasionally hire seamstresses to help me, and I need more room when I'm not working alone."

"I suppose we ought to write immediately, before changes are too difficult to make.

We'll send off a letter tomorrow."

"Thank you."

A moment of silence followed as they ate, then Virginia asked, "Does John say anything else? I suppose he's meeting with his clients at home until his building is available."

"Yes, he is. And Sarah's letter?"

She read it aloud, intending to do so in its entirety, and for the first two pages that was fine, even though her meal was likely growing cold. But on the third page, the paragraph she hadn't already perused offered a polite question about how she was adjusting to life in the country. After that Virginia cut herself short and read silently.

> . . . And how are things between you and Paul? I know he's an odd sort, him and his bees, and that he can go for days without saying a word. But he has a good heart, Virginia. If there is a way you could imagine yourself staying, perhaps making a life in the country, it might make you very happy. And me miserable, of course, to have my sister-in-law-and-heart too far away, but it's likely better for you to have someone in your life twenty-four hours a day than just the limited time any sister, no matter how fond, can have in your life.

"And?" Paul prompted, repeating the last word she'd spoken aloud. "And. . . Is that all?"

Virginia folded the letter, replacing it inside the envelope. "And she asks if I'm doing well away from the city."

"What will your answer be?"

"Well," she began slowly, carefully, "I'll tell her I miss my clients. I do like making bonnets, but they're easier to design when I have a specific face in mind."

"So you're eager, then, to go back? Perhaps in time to escape a brutal country winter."

She said nothing, because in fact she did not know how to answer. She'd been more than comfortable here. Mrs. Higgins and even Tim were already dear to her, and she suspected if she didn't have to sneak around to avoid positioning herself in Paul's company she might know the happiness Sarah hinted she might find. It would be a huge change from city life, and she had yet to experience the harsh winter even Paul himself seemed not to like, but there was something peaceful about living out here. She'd found most of her happiness in her work, just as she suspected Paul did. And that she could do under any roof, as long as she imagined for whom she was making her next bonnet.

They finished their meal, and she might have excused herself as usual but was in no hurry to do so. She had something else on her mind.

"Paul, I wonder if you might tell me sometime—whenever you feel like it, if you want to, that is—about your bees? I know nothing about them except they sting and produce honey, and other than liking the one thing and being terrified of the other, I imagine there is quite a bit more to know."

He eyed her as if trying to decipher whether or not she was just being polite or was in earnest about wanting him to answer a question he could likely have enough material to share that would take days to fully explore.

At that moment, she realized she wanted exactly that, to listen to him talk freely about something he was interested in.

She knew her request violated every intention of achieving invisibility, but she

couldn't bear not to take the risk by asking anyway. She was tired of being so careful around him. If he rebuffed her, she vowed to suffer through the rejection and return to her room. But if he didn't, she knew his companionship could make this remote farmhouse a home—even through the worst of Wisconsin winters.

Paul eyed her, managing to keep his pulse steady only with extreme caution. "Do you really want to hear about it? I've been studying bees for quite some time. I could find any number of ways to bore you with worker bees, drones, and queens."

She smiled. "How do you know I would find it boring? It already sounds a bit medieval, with workers and queens."

Just then Mrs. Higgins emerged again from the kitchen, carrying two plates of pastry puffs. But instead of delivering them to the table, she walked right past and entered the parlor.

Paul watched her then turned to Virginia, who appeared as surprised as he was.

"Mrs. Higgins?" he inquired, seeing her place the two plates on the table next to the bookshelf. There, she turned the lamp down a bit, lending a cozier feel to the room connected to the dining room.

"If you must know, I can easily hear each and every word spoken in that dining room, and up until this evening it's been downright boring. Now you're going to sit in here and share this treat, maybe have a cup of tea or coffee, and talk until one of you—or both— falls asleep. You've got some time to catch up on together."

Paul was nearly afraid to look at Virginia for fear of her being aghast at the idea of spending an entire evening with him. But she was already pushing away from the table, and so once again he escorted her into a room on his arm.

Whether or not she enjoyed hearing about how queen bees achieve their reign— as brutally accomplished at times as the worst human reign—Paul didn't think he was fooling himself to believe she was actually interested. She asked questions, gasped and laughed at the right times, and if she wasn't fascinated by some of the same things he was, she made a very good show of it.

The pastry and the tea were long since gone, and not a sound had come from the kitchen ever since Mrs. Higgins told them she was retiring for the evening. Paul hadn't shared everything he knew of the bees, or some of the tales he had from working with a university only by mail, but there was another topic he needed to address before Virginia—rightly so—excused herself out of pure exhaustion.

"Virginia," he said quietly, looking at the base of the lamp on the small table between them instead of at her, "why is it that you've so diligently avoided my company ever since I brought you here?"

It was the question he'd most wanted answered for some time now, but he'd been too cowardly to ask.

She hesitated so long he forced himself to look at her, hoping to read whatever it was she couldn't put into words. Her face beguiled him. In her eyes he found only welcome, but something else, too. Confusion.

"I—I've tried to be unnoticeable. I know your solitude is important, because you're dedicated to work not only in the fields, with the hives, or in the forests, but here, too." She tapped her temple. "The thinking that must go with formulating your reports for

your research's sake takes time. Your work is important to you, and you were more than happy living here without anyone underfoot."

"Underfoot? That's what you think you are?"

"I've been trying not to be."

He leaned back in his chair, never so tempted to laugh loud and hard. But he settled for a grin. "So it isn't because you miss the city so much you're miserable here, that you cannot tolerate my company, that you find me every bit as dull as countless other people do, my own brother included?"

To his astonishment, the glimmer of a tear shone in one of her eyes, and he had the audacity to welcome it if it meant he could take her into his arms again and comfort her. He really ought to find a way to do so minus the tears.

"I wonder," he began then cleared his throat and started again. "Virginia, if I promise to respect whatever decision you make, whether or not you can live so far from the faces you need to inspire your bonnets, will you allow me to court you? Properly?"

"Oh, Paul," she whispered, "I'd like nothing better."

Then they both stood at the very same time, and regardless of whether or not that single tear fell, Paul drew her into his arms and pressed his lips to hers. His only fear now was that he wouldn't be able to let her go.

Chapter 15

Virginia rose early the next morning and used the writing desk in her room as it was meant to be used—for letter writing instead of working on a bonnet. Her letters took considerably longer than she expected, being careful not to reveal too much to Sarah about her own myriad, but no doubt silly and overly romantic, hopes and notions for a future with Paul—her husband. She then set about the real work of a second letter in Sarah's care but directed to the builder. It took time to think up countless ways to complicate the rebuilding of her home in the city.

There was simply no way she planned to allow a choice any time soon of going back to the city or staying here. Not until she was convinced she was truly not a burden to Paul. There was no doubt about it. Having an option lurking for her to live elsewhere must be delayed. Only how was she to word this so not even someone as intuitive as Sarah could see through her ploy?

Paul sealed the letter he'd spent half the night composing—a night he couldn't have wasted sleeping anyway, with thoughts of Virginia keeping him awake. He supposed he should feel a bit guilty, if manipulation was a sin. Both Virginia and his brother had seemed to think themselves guilty after they'd manipulated the wedding vows. But he felt not an ounce of compunction.

It was, after all, every financial institute's responsibility to inspect the building process their good money worked to produce. Was he an unreasonable investor to expect someone to oversee every step of the way? So what if it delayed things? If the building was merely delayed one month or two or six, what of it? He might need every bit of that time to convince her to stay. But if she did decide to return to the city, at least she would live and work in the safest, most well-crafted building in all of Milwaukee. Thorough oversight would see to that.

It was Sunday, and even though only Mrs. Higgins and Tim had escorted Virginia to church last week, Paul intended to accompany them, at least today. The post office was closed for the Sabbath, but he knew the postmaster and could hand him the letters personally after services, along with a coin or two to cover the postage.

He fairly skipped down the stairs that morning, happy to see neither Virginia nor Mrs. Higgins had yet stepped outside to meet Tim with the buggy.

"Ah, Mr. Paul! You'll be delivering the tithe in person today, then?"

Holding out both arms to escort the women, he smiled. "I will indeed, Mrs. Higgins."

Epilogue

There they are! Oh Paul, they made it after all!"

Despite the unpredictability of December Wisconsin weather, Sarah and John had promised to come for Christmas, and it was just a day away. Little did they know their visit would include a celebration besides the birth of the Savior.

By the time Virginia rushed outside to wave at them still far down the lane, another buggy soon appeared on the horizon.

"Looks like Reverend DeWeis will be as punctual for us as he expects his congregation to be on Sundays for him," Paul said, drawing Virginia close and adding a wave of his own with his free hand. He hadn't promised to accompany Virginia to church every Sunday, but she'd visited Paul's cathedral in nature often enough for him to have convinced her he met God there with every bit as much reverence as she met Him at a conventional church. Paul had agreed, though, to occasionally attend church in the village with her, if only for her to claim progress on the task Pastor DeWeis had assigned to her.

"Oh Paul, it's perfect, isn't it? Having them here for an exchange of real wedding vows this time?"

He kissed her, and the familiar sensation of warmth and tingles spread throughout her. It had been marvelously difficult, this courtship under one roof, knowing legally and perhaps even spiritually they were already married. But Paul himself had suggested if they both wanted this marriage to be real they ought to exchange their vows for a second time. More than that, though she'd seen him fairly choke on the words, he admitted it was probably the high road to take if they waited until then before she moved into his bedroom.

They exchanged fierce hugs with Sarah and John, who were both surprised to see the reverend join them a few moments later.

"Oh Virginia! I'm so, so very happy for you! For you both!" Then Sarah beamed, smiling down at the infant in her arms. "Just wait, little Elijah, until I tell you how I arranged the marriage between your Aunt Virginia and Uncle Paul!"

The ceremony was every bit as brief but far more happily done than the first one out in the garden earlier that year, but Reverend DeWeis cheerfully repeated the vows for them to exchange.

That night, after all were abed—Sarah and John and the baby in the room Virginia had vacated only that morning—Paul held his wife and kissed her temple.

"The reverend was right, Virginia. God did use you to make this marriage a true ministry of marriage. You with your bonnets, me with my bees. After Christmas, I think we

ought to go back to the city with Sarah and John. Your place will be finished sooner if we stop pestering poor Mr. O'Shea. What do you say to splitting the months between here and there? Summer here, in the peace and quiet. Winters there? Everyone hibernates in Wisconsin winters, so what will be the difference?"

She sat up, and in the dim moonlight that filtered through the window above the bed, she looked all the more lovely. "Do you mean it? You wouldn't be too unhappy so far from the openness of life out here?"

"I've never liked the winter months. They're long without my bees. And with you. . .home is here, or there."

"Oh Paul, how I do love you!"

"And I you," he whispered, pulling her back into his arms.

Maureen Lang writes stories inspired by a love of history and romance. An avid reader herself, she's figured out a way to write the stories she feels like reading. Maureen's inspirationals have earned various writing distinctions including the Inspirational Readers Choice Contest, a HOLT Medallion, and the Selah Award, as well as being a finalist for the Rita, Christy, and Carol Awards. In addition to investigating various eras in history (such as Victorian England, the First World War, and America's Gilded Age), Maureen loves taking research trips to get a feel for the settings of her novels. She lives in the Chicago area with her family and has been blessed to be the primary caregiver to her adult disabled son.

A Groom for Josette

Gabrielle Meyer

Dedication

To my hero, David. Eighteen years ago
you took my hand and captured my heart.
Thank you for never letting go.

Acknowledgement

I couldn't pursue this dream without the love and sacrifice of my husband, David, and our four children, Ellis, Maryn, Judah, and Asher. Thank you for being my biggest fans and my greatest joy. My heartfelt appreciation also goes to my agent, Mary Keeley, from Books and Such Literary Management who diligently champions my work; to the wonderful editors at Barbour Publishers who have fulfilled my lifelong dream; to my amazing writing friends, Alena Tauriainen, Lindsay Harrel, and Melissa Tagg, who make me laugh and encourage me every step of the way; to my faithful beta readers, Andrea Skoglund, Angie VanRisseghem, Sarah VanRisseghem, Lindsay LeClair, Sarah Olson, Beka Swisher, and Kimberly Perry who put their lives on hold to give me feedback; and to my extended family members and friends who inspire me every day. A very special thank you goes to my parents, George and Cathy VanRisseghem, and my husband's parents, Virgil and Carol Meyer, who have been a constant blessing and support. I'm grateful God planted this dream in my heart and is allowing me to see it come true

Chapter 1

St. Louis, June 1856

Josette LeBlanc gripped her reticule as she stared across the expansive mahogany desk. "Did you say three weeks?"

Mr. Trestle's long mustache blew away from his mouth as he sighed. "I'm afraid so, Miss LeBlanc. Your father's will stipulates that if you're not married before your half brother turns twenty-one, the entire estate and business will go to him."

"But—" Her voice caught in her throat. "I'll be destitute."

"Surely your brother will provide for your well-being."

Stephen, provide for her? He could hardly provide for himself. Besides, Stephen had been poisoned against Josie years ago by her stepmother, Celeste. Josie would be turned out of the house at the stroke of midnight on Stephen's birthday—she was sure of it. For eight years, Papa's will had guaranteed an allowance and a place for Josie to live.

Until now.

She lifted her gloved hands to her temples and applied pressure. Sunshine poured into the wood-paneled office, illuminating the tall bookshelves and Josie's bleak future. "I don't understand. Why would Papa give Stephen control of his business? Stephen's. . .incompetent. He spends most of his time gambling on the steamboats."

Mr. Trestle's face filled with regret. "Your father had always hoped Stephen would outgrow his wild ways, but. . ." He shook his head. "He is your father's only son. If you were married, your husband could manage your share of the business. Since you're not, it's only right that your brother should manage it for you."

Manage the business for her? Josie straightened her spine. She didn't need Stephen's help. She had spent hours with Papa at the office learning about LeBlanc Shipping. Papa had said she was smarter than any businessman he'd ever met.

Josie wanted to pace, but she remained in her seat and took a deep breath. "Why wasn't I told of this stipulation before?"

Mr. Trestle shrugged. "Your father died when you were debuting into society. I'm sure he thought you'd be married by now. He didn't want you to marry in haste, just to secure your fortune."

Yet now she had no choice. Josie lowered her eyes and tried to hide the pain his words induced. Papa had always said she must marry for love, just as he had married her mama—a Chippewa maiden he had met as a fur trader in Minnesota Territory. The worst mistake of Papa's life was marrying Celeste just after arriving in St. Louis, a grieving widower with a little girl in need of a mama.

Mr. Trestle fiddled with a piece of paper and didn't meet her eyes. "Is there a special

young man who could be persuaded to marry you?"

Josie's cheeks filled with heat. At the age of twenty-six, society considered her an old maid, forcing her to give up on the idea of marriage. After her debut, there had been many prospects, but every time a gentleman became serious, Celeste made it known that Josie was the daughter of a Chippewa Indian.

Eventually, the gentlemen stopped calling.

She swallowed. "There is no one."

He looked as if he didn't believe her. "No one?"

Her chest squeezed with embarrassment, but she lifted her chin. "There is not a man in St. Louis who would have me."

Mr. Trestle cleared his throat. "I apologize, Miss LeBlanc."

She didn't want to bother with what she couldn't do—she needed to know what she could. "Can I fight this?"

"I'm afraid not—the only thing you can do is find a husband before your brother's birthday—in less than three weeks."

Hadn't she been searching since her debut, eight years ago? "Do you have any other ideas?"

Mr. Trestle opened his mouth and then closed it, as if he wasn't sure he should speak.

Josie leaned forward. "What is it?"

Mr. Trestle had been Papa's most trusted advisor over the years. If he had a suggestion, she would listen.

"I came across something that might work." He opened his desk drawer and removed a newspaper clipping, but then stopped, his blue eyes very serious. "If I thought there was any other way. . ."

Josie took the paper and scanned it with desperation—but her desperation soon turned to despair. This was his only idea? "It's an advertisement for brides?"

"It says there are a hundred eligible men for every single lady," Mr. Trestle said quickly. "The town is called Little Falls, and it's on the Mississippi six hundred miles north of here, in the center of Minnesota Territory. It's primarily a logging community, but with the water power at the dam, they expect industries to crowd their riverbanks. It's overflowing with prospects."

Josie held up the clipping, as if it were a poisonous snake. "What do you expect me to do with this information?"

"You could take a steamboat up the Mississippi to St. Paul and then go by stagecoach to Little Falls to make it known you are looking for a husband." Mr. Trestle pulled out a steamboat schedule, as if he had anticipated this moment. "If you leave tomorrow, that would give you a week to travel to Little Falls, a few days to find a husband, and then a week to travel back. As long as you present a marriage license to the judge before your brother's birthday, your share of the fortune will be secure."

Josie stared at him as if he had lost all common sense. "You're suggesting I travel to an uncivilized town, interview a handful of strangers, and then join my life to one of them—all within three weeks' time?"

Mr. Trestle nodded gravely. "That's exactly what I'm suggesting."

Josie looked at the advertisement again.

Wanted: good-looking women for the town of Little Falls, Minnesota Territory. We guarantee a hundred eligible bachelors for every single lady. If interested, please inquire with Philip Sommers at the company store.

"Don't they want their brides to stay in Little Falls? Who would agree to marry me and return to St. Louis?"

Mr. Trestle didn't blink. "A man who is interested in a shipping empire."

A chill ran up her spine. Why would she want to marry a person who was only interested in her fortune? It was a terrible reason to marry.

But what other choice did she have?

"You'll need to bring a companion," Mr. Trestle said, as if the plan was already in place. "Your lady's maid, or a relative."

"I have no relative."

"Then your lady's maid will do. I suggest you book passage immediately, as the steamboats are always full."

Josie imagined the look of triumph on her stepmother's face the day she could turn Josie out. Josie would have nowhere to go. And worse, she would have to watch Stephen destroy Papa's legacy.

Mr. Trestle watched her closely. "This is the only way, Josie."

The newspaper clipping dangled in her hand. She could hand it back to Mr. Trestle and face a future of poverty and hardship—or she could put it in her reticule, book passage to Minnesota Territory, and take her chances.

Either way, there was little hope.

Josie did the only thing a rational old maid would do. She folded the clipping, slipped it in her bag, and snapped it shut with determination.

Maybe now, for the first time in her life, she would gain control over her own destiny.

Chapter 2

Josie took a deep breath and pushed open the heavy front door of the Little Falls Company Store. A bell jingled overhead as she stepped into the bustling interior. At least two dozen men stood about the dusty store, some visiting around a game of checkers, while others shopped the disorganized shelves.

Josie's maid, Ruth, followed close behind, her confident blue eyes assessing their surroundings. Ruth had proven to be a valuable traveling companion. Though she was tiny, she was also spirited and unafraid. Her blond hair and fair coloring made her look sweet, but under her soft demeanor, she was ready for anything.

The men stopped their activities and stared at the new arrivals. The only noise in the room came from the pesky flies circling the salt pork barrels.

A well-dressed man stood behind the long counter, the pencil in his hand hovering over a thick ledger. His handsome face boasted a mustache and surprised blue eyes.

Here, at least, was a man who looked educated and clean.

"May I help you, ladies?"

Josie and Ruth maneuvered around a pile of rusted shovels and the two barrels of salt pork to reach the counter.

"I'm looking for Mr. Philip Sommers," Josie said.

The man grinned as he set down the pencil. "I'm Philip Sommers."

One of the men in the back of the store shouted, "No, I'm Philip Sommers!"

Then another shouted, "I'm Sommers!"

Soon, every man was claiming to be Mr. Sommers, and their laughter rang throughout the store. Josie's cheeks filled with heat.

Little Falls was as primitive as she had expected. Only two years old, the town had been built along the Mississippi River and consisted of fresh-cut lumber buildings, rutted streets, and grandiose dreams.

From the moment the stagecoach had stopped in front of the Northern Hotel, Josie had been in awe of the chaos of men. She had been convinced her prospects were good. . .until she inspected the rough men present.

"Please, excuse them, miss." Mr. Sommers lifted his hand to quiet the men. "If you can't act decent, boys, there's the door."

Thankfully, the room quieted, but everyone still stared.

"What can I do for you?" Mr. Sommers asked.

Josie swallowed hard, wishing she didn't have an audience for this important meeting—and hoping she was talking to the real Mr. Sommers.

Though Ruth stood by quietly, her presence bolstered Josie. With trembling fingers,

Josie opened her reticule and pulled out the slip of newspaper Mr. Trestle had given her. She handed it to Mr. Sommers. "I've come about this advertisement."

"What is it, Sommers?" called one of the men.

Mr. Sommers blinked several times as he stared at Josie. "Y–you've come to answer the ad?"

"Yes—" She cleared the nervous tickle from her throat. "I will be holding private interviews at the Northern Hotel this evening. Anyone interested may come at seven o'clock."

Mr. Sommers shook his head. "I never thought someone would actually answer our ad."

"Is she a prospective bride?" shouted a man with red hair.

Mr. Sommers grinned and looked her up and down. "She is!"

Pandemonium broke loose as the men rushed to the counter, climbing over tools and food supplies to get close to her. Josie squealed and bumped against the counter, while Ruth brandished Josie's parasol.

The men crowded around them, overwhelming Josie with the stench of dirty bodies and stale alcohol. Their questions and compliments rang in her ears as they reached out with grubby hands to touch her.

She put her gloved hand over her nose and tried to back away, but there was nowhere to go.

Josie barely heard the jingle over the front door. She glanced up as a new gentleman walked into the building. He towered over the other men, his brown eyes quickly assessing the situation. His clothes looked worn and dirty, and his rugged face needed a shave—but there was something different about him. Instead of hunger, his eyes were filled with curiosity—and then alarm.

He pushed his way through the crowd, his sheer size silencing the men.

"What's going on here?" His deep voice held a hint of a French accent and commanded attention.

The men backed away, and some had the decency to look contrite.

He stared at the crowd for a moment and then turned his intense gaze on Josie and Ruth, his demeanor softening. "Are you ladies all right?"

Josie lifted her unsteady hands to readjust her hat. "Yes, thank you. We were just about to leave."

He pushed two men out of their path and nodded for them to proceed.

Josie and Ruth walked past the men and around the shovels and salt pork.

The redheaded man jumped ahead of them and opened the door.

Josie nodded a thank-you as she and Ruth stepped out into the fresh air and sunshine.

"It's not too late to back out of this, Miss Josie." Ruth opened Josie's parasol and handed it to her, their boots clipping a solid beat on the wood boardwalk. "We can stay in our hotel room until the stagecoach leaves town."

A group of men across the street stopped pounding their hammers to watch Josie and Ruth pass.

"I can't go back until I have a husband." Josie secured her green parasol against the summer sun—and the men's stares. "We've come too far to turn around now."

"But those men—" Ruth shuddered and wrinkled her nose. "None of them would do."

"I'm not obligated to marry just anyone—I'll interview whoever comes to the hotel, and I'll pick the best candidate."

"What if there aren't any good ones to choose from?"

Josie stopped and put her hand on Ruth's arm. "There's no time to go anywhere else. I have to take my chances here."

"Mademoiselles."

Josie and Ruth turned at the sound of a man's voice. The tall gentleman from the company store strode toward them, his long legs covering the distance quickly.

"I wanted to make sure you're all right," he said.

Josie nodded. "Yes, we are, thank you."

He looked at their surroundings, at the men ogling them from the construction site, and his concerned gaze rested on Josie's face. "May I escort you home?"

Josie found herself smiling for the first time in over a week. His offer was very gallant, but she and Ruth had done fine by themselves—besides, they were a long way from home. "That won't be necessary."

"Please, I would feel much better if I could."

Josie glanced at Ruth, who looked quite taken with their hero. "If you insist. . . We're staying at the Northern Hotel."

"That's where I'm staying." With a dashing smile, he offered one arm to Josie and the other to Ruth.

They walked to the end of the street and turned left onto Broadway. Josie felt conspicuous with her expensive parasol and matching green gown—but even if she wore a plain brown dress, she would stand out like a cultivated rose in a weed lot.

The white clapboard hotel, standing proudly on the corner of Main Street and Broadway, was the one building in town with a bit of class. It came within sight, and Josie's shoulders relaxed. Inside the walls of her hotel room she would be safe from the stares and lewd comments—at least until seven o'clock.

The tall gentleman escorted them inside the hotel and then bowed. "Au revoir."

It wasn't until he was up the stairs and out of sight that Josie realized she hadn't asked his name.

Chapter 3

"Do you think this dress is too ostentatious for tonight?" Josie stood in front of the small mirror in her hotel room. She turned and looked at her anxious reflection from a different angle. "I want to make a good impression, but I don't want to draw too much attention."

Ruth's laugh was muffled as she knelt beside Josie's trunk, her blond head buried beneath the lid. "I think the time to worry about drawing too much attention has come and gone—aha! Here they are." Ruth stood with a triumphant smile on her face and a pair of white gloves in her hand. In her quest to find the gloves, she had strewn dresses, petticoats, and hats about the room, until Josie could barely discern where the bed, rocking chair, and dresser stood.

Josie pinched her cheeks for color and then inspected her dark hair in the mirror. Ruth had split it down the middle and combed it over her ears in puffs then gathered it in the back in ringlets. Every glossy strand was in place. She touched the pearl comb just above the ringlets, her palms sweaty. "What will I do if no one shows up?"

"I don't think that will be your problem." Ruth helped Josie put on her gloves and clucked her tongue. "I wish you had eaten something earlier. You'll need your strength."

How could she eat when her entire future depended on this one pursuit? She had less than two days to find a husband. The stagecoach only left Little Falls once a week—if she wasn't on it in two days, she would miss the steamboat back to St. Louis and wouldn't arrive in time to see the judge.

She needed to find a husband to gain control of her life. It was as simple, and as complicated, as that.

Ruth stood back and admired Josie. "I think you're ready."

Was she? Josie gripped the doorknob and took a steadying breath. Every inch of her body shook, and her corset strings pinched. What if she fainted?

Ruth gently pushed aside Josie's hand and opened the door. "You'll do fine. God isn't surprised by this turn of events. If He brought you here, He'll be faithful to complete the work He began. Just trust Him to bring the right man to the ballroom tonight. You might be surprised with His plans."

Josie offered Ruth a tremulous smile. She wasn't contemplating a happy ending—but could that be part of God's plan? It didn't seem likely, though a bit of hope tried to take root in her heart.

They stepped out into the long, narrow hallway, their footsteps echoing across the pine board floors. Fading daylight filtered into the corridor from a single window at the end of the hall.

THE *Convenient* BRIDE COLLECTION

Josie reached out and squeezed Ruth's thin hand. "Remind me to give you a big Christmas bonus."

Ruth squeezed back, her voice teasing: "I will."

They descended the open staircase and entered the hotel lobby. White wainscoting circled the large lobby and ran down the long hallway to the back of the hotel. A matching counter filled one corner of the room, while potted ferns sat in the opposite corner near a floral sofa.

The hotel proprietor, Mr. Churchill, stood behind the counter. His face lit with a grin when he saw them. "Good evening, ladies. I hope you had a pleasant afternoon."

It had not been pleasant waiting for this inevitable event, but Josie smiled. "Thank you. Are the parlors ready?" She had asked Mr. Churchill to reserve two parlors. One she would use to interview the prospective grooms, while the other would be for the men waiting to meet with her.

Mr. Churchill lifted his chin, as if to nod, and then he stopped. "Actually, there has been a change of plans."

A change of plans? "But I must have two rooms this evening."

"Oh, you will." Mr. Churchill squeezed out from behind the counter, his large belly making the task difficult. "The men are waiting in the ballroom."

"The ballroom?"

The front door opened and a group of six men entered, their boisterous conversation filling the lobby. "We're here for the little lady," one of them said to Mr. Churchill. He stopped when he saw Josie and Ruth, color filling his cheeks.

"Make your way to the ballroom, gents." Mr. Churchill rocked on his heels and grinned. "You'll find refreshments on the table."

Josie watched with wide eyes as the men sauntered into the ballroom, tossing glances her way. In the few seconds the door stood open, she glimpsed inside—and swallowed the horror.

Josie's hand went to her throat. "How many men are in there?"

"Oh, I don't know." Mr. Churchill rubbed his balding head. "I'd say there are at least a hundred, and they're still coming in."

The front door opened again, and another group of men entered. Mr. Churchill pointed them in the direction of the ballroom, and they slipped inside.

"A—a hundred?" Josie became light-headed. "How will I interview a hundred men?"

Mr. Churchill lifted his meaty palms and shrugged. "I'll keep the refreshments you requested coming, so don't you worry about that."

How much would it cost to feed over a hundred hungry men all evening?

Josie opened her mouth to protest, but the clock behind the counter chimed seven times.

"I'm right here beside you, Miss Josie." Ruth patted her arm. "You'll be fine."

Josie walked toward the ballroom. Sweat broke out on her brow and her dress felt heavy against her weak knees.

She opened the doors slowly.

Rowdy noise filled the ballroom and greeted Josie as she faced the men, all of them talking and laughing at once. Tall mirrors lined one wall of the room, reflecting the yellow walls and large chandeliers overhead. Light from the bright wall sconces made the room feel overly hot and stuffy. Josie licked her dry lips, suddenly wishing for a glass of water.

258

Her eyes quickly scanned the room, assessing her prospects. There were short men and tall men. Heavy men and thin men. Some were dressed in gentlemen's clothing, with ties and top hats, while others were dressed in grubby clothes that looked as if they hadn't seen soap in months. There were young men, with barely a whisker on their chin, and old men with beards down to their chest.

And all at once, every one of them turned their attention to Josie and Ruth.

Silence invaded the room—but then someone sent up a caterwaul, and the entire room burst out in cheers and foot stomping.

"Make way for the pretty ladies!" shouted the man with bright red hair who had been at the company store earlier. He pushed the crowd back, and the men made a clear path for Josie and Ruth.

This was what Moses must have felt watching the Red Sea part before him.

Josie forced her legs to move, and the entire room quieted again as she and Ruth walked to the front. They climbed the stairs until they stood on the stage, and then faced the room.

Over one hundred men stared back.

Now what? Where would she start? How did one go about such things?

"What're your names?" one of the men asked from the back of the room.

A chorus of voices repeated the question.

Josie's voice came out weak. "My name is Miss Josette LeBlanc, and this is my maid, Miss Ruth Hubbard."

"Is the maid up for grabs, too?" shouted a man close to the stage.

Ruth crossed her arms and shook her head, silencing the man.

"I'm the only one seeking a husband," Josie said.

"Well then, let's get on with it!" another man yelled.

Josie turned to Ruth. "Where do I begin?"

Ruth looked uncertain. "I don't know."

"What's all the fuss about?" A woman suddenly appeared at the ballroom doors, her deep voice sounding more like a man's. She quickly scanned the room and locked eyes with Josie. Without another word, she pushed through the crowd and climbed onto the stage. "Are you the one responsible for this circus?"

Josie took a step back.

The woman stood with her hands on her ample hips and her dark hair puffed out at the sides. She stared at Josie. "Well?"

"I–I've come to answer the ad for brides."

The lady threw her arms up. "Heaven help us. Until now, I thought I'd seen it all." She shook her head. "When I heard someone had answered that ridiculous ad, I rushed right over here to see for myself."

Would this lady try to stop Josie? Panic crept in at the thought. There wasn't enough time to go somewhere else.

"It looks like you're going to need some help, Miss. . ."

"LeBlanc," Josie said. "And who are you?"

"I'm Mrs. Cordelia Foreman. My husband and I were the second settlers in this town, and we care a great deal about what happens here." Mrs. Foreman turned to the men and they all stared at her, as if everyone knew exactly who she was. . .and maybe feared her, just a bit.

"First things first, gentlemen. Anyone over fifty years old—and under twenty—there's the door. Use it. The rest of you separate yourselves into groups by age. We'll do this thing up right, or we won't do it at all."

Josie could have collapsed in relief, but the sensation soon disappeared as she assessed the ragtag group of men. Was her husband among them?

Chapter 4

The savory scent of roasted chicken and mashed potatoes floated up the stairs to meet Alexandre Dugas as he descended the hotel staircase. A warm bath, haircut, and shave had done his body wonders, and soon his belly would be sated with a good meal. Tomorrow, he would go to Belle Prairie, his final destination on a yearlong pilgrimage up the Mississippi, and then his soul would be satisfied, too.

The *agréable* thought brought a smile to his face.

"Ah, Reverend Dugas." Mr. Churchill spoke from behind the lobby counter. "I almost didn't recognize you."

Alexandre rubbed his smooth jaw. He almost didn't recognize himself. It had been weeks since he'd had a good bath and clean clothes. He wanted to present himself to the directors at the Belle Prairie Mission as the clean-cut minister they were expecting.

"I've saved a place for you in the dining room." Mr. Churchill pointed down the hallway. "My wife boasts the best meals in the territory." He rubbed his protruding belly, as if to give his statement validity. "We'll soon be adding on to the hotel, to make the dining room bigger. People are pouring into town, and we can't keep up with the demand."

Alexandre had only been in town for a few hours, but he could feel the excitement in the air. The founding fathers believed Little Falls would rival any city on the Mississippi.

"The lots here in town are selling for over a thousand dollars apiece." Mr. Churchill rubbed his palms together. "If a man was smart, he'd buy one of the lots, build a store on it, and then sell it for a hefty profit to the settlers coming into town."

Alexandre began to calculate the costs of building a store. He had some money reserved in his saving's account. He could buy a lot, construct a building, and then sell it. With the profit, he could turn around and buy two more lots and build two more buildings. Within a year—

He brought his thoughts to a halt.

He'd left New Orleans to get away from business. After the mess Isobel had created, he had sought to give everything up and live a simple life. He'd had enough with investing—and love—to last a lifetime.

"What brings you to town?" Mr. Churchill asked.

"I will be taking over the church at the Belle Prairie Mission." He couldn't stop the grin from spreading across his face. After a year of traveling, he was only four miles from his destination. "The church has grown and they are in need of a preacher."

A group of men entered the front doors, their coarse laughter making them hard to miss. "Where can we find the gal?" one of them asked.

Mr. Churchill pointed his thumb behind him. "In the ballroom."

The men moved toward the ballroom. "Now don't forget," said the tallest man in the bunch, his eyes glossed over and the stench of whiskey in his wake, "if she chooses one of us, we've agreed to share her."

One of the other men slapped him on the back. "Not the first night!" They all laughed as they disappeared into the ballroom.

The crude comment made Alexandre's skin crawl.

Mr. Churchill's anxious eyes found Alexandre. "I'm sorry, Reverend—it's not what it sounds like. I run a clean establishment here. If the men want something else, they take their business to the Dew's place, near the river—" He stopped, his eyes widening. "Pardon me."

Alexandre waved the apology away. He'd heard and seen things along the river that could make even the coarsest criminal blush.

"I'll show you to the dining room." Mr. Churchill started to move away from the counter.

Alexandre lifted his hand and smiled. "Don't bother. I'll follow my nose."

The hotel proprietor gave an uncomfortable laugh and then wiped at the sweat on his brow.

Alexandre turned down the hallway and was immediately met by three or four dozen men leaving the ballroom.

"Out of my way," a man with white whiskers grumbled as he walked past. "Turned down, just because I'm seventy-one years old. I still got some vigor in me."

Alexandre moved out of the way, his curiosity mounting. What was happening in the ballroom?

He peeked in the room and found at least a hundred men standing in three separate groups. A robust woman was in the midst of them, calling out orders.

She turned, and her eyes narrowed on Alexandre. "How old are you?"

Alexandre pointed at his chest. "Me?"

The lady rolled her eyes. "Yes, you."

Why did she care? "I'm thirty."

"Then join that group." She pointed to a group of men near the mirrors.

"I don't think you understand—"

"I don't have time to understand anyone in this room. Join the group." She turned to the next man standing alone.

Alexandre's curiosity was even stronger now. He joined the group the lady had indicated, if only to discover what was happening.

That's when he looked at the stage and saw the other two ladies present. They were the young women he'd escorted to the hotel after the incident at the company store. He crossed his arms as he tried to make sense of what was happening. Who were these women, and why were they creating such a stir?

The little one with blond hair stood at the back of the stage, her eyes roaming the room like a sentinel on duty. The other one stood in the center of the stage, in a stunning rose-colored gown, which shimmered under the light of the chandeliers. Her black hair looked glossy and soft, and her beautiful brown eyes were wide in her pretty face. She stood with her hands clasped in front of her slender waist as she watched the older woman divide the men into groups.

"The rest of you might as well leave," boasted a man with bright red hair and freckles

in Alexandre's group. He had been at the company store earlier. "The lady is all mine. Once she finds out I'm gonna be rich someday, she'll fall at my feet."

A man with a dimpled chin cuffed him on the head. "Don't be an idiot, Clayton. She's mine. I already reserved a room here in the hotel for our wedding night—and what a night it's gonna be!" He let out a low whistle.

Alexandre had heard enough. He planted his feet and narrowed his eyes. "I don't think the lady would appreciate the way she's being talked about."

At least thirty men turned to Alexandre. The one with the dimpled chin crossed his arms, his voice low. "Then she shouldn't have answered the ad."

"Ad?"

Clayton shook his head. "Don't you know nothin', mister? Some men in town were lonely last winter and put out an advertisement for brides." Clayton's red hair stood straight on his head. "Miss LeBlanc is the first one to answer the ad. She's lookin' for a husband—but to tell ya the truth, I kinda like the maid a mite better."

Alexandre looked toward the stage. "Is Miss LeBlanc the one in pink?"

"That's the one."

She was here to find a husband? What kind of a woman would put herself on display like this?

But before the question fully formed, he knew the answer. A desperate one.

Chapter 5

Josie swallowed the lump of apprehension growing in her throat. There were so many men, and all of them were staring at her. Some looked lonely, while others looked ravenous.

Surely, there had to be a handful of decent men in the room.

Mrs. Foreman came to the stage and looked up at Josie. "They're separated by age. What's the next criteria?"

"Criteria?" Josie asked.

"Yes." Mrs. Foreman crossed her arms and tapped her foot. "What's the most important thing you would value in your spouse?"

Josie looked over the sea of men and her eyes locked on a towering man in the group of thirty-year-olds. His kind eyes looked familiar.

She pulled her attention back to Mrs. Foreman. "The most important thing is faith. I couldn't marry a man who didn't share my belief in Jesus."

Mrs. Foreman's face softened, and she nodded her head. "Good girl." Then she turned to the group. "You hear that, boys? If you're not a Bible-believing man, there's the door."

A handful of men mumbled under their breath, and then at least two dozen exited the ballroom.

"Now, Miss LeBlanc," said Mrs. Foreman. "What's next? There are about seventy men left."

Josie thought through her girlish hopes and dreams. She'd imagined her future husband a hundred times, but she had thought she'd get to know him on her parlor couch, or at a church picnic, or some other conventional way. How could she tell a group of men that she valued honesty and courage? Or that she'd always hoped to find a Frenchman, just like her papa?

Her eyes went back to the gentleman in the thirty-year-old group, and suddenly she remembered who he was. He was the Frenchman who had escorted her and Ruth earlier—only now he had a clean-shaven face and fresh clothing. He stood tall above the others, with broad shoulders and powerful arms. She had thought of him all afternoon, wishing she knew his name.

He stared back at her, his expression so different than the rest.

"Miss LeBlanc?" Mrs. Foreman lifted a brow.

"I—" She opened her mouth to speak, but the Frenchman broke away from his group and strode to the stage, confidence and compassion mingling in his dark eyes.

"Mademoiselle." He bowed. "My name is Alexandre Dugas."

Alexandre.

Josie felt awkward standing on the stage above him. She walked to the steps and descended to the dance floor, the whole room watching her every move.

She extended her hand to Mr. Dugas. "It's so nice to see you again. I'm Josette Le-Blanc."

His brown eyes lit with recognition. "Ah, *française?*"

"*Oui.*"

"Are you from France?"

Josie shook her head. "No. St. Louis. My father came from France. And you?"

"New Orleans, but my parents also immigrated from France."

Josie felt warmth curl through her belly, and it gave her courage to continue. "Mr. Dugas, I have a sitting room available to interview. . ." She paused, feeling heat rise to her cheeks. "Prospective husbands. Would you like to join me? My maid will act as chaperone."

His earlier familiarity disappeared, and a look of reservation filled his handsome face.

Had she said something wrong?

"Miss LeBlanc, I'm afraid there's been a misunderstanding—"

"What are you waiting for?" Mrs. Foreman asked. "There's a whole ballroom of men waiting to talk to this lady."

Ruth left the stage and joined Josie. "This way." She pointed toward a side door.

"But—" Mr. Dugas looked a bit panicked. "I didn't come here to get married."

Mrs. Foreman acted as if she didn't hear him. "You have five minutes."

"Five minutes?" Josie's eyes grew wide. "How will I know in five minutes?"

"Do you see how many men are waiting?" Mrs. Foreman swept her hand in an arc. "If you take any longer, you'll be here until next week."

"I don't have that much time. I need to get married as soon as possible."

Mrs. Foreman indicated the door. "Then get a move on."

Josie wished she had thought to bring a paper and pen with her to keep notes during her interviews. If she was going to interview seventy men, surely she'd need to keep notes.

Mr. Dugas followed her and Ruth out of the ballroom and into the cozy sitting room. A floral brocade sofa sat against the outside wall, where a window looked out onto the darkening street. Two chairs faced the sofa, and a colorful rug sat on the pine plank floor under their feet.

"Won't you have a seat, Mr. Dugas?" Josie took a seat next to Ruth on the sofa, wishing she had a glass of water, or punch—anything to ease the dryness in her throat.

Mr. Dugas stood by the door. "There really has been a mistake. I didn't come to find a wife."

"Then why are you here?" she asked.

"I just stopped here for the night to make myself presentable. My real destination is the mission church at Belle Prairie, about four miles north of here."

The mission? Josie sat up straighter. "An Indian Mission?"

He nodded, his face lighting up with excitement. "About a year ago, a missionary came to New Orleans from the Indian Mission at Belle Prairie, looking for a preacher to take over the church this summer. It took me all year to work my way up the Mississippi, finding odd jobs and learning to live as simply as I could. It was a pilgrimage

I needed to make after leaving my old life in New Orleans. Tomorrow I'll arrive at my final destination."

"So you're going to work with the Chippewa?" Josie's arms tingled as she waited for his answer.

"Yes, though I've heard the congregation now includes many settlers as well. I'm very eager to work with all of them."

Josie glanced at Ruth. Here stood a man she would be honored to marry. He was handsome, but more than that, he loved the Lord, was French, and wasn't prejudiced against the Chippewa.

How could she convince him to marry her?

Chapter 6

Alexandre loved the smile that bloomed on Miss LeBlanc's face when he spoke of his mission work. He often received mixed responses when he told people he was going to work with the Indians.

"Are you familiar with the Chippewa, Miss LeBlanc?" he asked.

She nodded, and her glossy black hair caught the light from the wall lantern and shone. Her dark brown eyes were even more beautiful close up, but especially now, when they glowed with warmth, and they drew him in.

"I'm very familiar with the Chippewa." She paused for a moment and then continued a bit hesitantly. "My father was a fur trader in northern Minnesota Territory when I was young. He spoke of the Chippewa at length."

She paused again, so he took a chair, hoping she would share more. He was eager to learn all he could about the people he would serve. "*Continuer.*"

"Papa would have stayed in Minnesota Territory, if my mother hadn't died."

"Was your mother French?"

She shook her head, and sadness permeated her dark eyes. "My mother was Chippewa. She was killed during a raid by the Dakota. I was only four years old."

Alexandre couldn't imagine losing his mother. She had been so much a part of his childhood and had shaped him in ways no other person had. "I'm so sorry. Have you been back to see your mother's people?"

"No, but I've helped to raise funds for the missions here in Minnesota Territory. It's the very least I could do."

"But doesn't Jesus say 'inasmuch as ye have done it unto one of the least of these my brethren, ye have done it unto me'? Your work, no matter how small, is valuable to God."

Her cheeks turned a delightful shade of pink.

"Your time is almost up," the maid said quietly.

Miss LeBlanc's eyes lifted to Alexandre's. "Do you not want a wife, Mr. Dugas?"

The simple question brought a deep and insatiable longing to his soul. Twelve years ago, he had left his parents' farm and gone to seminary school. When he arrived in New Orleans to preach, he had been sidetracked by Isobel and lured into her father's business instead. Last year, when Isobel had broken their engagement, he had finally answered God's call and made his way up the river. He couldn't allow another beautiful woman to cause him to stray once again—but maybe Miss LeBlanc was different. She was a believer and had a heart for the Chippewa—so unlike Isobel. He was going to Belle Prairie as an independent minister and wasn't required to be married—but it was desirable for him to have a wife.

Could he and Miss LeBlanc help each other?

The unexpected thought sent energy pulsing through his veins. "May I ask why you are here looking for a husband, Miss LeBlanc?"

Her eyes went to the clock on a parlor table, and she spoke rapidly. "I just discovered that when my half brother turns twenty-one in two weeks, he will become the sole inheritor of my father's estate and business." She swallowed. "But, if I am married, my father's will stipulates that my husband and I will retain half of everything." She paused, and her voice became grave. "If I'm not married, I'm at my brother's mercy, and I will be turned out on the street."

Alexandre stared at her. Was he crazy to even consider helping her? Surely there were other men who could better serve her purposes.

But then he recalled the men in the ballroom, and their coarse joking at her expense. What kind of a man could she possibly find who would treat her with the respect she deserved?

A knock sounded at the door, and the gruff woman stuck her head inside. "Your time is up. The next man is waiting to come in."

"Couldn't we have a few more minutes, Mrs. Foreman?" Miss LeBlanc pleaded.

The man with the dimpled chin strode into the room, his shameless stare settling on Miss LeBlanc. "I'm Amos Doolittle."

Alexandre needed more time and information. "How will you secure your inheritance?" he asked Miss LeBlanc.

Her eyes flew from Amos to Alexandre. "I need to travel back to St. Louis and present my marriage certificate to the judge."

"It's as simple as that?" he asked.

Mr. Doolittle nudged him on the shoulder. "Time's up, mister."

Alexandre stood, and then Miss LeBlanc stood, her eyes locked on his. "As simple as that."

Mr. Doolittle looked at Alexandre with steely eyes. "I said, time's up."

Alexandre needed more time to think. If they took the steamboat to St. Louis, presented the marriage certificate, and then traveled back by steamboat, they could be at Belle Prairie in about two and a half weeks. Surely the directors wouldn't mind waiting a bit longer.

Miss LeBlanc's face had become pale, her eyes pleading with Alexandre.

Why did he feel the sudden need to help her?

Lord, is this the right path to take?

"I need to ask you to leave," Mrs. Foreman said. "There are seventy other men waiting—and some of them are getting a bit unruly."

Miss LeBlanc's chest rose and fell quickly, and he imagined her heart was pumping as fast as his. He moved to the door, and Mr. Doolittle took his place on the chair, without waiting for Miss LeBlanc to sit first.

She bit her bottom lip, her brown eyes desperate.

His pulse thrummed in his body, making his head pound. He couldn't marry her—it would be ludicrous. Just a half hour ago he didn't even know the lady.

Non.

He tipped his head in farewell. "It's been a pleasure, Miss LeBlanc. Au revoir."

She slowly sank onto the sofa next to her maid, her shoulders slumped. "Au revoir, Monsieur Dugas."

Alexandre stepped out into the ballroom, regret making his legs feel like lead. The men had formed a line, with the redheaded man named Clayton at the front. Clayton turned to the man next to him. "The rest of us might as well go home. Amos will tell her whatever she wants to hear."

Alexandre looked back at the closed door.

"Doesn't he already have a wife?" asked the man behind Clayton.

Clayton shrugged. "What does it matter out here on the frontier?"

Mrs. Foreman stood in front of the door like a watchdog, her arms crossed and her eyes never resting.

Alexandre rubbed his sweaty palms against his pant legs. He couldn't leave Miss LeBlanc to face these men—what would become of her?

She hadn't been his concern half an hour ago, but during the course of their conversation, he'd begun to feel that God had brought him here to do something.

Before he talked himself out of it, he charged back to Mrs. Foreman. "I need to speak with Miss LeBlanc."

"Your time is up."

"But I need to ask her something."

"You'll have to wait in the back of the line to get another chance—"

"I need to ask her to marry me."

Mrs. Foreman's face lit with a smile. "Why didn't you say so?" She opened the door and Alexandre stepped back into the sitting room.

Miss LeBlanc rose to her feet, her eyes enormous. "Mr. Dugas!"

"Will you marry me, Miss LeBlanc?"

Her lips parted in surprise. "Truly?"

He prayed this wasn't the biggest mistake of his life. "Truly."

Mrs. Foreman shouted into the ballroom. "Send in the justice of the peace!"

Chapter 7

Josette walked slowly with Mr. Dugas—Alexandre—by her side. One lone kerosene lantern flickered on the wall at the end of the upstairs hall, offering scant light for their path. Their arms brushed against each other in the narrow passage, but neither said a word.

The past two hours had been like a whirlwind. The justice of the peace had been called in with a special license Josie had requested earlier in the day, and the ceremony was over before she could catch her breath. She had stood next to Alexandre and pledged her life to his, for better or for worse, in sickness and in health, until death parted them.

Her foot stumbled at the thought. Alexandre reached out and placed his large, steady hand under her elbow. Their gazes met, and her stomach filled with butterflies. She'd never been alone with a man before. It was both exhilarating and frightening—and to know this was her husband. . .

After the ceremony, Ruth had disappeared into their room, while Josie and Alexandre faced a ballroom of disgruntled men. Many left angry, but those that remained offered their reluctant well-wishes.

Now Josie stopped in front of her hotel door, realizing they hadn't discussed their sleeping arrangements. She suddenly felt overly warm, yet she shivered. "H–here's my room."

Alexandre turned, half his handsome face shadowed by the light. He stood tall and powerful before her, and she couldn't help but wonder why he had not been married before.

Another shiver ran up her spine. She didn't know much about him at all.

He studied her face, and she felt a flush creep up her neck.

Muffled noise seeped up the stairway, but the hall remained empty.

"My room is two doors down." His voice carried just above the noise.

She lowered her gaze to the tie at his throat. Would he ask her to go to his room? It was within his rights—but gooseflesh rose up on her arms at the thought. There hadn't been enough time to discuss their expectations. She had intended this marriage to be in name only. . . . What did he intend?

"The stagecoach will take us to St. Paul the day after tomorrow." Her voice caught, and she cleared her throat. "We will book passage on the first available steamboat back to St. Louis."

"I plan to go to Belle Prairie in the morning to tell them about the change of plans."

He stood so close, she could smell the fresh scent of soap on his clothes, and her thoughts became jumbled. "Of course. They must know."

"Would you like to come with me?"

Her gaze traveled back to his face. She tried to focus on his question and not how close he stood. "I would."

He looked pleased. "I'll rent a buggy, and after we visit the mission, we can go for a ride—if you'd like—to get to know one another better." His stilted words revealed his own discomfort, and Josie felt a measure of relief.

"I'd like that, very much."

"Could you be ready by eight o'clock, Miss—" He paused, his thoughts imperceptible. "Mrs. Dugas."

"Please, call me Josie."

The flickering light revealed half his smile. "May I call you Josette?"

Only her father and mother had called her Josette. Her stepmother had been the one to call her Josie, telling her it was more American—and Papa had acquiesced—like he had with so many other things. "You may. And what shall I call you?"

"You're my wife, non? You must call me Alexandre."

She was his wife—yet she had imagined being a wife would be so. . .different. For now, she carried his name. . . . Would she ever carry his child? The thought made her heart race, and she reached behind and fumbled for the doorknob.

"Wait, Josette." He placed his hand under her elbow, and a tingle of both pleasure and apprehension ran the length of her arm.

"In all the commotion, the justice of the peace forgot to have me kiss my bride."

Josie's breath caught in her throat. The ceremony had happened so quickly—she hadn't even realized. But he was her husband, and he deserved at least one kiss on his wedding day—didn't he? He had sacrificed his plans to help her manage her half of the inheritance. Surely he deserved more than a peck on the cheek. He deserved her heartfelt appreciation—for the rest of her life.

She let go of the doorknob and clasped her shaky hands. She lifted her gaze to his face and saw tenderness—and attraction—in his eyes. Heat coursed through her limbs.

Alexandre's eyes caressed her face. "You're a very beautiful woman, Josette. I'm proud to call you my wife."

The warmth from her limbs flooded her face. "Thank you," she whispered.

"May I kiss the bride now?"

Josie's backside pressed up against the solid door. She was thankful for something steady and certain at the moment. "You may." Her words were breathless, and she was afraid he hadn't heard her. "You may," she said a bit louder.

He grinned, and his eyes twinkled.

Clearly he'd heard her the first time. Oh, he must think her a silly, inexperienced young woman! She closed her eyes to hide her embarrassment—and wait for the kiss.

The door suddenly opened, and before Josie knew what had happened, she was on the floor of her bedroom, with Ruth standing above her.

Ruth gasped. "Oh, my goodness! I'm so sorry, Miss Josie. I heard talking outside the door and I thought maybe you'd forgotten your key." She scrambled to help Josie from the floor just as Alexandre stepped into the room and offered Josie his hand.

A lantern illuminated the room, and Josie was certain Alexandre could see her red cheeks. Her bottom stung, but nothing compared to the sting of humiliation.

She took his hand and stood to her feet. "*Merci*, Mr. Dug—"

"Are you all right?" he asked.

She forced herself to nod as she smoothed the front of her gown.

His eyes told her he didn't believe her, but he backed out of the room. "I'll return to collect you in the morning."

Josie couldn't wait for the door to close behind him.

Chapter 8

T he next morning, Josie sat in a single-horse buggy next to Alexandre, her embarrassment from the night before still fresh in her mind. The buggy was new, just like Little Falls, with a springy seat and shiny black paint. The small space forced them to sit close together.

It was an entirely new and wonderful feeling to be married.

She looked about the landscape and feasted on the untouched woods and prairies they passed. A long, low-lying bluff jutted out of the prairie to their right, and the Mississippi meandered to their left. The trees along the riverbanks reached toward heaven, unfurling their beautiful leaves like an offering to their Creator. She'd always marveled at nature's innate worship of God.

This place was a bit of heaven on earth.

"The country here is beautiful," Alexandre said into the quiet morning air. "I've always imagined living in a house along the Mississippi."

Josie couldn't hide her surprise—or delight. "I've always wanted to live near the river as well." When they returned to St. Louis, they could find a home on the Mississippi.

Alexandre smiled at her, and she returned the warm smile with one of her own.

"The Belle Prairie Mission isn't far from here, about four miles." Alexandre held the reins in his hands with ease, though his back remained rigid. Was he as nervous as she was? "I took the liberty of bringing a picnic lunch for us to eat before we go back to town."

It would be nice to picnic with him. There were so many things they needed to discuss about LeBlanc Shipping. He appeared to be intelligent and upright, but she needed to know more about the man who would help run her father's business.

Before long the mission buildings came within sight. To their left sat a large two-story house, with a wide front porch. To the north of the house was a New England–style barn, with pigs and chickens in the barnyard, and to their right was another building, which Josie assumed to be the school and church. Oat and wheat fields stretched out over the horizon, cultivated in the rich prairie soil.

Alexandre brought the buggy to a stop and didn't move for many moments. Josie turned to him and was caught off guard by the look of wonder on his face.

"It's taken me a year to travel here, but over twelve years to arrive at this moment."

Josie remained silent, unsure how to respond.

"I left my parents' home when I was eighteen to follow God's calling into ministry." He stopped for a moment, many emotions playing about his face. "But I allowed other things to get in the way—until now." He looked at her, amazement in his gaze. "Have you ever felt as if God was smiling on you? That's how I feel right now."

A funny sensation prickled up Josie's spine. What was he saying?

The front door of the mission house opened and an older man and woman stepped onto the porch. They lifted their hands in greeting, and Alexandre nudged the horse into motion.

"Hello," called the man when they stopped the buggy in front of the house.

Alexandre stepped out of the buggy and offered Josie a hand down. He grinned at her, and she offered a tentative smile in return. What would these people think when they learned about their hasty marriage and change of plans?

"Reverend Dugas, we presume?" the lady asked.

"Yes. And you must be the Greenfields."

"That's us." Mr. Greenfield's blue eyes shined in his whiskered face. "And who is this young lady?"

Alexandre turned his gaze on Josie, unabashed pride in his brown eyes. "This is my wife, Mrs. Josette Dugas. We were married yesterday."

"Congratulations," Mr. Greenfield said. "We had no idea you would be married."

"I didn't, either." Alexandre grinned once again. "Josette, this is Mr. and Mrs. Greenfield, the directors of the Belle Prairie Mission."

Josie shook their hands. "How do you do?"

"Not as well as you on this fine morning," Mr. Greenfield said with a chuckle.

"Stop that, Silas." Mrs. Greenfield swatted at her husband good-naturedly. "Come in and make yourselves at home."

Josie and Alexandre followed them into an airy parlor and took a seat on one of the sofas. Large windows looked out onto the prairie at one end of the comfortable parlor, and a shiny piano stood at the other end. Colorful rag rugs were scattered about the pine flooring, and fresh-cut wildflowers adorned tables and shelves, making everything feel homey.

"We're so happy you've come to join our little mission family." Mrs. Greenfield took a seat across from Alexandre and Josie, her eyes gentle. "We feel blessed to have another couple here to help. All of our teachers have married and left, save for one, Miss Smith.

With the influx of immigrants moving into the territory, our school and church have grown, but Mr. Greenfield is no longer able to preach, because of throat troubles."

Josie looked at Alexandre, hoping he'd stop Mrs. Greenfield. Surely the longer he postponed telling them about the change of plans, the more uncomfortable they would all be. But Alexandre allowed her to continue, and he even smiled, as if encouraging her.

"For now," Mrs. Greenfield said, "you're welcome to live with us, until you have a home of your own. We don't expect you to preach the first week, Reverend Dugas, but if you're willing, we're of a mind to hear you soon. It's been too long since we've had a service at the church."

"Actually, I have a bit of news to share," Alexandre said. "My plans changed unexpectedly last night."

Josie let out an inward sigh of relief—finally, he would tell them.

"Oh? What is that?" Mrs. Greenfield's pleasant gaze didn't waver as she looked at Alexandre.

He sat a bit straighter and turned his gaze on Josie. "I met Mrs. Dugas last night and learned she was in need of a husband, so we were married."

The Greenfields' surprised eyes turned to her, and her cheeks filled with heat. What

must they think of her, marrying a stranger?

"I felt God call me to marry her," Alexandre continued. "But it will require a change in my plans, of which I'm very sorry."

Mr. Greenfield was the first to speak. "You've only just met?"

"Yes. Less than twenty-four hours ago."

"How interesting," Mrs. Greenfield said. "Mr. Greenfield and I didn't know each other before our wedding, either."

Josie stared at the lady. She understood?

"We were both entering the mission field." Mrs. Greenfield turned her loving gaze on her husband and took his hand. "We were required to have a spouse, so Mr. Greenfield and I were paired. We married the day we met." She turned back to Josie and Alexandre. "What God has brought together, let no man put asunder."

Alexandre and Josie were quiet for a moment, and then Alexandre spoke. "We must return to St. Louis and present our marriage certificate to the judge. We'll leave on the stagecoach tomorrow morning."

Josie held her breath to see the Greenfields' reaction. There was disappointment on their faces, but they didn't say a word, allowing Alexandre to continue.

"It might take us a week or two to get all of Mrs. Dugas's affairs in order before we're able to return to Minnesota Territory. I hope it's not too much trouble."

Josie's eyes grew wide as she swiveled her head to look at Alexandre. What was he saying? She had no intention of returning! Hadn't she made that clear last night?

"It's not ideal," Mr. Greenfield said. "But you must do what is necessary. We'll look forward to hearing you preach when you return."

Josie opened her mouth to protest, but the kind looks on Mr. and Mrs. Greenfield's faces silenced her.

Chapter 9

Alexandre stood, and Josie followed, her stomach queasy. Dozens of questions raced through her mind.

"I apologize for the inconvenience," Alexandre said to the Greenfields. "Thank you for understanding."

Mr. Greenfield smiled. "We'll look forward to seeing you in about a month's time."

"Do you have a few moments to meet some of the students?" Mrs. Greenfield turned her hopeful eyes on Josie. "I know they'd love to meet you. They've been waiting eagerly for the new reverend."

The last thing Josie wanted to do was postpone her conversation with Alexandre. "I think it best if we go back to town and get our affairs in order. We'll be leaving on the stagecoach first thing in the morning."

"Oh, what a pity," Mrs. Greenfield said.

Alexandre touched Josie's hand. "We could spare a few moments, non? After all, the Greenfields have been very understanding."

If she denied his request, it would make a scene—and she didn't want to embarrass her new husband. "Of course." She tried to smile, though her lips trembled. "What was I thinking?"

Mr. Greenfield excused himself to tend to his chores.

They followed Mrs. Greenfield out of the house and across the rutted road to the school and church building. The day had grown hot, and the humming of the locusts buzzed from the prairie.

Mrs. Greenfield opened the thick oak door and led the way to the front of the stuffy classroom. At least three dozen students lifted their heads, their curious eyes assessing Alexandre and Josie. Many of the students looked to be children of local farmers and fur traders with their fair coloring, but the other half were Chippewa, with their dark hair and eyes.

A lump grew in Josie's throat. She hadn't spoken Chippewa since she was a child. Would she have a chance now?

A woman stood at the front of the room. Her eyes blinked behind spectacles, and her blond hair was pulled tight at the back of her head.

"Reverend and Mrs. Dugas, this is Miss Hazel Smith, our lead teacher at the mission." Mrs. Greenfield indicated the severe woman. "Miss Smith, this is the new reverend and his wife."

"Pleased to meet you," Miss Smith said with a curt nod of her head.

Josie nodded a greeting but cringed at the words *new reverend*.

"The reverend will be leaving but will be back in one month's time to take up his

duties," Mrs. Greenfield continued.

If Miss Smith was surprised at the change in plans, her stoic face didn't show it.

"I was wondering if the reverend and Mrs. Dugas might meet the children."

"Of course." Miss Smith indicated the classroom. "The children have been waiting for the reverend's arrival."

Josie's temples began to pound. She just wanted to leave and explain the mistake to Alexandre. Surely, once he realized she needed him to help manage her father's business in St. Louis, he would clear up the misunderstanding with the Greenfields. They would continue to support Belle Prairie financially, but the mission would have to find another preacher.

The students stood and introduced themselves. The girls gave a curtsy and the boys a bow. They all wore gray uniforms, with brass buttons and black boots.

When they were finished with introductions, Mrs. Greenfield encouraged Josie and Alexandre to walk among the students and look at their schoolwork.

Alexandre moved to the boys' side of the room, where he immediately engaged with a young boy about the sums on his slate.

Josie looked down at the first little girl. She sat with her legs dangling over the seat and no desk in front of her. She held a primer in her hands, but she couldn't keep her eyes on the book. She glanced up at Josie, her large brown eyes filled with curiosity. When she saw Josie looking at her, she dropped her gaze.

Mrs. Greenfield put her gentle hand on top of the girl's shiny black hair. "This is Claire. We've guessed her age to be around four or five, but we're not sure. Both of her parents died of the fever, so she was sent here."

Claire lifted her eyes again, and it was as if Josie was looking at herself, twenty-two years ago. The little girl was adorable, and all alone in the world. Josie suddenly felt overcome with the need to cry—but she put a smile on her face instead.

"Will she live here permanently?" she asked.

"Unless someone comes along to adopt her." Mrs. Greenfield smiled down at the child. "But we love having Claire here. She brightens up even the dreariest days."

Josie sank down to the girl's level. "Hello, Claire. I'm Miss—Mrs. Dugas."

The little girl dipped her head bashfully and didn't answer.

"She can understand English," said Miss Smith, "but she hasn't spoken a word of it. Shall I interpret for you?"

Claire blinked, and her large eyes drew Josie's heart. She wanted the little girl to know she understood what it felt like to lose her mama and papa.

"That won't be necessary," Josie said.

She reached back into the recesses of her mind for a simple phrase. Hello, I'm Mrs. Dugas. "*Aaniin. Niin* Mrs. Dugas *nindizhinikaa.*"

Claire's eyes lit with joy, and she bounced in her seat. Her words spilled out in Chippewa, and Josie tried desperately to keep up. She caught little snatches that she understood. "Hello! I'm Claire. . . .pretty lady. . .pretty dress. . .new teacher? . . .you sing?"

Josie's smile grew until she was fairly laughing. She lifted her hands to slow the child. "Slower, please."

The other children laughed with Josie, and for the first time in a long time, she felt real joy.

Chapter 10

A round of giggles brought Alexandre's head up from the conversation with the boy named Thomas.

Sunshine poured in through the windows, illuminating Josette's dark hair as she sat among the little girls. Her cheeks were pink and her eyes shining as she spoke in a language foreign to him. She said something, and all the girls laughed again. Clearly, she was mispronouncing her words, and the girls thought it great fun.

Alexandre couldn't help but smile himself.

Mrs. Greenfield stood off to the side with Miss Smith, but Alexandre couldn't take his eyes off his wife.

Wife. It was still a strange and wonderful word to him.

Mrs. Greenfield walked over to Alexandre, a bit of wonder in her eyes. "Your wife is a natural with the children, Reverend Dugas. The Lord knew what He was doing when He brought you together."

Josette laughed, and Alexandre realized it was the first time he'd heard her laughter. He liked the way it made him feel—warm and content, like a heavy quilt on a cold winter night.

He could hardly believe he would be blessed enough to hear that sound every day, for the rest of his life.

"God never makes mistakes," Mrs. Greenfield said, laying her hand on his arm. "Don't lose sight of that truth, no matter how hard life may get."

Alexandre looked at the older lady, seeing the years of hardship behind her wise words.

He hated to interrupt Josette, but they needed to let the children get back to their work. He crossed the room and touched her shoulder. "It's time to leave."

Her smile fell, but then the little girl named Claire wrapped her arms around Josette's neck. *"Baamaapii."* She looked at Josette, her brown eyes enormous. "Until later, Mrs. Dugas."

Josette's eyes shimmered with tears, but she managed to smile at the child's broken English. "Good-bye, Claire."

They said farewell and stepped outside. He helped her into the buggy, and then he climbed inside and snapped the reins. The horse trotted off across the prairie.

The nerves Alexandre had been feeling earlier in the day had dissipated. There were so many things they hadn't had time to discuss, but when he saw Josette with the children, he knew she was meant to be here.

The sun beat down on the prairie, reminding him that it was close to lunchtime. He pulled the horse off the road and parked the buggy under the shade of a large willow tree,

along the banks of the Mississippi.

Josette hadn't spoken a word, and he could see she was still overcome with emotion. "Shall we eat?"

"There is something we must discuss." Her grave voice surprised him.

His mind raced with all the possible things she might tell him, and his heart thudded hard within his chest. "*Très bien.* Shall we walk along the riverbank?" He didn't wait for her to answer but stepped out of the buggy and helped her down.

A flock of ducks landed nearby, their wings splashing the sparkling water as they found their resting place.

She finally spoke. "There's been a terrible misunderstanding."

Was that all? "It can't be that bad."

She swallowed and looked down at her hands. "Last night—before you agreed to marry me—I thought you understood that we would stay in St. Louis."

Stay in St. Louis? What—?

"I have my father's business to run." She looked at him, desperation in her eyes. "Didn't you realize this?"

Alexandre stared at her. "Stay in St. Louis? It took me a year to get here— I'm not going to move to St. Louis and run a business— I left all of that behind—"

"What did you think I was going to do with my half of the business?"

Alexandre opened his mouth to respond, but what could he say? He hadn't thought about what she would do with her inheritance.

He ran his hand down his face to try to clear his thoughts. "Everything happened so quickly last night. I just assumed you were willing to come back to Belle Prairie with me."

"And I assumed you were willing to stay in St. Louis with me." She looked like she might cry. "I can't leave my father's business in the hands of my brother—I just can't."

Alexandre fumbled for his clean handkerchief and put it in her hand. "Don't cry, Josette."

Surely, after spending the afternoon with the children at the mission, she couldn't deny that she belonged there. He'd seen it in her eyes, sensed it with every fiber of his being.

The water flowed by, moving driftwood and dead leaves with it. Hadn't he fought against this very river, pushing himself northward for over a year? How easily it could take him back to a life he didn't want to live.

He tore his eyes from the river. "I'll return long enough for you to secure your inheritance."

She swallowed. "But you will not stay?"

He had married her with every intention to live as man and wife—but he couldn't give up his calling, no matter how great the misunderstanding. "I will not stay in St. Louis, Josette."

She was silent for a moment, but when she looked at him, there was resolve in her face. "And I cannot return to Belle Prairie."

Frustration welled up in his chest. A part of him wanted to remind her that she was his wife and that she must go where he led. But the other part of him, the more rational part, knew that he could never force her—or anyone else—to do something against their will.

They watched the water flow by, each deep in thought. Alexandre had stayed awake

most of the night and allowed himself to imagine his life with Josette. He had counted himself a blessed man when he said his vows. Josette carried herself with elegance and grace, and she exhibited a gentle spirit, which he prized far above other qualities. Seeing her with the children had been the final confirmation that he had made the right choice.

He wanted to share his life with her.

He picked up a stick and tossed it into the water. The current grabbed it and pulled it away, and out of sight. He couldn't let the same thing happen to his calling.

He wouldn't force Josette to return. . .but maybe he could persuade her. They had a week's journey ahead of them—perhaps in that amount of time, he could convince his wife to return with him to Belle Prairie.

The ride back to Little Falls was painfully quiet for Josie. Alexandre didn't speak until they had finally stopped in front of the Northern Hotel.

"I imagine you and your maid have things to attend to this afternoon." He alighted from the buggy and tied the horse to the hitching post. He came to her side and offered his hand. She placed her hand inside his and felt it drown in the immensity of his palm.

His touch did strange things inside her stomach. Somehow, in less than a day, she had grown fond of the idea of having him in her life. There had to be a way to convince him to stay in St. Louis. She had a week with him on the steamboat—anything could happen. . . .

With renewed determination she stepped out of the buggy, and even managed to smile. If she was going to convince him to stay with her, she would need to muster all the charm she possessed.

She put her arm through his and they walked into the hotel lobby.

Ruth sat on the floral sofa near the potted ferns. She wore her hat and gloves, and her valise was at her side. She stood when Josie and Alexandre entered, her cheeks flushed. "Oh, I didn't think you'd arrive in time, Miss Josie."

"In time for what?" It was then that Josie noticed the man who had been sitting near Ruth. He looked vaguely familiar. Had he been in the ballroom the night before? He rose by her side.

Ruth's movements were awkward. She took a step forward but then stopped abruptly. "Miss Josie, th–things have transpired since you left this morning—things I didn't anticipate."

Josie still held Alexandre's arm, thankful for his steady presence.

"What's happened?" Josie eyed the strange man. He was pale and painfully thin, but he wore a well-pressed suit and a top hat.

"After you left, I came downstairs for breakfast, and this gentleman, Mr. Ashcroft, approached me. H–he made an offer I couldn't refuse." She lifted her hand and showed Josie a beautiful ruby ring. "He works at the land office, and owns a new house. We were married just an hour ago." Her lips quivered as she smiled. "I'm married now."

Josie blinked several times but couldn't say a word.

"Congratulations." Alexandre extended his hand to Mr. Ashcroft.

"Thank you kindly," the gentleman said with a bob of his head. "Never hurts to ask, is what I always say."

"I know this is a bit of a shock, and I apologize for the inconvenience," Ruth said to

Josie. "I realize this puts you in a bind—not having a lady's maid for your return to St. Louis. But now that you're married, I hoped Mr. Dugas would help you."

Josie thought of all that Ruth did—everything from tying her corsets to styling her hair. How could Alexandre possibly help with those things? But none of that mattered— she'd find a way to manage. She was more dismayed about losing her friend. "I'll miss you, Ruth. You've been the very dearest friend in the world." She reached out and pulled her maid into an embrace.

Ruth hugged her back, and Josie could feel Ruth's heart beating wildly in her chest.

"Are you nervous?" Josie whispered.

"Terribly."

Josie pulled back and tried to offer some encouragement in her smile, though her voice shook with emotion. "Thank you, for everything. You'll be sure to write?"

Ruth nodded as Mr. Ashcroft took her valise in hand.

"We must be off, Mrs. Ashcroft," he said.

Ruth offered Josie one final smile. "Good-bye, Miss Josie."

The pair left the Northern Hotel, and Josie stood motionless. "I can hardly believe it."

Alexandre held his hat in hand and studied her. "It looks like we're on our own."

Josie tried to hide her sudden anxiety.

"I don't think it's safe for you to sleep alone tonight," he said slowly. "This town is full of criminals who would do anything to take what they want. A small lock won't stop them."

Josie's eyes grew large. She didn't know what frightened her more: the criminals. . .or her attractive husband sleeping in her room.

Chapter 11

Josie stood on the Lower Landing in St. Paul, watching for Alexandre to emerge out of the noisy crowd. The morning sun hadn't yet crested the eastern horizon, and already there were dozens of steamboats lining the pier. Hundreds of passengers milled about the landing, with children running among the adults. Dockworkers walked up and down the gangplanks, loading and unloading cargo, while street peddlers hawked their wares. A whistle pierced the air as a steamboat backed out of the dock, on its way upriver.

Where was he? The *Northern Star* was scheduled to depart at first light. If they didn't get passage, they would have to wait for the next boat. For two days, they had tried to book passage on an available boat, but every stateroom had been taken.

Josie stood on tiptoe, straining to find him and willing the panic to subside.

Finally, Alexandre pushed his way through the crowd.

"Did you find rooms?" she asked, searching his face. They only had eight days before Stephen's birthday, and the trip would take at least six. If anything happened to stall their progress, they might not reach the judge in time.

Alexandre picked up her valise. "I was able to secure the last available stateroom, though it isn't much to speak of. I had hoped to find a room with servant's quarters for me, but there was nothing."

She followed him through the crowd, toward the steamboat, feeling both disappointed and thrilled. For the past three nights they had shared a room, and she had come to enjoy his company.

The first night in Little Falls had been awkward—until he opened his Bible. The book was common ground for them, so she asked him to read aloud. Soon they were engaged in a lively conversation that had lasted for hours. The awkwardness had dissipated, and she had loved the way his insights had challenged her.

Every night they had followed the same routine. He read a passage of scripture, and then they discussed what he read. After their conversations, Josie had slept on the bed and Alexandre on the floor. It was an entirely new experience to fall asleep listening to the steady rise and fall of his breathing.

Now, as he led her onboard the *Northern Star*, she felt her stomach flutter at the idea of spending an entire week in the same room with him. They were reading through the book of Proverbs—would they finish?

The *Northern Star* was a grand boat, with an ornate central stairway, a three-hundred-foot-long Grand Salon, and beautiful mahogany furnishings. It was reported to be one of the fastest ships on the Mississippi. Josie hoped it would live up to its reputation.

Alexandre showed her to stateroom number thirty-eight, and produced a key.

He opened the door and Josie stepped into the small room. Only eight feet square, it boasted a washbasin, slim dresser, and narrow bed. Two doors stood opposite from each other, one going onto the promenade deck and the other opening into the Grand Salon.

"There's just enough room for me to put a bedroll on the floor." Alexandre placed their valises on top of the dresser. His towering form took up a great deal of space, making the room feel much more intimate than their hotel rooms.

She made a pretense of studying the room, though she couldn't take her mind off him. "I'm sorry you must sleep on the floor."

"There are worse places to sleep." He smiled, and his brown eyes teased. "And there are better."

She didn't expect the heat that filled her cheeks. She dropped her gaze and began to fiddle with her hat pin to cover her reaction.

"The room will do," he said, "as long as we get to St. Louis on time." He leaned against the dresser, watching her. "On the way back, I'll have the whole room to myself."

She removed her hat and set it on the bed, smoothing down her hair. "I suppose you will." Unless she could convince him to stay in St. Louis.

He continued to watch her as she removed her gloves and took off her traveling coat. She tried not to let his perusal fluster her, but she couldn't keep her hands from trembling.

She glanced at him and couldn't deny the spark that flew between them. If she wasn't careful, she might fall in love with her husband. . . .

And that's when she realized how she might convince him to stay in St. Louis.

He needed to fall in love with *her*.

A knock sounded on the Promenade door. "I have your trunk," a steward called.

Alexandre opened the door and directed the steward to put the trunk in the only open space, between the washbasin and dresser.

"Breakfast is in fifteen minutes, ma'am." The steward bowed and left the room.

"Fifteen minutes?" Josie threw open her trunk and looked at her clothing in dismay. "How will I change into a clean morning gown in fifteen minutes?"

Alexandre suddenly looked uncomfortable as he shuffled his feet. "I suppose I could help you."

Josie clutched the lid of the trunk. "That won't be necessary. I can do it on my own. . .I'll just need some privacy."

Alexandre grabbed his valise and hurried to the door. "I'll meet you back here in fifteen minutes."

She closed the door behind him and leaned against the solid wood, taking a deep breath.

She might succeed in getting Alexandre to fall in love with her. . .but the real challenge would be guarding her own heart.

Josie stood beside Alexandre at the rail, watching the large red wheels churn in the muddy water. The delicious taste of warm pancakes and maple syrup still lingered on her tongue, and the quiet prayer Alexandre had spoken for their journey echoed in her heart. The timbre of his voice was as soothing as the sway of the boat.

She just wished the boat would move faster.

Conscious of her plan to win his heart, she stepped closer to Alexandre and put her arm through his. "When is the boat supposed to arrive in St. Louis?"

He looked at her, a bit surprised—but pleased. "Thursday evening."

"Thursday?" Her mind raced with the calculations. "My brother's birthday is on Saturday."

"We'll have two extra days."

"As long as we don't encounter any problems."

Alexandre placed his large hand over hers. "Don't borrow trouble, Josette."

"Reverend Dugas?" The captain appeared next to Alexandre, his blue uniform gleaming in the early morning sunshine.

"Yes?"

Captain Townsend was a young man, with dark hair and a well-trimmed beard. His gaze slid over Josie, and appreciation gleamed from his light blue eyes. He gave a slight bow. "Mrs. Dugas, I presume?"

Josie had not yet grown accustomed to the title, but she felt pride at being recognized as Alexandre's wife. "It's a pleasure to meet you, Captain."

Captain Townsend placed his hand over his heart. "The pleasure is mine."

The appreciation in his eyes fringed on something deeper, and Josie instinctively took a step closer to her husband.

As if reading her unease, Alexandre put his arm around her waist. "Can I help you, monsieur?"

The captain directed his gaze to Alexandre. "We will stop to observe the Sabbath the day after tomorrow. It has been my practice to find a reverend on board to lead our morning service. Would you do us the honor?"

Alexandre didn't hesitate. "Of course."

"Wonderful." The captain grinned, and his eyes landed on Josie once again. "I hope you'll sit with me as my guest of honor during the service, Mrs. Dugas."

How could she refuse? "I'd be honored."

The captain reached for her hand and placed a kiss on the top.

Alexandre's arm tightened around her waist.

"I will count down the hours." The captain stood straight and tipped his hat. "Good day to the both of you."

He walked away, but Alexandre was slow to remove his arm from around her waist—and she didn't mind.

The other passengers milled about the promenade deck, enjoying the mid-morning heat. Lush green vegetation grew along the riverbanks, and sunshine streamed down, creating a million sparkles on the river's surface.

A sudden jolt heaved across the promenade deck, tossing many people to the floor. Screams filled the air as a great noise ripped through the steamboat and brought it to a stop. Alexandre's arms tightened around Josie, helping her stay on her feet.

"What was that?" she asked, her heart thudding against her chest.

"My best guess would be a snag."

"A snag?"

"Sometimes the boats snag on dead trees in the water."

Josie stared at him. Had that terrible noise been the ship's bottom tearing off? "Will we sink?"

Officers and crewmembers rushed past, and Alexandre's eyes filled with concern.

"There is a possibility." He tried to offer a reassuring smile. "More than likely, it was a minor accident, and we'll stay afloat."

More crewmembers raced past on the promenade, their concerned faces not looking left or right.

Josie stood on tiptoe, trying to see what they were running toward.

Alexandre drew her gaze back to his face. "This may set us back a day or two."

It was then that she felt real panic.

Chapter 12

For a day and a half, the crewmembers of the *Northern Star* repaired the gaping hole in the bottom of the boat. On Saturday night, the captain announced they would not resume their journey until Monday morning, after observing the Sabbath.

Josie's insides wound up like a coil of rope, and for just a moment, she considered taking a lifeboat and rowing downriver by herself.

Alexandre spoke with the pilot, telling him of their need to arrive in St. Louis by Friday, and then he assured Josie that if the pilot pushed the steamboat hard, they would arrive in time, barring any other obstacles.

On Sunday morning, Captain Townsend escorted Josie to the front row of the Grand Salon, while Alexandre greeted the passengers who came to worship.

Captain Townsend indicated her chair and then sat next to her.

Alexandre strode to the front of the salon, in his best suit coat, and smiled at the congregation. The room was full of crew members, officers, stateroom guests, and deck passengers, many of them impatient from the recent delay.

"Welcome," Alexandre said, his French accent more pronounced in the pulpit. "It is good to come together on the Sabbath to refresh our souls, especially after the past couple of days." The calm look on his face put Josie at ease, and she felt the whole room take a deep breath. "Please bow your heads as I begin in prayer." He closed his eyes and lifted his voice.

Josie forgot about everything else as she watched her husband, unhindered. He prayed as if he had an audience with a king, his words reverent and beseeching. Josie had been raised with rote prayers, and had come to cherish the times Alexandre petitioned the Lord. His earnest communion with God caressed her tender heart and offered her hope.

He said amen and then opened his eyes—and caught her looking at him. A slow, handsome smile spread across his face. She smiled back, surprised at how intimate the moment felt, even among all these people.

Next, he led them in singing "Rock of Ages," and Josie was captivated by his melodic voice. It was deep and smooth, and as it rose to the roof of the salon, she could imagine it filling the very throne room of God.

After the hymn, the congregants sat on their chairs and Alexandre opened his Bible.

What followed was the most intriguing sermon Josie had ever heard. Alexandre was a naturally talented speaker, but it was the context of his sermon that drew her attention and made her heart pound. He spoke of the apostle Paul and how he sacrificed everything to run the race God had set out for him. His words were comforting yet compelling,

drawing her to ponder the weight of the scriptures and the power of God's Word.

Josie was mesmerized by his deep and abiding conviction, and she recalled the look of awe on his face when they'd arrived at Belle Prairie.

No wonder her husband felt God smiling on him.

How could she possibly ask him to stay in St. Louis to run LeBlanc Shipping, when he was clearly meant to preach?

As she sat in her chair, absorbing his words, the truth settled over her heart.

She would have to let him go back to Belle Prairie.

But even as she realized this truth, a new question took her by surprise.

How could she let Alexandre go, now that she was falling in love with him?

Alexandre loved the feel of Josette's body pressed close to his as they waltzed. It was the last night on board the *Northern Star*, and she wore the pink dress he had come to think of as her wedding gown. Her hair was styled in a simple fashion, but it shone under the flicker of the chandeliers. She smelled of fine perfume, and he took a deep breath, savoring every moment with her.

Throughout the day, storm clouds had gathered in the sky, and now thunder reverberated throughout the Grand Salon, rattling the massive chandeliers overhead. The noise was masked by the orchestra as they played "Tales of the Ball," by Johann Strauss II.

Alexandre leaned close to Josette's ear as he led her about the dance floor. "You're quiet this evening. Is everything all right?"

"I'm praying."

"About what?"

"I'm praying we don't encounter any more snags."

He laughed and held her closer as they spun about the parquet floor. They had made good time and would arrive in St. Louis on Friday afternoon, if all went as planned.

The end of their week was in sight. Suddenly, he felt melancholy.

Neither one spoke of the impending separation, and Alexandre felt that maybe they both wanted to pretend it wasn't going to happen. Josette had not spoken of going to Belle Prairie, and Alexandre had refused to ask her again.

Instead, he had spent the week wooing his wife.

They had danced and played games and walked along the promenade under the stars. Every night he read to her from the book of Proverbs, and they spent the last few hours of their day discussing the scriptures. Alexandre never tired of Josette's company. He learned more about her in that week than he had learned about Isobel in years.

But in the process of wooing Josette, he had fallen in love, which he had tried so very hard not to do. He didn't want to leave her in St. Louis. He had married her for better or for worse and had fully intended to take care of her for the rest of her life.

He couldn't stay in St. Louis, and he wouldn't force her to go to Belle Prairie. That only left one option. They would have to live separate lives, as husband and wife.

Another clap of thunder boomed across the sky, and a gust of wind sent the boat listing to the side.

The orchestra came to a halt as Captain Townsend stepped onto the stage. "I must ask all of you to return to your staterooms as we navigate through these choppy waters.

The storm is gaining in intensity, and we must continue on until we come to a proper landing."

The boat rocked back the other way, and Josette lost her balance. Alexandre reached out to steady her.

"Will this delay us, again?" Her large brown eyes filled with anxiety.

"Don't worry. Let's do as the captain says."

The rain pounded the roof of the Grand Salon, and the wind rocked the boat back and forth. The noise from the storm followed them into their stateroom.

Alexandre closed their door.

Josette lit the lantern on the wall and light flooded the small room, illuminating her solemn face.

Alexandre stood by the door and watched her. The boat continued to sway, but she held her footing as she blew out the match and set the chimney back on the lantern.

When she turned to him, their gazes collided, and it felt as if the air tingled with electricity.

"What shall we do to pass the time?" she asked, just above a whisper.

The room felt much smaller on this dark, stormy night, but the distance between them was still great.

"Shall we talk?" he asked.

She studied his face. "I feel as if maybe we've said all there is to say."

He took a step closer to her. "We haven't said everything."

The lantern flickered as the boat tilted to one side and then rolled back to the other.

She braced her hand on the washbasin. "Our journey is about to end. What more is there to discuss?"

He took another step toward her, balancing with the sway of the boat. "Our journey doesn't have to end tonight, Josette." He reached out and touched her cheek. "You're my wife."

She swallowed. "In name only—not in any other way that truly matters."

He traced the edge of her cheek. "Our marriage doesn't have to be in name only. It can be much more."

She drew her eyebrows together. "It can't be anything more than it is right now. I cannot give my heart to a man I'll never see again."

Alexandre reached up and touched the other side of her face, searching her eyes. There was only one day left. One chance to convince her to go back with him. "I think you've already lost your heart. . . . I know I have."

The lantern light flickered in her eyes, and all he knew was this moment in time. Before he had a chance to contemplate his actions, he bent down and placed his lips upon hers.

He sensed she was surprised, but she didn't pull away. He drew her into his arms and kissed her deeply.

She responded to his kiss and allowed him to let the moment linger. The boat rocked under their feet and the rain pounded on the roof, but all he knew was her lips. She tasted as sweet as he imagined.

He finally pulled back, just as a tear escaped her eye.

The world came crashing back in all its agonizing reality as he wiped her cheek. "Why are you crying, *ma chérie?*"

"Oh, Alexandre." She buried her face in his chest and wrapped her arms around his waist. "It's impossible."

He rubbed her back. "What's impossible?"

"Us."

"But it doesn't have to be. I know we could be very happy. God brought us together, non?"

"Through a misunderstanding." She pulled back and met his gaze. "Had we known the plans of the other, we would never have married."

"Maybe that was why He allowed the misunderstanding." He tried to pull her close again, remembering Mrs. Greenfield's words. "God doesn't make mistakes."

She resisted his comfort and separated herself from him completely, walking across the short distance of the room. "No, but humans do. And I believe we did. Neither one of us is willing to sacrifice for the other."

"But weren't you happy at Belle Prairie? You came alive there."

Her face filled with a myriad of emotions. "You asked me once if I've ever felt God smiling on me—and my answer is no. I've never had the luxury of following a dream—until now." Her eyes pleaded for him to understand. "Operating LeBlanc Shipping is my calling—I can't ignore it, just as you can't ignore your calling—it's what God created you to do. Even if you wanted to, I wouldn't let you."

Her words sobered him. She had come to realize that preaching was a part of who he was, and she wouldn't ask him to give it up.

Shouldn't he be just as selfless for her?

"I'm sorry, Josette." He stared at the cold floor, which would be his bed once again tonight. "It's been wrong of me to hope you'd give up your father's business."

"It's more than his business—it's his legacy, the only one he left." She sank onto the bed and lowered her head onto her hands, her voice forlorn. "Our marriage is impossible—isn't it?"

Maybe it was, and maybe it was time they both admitted it. "Oui. After we present the marriage certificate to the judge and I help you get settled, I'll return to Minnesota."

Alone and miserable.

Unless the storm delayed them and they didn't make it to the judge in time. Only an act of God would allow Josette to be his.

Chapter 13

The following day, Alexandre sat beside Josette as they made their way to her family home in a rented cab. He felt void of emotion as they sat in silence. The steamboat had arrived in St. Louis mid-afternoon, and they had just enough time to visit the judge and present the marriage certificate. Their time together was quickly coming to an end.

God had chosen not to intervene.

"We've arrived," Josette said.

Alexandre looked out the cab's window, unprepared for the grandeur of her childhood home.

Sitting on a little rise above the street, the tall redbrick house towered over the neighboring homes and stood like a gothic sentry.

"This is where you grew up?" The cab stopped in front of the house, and Alexandre's head fell back as he looked up at the monstrosity.

Josette looked past him out the window, no trace of warmth in her eyes. "I lived most of my childhood at a boarding school and only returned here for a few weeks each summer. My stepmother often went into fits of jealousy when Papa showed me any special attention, so he and I spent a lot of time at the shipping office."

Alexandre thought of his humble farmhouse in Louisiana. It was a cozy home with nothing ornate or ostentatious about it, but it was full of love and happy memories for him. He wished his wife could say the same.

The butler opened the door, his surprised face quickly masked with indifference. "Miss Josie, your mother will be eager to see you."

Josette removed her gloves and hat and handed them to the butler. "Tell her I'll be in the south parlor, Mr. Warren."

"Very good." Mr. Warren bowed and closed the door behind them without another word.

Alexandre followed Josette through a magnificent foyer and into a flamboyantly decorated parlor. Gaudy gold drapes hung at the massive windows, and intricately patterned rugs covered the floors. Oversized furniture filled the room to overflowing, yet nothing looked comfortable.

Josette stood in the middle of it all, looking as out of place as he felt. Her eyes met his, and he could see she was bracing herself for a battle.

"Will your brother be at the loading docks?" he asked, hoping to spare her from at least one unpleasant encounter.

Josette shook her head. "He never goes there. No doubt he's on a steamboat,

gambling away Papa's money."

She became silent then, so Alexandre did the same.

A clicking noise soon filled Alexandre's ears, and he sensed Josette stiffen.

"Josie!" The woman who entered the room looked as if she could be Josette's sister, not stepmother. Luxurious brown hair, with nary a gray streak in sight, was coiled in a large twist at the back of her head. Her smooth skin and slender body were no indications of her age.

But it was her eyes that made Alexandre take a protective step closer to Josette. She looked at him, running her icy blue gaze up and down his frame. An indecent smile tilted her lips, and she lifted a brow.

"Who is this handsome young man, Josie?"

Josette lifted her chin. "This is my husband."

Her eyes darted to Josette, and she glared. "Husband?"

"Yes, Celeste."

"Is that where you've been these past three weeks? Finding a *husband?*" She said the word as if it were tainted.

"That's precisely where I've been."

For a moment, Celeste was speechless—but then her tongue let loose, and she advanced toward Josette. "How dare you leave my home and not tell me where you went! I had to engage the police to help look for you. And where is Ruth?"

"She's also married."

Celeste narrowed her eyes, her breath seething out of her mouth. "And what, pray tell, caused this sudden move on your part?"

Josette's face held no emotion, and Alexandre's chest tightened at seeing her this way. Gone was the joyful young lady on the steamboat, who had danced with him and strolled under the starlight.

Had her laughter ever filled these rooms?

"I was informed that I would lose everything if I wasn't married before Stephen turns twenty-one—but you knew that, didn't you? It's the reason you worked so hard to turn away the gentlemen who called on me."

Celeste's eyes grew wide, and for the first time since they arrived, she lost her bluster. "How dare you accuse me—"

"I'm here to collect my belongings," Josie said, her spine stiff. "I expect to see Stephen at the office first thing tomorrow morning. I'm now co-owner of LeBlanc Shipping, and I intend to make immediate changes."

Celeste only stared, her face frozen in shock.

Josette took Alexandre's arm, and they left the parlor.

Josette was shaking.

"I'm proud of you," he whispered into her ear.

"I've been waiting to stand up to her. Until now, I didn't have the authority to do it."

Again, Alexandre understood how important Josette's inheritance was—not only to continue her father's legacy but to give her control of her life for the very first time.

Chapter 14

Josie stood looking out the front window of her rented home. The narrow three-story brick house looked identical to the other homes standing next to it. An ornate wrought-iron fence encircled her small front yard, and just beyond it, Lafayette Boulevard teemed with fancy buggies as evening set in. People were driving about socializing, but she had no desire to join them.

The savory scent of gumbo filled the cozy rooms as she looked at the grandfather clock once again.

Alexandre was late.

The table was set, the meal prepared, and she was waiting to greet him in her pink gown.

Tonight had to be perfect—it was Alexandre's last night in St. Louis. After two weeks of helping her organize LeBlanc Shipping, he would be leaving before the sun rose in the morning.

Having him close gave her an edge of confidence she had never felt on her own. He made her believe she could do what she set her mind to.

The sun sat low in the sky when the carriage finally pulled up to the house.

Josie opened the heavy front door as Alexandre walked slowly up the sidewalk, his brow crinkled and his gaze on the ground. He looked as if he carried a great burden on his shoulders.

If only she could rub the cares away.

Gone were the days when she thought she might convince him to stay. She knew, deep in her heart, that he didn't belong in St. Louis. He belonged in Belle Prairie.

He lifted his head and she was rewarded with his smile, which erased all the cares from his face. "Josette, you look lovely—and what is that heavenly smell?"

She took his hat and gloves and closed the door behind him. "It's gumbo, your favorite."

He hadn't taken his gaze off her, and she felt her cheeks warming under his appraisal. "For as long as I live, I'll always remember the first moment I saw you in that gown."

They faced each other for a long time, her arms aching to wrap around his waist. But she refrained, not wanting to make this parting harder than it should be.

"Are you ready to eat?" she asked.

"I'm famished."

He followed her into the dark-paneled dining room. The table was set with fine china, crystal, and silver. Two tall candelabras were filled with white candles, flickering on either side of a fresh-cut bouquet of flowers.

They took their places and Alexandre offered grace. The cook, Mrs. Anderson, entered the room and quietly placed fresh bread and steaming bowls of gumbo in front of both of them.

"I hope you don't mind, but I thought we'd keep the meal simple tonight," Josie said.

"Mind? I wish I could eat like this every night. It reminds me of home."

Warm pleasure filled Josie's stomach as she dipped her spoon into the creole stew—but a thought soon made her grow sober. "Will you make your own meals when you return to Belle Prairie?"

"I'm sure the mission workers will provide my meals until I find my own place." He stared at his bowl and then finally lifted his somber gaze. "After that, I'll have to fend for myself."

Josie tasted the gumbo, but the flavors fell flat on her tongue.

They sat in silence for a moment, and then Josie took a deep breath. She didn't know how to broach the topic that had been niggling at her conscience. Maybe it was best to just say what needed to be said. "What happens if you meet someone else?"

He lifted his brown eyes slowly, until his gaze settled firmly on her face—but he didn't say a word.

Josie set down her spoon, suddenly unable to eat. "What happens if you want to marry someone else? Will you ask me for an annulment?"

Alexandre studied her for a moment and then slowly rose from his chair. He stepped over to her and took her hand in his, gently pulling her to her feet.

She looked up at him, her knees trembling.

Alexandre put his hands on either side of her face and placed his lips on hers. The kiss was tender, yet bold, and it took her breath away.

When he pulled back, his eyes were as serious as she'd ever seen them. "I want you to know, Josette Dugas, that as long as my body draws breath, I will never love another woman the way I love you. Even if I cannot be with you, I will honor our marriage vows every day of my life."

Josie couldn't move as she stared back at him. No one had ever looked at her the way he looked at her now.

He pulled her into an embrace and whispered into her ear, "Come with me, ma chérie. Let me love you the way I was born to love you."

She clung to him. "Oh, Alexandre—if it were only that simple."

"What is simpler than a man loving a woman?"

"But my father's legacy. . ."

She could hear the frustration in his voice. "And what of your mother's legacy?" He took a deep breath and pulled back, his eyes no longer frustrated, but probing into the recesses of her soul. "And what of our legacy, Josette?"

Josie clutched the back of his coat, never wanting to let go. But then she thought of Stephen and Celeste, and how they would destroy everything if she left.

She couldn't let them win. Josie finally had the control she'd always wanted. It might mean she would have to sacrifice her own happiness to protect her father's business—but she was the only one willing to do it.

She stepped away from Alexandre, putting space between them. She held on to the back of her chair and couldn't look him in the eyes. "I'm sorry. I can't give up on my father.

He was a miserable man, and the only thing that brought him happiness was his business. If I hand that over to Celeste, it will be the final nail in his coffin."

Alexandre took several deep breaths before he spoke. "Then I will not ask you again. I'll leave the house in the morning—but please don't see me off. I don't think I'll have the power to say good-bye."

And with that, Alexandre left Josie alone in the dining room.

Chapter 15

Josie sat behind her father's massive oak desk and stared absently out the window overlooking the bustling docks along the Mississippi. Her forefinger traced the edge of a stack of invoices, while her mind traced the memories from the past couple of months. Always, she returned to the image of Alexandre, preaching from the pulpit on the *Northern Star*.

It had been three weeks since Alexandre had left, and Josie had done nothing but work. She had mistakenly thought she could bury herself in her work to forget about him, but she soon realized there was nothing that could distract her from the aching void left in his wake.

Her father's business was running smoothly, though she left most of the daily interactions in the hands of her general manager, Mr. Thompkins. She stayed in the office for hours on end, telling herself she was exactly where she had wanted to be.

A knock at the door startled Josie from her reverie. "Come in."

"I never thought you'd actually do it."

Josie stared at the blond-haired lady who poked her head into the office.

"Ruth!" Josie rose from her chair, incredulous. "What are you doing here?"

Ruth entered the office, a grin on her familiar face. "Mr. Ashcroft and I are on our way to the goldfields in California."

"The goldfields?"

"We're going to take our chances out west. Since we're in St. Louis for a few days gathering supplies, I thought I'd say hello."

Josie came around her desk and embraced her old friend. "I'm so glad you did."

Ruth hugged her back but pulled away to frown at Josie. "What are you doing in St. Louis?"

"What do you mean? You knew I was going to manage my father's business."

"I didn't think you'd actually go through with your plans after marrying Mr. Dugas. Why didn't you go back to Belle Prairie with him?" Ruth took a seat and set her reticule in her lap. "Mr. Ashcroft and I crossed his path the day he arrived in Little Falls. I was shocked to see him alone."

"It's actually quite simple." Josie sat and rested her hands on top of the desk, trying to convince herself. "Alexandre was called to preach at Belle Prairie and I was called to manage my father's business."

"But you're still married?" Ruth's brows came together, clearly confused.

"Yes."

"I don't understand. Aren't you concerned about what God thinks?"

God? Josie blinked several times before she spoke. "What about God?"

"Marriage is a sacred trust, between a man, a woman, and God. He intended marriage to bring a couple together, to make them one—not to live separate lives."

Josie was silent as she contemplated Ruth's words.

"Why did you stay here?" Ruth asked quietly.

"To honor my father's legacy."

Ruth tilted a brow. "I mean no disrespect, Miss Josie—but your father is in glory, singing with the angels and dancing with your mama—but Mr. Dugas is still very much here on earth—and he's not singing or dancing with anyone." She leaned forward. "Last time I saw him, I said to Mr. Ashcroft, 'I've never seen a more miserable soul.'"

Alexandre was miserable? Josie's own pain increased at the knowledge. Her father had been miserable because of Celeste. . . . Was Josie now responsible for inflicting misery upon her own husband? How had she not realized?

She looked about the office, her eyes trailing over the things her father had collected as a fur trader. He had been happiest in Minnesota, with her birth mother, and had only come to St. Louis when he thought it a better life for Josie. But it hadn't been a better life—for either of them. Wouldn't Father want her to be with the man she loved, free from Celeste and the life that had brought both of them so much heartache?

Josie's eyes wandered back to Ruth, and it was as if she could see clearly for the first time in her life. "I've wanted so desperately to prevent Celeste from having control, that I sacrificed everything to become a slave to my father's business." She waved her hand around the room. "My father wouldn't want me stuck here in this stuffy office, fighting to keep Celeste away from LeBlanc Shipping. He would be happy knowing I was with the man I loved." She stood, her heart beating rapidly. "Celeste and Stephen may come in here and take over if I'm not here to stop them, but they can no longer hurt my papa. He's long done with this earthly life—but I'm not."

In giving up control of the business, she would be gaining control of her life.

Ruth scooted to the edge of her seat. "What will you do?"

Josie picked up her hat and put it on her head. "I'm going to Belle Prairie, to be with my husband."

Ruth jumped to her feet. "You'll need a companion to travel with."

Josie stuck her hat pin in place and stopped. It would be foolish to travel alone—but who would go with her?

"If you're looking for a maid, my sister Roxanne is looking for a husband. . . ."

Josie laughed and threw her arms around Ruth. "Could she be ready to leave in the morning?"

"I can guarantee it."

"Good! Have her meet me here tomorrow before sunrise."

Ruth squeezed Josie's hand. "I'm happy for you, Miss Josie."

Josie stopped suddenly and felt a deep peace overwhelm her soul. "Ruth, have you ever felt like God was smiling on you?"

Ruth grinned. "I have, indeed—and I think you have, too."

It would be a long week aboard another steamboat, but the reward at the end of the journey would be worth the wait.

Josie was going home to Belle Prairie—and to Alexandre.

Chapter 16

It was good, on days like today, for Alexandre to have a place of his own. It had been a month since he had left Josette, and though he was on the prairie, surrounded by wide-open spaces and windswept grass, he still felt as if he couldn't take a deep breath.

He sat on the front porch, his Bible in hand. It was Friday, which meant he only had two days to finish his sermon. He planned to speak about the prodigal son, but he couldn't take his eyes off the second chapter in Genesis. He read the words aloud, knowing he would find no comfort, but reading them anyway.

"And the Lord God said, It is not good that the man should be alone; I will make him an help meet for him." He stopped, his voice cracking from the weight of his loneliness. "Therefore shall a man leave his father and his mother, and shall cleave unto his wife: and they shall be one flesh."

He closed the Bible and leaned his head back against the rocking chair. He could not stop thinking of Josette. Even in the pulpit, while his mouth spoke the sermon he had prepared, he thought of his wife. At least a dozen times, he had started to compose a letter to her—but he didn't know what to say. He couldn't bring himself to ask her to come to him—and he knew, with every fiber of his being, that he couldn't go back to St. Louis.

Fragrant wildflowers blanketed the August prairie and butterflies flitted about, but the joy of the day was lost to Alexandre. He had tried to keep a happy face for the others living at the mission, but he failed. He'd told them Josette had stayed behind to manage her father's business, and he was sure the Greenfields would ask him to leave, but Mrs. Greenfield only smiled and reassured Alexandre that God didn't make mistakes. Her confidence was something he struggled to feel himself. He needed his own space to put his life back together, so shortly after his arrival he had bought a two-story clapboard house close to the mission and the Mississippi. A clothesline and chicken coop sat in the back and an oak tree sheltered the front, with a picket fence encircling the whole yard.

He often sat on the porch and watched the water flow by. It was the same water that would one day pass St. Louis, and then go on to New Orleans. It was a tangible connection to the people he loved most in the world.

Alexandre set his Bible on the little table next to his rocker and stood. Maybe he would take a walk and clear his mind, so he could prepare his sermon.

He put his hands in his pockets and walked to the riverbank, staring into its murky depths. Summer was at its peak, and the prairie was alive with life. Birds sailed through the air, singing to one another, while ground animals scampered on their quest to put up food for the winter. But all Alexandre could focus on was the prayer he had uttered every day since leaving St. Louis: "God, please ease the pain in my heart, and let Josette fade into a distant memory."

Instead of fading away, his love only grew, until he thought his soul would jump out of his body to seek after Josette.

A rattle on the road startled him out of his melancholy. The stagecoach passed by on Friday afternoons, and Alexandre usually waved at the driver as he sat atop the shiny red vehicle.

But today, the stagecoach didn't drive by. It stopped.

Alexandre turned from the river and strode through the tall grass to the front of his home. Hopefully no one was sick, or injured. Maybe the driver just wanted to chat for a few moments.

A movement in the back of the stagecoach brought Alexandre to a sudden halt. Through the small window he could see two women. The one closest to him was a stranger—but the other looked just like Josette.

His heart raced. Was he imagining? Had his grief taken him too far?

The driver jumped down and shouted howdy before opening the stagecoach door.

Alexandre held his breath as one of the women stepped to the opening.

She wore a beautiful blue traveling gown with a matching hat, and when she lifted her face, she offered Alexandre the biggest smile he'd ever seen.

"Josette." He said her name like an answer to prayer. He raced to the stagecoach and lifted her off the step, hugging her in a massive embrace.

She threw her arms around his neck and kissed his face, over and over, until she was giggling and breathless. "Alexandre."

Her laughter was like a balm to his weary soul. "Why are you here?"

She smiled, tears glistening in her beautiful brown eyes. "Because you're here."

He wanted to believe what he was hearing—but he had to be sure. "Ma chérie, are you here to stay?"

She smiled and then leaned down and whispered into his ear. "If you'll have me, I'm here forever."

Alexandre didn't care if he had an audience—he wanted to kiss his wife.

And that's exactly what he did.

Gabrielle Meyer lives in central Minnesota on the banks of the Mississippi River with her husband and four young children. As an employee of the Minnesota Historical Society, she fell in love with the rich history of her state and enjoys writing fictional stories inspired by real people and events. Gabrielle can be found at www.gabrielle-meyer.com where she writes about her passion for history, Minnesota, and her faith.

WEDDED TO HONOR
Jennifer Uhlarik

Dedication

To Colleen S., Ginny H., Joy M., Michele M., Ruth R., Sarah H.,
and Shannon M.—thank you all for the prayer support, encouraging words,
critiques, and reminders of God's faithfulness through the process
of writing this story. I could not have done this one without you.
And to my husband, who has graciously put up with frozen meals, takeout,
and a wife who has been MIA for a month while I finished up the story.
You are a blessing!

Chapter 1

S oft hands. Far smoother than *her* calloused palms. With hands like those, the man couldn't have worked a single day in his life.

Honor Cahill squeezed her eyes shut. *Stop it. You asked for this.*

If she'd had more time, perhaps someone better would have replied. Someone more suited. She shook her head. This Eastern-bred dandy was the only one to answer her *Matrimonial News* ad, and she had no time to waste. This all had to be accomplished *today*.

She stared up at the stranger before her. His brown eyes narrowed in response, his thick dark hair falling in soft waves across his forehead. At least he was handsome.

Honor adjusted her grip on his sweaty palms. The preacher's voice droned on like the buzzing of a bee until, finally, it landed.

"I now pronounce you husband and wife. You may kiss the bride."

A vise cinched tight around her chest. She was someone's wife. And her husband was nothing more than a stranger in a fine suit.

An uncomfortable stillness swelled as Ashton Rutherford leaned in. Honor drew back, and the preacher arched a brow. Her stomach knotted. Oh, botheration. She inhaled deeply and, heart pounding, pecked him on the lips. When she pulled away, he lingered there for an instant then straightened, an amused grin painting his mouth. The preacher and witnesses—all strangers—stared.

Her new husband chuckled. "My bride must have a few wedding day jitters, Reverend. I'm sure she'll kiss me more soundly in private. Won't you, sweetness?"

Heat leaped to her cheeks. How dare he—

A perplexed smile flickered across the man of God's face. "Um, congratulations, Mr. and Mrs. Rutherford."

Mrs. Rutherford. The weight of the name descended like a shroud. She'd never dreamed she'd marry. Her. . .backward Honor Cahill. And it had all happened so suddenly. Surely, there had to be another way to save her beloved ranch.

Honor huffed. No sense kidding herself. There was no other way. She tugged at her dress, smothered by petticoats and corset. A lump swelled her throat.

The deed was done. No turning back.

Her new husband shook the preacher's hand, and after signing the marriage certificate, they excused themselves. His hand at the small of her back, he guided her toward the church door and out into the late-morning sun. Honor shielded her eyes.

"So, sweetness, where are we off to now?"

"My name is Honor Cahill. I expect to be called that."

"Rutherford." He smiled.

Honor stilled. "I beg your pardon?"

"Your name is Honor *Rutherford*, sweetness." The cleft in his chin deepened.

"Call me that again," she dared.

His brows shot up. "Call you what? Rutherford or sweetness?" Oh, but he and that stupid cleft in his chin were mocking her.

Honor drove the heel of her boot onto his instep, and he howled.

"Call me sweetness again, and I'm liable to shoot you." She strode to her wagon and climbed aboard. "Now get your sorry hide over here, or find your own way to Rancho Regalo de Esperanza."

His young bride knew her mind and wasn't afraid to speak it. A far different kind of woman than he was used to.

Ash hobbled to the side of the wagon. At least they'd had the foresight to load his trunks before the impromptu ceremony. That chore would've been more difficult with his recently acquired limp. Now they could get on to Rancho whatever-she-called-it and figure out what to do next. After one brief stop.

He clambered up beside her, reaching for the reins. His new bride turned a heated blue-eyed gaze his way, and he stilled, hands in mid-reach. "You don't want me to drive?"

Annoyance flitted across her pretty features. "Do you know where you're going?"

"No, but you could direct me." Sweetness.

She snorted. "I'll drive, thank you very much."

"Then by all means, Mrs. Rutherford. Proceed." He grinned at her clenched teeth. "Although I have one brief errand to run before leaving town."

"You couldn't have run your errands on Saturday? It's several hours' drive to Santa Rosa, where we have a four o'clock appointment."

Ah, yes. The reading of her father's will. She'd mentioned it moments after they met the previous day. Given his recently awarded law degree, it would be interesting to see the workings of the California court system, especially since Santa Rosa was the county seat. "I'd like to stop by the telegraph office and send the news of our nuptials to my parents. Not something I could have done previously."

His bride's face softened, and her cheeks paled. "You have family?"

Ash nodded. "Mother, Father, and three sisters—one older and two younger."

"Oh." She turned the wagon toward the heart of town. "How do you expect this news to be received?"

"Not well." Ash chuckled. "Father will be livid, and Mother, wounded."

"Why would you agree to marry me if it would hurt your family?"

"I'm tired of having every detail of my life planned for me." Ash was his parents' only son, and his father had taken great liberty in dictating his friends, courses of study, and career path. Despite Ash's protests, he'd been groomed to become just like Father. He wanted to make his own way in the world, and that didn't include returning to Philadelphia.

He eyed his bride, a smile playing about his lips. Her *Matrimonial News* ad had said she was "a woman of some means." She was handsome enough, with delicate features and mounds of light brown curls arranged atop her head. Her only flaw was her

sun-kissed complexion, though the color looked fetching on her.

"What?" She shot him a sidelong glance. "Have I got dirt smeared on my face or something?"

Ash couldn't help but laugh. "No."

"Then quit gawking at me like I wallowed in pig slop. You're making me uncomfortable."

Wallowed in pig slop? He faced front again, chuckling. Yes, she had spunk. The very opposite of every woman Father had paraded before him in Philadelphia. Each was from a wealthy family, hand-selected for her father's status or wealth, and each had carried herself with perfect comportment, just like Mother. Any one of them would have made a proper wife, but he'd seen the cold, loveless marriage his parents shared—and the sterile, businesslike union his eldest sister shared with her husband. If he was to be relegated to such a union, he wanted the selection of a bride to be *his* choice. By marrying the spirited Honor Cahill, he'd assured it was.

Certainly, he could have chosen not to return to Philadelphia without marrying Honor, but Father would spare no expense in finding him and persuading him to return. By marrying her, Ash provided himself an unequivocal reason to remain out west. His bride's home was here, and she had no desire to leave.

She turned down another street and stopped in front of the building on the far end of the little road. "There's the telegraph office."

"Thank you." He climbed down. "This shouldn't take long."

Ash stashed the marriage certificate beside the edition of the *Matrimonial News* containing her ad, as well as their brief letters, in the nearest trunk, then stepped into the dismal little building. The telegrapher offered a dull greeting as Ash retrieved paper and pencil and wrote out his brief message.

> *Not returning to Philadelphia. Married a woman of some means.*
> *Residing near Santa Rosa.*
> *A.W.R.III*

As the telegrapher took the message, Ash gripped the wood counter. There was no doubt that Ashton Wendell Rutherford Junior would become furious at the abrupt message. Ash was prepared to deal with the consequences, as well as the guilt his mother would serve him. What gnawed at him was the thought of his beloved younger sisters, Lucy and Eliza, finding out that he had broken his promise to return home soon.

Chapter 2

Santa Rosa, California
That Afternoon

J udges don't like to be kept waiting." Her groom snapped the cover of his pocket watch closed and looked at her. "Shouldn't we go inside?"

"Where's the marriage certificate?" Honor peered around his trunks and stopped short when she caught sight of the family Bible she'd brought from home. Nausea threatened to overtake her as she gripped the side of the wagon box. She'd toted the precious tome all the way to Petaluma in order to record their names on the marriage page after the wedding, but the thought of doing so set her to trembling.

"It's in here." Ash tapped a trunk lid.

She opened the lid and snatched the folded document as if it were a lifeline.

"Slow down there. Why do you need the certificate?" Ash caught her trembling hands in his steady ones. His brown eyes brimmed with compassion.

Honor gulped. "It's. . .very important. We should take it with us for safekeeping."

He shook his head. "What has you so scared?"

Honor squared her shoulders and pulled her hands from his grasp. "I'm most certainly *not* scared." Terrified more like, but she wasn't about to say that to him. She tugged at her restrictive bodice for the hundredth time and stared at the courthouse. "It's just that the reading of Papa's will is so. . ."

"Final."

Her breath hitched and her throat knotted. She clamped her eyes shut.

Ash drew her into his arms. Despite her better judgment, she couldn't resist. The warm embrace soothed something deep within her.

"I'm sorry. This must be very hard for you."

At his gentle words, she pulled away and gulped down her emotion. Confusion clouded his expression.

Pull yourself together, Honor.

Again, she tugged at her restrictive clothing. If only she could have worn her trousers and shirt, rather than the confining dress and underthings. She swallowed down the threatening tears. "I'm ready."

"Are you sure?"

She nodded. As ready as she could be.

Ash tucked the marriage certificate into his coat pocket and offered her his arm. "I know we're all but strangers, but would you allow me the pleasure?"

Honor's smile wobbled as she slipped an awkward hand into the crook of her groom's

elbow. They crossed the street and marched through the doors of the large courthouse. Now just to find the right courtroom. . .

Few people were in the stuffy hallway, but at one end of the corridor, two boys stood guard outside the courtroom. Levi and Sam Donovan. When they caught sight of her, Levi beckoned. Both boys disappeared inside. Surely they had been stationed there by their father when she hadn't arrived on time. Honor stopped and pulled free, heart hammering. Had they noticed her hanging on a stranger?

Ash stalled mid-step. "What's wrong?"

Beyond that door, her lifelong friends waited, and in moments they'd know she'd secretly married. "For now, please. . ."

At her hesitation, his eyebrows arched. "Please *what*?"

Don't let on that we got hitched.

"Nothing. It's not important." Silly, actually. Honor swung the door open.

With his hand at the small of her back, Ash ushered her into the room. Judge Sutton eyed them from his bench. On the right side of the courtroom, her half brother Nate sat alone. On the left, Teagan and Ellie Donovan, along with their four children, filled the second row. All eyes focused on her then shifted to Ash, half a step behind. She made eye contact with no one.

"Nice of you to join us, Miss Cahill." The judge's stern tone sent a shiver through her. She'd always found the man unsettling, the little she'd seen of him. Now, he was downright off-putting.

She stepped into the front row and Ash slid in beside her. She remained standing. "Please forgive me, sir. I had important business in Petaluma and only just returned."

"Your father made the unusual request that I sit in on the reading of his will. Was your business so important that it required delaying my last case for the day?"

She fidgeted. "It had to do with the reading, Your Honor."

"Oh? How did business in Petaluma relate to the reading of a will in Santa Rosa?"

"This is Ashton Rutherford." Honor fidgeted with the folds of her dress. "He's a lawyer. I went to Petaluma to meet with him." *Please don't ask more. Not yet. . .*

Judge Sutton shifted his attention to Ash. "Is that correct, Mr. Rutherford? You're Miss Cahill's attorney?"

Please, don't say too much. . . .

"I suppose that is correct, Your Honor." Ash gave a genteel nod. "And please accept my sincere apologies for our tardiness as well."

"You suppose. . ." The judge huffed. "Fine. Let's get this done." Honor and Ash sat. "We are here today for the reading of Orrin Cahill's last will and testament. Is the executor present?"

Behind them, wood creaked. Her father's longtime friend, Teagan Donovan, rested a hand on her shoulder as he stood. The simple gesture warmed her.

Teagan cleared his throat. "I am, sir."

"Are all the parties now present?"

"Yes, sir." Teagan gave Honor's shoulder a little squeeze.

"You have the will?" When Teagan held up an envelope, Judge Sutton beckoned. "Bring it to me, please."

Teagan walked the envelope up to the judge, who broke the seal and looked the contents over. Nate shot a cold glare her way. She faced front and avoided Ash's gaze.

After a long moment, the judge handed the papers back to Teagan. "All appears in order. You may read the document."

Teagan cleared his throat and caught Honor's eye before beginning. "I, Orrin Augustus Cahill, do solemnly swear that the following words shall serve as my last will and testament, dated November 14, 1874."

Honor's heart lurched, and she closed her eyes. Papa wasn't coming back, and life wouldn't ever be the same. She had only vague recollections of her mother, who died before Honor turned four. Papa had been the central figure in her world ever since. How would she carry on?

A warm hand covered hers. Startled, she looked at Ash, who twitched a smile at her and winked. Bother! Ellie and Julia were seated on the row behind. What would they think, her holding a man's hand?

"I have had difficulty in trying to fairly divide my property between my two children, as I love them both equally. It is my desire for Rancho Regalo de Esperanza to stay in my family line for generations to come, but as of this writing, my son, Nathaniel Acacio Cahill, born February 16, 1843, has proven a poor manager of the twenty-five-hundred acres I gifted him in 1864. I fear that giving him more would end in the same result."

From Nate's direction, a loud huff broke the stillness. Honor bit her bottom lip. Papa had tried for years to get her half brother to take proper care of his ranch. He'd offered Nate his help, instruction, and even money, but Nate had been determined to live life by his own terms and had distanced himself from Papa even more.

Teagan continued reading. "On the other hand, my daughter, Honor Katherine Cahill, born September 1, 1854, is a capable rancher and has been invaluable in running Rancho Regalo de Esperanza these past years. However, I fear that inheriting the remaining fifty-five hundred acres will be too much for her to handle on her own."

The words cut Honor to the quick, just as they had months ago. She didn't need help to run the ranch. She could do it with her eyes closed. But Papa had spoken, and she would abide by his wishes. Thank God, she'd found the copy of his will before he filed it away out of sight. Otherwise, her beloved ranch, the only home she'd ever known, might have been lost to her forever.

"After much deliberation, I choose to give the remainder of my land to Honor, under the condition that she is married upon the reading of this will."

Ash squeezed her hand and shot her a glance. She wiggled free of his grasp and avoided his eyes. She'd done what Papa asked. She'd married before the will's reading. So why did she feel like she'd done such wrong? Was God pleased with her honoring her father's wishes, or angry she'd married a stranger?

"If Honor is unmarried, my executor, Teagan Donovan, should sell the land and cattle within sixty days at a fair value determined by the court. Proceeds from the sale of the land should be used to pay my debts, of which there are few, and the remaining monies should be split evenly between Nathaniel and Honor. The contents of my home should go to Honor, as well as my saddle horses. If a suitable buyer cannot be found within sixty days, only then may Nathaniel purchase all or part of the land at half the court's assigned value. Should he choose to do so, the proceeds of the sale should go to Honor. Signed, Orrin Augustus Cahill on this day, November 14, 1874."

As Teagan finished reading, silence enveloped the courtroom. Across the aisle, Nate

scowled and shook his head.

Judge Sutton cleared his throat. "Since Miss Cahill is unmarried, I will assess a fair price for the sale of—"

"Excuse me, Your Honor. . ." Heart pounding, Honor snatched the certificate from her husband's pocket and shot to her feet.

The judge scowled. "What is it?"

"I *am* married, sir."

Honor's brother bolted up. "Liar! You ain't married!"

Behind them, surprised murmurs filled the air.

Ash stared up at his pretty bride, his thoughts reeling. No wonder she'd seemed full of trepidation. Honor had married him without telling a soul—at least in this room. He'd known her desire to marry had to do with keeping her ranch, but he hadn't realized their union was such a secret until that moment.

She was bold. The young woman had a determination like no woman he'd met before, but a question suddenly lodged in his mind. Once the ranch was legally hers, would she remain his wife or seek to annul their marriage? Hopefully not the latter. He hadn't married her just to end their union a matter of weeks later.

"Come to order." The judge banged his gavel once.

The room dulled to stunned silence.

"Based on the reaction in my courtroom, I take it this is recent news." The judge leaned forward. "Explain yourself, Miss Cahill."

She reached for Ash's hand and tugged him to his feet. His face flushed at the judge's glowering expression. Not a good idea to anger judges. . .though he'd answered the man's question honestly. As her husband, he *would* act as her counsel.

"I have a signed certificate that says I am Mrs. Ashton Rutherford, if you'd care to see it."

The judge's scowl deepened, and he beckoned her forward. "Bring it to me."

Ash stepped into the aisle, feeling the weight of everyone's gazes. He pinned his focus on his bride as she slipped out and turned toward the judge's bench. The man's jaw muscle popped as he spread the document out and read, then refolded the paper.

"Sit." The judge handed Honor the certificate then looked Mr. Donovan's way. "May I see the will, please?"

Ash slid back into the row, and Honor retook the seat beside him. Nathaniel glared their way, throwing enough heat to melt the ice from a Pennsylvania winter.

The judge folded the will and cleared his throat. "It appears Miss Cahill and Mister Rutherford married this morning in Petaluma. The will stipulates that Miss Cahill be married before the will's reading, which she was, so Rancho Regalo de Esperanza is legally hers. As with any will, the parties involved may contest the decision when this court reconvenes on the first Monday of the next month. We're adjourned." He banged his gavel and rose.

Honor grabbed Ash's hand and dragged him into the aisle, speeding past everyone and ignoring the calls from the family who'd sat behind them. They were nearly to the door when her brother caught up, grabbed her arm, and jerked her to face him.

Heat washed through Ash, instincts on alert. "Unhand my bride." He forced his way

in front of Honor, stepping toward Nathaniel to create distance between brother and sister.

Though Nathaniel had no choice but to release her, he drew himself up and stood nose to nose with Ash.

"Nate!" Donovan's sharp voice rang out.

Honor pulled at Ash's forearm. "Ash, please. Don't give him a thought."

Ash and Nate exchanged glares. *Don't give him a thought?* The man had just threatened his wife.

Nate cursed. "This won't work. Rancho Regalo de Esperanza is rightfully mine, and I will have it."

Chapter 3

Still gripping Ash's forearm, Honor stared at his back. How quickly he'd stepped in to defend her, and against *Nate*. No man, save Papa and Teagan, had done that before.

"That's enough, Nate." Teagan's voice rose as he stormed down the aisle. "You heard your father's wishes. The ranch is *not* rightfully yours. It's time you leave."

Nate's cold-eyed glare chilled Honor to her core. Growing up, she'd borne the brunt of his meanness and knew what he was capable of. Teagan, though, seemed unaffected. Her half brother scowled in Teagan's direction before he shifted a fierce gaze her way. "This isn't over." He stomped out of the courtroom.

Teagan looked at her then at Ash. "Are either of you hurt?"

"No." They spoke in unison.

Honor avoided Teagan's eyes. She hadn't wanted to face him and Ellie yet. Silly of her to think they'd be able to escape the courtroom without speaking to them. Even if they had, Ellie and Teagan would have simply followed them home.

Teagan offered Ash a reserved smile. "The name's Teagan Donovan." He waved for the rest of the family to join him. "This is my wife, Ellie, and our children, Julia, Ben, Levi, and Sam. We're longtime friends of the Cahill family." He thrust a hand toward Ash. "And you are. . .?"

"Ashton Rutherford the Third, sir, though I prefer to be called Ash." Her groom's Adam's apple bobbed as he shook the man's hand and nodded to the rest.

"A pleasure." Teagan turned to his children. "Julia, boys. . .wait for us at the wagon, please. Your mother and I will be along directly."

"Yes, sir." As the boys slipped out the door, Julia gave Honor a lingering hug. "Are you all right?"

Honor answered her best friend's question with a nod.

Ellie Donovan stepped closer. "Do as your father asked, Julia."

The beautiful blond pulled away and slipped out the door.

Teagan's gaze sharpened. "You want to tell us what's going on here?"

Honor's jaw went slack. "You just read what's going on here. Papa's will said I had to be married in order to keep my home."

"I'm confused, darlin'. Orrin had Ellie and me act as witnesses to his will, but he didn't let us read it. How'd you know what was in there?"

She hung her head. "I didn't mean to, but I found a copy one day last year. I went into Papa's office to fetch paper and ink, and his will was there. He must've just been writing it. I didn't know what it was at first, so I read a few lines. Then I couldn't stop."

Ellie and Teagan exchanged silent glances. She rubbed her lips together. *God, please, don't let 'em be angry.*

"So tell us," Ellie said, "how, or where, did you two meet?"

Honor looked at Ash then closed her eyes. "I placed an ad in the *Matrimonial News*. . . ." In all her days, she never thought she'd *advertise* for a husband. No man in his right mind would look twice at a backward girl like her. Were it not for Papa's stipulation, she would not have married now—and probably never would.

"Oh, child." Ellie pulled her into an embrace. "Honey, Teagan and I could have told you there are far worse things than losing your home. We'd never allow you to be without a roof over your head."

"But don't I deserve something? I've worked that ranch since I was barely big enough to sit a saddle." She clung to Ellie, her eyes burning. It was the only life she'd known, and the only life she wanted.

"Of course you do. I can only guess why your papa wrote his will the way he did." Ellie twisted toward her husband.

"Darlin'," Teagan said, "your papa was my best friend, but he was a fiercely private man. He didn't share his thoughts on this matter, and out of respect, I didn't ask."

No, Papa wouldn't have shared such details with anyone.

"Well, son?" Teagan shoved his hat to the back of his head. "Tell us about yourself."

Ash cleared his throat. "My family lives in Philadelphia, where my father has a law practice. I recently graduated from Harvard after studying law."

"And what brings you to California?"

Honor pulled out of Ellie's grasp. "The trip was a gift from his parents to celebrate his graduation."

Ash nodded. "Honor's correct. I was to stay a couple of months, though I'll be extending my stay indefinitely now."

Teagan's eyes narrowed. "And what are your intentions toward this young lady?"

"I assure you, Mr. Donovan, they're nothing but honorable."

A stranger stepped into the courtroom and shooed them out. Ash smiled inwardly. At least the questions would end.

Mr. Donovan turned to his wife. "Ell, why don't you take Honor to see Julia for a minute. Ashton Rutherford the Third and I have a few things to discuss."

Ash's nerves jittered. Honor shrugged almost imperceptibly as Mrs. Donovan ushered her into the hallway beyond.

Heart pounding, he trailed after Mr. Donovan. They crossed the street to the large grassy square, Honor and Mrs. Donovan turning toward a parked wagon where the Donovan children waited.

Mr. Donovan stopped and, for several uncomfortable seconds, sized Ash up. "I don't mean this to be insulting, but what do you know about running a ranch?"

Ash searched for his voice. "Not a thing in the world. . .sir."

"Then what are you doing? What are you getting out of this?" Mr. Donovan pointed a finger at him. "And before you answer that, keep in mind that Honor Cahill is like a daughter to me."

Honor Rutherford. He bit his tongue to keep from correcting the man. "May I speak plainly, Mr. Donovan?"

"Is there another way?"

Ash chuckled but sobered quickly. "Sir, my father is a controlling man. All my life, he's dismissed my dreams in order to mold me into his vision of the perfect son. Life with him is stifling. He forced me to attend Harvard and study law. It didn't matter to him that I hated it. From the time I was a baby, he has had my whole life planned out—from what I would study to where I would work. Even what type of woman I should marry." He shrugged. "The longer I've been away, the more I've realized I want to find my own way."

Teagan Donovan folded his arms. "I can respect a man wanting to make his own way, except *your own way* involves a young lady who my family and I care for. If I were a sharp-tempered man, you'd be staring at the business end of my scattergun about now." He speared Ash with a glare. "If you hurt her, you're likely to get me and that scattergun riled. Understand?"

Cold sweat broke out across Ash's skin. Mute, he nodded.

"I'm glad we're clear." Mr. Donovan scanned the street. "You'll need to keep your eyes open for Nate. Right now, he's in the alley across from your wagon. If you want, my family and I can follow you home to be sure he won't try anything along the way."

Every fiber in him wanted to look. Instead, he stared at Mr. Donovan. "Do you actually think he'd try to harm us?"

The man chuckled. "This isn't Philadelphia, son. One thing's for certain. Nate's an ornery cuss, and losing that ranch has him plenty riled."

Ash's heart stuttered. No, this wasn't Philadelphia. The people here were rough and brash. This would take some getting used to. "I would appreciate the escort, sir."

"Done." Mr. Donovan motioned, and Honor hugged Julia, as well as Mrs. Donovan, waved to the three boys, then traipsed toward them.

Ash held out his hand. "Thank you, sir."

A wry smile crossed Mr. Donovan's face as they shook hands. "Best of luck. Ellie and I'll be checking in on you two now and then."

Honor joined them as Ash gave a sober nod.

"Wait until we pull around."

Ash nodded. "Yes, sir."

They parted company, Ash offering Honor his arm.

Honor hesitated. "Why are we waiting?"

"Your brother is watching us, and Mr. Donovan offered to follow so he wouldn't attempt anything."

"*Half* brother. And that's probably wise. There are lonely stretches of road between here and home."

Ash scanned the street. In a waning patch of sunlight, Nate sat on his horse across the way, arms resting on his saddle horn as he glared at them. At the wagon, Ash turned and drew Honor to himself. Their bodies close, he brushed her lips. She stiffened, tried to pull back, but he shifted one hand to the nape of her neck, the other to the small of her back, and gently held her. His mouth inches from hers, he looked into her deep blue eyes.

"Relax, sweetness." He brushed her lips a second time. "He's watching. Let him think we're in love."

She remained rigid a moment longer. When he sought her lips a third time, she closed her eyes and responded, kissing him in return for half a breath before she tucked her chin and tried to draw away. Pulse racing, Ash angled his head and followed her mouth. Her lips were soft and yielding, her body a perfect fit in his arms.

His bride.

At the rumble of an approaching wagon, she broke the kiss but lingered, head bowed against his shoulder. Ash breathed in the scent of her. Perhaps this wouldn't be a cold marriage after all. . . .

Teagan Donovan's wagon stopped as she shifted a red-hot gaze to meet his. "This"—she stomped his foot, and he grunted, balancing on the other—"is for presuming to kiss me. And I already told you what would happen if you keep calling me sweetness."

She wiped her mouth on her dress sleeve then scrambled onto the wagon bench and sat, spine rigid and jaw set.

Foot throbbing again, Ash struggled onto the wagon bench beside her. "I thought only to convince Nate that our marriage is one based on love."

"I don't care what Nate thinks. Papa's will states only that I must be married. It doesn't say anything about love."

Chapter 4

The sun-dappled meadow was Honor's favorite spot on the ranch, her thinking place. Water gurgled in the small creek, and tall trees lined its bank, offering cool shade without completely blocking the sun. She and Papa had often shared noon meals together in this serene corner of the ranch, and she came here by herself to reflect.

Was she ever in need of quiet reflection lately.

She dismounted beside the little brook and shucked her boots and socks. A couple of quick turns of her trouser legs, and she set off along the bank. The lush grass was cool underfoot. She dipped a toe in the tepid water.

Three weeks had passed since she and Ash had married, three weeks since she'd gained possession of Rancho Regalo de Esperanza. Except for that ridiculous kiss in Santa Rosa, Ash had been a perfect gentleman. He'd attempted nothing further, though she sensed he hoped for more than separate bedrooms in the rambling ranch house. She owed the man for helping her keep her beloved ranch, but she wasn't yet ready to cross that line.

It wasn't that she didn't like him. Ash was kind. Good-hearted. The way he'd stepped in to protect her from Nate in the courtroom still warmed her heart. But ranch work was as foreign to him as living a pampered life back East would be to her. At least he'd attempted the tasks she'd asked him to do.

Add to that Ash's seeming frustration with her favorite choice in clothing—men's trousers and Papa's large shirts. She could tell he didn't approve, though in her estimation, women's clothing was completely impractical for ranch work. Papa had understood and dressed her accordingly when she was a little girl. If Ash didn't care for it, *he* should attempt to ride horseback, herd cattle, or deliver a calf in a dress, petticoats, and corset.

The image of her husband in such a getup brought a giggle to her lips, and it blossomed into a full belly laugh. She kicked the water, the fat drops catching the sunlight as they arced through the air.

Honor sighed. As unknowledgeable as Ash might be about ranch work, they *had* managed to find a little common ground. They shared a love of books, of which Ash had many. During their first week, he'd seen Papa's checkerboard in the corner and challenged her to a game. She'd beaten him soundly. Then he'd introduced her to chess. He'd proven himself clear and patient in teaching her the game's intricacies.

She meandered along the bank, ending up under a big oak. There in the shade, the grass had grown thin, and the chuckling water lapped at the bare earth to create a little eddy that formed a mud puddle. *This* was why she liked coming here. When she was a child, Papa had promised that sticking her toes in the mud could fix nearly

any problem—and back then, it pretty much had. Something about it loosened all her bound-up thoughts, and after a while everything seemed better.

She stepped into the puddle and spread her bare toes. Could it work this time? As the goo squished between them, her chest ached.

Papa. I miss you. The ranch just isn't the same without you here.

She lifted her father's shirt to her nose and tried to catch a hint of his scent. It was gone.

Forever.

Ash pushed the wheelbarrow full of soiled straw behind the barn, dumped the contents, and paused to wipe away the sweat beading across his forehead.

He was under no illusions. Honor and her hired men had given him the menial tasks, those requiring the least skill or know-how, like mucking stalls. If he was honest with himself, it was probably a good thing. At least for now.

In the weeks since they'd married, Honor had taken him out riding several times to become familiar with the sizeable ranch. Being unaccustomed to the long hours of riding and physical nature of ranch work, his muscles quickly grew sore. He had not complained, though if he read her correctly, Honor had become impatient, more with his lack of knowledge than his obvious discomfort. She'd tried to hide her aggravation, but it hadn't escaped his notice.

He rolled the wheelbarrow to the front of the barn and stopped short at the sight of a large gray horse. The saddled mount stood in the middle of the yard, no rider in sight. He left the barrow by the barn door and walked into the yard. "Hello?"

A man stepped away from the front door of the house. Warnings clanged in Ash's brain.

Nate.

"What do you want?" The words flew out of Ash's mouth unchecked.

"That's no way to be neighborly."

"After the threats you made at the courthouse, I've no confidence that *you* will be neighborly. Please leave."

Nate stepped down from the porch and shrugged. "Just figured to come by and visit my sister and her new husband, but if you want me to go, I'll go."

He crossed to the big gray horse and swung into the saddle then reached back and pulled a burlap sack from one of his saddlebags. "By the way, I brought a gift for the happy couple." He flung the sack across the distance. It hit the ground with a solid thump, only inches from Ash's foot. Nate spurred his horse and rode away.

From the mouth of the sack, a triangular head emerged, followed by a long slithering body. A warning rattle sounded. Ash's heart and breathing seized.

Seconds ticked by. He stayed frozen as the rattlesnake coiled and adjusted, tail rattling. The thin black tongue flicked over and over until the reptile dived for the open space beyond Ash and slithered into the lush grass.

Ash watched it until it was out of sight, then wobbled toward the front porch. With a huff, he sank into the nearby chair, heart racing and limbs trembling. It took a couple of moments before his mind engaged in logical thought once more.

Nate had some nerve. If he'd be so bold as to openly try to harm Ash, what things

had he done to Honor, and what might he yet try? Thank goodness, she wasn't there when the rogue threw that bag at him. Ash wouldn't be quick to forgive if his *half* brother-in-law endangered his wife.

The rumble of wagon wheels drew his attention, and Ash looked up to see the Donovans approaching.

Mr. Donovan drew the team to a halt in front of him. "Morning. Thought we'd stop by since we didn't see you at church today."

Sunday again, already? Somewhere in the past three weeks, he'd lost track of the days. Ash rubbed at the ache developing behind his eyes. He and Honor had yet to make a church service in the weeks since they'd married, and now they'd have to wait another. He shuffled to his feet, knees still soft like warm butter, and stepped off the porch. "Good morning."

Mr. Donovan glanced around the ranch yard. "Where's that bride of yours?"

"She rode off up the hill behind the house about an hour ago." He waved in the path's direction. "I stayed behind to work on a few chores."

"Oh, she probably went to the meadow," Julia chimed in.

Ash looked at her. "The meadow?"

"She hasn't taken you to the meadow yet?" The young lady's brows arched.

Ash shook his head slowly. "I don't believe so, no."

"Oh. . .it's, well. . .she's quite partial to that spot. Stay on that path and you'll run right into it."

"Thank you."

Mrs. Donovan grinned at him. "Has she mentioned that her birthday is Wednesday?"

Her birthday. "No, ma'am."

"It's been our tradition to invite Honor and her father, as well as Teagan's brother Cody and his family, and Reverend Pritchard and family over for dinner on her birthday. We don't want to impose, but if you'd like, the offer stands."

"We accept. I look forward to meeting everyone."

"Believe me, folks are anxious to meet the man who claimed Honor's heart."

He hung his head. If only it were true. . . .

Mr. Donovan set the wagon's brake and turned to his wife. "I'll be back in a moment." The man swung down and motioned for Ash to follow. He was silent until they reached the barn.

"You all right, son? You're lookin' a little peaked."

Better that his bride's friend didn't think him weak or ill-equipped for the life he'd chosen with Honor. Ash smiled. "I'm fine, thank you for asking."

Mr. Donovan turned a wry grin on him. "You want to put all those Eastern pleasantries aside and tell me what's going on? You look pale as a ghost." His voice filled with concern.

Ash chuckled. Mr. Donovan might not have the polish of an Easterner, but he was nobody's fool. "Nate just paid us a call. I asked him to leave, and before he did, he tossed a sack containing a live rattlesnake at my feet. He said it was a wedding gift."

Mr. Donovan's expression turned grim. "Didn't get bit, did you?"

Ash shook his head. "It certainly made my heart pound, though." He shrugged. "I'm just glad Honor wasn't here when it happened."

"Agreed."

Ash folded his arms and leaned against the wall. "Can I ask you something about Honor?"

"Reckon you can."

He stared at the barn floor. "I don't mean to be indelicate, sir, but is there a reason she's so averse to wearing the types of attire befitting a lady?"

A humorless chuckle spilled from Mr. Donovan's lips. "There's something you should understand about your wife, Ashton."

"Sir, I prefer Ash."

"Then call me Teagan." He folded his arms. "Honor's mama died when she was just a little thing. Three, maybe four. Her papa raised her by himself. When she was just a wee thing, her papa would put her in the saddle in front of him while he was working. As she got older, she'd go to school during the day then rush home to work alongside her papa and the vaqueros until sundown. Every year, Ellie made her two dresses for school and church. The rest of the time, she wore Nate's hand-me-downs."

Honor had told him that her father raised her alone, though it hadn't occurred to him just how immersed in ranch life she'd become as a result.

"You need to understand," Teagan continued, "she's been raised in a man's world, doing a man's chores. Her father loved her dearly, but he never paid much mind to the fact that she was a young lady. Don't reckon he knew how to nurture that in her. She may never fit with your high-society friends, but she's got a good heart, and if you pray and you're willing to work at it, I'm betting you'll discover there's a lady hiding deep inside her, wanting to be found."

Chapter 5

At the sound of hoofbeats, Honor turned toward the trail from the ranch house. Her brow furrowed. *Ash?* Not that she was trying to hide, but. . .how had he found her? She swallowed the lump of emotion that often accompanied memories of Papa, then dabbed her eyes to remove any telltale signs of tears.

Ash eased back on the reins and stared, his gaze traveling from her head to her mud-drenched toes. A bemused grin crossed his face. "What on earth are you doing?"

She shrugged. "I come up here to think."

Saddle leather creaked as he dismounted. He approached and looked down at her feet. "You're thinking. . .in mud."

"That'd be about the size of it." She wiggled her toes. "You sound surprised."

"Shouldn't I be?"

"You ever tried it?"

Ash guffawed. "No. Ashton Junior's children were never allowed near mud."

Her jaw went slack. A man who'd never played in mud. . .she'd never heard of such a thing. What had his childhood consisted of, if not getting dirty in work and play? "Come try it. You don't know what you're missing."

Again, he laughed. "I can think just fine without making a mess."

She took a long look at him. His work clothes still bore the creases they came with from the seamstress's shop. While they were a bit dusty, they weren't soiled. Not in the way Papa's clothes—or hers—got when they'd been working hard. Could it be that Ash didn't know how to get dirty? Hard to believe, but sometimes the truth of things took a strange turn.

"C'mon. It's fun."

Her husband shook his head, smiling as if she were daft. "I thought you'd want to know the Donovans came by a bit ago."

"Are they still down there?"

"They went home, but when Julia heard you'd left, she said you had a special place up here." He turned to look around the sprawling meadow. "I can see why. It's quite beautiful."

Yes, it was. . . .

While his back was turned, Honor bent and scooped a small handful of mud and molded it into a ball. "Ash, would you help me a minute? I need to clean up in the creek, but I don't want to slip."

"Of course." He hurried to her and offered his hand.

"Thank you." With a sweet smile, she slid her hand into his and squeezed. Mud oozed between their fingers

Ash's eyes widened, and he yanked away.

Honor held back a chuckle. How would he react? He stared at his dirty hand, and she bit her lip. Was he angry? She'd meant it only in fun. . . . "Ash, I'm sor—"

His brown eyes met hers. A wicked grin sprouted on his lips as he reached over—and smeared the mud across her cheek and down her neck.

She cackled and stretched one mud-laden finger out to fill that annoying cleft in his chin. He twisted away, smearing the mud across his jawline instead. Honor snatched another handful as he ducked and raced several steps out of her reach.

They darted around the meadow, Ash ducking and weaving every time she got close. He sprinted back to the mud, grabbed a handful, and held it as if ready to lob it at her. Honor squealed and darted behind another tree.

Footsteps whispered in the grass. Her back pressed to the trunk, she waited. She attempted to quiet her breathing as the whispering footsteps ceased. She twisted to her left and peeked from behind the tree—not there—then looked right. They were nose to nose. She gasped.

Ash caught her wrist and held up the mud ball with a devilish smile. "Do you yield?"

She matched his grin and smeared muck across his chin. "Never."

Eyes narrowed, he looped his hand around the back of her neck, grinding the sludge into her skin.

His thumb brushed against her cheek, lingering there. Their eyes met and held, and his expression softened. A second passed before he swiped the back of his hand across his mouth, smearing the mud away from his lips. He bent.

Honor's eyes closed, and she held her breath as his lips touched hers softly, sweetly. Her lips parted of their own accord. A stuttering little sigh escaped as he shifted closer. Her arms circled around him. Suddenly dizzy, she twisted her chin down and away as she melted in his arms, her head resting against him.

Ash held her, his hands shifting to her rib cage. "Are you all right?"

She blinked and closed her eyes again.

"Honor?"

"Do that again. . . ." The words were a breathy whisper.

"The last time you dared me to do something again, I got my foot stomped."

Honor smiled. "This wasn't a *dare*. It was a *request*."

A throaty chuckle escaped him, and he pushed away just enough to peer into her eyes. "Are you sure?"

With a shaky smile, Honor nodded.

The timorous look in her astonishingly blue eyes sent Ash's heart into a gallop. He grinned and leaned in. This time, she met him halfway. With her arms still circling his body, Ash drank in the feel of her. Soft. Warm. Perfect.

All woman. His bride.

He settled her back against the tree trunk, and his hands skimmed her sides toward the curve of her hips as he deepened the kiss.

Honor tensed and pushed him away. Eyes huge, she took a big step sideways.

"What's wrong?"

"I. . .I'm not ready for. . ." She straightened her shirt, eyes averted.

"You're not ready to kiss me?" Ash arched a brow. "You just did, and you asked me to do it again."

Even the mud caked from her hairline to shirt collar couldn't hide the flush brightening her face. "I don't mean that part." Her voice dropped to a hushed tone, and she shot him a sheepish gaze. "I kind of liked that."

Well, that was a start.

"Then—?"

"I'm not ready for where that can lead."

Ahh. His shoulders slumped. Just when they were making progress, she put up another wall. "Honor, we've lived under the same roof for several weeks. Have I not been a gentleman thus far?"

She nodded. "You have."

"Why would you think that would change?"

"I'm your *wife*. Was I wrong to assume you'd expect. . ."

Ash closed his eyes, memories of his parents flashing through his mind. "We are husband and wife, and I would be lying if I said I didn't hope for more." He looked at her. "But I won't force you where you're not ready to go. I want both of our hearts to be in it when we cross that line." He wouldn't allow himself to become like his father.

She looked away but let out a breath. "Thank you."

He pulled her into his arms again and settled his cheek against her temple. "What do you say we head home and get cleaned up. Or were you in need of more thinking time in the mud?"

She chuckled. "I've had enough mud for now."

They washed up in the creek, though neither of them got truly clean. After Honor put on her socks and boots, Ash helped her into the saddle and mounted up as well.

"Nate stopped by." Ash made the announcement as Honor led the way down the narrow path toward home.

She looked over her shoulder at him. "Oh?"

"I'd just finished with the stalls and found him on the front porch. He brought us a wedding gift."

Without stopping her horse, she twisted in the saddle to stare at him. "That doesn't sound like Nate."

He locked eyes with her. "It was a live rattlesnake in a flour sack."

She spun her mount to face him. "You weren't hurt, were you?"

"No." *Scared*. But he wasn't ready to admit that to his bride. "I was very glad you weren't around for that episode."

"Nate should be glad I wasn't around. . . . ." Though she mumbled, her words were plenty clear. "I'm glad he didn't hurt you."

"Thank you." He took another good look at her and stifled a chuckle. She was a mess. A truly beautiful one.

Honor headed down the path again, and as they continued in quiet conversation, his thoughts rattled between Nate's visit, their muddy encounter, and their kisses. When the path widened out toward the bottom, he urged his mount forward and came alongside her.

"I had fun with you, Honor Cahill."

An impish sparkle lit her eyes. "That's Honor *Rutherford* to you."

He snorted. "Why, yes it is."

They laughed as they rounded the barn into the yard. Both drew to a halt at the sight of an empty carriage standing near the house.

"Ash!" Familiar squeals split the air as his younger sisters, Eliza and Lucy, bolted from the porch. Behind them, Mother stepped down, her eyes wide. And behind her, stoic and scowling as usual, sat Father.

Chapter 6

Who are these people?" Honor looked at Ash, who'd gone rigid as a fence post.
"My family."

Her stomach flip-flopped. "But I'm not ready for visitors." Least of all
them. Mud coated her shirt and her neck, having dripped between her shoulder blades
and adhered the fabric to her skin. She must look a fright.

Lord, You're punishing me, aren't You? If they'd gone to church that morning, they'd be
arriving home in their Sunday finery to prepare the noon meal. Instead, both she and Ash
were covered in sludge, with their recent fun a distant memory.

"I'm sorry. I should have expected this. I'll handle it." He nudged his horse into
motion.

A shiver raced through her. She urged her horse forward, following Ash. "That was
rude of me. They're your family." But this was *hardly* how she wanted to meet her in-laws.

Her eyes flashed to the flour sack on the ground then to her guests. The two young
ladies, dressed in fancy, bustled traveling dresses, grinned and clapped, though their
excitement waned the nearer she and Ash came. When Ash dismounted, his mother
dragged the girls back by their elbows, as if protecting them from some vile evil.

The man on the porch stepped out of the shadows. His suit, made from fine material
in what looked like the latest style, was just like the one Ash wore on their wedding day.
His posture and expression bespoke disapproval. "Ashton."

The hairs on the back of her neck rose at his clipped tone. She'd addressed ornery
livestock in friendlier ways.

"Father." Ash's mouth twitched into a half smile, pinched and awkward. "Mother.
Eliza, Lucy." His easy grin returned as he looked at the two girls. "Please, forgive us. My
bride and I could both do with hot baths before offering you a proper greeting." Ash
stepped around to her side as she dismounted, then laced his fingers with hers.

"*This* is your wife?" Ash's father's gaze raked her up and down.

Heat flooded her.

"Yes, sir. I'd like you to meet your daughter-in-law, Honor." Ash pulled her forward a
step. "Honor, please meet my father, Ashton Rutherford Junior; my mother, Gwendolyn;
and my sisters Eliza and Lucy."

The girls mustered somewhat genuine smiles. Ash's mother looked as if she might be
ill, and his father's disapproval oozed from every pore.

Her mouth dry, Honor's nerves sizzled with the desire to swing into the saddle and
ride right back to her quiet little meadow. Or anywhere, so long as it wasn't here.

Yet here she was.

"It's a pleasure." How she'd managed to find her voice, she didn't know.

"The pleasure is ours, Honor." The older girl smiled warmly, though her smile faltered when Mr. Rutherford cleared his throat.

"What are you all doing here?" Ash asked.

"After that cryptic message, you left us no choice but to check on you. Now, might we go inside, or will you continue to make us wait in this heat?"

Honor gritted her teeth. Perhaps these were Ash's parents and sisters, but the rudeness—particularly of his father—grated on her nerves.

"And I assume, in a home this size, you'll have rooms enough that we can stay?"

Stay? With only three bedrooms, there weren't rooms enough. . .not as long as she and Ash inhabited separate quarters.

Ash offered a hesitant smile. "I'm sure we can make do."

Honor's face went pale beneath the residue of mud, and she disentangled her fingers from his. Ash reached for her hand, but she slipped away before he could get it back. Without a word, she stomped to the front door. Mother's eyes grew wide, and again she dragged Eliza and Lucy out of the way. Father's eyes followed Honor as she walked. Her back ramrod straight, she turned toward Father, eyes flashing, and bared her teeth. She turned her head one way then another.

Ash watched in horror. Had she gone mad?

Father stiffened, drew back. "What in heaven's name are you doing, young lady?"

She opened her mouth as wide as she could, again turning this way and that.

Ash's stomach churned. *Oh, Lord, help me. . . .*

"That is quite enough!" Father turned toward him. "What is this all about?"

Honor snapped her jaw closed and settled her fists on her hips. "The way you keep looking me over is reminiscent of the way Papa used to size up horse flesh. I just figured to save you the trouble of asking to see my teeth." She whirled to glare at Ash. "Let me know if I pass inspection, will you?"

She disappeared into the house. Fifteen-year-old Lucy tittered behind her hand, but both Ash and their father shot her heated glares.

Father turned on him. "She's simply charming, Ashton. Just what are you trying to prove by marrying someone like her?"

Heat flooded Ash's body, and he gritted his teeth. "I will thank you not to insult my wife. Honor is quite charming when you get to know her. Now if you will excuse me, please make yourselves comfortable on the porch while I check on my bride."

He stormed past them all. Father grabbed for his arm, but Ash cut around him and scooted through the door. Honor stood in the middle of the room.

"I'm sorry. My father was very rude. Are you all right?"

Back to him and posture completely unbending, she shook her head.

"Please, look at me."

Honor turned slowly, her muddy face a sickly shade of white, and held out a burlap sack. "Perhaps you can tell me why this gunnysack was on the floor."

He stared at it a moment. "That's the bag Nate kept the snake in." Wasn't it? But how had it gotten—

"That bag is still in the yard. I saw it when we rode up."

Come to think of it, he had, too—and this one was larger. He looked from Honor

to the floor, his nerves sizzling. In the amount of time since Nate's fateful visit, a snake could have hidden itself *anywhere*.

"I'll kill him."

Ash barged from the house, mounted his horse, and spurred the animal toward Nate's ranch.

Chapter 7

Nerves jangling, Honor drew her horse to a sliding stop as she reached the edge of Nate's ranch yard. Already off his horse, Ash strode up to her half brother.

"Nate, you and I need to settle something, man to man." Ash threw the empty gunnysack, hitting Nate square in the chest.

No, no, no...

"I reckon you found those extra wedding gifts I left ya."

Gifts... More than one? A sensation akin to a thousand crawling spiders rolled down Honor's spine.

"So you've come to thank me?" Nate's sneer deepened.

The sound of carriage wheels and clopping hooves filled the air. Behind them, Ash's family rumbled up in the carriage, despite the fact Honor had warned them to stay put and *not* to enter the house.

"I've come to teach you a lesson." Ash squared off in a boxing stance, fists raised and feet spread.

"Ash, don't!" Honor dismounted, though her feet instantly rooted to the ground.

Nate laughed as he circled. "Yeah, Ash...*don't*. Wouldn't wanna thrash you in front of your wife."

"I'll have you know, I was a boxer at Harvard." Ash jabbed, catching Nate on the cheekbone.

Nate scowled, as if the snapping blow was only a buzzing insect.

"Never lost a match." Ash jabbed again and followed it with a solid right cross. Nate stumbled backward. Her husband moved in, fists flying. He landed several resounding punches, rocking Nate onto his heels.

"Ash, stop!" He didn't know what he'd stirred up. Nate was vicious when riled, and from the look in his eye, riled he was.

Her half brother caught himself, ducked low, and rushed Ash. Both men toppled into the dirt, Ash landing with a thud on his back. Nate straddled Ash's body, knees pinning his arms. He struck blow after blow.

The sickening punches sent nausea spiraling through Honor. Forcing her feet to move, she yanked her Spencer repeating rifle from its scabbard. As Nate continued to pound Ash, she ran to the two men and leveled the long gun at Nate's face. "Stop it. *Now.*"

Nate stalled, shot a frigid scowl her way, and batted the gun barrel aside like a toy. He returned his attention to Ash.

Lord, help me, please.

Honor stepped in and smashed the butt of the rifle above Nate's ear. He toppled

sideways, grabbing his head. She cocked the hammer and shouldered the rifle, hand on the lever.

"Don't make me shoot you, Nate." *I will if I have to, Lord. . .but I hope You know I don't want to.*

One hand braced against the ground, he glared.

Ash groaned and shoved Nate off then rolled to his knees. Face bloodied, he stood but nearly fell again. She sidled up to him, and he steadied himself against her shoulder.

"Can you ride?" she whispered as he got his feet under him, her eyes focused on her half brother.

"Yes." Ash staggered toward his horse.

"How many?" She ground out the words. "How many snakes did you set loose in my house?"

Nate chuckled. "A few."

She leveled the Spencer with his nose and worked the lever. "You better be more specific than that."

His face paled and his Adam's apple bobbed, though the cold glare never left his eyes. "Five."

Lord, have mercy. She gritted her teeth. "Be thankful Papa raised me right, or you'd be bleeding to death about now." She backed up before glancing over her shoulder.

Ash had mounted his horse, apparently with the help of his father.

Honor turned on Nate. "Don't come around my house or property anymore. You're not welcome." She kept the rifle leveled on Nate until she was beside her mount.

Nate smirked. "Don't forget what I said, you little brat. That ranch is rightfully mine, and I'm gonna have it."

"I'd like to see you try." Honor swung into the saddle. Once Ash had headed out, followed by the carriage, she spurred her horse after them.

⁓

Ash had taken some hard hits in the boxing ring, but none had prepared him for the brutal and dirty way Nate brawled. If he'd only fought like a gentleman and let Ash do the same, rather than knocking him to the ground and pinning him. . . .

In front of Father, Mother, his sisters. And Honor.

He should have kept a level head, found a better way to deal with Nate, though his family's unannounced appearance, and especially Father's rude comments about Honor, had added to his ire.

Rifle in hand, Honor raced up beside him and slowed her horse to match his pace. "Are you hurt?"

Head throbbing in time with his horse's hooves, he took stock of his other aches and pains. Blood trickled down his left cheek from a cut along his cheekbone. His left eye had swollen quite a bit. His jaw along the right side was tender, possibly swollen. Lips were raw. Nothing life-threatening, though he was a little dizzy and his muscles shook after the surge of adrenaline.

He kept his focus on the horizon. "I'll live."

Though his pride might die a slow and humiliating death.

"I'm glad." Her voice rasped.

Ash looked her way. As she stowed the rifle, her chin quivered and her eyes glistened.

Tears. . .for him? He furrowed his brow, though the movement sent pain rattling through his skull. He groaned and cupped his forehead in his hand.

"We need to get you cleaned up."

He couldn't help his sudden grin. They *both* needed cleaning up. They still sported the telltale signs of their mud fight.

When they reached the ranch yard, Ash and Honor both turned to face his family as their carriage rumbled up and stopped.

"What is going on?" Father's voice was stern. "Why did you pick a fight with that man?"

Ash leaned on the saddle horn, his strength waning. "I don't mean to be rude, Father, but it would be best if you all went back to town."

"We've come all this way to see you, and you're sending us away?" Mother gave him a pitiful look.

Honor lifted her chin. "You're welcome to stay, Mrs. Rutherford. Just be aware. . .we have five rattlesnakes loose in our home, and until I can attend to Ash's injuries, I can't go snake hunting. The best we might offer you and your family for the night is some hay and blankets in the barn loft."

Ash turned to her. "Please don't think you'll hunt those snakes by yourself. I don't want you hurt." His whispered words elicited only a sigh from her.

Mother's eyes widened, and her cheeks paled. "Oh." She turned to Father. "Perhaps we *should* go back to town, Ashton."

"I would say so." Ashton Junior looked them both over, his disdain for Honor apparent. He pinned Ash with a glare. "However, expect us to return tomorrow."

Of course. He'd expect nothing less.

As they drove off, Eliza peeked out from the back of the carriage, offering a little wave. Ash nodded at her. He *did* miss his sisters, if not Mother and Father. Theirs would be a welcome visit, when it finally came.

"C'mon." Honor headed across the ranch yard.

Ash followed. "Where are you going?"

"Until we can get those snakes out of the house, I figure we could use the bunkhouse stove to heat some water and get you cleaned up."

His bride took charge, seating him on an unused bunk near the door. Ash gingerly stretched out, back propped against the wall. Honor rummaged around until she found rags and a small pot and pressed a cloth to the cut on his cheekbone.

"Hold this. I'll be back in a few minutes." She guided his hand to the cloth then disappeared outside. The squeak of the well pump broke the stillness.

Ash closed his eyes. He must have dozed off, for when he opened them again, Honor was seated beside him, cloth in hand. With a tender touch, she washed his face and ministered to his cuts and bruises. "Manuel returned from the south pasture a bit ago."

"Yeah?" The head vaquero's comings and goings weren't a usual topic for conversation. The old Mexican knew his job, did it well, and kept the rest of the vaqueros in line for Honor, just as he'd done for her papa for many years.

"When I told him what Nate had done, he offered to hunt down the snakes for us. He's taking care of that now."

Relief washed through him. Tired and sore as he was, he'd be little use in searching out the reptiles today, and he didn't want her doing it by herself. Not that she wasn't tenacious enough. She'd faced down the two-legged snake, Nate, with courage. There was

no doubt she'd do the same with the belly-crawling variety, but he didn't want her hurt.

"I got some clean clothes for you, if you want to change from those muddy things."

As she dabbed at his injuries, he took a better look at her. She'd washed and changed into a dark blue skirt and white blouse. Women's clothes. That was a welcome sight. She'd even redone her hair, with soft curls piled atop her head in a fetching arrangement.

"You're beautiful." The words rolled off his tongue, unbidden.

Her hands stilled, and as she rewet the cloth, her cheeks flushed a pretty pink. "You're delirious. That, or you can't see straight with that eye swollen up like it is."

He caught her hand as she reached to dab at the corner of his mouth. "I see just fine. You're beautiful, strong, tender. . ."

Her cheeks blossomed red. "Stop that." She pulled her hand from his grasp and carried on.

He didn't want to stop. The same protectiveness he felt for Eliza and Lucy welled in his chest when he looked at her, only mixed with something more. A warmth, a depth he didn't feel toward his little sisters.

Was he falling in love with his wife?

Chapter 8

Coffee cup in hand, Honor stared at the big Bible on the bookshelf. She touched the spine, drew her hand back, chewed her bottom lip. Ridiculous. She was a married woman, Ash was her husband. Why couldn't she bring herself to write their names below Mama's and Papa's on the marriage record page of the Bible? She wheeled away from the shelf and paced to the door.

She'd planned to work on the far side of the property that day, but with Ash recovering from the fight and his family's impending return, she hadn't dared wander too far afield. Instead, she'd tidied the house after Manuel routed the snakes the previous evening. Then she'd returned to her room and changed into a dress to entertain her new in-laws, much as she loathed the idea—of entertaining *and* wearing a corset and frilly petticoats.

She had to admit Ash's compliments the previous afternoon had been nice, though they'd set her head to spinning. She'd wanted to bolt out of the bunkhouse just to get some air. Her cheeks warmed at the memory.

The boys she'd grown up with had never treated her like she possessed any girlish qualities. It didn't help that she felt more at home in a saddle than skipping rope or picking wildflowers. It was far more natural to her to run and chase with Ash, which was precisely why she'd started the mud fight.

But there was something pleasant about the way his face lit up when he noticed her skirt and blouse yesterday. Perhaps wearing dresses and fixing her hair was worth his kind words.

"Good morning, Mrs. Rutherford."

She started and stepped back into the house.

"Sorry I slept so late." Ash descended the stairs as if it hurt to move. A reddish-purple bruise marked his jaw, left eye nearly swollen shut. The cut on his cheekbone was red and angry.

"Morning." She smiled. "You look—"

"Terrible." He nodded.

"I was going to say sore."

"That, too." Focusing on her coffee, he approached, grasped the cup still in her hand, and inhaled the aroma. "That smells good." He took a sip, a playful glint in his good eye.

A thrill raced through her as he pulled her close. She shifted the coffee cup to her other hand.

Ash gingerly pecked her on the cheek. "You look fetching this morning."

Warmth spiraled through her. Definitely something pleasurable about his notice.

She smoothed her tan and brown dress and shot him a shy smile. "I thought I should

try to make a better impression on your family. Sorry I don't have anything more fashionable." As if she would know how to wear the fancy dresses Ash's mother and sisters had worn.

He cupped her cheek and smiled. "Just be yourself. That's all that matters."

"I did that, remember? It didn't go over real well." She bared her teeth at him as she had to his father.

Ash laughed but grimaced and worked his jaw from side to side. "That's not a moment he'll soon forget."

"I'm sorry. The way he was staring rattled me."

"No, *I'm* sorry. He's an exacting and difficult man. I wish I could tell you he might act more respectfully today, but I wouldn't count on that." Ash pulled away and turned toward the kitchen. "His whole purpose in coming is to force me to return home."

Return? Her grip on the cup loosened, and it hit the floor with a clatter. "Oh."

Limbs trembling, she darted around the spill and past Ash into the kitchen. He couldn't return. He was her husband. She grabbed several towels and turned, gasping when he stood just feet from her.

"What's the matter?"

She shook her head. "Nothing. Just clumsy." She shot past him, barely making eye contact as she rushed back to the mess, shook the folds from a towel, and tossed it over the spill.

He wouldn't actually leave. . .would he?

Lord, I haven't had a lot to say lately. I reckon You're angry at the way I got married. . .and for playing hooky from church these last weeks. Maybe I have no right to ask, but please—

"Let me help you." Ash braced one hand carefully against her shoulder and acted as if he would kneel.

"It's fine. I don't need any help." She shook out another towel. The sound of an approaching carriage broke the stillness, and she waved toward the yard. "Go welcome your family. I'll be along."

Ash looked unsure but finally stepped outside. He pulled the door closed, though not before the carriage rattled within view of the door.

A knot clogged her throat, and she gulped air around it. *God, please, don't let him go back with his family. Ash and I are married. And besides that, I think I'm falling in love with him.*

Her muscles went weak at the realization. She was falling in love. . .and his family was here to snatch him back to Philadelphia.

Without her.

Greetings, startled comments about his bruises, and questions about the snakes carried in from outside. Biting her lip, Honor sopped up the spill and listened until the door hinges squeaked softly. With a start, she looked up in time to see the older of the two girls slip inside. The young woman knelt and reached to help.

"Oh, please don't. I'd hate for you to dirty yourself."

The girl grinned and pushed the sopping towel toward the center of the puddle. "This is just the sort of thing I would do. Spill something just as company arrives." She met Honor's gaze and smiled. "I'm Eliza."

"I'm Honor."

"Pleased to make your acquaintance." Eliza's smile widened. "Welcome to our family."

Mute, Honor quirked an unsteady grin Eliza's way. Their gazes held, a friendly understanding passing between them. Honor's stomach eased just a little. There was at least one friend among Ash's family.

But did that really matter, if Ash left?

❦

"May I hug you? You look like one big bruise." Lucy's face twisted into a grim mask, yet her big eyes glinted with hope.

"I *am* one big bruise, but if you're gentle..." Ash opened his arms, and his baby sister slipped into them.

"I've missed you, Ash."

Her soft words pricked his heart. He pulled her a little tighter. "Missed you too, Luce."

"Then come home." Father's voice was firm, his expression dour.

"Ashton, please." Mother laid a hand on Father's arm. "You promised we wouldn't do this, that we would see the type of life Ash has made for hims—"

"What I see is my only son making very unwise choices." Father shrugged off Mother's hand. "I paid for a Harvard education so you would learn to fight with your mouth, not your fists, and you've thrown it away. From what I saw yesterday, you were no better than an unsophisticated street tough in a schoolyard brawl. And you couldn't even defend yourself."

Despite the pain in his jaw, Ash ground his teeth.

"I've given you the prestigious life of a gentleman, and you've thrown it away in exchange for backbreaking labor...or whatever it is one does on this God-forsaken piece of dirt."

The dull ache in Ash's skull grew to a steady pounding beat. Lucy tensed in his arms, and Ash released her, pulled her around behind him.

"I wouldn't expect you to know this, Father, but Rancho Regalo de Esperanza is a fifty-five-hundred-acre cattle ranch, one of the largest in the county. That carries a fair amount of prestige in these parts."

"Hardly the notoriety I've tried to afford you."

"You're right. It's different, but not any less respectable, and I can only hope that Lucy and Eliza will see my example and realize that they can make their own choices."

Mother looked around the porch and back to the carriage. "Where is Eliza?"

Ash pivoted, searching. Not finding her, he pushed the front door open. Eliza and Honor both looked up from the coffee spill, a smile on his sister's lips.

Eliza always had been the gracious one.

"Get up from there." Father stormed to his daughter's side and dragged her up by her arm. "What do you think you're doing?"

"I was helping Honor clean a—"

"You're not some common chambermaid. Let her handle it."

Honor flinched as if struck, and her cheeks flushed crimson.

Ash's jaw loosened, and, stunned, he turned on his father. "Say what you will to me...but you have no right to speak about my wife that way."

Father's eyes narrowed. "It seems I just did. She and this life are beneath you. I raised you to be more than some dirty farmer."

Ash fisted his hands, heat boiling up from his gut. "Get out!"

Father quirked a brow. "You had better be sure this is what you want before you say that to me. You may not like the consequences."

Familiar fears threaded through Ash at Father's threat, but he shoved them away. "I've spent years considering this moment, Father, knowing it would come. If you are unable or unwilling to respect my wife, my life, and the choices I've made, then you need to leave."

Ashton Junior's face blanched. "You'll be sorry."

Ash looked at Honor, her face stained with tears. "No, as long as I have Honor, I won't."

Father went rigid. "Gwendolyn. Girls. Get in the carriage."

Mother's face went deathly white, and her eyes widened. "Ashton, please, don't do this. He's our son."

"I've done nothing. He's done it all. Let's go."

One by one, Mother and his sisters filed out, Eliza stopping to give him a quick hug, tears pooling in her eyes. "I love you, and I really like Honor." She breathed the words in his ear.

He held her tight. "You and Lucy write me if you can."

"Now, Eliza," Father prodded.

She slipped out of Ash's arms and into the carriage beyond.

Father turned on him once more, poking a finger in Ash's chest. "You've brought this on yourself."

"If that's what lets you sleep at night, Father, so be it."

The elder Rutherford walked out, slamming the door after him.

His knees weak, Ash took a seat in the nearest chair.

"Ash?" Honor knelt next to him. "Are you all right?"

Was he? He was. . .numb. He'd tried to prepare himself for what he knew would come. Of course Father would react as he had, but knowing it hadn't prepared him for the ache of watching Eliza and Lucy, even Mother, walk out of his life, possibly for the last time.

Honor carefully slid into his lap. Her touch gentle, she pulled him close and wrapped her arms around his shoulders. "I'm so sorry. . . ."

Chapter 9

Honor looked at her husband as he drew the team to a halt in the Donovans' yard. "Are you sure you're up to visiting?"

Ash shot her a lopsided smile. "It's your birthday. I don't want you to miss out on your tradition."

A kind sentiment, but. . . "You still look so—"

"Awful?"

"No." She swatted his knee gently. "Achy."

He laughed. "If it gets to be too much, I'll say so, but I want to meet your friends."

The other guests had already arrived. Adults and older children gathered on the porch while the youngsters ran and chased each other in the yard, their delighted squeals filling the air.

Teagan and Ellie broke away and ambled toward them.

"What'd you tangle with, son?" Teagan called as they neared.

"*Who* is the better question." Honor looked Ash's way. "He fought Nate."

Honor scrambled down, and Ellie received her with a lingering hug.

Teagan narrowed a glance as Ash climbed down after her. "He came back after we left?" The men shook hands.

"No, but we discovered he'd turned five rattlesnakes loose in our house." Ash sounded far more casual than she could.

"You're joshin'." Teagan shook his head.

Ash shrugged. "It was foolish of me, but I rode out to his place and picked a fight."

Ellie released Honor. "Hope he looks worse than you."

The sheepish tilt of Ash's head elicited a grunt from Teagan.

"Perhaps not, but Ash was *very* brave." Honor squeezed her groom's hand.

Teagan and Ellie exchanged amused smiles, and Teagan wrapped Honor in a warm hug.

"Happy birthday, darlin'." He kissed the crown of her head as he'd done every birthday for years. The familiar gesture brought memories of birthdays past rushing back. Memories of Papa. A deep ache stole through her. Limbs trembling, she clung to Teagan and tried to draw a breath, though her lungs wouldn't cooperate.

An uncomfortable silence hung in the air.

Teagan shifted toward Ellie. "What'd I do?"

"She's probably missing Orrin." Ellie's voice cracked with emotion.

Honor squeezed her eyes shut and nodded against Teagan's chest.

Teagan held her a little tighter. "It's all right. We all miss him."

"Sir?" Ash's voice broke the stillness. "May I?" He looked at Teagan before meeting Honor's teary gaze.

"I reckon it's a man's right to comfort his bride."

Eyes misting, she slid easily into Ash's waiting arms and buried her face in his chest. He engulfed her in a warm embrace. The soft rustle of grass was the only indication that Ellie and Teagan walked away.

"I should have thought to ask if *you* were up to visiting tonight."

Honor balled his shirt in her fists. "I miss Papa." Fiercely. So much it nearly suffocated her sometimes. "Too many memories of him involve the people on that porch."

"Would you rather go home? I'll make our apologies, if you'd prefer." He rubbed her back gently.

More than she realized, coming here had driven home the loneliness she felt without Papa. But Ash's tender affections soothed her rattled nerves, and as he continued to hold her, the tightness in her chest eased.

"No." She shook her head. "I just need a minute. . . ."

Silence fell between them, and Honor fought to still her trembling limbs.

Ash kissed her forehead softly. "You're very brave."

Something between a laugh and a sob boiled out of her, and she clung all the harder to him. "I don't feel very brave. If you weren't holding me up, I'd melt into a big puddle on the ground."

His hand settled at the small of her back. "Then maybe we're starting to understand things."

"What do you mean?"

"Maybe this is what marriage is supposed to be. Being strong for each other."

She eased her grip on his shirt, smoothing the fabric.

"My parents' marriage was a business arrangement, nothing more. Father married Mother for her family connections and her money. In exchange, Mother received a very comfortable lifestyle, trips abroad whenever she pleased, and children—though she left us to be raised by nannies and governesses most of our early lives. I never sensed they truly cared for each other. When we married, I expected some version of their marriage, though more amicable, I hoped."

She drew back to look at him. "You did?"

Ash hung his head a little. "That's not what we have, though. When you were tending to me after the fight, you were caring and compassionate. After my parents' last visit, I could tell it grieved you, what had happened—and not just because of what Father said about you."

"I hated that he spoke to you that way." His father's sharp words had stung her. How much worse were the man's well-aimed darts when pointed at Ash's heart?

"Unfortunately, that's commonplace behavior with Father. I vowed long ago I wouldn't be like him."

She grinned. "It's working. I feel safe with you."

His intense gaze set her belly aflutter. "Honor, you stir things in me I've never felt before. I want to protect you and give you everything you could ever want. I like that when I needed you, you were there, strong and unwavering. I want to do the same for you."

"You already do." She bit her bottom lip.

Ash stroked her cheek with his thumb. "I love you, Honor."

He loved her? For the second time that afternoon, her lungs wouldn't expand. She

loved him, too, but her tongue froze in her mouth and refused the command to speak. Silence lingered.

Pain—there and gone—flashed across his face. Slanting sunlight made his brown eyes fairly glow, and her belly's fluttering grew as he leaned in for a featherlight kiss. Instead, she cupped his cheek and met his lips with intensity that set her heart pounding.

Laughter and cheers erupted from the direction of the house. She jerked toward the clamor, as did Ash, and heat washed through her at the ridiculous grins on the faces of her friends.

Teagan waved. "C'mon, you two. The food's getting cold."

⌘

"You enjoyed your evening?" Ash asked as they turned the horses into their stalls.

She beamed. "Oh, yes. Did you?"

"I laughed so much my face hurts." He probed the large bruise along his jaw, the dull ache radiating into his skull. "But it was nice."

At the front of the barn, they collected Honor's gifts—among them, two new dresses from Ellie and Teagan—and shut the doors. He tucked the bundles under one arm and offered her his other. "Mrs. Rutherford. . ."

She dipped her chin. Perhaps with more light, he'd see that pretty blush creeping across her cheeks.

Honor cuddled close as they walked toward the house. "You made tonight very special, Ash."

After depositing the gifts in the nearest chair on the porch, he pulled her into his arms. "I meant what I said. I love you."

I love you, too. He held his breath, hoping to hear the words. The fervor of her earlier kiss said she did, but. . .

The moon cast just enough light to outline her upturned face. A hint of moisture glinted against her lower lids. *Tears?*

"Never thought I'd find love," she whispered.

"Why would you think that?"

She snorted. "I'm backwards. I wear men's clothes, I do ranch work. I play in the mud."

"You're far from backward." He smoothed her silky hair and kissed her cheek. "And I *liked* playing in the mud with you."

She chuckled but sobered. "When I was younger, I was always more interested in racing or wrestling with the boys than being sweet and demure, playing with dolls." She shrugged. "Because of that, nobody ever gave me a second look."

Ash's heart pounded. Oh, but he would *like* to wrestle with her, perhaps yet tonight. His body warmed with the thought. "You're far sweeter than you give yourself credit for. And I gave you a second look."

"Would you have if we'd met under normal circumstances?"

"I don't know. Perhaps not, but would you have given a citified dandy like me more than a look?"

She nuzzled against his chest and giggled. "No."

"Maybe that's why God had us marry when we were still strangers. So we didn't miss each other. Honor, you're beautiful and charming. If I hadn't looked twice, I'd have missed out."

From somewhere out in the yard, a voice cut the stillness. "Ain't that sweet."

Nate.

Honor jerked away to face the yard.

Ash stepped around her, blocking her from the intruder. "I thought we told you not to come on our property again."

"Just came to bring Honor her birthday gift." He shook what looked like a piece of paper.

Gift? Ash shivered. "We don't want anything you've got to offer. Now get off our ranch."

"This one's harmless enough. I'll just leave it here." Nate stepped toward the porch, produced something else from his pocket, and speared the paper onto the nearest wooden post. "Have a nice evening. I'll see you Monday. Oh, and. . .happy birthday, Honor."

He faded into the darkness, and after a moment, hoofbeats thundered away.

Behind Ash, the click of a lock and the rattle of a door signaled Honor was headed inside.

"Wait." Ash grabbed her arm. "Let me go first." They'd started locking the door after the snake incident, but with Nate. . . "Just in case."

Ash slid past her, lit a match, and touched it to the nearby lantern. Both glanced around the room.

Honor looked at him. "Everything seems in place."

Ash snatched the lantern and stalked back to the porch. A small knife protruded from the post, tacking a folded paper in place. He worked it loose and, paper and blade in hand, returned inside.

"What is it?" Honor's eyes shifted between his face and the paper.

He skimmed the official-looking contents of the page.

"Well?"

"It's a summons to appear in court. Nate is contesting your father's will."

Chapter 10

Honor folded her hands in her lap, knuckles whitening. She stared ahead, spine rigid as Nate took a seat across the courtroom.

Her husband looped his arm around her shoulders. "You have no reason to be nervous. Remember, you married a lawyer."

She gave a hesitant nod. Beyond him, Nate stared at her, wearing an arrogant smirk. Blast him, but he seemed far too pleased with himself.

Teagan and Ellie arrived, and Ash rose to greet them. Ellie touched Honor's shoulder, but before she could turn, they were told to rise.

Judge Sutton entered and took his place. "Be seated."

Honor sat, muscles twitching, and ran her palms over her dress.

Ash took her hand. "Stop fidgeting," he whispered. "This is nothing."

After shuffling papers, the judge looked out. "Nathaniel Cahill, on what grounds do you wish to contest Orrin Cahill's will?"

Nate stood. "My sister's marriage is a fraud. She got married just to keep the ranch from me."

Her heart froze.

"That is a strong accusation, Mr. Cahill. Can you back it up?"

"I got proof." Smug grin sprouting once more, he produced a stack of papers. "Here's the *Matrimonial News* from the week after Pa's death. Inside, there's a circled advertisement matching Honor's description. I got letters written between Honor and Ashton Rutherford, dated between Pa's death and a few days before the will was read. The letters reference the advertisement and their plans to meet. And they got married the same day as the reading of the will. That says a lot right there. I think she knew what was in the will and got hitched just to keep the land from me."

Honor leaned against Ash as the room tilted. Their letters? When—or where—could he have gotten those? She'd last seen them on—*their wedding day*. They'd been in the trunk with their marriage certificate, which she retrieved before entering the courthouse. Come to think of it, she'd not seen them since.

Ash stood. "I object to this evidence, Your Honor. If he has our private correspondence, then it was illegally obtained."

"Overruled. Bring those to me." Judge Sutton beckoned Nate forward.

Silence fell as the judge perused the papers.

Honor clutched Ash's arm. If only he could hold her. The comfort of his embrace would soothe the quaking of her heart.

After long minutes, the judge looked at her. "Honor Cahill, come forward." He nodded to the chair to his right.

She gripped Ash's hand.

Ash squeezed her fingers in return. "Go on. Answer him honestly."

Thoughts whirling, Honor faced the judge. "Sir?"

"Yes?"

"My name is Honor *Rutherford*."

Irritation flashed across his face. "My apologies. Take a seat, please."

Ash squeezed her hand one last time as she stepped away and seated herself where directed. Heart pounding, she stared at her husband.

"Based on these letters, it seems you had no intention of marrying until after your father's death. Is that true?"

"No...yes...." Her body zinged as if lightning coursed in her veins. "It's true. I had no intention to marry until after Papa's death."

"Why did it become important then?"

Her mouth turned cottony. Ash nodded his encouragement.

"Last year, I went into Papa's office to fetch paper and ink and found a copy of his will. Not knowing what it was, I read a few lines...." Her eyes stung. She looked at the judge. "Papa was always so strong. It horrified me to think about him dying, but I couldn't quit reading what he wrote."

"You admit to having read the will before I unsealed it last month."

She swallowed. "Yes."

Nate slapped the table, and Judge Sutton glared his direction then refocused on her.

"So you found a man willing to marry you quickly so you could keep your father's ranch." His tone was accusing. "Did you plan to remain married after you'd secured the property?"

Remain married? Dizziness swept her. She gripped the edges of her chair and looked at Ash.

"What's your answer, Mrs. Rutherford?" the judge prodded.

Honor looked at him. "Of course. Marriage is nothing to trifle with."

"No, it's not. And yet I understand why your brother believes your marriage to be a fraud."

Her heart pounded. She wasn't the first woman to marry for such reasons. Probably half the women advertising in the *Matrimonial News* had similar purposes.

Ash stood. "Your Honor, I object."

The judge threw Ash a heated gaze. "On what grounds?"

"If I might see Orrin Cahill's will, I will explain."

Judge Sutton held out the paper to Ash. He stepped out from behind the table, tall and handsome, despite the green-hued bruises he still wore. He twitched a little smile at Honor and took the paper.

After skimming the page, he looked up. "The will states, 'After much deliberation, I choose to give the remainder of my land to Honor, under the condition that she is married upon the reading of this will. If Honor is unmarried, my executor, Teagan Donovan, should sell the land and cattle within sixty days at a fair value determined by the court.'"

"And?" the judge barked.

"Orrin Cahill never stipulated that his daughter be in love, or how long she'd have to have been married, just that she be married prior to the will's reading. She met the condition. There's no purpose in proceeding with this."

Honor closed her eyes, her chest swelling with pride. Surely that would be enough. *Thank You, Lord.*

"Overruled, Mr. Rutherford. I'm the one wearing the title of judge. I certainly don't need some Harvard upstart telling me how to run my courtroom."

Honor flung her eyes wide, thoughts reeling.

Ash frowned. "I meant no disrespect, Your Honor."

"Then watch yourself, young man."

"Yes, sir." Ash gave a conciliatory nod. "But as my wife's counsel, may I ask her a few questions?"

The confidence in his voice quieted the lightning coursing in her veins.

Another flash of irritation from the judge. "You may."

"Thank you, sir." Ash turned to Honor. "The day we married, did you love me?"

Answer honestly. "No. I didn't even know you."

"How long did you plan to stay married to me?"

"I vowed until death do us part."

The cleft in his chin deepened with his smile. "So you meant those vows?"

She could drown in his dark gaze. "I wouldn't have taken them if I didn't."

"At the risk of sounding self-serving, have you developed feelings for me since we married?"

Heat swept over her, warming her to her toes. "Yes. I've fallen in love with you."

For one breathless moment, all was still. Then, spell broken, Ash walked back to the table. "I'm done, Your Honor."

The judge dismissed Honor.

"Mr. Cahill, do you have anything to add?"

"Nope. She confirmed my point."

"Then we'll recess for a half hour while I consider my verdict."

Head pounding, Ash drew the team to a halt in front of the house. Honor raced to the door, sobs wrenching her slender frame, and fumbled to pull the key from her pocket.

"Honor, wait." He set the brake and stood.

She yanked the door open and disappeared inside.

His shoulders slumped. He couldn't blame her for not wanting to talk to him. She had counted on him to outmaneuver Nate in the courtroom, and he'd failed.

His thoughts spiraled. It made no sense. She'd met the requirement of her father's will. She was married prior to the reading. That should have been enough for her to keep the ranch. Even Judge Sutton said so at the will's reading. But. . .

"Mrs. Rutherford, your foreknowledge of the contents gave you unfair advantage. You worked your circumstances so the will would favor you. Therefore, I rule in Nathaniel Cahill's favor. The ranch shall be sold under the provisions set forth in the will."

Ash rubbed at his throbbing forehead. Nate had threatened to get the ranch since the reading a month ago, but by contesting it, he'd only forced Rancho Regalo de Esperanza to be sold. It wouldn't transfer into his hands. The only way Nate could get the land was if it failed to sell within sixty days, and it was doubtful a prime piece of land like this, offered at a reasonable price, would fail to sell.

So why contest the will? Was Nate so selfish that if he couldn't have it, he'd keep

Honor from having it, too?

Ash collected his suit coat from the wagon and trudged inside. His eyes strayed to the worn settee where Honor often curled up to read of an evening. Empty. Dare he head upstairs to comfort his wife when he had no answers?

Before marrying her, he knew nothing of lack and little of physical labor. He'd thought himself a good boxer and lawyer, but Nate had beaten him soundly in both. He wouldn't blame her if she never spoke to him again, especially since she'd married him to keep her ranch, and it was lost. Would she reconsider their marriage? Iron talons gripped his chest until he couldn't draw breath.

Lord, no, please. As long as I have You—and her—I can make it. Please let her feel the same way.

The telltale sounds of her crying met his ears. He laid his coat over the back of the settee and paced to the stairs.

Lord, does she want me?

He wanted her. If her feelings were the same, they could find a way. Muscles weak, he climbed the stairs.

"Honor?" He knocked on her half-closed door. No answer, so he peeked inside.

She lay on her bed, shoulders trembling, brown curls loosed from their pins.

"May I come in?"

Tear-filled blue eyes turned his way, and she nodded.

An unadorned vanity, a small writing desk, a cedar chest, and her bed furnished the only room he hadn't yet entered. Halfway to her bed, he shoved his hands in his pockets.

"I'm sorry. I. . ." He gritted his teeth. "I don't know what to say."

He'd promised it was nothing. He'd delivered. . .*a whole lot of nothing*. No home. No livelihood. In one stroke.

"I was born in this house. Everywhere I look, there are memories."

Searing pain like a red-hot knife slashed through his chest. He swallowed. "I know." He'd been here only a month, yet it held some good memories for him. How many more for her?

"Where will we go now, Ash?"

We. . .? A tendril of hope sprouted in his belly.

She pushed herself up, curls framing her face. Striking blue eyes full of fear and expectation met his.

"Say that again."

Confusion etched her features. "Where will we go now?"

We. So she *did* want him. The talons eased their grip. "We'll figure something out."

Her face contorted. "Please hold me."

Gladly. Ash sat, back against the headboard, and Honor crawled into his arms and rested her head against his chest. She trembled.

He smoothed her hair and twined his fingers into the curls. *So soft.*

She dragged in a big breath and ran her finger over the buttons of his shirt. "Is God taking the ranch because of how we married?"

His heart stalled. "Do you think He's punishing us?"

She shrugged. "We just did everything so fast. We didn't get to know each other at all before we tied the knot. It's not the usual way."

No, it wasn't. But he'd come to love her in a short time, and she'd just said she loved

him. "Perhaps that's the wrong perspective."

"How so?"

"If we hadn't married, you would have lost the ranch, and you'd be on your own. Ellie and Teagan would do all they could for you, but for how long? At some point, you'd have to stand on your own." He brushed her hair back again, drinking in the curves of her face and her full lips. "What if God brought us together, even by unconventional means, so you wouldn't face losing the ranch by yourself?"

Honor's chin quivered. "So you think God meant to bring us together. . .to get through this."

"Not just this." He cupped his hand behind her head. "Everything."

Their lips met, a deep, lingering exchange that made his heart race. His free hand skimmed toward her hip, though he let it range no farther. Honor broke the kiss but remained close, exposing her neck as if inviting him to trail his lips across her tender flesh. He blinked, tried to resist, but her warmth and softness overrode thought. His lips against her throat, a stuttering gasp spilled out of her. Shivers cascaded through him, and he pulled her into his lap. As his mouth reached the neckline of her dress, she fumbled to unfasten the top button.

Reason returned, and he pushed her away. They locked eyes. "Are you sure you want this?"

Eyes sparkling, she smiled shyly and reached for the button. "My hands are trembling. Would you help me?"

His own hands shaking a little, he assisted her then unbuttoned his own shirt. He slid his fingers beneath her dress bodice and slowly revealed her collarbone, the curve of her shoulder, and more.

Chapter 11

Another empty crate in hand, Honor turned back inside. The once-homey room stood stark and empty, shelves and furnishings nearly bare. Her eyes misted. She didn't want to remember it this way.

Pull yourself together, Honor. You've got work to do.

Thanks to Teagan and Ellie, they wouldn't be homeless. The one-room cabin on the far reaches of the Donovans' ranch would suit until they could find something permanent.

After placing the box on the floor by the shelves, she reached for the old family Bible. She paused, opened to the record pages in the front. There, Mama and Papa's marriage was listed among other family members'. The blank lines below Mama's and Papa's names stared up at her. Their names—hers and Ash's—belonged there now. It finally felt right. She closed the cover and headed upstairs to the office, Bible in hand.

Ash sat at Papa's desk, feet propped on the corner, stacks of papers covering the surface. Hands stilling on the stack in his hands, his eyes lit up as she entered. "What are you doing?"

"Thought I would record our marriage in the Bible before I pack it away." Her eyes misted again. She gulped back the emotion and marched toward the desk.

His feet on the floor, Ash tugged her into his lap. She giggled, and as she lifted the book onto the desk, Ash nuzzled her neck. His whiskers tickled her skin, and the Bible fell flat on the desktop. Papers skittered in all directions, cascading to the floor.

Ash chuckled. "Oops. Sorry about that. . .*sweetness.*"

Honor twisted toward him, her eyes narrowing.

Mock concern flashed across his face. "Uh-oh. You're not going to stomp my foot again, are you?"

Honor stifled a giggle and tried—failed—to look threatening. "Not this time." *Not ever.*

"Good. Then clean up the mess you just made." A devilish smile brought out the cleft in his chin.

She planted a fist against her hip. "Oh no. You made that mess. You deal with it."

Ash laughed. "If you state it that way. . .yes, ma'am."

She twisted forward and opened the Bible. Ash wrapped his arms around her waist, peeking around her as she retrieved Papa's pen and wrote their names.

"There." Honor bent to blow on the wet ink. Ash also bent and puckered, only his warm breath caressed the back of her ear and stirred a loose tendril of her hair. She laughed and squirmed as shivers raced over her skin.

"You, Mr. Rutherford, are an incorrigible tease."

A roguish glint lit his brown eyes. "And you like it."

Honor bit her lip. Yes, she did. But it wasn't conducive to getting any work done.

She peeled his arms from around her middle and stood. He grinned playfully as he rose, and she ducked away toward the door. Rather than follow her, he bent to retrieve the papers.

"I'll be downstairs if you need me." She rounded the corner into the hall and started down the steps.

She was nearly to the bottom when he called. "Honor? You might want to see this." The teasing tone had disappeared.

Concern overshadowed her thoughts. Setting the Bible on the step, she scrambled back to the office. "What's wrong?"

"I found something among the fallen papers." Expression serious, Ash handed her an envelope.

Her father's distinctive scrawl embellished the front.

To Honor on your 21st Birthday. Love, Papa.

His voice rang in her mind as if from the grave. She covered her mouth with a suddenly trembling hand.

"Come sit with me." Ash guided her to the chair, settled himself, and pulled her into his lap again.

She could only stare at the paper, head resting on Ash's shoulder.

"Are you all right?"

She nodded, eyes moistening. "Maybe it's foolish, but this is the last gift I'll ever get from him. I want to make it last forever."

He rubbed her back. "I understand, but what good is an unopened gift? Open it."

Ash was right, yet still she hesitated. She ran her finger over the scrawled words then heaved a breath and broke the seal. She removed the papers, smoothing them before she began to read.

I, Orrin Cahill, deed the 2,500-acre parcel of land shown, now currently part of my holdings on Rancho Regalo de Esperanza, to my daughter, Honor Katherine Cahill. The property shall be hers solely, with no restrictions or liens. Also, she may select eighty head of cattle from my herd. The transfer of all notated properties shall become effective on September 1, 1875, Honor's twenty-first birthday.

Signed, Orrin Augustus Cahill, on this day, June 25, 1875.

She stared at the bold script, thoughts moving like cold tar. The map of Rancho Regalo de Esperanza indicated the parcel with a thick line and shading to set it apart.

"Ash..." Hands trembling, she held the paper up.

"I read it."

Papa gave her land? But... "What does this mean?"

"It seems pretty straightforward."

"I mean in light of the will and the outcome of the hearing...the land being sold."

After a moment, Ash pushed her up and scrambled after her. "It means we need to get over to Teagan's place and make sure he doesn't sell the ranch before we can get to town to see a judge."

Lord, please—please—let us get in to see the judge today. Honor deserves a proper home, even if it's not the one she's always known.

Ash turned the wagon toward the courthouse. On horseback, Teagan rode beside them. The fact their friend had come along was a comfort. Perhaps the judge would look more favorably on him, a longtime resident of the area and executor of the will, since he had seemed unimpressed with Ash and his education during the recent hearing.

"Ash!" A familiar voice rang above the noisy streets.

He slowed the wagon and looked around. From an open second-story window in a nearby building, Eliza and Lucy waved.

Jaw slack, Ash stopped, and Teagan drew up just ahead of them.

"Who's this?" Teagan called.

"Ash's sisters," came Honor's answer.

Eliza and Lucy. . .here. "What are you doing?" His voice echoed against the building.

They motioned for him to wait, then disappeared. His heart pounding, he parked the wagon beside the huge town square. The girls exited the quaint boardinghouse and dashed across the street.

He met them each with a hug. "What are you doing here?"

Eliza's expression grew serious. "We never left. Father is—"

"Girls!" Father's voice tolled sharply, and both Eliza and Lucy stiffened. Jaw set, the man marched toward them. Once he reached them, he clamped a hand around each girl's shoulder and turned them toward the boardinghouse. "Inside. Now."

Acid rose in Ash's throat as he watched them go, straight into Mother's beckoning arms.

Ash looked at the elder Rutherford. "Father. What are you doing here?"

"I'm glad you've come. It saves me the trip." Ashton Junior turned a steely-eyed gaze his son's way. "It's time you return home."

Ash's thoughts spun. "I thought I made myself clear. I am home."

"How long are you going to pursue this ridiculousness? You have a life of opportunity waiting in Philadelphia. You have nothing here."

Nothing? "My *wife* is here, and therefore, my life is here. And lest you forget, California is a land full of opportunity, Father."

The man snorted. "Not like I can offer. I'll hand you everything you could dream of—and more. Out here, you'll toil for whatever little bits you get."

"But I'll respect myself, Father. There's nothing wrong with working with your muscles." He looked back at Honor. "It's a challenge." One he liked.

Father grabbed his arm. "This is sheer stupidity. You have *nothing* here. I made sure of it. No ranch. No reason to remain in that sham of a marriage. Wise up and end this foolishness now."

"You did *what?*" He'd made sure they had nothing? Ash's thoughts churned.

"I've spoken with Judge Sutton about annulling this marriage. Once that's done, you *will* return to Philadelphia and marry—"

Adrenaline poured through his veins, and Ash threw one solid punch. Father stumbled backward, lips spouting blood, and landed in the dirt. Instinct drove Ash forward, but Teagan darted between them and pushed him back.

"You don't want to do this, son."

He glared around Teagan as Father tottered to his feet. "Get out of my way."

Teagan pushed him back, a restraining hand against his chest. "Walk away. Catch your breath. You don't want to fight your father."

Oh, but he did. . . .

"Especially not here." Teagan nodded at the public square.

Honor slipped in front of him, her arms around his torso, blue eyes pleading.

"Ash, please, come with me."

The urgency in her voice drained the fight out of him. She pushed him back until he finally turned and walked away of his own accord. Thoughts reeling, he replayed his father's words.

"Are you all right?" She stared up at him.

"I never told Father how or why we married, yet he called our marriage a sham."

Honor's brow creased.

"And he said *he* had made sure we have nothing. Like the ranch." He chewed on the information and locked eyes with her. "And the judge called me a Harvard upstart. . .?"

"I remember that. You made a valid point, and he overruled you, called you an upstart."

"A *Harvard* upstart." He glared across the square at Father and Teagan, exchanging what appeared to be heated words as they separated. "Teagan and Ellie are the only ones I've told about my schooling, and I don't think they'd pass that news around."

"They wouldn't."

Teagan stalked up, face grim. "Your father is something."

Ash glared after Ashton Junior. "You have no idea. . . ." He detailed the little evidences to Teagan. "I think my father and Judge Sutton are working together to ruin Honor's inheritance—and our marriage."

Teagan looked toward the courthouse. "Leroy Bowen, the judge over the District Court, is a friend of mine. I'll see if we can't get an audience with him. Maybe he can call for an appeal about the will."

Epilogue

Two months later

Today, they would finally learn the fate of her beloved Rancho Regalo de Esperanza. Honor gripped Ash's hand in eager anticipation.

"Be seated," Judge Bowen said as he shuffled some papers then looked out at them. "I want to apologize for the delay on the appeal to Orrin Cahill's will. I know it has affected some of you more than others." He looked directly at Honor.

Judge Bowen rested his elbows on his desk and steepled his fingers. "The serious accusation against Judge Carl Sutton required careful investigation. He made more than one questionable verdict or performed dubious actions during court cases, including that of Orrin Cahill's will. Therefore, he has been removed from his position, pending further examination."

The judge looked directly at Ash. "Mr. Ashton Rutherford Junior admits he offered a bribe to Judge Sutton, though no money actually changed hands. Mr. Rutherford has cooperated with my investigation in every way, so this court has issued a stern warning but will take no further action at this time."

With a grim expression, Ash nodded to Judge Bowen.

Honor sighed. The Rutherfords had stayed in Santa Rosa while the court investigated. Twice, she and Ash had attempted to make contact with his mother and sisters but were turned away at the boardinghouse door. Soon after the second attempt, they learned that Judge Bowen granted Ash's father permission to return to Philadelphia for a family emergency, and the family left.

"Now. . .on to the decisions at hand. Honor Rutherford, I have found the deed, written and signed by your father, which gives you twenty-five-hundred acres and eighty cattle, to be valid. That land and herd are yours. All further discussions will reference only the remaining three thousand acres."

Ash squeezed her hand, and she returned the gesture, thankful that part of her father's wishes would be honored.

"Nathaniel Cahill, you contested your father's will on the grounds that your sister's marriage was fraudulent. I disagree. They were married before God in a Petaluma church. Their marriage certificate was signed by a reverend and two witnesses. It's a legitimate union, though the timing is questionable in light of the reading of the will. However, there's no reason that should negate the provision of the will. Thus, I award the final three thousand acres of Rancho Regalo de Esperanza to Honor Cahill Rutherford."

A grin exploded across Honor's face, and tension drained from her body. Ash looped his arm around her shoulders.

Lord, thank You. You've blessed us greatly, despite our quick beginnings. I love You, and I

love this man—more than I thought possible.

Across the aisle, Nate grunted, and the judge speared him with a fiery look. "I've been informed of the intimidating actions you've taken against this couple. . .poisonous snakes thrown at their feet or set loose in their home, sneaking around their property after dark, and the like. If I get word of any more, shall we say, uncharitable behavior by you—or those working for you—I will take a long, hard look into your history. I am fairly certain to find things, knowing the man you are. Be warned, Nathaniel Cahill: you don't want to be on my bad side." Judge Bowen paused to look over the room. "Now if there is no further business. . ." He reached for his gavel.

Heart pounding, Honor nodded to Ash.

Her husband stood. "Your Honor?"

Judge Bowen stilled. "Is there a problem, Mr. Rutherford?"

"No, sir." He reached for Honor's hand and tugged her to her feet. "My wife and I would like to make Mr. Cahill an offer, and we wanted to do it in front of the court, for the record."

Surprise registered on the judge's face, and suspicion on Nate's.

"What offer?"

Honor cleared her throat. "Sir, we'd like to offer Nate fifteen hundred acres." She turned toward Nate. "As a peace offering. We're neighbors. . .and family. Papa would have wanted us to be on friendly terms."

Stunned silence fell. "You're giving me fifteen hundred acres. Free and clear?"

"I ask nothing except that we work at being neighborly."

Nate's expression shifted from suspicion to confusion.

Judge Bowen leaned forward. "Mr. Cahill, will you take the land?"

Nate nodded. "Reckon I will."

The judge turned to them. "Do you have particular boundaries in mind for the division of the land?"

Ash looked Nate's way. "We have some thoughts, but we're willing to negotiate privately."

Judge Bowen looked at Nate as well. "They're giving you a gift, Mr. Cahill. Be grateful, and don't let greed rule your negotiations."

"Yes, sir."

"We're adjourned." One bang of Judge Bowen's gavel set the courtroom in motion.

Nate ambled their way. "If you were so hell-bent as to marry a stranger to keep all the land, why'd you give me some of it?"

Honor shrugged. "I never wanted *all* of it, Nate. But the will said I had to be married to have *any* of it. You had the land Papa gave you. I wanted a piece, too, to feel connected to Mama and Papa. By giving you these acres, we both have equal parts. I'm hoping it might end some of the bitterness between us." After much discussion and prayer, she and Ash had decided to offer Nate the olive branch, hoping it could soften his heart—toward them and God.

His jaw muscle popped. "It might. . .we'll see."

Honor smiled. The begrudging statement gave her a kernel of hope for bigger changes to come, though she knew it might take years for true reconciliation. "Come to dinner tomorrow. We can talk about dividing the land."

After arranging the details, Nate departed. Teagan and Ellie waited near the door,

and as they all exited the courtroom, Teagan shook Ash's hand and winked at her. "Congrats. Hope you two can get settled once and for all."

Honor laced her fingers with Ash's and smiled. "We have some work to do, but it'll be nice to make the house *ours*."

Ellie sidled up next to her. "Julia and I are available if you need help."

Outside, they talked briefly before parting from the Donovans.

"Ash?" A woman's voice called as they headed toward their wagon.

They both turned. Near the corner of the courthouse building sat Gwendolyn Rutherford and her two daughters.

"Mother?" Ash released Honor's hand and hurried toward them. Both Eliza and Lucy launched into his arms.

Hanging back to give them a moment, Honor smiled at the warmth with which he hugged his sisters and mother.

"We heard you'd gone back home."

"We did. . .and your sisters and I have returned."

"Without Father. . ." His tone held a twinge of sadness.

Tears pooled in Ash's mother's eyes. "You know how fiercely prideful your father can be. But don't lose hope. When he saw how heartbroken the girls have been, he grudgingly agreed that we could return for a lengthier visit."

Ash offered a solemn nod. "It's a start."

"It is. Now. . ." With a genuine smile, Gwendolyn approached and drew Honor into a warm embrace. "I'd like to know the brave young lady who captured my son's heart."

Dear Reader,

As an author, each new story presents a cast of characters that are waiting to be discovered. Some come bursting forth on page one in all their glory, and others are shy and reserved, not wanting to reveal themselves fully until well into the story. No matter what type of character, though, I find that they all live on in my heart after I write "The End."

Some characters just demand more "page time" than what a single story can contain. This was the case with Ellie and Teagan Donovan. If you are interested in learning the history of this couple, you can find their story in my novella, *Sioux Summer*, which appeared in Barbour's *The Oregon Trail Romance Collection*. I hope you'll check it out.

Blessings!
Jennifer Uhlarik

Jennifer Uhlarik discovered the western genre as a preteen, when she swiped the only "horse" book she found on her older brother's bookshelf. A new love was born. Across the next ten years, she devoured Louis L'Amour westerns and fell in love with the genre. In college at the University of Tampa, she began penning her own story of the Old West. Armed with a BA in writing, she has won five writing competitions and was a finalist in two others. In addition to writing, she has held jobs as a private business owner, a schoolteacher, a marketing director, and her favorite—a full-time homemaker. Jennifer is active in American Christian Fiction Writers and is a lifetime member of the Florida Writers Association. She lives near Tampa, Florida, with her husband, teenage son, and five fur children.

A BRIDE FOR BEAR

Erica Vetsch

Dedication

For Peter as always. You are the hero in my real-life romance.

Chapter 1

S omeone has made a big mess here, and I am not going to clean it up. This is not my problem. Please, Lord, don't let this be my problem.

Bear McCall pinched the bridge of his nose, rubbing his thumb and forefinger into his eyes, and then looked across the depot once more, praying what he'd thought he'd seen would turn out to be a mirage or hallucination or something.

"There has to be some mistake. I'm here to pick up a *package*." The telegram his neighbor, Charlie, had delivered yesterday said clearly that a package would arrive for him on the noon train and he must pick it up in person that day.

A package from Chicago. The only person he knew in Chicago was his cousin, Isabelle, and he hadn't seen her in a score of years, not since he'd headed west when he was sixteen. What she would be sending him, he couldn't imagine, but his curiosity had been piqued enough to make him travel down his mountain and into town to find out.

The station clerk looked up from his puttering and gave him an I-already-told-you-once stare. "If your name's McCall, *that* is what was left for you. And I'd appreciate it if you'd take delivery so I can go to lunch. Been waiting all morning for you to show up." He went back to punching and stamping and tapping cards together.

The skinny clerk must've felt safe behind the metal grill and high counter. Most men didn't have the nerve to brush Bear off like that. He hunched his shoulders inside his flannel jacket and flexed his hands. No matter what the dunderhead behind the counter said, there had to have been a mistake somewhere along the line.

He approached the bench along the far wall as he would a pint of nitro.

If there was one thing that made him more uneasy than a woman, it was a little girl. And here sat three of them looking at him like they expected him to pound them to powder like rocks in a stamp mill.

Hair red as fire, and those eyes. Big as globeflowers in high summer. And pinned to each of their coats was a paper that said "Deliver to Mr. C. McCall, Idaho Springs, CO."

The biggest one—who still looked mighty small to him—stood and locked eyes with him, her chin coming up. She was pale and tight as a bowstring, but she didn't run away. Bear almost smiled. Grown men had been known to avoid looking him right in the eye, but this little sprite held his stare like a stone-cold gunfighter.

"Are you Mr. McCall?"

Scratching his beard, Bear shrugged and nodded.

Her wrists stuck out a good few inches from the sleeves of her thin coat, and one of her black stockings had a sizeable ladder running up the outside. Her shoes had seen better days, too. She was probably about ten—not that he had much practice in guessing

little girls' ages—but her face had a world-weary look to it, as if she'd seen too much hardship for her years. With a quiet dignity, she opened her coat and tugged out a battered envelope.

"I'm supposed to give this to you."

He took the envelope, careful not to let their fingers brush.

The middle one jumped up like she'd been sitting on a coiled spring. Her braids bounced on her shoulders, and sprouting up all over her head, wispy strands escaped, making a red halo.

"You took a long time. We been here *forever*." Her hands went to her narrow hips and she tilted her head to the side, squinting up at him. She had more freckles than a speckled pup. Her greeny-brown eyes accused him.

"Sorry," he mumbled then scowled. Pint-sized they might be, but they were women for sure, already putting him in the wrong.

The smallest one, her hair a mass of strawberry ringlets, stuck her finger into the corner of her mouth and stared at him like he was a freak in a sideshow. Her hair was the lightest of the three, and her eyes, though still hazel, were more green than brown. Her feet swung from the edge of the bench in impossibly small buttoned-up boots. This one scared him more than the other two combined. The kid was practically a baby.

Number One picked up a battered valise and motioned to the other two. "Come on."

"Hang on a minute. What are you doing here in Colorado, and where's your ma? Is she gonna be back soon?"

"Ma's dead." Number Two crossed her arms. Her bottom lip trembled in a way that made Bear's knees wobble and his chest cave in. *Please don't cry. Please-don't-cry. Please-don't cry!*

Then it hit him. Isabelle was dead?

And her girls were here.

Staring at him.

Panic clawed his chest like a hungry badger.

"Ma died last week, and she left a paper that said we was to be sent to you," Number One said.

Her matter-of-fact tone did nothing to lessen the mule-kick her words delivered. Before he could grab hold of this bit of news, Number Three scooted off the bench, reaching for the floor with one toe before slipping off the edge. She sidled up to Number One and tugged on her sleeve.

"I gotta go." Her version of a whisper filled the room.

"Again?"

"You just went, not even half an hour ago." Number Two's eyes rolled, and her trembling lip firmed up into a sneer. "You're leakier than an old bucket."

The little one tugged on the big one's sleeve again. "I gotta go potty."

His palms began to sweat.

Number One handed the bag to Number Two. "Here. Don't lose this. We'll be back." She held her hand out for Number Three, and they disappeared through the side door. Bear breathed a sigh. Talk about sidestepping a cannonball.

Number Two gave him a hard look. "Are you my uncle?"

He rubbed the back of his neck and pulled his hat down. "No. Your ma was my cousin."

"So what's that make us?"

Pure trouble. Times three. "Blamed if I know."

She flipped her braids over her shoulders and hiked the bag higher. "You're kinda big, aren't ya?"

He grunted, his mind still reeling.

"You always this grouchy? 'Cuz if you are. . ." She didn't finish the sentence, but her freckled face said volumes. "Is your wife grouchy like you?"

He scowled and jerked like she'd kicked him in the shin. "Don't have a wife." *Thank the Lord.*

"Just as well, if you're always this cranky."

"You're kinda mouthy, aren't ya? I thought kids were supposed to be seen and not heard."

"Yeah, I get told that a lot."

A smile quirked his lips at her long-suffering expression.

Number One and Number Three returned. Number One squared her shoulders, checked that Number Two still had hold of the bag, and said, "We're ready."

Well, he sure wasn't. There was no way. He was *not* being saddled with three little girls.

"What about your pa? Where's he?"

Number One shrugged. "He's been gone a long time. Ran off. Ma didn't know where he was, and she didn't want him back, nohow."

Bear felt as if he were grasping for any handhold or tree root to keep himself from falling off this particular cliff. He thrust his hands into his pockets. How had he gotten into this mess? He had a claim to run. The nip in the air said he should be greasing and preparing his traps for the winter, not nursemaiding a gaggle of girls he'd never seen before.

They looked up at him with expectant eyes, and his gut twisted.

There was no help for it. He couldn't just leave them here, and sending them back where they came from didn't seem to be an option, either. He'd have to find somewhere else to park them. They certainly weren't coming up to the cabin with him. He had a strict policy when it came to females invading his home: they weren't welcome. Period.

Stalking over to the ticket window, he banged on the counter. "Hey, I want some service!"

The fussy clerk stuck his head out of the back room, a sandwich in his hand. He finished chewing and swallowed. "I'm on my break."

"You're going to know the meaning of the word 'break' if you don't get out here." Bear grabbed the grillwork window and shook it.

The man flinched and edged to the counter, his thin eyebrows bunching under his green visor. "What do you need?"

"Four tickets to Denver. When's the next eastbound?"

The clerk fumbled with some papers. This guy must be new. Bear had never seen him before. Not that Bear came into town that often. Twice a year was enough.

"Half an hour."

"How much?" Bear reached into his coat. Blamed nuisance, having to go to Denver. Good thing he'd secured everything at the cabin before he came down. This little errand shouldn't take more than a day or two, and Charlie would probably check on the place

anyway, nosy as he was.

The clerk told him the price, and Bear forked it over.

He shoved the tickets and the envelope Number One had given him into his coat pocket and turned back to the girls.

All three girls sat side by side on the bench once more, and all three of them stared at him, Number Three with fascination, Number Two with accusation, and Number One with resignation.

Emmylou Paxton had never been so humiliated in all her life, and that was saying something, considering where she'd come from.

Every ounce of hope drained out as she stood in the Denver depot.

"So that's how it is. Bertha showed up first." Cletus Bloggett shrugged. "I went ahead and married her yesterday. We're leaving for my claim on the next train."

His new bride, a buxom blond with pink cheeks, blinked wide blue eyes and took his arm as if staking a claim.

Emmylou gulped. "But you're betrothed to me. I have your letter." She dug in her reticule.

"Well, I figured I'd better my chances by answering mor'n one ad in the *Matrimonial News*. Thataway I could have my pick of brides." Cletus tucked his thumbs under his suspenders and nodded as if his words and his plans made perfect sense. "You and Bertha both answered the ad, and when she stepped off the train, I knew she was the one I wanted. I mean, look at her, with all that blond hair and all those curves. I had both your pictures, but I wanted to look you over myself. Now that I see that you're kinda skinny, and redheaded to boot, I'm thinking I made the right choice. But you'd already set off from Harrisburg, and I didn't have no way of calling you off."

Hot tears burned the backs of Emmylou's eyes and tingled down the inside of her nose, but she blinked hard to fight them off. All the accusations Aunt Ida had hurled at her about being skinny, redheaded, and a flaming nuisance to have to care for came back like an avalanche.

They were drawing a crowd of onlookers, and shame swirled into her cheeks. Why didn't they mind their own business? Didn't they have something better to do?

She straightened. "I've spent the last of my money just getting here. I have none for a return trip." Not that she wanted to go back to Pennsylvania, ever. "What am I supposed to do now?"

"I dunno." Cletus dug in his back pocket and pulled out a much-folded newspaper. "You could always take out another ad or two."

"I could always sue you for breach of contract. You promised me marriage, and you've reneged on that promise."

Bertha squeezed his upper arm, her doe-eyes widening.

Cletus—the rat—grinned and shook his head. "If you don't got money for a train ride, then you don't got money for no lawyer. Anyway, even if you did sue me, what'd you get? I ain't rich. I got enough for me and Bertha, but if you're hoping to squeeze me for cash, you're gonna be disappointed."

A train whistle sounded, and Cletus tipped his hat brim. "Gotta go. Sorry it didn't work out." He hefted a couple of suitcases, and with Bertha scurrying in his wake, left

Emmylou standing in the middle of the depot with her bag at her feet and her dreams in shards on the floor.

The ring of onlookers glanced at one another. Some looked on her with pity, others with wry amusement, as they dispersed.

With no idea where she was going, Emmylou hefted her bag and headed for the stairs leading up to street level. She didn't have to look in her reticule to know that she had exactly five dollars to her name. No going back, but no clear way forward, either.

Lord, now what am I supposed to do? I thought Cletus was an answer to prayer, a way out of a bad situation, but this is much worse.

The street was a morass of muddy ruts. Wagons trundled by, and pedestrians, heads down against the brisk wind, passed without looking up. Smoke blew on the air, and as she took a firm grip on the handle of her valise, she looked up at the mountains.

"I will lift up mine eyes unto the hills, from whence cometh my help." The verse came unbidden from her memory, and she swallowed. *All right, Lord. Where do I go now?*

"Hey, lady, somebody meeting you, or are you looking for a place to stay?"

A man in a bowler hat and checked suit leaned against the depot wall. He had a drooping moustache and eyes so dark they looked black. . .like a rat's. He shoved away from the bricks and came toward her. Something about him repelled her, but she couldn't say what. She was probably just jumpy because of Cletus leaving her stranded.

"Could you direct me to a boardinghouse or hotel?" Someplace where she could examine her situation and her options and decide what to do.

"I know a place. It's not too far from here. I'll walk you over."

He didn't offer to carry her bag, but he set off at a pace that made it easy to keep up, even in the thin air. After a quarter of an hour though, she began to wonder what his definition of *not too far* meant.

Finally, he turned up a short walkway. "This is the place. The landlady is a friend of mine. Her name's Pauletta. I imagine she can find a place for you. She's been looking for a few more boarders."

The three-story brick house looked tidy enough. In fact, it was nice enough she wondered if she could afford a room. The man rang the bell, and a girl of about twelve opened it.

"Is Pauletta awake yet?"

Awake? It was almost midday. What kind of woman slept till noon?

The girl's head bobbed, and she stepped back, inviting them in. She wore a ragged dress and a mob cap from which dirty-blond hair escaped. Emmylou followed the girl into a parlor that was positively opulent. A chandelier, fancy red wallpaper, a piano, and lots of tables and settees and ferns.

The man went to the bottom of the stairs and hollered up. "Paulie, c'mon down. I got a live one for you." He grinned and reached into his coat pocket, withdrawing a cigar. He bit the end off, showing a lot of fierce white teeth, and spit the tobacco into a nearby fern.

Something was wrong here. The way he looked at her, sizing her up like an item in a store window, sent a chill through her. Footsteps on the stairs drew her eyes away from his, and the moment Pauletta came into view, Emmylou realized the nature of the house.

The woman was scantily clad, with a pale blue silk robe, open down the front, trailing behind her. Her black hair hung to her waist, and her cloying scent hit Emmylou even before she reached the bottom of the staircase.

"Morning, Hank."

"Afternoon, you mean. I found this one at the station. A mail-order bride that got left high and dry. Heard it all myself. She ain't much to look at now, but with some makeup and a different dress, she might be something. You don't have a redhead."

"Excuse me, but there's been some kind of mistake. I am looking for a boardinghouse not a. . .a. . ." Emmylou couldn't even get the word out.

Pauletta looked her over, tapping her front teeth with her long fingernail. "Spruced up, she could be something. Bit on the skinny side, but with some good food, we could fill her out. Got nice eyes and cheekbones. Right now, she'd make a nun look flamboyant, but in the right clothes. . ."

Emmylou, not wanting to hear another word, headed for the door where the girl waited.

As she passed, the girl touched her wrist and whispered, "Try a place called the Front Range Hotel back near the depot. It's clean and cheap, and you should be safe enough there."

Making her escape, shaking, Emmylou hurried up the street. They must be laughing at her now, saying she was as raw as unshucked corn. She should've trusted her instincts. Something about the man had been wrong. What if they'd tried to keep her there by force?

When she was out of sight of the house, she stopped and leaned on an iron-rail fence. The desire to weep made her stomach quiver and her throat ache.

The Front Range Hotel. Near the depot.

Chapter 2

The orphanage wasn't much to look at, but he'd rather stare at the ugly building than look into the eyes of those three little girls any longer. When he'd delivered the news about their destination, none of them had said a word. Not even Number Two, though she set her mouth in a hard line and crossed her arms, staring at him like she wanted to bore him through with a rock drill.

Number One had nodded, bitten her lip, and turned to stare out the train window as if she expected nothing more of life than to be knocked down and kicked a few more times.

And Number Three had slipped her hand into her eldest sister's and stared at him with those enormous eyes until he felt lower than a worm in a mineshaft and meaner than a wounded wolverine.

But he was doing the right thing.

No way should they live with him, a bachelor alone on a mountain. They should have a family. They were cute enough, surely someone in town would adopt them.

Bear told himself this as he mounted the stairs and opened the door. Inside, the foyer smelled of wool and cabbage and kids.

"Wait here." He pointed to a bench. As he put his hand on the knob to the door marked OFFICE, a row of silent little girls marched down the staircase like soldiers and headed down the hall. Not one of them smiled.

A boulder took up residence low in his innards.

The orphanage matron sat behind her desk, a frowsy gray-haired woman. Papers littered the desktop and poked out of filing cabinets. A nameplate in danger of being pushed off the edge of the desk read MRS. ALBERTSON.

He told her why he was there, and she began shaking her head even before he was finished.

"Mr. McCall, let me ask you a few questions. You said you are the girls' only living relative?" She folded her hands and leaned her elbows on the desk. All around her mouth, soft whiskers stuck out like a colt's, and her faded blue eyes regarded him.

"They've got a pa somewhere, but he ran off awhile back. At least that's what the girls told me."

"Do you have a home?"

"Sure, a cabin. Built it myself. But it's no place for little girls. I live there alone."

"How do you support yourself, sir?"

"I'm a miner and trapper. Look, what has this got to do with these girls?"

"And it was the mother's wish for you to take the children? How old are they, and what are their names?"

smoothed his beard and looked out the window. He didn't even know their nahe sent the girls on to me, yes, but I'm not keeping them. I told you, I live alone. a mountain. I don't know anything about little girls, and I don't want to learn."

She was shaking her head again. "I'm sorry, Mr. McCall, but we have no room for more children, especially not ones with relatives who can support them. This orphanage is for the truly destitute, not those considered merely the inconveniences of life. I would suggest, if you have the means, that you place the girls at the boarding school across town. Miss Miniver's Academy might solve your problems. I warn you, the tuition is steep, but the girls would be cared for and well educated."

He grasped at her suggestion like a rope thrown down a deep shaft. Boarding school. That would work. And it would ease his conscience about dumping them in an orphanage.

The girls sat in a row, just as he'd left them.

"Come on. We're going somewhere else."

"They don't want us, neither, do they?" Number Two—he really was going to have to find out their names—jumped off the bench and dragged their valise out from under it. She turned to Number One. "I told you."

Bear led the way outside, and they followed, for all the world like ducklings after a mama duck. God was playing some kind of awful joke on him. He'd sworn off women for life, and here he was saddled with a trio of them. *Very funny.*

Hiring a cab solved the problem of getting them across town. It rolled through the gates of Miss Miniver's Academy for Young Ladies and up the curving drive. Someone had planted dozens of saplings, tying and staking them. In about ten or twelve years, this place would be beautiful. For now, it had a raw look about it, all sharp edges and new paint.

When he laid eyes on Miss Miniver, he could see why she was a spinster. With a mouth tighter than a miser's purse, and eyes like knitting needle points, she'd give any man the shivers.

"My name's McCall, ma'am." He swept his battered wide-brimmed hat off his head and shoved his hair back and out of his eyes before extending his hand to her.

Her brows arched, and she barely let her fingertips graze his, as if she thought he might have something catching. She sized him up, from his calf-high laced boots to his flannel jacket and shaggy beard.

"What can I do for you, Mr. . . . .McCall?" Her very British voice sounded like she had dumplings stuffed in her cheeks. . .razorblade-filled dumplings.

"I've got three girls I'd like to enroll in your school." He motioned them forward. Number Two stared at the crown molding and plaster medallion above the chandelier, her mouth hanging open and the valise dangling from her fingertips. Number Three hid behind her sisters, peeking out, her finger stuck in the corner of her mouth, and Number One studied Miss Miniver, as if envisioning the future under her tutelage and not finding it to her liking.

A small facial jerk that he supposed passed as a Miniver smile contorted the woman's face for an instant. "There appears to be some mistake. Your daughters are hardly our desired demographic."

Desired demographic? What was that supposed to mean?

She rounded her desk and sat, nodding for him have a seat. His chair was harder than permafrost, her look was twice as cold, and Bear got the feeling she was using the desk as some sort of barricade.

"Mr. McCall, we have a screening process for all new applicants. Do you perhaps have references? We accept students by recommendation only."

"References? From who? I just got saddled with them this morning. The orphanage wouldn't take 'em and said I should try this place. And I'm not their daddy. Just a sort of cousin, I guess."

She winced. "This academy is for the education and edification of young ladies of the highest caliber. We don't allow just any urchin off the street to enroll. We are exclusive." She said it with her chin in the air, staring down her narrow nose as if she'd just smelled something bad. Bear took a tight grip on his temper, aware that she had him betwixt the tail and the snoot. If she turned him down, he was fresh out of ideas.

"They're bright girls, smart, and obedient." He didn't know if this was true, but it sounded good, and he was desperate. "They came all the way from Chicago on the train by themselves. They've got grit."

"Perhaps, but 'grit,' as you so delicately put it, is hardly a selling point in this instance. I'm afraid we cannot accept them. Parents enroll their daughters here expecting us to maintain a certain clientele. Our establishment is like a rose garden, if you will, where the girls are tended and sheltered and kept from contact with. . .shall we say, ragged little weeds."

He glanced at the girls, his ire rising. There in the fancy front room, they looked as out of place as tin cups at a tea party, but by sugar, they didn't deserve to be called weeds.

The tears on Number One's lashes and the bucky set to Number Two's jaw tore things completely. He slowly rose, planted his palms on the desk, and loomed over the dried-up old stick of a headmistress.

"Lady, those aren't weeds. They're little girls. Girls who just lost their mother. You're about as sensitive as granite and twice as hard. I need someplace to put them, but I'd rather leave them with a pack of wolves then under your 'tender' care."

She shrank back, flinching with every word and jumping when Bear cracked his fist on the desktop hard enough to make the inkwell hop. Gathering her dignity, blinking, and pushing her chair away from him, she stood.

"Mr. McCall, get out. Neither you nor these ragamuffins are welcome here. I suggest you find yourself a wife to care for them instead of trying to farm them out. Though I pity the poor woman who would marry you. You come in here dressed no better than an Indian, with your animal skins and wild hair and a beard that would make a billy goat proud, demanding that we take your problem off your hands. Well, we're not going to do it, so you might as well be on your way. And don't come back."

At the mention of a wife, Bear's blood boiled right over. "I'd rather poke a rabid mama grizzly in the eye than get married, but even that's preferable to leaving the girls here with you, you old viper. Calling them weeds and saying they don't measure up to your lofty standards. Well, I'm glad they don't, because I'd be ashamed to be related to anyone who resembled you. I wouldn't leave a dog I didn't like in your care." He whirled, upsetting his own chair and not bothering to pick it up. "C'mon, girls. We'll find somewhere a little more fitting to *our* lofty standards."

Slamming the door hard enough to rattle the windows gave him immense satisfaction.

As he stalked down the drive in the dusk of early evening with the girls scampering to keep up behind him, Bear had a mental image of his last bridge turning to a pile of embers.

Emmylou trudged up the steps to the Front Range Hotel, weary to her marrow. The white-clapboard building looked neat enough, though after her latest experience, she was on her guard. She entered the lobby. Doors opened on her left into a restaurant where plenty of noise emanated. Smells of baking bread and roasting meat hit her, reminding her that she hadn't eaten all day. The sound of breaking crockery shot through the first floor, followed by a shout.

"Forget it. I quit." A petite dark-haired woman stomped out, yanking off her apron and tossing it behind her. "I refuse to be treated like this." She hit the door and didn't look back, leaving Emmylou staring after her.

A short, hand-wringing man shuffled into the lobby, peeling the apron from around his neck. He flung it down on the counter. "Dinner is about to start, and I've no waitress." He muttered and twisted his hands. "That's the third waitress I've lost this month. Seems no matter how much I pay, they won't stay." He sighed. "Can I help you? Do you want dinner or a room?" His droopy eyes looked up at her, as if hardly daring to hope.

"How much are your rooms?" *Please, Lord, don't let them be too expensive.*

"Two dollars a night. Food in the restaurant is extra."

Her heart sank. At that rate, she would be broke in two nights.

He looked her up and down. "Say, you wouldn't want a job, would you? I need a waitress. You ever waitressed before?"

A spark of hope flickered in her chest. "Does the job come with a room?"

He scratched his cheek. "I guess I can spare you a room, but it won't be much." He named a paltry wage. "Best I can do if you're gonna be boarding here, too."

She could hear her aunt deriding her as she packed her bag. *"A mail-order bride? You're going to regret this. You never look before you leap, expecting somebody to catch you when you fall. You're impulsive and reckless, and it will land you in trouble one of these days."*

"I'll take it." It wasn't as if she had a lot of choices, and sometimes when the Lord gave you an opportunity, you had to leap at it or it would pass you by.

An hour later, she was sure she'd made a mistake. The cook was a surly Russian who spoke almost no English. He knew the words *beef* and *chicken*, and that sufficed to prepare the orders. Emmylou scribbled on her order pad, sliced pie, dished up green beans, and juggled hot rolls. She sloshed coffee into cups, poured a hundred glasses of water, and trotted up and down the dining room a thousand times.

Her baggage sat in a cramped little cubby off the pantry where the proprietor, Mr. Luverne, had shoved a cot. The window was bare of any covering, something she would have to remedy before bedtime.

But first she would have to make it through this dinner service. There were so many tables, and she was only one woman. Most of the customers were males, and the longer the wait, the more rowdy they became. She worked as quickly as she could but fell further and further behind.

Then it happened. After setting down four plates of roast beef swimming in gravy, trying desperately not to spill on the tablecloth, herself, or her customers, one of the men at the table reached out and swatted Emmylou on the bottom. She yelped, plunking the last plate down so hard the gravy shot up and splattered her in the face.

The men roared as she jumped back and swiped at the brown sauce dripping from her nose.

"Hey, darlin', why don't you come over and sit here. I'll help you clean yourself up." The offender leered and patted his lap. His buddies laughed again.

Using the hem of her apron, Emmylou cleaned the droplets off her forehead and cheeks, marshaling her dignity. "Sir, I would thank you to kindly keep your hands to yourself."

"Aw, c'mon, sister. I bet it's the most attention a man's ever shown you." He smirked, licking his lips.

Emmylou began to get an inkling why the other waitress had quit. "I can do without your attentions. Enjoy your meal." *And get out.*

"Say, ain't you that gal that got ditched over at the depot today? A mail-order bride or somethin'? I saw the whole thing." He then told the story to the rest of the men at his table and quite a few others around him, including Mr. Luverne, who was seating yet another group of diners.

Emmylou balled her fists and lifted her chin. At the rate the tale was spreading, she'd be surprised if it didn't appear as the lead article in the local newspaper tomorrow.

Her dignity suffered several more times as she wove through close-packed tables with her hands full of plates raised high. One man even pinched her! The male patrons seemed to think she was an object for their amusement. Her cheeks burned, and her hands itched to slap their smug faces. *When will this shocking, degrading day end?*

The rush finally became a steady flow, which became a trickle. Emmylou cleared tables and refreshed tablecloths while the cook went out back to smoke a vile-smelling cigar. Her back ached, and her feet protested every step. How many miles had she walked in the last three hours? It felt like a hundred.

Mr. Luverne directed another group of diners into the almost-empty room. "It's late, but I reckon we can accommodate you, since you're taking a room, too." He pointed her way. "Hey, tell the cook there's four more."

And just how was she supposed to do that when he didn't speak English? If she said anything other than "beef" or "chicken" to him, he scowled and growled.

A mountain of a man entered the room, and her heart sank. He wore flannel and buckskins, had hair that hung over his shoulders, and had a beard sorely in need of a trim. If he was bringing three more friends like himself, she would insist Mr. Luverne serve them. She'd had enough patting and pinching to last her a lifetime. Tomorrow, she'd carry a wooden spoon with her and whack the wrist of any man who dared lay a hand on her, that was what.

To her relief and surprise, the man stepped aside and let three children come before him.

"Pick a table." His voice was rumbly and deep.

Three darling little girls with hair as red as her own. The oldest boosted the youngest into a chair and scooted it in for her before taking a seat herself, and the middle one climbed up and knelt on her chair, examining every corner of the room. Emmylou had a

feeling that one didn't miss much.

Glancing down at her stained and rumpled apron, Emmylou grimaced. Her hair was probably a rat's nest, and her dress was limp.

The eldest girl looked as tired and defeated as Emmylou felt. Poor thing. Where was their mama?

Their father removed his hat and hung it from the back of the littlest one's chair and slid out of his coat. His elbow poked from a tear on the sleeve of his flannel shirt, and the well-worn fabric stretched across a pair of brawny shoulders that would've made a buffalo proud. He meticulously rolled up his sleeves, revealing strong forearms dusted with reddish-brown hair.

Realizing she was staring, Emmylou composed herself and approached. "Evening. I'm afraid, late as it is, there's only roast beef left, but there's plenty of beans and bread. And there's coffee, milk, or tea to drink." She held her pencil ready over her order pad.

"Guess we'll take the roast beef then." He flipped his coffee cup over. "And coffee."

"Coffee for the girls?"

He frowned. "I guess milk for the girls." He crossed looks with the oldest one. "That work for you?"

She nodded.

Emmylou didn't bother the cook. She loaded the plates herself from the pots and pans still on the stovetop and carried them to the table. When she'd served them, she prepared a plate for herself and brought it to a table near her last customers so as to be handy if they needed something.

Sinking onto the ladder-backed chair, she took a moment to say grace before opening her napkin and spreading it on her lap. Her feet screamed inside her high-buttoned shoes, and her back and head ached. But not as much as her heart. One blessing of being so busy was that she didn't have time to grieve her lost marriage. Not that she had been in love with Cletus. But she had been prepared to learn to love him if at all possible. To make a new life for herself far different than where she'd come from.

"Are we really going to stay in a hotel?" The middle girl tore off a big piece of bread and stuffed it into her mouth. "I ain't never slept in a hotel before."

The man grunted. "Got to. No trains until morning."

The oldest girl cut her littlest sister's food for her, but the tiny child only managed a couple of bites before she pushed her plate aside and laid her head on the table.

"What's wrong with her? Is she sick?"

Emmylou couldn't miss the panic in the man's voice.

"No, she's just tired."

Emmylou knew just how she felt. Poor little mite. Her own plate looked none too appetizing. All she really wanted was to go to bed and try to forget this whole day.

The man shoveled food into his mouth as if he were stoking a furnace. "You girls can have dessert if you want."

The middle child froze, her eyes widening. "Really?"

"Sure. There's bound to be pie. Pick out what you want."

Emmylou pushed herself up from the table and forced a smile. "What will it be, ladies?"

Apple won the day all around, and Emmylou cut three extra-large pieces. No sense bringing one for the baby. She was sound asleep.

When Emmylou set the plates on the table, the oldest girl looked up at her. "Are you married?"

Emmylou flushed. "Um. . .no, I'm not."

"Do you want to be?"

"Excuse me?" She blinked.

"Do you want to be married?"

The man let his fork clatter to his plate. "Hey, stop that."

"What?" The girl turned innocent eyes his way.

"You know what."

"The lady at the boarding school said you need a wife. I like this one." She pointed up at Emmylou, who stood frozen to the spot like a lamppost. The child turned to her. "Our mama died, and we have to live with him now. He needs a wife in a hurry to look after us girls. He's about had it with us and has been trying to get rid of us all day. If he doesn't find a wife, then he's gonna have to take care of us himself, and *none of us* want that."

When the man snorted and shoved his plate away, the girl looked at him like a teacher reprimanding a child. "You know it's true. You need a wife, even if you don't want one. You're a parent now. That means you have to do what's best for us girls, even if you don't like it."

He looked like he'd swallowed a wasp.

Emmylou's knees gave out, and she plopped into a chair. "That's very kind of you, dear, but I couldn't possibly marry your father. He's a complete stranger."

A snort came from the doorway. The Russian cook leaned on the jamb. "You were mail-order bride, yes? Going to marry a stranger? But groom—how do you say it?— ditched you at train station? Is talk all over town." He shrugged. "You marry this one. Get out of keechen and hotel. You make better wife than waitress, I think." He straightened and sauntered through the dining room, letting the kitchen door flop in his wake.

Was she awake? Was this a dream? Perhaps she was still in her bed in Harrisburg, Pennsylvania, and at any moment she'd wake to the caustic demands of her cranky aunt, and this horrible day would disappear. She'd been jilted by her intended, proposed to by a child on behalf of her. . .cousin? . . .and found that the Russian cook who had said not a word to her all evening spoke somewhat comprehendible English.

The middle girl bounced out of her chair and came over to take Emmylou's hand. "Please say yes. You look a little like our mama. And you won't mind that we have red hair, since you have red hair, too."

Chapter 3

B ear liked the way the woman cupped Number Two's head. She looked tired to death, and she'd been jilted by the man who was supposed to marry her, but she still took time to be nice to the girls.

Not that he wanted to get married. No sir. But if he *was* going to get married, it would be to someone who understood heartbreak.

And he did need someone. Number One looked at him with pleading eyes, and Number Two inclined her head toward the woman as if telling him to make an offer before she disappeared.

He started to wipe his mouth with his sleeve then remembered his manners and used his napkin.

"Ma'am, what the girls say is true. I do need a wife in a powerful hurry. They got sent to me completely out of the blue, and I don't have the foggiest notion what to do with them. I tried to find a place for them, but that didn't work out so well. If you were prepared to become a mail-order bride, then I guess you aren't one of those women with their heads all full of romance and nonsense about courting and love and such."

Her lips twitched, and he thought she might be trying not to smile. Had he been too blunt?

"Anyway, I live up past Idaho Springs. I have a cabin and a claim, and I have enough money to support you and the girls."

The woman moistened her lips, and her hand crept up to smooth her hair into the knot at the back of her neck. "Sir, I don't even know your name."

"You can call me Bear. Everybody does."

She had blue-green eyes, the same color as the mountain lake just below his cabin. "Bear?"

"He growls like one, doesn't he?" Number Two tugged on the end of her braid. "You should've heard him when that lady at the boarding school called us weeds. I'm glad she didn't want us. I didn't want to stay there."

Trying to drag the conversation back to the point at hand, Bear glared at the girl before turning back to the woman. "Look, I know this is all kind of sudden, and you don't have to decide tonight. We don't leave until nine tomorrow morning. For now, I'd best get these girls up to their room. Number Three's already asleep, and the other two should be, too."

"Number Three?"

Glad that his beard hid the red he was sure crept up his neck, he shrugged. "That's what I've been calling them. Tell her your names."

Number One stood and gravely held out her hand. "My name is Miriam DeWitt.

I'm pleased to meet you."

"I'm Emmylou Paxton, Miriam."

Number Two bounced up on her tiptoes. "I'm Deborah. And that"—she pointed to Number Three—"is Tabitha. Can we call you Emmylou? I like that name. We have Bible names, because Ma liked Bible names. Is Emmylou a Bible name?"

"No, sweetie. It's a combination of my parents' names. My mother was Emma and my father was Louis."

"My ma's name was Isabelle. And my pa's name is Oscar." She wrinkled her nose. "If I was named after both of them, my name could've been Isacar or Osabelle." Her giggle hunched her shoulders.

"Bedtime." Bear cut across the giggles. Little girl giggles made him uneasy.

Number Two—Deborah—clung to Miss Paxton's hand. "I want *her* to put us to bed."

"She's got work to do, I'm sure. She doesn't have time for that."

"Please, Miss Emmylou? It'd kinda be like when Mama would tuck us in and hear our prayers."

Again Emmylou caressed Deborah's head. "I don't mind, if it's all right with your. . . with Mr. Bear."

Truth be told, it would be a mighty relief. "Sure. If you want to."

Emmylou and Deborah started toward the foyer, and Miriam took a couple of steps after them before turning around. Number Three—Tabitha—he needed to start calling them by their names—still knelt on her chair, her head on the tablecloth, sound asleep.

"Do we wake her up?"

Miriam shook her head. "You couldn't wake her up if you tried. Once she's asleep, she don't wake until morning. You'll have to carry her."

His stomach muscles clenched. Bending, he moved his hands first one way then another, trying to gauge the best place to grab hold of her without breaking her. She was so tiny, his hands looked like ham hocks next to her. Eventually, he had her cradled in his arms.

Her head rested on his upper arm, and her little feet dangled over the opposite forearm. She snuggled in like a kitten into a quilt, her mouth pursing then relaxing. He stood for a moment contemplating how she didn't weigh more than thistledown and how her lashes looked dark against her cheeks.

What on earth had Isabelle been thinking to put them in his care?

Emmylou couldn't believe she was even contemplating accepting his offer. She felt all shaken up inside, like a marble in a canning jar.

The cook had a point, though. She had come out here intending to marry a complete stranger. That had taken some gumption. But did she have enough gumption to marry a surly mountain man?

Deborah chattered all the way up the stairs, still holding Emmylou's hand. Miriam followed behind, and Bear. . .surely that wasn't his real name. . .brought up the rear carrying Tabitha.

The hotel room had one bed.

Bear stood in the doorway. "Where do you want her?"

"Tabitha sleeps in the middle so she don't roll off." Deborah dragged a battered valise

up onto the bed. "Her nightgown is in here."

Bear eased Tabitha onto the mattress and backed up. "I'll wait in the hall." He scooted out like his tail was on fire, and Emmylou smothered a laugh. He might be as big as a mountain and twice as rough, but that man was flat-out scared of these little girls.

She helped them brush and re-braid hair, scrub faces and hands, and change into nightgowns. Miriam could use a new one, and hers should be passed down to Deborah. The girls were thin, their clothes threadbare, but she could see where the gowns had been carefully mended. They might not have had much money, but their mother clearly loved them and cared for them as best she could.

"You gotta sit in the chair while we say our prayers." Deborah led her to the rocker in the corner then knelt and put her head on Emmylou's knee, squinching her eyes shut and folding her hands into a ball.

"Dear Jesus, thanks for the good dinner tonight and that Cousin Bear didn't like that lady at the boarding school. Please help Emmylou to like us so we don't have to live with him all by ourselves. Amen."

She popped up and skipped over to the bed, diving under the covers next to Tabitha. "Miriam?"

"I'll say my prayers by myself. I'm big enough." Miriam folded her dress and laid it in the valise. She'd been quiet since coming to the room, her face drawn and her eyes troubled.

"That's fine." Emmylou stood. "Climb in, and I'll tuck the covers for you."

When they were lined up, three little red heads on the pillows, Emmylou turned down the lamp and went into the hallway, leaving the door cracked.

Bear stood at the end, looking out the window, his hands jammed in his pockets and his hat shading his face from the moonlight falling through the glass. He turned. "They asleep?"

"Nearly."

"Thanks."

"You're welcome."

He shifted his weight, took off his hat, and shoved his fingers through his hair, which fell just below his shoulders.

"I don't want a wife."

She sucked in a quick breath.

"I mean, I *need* a wife to take care of those little girls, but I don't want a wife-wife, not a real wife. If you go ahead and marry me tomorrow, I promise I won't...pester...you in any way."

This time he took her breath completely away. She fumbled for words, but nothing came out.

"If it wasn't for the girls, I wouldn't ever have a woman in my house again. But I'm backed into a corner. It sounds like you are, too. You'd sure be helping me out of a tight spot, and the girls seem to like you. I can provide for you. I'm not poor. And like I said, all you'd have to do is take care of the girls."

Tugging on her lower lip, Emmylou studied him. He might be intimidating at first sight, but she'd caught glimpses of something vulnerable inside that big frame. How he'd let the girls have any dessert they wanted, the way he'd carried Tabitha up the stairs as if she were made of spun-sugar icing, how, though scared, he was willing to take on the care and raising of three little girls.

Still, she'd made one bad decision in becoming a mail-order bride already. Perhaps she should at least sleep on it.

"I'll give you my answer in the morning. Good night, Mr. . . .Bear."

By morning, she'd made up her mind to say no. The girls were very sweet, and he did need someone to help him, but marriage was too much. Emmylou had dodged one catastrophe with Cletus Bloggett. She wasn't of a mind to walk into another by marrying Bear. . .she didn't even know his last name.

At five, she was up and tying on her apron. The cook was back to mumbling in Russian and pretending he didn't understand anything she said. Fortunately, the dining room wasn't nearly as full as it had been the night before, and the customers were more subdued. She carried plates of biscuits and gravy, hotcakes, and scrambled eggs without trouble. Perhaps the job wouldn't be so bad after all.

Then Bear and the girls came in.

He had a haggard, stressed look as he directed them to a table. Emmylou grabbed a coffeepot.

"Good morning." She poured him a cup.

Miriam gave her a nod, and Deborah beamed, her smile splitting her face and making her eyes into crescents. Her braids were askew, as if she'd tried to do them herself, and Emmylou longed to fix them for her. Tabitha's sweet smile chipped away at Emmylou's resolve.

Still, she needed to stay her course and not let emotions sway her. Balancing several plates, she brought them their breakfast. Things were going much better than yesterday.

A commotion in the doorway drew everyone's attention, and Emmylou's heart sank. It was a few of the rowdy men from last night. Maybe she'd best get a wooden spoon. They jostled past her as she set the plates before the girls and Bear, and as she went back toward the kitchen, the rudest of the men reached out and swatted her on the behind.

She yelped, but the sound was drowned out by a roar and breaking dishes. Hand to her chest, she whirled in time to see Bear grab the man who had smacked her, haul him out of his chair and up so that his feet dangled inches from the floor. Though the man struggled, Bear seemed to have no trouble keeping hold of him.

"If you ever touch her again, I'll break every bone in your miserable body. Is that understood?" The words were all the more fierce for being whispered an inch from the man's nose.

Emmylou's mouth went dry. Bear's eyes bored holes through her assailant, and his grip on the man's collar was so tight, the man's face went red.

"Is. That. Understood?" With each word Bear shook the man like a dusty rug.

The girls stood together beside their table, eyes wide, faces pale. Emmylou stepped close to Bear and spoke softly. "He can't answer you until you turn loose of his neck." She put her hand on Bear's massive forearm, conscious of the muscles and heat. When he didn't ease up his hold, she said, "You're frightening the girls."

At that he let go, and the man sank to the floor, gasping and choking. Standing over him, hands clenched, legs braced, Bear growled, "Apologize to the lady."

"Sorry." The man scrabbled at his throat, inching back until he hit a table leg.

"Now get out of here. Find somewhere else to eat."

The beaten man and his companions crowded out, and Bear finally relaxed. He ran

his fingers through his hair and down his face. "That tears it, doesn't it? I could tell you were going to turn me down when we came in this morning. Guess this didn't help."

"Actually, I've decided to take you up on your offer." The words slipped out before Emmylou could call them back, but the sight of him standing there like an avenging angel, defending her honor, had tipped the scales in his favor. Nobody had looked out for her in such a long time. It made her feel. . .safe. "If you're still willing, I will marry you."

Deborah hopped in place, and Miriam sighed, some of the tension going out of her face.

Bear's lips parted, and his eyes widened. "You sure?"

Emmylou nodded. The girls needed her, and living with Bear couldn't be as bad as waitressing here for a wage that would barely keep her.

"We'll take care of things as soon as the girls finish eating then." He turned back to the table.

"Boy, are we lucky. I didn't think you'd find *anyone* to marry you." Deborah climbed back into her chair and dug into her hotcakes.

In what seemed an indecently short amount of time, Emmylou found herself married to Bear McCall.

No, not Bear.

Courtney.

His given name was Courtney, but the warning glare in his eye told her she must never use it.

Deborah had giggled then clapped her hand over her mouth while Miriam nudged her.

Barely waiting for the ink to dry on the marriage certificate, Bear hustled them to the depot and aboard the westbound train. In order to save time, they'd found a justice of the peace rather than hunting up a preacher. Emmylou felt the loss of not having even a minimal church wedding, but considering the circumstances, she didn't complain. Tickets, luggage, one last trip to the facilities for the girls, lots of growling, and they were aboard.

Miriam chewed her bottom lip and kept constant tabs on her sisters. Deborah bounced up onto the seat on her knees to stare out the window. Tabitha slid onto the seat next to Miriam, keeping a tight grip on her sister's sleeve with one hand and chewing on the index finger of her other. Every few moments she peeked at Bear.

Bear sat across from Emmylou, his knees bumping hers occasionally in the cramped space. Every so often he would look at all of them and shake his head, as if he had no idea how he'd gotten in this predicament.

Now married and on the train with them, Emmylou knew just how he felt. Still, she'd put her hand to the plow, and she wouldn't look back.

"Why does she keep doing that?" Bear crossed his arms and frowned.

"Who?"

"Number Three. She keeps staring at me like she thinks I'm going to pounce on her or something."

Tabitha ducked behind Miriam's shoulder, one round eye peeping out.

"She probably does. You're a very large man." *Not to mention gruff and forbidding.*

His brown eyes widened, and his thick brows rose. "I'd never do that. What kind of man do you take me for?"

"Since we hardly know each other, I can't really judge, but if you try a little kindness,

you might be surprised at the results."

"I've been kind. I fed them, put them up in a hotel, and to top it all off, I married you. That's a heap of kindness in my book."

She fell silent. He *had* gone out of his way to look out for them, and most likely trying to change him the first hour of their marriage wasn't the best idea. He'd said he would leave her alone. Perhaps she would extend him the same courtesy.

By the time the jolting, rocking train arrived in the town of Idaho Springs, Emmylou was so tired she could barely think. She hadn't slept well in days, and last night she'd spent hours wrestling with Bear's proposal. She smoothed her hair and gathered her reticule. Bear hefted down their bags from the overhead rack, and Miriam herded the girls behind him up the aisle.

"Have we far to go?"

"Couple of hours." He dropped the bags on the platform and swung each of the girls down from the train before reaching up for her.

His huge hands spanned her waist, and before she could protest that she was more than capable of walking down the iron steps, he set her beside Miriam. The top of her head came to just below his chin, surprising since she was a tall woman. He made her feel small, even delicate.

She liked that altogether too much.

Perhaps this was the start of a new life for her and these girls.

Three hours later, she wanted to throttle him.

Her mule balked at every turn, her backside was killing her, and Deborah hadn't stopped talking the entire way up the mountain. Emmylou had never ridden an animal before, much less astride a blockheaded beast with no notion of what it meant to obey. Bear had gotten so frustrated, he'd taken the reins from her and tied them to his saddle horn.

Bear, with Tabitha in front of him and Miriam hanging on behind, never looked back, doggedly winding his way up the precipitous trail.

"I thought you said two hours." The words she'd been determined to keep to herself flew out as the mule scrambled up a rock-strewn incline, bouncing her hard against the saddle.

"Takes *me* two hours." She didn't miss his inflection that more than suggested that she and the girls were slowing him down.

"Are we there yet? Look at that squirrel. It's as big as a cat. Sure is a long way down, isn't it?" Deborah leaned to her left, and Emmylou reached behind to grab the little girl.

"It is, and if you fall, you'll bounce all the way to the bottom. Sit still." Her other hand gripped the saddle horn so hard she was sure her fingers were imbedded in the leather.

"I'm tired." Deborah swatted a mosquito and wrapped her arms around Emmylou's waist again.

"If this is you tired, I'm afraid of what you truly rested might look like."

"I know. Mama said I'm jumpier than a grasshopper in a frying pan. I just can't seem to be still. Miriam says I wear her slap out sometimes."

When they'd climbed for another half hour or so, Bear led them through a high cleft of rock and pulled up.

Emmylou sucked in a breath. Before them, in a bowl surrounded by peaks, lay a mountain lake, flat as a mirror, reflecting the puffy clouds and perfect blue sky overhead. Aspens stood like golden torches along the lakeshore, and in a glade, a sturdy cabin sat under the pines.

"Is this it?" She didn't mean to sound disparaging, but the square building looked so small, dwarfed by the towering mountaintops and trees. She scanned the grassy meadow and could see no other signs of habitation, no other people.

"What were you expecting, downtown Denver?" He kicked his horse and tugged on the mule's reins. They finally halted in front of the cabin, and before he dismounted, the door swung open.

"That you, Bear? Where you been? I expected you back before now. Figured I'd best keep an eye on the place for you till you got back."

Emmylou blinked. It was as if a hairy stump had sprung to life and started talking. Mounds of white hair and beard, inky eyes, and leathery wrinkles.

"Who's that with you?" The black eyes grew round and the mouth hung slack. "Is that a woman?"

Bear helped Miriam slide to the ground and swung down himself, a drowsy Tabitha in his arms.

"By sugar, there's more of them." The old man scrubbed his eyes and leaned forward.

Deborah used Emmylou's leg as a ladder to climb down, not waiting for Bear's assistance. "Who are you?" She hopped over to stand before the man. "Are you Bear's pappy?"

The man snorted and shook his head. "Don't believe Bear had a pappy."

"Knock it off, Charlie. These are my cousin's kids. *This* is what I was supposed to pick up at the train station." Bear began unsaddling his horse.

"Well, if that don't take the biscuit." Charlie scratched the hair over his ear and squinted at the girls. Tabitha took refuge behind Bear's leg, peeking out from beyond his knee. Miriam edged away from the stamping and blowing horse.

"This one of your cousin's kids, too?" Charlie eyed Emmylou, still atop the mule.

Bear let the saddle thump to the ground and turned. His raised eyebrows seemed to ask what she was still doing up there. Emmylou continued to grip the saddle horn for dear life.

" 'Smy wife." He stalked over, grabbed her by the waist, and hauled her down. She shifted her grip to his shoulders as her heart lurched.

"Your wife?" Charlie choked on the question.

Emmylou's legs quivered, and her back felt as if she might break in two. Bear seemed to sense her distress and didn't let go.

"I've never ridden a horse before—or a mule," she whispered.

"I could tell." His voice this close to her ear, held a hint of humor and rumbled in his chest, sending a strange sensation through her middle. "You think you can stand now?"

She nodded and stepped back, letting her arms fall to her sides. Scanning the area, she gasped. "Deborah, get down from there this instant."

"But I can see a long ways up here. I can see clear across the lake." Using the log ends jutting from the corner of the cabin, Deborah had shinnied up to the eave and now hung on like a squirrel.

Bear reached up and plucked her down. "Stay on the ground." He gave her a frown as if that settled the subject.

"Three kids *and* a wife?" Charlie repeated, tugging on his earlobe. "You're not joshin' me?"

Bear's grim look did nothing to make Emmylou feel more welcome. "I'm not joshin'. Help me unload this gear. You girls can go inside."

Deborah was the first into the cabin, and Emmylou followed with Miriam and Tabitha behind.

"Look at this place." Her hands on her hips, Deborah turned a slow circle in the crowded space. "Mama would have a conniption."

Emmylou took the pins out of her hat and let her eyes adjust to the dimness. She bit her lower lip and surveyed her surroundings. The place wasn't exactly a mess, but it was crowded. Every inch of wall and most of the floor space was taken up with Bear's possessions. Traps, snowshoes, a buffalo coat, shelves of foodstuffs, three long guns, a pistol in a holster, and the one thing that gave her a little ray of encouragement. A row of books ran along a high shelf.

Bear was a reader.

"Where are we supposed to sleep?" Miriam fingered her collar. Two bunks stood against one wall, each spread with a striped wool blanket. Deborah squatted before the fireplace to stare into the glass eyes of a grizzly bear head. The rest of the bearskin covered the floor of the cabin.

"Lookit his teeth." She touched one of the ivory spikes. "I bet he could bite your head clean off."

Tabitha took one look at the bear's frozen snarl, gave a yelp, and ran toward the door, only to collide with Bear's leg. She bounced off, landed on her bottom, and burst into tears. Bear backed off, guilt and confusion clouding his expression.

"What's wrong with her?" His voice caromed around in the cabin as if looking for a way out, and Miriam clapped her hands over her ears.

Emmylou rushed to Tabitha and picked her up, cuddling her close and whispering against her curls. "It's all right, sweetie. Shhh."

Bear slung the bags onto the bottom bunk, ripped his hat from his head, and thrust his fingers into his hair. "Can't you make her stop?"

"I'm trying," Emmylou snapped. "Do you think this is easy for any of us? We're tired and hungry. We've been dragged up a mountain far away from everything we've known, and then to wind up in this...storage shed..." She turned her back, lest he see her tears, only to come face-to-face with a giant mounted elk head. She squeaked and closed her eyes, trying to hold on to the last shreds of her composure.

"This place is full of dead things, ain't it?" Deborah made her observation from the top bunk.

Emmylou locked eyes with Miriam, who seemed to be searching for reassurance.

Too bad Emmylou had none to give.

That evening, Bear laid out his expectations, and it was all Emmylou could do to bite her tongue as he paced the narrow open space in the center of the cabin.

Emmylou was to confine her attention to caring for the girls. The only reason he married her was for the sake of his cousin's children. There was to be no hen-pecking, no nagging, no crying, no moods, and no manipulation. If she or the girls needed something, she was to tell him in plain English. She should not expect him to read her mind, and she would absolutely not say one thing when she meant another. He would mind his own

business, and she would mind hers.

As for the girls, they were to mind Emmylou and not get into his things. They were to stay within eyesight of the cabin and not wander off. They would not touch his guns or his traps.

"And I want them to stop giggling and crying. I don't like it."

Emmylou boggled. "You don't want them to giggle or cry?"

"No."

"And how do you propose they go about doing that? Both are natural, especially to little girls. It sounds like you'd prefer to stuff them and mount them to the walls." She knew she was being snappish, but it had been such a long, confusing day, she didn't seem to be coping too well.

His scowl would scare a statue. "I'm just telling you the way things need to be."

And I'm telling you the way things are going to be. Some of his rules made sense, and some were downright silly. It would be up to him to discover the difference.

Following a dinner of cold biscuits and canned beans, which nobody was too enthusiastic about, the sleeping situation was solved by putting Tabitha and Miriam in a quickly fashioned trundle bed, Emmylou on the bottom bunk, and Deborah on the top bunk. Bear removed his bedroll from a hook on the wall.

"I'll bed down in the toolshed for now. We'll have to figure out something different before the snow flies."

At Emmylou's gasp, he rolled his eyes. "I mean something like adding a room or two to the cabin." He slammed the door behind himself.

Tabitha was the first to fall asleep, having cried herself out and been reassured time and again that neither the bear nor the elk would suddenly leap to life and harm her. Or the bobcat on the mantel or the turkey in frozen flight on the wall. Miriam curled beside her little sister, and her lashes soon fanned her cheeks in deep sleep. Deborah didn't settle as easily, popping her head over the edge of the bed every few minutes.

"Bear's awful grumpy, isn't he? I guess I would be, too, if four people moved into my house and I had to sleep in the toolshed."

"Go to sleep, Deborah."

Emmylou's brain whirled as she tried to get comfortable on the lumpy mattress.

"Do you think he shot that bear? It sure has big teeth. I'd hate to meet up against something like that, wouldn't you?"

"Deborah." Emmylou's voice sharpened. "That's enough. Not another peep. You might not be tired, but the rest of us are. Go to sleep."

With a huff, Deborah's face disappeared.

With Deborah finally silent, Emmylou had time to contemplate just what she'd gotten herself into. In the space of two days, she'd gone from jilted spinster to wife and mother.

The feeling of water closing over her head made her sit up, taking deep breaths. In the dim glow of the banked fire, the eyes of the elk gleamed at her, and she slammed her eyes shut, dropping back on the pillow.

But if she was feeling unsettled and panicky, how must Bear be feeling? He'd had four women dropped into his life like baggage, and now he was ousted from his home and his normal existence. No wonder he was a bit grumpy.

Perhaps tomorrow, when they got their bearings, things would be better.

Chapter 4

After two weeks Bear would swear there were more than three of them. Every time he turned around, a pint-sized redhead was asking him a question or poking into his stuff. Miriam had organized his traps on their hooks by size, and his books on the shelves by author. Tabitha had taken to playing dress-up with his hat, his winter gloves, his heavy boots, any part of his clothing she could get her hands on. And if Deborah ever stopped talking or moving, he'd never witnessed it. She stuck to him like a cocklebur from sunup to bedtime.

"What's that?"

"Why do you have such a long beard?"

"Why do people call you Bear? Is it because you growl so much?"

"Can I ride your horse?"

"Why do you have so many guns?"

"Why can't I try cutting wood with the ax?"

"Can I have a skunk for a pet?"

"Why can't I go fishing with you?"

All day long, yammer, yammer, yammer. A man had sticky work to escape without one of them following him. And yet, he found himself not minding so much. Their giggling and chattering didn't set him on edge as often as it had at first.

Bear shouldered his rifle and shifted his grip on the turkey he'd shot for supper. With the leaves turning and the nip in the air, it would be time to bring down a couple of deer or elk and get them smoked before winter set in. With more mouths to feed, he'd have to be sure not to run short.

The cabin came into view as he broke the tree line, and the now-familiar battle set up in his chest. The smoke wafting from the chimney and the knowledge that he wouldn't be coming home to an empty house warred with the uneasy awareness that he was growing much too fond of the girls.

And not just the girls.

Emmylou had followed his rules to the letter, and yet somehow she still managed to invade nearly every corner of his life, including his thoughts and even his nocturnal dreams. She'd lost that tight-strung look, and though she worked too hard, she had a healthy glow in her cheeks and a sparkle in her eyes. Especially when she was with the girls.

The changes she'd wrought in the cabin were amazing. At first he'd resented every moved item, every sign that he wasn't the sole proprietor longer. He'd barely held on to his temper when he'd walked into a clothesline of damp little-girl dresses strung across

the cabin one day. And when he saw it was strung from the top bunk to the antlers of his trophy elk, he'd had to walk right back out into the rain. But he'd started coming around to his new way of life. For the first time in a long time, he had a clean shirt whenever he wanted it. He had delicious meals eaten in congenial company. He had companionship that drove away a loneliness he hadn't known he'd felt.

"Bear's here!" Deborah bounded from the cabin doorway and skipped down the path. "Lookit that turkey. He's a whopper."

He stopped and set his rifle butt on the ground, propping it against his side as he ruffled her hair. "Were you good today?"

Her nose wrinkled, and she squinted up at him. "No worse'n usual."

It was her customary reply, and he couldn't help but grin. She was so much like him, it was scary. Bear dropped his hat on her head and hefted his gun once more. Emmylou and the rest of the girls stood in the doorway, and his heart beat a little faster.

"A successful day." Emmylou reached for the bird, but Bear held it away.

"I'll pluck and clean it first. That's no job for a lady." He handed her the rifle. "If you could get a fire going under the washtub, I'll scald it."

Her nod and smile made him feel like the sun had just burst through the clouds. Shaking his head, he rounded the cabin and drew his knife from his belt. How had things changed so quickly? He'd vowed long ago to steer clear of women. He'd long thought himself cured of every ounce of romance or relationship. But now he found himself eager to spend time with "his girls."

Returning to the cabin with the cleaned bird, Bear handed it over and sank into his chair. He'd made the slat-backed rocker to fit his large frame and draped it with wolf pelts for comfort and warmth. As he leaned back, he waited. Sure enough, little Tabitha—with one of his mufflers draped around her neck and dragging the floor—left the bunk where she'd been playing with the rag doll Emmylou had fashioned for her, and sidled over to him. Her finger went into the corner of her mouth, and she turned her big eyes up to his face.

"What do you want?" He eyed her, pretending to be stern.

"Story." The little sprite had seen through his gruff exterior before any of the others, and he had a feeling if he didn't steel himself against it, he'd spend the rest of his life wrapped around her little finger.

"Story, huh?" Leaning down, he lifted her into his lap, where she cuddled back against his chest. It had become their ritual before supper each night. He started in on a continuation of the lives of a family of squirrels he'd made up a week ago.

While he talked, Miriam set the table. Bear couldn't miss how she took extra care with his place setting, nor how she gave him the biggest slice of bread from the basket.

A man could get used to this.

Deborah hopped around like a flea at a dog show, not appearing to listen to the story but commenting whenever he stopped for a breath.

Firelight bathed Emmylou's face as she bent over the coals to slide the Dutch oven over the heat. The ease with which she'd sliced up that turkey, made a quick gravy, and whipped up dumplings fascinated him. She sure knew her way around a cook-fire. He'd have roasted that bird whole and had to wait until near midnight for it to be done.

Maybe he should think about dragging a stove up the mountain.

Her skirts swayed with her movements, and fine wisps of hair teased her cheeks.

Funny how he'd not thought her much to look at when he first met her. The truth was, Emmylou Paxton. . .McCall was worth more than a second glance.

Yep, he had a few things to be thankful for.

Best of all was when the girls were ready for bed. Deborah insisted that Bear be a part of tucking them in and hearing their prayers. He was clumsy when it came to brushing hair and tying nightgown strings, but Deborah squealed when he tossed her up on her bunk, and Tabitha giggled when he chucked her under the chin. Miriam was more reserved, but she smiled when he patted her shoulder and tugged the blanket up.

When they were settled, Emmylou poured him another cup of coffee then seated herself near the lamp with one of his shirts and a needle and thread.

"Seems I've been pretty hard on my wardrobe." He settled into his chair with his book. "You've been patching and mending every night." Mostly he just wore something until it wore out, then got a new one. Having her wash and mend his things was a kind of intimacy he hadn't been prepared for when he'd jumped into this marriage.

"I haven't even started on the socks." She smiled, her hands quick as she turned the plaid collar to hide the worn spots. "You're hard on those, too, and darning isn't my forte."

He turned the book to catch more of the lamp and firelight. "It'd be the first thing you weren't good at. I guess I got the better end of the deal marrying you."

She was quiet for a moment, and the color in her cheeks entranced him.

"I wouldn't say so. Compared to where I came from, and compared to what waited for me in Denver, this is very nice." She didn't look up.

"Where did you come from?" He set his book in his lap. "I don't know much about you."

"Nor I you." This time she favored him with a quick glance. "I'm from Harrisburg, Pennsylvania. I was orphaned when I was about Miriam's age and sent to live with my aunt and uncle. They had no children, nor any clue what to do with one. Aunt Ida is stern and exacting, and Uncle Henry is cold and remote. I always knew I was a burden to them, that I wasn't really wanted there. When I saw a copy of the *Matrimonial News*, I thought it was my way out."

"Then you got jilted at the train station." Guilt at his bluntness pricked him when she winced. "I know how you felt." He rushed on to cover his gaffe. "I got jilted, too. Left at the altar in a new suit and tie. My bride hopped it with the best man at the last minute. He'd come into some money, and I guess she figured the grass was greener on his side of the fence."

Her hands stilled. "That's terrible."

"Sure hurt at the time, but now I'm glad. Meredith was a mistake."

"What did you do?"

"Sold my farm, left Indiana, came to the mountains to get away from people, women especially." He chuckled, looking over at the three cherubs who had invaded his life. "I guess God's got a sense of humor, huh?" He opened his book again.

"Would you mind reading aloud?" Her lower lip disappeared behind her teeth, and she dropped her gaze back to her work.

It was the first time she'd asked him for anything. That strange warm feeling in his chest expanded.

Emmylou shook the rug, sending dust billowing into the crisp morning air just outside the doorway. Behind her Tabitha swished the dishrag around in the washtub water while Miriam swept the cabin floor. Golden aspen leaves floated down around Emmylou. She drew in a deep breath, rejoicing in the peace of this place. Here, no one belittled her. No one made her feel unwanted—not even Bear, who had every excuse to do so. For the first time in her life, she had a purpose, plenty to keep her busy each day, and three little girls she was coming to love dearly.

Then there was Bear.

Even now the ringing of his ax told her where he was, felling logs and dragging them up to begin adding two rooms onto the cabin, one for her and one for him. Once those were completed, she could stop feeling guilty that he had to spend his nights in the toolshed on a hard bedroll. Everything he'd done since she met him had been to provide for her or the girls. He was a provider and protector by nature, even if a gruff one.

And from the moment he'd shared his own ill-fated brush with matrimony, she'd felt a kinship that went beyond their marriage of convenience. He understood the humiliation of being jilted. He understood wanting to get away from the past. He understood what it was like not to be wanted.

Maybe that was why, in spite of his growling and grousing, he made room for the girls in his life. He snuggled Tabitha, answered Deborah's thousand-and-one questions every day, and made time to compliment and encourage Miriam. It was as if he knew how desperately each of them wanted to be somebody's little girl.

And the girls were blossoming. All day long it was "Bear" this and "Bear" that. She'd even caught Tabitha telling her dolly the squirrel stories and trying to imitate Bear's growl.

Then there was the eager, flighty feeling Emmylou got every evening after the girls were asleep and she and Bear settled in front of the fireplace and he read aloud to her. He had a rich, mellow voice, and he'd obviously had good schooling at some point, because his diction was perfect. But more often than not, Emmylou would lose track of the story as she watched the firelight flicker in his brown eyes, the way his big hands held the spine of the book, the way he lounged in his chair, so masculine and certain of himself. That easygoing confidence in his abilities was very appealing to her.

She held the rug to her middle as she surveyed the glade. It would be time to call Deborah in for lessons soon. Miriam and Deborah did schoolwork each day, something Miriam thrived on and Deborah endured.

Emmylou scanned the high meadow. A glimpse of bright color flashed under the trees on the far side of the meadow. Deborah in her blue coat. The cabin never seemed big enough to hold Deborah. What it would be like in winter when she had to stay indoors, Emmylou couldn't imagine. She'd give her a few more minutes to play.

"Emmylou, can we make cookies for Bear today?" Miriam whisked the dirt over the threshold and stood the broom in the corner behind the door.

That was her Miriam, always looking for ways to serve, especially Bear.

Emmylou paused. *Her* Miriam. How had these girls snuck into her heart so quickly? Because she really did feel as if they were hers.

Tabitha, with a dish-towel apron slung around her neck, finished "washing" the tin plates while Emmylou gathered the ingredients for cookies. They were just about set to begin mixing when a faraway scream rent the air.

Deborah!

Emmylou dropped the flour sack, sending a cloud of white du... for the door. "Girls, stay here!" Slamming the door behind her, she... Deborah.

Another scream rent the air, nearly drowned out by a ferocious ro... fabric darted through the trees. Scrabbling up into a slender aspen, Del... fast as she could.

A monstrous grizzly rose on its hind legs below her, swiping up into th... mouth open and snarling.

Emmylou's heart slammed into her throat.

Not knowing what else to do, not thinking, only knowing she had to pro... rah at all costs, Emmylou hiked her skirts and ran straight across the meadow... flew over the logs spanning the creek, and her hair streamed out, falling from its... draping across her eyes like a shawl. She shouted, her voice barely clearing the l... her throat.

The bear ignored her, planting its huge paws against the tree trunk and shoving... entire aspen shuddered, and Deborah screamed again.

"Hang on! I'm coming!" The words were snatched away from Emmylou as she ra... Though what she would do when she got there, she didn't know. All she knew was she... had to get to Deborah.

She stumbled in the grass and fell headlong, sprawling and tumbling. Bouncing up, her legs tangled with what had tripped her. A branch. She snatched it up and raced on. Behind her came a masculine shout, but she didn't stop.

The bear shook the tree again, sending a cascade of leaves floating down. It was so focused on Deborah, it didn't even notice Emmylou until she swung the branch and cracked it across the bear's back.

With a roar, the animal dropped onto all fours and swung its boulder-sized head around. Lips snarling, teeth dripping with slobber, another meaty bellow blasted from its throat.

Stunned, Emmylou dropped the branch and backed away. The animal rose again and swatted as she dodged, barely missing her with its rapacious claws.

Deborah's first scream made Bear drop his ax onto the woodchips at his feet. Emmylou's shout had him snatching up his rifle and racing across the grass. He spied Emmylou, hair like a red flag behind her, running for all she was worth—toward a grizzly! Was she out of her mind? He thundered after her. Not bothering with the bridge, he leaped the creek. Emmylou tumbled to the ground, arms flailing, but she popped up again, this time dragging something behind her.

"Get down! Lie down and curl up!"

She appeared not to hear him, instead swinging a stick—a stick!—at the angry beast as if she could slap it away like a fly.

She managed to dodge the first swing of a paw, ducking behind the tree trunk, but he knew she wouldn't get so lucky again. Though farther away than he would've liked, he had run out of time. He knelt in the grass a hundred yards away, bracing his elbow on his knee and sighting down the barrel of his rifle.

ne gunshot reverberated through the glade. His shoulder absorbed the recoil as he
d another shell into the gun breech and fired again. The sow bear jerked, but she
t stop her pursuit. She swung her head, jaws slavering, darting around the aspen and
ering toward Emmylou.

Two, three, four shots. One splintered off a tree trunk, but he was sure the others had
ched their target. Why didn't the animal go down?

Emmylou quit dodging and leaped at a spruce tree, climbing the branches, hindered
her skirts. Her sobbing reached him, sending a chill into his core. He snapped off
another shot then stood and waved his arm, shouting at the grizzly.

She turned toward him, snarling, and started his way. Fat from a summer of grazing
and berry picking, her coat rippled with each ground-eating bound.

Now that she faced him, he knew he would have to break her down in order to stop
her. His rifle would never penetrate that skull, not even at this distance. He dropped to
his knee again and shot at first one forepaw and then the other.

With his second shot, the bear tumbled, her momentum sending her tail over tip.
Before he could relax, she was getting to her feet once more.

He ejected the spent shell. "Stand up, stand up, stand up. . . Please, God, make her
stand up." Praying that Emmylou and Deborah had the sense to get higher in their trees
and stay there, he aimed.

Just as he prayed, the grizzly rose on her hind legs, exposing her belly. This time he
paused, let out his breath, held it, and squeezed, aiming just right of center, where her
heart would be.

The bear sank to the ground as if her bones had melted. He lowered his rifle, bracing
it against the ground and leaning his forehead on his hands where they grasped the warm
barrel. His breath came in gulps, and his heart pounded in his ears.

"Boy howdy, did you see that? You sure saved us, didn't you, Bear? Hey, Bear saved us
from a bear." Deborah shinnied down the tree like a chipmunk, dropping the last couple
of feet. She had a leaf in her hair and a dirt smudge on her cheek, but her eyes sparkled,
and she grinned at him as if she hadn't nearly been killed.

Bear's hands shook, and he swallowed, unable to speak. He felt cold all over, shaky,
as if he'd been ill for a long time. The little horror didn't even know the danger she'd been
in. Just thinking of her big eyes and tiny bones, all that life and chatter and motion in the
clutches of an angry grizzly, made his knees wobble.

Emmylou descended more slowly, looking as shaky as he felt. A trickle of blood
stood out boldly from a cut on her pale temple, and her hair spilled down her shoulders.
Spruce needles, twigs, and grass caught in the fiery locks.

He'd almost lost them.

The chill in his belly turned to fire.

"What in thunder did you think you were doing?" His knees firmed up, and he
jumped to his feet, towering above them. "That grizzly almost killed you! If I hadn't come
running, you'd be dead right now, the both of you! What were you thinking charging
across the meadow like that?"

Emmylou blinked, freezing in her tracks. "I. . .I. . .don't know."

"You don't know?" He yanked the knife from the scabbard on his belt. He pointed it
at Deborah, who was far too unabashed for his sanity. "I *told* you not to wander, didn't I?
My rules aren't just suggestions for you to consider. You're too wild for your own good,

and it's going to stop even if I have to chain you to a chair. Now get back to the cabin and bring my horse and a rope, and don't you stop to lollygag or chat with the birds, got it?"

Deborah's lip trembled, and her chin came up a notch. She fisted her hands and blinked hard, turning on her heels and marching toward the house. Bear felt like a heel yelling at her, but by sugar, she needed to be more careful. What if he'd been up at his claim, or walking his trap line?

The moment Deborah was out of earshot, Emmylou gave him an earful he was in no mood to hear.

"You didn't need to shout at her. She didn't do anything wrong. She was just playing under the trees. It isn't as if she enticed a bear close and poked it in the eye." Emmylou tried to smooth her hair out of her face, but her hands were shaking. She came away with a smear of blood on her hand.

"You were both nearly killed!" How could he make them understand?

"I know. But your rule was to stay within sight of the cabin. Deborah did that. It isn't her fault that a bear chased her."

He didn't know whether to grab her up tight and hold her until he stopped being afraid or shake her until her teeth rattled for scaring him in the first place. To avoid doing either, he began field-dressing the carcass. The sow grizzly would go a good four hundred pounds if she weighed an ounce. Her claws were inches long, capable of eviscerating an elk, and her teeth... His hand shook so that he nearly dropped the knife.

The words wouldn't stay behind his teeth, no matter how tight he gritted them. "That doesn't explain what you were doing running right at a grizzly. Talk about a babe in the woods. You need a full-time minder. I never should've brought you up here. Not any of you. You had one job to do, look out for the girls, and what do you do? Let one get chased up a tree then put yourself in danger by smacking a bear with a switch. I should've sent those girls right back where they came from, and you, too."

She gasped and flinched as if he'd slapped her. Moisture gathered on her lashes and plummeted down her cheeks. Without a word she lowered her head and turned toward the cabin. He regretted his words before they'd even died away in the crisp air, but he didn't call her back.

Chapter 5

B ear gave a mighty heave and sank the ax deep into the tree trunk, taking his frustrations out on the wood. Two more arcing whacks and the branches began to quiver. He moved away to avoid any kickback and watched as the pine landed within a foot of where he'd intended.

But there was no satisfaction in the accomplishment. Around him stillness invaded the forest. No happy chatter, no questions, no endless movement. In the two days since the bear attack, Emmylou had kept the girls at the cabin with her.

Which is just what he'd told her to do, so his getting twitchy about it made no sense. Not that much had made sense ever since the girls had barged into his life.

But this time he was to blame. He'd blown it. He'd let his temper get the best of him, lashing out because he'd been scared, saying things he didn't really mean. And he had no idea how to fix it. It wasn't like he could unsay the words, erase the hurt that shone out of four pairs of eyes.

Bear's pa had been of the "least-said-soonest-mended" school of thought. No profit in dragging it out and examining it all over again. Just put it away and go about your life. Folks got over things, right?

Except nobody seemed to be getting over it, not even him. Every time he returned to the cabin, they scattered like quail. Tabitha ran to the bunk and grabbed up her dolly, Miriam watched him from the corner of her eye as she went about her tasks. Worst of all, Deborah crept around with her chin on her chest, her feet dragging. His little I-can-whip-my-weight-in-wildcats Deborah had disappeared.

And Emmylou. His conscience kept kicking him in the backside every time he looked at her. The light had gone out of her eyes, the spring from her step, and worse yet, she had stopped talking to him. The evenings were silent as she mended. He couldn't concentrate on his reading. He didn't work on his traps. He didn't do anything.

Lopping branches off the fallen tree, he pressed his lips together. Well, tonight things were going to change. If he'd broken it, he could fix it, that was all. He'd tell them to stop skulking around and go back to the way they had been.

"McCall, where you at?"

Charlie.

Bear picked up his rifle, shouldered it along with his ax, and picked his way down the mountainside. "Coming!"

Charlie sat atop his mule, his white beard poking out every which way, and his buckskins greasy and dark. As always, he scorned a hat, his hair straggling down his shoulders

and mingling with the fringe on his jacket. He dug inside his shirt and pulled out a battered envelope.

"Don't know when I became your personal Pony Express, but there's a letter for you. Some lawyer in Denver. Figured I'd best bring it up since it looked so official and all."

A chill hit Bear's gut. The last time Charlie brought him a letter it had turned his world upside down. He took the envelope.

"You got time for supper?"

"That gal cookin'?" He cocked his head.

"Yeah. And she has a name. Emmylou." Bear continued past Charlie, who whirled his mule and followed.

"How's that workin' out? I never thought I'd see the day you got hitched, much less had a passel of little girls runnin' around. Not after listenin' to you spout off about how there was no place in your life for a woman, not ever again, amen." Charlie chuckled.

Bear grunted and lengthened his stride. The cabin came into view, and his chest swelled a bit at the sight of smoke coming from the chimney and a line of little girls' clothes drying in the autumn sun. Deborah sat cross-legged on his splitting stump, a crown of leaves on her head, plucking berries from a twig. When she spied him and Charlie, she hopped up and hustled inside. Emmylou came to the door, a sack-apron at her waist.

Charlie slid off his mule.

Bear gripped his rifle stock. "I invited Charlie to supper. Hope you don't mind."

"Of course not. It's your house." She stared at the mountain over his shoulder.

So she still wasn't past it.

"How are the girls?" He leaned his rifle and ax against the side of the house and dunked his hands in the washbasin on the bench by the door.

"Fine. They all stayed close." Her hands knotted in her apron. "Just like you wanted."

He didn't know whether to be irked or relieved that she had a bit of snap to her voice. Much better if she stormed at him a bit, then they could hash it all out and be done. But she pressed her lips together and disappeared into the cabin.

"Girls, company for dinner, so I'll need some help. Deborah, fetch me an armload of wood. Miriam, whip me up a batch of biscuit dough for dumplings, and Tabitha, can you set out the cups and plates?"

They did her bidding, though when he came inside, they all stilled for a moment before continuing on with their tasks. He felt like a grouchy old badger at a tea party.

When they all sat at the table, he said grace, though it was gruff and rushed. Truth was, he was embarrassed to be talking to God when so many people—females—were upset at him. . .and not just upset, but rightly so.

"So, what's in the letter?" Charlie shoved a dumpling in his mouth. "Best food I've et in a while, and that's includin' what I had at the café in Idaho Springs this morning, ma'am. If Bear ever tosses you out, you could start a restaurant."

The girls' heads swiveled from Bear to Emmylou, who forced a chuckle. "Thank you, Mr. Charlie. I'll have to remember that. What letter?"

Bear dug it out and opened it, holding the single page toward the lamplight in the middle of the table. Scanning the first paragraph, his mouth went dry and a fist squeezed his throat. He quickly read the rest before tucking it back into his shirt pocket. He gave a quick shake of his head to Emmylou, who took his cue and didn't ask. Putting his spoon in his dish, he pushed his plate away, appetite gone.

Whatever it was, it was bad. Emmylou wanted to snatch the letter from Bear, but the girls were watching and they had a guest at the table, and Bear's eyes clearly said "later."

"Later" turned out to be much later. The girls, catching the jump in tension, had been fractious and out of sorts. And Charlie stayed forever, sitting by the fire and keeping up a running commentary on every person in Idaho Springs. Bear stared at the flames, nodding occasionally, but not listening any more than Emmylou, who sat on her bunk, fingers laced in her lap, waiting.

At last, Charlie heaved himself up and shuffled to the door, bobbing his head in Emmylou's direction and thanking her again for the dinner. "Thanks for the bed. Don't wait breakfast on me. I'll be gone before sunup."

"He's putting his bedroll in the toolshed." Bear got up and threw another log on the fire.

Emmylou blinked. "Is there enough room for both of you?" Bear was a big man, and it was a small shed.

"Don't worry. I'll sleep out." His voice was dry as chaff.

"Won't you be cold?"

"Not any colder than the shed." He dug the letter out of his pocket. "Don't worry about that; worry about this."

She read it, her fingers going to her lips and her heart dropping to her heels.

"Is this legitimate?"

"Dunno." Bear scratched his beard and leaned forward, planting his forearms on his knees, hands hanging limp. He shrugged. "It sure sounds like it. Official lawyer letterhead and lots of legal-sounding words."

"What are you going to do?" She didn't say *we*. His tirade of a couple days ago had made it quite clear that there was no *we*.

"Reckon I'll have to go to Denver and sort it out."

Emmylou felt as if she'd walked off a cliff in the dark. Here in her hand she held Bear's ticket out, his way of escape from a burden he'd never wanted.

The girls' father had shown up and wanted his children back.

Chapter 6

In the end, they all went. The ride down the mountain was much worse than the trip up, and Emmylou wondered if the mule felt the burden of her heavy heart. She'd hoped Bear would go alone, leaving her and the girls at the cabin, fearing if they all went, it would be too easy for him to leave them in the city.

The train ride seemed endless, lurching down the track toward Denver. Bear sat hunched in his flannel jacket, one boot propped up on the seat opposite him, as if penning Emmylou and the girls into their seats. He had what Emmylou had heard described as a "thousand-yard stare" going that didn't invite comment.

Miriam said nothing. Her little mouth was pinched and her eyes sad, looking much like she had the first time Emmylou had seen her, as if she'd seen too much of life and had no expectation that it would get better. They had told her and Deborah about their father and the lawyer's letter and that they were going to Denver to see what was to be done. Bear had made no promises about fighting to keep the girls, no matter how much Emmylou wanted him to, and she hadn't made any, either, since everything hinged on him. She couldn't take the girls herself, not without some way to support them, and even if she could, the court wouldn't let her, not with blood relatives in the picture.

Deborah wedged herself into the corner of the seat by the window, arms crossed, staring daggers at Bear and Emmylou. Anger and helplessness etched her features. She was such a fighter, but there was no one to fight, no way to gain even a measure of control over her life. Emmylou's heart broke for Deborah, but when she tried to touch her, the child wriggled away and turned her face to the window.

Tabitha, keyed in on the tension, tucked her finger into her mouth and nestled into Emmylou's arms. From time to time she popped upright and looked from one sister to the other then at Bear and Emmylou before snuggling once more. Emmylou wrapped her tight in her arms, lightly rubbing her chin across Tabitha's russet curls, her heart aching at the thought of losing these precious girls.

The train lurched to a stop, and Bear roused. "Don't straggle. There will be a lot of people here, and I don't have time to hunt for you if you get lost."

"Ain't like we never been in a train station before." Deborah's mutter was just loud enough to be heard.

Bear took Tabitha from Emmylou and hoisted her onto his arm. "Then you know better than to wander, don't you?"

Miriam slipped her hand into Emmylou's, and they filed down the aisle and into the depot. Bear carried the girls' valise, and Emmylou her own suitcase. Bear had told her

to pack all the girls' things, just in case, and with that in mind, she'd packed all her own belongings as well.

"We'd best head right to this lawyer's office. There's a westbound train at five, and I'd like to be back on it." Bear shouldered his way through the depot door and tossed the girls' bag into a waiting cab.

Their shoes sounded loud on the narrow staircase as they trudged up to the second-floor lawyer's office. Emmylou's heart throbbed, and she found herself taking deep breaths every few minutes, as if there wasn't enough air in the building.

They filed into the office. An ordinary table, a single file cabinet, and four hard chairs filled the cramped space. A disheveled man with a soup-strainer moustache and wispy thinning hair hunched behind the paper-strewn table.

"What can I do for you?"

Bear handed Tabitha to Emmylou and dug in his pocket. He pulled out an envelope, frowned at it, and stuffed it back in, digging in the other pocket and producing a crumpled page. "We got this letter from you, and we're here to talk about it."

The man smoothed his rumpled lapels and swiped his hand across his sparse dome. "Let's see here," he said, picking up the paper and scanning it. "Ah, yes, I remember now. The matter of Oscar DeWitt's children." He eyed the girls as if examining scientific specimens. "Mr. DeWitt arrived last night and is most anxious to be reunited with his daughters. If you would like to leave them here in my care, I'll be happy to turn them over."

Tears burned Emmylou's eyes, but she fought them back. She didn't want the girls to see her cry. She had to be brave, for them.

Bear scowled, hands on his hips. It was hard not to be angry with him in spite of the fact that he hadn't asked for any of this, not to have the girls dropped into his life, not to have to marry a stranger, and not to have his life disrupted by lawyers and train trips and all the rest. She couldn't blame him for wanting to be rid of them.

"Just hold on a minute. I'm not leaving them here. I don't even know you."

The lawyer, Mr. Twigg according to the name on the door, tapped his chin with one long finger. "You want to deliver the children to the hotel where their father is staying?"

Bear loomed over the desk and planted his hands on the papers, making Mr. Twigg lean back, his eyes widening. "I don't. I want to see this DeWitt fellow face-to-face. I want to hear why he abandoned his family. I want to know why he's sashaying back into their lives now. That's what I want." He straightened. "You tell DeWitt we'll meet with him at the Front Range Hotel tonight."

Twigg fussed with his rumpled clothes and shook his head. "I can't allow my client to converse with you regarding the children unless I am present."

"Then I guess you'd better show up, too, huh?" Bear grabbed both suitcases, jerked his head at the door, and stalked out.

As Emmylou followed him out with Tabitha on her hip, she didn't know whether to be grateful or crushed. Bear had put off turning the girls over for a few hours, but had he just prolonged the agony?

❦

Bear strode along the boardwalk toward the Front Range Hotel.

Looks like the five o'clock train is out of the question.

Every time he looked at Emmylou she was blinking back tears and touching one of the girls, cuddling Tabitha or squeezing Miriam's hand or smoothing Deborah's hair. He could use a little comforting himself, not that he was getting any. She saved it all for the girls.

He stopped and turned. Where were they, anyway? Several yards behind, they trotted along. Deborah reached him first.

"You going to a fire?" She panted and tossed her braids over her shoulders. "Or are you just in that big a hurry to get rid of us?"

He took a deep, calming breath. She was always trying to twist his tail, but at least she was talking to him again. "Forgot your legs are shorter than mine." He handed her the valise. "Here, you take this, and I'll take Tabitha." When Emmylou caught up, he reached for the little girl. "C'mere, punkin. You're about too big for Emmylou to carry."

Tabitha's arms wrapped around his neck, and a dull pain hit his chest. She smelled like sunshine and little girl and Emmylou's soap. He tightened his hold and entered the hotel.

An hour later, the dining room was crowded, and they had to wait for a table. As the harried waitress squeezed between the chairs, arms holding plates high, Bear could only be thankful he'd gotten Emmylou out of that job.

Nobody seemed to want the meals they ordered. Bear had just about decided to call it quits and head back to their room when Miriam stiffened as if someone had poked her with a stick. Her big eyes tracked to the doorway, and Bear turned in his chair.

A wiry man with a scraggly goatee and a checked suit stood there surveying the room. He stopped when he spied their table. His eyes glittered, and he grinned, advancing toward them.

"I thought I'd never find you." He squatted beside Miriam's chair, but when he moved to hug her, she backed away, off the chair and into Bear's side.

Bear's arm came around her. In a flash, Deborah was ducking up under his other arm. Tabitha, perhaps too young to remember her father, sat still, watching.

"Come here and say hello to your father." The man straightened and frowned.

The girls remained where they were. Emmylou's eyes clashed with Bear's. Miriam trembled, and Bear's senses went on alert.

"You DeWitt?"

"That's right. These are my daughters."

"Where's your lawyer?"

"He'll be along directly. I didn't figure I needed him first thing." He jammed his hands on his hips. "I gotta say, girls, this is a fine greeting. Your mother would be ashamed." He narrowed his eyes. "You're lucky I don't backhand you for being so rude." His hand came up, and he made a slapping gesture. "I can't abide an uppity kid."

Miriam flinched. The muscles in Bear's chest tightened.

"I can't abide you," Deborah muttered, her chin in her chest.

"Emmylou, maybe you'd best take the girls upstairs. I believe Mr. DeWitt and I have a few things to talk about." Bear struggled to keep his voice even. His fists itched to grab DeWitt and shake him till his pea brains fell out. How dare he threaten these children?

Emmylou took Tabitha's hand and directed the girls out of the room, throwing a pleading glance back over her shoulder as she went.

DeWitt didn't try to stop them, instead turning Emmylou's chair around and straddling it, crossing his arms along the back. "Good thinking, McCall. Get the womenfolk out of the way so they aren't horning in where they ain't wanted. Now we can talk man-to-man."

Bear crossed his arms and waited, his teeth clenched. His pa had always said a fool can't abide the sound of silence.

Sure enough, DeWitt started blathering. "A shame I couldn't get home to Chicago before my wife dumped the girls on you. It's all over town about how they landed on your doorstep and you had to marry that skinny redheaded spinster. Drastic step. Is she a good cook at least? 'Cuz she sure ain't much to look at." He grinned. "Still, there might be other compensations, if you know what I mean." His leer nearly got his teeth shoved down his throat. "Anyway, my wife was dumber than a sack of hammers sometimes. Always ailing, always needing something. I'd plumb had it when she dropped another girl. Hope you have better luck than I did when it comes to kids. Three mouthy redheads like their mama. Course, you marrying a redhead don't improve your chances much, but at least yours didn't seem too gabbity. Uppity kids and gabbity women are the bane of a man's existence, ain't they? No wonder I had to clear out for a while."

Bear flexed his fists and pressed his tongue hard against the back of his teeth.

"Anyway, I can take the brats off your hands tomorrow. We don't need to involve the lawyer. I told him to stay away. I just needed his clout for the letter so's you'd know it was all official-like. Just have the girls at the depot in the morning and you'll be a free man." He slapped his hands against the top of the chair and made to rise. "Bet you can't wait to be shut of them. I can't say I'm all that eager to get saddled with them again myself, but a man's gotta do what a man's gotta do, I guess."

Bear leaned forward and braced his forearms on the edge of the table. "We're not through here. I'm not just dropping the girls off tomorrow. If we're going to do this thing, it needs to be legal. You drag your lawyer to the courthouse tomorrow, and we'll go before a judge and get this all straightened out."

DeWitt's shoulders sagged, and then he shrugged. "If that's the way you want it. I suppose I can stay another day. But the only one who will profit will be my lawyer, 'cuz he'll charge me a fee for appearing in court."

Bear followed him out of the hotel, headed for the telegraph station in the depot. Then he hurried to a neighborhood south of the downtown area and, after a brief visit with a friend, returned to the hotel.

He tapped on the door and Emmylou opened it a crack, then, seeing him, she slipped out, closing the door behind her. She had a tight-drawn look, and she twisted her fingers at her waist.

"The girls are in bed, but Miriam and Deborah aren't asleep yet." She kept her voice low, drawing him toward the window at the end of the hall, the same place where he'd laid out his proposal the night he'd met her. The moonlight picked out the fiery highlights in her hair and gave extra luster to her eyes. The curve of her cheek was so satiny-perfect, he wanted to brush it with his fingertips.

"Bear, what are we going to do? The girls are afraid of that man. I can't stand the

thought of turning them over to him. He doesn't love them, you can tell. He won't care for them properly. I know you're tired of us, I know you don't want us invading your life, and I know you were looking forward to getting free from this burden, but please. . ." She gripped his arm. Her voice shook, and her lashes fell. "Please don't do anything hasty. I don't trust Oscar DeWitt, not after the way the girls shied away from him. Miriam told me he slapped them around when he got angry, and Deborah said he was meaner than second skimmings, never giving her mother enough money to run the house, or buy food or clothes for the girls. Please, give me a few days to figure something out. Maybe I can find a way to take care of the girls myself here in Denver. Don't abandon us yet."

He covered her hand with his, ducking to force her to look him in the eye. "What are you talking about? Who said I was abandoning you?"

She slipped her hand from his grasp. "You. You said you wished you'd never taken us up the mountain in the first place, that you should've sent us right back where we came from. And then the letter came and you bundled us up with all our things and hustled us down the mountain. I know you want to be rid of us, but I'm asking for just a few more days so I can try to find a way to keep the girls."

He stepped closer, backing her up. "Emmylou McCall, what on earth are you talking about? I don't have any intention of abandoning you." Placing his hands on the wall on either side of her, he penned her in. "What kind of man do you take me for? I just traipsed all over town sending telegrams and consulting my lawyer. Tomorrow morning we meet him at the courthouse and fight this thing."

Her tongue darted out to moisten her lips, and he sucked in a breath. "But you said. . ." She stared up at him, the pulse beating in her throat. "I thought. . ."

Leaning down, he pressed his forehead to hers, closing his eyes and inhaling her scent—flowery soap, sunshine, and woman. "Emmylou, I'm sorry. I never should've shouted at you. I was just so scared. I saw how close I came to losing you and Deborah, and I realized how deep you were imbedded in my life and in my heart. I've been alone for so long, and I didn't even know how lonely I was. Then you girls busted in on my life, scattering everything every which way, bringing noise and chatter and joy." His hands went to her shoulders then down her back, bringing her into his arms. He rested his chin on her hair, savoring the feel of her against him. "I couldn't stand the thought of not having you in my life, you and the girls." His embrace tightened. "I'm so sorry for hollering at you. I wanted to take it all back the minute I said it."

Her arms came around him, and she pressed herself further into his hold. His throat grew thick, and he knew this was as close to heaven as he was going to get this side of glory. Then she leaned back, her eyes searching his face, and he bent his head to brush her lips with his, sending his heart soaring to new heights.

Slowly, softly, he explored her lips, cupping her cheeks, letting the tendrils of her hair curl around his fingers, reveling in the texture of her skin. Like a starving man, he longed to snatch her up and devour her, but he held himself in restraint, not wanting to scare her, aware that they stood in a hotel hallway with three little girls nearby. Easing back, he searched her eyes, trying to gauge what she was thinking about this turn of events. Had he scared her? Had he crossed a line? She hadn't resisted, but. . .

"Emmylou?"

She sucked in a quick breath, her eyes full of wonder and her cheeks flushed.

"Bear. . ." Her fingertips brushed her lips then rose to touch his, as if she couldn't quite take things in. He knew just how she felt.

He took her hand and pressed it to his thundering heart. "I know this isn't the time or the place, but we're going to talk. For now. . ." He kissed her fingertips. "I don't want you to worry. My lawyer will meet us at the courthouse in the morning. We're going to fight DeWitt. There's no way he's getting the girls."

The girls.

Miriam, Deborah, little Tabitha.

His girls.

His and Emmylou's.

Chapter 7

Emmylou hardly slept that night, sitting in the rocker beside the bed. Bear had opted for the bench at the end of the hall, leaning back in the corner, his rifle propped beside him.

Every time she closed her eyes, she was back in his embrace, his arms holding her, his lips on hers, the rough softness of his beard brushing her cheeks, his outdoorsy-piney-masculine smell enveloping her.

He cared for her, and he was going to fight for the girls.

Thank You, Lord. You've given me so much more than I ever expected. Please, help us find a way to do what is best for the girls. Protect them, surround them with Your love. Go before us, prepare the judge and the lawyers, help us and show us what Your will is for us and for these precious children.

She didn't say amen because her prayer didn't end, cycling through the night, begging for guidance and strength for the next day.

By the time they reached the courthouse, she was an exhausted bundle of nerves. The girls were so good, quiet and watchful. Even Deborah hardly said a peep, keeping hold of Bear's hand and watching everything, but keeping her thoughts to herself.

Mr. DeWitt and his lawyer, Mr. Twigg, showed up. Oscar DeWitt gave Emmylou such a sneering, superior glance, she gasped, but when Bear stepped forward, she put her hand on his arm.

"Bear, this must be your family." A man strode toward them, his shoes loud on the hardwood floor. He shook hands with Bear and turned to Emmylou.

"Greg Snyder. I'm Bear's attorney. You must be Mrs. McCall."

He had a friendly face, with intelligent eyes and quick mannerisms. Squatting, he greeted each of the girls by name. "Ladies, it's a pleasure to meet you."

Drawing Bear and Emmylou aside, he lowered his voice. "I've met with the judge already, and he's going to squeeze us in. And I burned up the telegraph lines between here and Chicago. I wish we had some eyewitness testimony, but we'll have to go with what we have. Now, I have to confer with my colleague. Twigg's a sharp operator. Don't let his rumpled appearance fool you. He's no slouch. DeWitt has the upper hand at the moment. He *is* the girls' father, after all."

He left them, and Oscar DeWitt sidled over. "I hate that we're dragging this all out in court. Why don't you just turn the girls over? I'm their pa, and you know the court is going to award them to me."

Emmylou's already erratic heartbeat stumbled, and she tried to work some moisture into her dry mouth.

"Still, there might be a way we could both win here." DeWitt stuck his hands into the pockets of his checked suit and rocked on his heels. "I could always sell the girls to you if you are that set on keeping them."

Her breath hitched and stuck in her throat, and hope bloomed in her chest.

"How much?" Bear's voice grated low.

"For, say, a thousand dollars apiece?" He sniffed and shrugged. "They ain't worth it, but you seem awful set on having them."

Emmylou let out the breath she'd been holding, her shoulders sagging. A thousand dollars apiece? Might as well be a million.

Bear nodded and stroked his beard. "Three thousand dollars and you clear out and leave them alone?"

"You pay me three thousand dollars, and you'll never hear from me again, that I can guarantee."

The lawyers returned. "It's time." Mr. Snyder led them into the courtroom.

The judge sat behind his bench, his black robes settled around his shoulders like a cape. He had a seamed face, and his hands were gnarled and knobby.

"Let's get down to business. I have a busy docket today." He folded his hands. "I understand this is a custody issue?"

"Your Honor." Mr. Twigg stepped forward. "My client is these girls' father, and he's come to claim them. Mr. McCall is contesting his claim."

"That so?"

Mr. Snyder seated Emmylou and the girls in the first row and motioned to a chair for Bear beside him at a table. "Good morning, Judge. My client, Mr. McCall, was given custody of the girls by his cousin, the late Mrs. DeWitt. Her husband had abandoned her and the girls, and when she knew she was dying, she made arrangements to send her children to her only known surviving family member. Mr. McCall and his wife have been caring for the children." He drew several papers from his attaché case. "I have here telegrams from neighbors of Mrs. DeWitt in Chicago where she died, attesting to the fact that Mr. DeWitt abandoned his family more than three years ago, leaving them destitute. The only reason he's come after them now is that another distant cousin, one Mrs. DeWitt wasn't aware of, has recently passed away and left his money to the DeWitt girls, Miriam, Deborah, and Tabitha. We contend that Mr. DeWitt has no intention of caring for his daughters once he gets his hands on their inheritance, modest though it might be."

"That's a scurrilous assumption, Your Honor." Twigg shook his head as if such a notion was preposterous. "My client left his family in search of employment so he could support them. When he returned to Chicago, having procured a job in Indiana, he found his wife dead and his children gone. It has taken him several weeks just to track them down. Now all he asks is to be reunited with his family. He has no notion of any inheritance. He loves his daughters, and their rightful place is with them."

"I ain't going with him." Deborah's voice carried across the room.

The judge's head snapped up from reading the telegrams. "What's that? Young lady, you are not to speak here. This is a matter for grown-ups."

"I don't see why. We're the ones everybody's bickering over. Don't we get a say? You send us away with him"—she jerked her thumb at her father—"and he'll just smack us around for a while then skite out and leave us again, or dump us in an orphanage somewhere."

Emmylou put her arm around Deborah and drew her down into her chair. "Shh, let Bear handle it."

"Your Honor." Bear stood. "What Deborah says is true. Just a few minutes ago, out in the hallway, DeWitt offered to sell the girls to me for a thousand dollars apiece."

Twigg's mouth fell open, and he glared at DeWitt. "You did what?"

"That ain't true, Judge. He's making that up to make me look bad."

The judge removed his glasses and chewed on one of the ear stems. "What I wish was that we had the testimony of the children's mother. These telegrams are quite damning, Mr. DeWitt, but you are the children's father. I'm inclined to award you custody, as I am reluctant to separate children from their parents."

Emmylou's fingers hurt, she gripped them so hard. The girls were slipping away.

Bear jammed his hands into his coat pockets and sank into his chair once more. Then his head came up with a jerk, and he yanked his hand out, holding a crumpled envelope. "Snyder, wait a minute." Tearing open the envelope, he scanned the page then handed it to his lawyer.

"Your Honor, you asked for the testimony of the children's mother. I have it here." Snyder read as he spoke. "Here in her own handwriting." He passed it to the judge and turned to fire a hopeful look to Bear and Emmylou.

"Wait a minute, we're supposed to just accept some bit of paper?" Twigg protested. "How do we know that's legitimate? It could be a forgery."

The judge held up his hand, reading the letter. When he finished, he lowered the paper and stared hard at DeWitt, who squirmed under the scrutiny.

"Mr. McCall, where did you get this letter?"

Bear motioned to Miriam. "It was pinned inside Miriam's coat when she showed up in Colorado. Her mother had given it to her just before she died. I clean forgot I had it in my pocket, what with being surprised by getting three girls in the mail and all. If half that stuff is true, a man would be a criminal to give custody of those girls to a scoundrel like DeWitt."

"That's for me to decide. Now, where is this Miriam?"

Miriam slid off her chair, her face pale, her eyes uncertain.

"Young lady, did your mother write this letter, and did you give it to Mr. McCall yourself?"

"Yes, sir. Mama said not to give it to anyone else. She told us Bear would take care of us girls and not let anything bad happen to us."

"And did your mother speak of your father?"

Miriam nodded. She looked fragile and resilient at the same time, needing someone to take care of her and yet so ready to care for her little sisters. Emmylou pressed her lips together to stop them trembling.

"Mama said we needed to go to Bear because if our pa ever came back, it would be bad for us. I don't think Mama knew about any inheritance, but she wanted us to be safe. She knew we wouldn't be if our pa got a hold of us. He's mean, and he hits us. I was glad when he left."

The judge nodded. "This is a weighty matter. I want you all to clear out and come back at noon, when I will have made a decision. Twigg and Snyder, if I have any questions, I'll send my clerk to your offices."

Emmylou's knees wobbled as she rose and took Tabitha's hand. It was nine o'clock

now. Three more hours until they would know. She didn't think she could stand it.

Bear lifted Tabitha onto his arm. "Let's get out of here."

He led them outside. Greg Snyder settled his hat on his head. "I'll be at my office. You can wait there if you want."

"No, thanks. We have a few errands to run. We'll be back here at noon."

They set off away from the courthouse. "Where are we going?" Emmylou asked.

"Figured we'd better do some shopping. The girls need new winter clothes, and so do you." Bear hitched Tabitha higher. "And I want to buy some things for the cabin. We have a couple of new rooms to furnish, and I want you to have a stove so you don't have to cook in the fireplace anymore."

Emmylou trotted to keep up. "But don't you want to wait until we hear from the judge?"

"Nope. He's going to do the right thing."

"How can you be sure?"

"The letter. If I'd only read the letter a long time ago, I would've gone straight to a judge and adopted those girls outright first thing." He nodded toward the girls, who were looking in a store window. "We can talk about it more later, and you can read the letter, but I imagine the judge is doing some checking, and when he does, things will shake out the way we want."

They entered the store, and Bear set Tabitha on the floor. "Buy what you need for the girls, and don't skimp. I want them to have warm clothes and toys and books and whatnot. They've done without long enough."

"Can we afford it? I'll admit, for a minute I seriously thought you were going to take DeWitt up on his offer to sell you the girls, but then he named his price and I wanted to cry."

Bear rubbed his chin, ruffling his shaggy beard. "Emmylou, there's something I've been meaning to tell you. I figured I'd get around to it once I was sure of you, and last night. . ." A gleam entered his eyes, and she put her hands to her cheeks. "Well, last night, I decided I *was* sure of you. Sure enough that I'm pretty eager to get those new rooms finished on the cabin." He winked, making her cheeks heat even more. "Truth is, I have more than enough money for you and the girls. I have a good claim. Been banking the gold I've been pulling out of the mountain a little at a time so as not to rouse too much suspicion that I'd hit a good strike."

She blinked.

"You remember how I told you the woman I was supposed to marry left me at the altar for a richer guy? Well, I never wanted to be married for my money, so I just didn't tell you. Truth is, you're married to a rich man."

Shaking her head, she grasped his fingers. "You're a wonder, do you know that? Why didn't you take DeWitt up on his offer then?"

"Because he never would've left us alone. What he wanted was tantamount to blackmail. A blackmailer never quits until he's bled somebody dry. Don't you worry. DeWitt will get what's coming to him."

Bear was lavish in his buying: laughing when the girls squealed over toys and books and candy and new clothes; insisting that Emmylou get herself a fancy dress in addition to more practical gear; and huddling with the girls, whispering and plotting something while Emmylou sorted through household goods and supplies to carry them through the winter.

The hands of the clock crawled toward noon, and they assembled at the courthouse half an hour early.

Bear paced the hall, and Emmylou fidgeted, half listening to Deborah as she sounded out the words in one of her new books. Emmylou prayed she'd get to take it back to the cabin.

When the judge called them in, Emmylou thought she might faint.

Everyone took their places, Bear and Mr. Snyder at one table, DeWitt and Mr. Trigg at the other. The judge wore a stern expression and nodded when a man slipped in the back and stood with his hands folded at his belt.

"I've gone over the evidence, and I've sent a few telegrams myself this morning. What I've discovered is disturbing." He lifted several sheets of paper. "Mr. DeWitt, based upon your late wife's handwritten testimony, I'm awarding custody of Miriam, Deborah, and Tabitha DeWitt to Mr. and Mrs. McCall, and I'm placing you under arrest." He nodded to the man in the back, who stepped forward with a pair of handcuffs. "I'm holding here a telegram from a Sheriff Kannick of Gary, Indiana, where you resided before coming here. According to him, you are wanted for embezzlement and fraud in Lake County, and will be held in jail here until such time as they can escort you back there to face charges."

The sheriff slapped on the cuffs and dragged a protesting DeWitt from the room. Emmylou sagged into her chair, boneless with relief and surprise. Bear turned in his chair, grinning as he shook Mr. Snyder's hand.

The judge wasn't finished, however.

"Mr. McCall, in order to safeguard those children from having to go through something like this again, are you prepared to legally adopt them?"

"You bet your life, sir." His confident voice rocketed around the room.

"Mrs. McCall?"

"Yes, Your Honor. I'd like nothing better."

"Bring those young ladies up here."

The girls filed through the swinging gate and stood in a row before the judge, in new dresses and shiny new shoes.

"This is permanent, you realize. You'll be a family forever."

"We want nothing more, Judge." Bear put his arm around Emmylou's waist.

The judge motioned for his clerk, who set a document on the bench before him. "I figured you'd agree, so I had my clerk prepare the paperwork." He dipped his pen into his inkwell and scrawled his signature. "You two sign here and they're all yours."

Bear took the pen and signed then handed it to Emmylou. She wrote her name, Emmylou McCall, smiling when she saw "Courtney McCall" in bold letters above hers.

When the judge and the clerk left them alone in the courtroom, Bear scooped her up into his arms and kissed her, swinging her around. His laugh filled every corner.

"Does this mean you are going to be in love and be really married like regular folks?" Deborah rounded the judge's bench and climbed into his chair, picking up the gavel and eyeing it.

Bear reached over and plucked it from her hand. "It sure does. You girls ready to do what we talked about?"

"Yep. We're ready."

"What are you up to?" Emmylou tried to smooth her hair and calm her heart. Bear kept her clamped to his side.

"Me and the girls have a plan we'd like to run by you."

"At the moment, I'd do anything you asked." She hugged his arm. "I'm so happy, I could burst."

"Well, we thought it might be nice if we had a proper church wedding, now that..." He shrugged and scratched his whiskers. "Now that we've reached a sort of understanding. Now that we're a family. You got cheated out of a church wedding and all the fripperies, and I want to make that right."

Emmylou's heart swelled, and happy tears pricked her eyes. Deborah hopped off the judge's chair and grabbed Bear's free hand and swung it, and Miriam laced her fingers under her chin, her eyes full of hope.

Deborah nodded. "Bear said we could wear our fancy dresses and that you would, too, and that you would look beautiful."

Bear's grin widened. "That's right. I'll be the envy of every man in town. You girls go get gussied up, and I'll find the preacher. Just don't keep me waiting too long. I might get nervous." He winked and kissed her again.

Two hours later, Emmylou followed the girls up the aisle of a pretty white church. She couldn't take her eyes off the handsome man at the altar.

He'd cut his hair and trimmed his beard, and he wore a suit and tie. But when she got close and looked into his eyes, so full of pride and love, she recognized her Bear. He took her hand in his and faced the preacher.

They said their vows, this time with conviction, because they wanted to, not because they were desperate. This time, love filled their voices as they became a family, their promises witnessed by the girls who had brought them together.

Erica Vetsch is a transplanted Kansan now residing in Minnesota. She loves books and history, and is blessed to be able to combine the two by writing historical romances. Whenever she's not following flights of fancy in her fictional world, she's the company bookkeeper for the family lumber business, mother of two, wife to a man who is her total opposite and soul mate, and avid museum patron. Erica loves to hear from readers. You can find Erica on the web at www.ericavetsch.com. And you can email her at ericavetsch@gmail.com.

HAVE CASH, WILL MARRY
Renee Yancy

Chapter 1

New York City
April 28, 1899

The Honorable Robert Alexander Radclyfe observed the promenade of young women as they sauntered up the stairs of the Metropolitan Opera House, gorgeously gowned in satin and silks like strutting peahens. Diamonds glittered from tiaras and feathered aigrettes in their hair, flashed from their waists, and adorned the deep décolleté of their bodices.

It reminded him of the summer cattle fairs in England, except the females were dressed in silk and glittering jewels instead of sporting iron nose rings.

"There, Rob—that's the Goulet heiress."

His best friend, James George Epperson, Baron DeVille, who had joined Rob for the scouting trip to America, casually tipped his head toward the shining creature swathed in clouds of pink tulle descending the staircase. "Her father made a fortune in silver mining in Colorado. She's worth millions."

Rob shook his head, amazed. "How the deuce do you know all this? Especially since you're a confirmed bachelor?"

DeVille shrugged. "I read the American papers." He grinned and poked Rob in the shoulder. "I'm looking out for you, old chap."

Miss Goulet gave them a flirtatious smile as she passed, leaving a drift of jasmine scent in her wake.

"Her dowry," James whispered, "is five hundred thousand."

"Hmmm." Rob considered this startling sum. Half a million dollars would buy a lot of stone, timber, plaster, and roof tiles to refurbish Donalee, his family's crumbling ancestral seat in southeast England. Not to mention carpets, drapes, and mullioned glass panes for the hundreds of windows in the castle. Then he winced. What made him any different from the lynx-eyed American mothers at the ball who had diligently perused periodicals like *The Titled American* before they made their plans? It contained a register of available and eligible titled bachelors, with descriptions of their age, accomplishments, and prospects. Page ninety-two held his entry:

> *The Honorable Robert Alexander Radclyfe, eldest son and heir of the ninth*
> *Earl of Wentwater. Entailed estates amount to 15,000 acres, but due to*
> *large mortgages do not yield their nominal value of $200,000. Educated at*
> *Oxford.*

Not exactly complimentary.

"You're attracting attention, Rob," murmured DeVille, gallantly stepping aside for a stunning blond in white cut-velvet and flashing sapphires, led by her mama, who swept toward the staircase, corseted to the extreme and resembling the prow of a battleship at full speed ahead.

"I think she likes you." DeVille raised a discreet eyebrow toward the girl, who had slowed and cast an inviting glance over her bare shoulder at Rob.

Rob shrugged and forced a smile in the girl's direction. His father had ordered him to New York for the sole purpose of finding an American heiress for a bride, with a dowry large enough to pay for the restoration so badly needed to bring the estate into the next century.

But he hadn't met the right American heiress yet, and this was the last ball of the New York social season. As his father's heir, he had a responsibility to marry well, but most of the English aristocrats occupied the same precarious position as his father, land rich and cash poor. The only heiresses with considerable dowries lived in America. So he had dutifully traveled to New York with the understanding he wouldn't return until he'd found the right girl. He'd already had several irate letters from his father, wondering why he wasn't engaged yet.

Soon the cream of New York society would be off to Newport to summer at their "cottages" on the Atlantic Ocean, or go yachting to exotic foreign ports. If only he could leave as well. Summer was short in England, and Donalee was at its loveliest then.

Several American debutantes had shown interest in him. But though he had to do his father's bidding, he had one firm criterion unknown to his father.

Rob was determined to find a woman he could marry for love first and money second. He'd been in love once in his life, five years ago, at the tender age of nineteen. And then scarlet fever had struck England, and Lady Alice Mary DeVere survived its initial onslaught only to perish days later from a weakened heart. He sighed. Even now the memory pained him.

"The supper rooms are upstairs," said DeVille. "Is it too early to have a bite?"

The ball would begin in earnest afterward, on the main floor of the Met. The crush of people upstairs was worse, and Rob resisted the urge to disappear. The blond debutante with the sapphires headed directly toward him, and he ducked through a slim door behind a velvet portiere. Immediately the roar of the ballroom crowd diminished, and he sighed, enjoying the moment of peace.

A row of mirrored tables lined the wall, with hooks opposite for capes and cloaks. A dressing room for the singers of the opera house.

Then he blinked. At the back of the narrow room, a gorgeous red-haired girl in a gown of apple-green silk intently read a book and hadn't noticed his entrance. Curious, he crept closer, hoping to catch a glimpse of what it was that held her rapt attention. Her red hair was a mass of curls tied up most becomingly at the back of her head. Rather than the multiple diamonds and precious stones the other women wore, only a jeweled dragonfly pendant on a gold chain adorned her creamy décolleté.

Then the title of the book loomed into view. *The Picture of Dorian Gray.* He snorted at the idea of a young lady secretly reading a controversial novel, and, like a shot, the girl sprang out of her seat, with hands clenched on her hips and her glorious eyes blazing at him like green fire.

"How dare you! What do you mean by sneaking up on me?"

Rob stepped back and held up his hands. "I didn't mean to startle you. Please accept my apologies."

"Why should I? Of all the nerve." She turned away, opened the table drawer, and slipped the book into it.

Rob cleared his throat. "I wanted to see what you were reading. You seemed so captivated by it. You must admit, it's a rather curious choice for a young lady."

Her brows slanted downward in a fierce frown. "I'll admit no such thing. Do you always go around spying on women?"

Rob blinked at her accusation. "Of course not." He smiled, trying to turn on the charm. "I stepped in here for a moment of peace. You know, 'far from the madding crowd'?"

She almost smiled then. He was sure the hint of a dimple lurked near that pretty mouth.

He held out his hand. "I say, we've rather gotten off on the wrong foot, as you Americans put it. I'm Robert Radclyfe."

She ignored his outstretched hand. "Please, allow me to pass. An unmarried woman must never be alone with a man."

He slapped his forehead. Of course. If he hadn't been so bewitched by her, he'd have understood at once the precarious position he had placed her in.

"Forgive me, Miss—?"

She didn't answer—merely flounced past him in a flurry of silken skirts and mimosa perfume, opened the door, and slammed it hard behind her.

Rob took a deep breath and smiled. The evening had just become far more intriguing.

Chapter 2

Anna walked toward the supper rooms as fast as her corset would allow. Thank goodness they planned to leave New York for the country next week. Her father insisted on attending every ball and party of the season, trying to find her a husband.

But after Stuart. . .

Her heart clenched painfully. She knew that she should have listened to her father when he raised objections about her engagement to Stuart Maxwell Gordon a year ago. But she had been in love. And too blind to see he cared more for her dowry than for her.

She pushed the thought of her former fiancé firmly out of her mind and reached the foyer to the supper room in time to see her father searching for her, elegant in his black tailcoat and the vest of MacDougall tartan plaid that he insisted on wearing in public. His full head of silver hair matched the clan brooch bearing the MacDougall motto: *Buaidh No Bas*—Victory or Death—and she smiled at the attractive picture he made.

"There ye be, lassie." His wide smile replaced the frown. He pulled her gloved hand through her arm and patted it. "I am more than ready to sit," he said as he loosened his cravat. "Rather warm in here tonight."

His face looked drawn, or was it the shadows cast by the candlelight? "You're not feeling well, Papa?" A sudden stab pierced her chest. Her father had never been ill a day that she could remember.

"A wee bit tired. Don't worry, lassie. I've been workin' too hard—that's all."

Anna stepped out of the line queuing for supper and led her father to a small table near the windows. "Sit and rest, Papa. I'll get your supper."

He nodded. "Thank you, lass."

She turned to check on him as she filled a plate with roast squab and beef Wellington. He was gazing out the window toward the New York City skyline, lit up like chains of diamonds. As she fumbled with the dishes, a gloved hand intervened and deftly retrieved a plate before the squab tumbled to the floor.

"Allow me to help you, miss."

The dark-haired stranger from the dressing room beamed down at her and offered his other arm. She bit her lip and then accepted his help with a gracious nod. "Our table is near the windows, sir."

He did cut a fine figure in his evening dress, and evidently other ladies thought so, too, as their heads turned as he passed, like hunters following the scent of prey.

As they neared the dining area, he raised an eyebrow. She moved ahead of him and walked to the table where her father sat staring out the window into the night.

"There you go, sir," he said as he placed the plate before her father. He pulled out a chair for Anna and nodded at her. What did he think he was doing? They hadn't been properly introduced.

Anna sat in the chair, murmured her thanks, and faced her father. But the young man didn't leave as any other gentleman would do. Instead, he stood with a ridiculous smile on his face.

"May I introduce myself, sir?" He bowed deeply. "Robert Alexander Radclyfe, son and heir of the ninth Earl of Wentwater, at your service."

Her father stood and bowed. "Philip Henry MacDougall. I see ye've met my daughter, Anna."

"I haven't had that honor yet." He turned to Anna and bowed again. "Delighted to meet you." He paused. "Miss MacDougall."

He had almost said "again." She could tell it had been on the tip of his tongue. And that enigmatic smile—as if they shared a secret. Such impudence couldn't be tolerated. Anna pasted a frosty smile on her face and inclined her head, ignoring the twinkle in his eye.

"Would ye like to fetch your supper and join us, laddie?" her father asked.

"That would be lovely, Mr. MacDougall. Thank you so much."

The Englishman left, and Anna scowled at her father. "Really, Papa."

Her father shrugged. "He's a verra nice chap. That's why we're here, aye? To find ye a husband."

Anna wrinkled her nose. "You are much more anxious that I, in that department."

"I'd like to see ye settled before I go the way of all flesh."

Anna sighed. "Papa, you always say that."

"Because it's true." He hesitated then reached across the table and took her hand. "Anna...sometimes I dinna think I will see seventy—"

"Please, Papa, I don't want to think about—"

"Here we are." Mr. Radclyfe seated himself and shook out his napkin. "I shall be quite interested to see whether the beef Wellington on this side of the ocean is as delicious as that served in London."

Her father released her hand and smiled at him. "Is this your first trip to New York then, laddie?"

"It is."

"And how do ye find your neighbors across the pond then?"

Mr. Radclyfe studied Anna. "Enchanting."

Anna resisted the urge to roll her eyes. Her father glanced in her direction and ever so slightly raised an eyebrow. Certainly he was wondering why she didn't enter the conversation, but she had nothing to say to this particular young man, no matter how devastatingly handsome. She smiled prettily instead, kept her mouth shut, and stood. "Please excuse me."

Both men got to their feet as she swept away. A peek over her shoulder revealed Mr. Radclyfe gazing after her with a puzzled smile on his face. Then he winked.

Anna whipped her head around and exhaled hard. Winking was considered insufferably rude. A gentleman should never wink in the presence of a lady, nor cross his legs, shrug, or laugh immoderately. *But then*, said a voice in her head that sounded suspiciously like her maid, Winifred, *a lady should never turn to look back after a man, either, whether in*

the ballroom or on the street.

A swarm of excited voices swirled over her as she opened the door to the ladies' refreshing room.

"...the most divine smile!"

"...and his accent. I almost swooned...."

"...my mother will settle for nothing less than an earl...."

Anna sighed and pushed her way to the mirror. She didn't enjoy this social scene. Then she grimaced.

Be honest. You did enjoy it. Until Stuart.

She shook her head irritably as a maid approached with a tray of scent bottles. There was already enough fragrance in the air to perfume all of Central Park. She was turning to leave when she saw an old friend enter the lounge, in diamonds and ice-blue satin.

Anna hastened to meet her with an embrace. "Nora! What a wonderful surprise. I didn't know you were in New York."

"My husband said he needed a change of scenery. It was a last-minute thing. But it's good to be back in New York. Living in England has been a nightmare."

A pinched look about her friend's lips alarmed Anna, and her normally rosy complexion had paled. Nora's eyes brimmed with tears.

"What is it, Nora?"

Nora shook her head. "Everything." Her lips trembled. "But I can't speak here," she whispered, glancing at the giggling young women around them.

"Come with me. We'll find a place."

Anna took Nora's arm and found a quiet corner screened by potted orange trees. Sitting close to her friend, she took her hands and gave them a gentle squeeze. "Now tell me. Are you ill?"

Nora hunched her shoulders. "I might as well be. I'm so miserable."

"Are you having...marriage troubles?"

"I suppose you could call it that." She gave a languid toss of her head, the corners of her lips turning down into an unattractive scowl.

"What's wrong? Can you tell me?"

Nora twisted her handkerchief into knots. "I've made a terrible mistake." She dabbed at her eyes with the limp hankie. "I never should have married Peter."

"Why do you say that?"

Nora bit her lip. "I believed my parents—that love would come after the marriage. But it didn't happen. Peter despises me."

Anna gasped. "That can't be true. You are the sweetest girl I know."

"He cares nothing for me. It was all about the money."

"Your dowry?"

Nora nodded, and fresh tears cascaded down her wan cheeks. "As soon as he got his hands on it, he didn't bother with me at all, except for the business of getting an heir. And when I didn't become pregnant after a year of trying, he began living at one of the other family estates in London. I'm out in that drafty old house on the moors, alone, with a skeleton staff that treat me with condescension and laugh at me behind my back."

Anna blinked, unable to believe her friend could be in this position. "How awful for you. Can't your father speak with him?"

"How can I tell my father?" Nora's red-rimmed eyes stared piteously at Anna. "He'd

tell me to do my duty and be a good wife. But I tried, Anna, I tried." She broke down sobbing.

Anna rubbed her friend's shaking shoulders, at a loss as to how to comfort her. Nora had become engaged two years ago and then married Peter Marlborough, the Count of Dorset, in a spectacular wedding a few months later. Anna contrasted the beaming bride of that day to the weeping woman in her lap. How had it gone so wrong?

"Where is Peter now?"

Nora sat up and wiped her eyes. "He went down to Newport. Some sailing party." She lifted her chin. "I haven't told you the worst of it." Her lips trembled. "I think he's. . . I think he's meeting another woman. On the yacht."

"Oh, Nora." Anna shook her head. "How terrible." She thought a moment. "I'm surprised he brought you to New York."

Nora laughed bitterly. "Appearances, darling. It's all a show."

"What are your plans then?"

"Probably visit my parents, although I'd rather eat nails. Father's here with me tonight."

"We're going to Longmeadow Monday. Why don't you come with us?"

The glimmer of a sparkle returned to Nora's eyes. "That would be marvelous. Like old times. But enough about me." She tilted her head and scrutinized Anna. "Is there. . .anyone special in your life?"

Anna shook her head. "Papa is still looking for the right one. But I don't think it's possible for a woman in my situation to marry for love." She had tried it once. Remembering the day of her engagement to Stuart Maxwell Gordon sent a shiver of pain and regret through her chest. She would never make that mistake again.

"You think that because of Stuart?" said Nora.

"I can't talk about it." Anna swallowed hard and shook her head. "It's still too distressing. Soon we'll be off to Longmeadow, away from all the gossiping harpies."

Nora sighed. "It's not fun to be the target of gossip, is it? I'm sure the same thing will happen to me, once word gets around that Peter most likely has a mistress."

"Then say you'll come to Longmeadow. You know my father adores you. And we can go to all our old haunts and search for fossils in the riverbed."

Nora face brightened. "I think we're too old for that, dear. But I would like to come."

"Do you want to travel with us?"

"No, I'll come on the late train Tuesday, in time for dinner. I'll need to cable Peter first." She smiled grimly. "I wonder how he'll enjoy that." She got to her feet and smoothed the flounces of her ball gown. "Father will be wondering where I am. I must go."

She kissed Anna's cheek and left as the notes of a waltz wafted through the air. The Englishman remained at the table when Anna returned, deep in animated discussion with her father. She didn't know whether to be irritated or pleased.

"Split cane?" Robert Radclyfe stared intently at her father.

"Cane, definitely." Papa nodded. "Ye canna beat the lightness, nor the strength."

"Dry? Or wet?"

Papa chuckled. "I'm progressive in my politics and my business, Mr. Radclyfe, but I'm old-fashioned where fishing is concerned. None of those newfangled 'dry' lures for me."

"Perhaps I could persuade you otherwise. Do you know a good fishing spot?"

"Not here, but my country estate in Hyde Park has some excellent ones."

Oh, no. In the next instant Papa would be inviting the Englishman down for a fortnight visit.

She hastened to the table, and both men rose. "You two look to be in agreeable conversation." She patted her father's hand. "But the dancing is beginning, Papa."

Mr. Radclyfe's gaze fastened on the silver booklet that hung from a ribbon at her waist. "Might I have the honor of a dance, Miss MacDougall? If your dance card hasn't already been filled, that is."

"Oh, I'm so sorry, Mr. Radclyfe," she said, managing to sound as if she wasn't sorry at all, "but I haven't any openings."

Alex Vanderbilt, dapper in his evening dress, with his blond hair slicked off his forehead, popped up behind Mr. Radclyfe. "My dance, I believe, Miss MacDougall?"

"Yes, indeed." She took Mr. Vanderbilt's arm and flitted away.

Alex was an excellent dancer, although most of his other attributes left something to be desired. He'd obviously eaten some pickled onions earlier, and she turned her face away to escape his halitosis, when someone tapped Alex's shoulder.

"May I cut in, old chap?"

Alex's mouth opened in a round circle of surprise, and in the next moment Robert Radclyfe had smoothly taken Alex's place, gazing down at her with an impertinent gleam in his eye.

"You're quite persistent, aren't you, Mr. Radclyfe?"

"In some things, yes." He smiled, and a funny shiver went through her. He was definitely handsome in a roguish way, with that head of dark hair and olive skin. One stray lock curled over his forehead, begging to be smoothed back. She gave herself a mental shake and straightened her shoulders, creating more room between them.

She had thought Alex Vanderbilt a good dancer, but he wasn't in Mr. Radclyfe's class. They were attracting attention as he expertly whirled her through the swooping turns of the waltz, one with the music and light as down on his feet. And the way he looked into her face made her feel so faint she had to look away, with her pulse hammering like hummingbird wings.

She was out of breath as the waltz finished. He didn't release her as quickly as he should have, but instead stood for a brief moment with his hand at her waist. She took as deep a breath as her corset would allow, and the essence of bergamot from his linen filled her nose.

"Thank you, Miss MacDougall. I hope to have the honor of dancing with you again this evening." He removed his hand from her waist and offered her his arm. "May I escort you to your father?"

She nodded and took his offered arm, thinking she might find an opening on her dance card after all, when the Hungarian orchestra went into the strains of a schottische, and she stopped. "This is my favorite," she blurted out before she could stop herself.

"Then we must dance it, Miss MacDougall." Mr. Radclyfe led her back to the dance floor, where he partnered her in the steps, turns, and hops of the old German folk dance. "I had the distinct impression earlier that you didn't care to dance with me, Miss MacDougall." His hand met hers before the gliding turn.

"You are correct, sir." She turned in the opposite direction before he captured her hand again.

"Why did you change your mind?"

"Do you know Robert Burns?"

"The Scottish poet? Yes."

"Aye, then," she said. " 'Women's minds, like winter winds, may shift, and turn at that.'"

"Very good, Miss MacDougall. I did perceive the brogue in your father's speech."

"He grew up in Scotland and immigrated here as a boy."

"So you were born here in New York?"

"Yes."

Mr. Radclyfe gave her a sly wink. "And what a pretty lassie ye are then."

"Don't play with me, Mr. Radclyfe. You and I have nothing in common."

"I wouldn't be too sure. I love to read as much as you do."

Anna stiffened. "I trust that you will not bring that up again, sir."

"Why not? I find it fascinating that you secreted yourself away in a dressing room to read a novel in the middle of a ball."

"I wasn't—" She broke off. She didn't like the fact that she'd been found doing something unladylike. "I don't wish to discuss it."

"But you agree it's a rather mutinous act."

"I agree to no such thing. I find this conversation outrageous. You know nothing about me, yet you presume to pass judgment. As I said before, we have nothing in common, and I think this dance must end. I generally find these affairs distasteful."

"Then we do have something in common, as I also usually avoid balls."

"Then why are you here?" She sniffed. "Wait. Don't tell me. You're looking for a wealthy American wife."

He gulped. "I—"

"I've called you out, sir." She stopped dead in the middle of the ballroom floor, while the dancers surged around them. "I wish to return to my father."

He sighed and offered his arm. Several times he started to say something then stopped.

It didn't matter how handsome or charming he was. A year ago she had been down that path, and nothing would compel her to tread it again. She mentally practiced the stinging words with which she would bid him an icy adieu. But she forgot them in a flash as they arrived at the table and she noticed her father's face. Cold tentacles of fear gripped her throat.

"Papa, what's wrong?" He had developed a dreadful pallor, and a bluish shadow edged his lips.

"I dinna ken," he said hoarsely. "A terrible weakness has crept over me."

Anna took the chair next to him and laid her hand on his forearm. "Are you in pain?"

"No, lassie. Just dreadfully tired."

She let out the breath she'd been holding, feeling weak herself. "We're going home at once."

She turned to ask Mr. Radclyfe to send for their carriage but he had disappeared, just when he might have proved useful. But a moment later, he pushed through the crowd with a silver-haired gentleman who looked vaguely familiar.

"Miss MacDougall, this is Dr. DeVries."

Anna threw a look of gratitude toward Mr. Radclyfe and stepped aside for the physician, who quickly assessed her father.

Mr. Radclyfe gently touched her shoulder. "I'll see that your carriage is brought round at once and return to assist you." He disappeared into the throng.

"Papa, can you walk?"

Dr. DeVries shook his head. "Let him rest."

A fine sheen of perspiration broke out on her father's forehead. He groped for his handkerchief and mopped his face.

Anna loosened his cravat and fanned him. His face had lost some of the greenish-gray pallor by the time Mr. Radclyfe returned. With his strong arm around her father's waist, they negotiated the halls and steps of the opera house to the waiting carriage.

Her father took a deep breath of the cool spring air. "Better already. I think it was too close in there. Sorry I spoiled your fun, lassie."

"Please, Papa. . ."

Mr. Radclyfe helped him into the carriage, closed the door, and then turned to her, his breath misty. "Miss MacDougall, please forgive—"

"There's nothing to forgive. As it's likely I will never see you again, good night."

The footman opened the carriage door and assisted her inside. Then her father rolled down the window. "Don't forget my invitation, Robert. Next week. Hyde Park. I have a few things I can show ye about fly-fishing. Bring a friend if you like."

Anna's heart sank. What a kerfuffle. Now she'd have to face him for two weeks or more.

Mr. Radclyfe smiled and looked past her father to meet her eyes. "It will be my pleasure. Looking forward to it."

❧

Baron DeVille pounced on Rob when he returned to the ballroom. "Where the deuce have you been, Rob? I've been hunting for you all evening."

"I've met an interesting girl."

"It's about time." DeVille grinned. "What's her fortune?"

Rob shrugged. "I've no idea."

"What?" DeVille choked. "Who is she?"

"Anna MacDougall."

DeVille's eyes widened. "MacDougall? As in Philip MacDougall?"

Rob nodded.

DeVille put his hand over his heart. "You've hit the mother lode, my dear man. Anna MacDougall—she's worth millions."

Rob gasped. "Huzzah!"

"He's the MacDougall in the MacDougall Sewing Machine Company. Single-handedly revolutionized the industry and cornered the market for twenty-five years. Very shrewd man, that MacDougall. Bought out every smaller company until he was the main manufacturer."

"My word." He'd had no idea, and the thought of his need to marry for money had vanished when he had seen Miss MacDougall's face.

DeVille blinked. "You truly didn't know who she was?"

Rob shook his head and smiled.

"Who introduced you?"

"No one."

DeVille groaned. "Don't keep me in suspense, my good man—how did you meet her?"

"I slipped into a dressing room to avoid that blond in the white velvet. And tucked away at the back, I found a striking redhead in green silk reading a book."

DeVille rolled his eyes. "Please tell me you didn't approach her."

"Unfortunately, I did."

"You know better." DeVille frowned. "So what happened?"

"I spoke to her." Rob shook his head. "She wouldn't accept my apology or give me her name. So I watched for her and offered my assistance at the supper table, and managed to worm my way into an invitation to visit their country estate."

DeVille clapped his hands. "Well done."

Rob shrugged. "Not really. She can't abide me."

DeVille pursed his lips, thinking. "I'm trying to remember... I think she was engaged last year. But then it was called off."

"Do you know why?"

"I think the chap was after her money."

Rob groaned. "That doesn't bode well for me then."

DeVille grinned. "Unless you can make her fall in love with you."

They reentered the ballroom, and though Rob dutifully danced with a bevy of young ladies eager for his attention, his thoughts kept returning to the girl in the apple-green silk.

The ball ended at one a.m. Before he and Deville left for their hotel, Rob slipped into the dressing room and retrieved the copy of *Dorian Gray* from its hiding place.

Chapter 3

Anna sent an urgent message to her father's physician upon their return home at midnight. Fortunately their mansion on Fifth Avenue stood just a few blocks from the opera house. Two of the burlier footmen assisted her father up the curving flight of marble steps and into the east wing, which contained his suite of rooms.

Her father asked for privacy while the doctor examined him, so Anna paced the hallway outside his bedroom door until the pattern of ribbons and scrolls in the Aubusson rug had been burned into her brain. Winnie hovered nearby, along with Mrs. Ludley, the housekeeper, and their butler, Mortimer, and some of the other maids and footmen.

Mortimer approached. "May I get anything for you, Miss Anna?"

"No, thank you, Mortimer."

She'd clenched her teeth for so long her jaw ached. The grandfather clock downstairs chimed one a.m. when the door opened and Dr. Buchanan exited the room, frowning as he rolled down his shirtsleeves and pocketed his stethoscope.

"Is he well?" Anna clasped her hands and waited for the doctor's pronouncement. "Spare me nothing."

Dr. Buchanan drew her to a sofa in the hall and carefully chose his words. "He is stable, for the moment, Miss MacDougall." He hesitated, fumbling for words. "But. . .he isn't a spring lamb anymore."

"He has always been hale and hearty."

Dr. Buchanan nodded sympathetically. "My dear, sometimes our bodies tell us it's time to rest."

"What's wrong with him?"

The doctor avoided her gaze and stood. "He prefers to tell you himself, Miss MacDougall."

Dread rose into the back of her throat, and she swallowed hard. "May I see him?"

"Briefly. I left some medications for him and administered a mild sedative. I'll be back to check on him tomorrow. Good night, my dear." He stroked his gray mustache and gave her an appraising look. "You need some sleep as well. I'll see myself out."

"Thank you, Doctor."

Anna opened the bedroom door and quietly slipped inside. Her father lay propped up on pillows, and he opened his eyes when she entered the room and pulled a chair to his bedside. His face had regained his usual ruddiness, and the blue shadow around his lips had disappeared. Two corked brown glass bottles stood on the nightstand labeled "Digitalis Leaves" and "Nitroglycerin."

"You're feeling better, Papa?"

"Aye." He sighed. "But it's to be expected, lass."

"What is?"

"That my life is nearly over."

"Don't say that. I can't bear it.".

"But I must say it." He took her hand and held it tightly. "It's my heart, Anna. It's failing. I'm nearing seventy, ye know. I willna be here forever. We must talk—"

"Don't, Papa!" She jerked her hand out of his and stood up. "I can't." Her throat swelled, and she pressed her hand over her mouth, shaking her head to hold back the tears.

He gazed at her, his eyes deep and soft in the lamplight, and nodded. "Another day then, lass. Kiss me good night, and then off with ye. Let an auld man sleep."

She rested her face against his and then kissed his cheek. Instead of going down the hall to her own bedroom, she stopped at the door to the bedroom that adjoined her father's. Her mother's bedroom hadn't been touched since her death seven years ago on a snowy December night. Crystal perfume bottles waited on the sterling silver tray, and all her mother's gowns still hung in the huge mahogany wardrobe. Every eight days, a maid dusted the room and wound the little French ormolu clock on the mantelpiece. The faint fragrance of Guerlains's Jicky still lingered in the elegant room. Her mother had adored its classic sweet hay and lavender scent.

Anna sank to her knees beside the bed and grasped the counterpane. She laid her cheek against the silk and uttered a great sobbing breath. Losing her mother at the age of twelve had been the most difficult event of her life, compounded by witnessing her father's deep pain and sorrow at losing his beloved wife. Now she had to face the fact that her father was growing older and it would only be a matter of time before she lost him, too. Why did it have to be this way?

Her mother had been fond of quoting Ecclesiastes, and one of her favorite verses came to Anna's mind. *"To every thing there is a season, and a time to every purpose under the heaven: a time to be born, and a time to die. . .a time to weep, and a time to laugh; a time to mourn, and a time to dance. . . ."* Oh, how her mother had loved to dance!

"I wish you were here, Mama," she whispered into the darkness. She closed her eyes and thought of her mother's beautiful face and cornflower-blue eyes, and most of all the way she would laugh—not politely, but throwing her head back with a deep belly laugh when something amused her.

Anna swallowed the lump in her throat. Elizabeth Mary DuPont MacDougall had firmly believed in her Lord Jesus Christ and the eternal life He had given her. Anna knew her mother was alive somewhere with Him and that one day they would be reunited, and that comforted her.

Anna turned her attention to the Lord. "Father, thank You for getting Papa home safely. Thank You for what a wonderful parent he has been." She swallowed hard. "Please, let me have him a little while longer."

Anna woke at dawn after a restless night and came down to breakfast early. Her morning tea arrived as her father entered the room fully dressed but walking slowly and holding on to the chair backs as he slipped into his seat across from her. "Good mornin' to ye, lassie."

"Papa!" She dropped her spoon, and it clattered against her teacup. "I didn't expect you downstairs."

He rang the silver bell beside his plate. "Can't stay in bed. . .all day."

Here in the sunny light of the breakfast room, the gray pallor had returned and the stubborn blue shadow ringed his lips again.

"Have you taken the medicine Dr. Buchanan left you?"

"Not yet." He placed two tiny pills on the table.

The butler entered the breakfast room.

"Coffee, Mortimer," her father instructed.

"Very good, sir." Mortimer nodded and left the room.

Anna frowned. "Take your medication, Papa."

He nodded and slipped one of the pills under his tongue and then the other when Mortimer returned with the coffee.

Mild spring air filtered in through the floor-to-ceiling windows, and with it came the sounds of traffic on Fifth Avenue below, the *clip-clop* of horse's hooves, an occasional shout, and the clattering of wagon wheels on the cobblestones.

Her father mopped his forehead, where a faint sheen of perspiration had broken out. "Have ye ever heard such a clishmaclaver? I'm ready to get out of the city, Anna. I'm pinin' for Longmeadow. Let's go away tomorrow, earlier than we'd planned."

The thought of their country estate in Hyde Park immediately brightened her spirits. "We need to give the servants a day to prepare, Papa. And I forgot to tell you that Nora's in town. I invited her to stay with us at Longmeadow."

"Wonderful. We'll have a full house then, won't we?"

Anna bit her lip. "Shouldn't you rescind your invitation to that Englishman?"

He raised an eyebrow. "Why? He's a canny lad. I like him. Ye might, too, if ye give him a wee chance."

"Papa." How could she make him understand? "I don't want to marry. Ever. I can't. . . Stuart. . ." She floundered, helpless to push away the waves of panic that threatened to engulf her at the thought of trying again.

Her father laid his hand over her trembling fingers. "I know, lassie. But you'll have to humor me. I haven't given up hope, even if you have."

Chapter 4

Longmeadow, Hyde Park, New York
May 1, 1899

The MacDougall carriage entered the towering stone and iron gates of Longmeadow as the purple shadows of late afternoon lengthened across the wooded lawns. Flowering white dogwoods and redbuds bloomed among the stands of maple and oak. The mansion stood at the end of a long green park like a perfect jewel, simple yet magnificent with its colonnaded front portico and walls clad in creamy limestone.

Before her father could exit the carriage, Anna ran up the stone staircase, burst through the heavy front door past the waiting staff and on through the octagonal solarium, then pushed through the french doors to the south portico that overlooked the Hudson River. From her vantage point she had a grand view of the Catskill Mountains, the sloping green lawns, and the river below. The crabapples that edged the bluff mingled rosy blossoms with the pale spring green of newly leafed trees. She took a deep breath and sighed luxuriously as her father came onto the veranda and put an arm around her shoulders.

"I agree," he said, breathing hard. "It's a bonnie place."

"It never changes."

Her father laughed. "It's changed, lassie. At one time the river was as high as the bluff there." He pointed to the edge of the lawn. "And don't forget all the arrowheads ye gathered as a child. We aren't the first to live here, and we won't be the last." He gave her waist a squeeze. "Let's have tea in the garden?"

"Of course, Papa. I'll go change."

Her maid, Winifred, a petite brunette with hair wound in a braided coronet, was already hard at work unpacking in the bedroom when Anna came in.

"Help me change, Winnie, and then take the rest of the afternoon off. This can all wait until tomorrow."

Winnie turned her mistress around, undid the tiny buttons on the back of the bodice, and helped her out of the skirt. "One of your tea gowns?"

Anna nodded. This was her favorite time of the day, when she could leave her corset off and wear loose dresses with no train. "Take my hair down, too, Winnie. It's only Papa and me for dinner tonight."

Feeling light and refreshed, she skipped downstairs like a little girl as the French revolving clock chimed four. Her father was waiting for her, and together they passed through the french doors of the breakfast room and down the tidy graveled paths to the huge flowering crabapple in the center garden, so loaded with pink blossoms, that barely a bit of green could be seen. Underneath its spreading branches stood an old cedar bench, weathered to a silvery gray. The tea table had been set up among the gauzy carpet of pink

petals and covered with a snowy damask cloth.

Birdsong floated on the warm breezes of the balmy afternoon. Honeybees buzzed among the roses, and hummingbirds darted in and out of the trumpet flowers, the drumming of their tiny wings adding to the musical notes of water falling in the fountain. Her father sank onto a bench and exhaled a long deep breath as the perfumed peace of the garden washed over them.

"Anna," he said, taking her hand and looking deep into her eyes. "My darlin' girl. We must speak of it. My heart is failing. It's gotten auld, along wi' the rest of me."

"Oh, Papa," she said. Tears brimmed in her eyes.

Her father put an arm around her shoulders and drew her close. "Weel, then. . ." he said. "I'll be fair sorry to leave ye, lassie."

"How long?"

"Dr. Buchanan didna say. But I've a wee feelin' it won't be long."

Anna swallowed hard. "What shall I do without you?" She searched the pockets of her tea gown for a hankie, to no avail.

"As usual, lassie." He shook his finger at her and pulled a starched handkerchief from his vest pocket. She blew her nose and then put her arms around him.

The guests arrived at Longmeadow the next afternoon on the train.

Nora arrived first, and Anna and her father greeted her in the octagonal solarium, along with Mortimer, the head housekeeper Mrs. Ludley, and most of the servants.

"Och, lassie," said Philip MacDougall as he welcomed Nora with open arms. "Ye're a sight to see. Bonnie as ever." He embraced her and gave her a hearty kiss on the cheek.

"Darling," said Nora, "I'm reinvigorated already. This country air." She wore a royal-blue traveling suit, with a pert hat trimmed in snowy egret plumes and a tiny bluebird, the breast of which matched the rose of her blouse.

"You're looking very chic," said Anna, returning the hug. "We'll speak later."

Nora nodded and followed Mrs. Ludley up the grand staircase to her guest bedroom on the second floor, followed by a parade of footmen bearing trunks, hatboxes, and even a tiny yellow canary in a round brass cage.

When the gateman notified the house two hours later that their remaining guests had arrived, Anna put on a gracious smile as she joined her father in the solarium.

"It would have been wonderful to have you to myself this visit," she murmured under her breath as they stood side by side in front of the staff.

"Too boring with just your old da for company." He smiled as the great front door opened to admit their guests. "Dinna fash yerself, lassie—it will be fine."

Anna smiled. "If you say so, Papa."

Mr. Radclyfe entered first, followed by his friend. Anna choked when the man pulled off his hat and stepped forward. A tall, tawny blond, with a neat mustache and a rakish expression, he looked so much like Stuart Maxwell Gordon it took her breath away.

Mr. Radclyfe shot her a concerned look, and she smiled quickly to cover her gaffe. Her father held out his hand to Robert. "Mr. Radclyfe, welcome to Longmeadow."

Mr. Radclyfe doffed his top hat and bowed. "May I introduce my good friend, James George Epperson, the Baron DeVille."

The men shook hands with her father then turned to her.

"Gentlemen," she said smoothly, having recovered her composure, "I echo my father's gracious sentiments. Welcome to Longmeadow."

The men bowed in return. She had forgotten how tall Mr. Radclyfe was. He topped her father by a good three inches, and his broad shoulders agreeably filled out his traveling suit.

"Mrs. Ludley will show you to your rooms," she said. "Aperitifs in the library at seven?"

They nodded, and she hurriedly took her leave. The baron's close resemblance to her former fiancé had shocked her badly. It was difficult enough to be worrying about her father's health while entertaining guests—and now to be reminded of her failed engagement every time she looked at the baron. How would she bear it?

But she couldn't think about it now. She still had to choose the china and silverware, write the place cards on thick vellum edged with gilt, and do the flowers.

In the lower-level flower room, Anna considered the pink roses and delicate white lilies heaped on the marble table. From the glass-lined cases against the wall she chose a silver epergne and assembled the roses and lilies asymmetrically, allowing a spike of the lilies to be the main focal point, with delicate ferns at the back and ivy trailing over the sides.

"Lovely, Miss Anna," said Mortimer, entering the room from the kitchens. "The table is finished. Would you care to see if all is arranged to your liking?"

"Certainly, Mortimer. But if I know you, everything is perfect."

Mortimer inclined his head at the compliment. "Thank you, miss."

The dining room lay at the opposite end of the mansion from the guest bedrooms. The immense walnut table that could seat seventy-six guests when fully opened had had most of its leaves removed for the small dinner party of five. She had chosen an Old Crown Staffordshire pattern with green chinoiserie landscapes and twiggy handles, fitting for a country dinner on the estate.

Anna clapped her hands as the French revolving clock in the solarium chimed six thirty. "As I said, Mortimer, it's perfect. Thank you. And now I need to get upstairs."

"Yes, miss."

She ran up to her room and paused on the threshold, out of breath.

Winnie turned away from the wardrobe and tsked. "Now you know better than to run in the house, Miss Anna."

"I do, Winnie," she gasped, holding her side, "but I'm going to be late if we don't begin soon. And I absolutely must take my corset off."

"We don't have time for that."

Anna made a face. "It's pinching me like the dickens."

Mumbling under her breath about the lateness of the hour, Winnie obligingly came and undid the bodice of the day dress, helped her out of the skirt and petticoats, then unlaced the corset.

"Ohhh, that's heavenly," said Anna as the restrictive garment fell away and she could take a deep restorative breath.

"Don't you be getting too happy, Miss Anna. You know you're going to have to put it right back on."

Anna scowled at Winnie. "Don't remind me."

"Come here. I'll take your hair down and brush it good."

"Anything to delay putting that horrible thing back on."

Anna relaxed against the padded bench as Winnie took the pins out of her hair and let the long coils and braids down.

Anna closed her eyes and let the hypnotic rhythm of the brush take over. "Mmm. Oh Winnie, that's wonderful. One of those pins was stuck into my head all day, and I was so busy I never had the time to fix it."

"I guess I know you pretty well after all these years, Miss Anna. And I s'pose you're going to take me along with you when you get married, too."

"Humph." Anna sniffed. "I don't think that's going to happen."

"Then why are two handsome men in the house?" Winnie held her arms akimbo and glared at Anna in the mirror. "Surely they aren't merely decorative?"

Anna shook a finger at her maid. "Winnie, have you been spying?"

Winnie smiled slyly. "I did stand upstairs and watch as the gentlemen came in."

"And what did you think of them?"

"I liked the dark-haired mannie."

"Why?"

Winnie snorted and flapped her apron at Anna. "A blind man could see he only has eyes for you."

"Indeed." Anna frowned. "Heavens," she said, getting to her feet. "Look at the time."

White tie and tails. Rob checked his appearance in the mirror.

"You're looking well, sir. Fits you like a glove." His valet, Jackson, stood back to admire him then flicked one microscopic piece of dust off his lapel. "Top-notch, sir."

"Thank you, Jackson." Rob hoped Miss MacDougall would think so. Could he persuade her not to look at him as a fortune hunter? He had to try. None of the other American women he'd met held half the attraction for him that Miss MacDougall did.

He left the bedroom and made his way down the grand staircase, admiring the marble busts in the wall niches and pausing to examine a tapestry over the hall table. The Medici coat of arms. Probably priceless. It would be wonderful to see Donalee restored to its previous grandeur like this amazing house.

The library lay off the solarium hall, filled with thousands of leather-bound books In glass-fronted bookcases. Carved wooden ribs ran along the vaulted ceiling and met at the center brass medallion in an elaborate crystal chandelier.

Philip MacDougal stood near the fireplace in the necessary white tie and tails, but Miss MacDougall was nowhere to be seen. "She'll be down in a wee moment," MacDougall said.

Was it that obvious? Rob cleared his throat. "Is that an elk over the fireplace, sir?"

"Caribou."

Self-conscious, he examined a collection of guns on the wall opposite the fireplace.

"Antique Swiss wheel locks," said MacDougall. "Do ye hunt?"

"Of course. But I prefer fishing. Don't tell anyone." It was considered unmanly not to love hunting.

"Aye." A gleam sparkled in MacDougall's eye. "I havena forgotten, lad. Ye brought your rods?"

"Of course—" he started to say, when Miss MacDougal swept into the room.

"I'm sorry I'm late, Papa." Then she caught sight of him, and the initial look of pleased surprise transformed into a cool and watchful demeanor.

"Good evening, Miss MacDougall," he managed to say, surprised at the coolness of his own voice, and bowed.

She was breathtaking in deep purple silk, her neck and shoulders bare, the gown fashionably décolleté. Slim diamond straps adorned the bodice, and the fiery mass of her hair had been swept up in a heavy chignon. Amethysts sparkled in the lamplight, in her hair, and at her wrists and throat.

"Good evening, Mr. Radclyfe," she said and extended her arm, encased in long silk gloves.

He kissed the back of her gloved hand, and then they stood there for an awkward moment.

"Let's have a sherry," said MacDougall. He went to the silver tray near the fireplace and poured three small glasses. In the next moment, James and the other guest arrived, a striking blond, and Philip MacDougall made the introductions.

"Good evening, all." Leonora Singer Marlborough, Countess of Dorset, radiated warmth in an evening dress of garnet-red satin, with rubies and diamonds as her jewels and an enormous feathered aigrette in her hair that threatened to take out the eye of anyone who stood too close.

With the entrance of the countess and DeVille, conversation flowed, and before long Mortimer appeared to announce that dinner was served. MacDougall escorted the countess, DeVille escorted Miss MacDougall, and Robert followed.

The dining room was a grand space in a Renaissance style, with full-length casement windows. A huge antique Oriental rug covered the floor, and Flemish tapestries hung on the walls between walnut panels, and the ceiling. . . He tilted his head back to take in the enormous painting of cherubim.

"From Venice," said McDougall, noting his interest. "Seventeenth century."

"Amazing." Rob gestured to the chandelier overhead. "And you have electric lights throughout the house."

"Yes. I constructed a hydroelectric plant on the property before we built anythin' else."

"I'd like to see it."

"Of course. Tomorrow? And then ye must plan a day to fish with me."

"Whenever you say, sir," Rob said. MacDougall was affable and easy to talk to. How could he convince the man that he was a worthy suitor, despite his lack of money?

At dinner, Rob couldn't keep his gaze off Miss MacDougall, by far the loveliest ornament in the glittering room. The butler gave a nod to the footmen to serve the first course, which turned out to be a delightful lobster bisque.

MacDougall cleared his throat. "Now, gentlemen," he said, picking up his soupspoon, "I know ye're accustomed to dinner conversation being restricted to polite observations of the weather, but at my table, ye have leave to discuss anythin' of interest, as long as it's not offensive to the ladies. At Longmeadow, it's a much greater offense to be boring."

DeVille spoke up. "Capital, Mr. MacDougall."

After the soup dishes had been removed, footmen brought in the salad course of celery and chestnuts, and DeVille spoke up. "Mr. Radclyfe and I went to see 'The Importance of Being Earnest' last week in the city"

Rob narrowed his eyes and shook his head slightly at DeVille, who ignored him.

"Do tell us, Baron," said the countess, with a languid wave of her jeweled hand. "Do you recommend it?"

"It depends," said DeVille.

"On what, sir?"

"Your thoughts on marriage." DeVille pursed his lips and glanced around the table. "Whether marriage is a pleasant or an unpleasant undertaking is debated throughout the play."

"It makes a mockery of marriage," Rob retorted.

"Indeed," said DeVille with a wicked grin. "Inform us of your thoughts on marriage, dear boy. Pleasant? Or unpleasant?"

Rob glared at his friend. And then the lights in the dining room flickered and went out, plunging the room into darkness.

"Oh!" exclaimed the countess.

Only two candlesticks lighted the massive room now, revealing surprised faces in the tiny circle of light.

MacDougall rose. "Dinna fash, it's the hydro plant. I'll go see what's wrong."

Miss MacDougall put a restraining hand on her father's arm. "No, Papa, let someone else do it."

DeVille plucked a chestnut from his plate with a tiny silver fork. "Don't you have a man to do that, sir?"

"Aye, a man during the day, but most of the time there's no need; it runs itself."

Rob stood, too. "May I go with you, Mr. MacDougall? Perhaps I may be of assistance."

MacDougall nodded, and patted his daughter's hand. "I'll be fine, lassie, with such a fine braw lad to help me. Come along then, Mr. Radclyfe."

Miss MacDougall threw him a look of gratitude. "Thank you," she mouthed.

James piped up. "I'll stay here and protect the ladies."

"Aye, ye do that," said MacDougall. "I'm off to find a hand torch."

Mortimer met them at the door with two flashlights. Footmen had kerosene lamps already lit in the solarium as Rob and MacDougall exited the mansion. The moon hadn't risen yet, and it was as dark as pitch as they walked to the powerhouse a quarter mile south—a fieldstone building with a slate roof, a deep porch, and leaded glass windows.

"There's a battery room and a pump room," said MacDougall as he unlocked the door and set the kerosene lantern down. "Wait a moment." He pulled a small vial from his waistcoat. "Just a precaution. All this excitement, ye ken." He put the pill under his tongue and motioned for Rob to follow him. "Bring your light in here," he said, opening another door. The smell of dampness and wet wood enveloped them like a cloud. In the yellow light of the torch, the waterwheel loomed large in the semidarkness. "How big is it?" Rob held his lantern high to scrutinize the huge wheel.

"Eleven feet," said MacDougall, "on a twenty-five-foot head."

"Overshot or undershot?"

MacDougall threw him a keen glance. "Under." He arched a silver eyebrow. "It's surprised I am, laddie, that ye ken the difference."

"We've a waterwheel on the estate at home." Rob shrugged off his frock coat and removed his tie. Rolling up his shirtsleeves, he approached the massive wheel. "Looks like

the buckets are worn." He tapped the nearest one. "Need to be replaced soon."

"Ye've a sharp eye."

Rob knelt by the side of the pool, strained his arm as far as it could go, and scooped up some standing water. "Here you go," he said, offering his hand. "Sediment." He rolled up his trouser legs and pulled off his shoes. "No help for it. I've got to go under. Hold the lantern close."

MacDougall scrutinized him. "No need for this tonight, lad. I'll send for my pump man in the morning."

"What? Deprive James and the ladies of their hot baths? I wouldn't think of it." He hesitated a moment. "If the truth be known, sir, I'm far more comfortable fixing something and getting my hands dirty than trying to make witty conversation."

He slipped off his shirt, sat at the edge of the sluice gate, and took a deep breath before he dove underneath the wheel. The icy water hit him like a thousand painful needles, and he exhaled a hard stream of bubbles to the surface. MacDougall's lantern light barely pierced the murky water, forcing him to use his hands to check the buckets at the bottom of the wheel. He resurfaced with a gasp and refilled his lungs with oxygen.

"I have to clean out the buckets," he said. "Do you have a bag or another pail to empty them into?"

MacDougall smiled and fetched a stout bucket. Rob went down again, holding on to the wheel rim with one hand and scooping the detritus out with the other. With repeated returns to the surface for air, he cleaned the buckets one by one until the wheel lurched then lumbered forward, slowly at first, and then more rapidly. The wire-covered lights on the ceiling flickered back to life. By then Rob's fingers and toes were numb, and a glacial finger of ice had settled between his temples

"B–b–back in b–b–business, s–sir," he said. "Whew! That water's c–colder than an iceberg in the A–Arctic."

MacDougall hauled him out of the freezing water and covered him with the frock coat as Rob's teeth chattered. "Ye're a fine strong laddie, that's certain," he shouted over the roar of the wheel and the splashing water. "Well done."

"Th–thank you, s–sir."

"You see a problem and tackle it like a man."

"G–glad to be of service, sir."

"Let's go back. Can't have ye freeze now, can I?"

MacDougall supported him as they loped back to the house, where light glowed warmly from every window. By the time they arrived, Rob was shaking so hard he couldn't speak.

"Oh my goodness!" shrilled the countess. "What happened?"

"He repaired the waterwheel for you ladies. And nearly froze in the process." He turned to Mortimer. "Get a hot bath started, and bring some tea immediately."

DeVille and MacDougall lugged Rob upstairs and into his bathroom, where the tub was nearly full. Together with his valet, the men stripped him of his wet clothing and got him into the tub. It was pure bliss to sink into the hot water and relax his cramped muscles.

The tea arrived, and MacDougall pressed the hot mug into Rob's hand. "Drink this, laddie," he said. " 'Twill warm ye. Then come to the library when you're ready."

Rob laid his head back as steam swirled through the room and misted the mirrors.

Although he'd barely been able to speak when he arrived back at the house, he did remember seeing Miss MacDougall's admiring look as he stumbled past her.

His fingers had wrinkled by the time he got out of the bath and dressed in a fresh outfit. He came down to the library to find everyone waiting for him.

"Quite the stunt, Radclyfe," said DeVille, jumping to his feet and clapping his hands.

The countess stood and curtsied. "You're the hero of the hour, dear boy. I certainly couldn't do without hot water."

MacDougall got up from his chair. "Take mine—it's closer to the fire."

Rob waved his hands in protest. "I'm perfectly fine, thank you." But at MacDougall's insistence, he took the seat the older man had vacated.

"Papa told us what you did. So I must add my thanks to his." Miss MacDougall drew closer, and the scent of mimosa drifted to him. "Are you quite recovered, Mr. Radclyfe?"

The firelight touched off glimmers of gold in her red hair, and when she leaned toward him, it was all he could do not to touch her lovely face.

"Quite so, tip-top." *With you near*, he wanted to say. "I adore a midnight swim, don't you?"

Chapter 5

Anna woke before dawn to the robins singing outside her window and opened the french doors to breathe the jasmine-scented air.

She wrapped herself in her dressing gown, found her Bible, and sat on the balcony to think and pray. The Bible fell open at Jeremiah, where the familiar, well-read page had detached itself from the binding. *"For I know the thoughts I think toward you, saith the LORD, thoughts of peace, and not of evil, to give you hope in your latter end."*

"To give me hope," Anna said. She bowed her head. *Thank You, Lord, that Your thoughts toward me are like the sand of the sea and the stars of the sky. So many I cannot count them. Please direct my path as I put my trust in You.*

The pale mist over the river vanished as she meditated on the verse. When a soft knock sounded at her door, Anna turned to find Nora peeking in. Her friend tiptoed through the bedroom in a dressing gown, her hair in a thick braid down her back. "So you're awake, too?" She had dark smudges under her eyes and a worried line between her eyebrows.

Anna smiled. "I usually wake at this time, sleepyhead. What are you doing up?"

"I couldn't sleep." She sat down and gave Anna a searching look. "I'm worried about you, dear." She pulled her braid over her shoulder and fiddled with the end of it. "I don't want you to make the same mistake I did. I can see you're warming to Radclyfe." She dropped the braid and grasped Anna's forearm. "You can't believe anything he says." She clutched Anna's arm as if she could physically prevent her from falling in love with Mr. Radclyfe.

Gently, Anna disentangled her arm. "Nora, the memory of what happened with Stuart is enough to stop me."

"What did happen? You never said."

Anna hesitated. A sick pang gnawed her insides whenever she reflected on the hurt and humiliation she had suffered at his hands. "Papa overheard him boasting at the club, saying he'd made the deal of the century and couldn't wait to get control of the dowry." She stopped and cleared her throat. "Papa confronted him, and Stuart tried to talk his way out of it. But Papa told him the engagement was off and that he was lucky he didn't get challenged to a duel."

"Oh my."

Anna nodded. "When Papa first voiced objections about Stuart, I wouldn't listen. I was over the moon in love." She sighed. "I know now Papa was correct. And it's ruined me." She patted Nora's hand. "So you see, my dear, you don't have to worry. I've been fooled and betrayed once. Never again."

Anna shut the bedroom door after Nora left and returned to the balcony. A robin lighted on the rail and gave Anna an inquisitive look. Anna sighed. "It's true, isn't it?" she said to the bird. "I am warming to him." She shook her head hard, and the robin flew off. "Dear Lord, help me."

Rob woke late the next morning and breakfasted alone after Mortimer informed him the baron and the young ladies awaited him outside on the bluff. Bacon, eggs, and coffee swept away the last vestiges of exhaustion from his impromptu swim the previous evening.

Miss MacDougall and the countess sat in wicker chairs, holding sun parasols, while DeVille lounged at their feet on a plaid blanket. The whistle of a steamship echoed faintly on the Hudson River below as a warm breeze brushed his face. A beautiful morning to be alive. And to pursue Miss MacDougall.

Miss MacDougall and the countess turned in their chairs to greet them, both attired in summery white lace dresses. Rob took a chair between them. Was it his imagination or had Miss MacDougall's eyes brightened as she greeted him?

"Have you quite recovered, Mr. Radclyfe?" she asked.

"Yes, thank you. But I interrupted your conversation with DeVille. You were saying?"

DeVille sat up. "I wondered what we could do for fun when there's no need for a hero to rescue the day." He gazed into Miss MacDougall's face and then playfully flung daisy petals into her lap. She stiffened, and Rob noted her fingers clenched white on her parasol handle.

Then she tossed her head. "You may do anything you please. Tennis, croquet, cards. You can ride any horse you like from the stable."

"Fresh air and sunshine then." James looked disappointed. "What other bucolic delights await us at Longmeadow?"

"Witty conversation. Erudite speech." Miss MacDougall arched an eyebrow. "You're quite fond of the latter, aren't you, Baron?"

DeVille sprang up with a mock look of dismay. "Did you hear that, Rob? I've been insulted."

Rob shook his head. "Miss MacDougall is an astute observer of human nature."

DeVille took a seat next to Nora. "And what do you think, Countess?"

When DeVille smiled at the countess, Miss MacDougall turned away, an odd look on her face. Rob frowned. Something about DeVille bothered her.

Nora's eyes sparkled. "Perhaps you should challenge her to a duel."

"Excellent idea! What do you propose? Walking shoes or riding crop?"

Miss MacDougall laughed. "You're on your own there, Baron. I don't ride."

That surprised Rob. "Why?"

"I had a bad spill as a child and never wanted to ride after that. But the horses would welcome some hard exercise. Why don't you go down to the coach house and choose a mount?"

DeVille bowed to Nora. "May I escort you, Countess?"

Nora nodded. "You may. Coming, Mr. Radclyfe?"

Rob shook his head. "I'll remain here, thank you." He glanced at Miss MacDougall's

maid, who was reading a book and sitting close enough to chaperone but not quite near enough to hear their conversation. The blue peaks of the Catskill Mountains shimmered against the northeast horizon. The wind sang through the ancient pines, accompanied by the warbled melodies of the robins. He laced his fingers behind his head, stretched out his legs, and let out a long, slow breath. It was so peaceful. It reminded him of Donalee, and a spasm of homesickness went through his gut.

"You enjoy the country, Mr. Radclyfe?"

Rob sat up and brushed pine needles off his coat. Now here alone with her, he couldn't think what to say next. The silence grew as he frantically searched his brain and tried to decide how to press his suit.

She examined him with the hint of an amused smile on her lips. "Would you like to see the gardens?"

Perhaps it would be easier to have a conversation if he didn't have to face her. So he stood and offered his arm while she raised her parasol. He was acutely aware of her mimosa perfume and the touch of her fingers as they walked the paths of crushed gray stone, followed at a respectful distance by the maid. On the lowest level, a reflecting pool led to a shady pergola, where a marble statue of Orpheus, the Greek god who could charm wild animals with his sweet singing voice, stood guard. *If only some of that charm could rub off on me*, Rob thought.

"Shall we sit awhile?" Miss MacDougall gestured to a stone bench built into the brick wall underneath an arch covered with wisteria trailing long purple panicles.

"Of course."

Other stone benches had been built into the walls and under the trees, perfect for viewing the garden at all its levels. Miss MacDougall closed her parasol and looked at him expectantly. Her maid took a seat not far away and buried her nose in her book, which reminded him he'd been keeping the copy of *Dorian Gray* in his pocket for the last few days, trying to find the right time to give it back to her.

He pulled it from his frock coat and laid it in her lap.

Her face flushed pink. "I hope you don't mean to needle me about this again."

"No. But I'd like to discuss it." He glanced at her with a tiny smile.

She gritted her teeth, and Rob held up his hands. "May I try to explain?"

She gave him a short, tight nod.

He leaned toward her. "Most English girls I've known would never be interested in such a novel, nor any of the American girls to whom I've been introduced." He sat back. "It tells me you have curiosity, Miss MacDougall, and an interest in the world around you that extends beyond the confines of the ballroom and the boudoir."

She sniffed. "Indeed, you're rather peculiar yourself, Mr. Radclyfe. Because no ordinary young man would dare to use the word 'boudoir' to a young lady."

His mouth fell open as his cheeks flushed bright red. "I. . .I didn't mean—"

She waved her hand. "Quite all right. It's marvelous to know I can disconcert you as easily as you can me."

His shoulders relaxed, and he smiled tentatively. "Then may we continue our discussion?"

She smiled for the first time during their exchange. "Yes."

He crossed his arms and glanced at her skirt, where the outline of a book clearly showed in a pocket. "What are you reading now?"

She smiled faintly and pulled the book out.

"*Frankenstein*." He blinked then shook his head. "My word. You're a Pandora's box of surprises. How do you like it?"

"I've almost finished. One chapter to go." She sighed. "I know how it's going to end, though. Sadly."

"You feel for the monster?"

"Didn't you? He isn't much different from a child rejected by his own father and then society. And then after the creature experiences pain and suffering, he turns bitter and murderous."

"Do you think he was evil?"

She considered his question. "His evil had a focus. Vengeance against Dr. Franken-stein." She replaced the book in her pocket. "I blame his maker, the good doctor—who wasn't so good after all. Creation of life belongs to God the Father."

"I agree. And not everyone who is rejected by his father turns evil."

His morose tone caught her ear, and she studied him thoughtfully. "Are you thinking of your own father?"

Mr. Radclyfe grimaced. "You're very perceptive, Miss MacDougall. I've had few con-versations of significance with my father in my entire adult life. He's rather a cold man."

"I'm sorry for that." She smiled ruefully. "I'm fortunate to have a loving father. Not everyone does."

Rob shook his head. "I've spent my life trying to please him. In hopes of gaining his approval."

"And that's why you're here in America." She regarded him thoughtfully, her head tipped to the side.

The spring sunshine had brought out tiny freckles on her nose and cheeks, and she was so lovely he could sit and gaze at her forever. He hoped she was developing a view of him as a dutiful son rather than a fortune hunter.

"I find it odd, Mr. Radclyfe, that you haven't been able to find the right woman the entire season." She blushed then. "What I mean to say is. . ." She hesitated. "I know there are many willing young women who desire what you can offer: a title."

He might as well come right out and say it. "My search has been difficult because I have one firm stipulation my father knows nothing of."

Her eyes narrowed, and then curiosity got the best of her. "And what is that?"

He smiled, leaned toward her, and gazed into her beautiful green eyes. "I must be deeply in love with the woman I marry, Miss Radclyfe. Above all else, that is most important to me."

Chapter 6

Rob rose at four, dressed quickly, and packed his waders and gaiters into the wicker gear box with his tray of flies. His rods were already downstairs. Normally the prospect of fishing in beautiful new country gave him a sense of great expectation, but his gut clenched every time he thought of having a private discussion with Philip MacDougall.

He left his bedroom to find MacDougall waiting in the darkened solarium. "Ready, lad?"

"Yes, sir." He took his rod case and followed MacDougall outside. A light one-horse gig waited on the drive, with no servants in sight.

"Climb in, lad," said MacDougall as he plucked the whip from its stand. "Just the two of us. We can dispense with all the folderol and get right down to it."

Rob blinked. Was MacDougall speaking about fishing or. . .other things? The older man remained silent as the gig exited the gates of the estate, traversed the sleeping village, and turned onto a dirt trail into the forest. Rob decided to say nothing, enjoy the drive, and take his cues from his host. Squirrels skittered in the trees overhead, and a red fox dashed across their path. Rob relaxed, and the peace of the dawn washed over him like a healing balm.

"I hope that's a sigh of contentment," said MacDougall, giving him a sideways glance.

"Very much so. I forget how much I miss being in the forest until I'm there again."

MacDougall nodded and turned the gig off the dirt path and down a trail wreathed by clinging vines. He let the mare walk slowly, urging her on with his voice until they arrived at a small clearing. He tied the horse to a tree and left her a bag of oats.

"It's a wee bit from here," he said, pointing to a faint trail that led off into the green darkness. Somewhere to their left, a stream rushed pell-mell downhill. But MacDougall led him away from the brook, their footsteps muted on an animal trail thick with leaf loam. Rob frowned, as MacDougall had to stop several times to rest and catch his breath. His face had gone pale.

"Sir? Are you unwell?"

MacDougall gasped and fumbled inside his pocket for a tiny vial. Quickly, he slipped a pill under his tongue and bent over, waiting. His agonized breathing eased a moment later, and he straightened.

"Right as rain now, laddie."

"Perhaps we should go back." If MacDougall had a heart attack out here, Rob wouldn't be able to get help quickly.

MacDougall snorted. "And miss our day to fish? Nay."

He gestured to Rob to follow down the trail until it widened and a pool of water

ringed by moss-covered rocks opened up before them. White violets poked their heads up among the stones, and at the far end of the pool, a surging freshet emerged from a rock wall to tumble merrily into the pool. A fairy glen, tucked away among the rocks.

Breathing hard, MacDougall put his hand on Rob's arm and pointed to a doe and two tiny fawns drinking at the water's edge. The doe's ears flicked, and with one bound the trio disappeared into the ancient oaks surrounding the dappled glen.

"It looks shallow, lad," MacDougall whispered, "but there's many a deep place where the trout like to hide."

Rob nodded and readied his rod. Quiet water worked best to fly-fish, so this was the perfect time to demonstrate the use of the "newfangled" lure to MacDougall. But he didn't announce his intention, having already surmised that words didn't mean much to the man. He hooked his fly, threw his rod forward, back, and forward again as the line spun out in an elegant arc and dropped onto the surface of the pool without a ripple. A moment later there was a splash as a fish took the fly with a mighty tug on the line, and before he could say "Jack Robinson," a fine fat brook trout squirmed on the bank.

MacDougall stared at the fish and then looked up at Rob, a wry grin on his rugged face. "And that would be the dry fly, laddie, I'm thinkin', no?"

Rob laughed and attached a fly made with the striped under-feathers of a rooster. He cast again, a wide beautiful arc that allowed the line to settle delicately on the water. A moment later a second plump trout joined the first. "Dinner," said Rob. Unfortunately, it wouldn't be this easy to persuade MacDougall of his other talents. Or Miss MacDougall.

MacDougall laughed. "Ye've sold me, laddie. Show me how it's done, then."

A few hours later, after MacDougall had mastered the art of the cast quite well for a beginner, they had a bag full of trout.

The day had grown warm, and they basked in the sun as they sat on the bank and tucked into lunch: roast beef sandwiches with horseradish, lemonade, and apple tarts.

"This is beautiful country, Mr. MacDougall," said Rob between bites of roast beef.

"Aye. Almost as fair as Scotland."

"Do you miss it? Scotland?"

MacDougall nodded, his gaze fixed on the blue mountains in the distance. "Aye. In some places it's verra like it. But I made my choice long ago, and America is my home now. And what about ye? Are ye missin' your home?"

Rob set his sandwich down. "No, I'm quite enjoying my stay here. For more reasons than one."

MacDougall smiled. "I can see my daughter has captivated ye."

"Yes." No use hiding it. He was like a stone pulled to earth by gravity as soon as she walked into the room.

"I understand your family is in a bit of a difficulty with the estate."

"Yes, sir. Most of the grand estates and manors in England are trying to find ways to survive. With the industrial changes and the rise of the railroads, young men and women are flocking to the cities to find work. This is the first time in almost five hundred years that Donalee is no longer self-supporting."

MacDougall nodded. "And so America has come to the rescue. With its wealthy heiresses and their mamas, all wanting a title in the family. The one thing money can't buy."

"Yes, sir."

"Your parents. Are they happily married?"

Rob fidgeted with the remains of his sandwich. MacDougall was all business now, and Rob couldn't wiggle off the hook. "No, sir. They live apart."

"And what do ye think of that?"

"I'm sad for them."

"Indeed. I've been married twice myself. I thought my first wife loved me, but she loved my fortune more."

Rob squirmed in his seat. This was too close to home. What was MacDougall driving at? "I feel awkward, sir, discussing this with you, as you are plainly aware of my family's financial difficulties and my need to. . ." He couldn't quite bring himself to say it.

"Ye need a substantial dowry from your bride when ye do marry."

Rob swallowed. That was plainspoken. And blunt. "Yes, sir."

"I appreciate your honesty. I know all of Anna's suitors have wanted or needed her dowry. But I'm looking for the man who wants my bonnie Anna for herself."

Rob nearly lost his perch on the rock. MacDougall had given him the perfect entrée into the discussion.

"Then I may as well be bold and come right out with it, sir." He put his sandwich down and faced MacDougall. "I'm falling in love with your daughter."

"Have ye quite recovered from your dunking a few nights ago?"

So MacDougall wasn't going to give him a straight answer. "Yes, sir, quite recovered."

"Ye impressed me, Mr. Radclyfe. And that's a verra hard thing to do, mind."

"Yes, sir," said Rob, wondering where the conversation was headed.

"Ye've a mind inclined to mechanical things then." It was a statement, not a question.

"I studied mechanical engineering at university, sir. Thought it would come in handy on the estate."

"So ye're not a gentleman of leisure?"

"Far from it."

MacDougall sat back. "I'll share a wee secret with ye, Mr. Radclyfe. Anna suffered a severe disappointment a year ago, at the hands of an unscrupulous fortune hunter."

Rob winced at the description. "Sir, I—"

"Let me finish." MacDougall lowered his chin and examined Rob intently. "I have no quarrel with your need for money to restore your family's estate. Ye've a responsibility to your father, as his son and heir, to marry well. I would expect no less from my own son, if I had one." He sipped his lemonade. "Anna has decided she will never marry. She doesn't think it's possible in her situation to know for certain a man loves her for herself and not her money." He smiled wryly. "That's your challenge, laddie. You're going to have to prove to Anna you do."

❧

Rob went for a long walk after he and MacDougall arrived back at the mansion. Miss MacDougall, the countess, and DeVille had gone into the city to see a play and would return late. MacDougall had a business appointment in the village. Rob had the rest of the day to mull over MacDougall's revelation regarding his daughter.

He had to make something happen soon. Another acrimonious letter from the earl had arrived, demanding to know what was happening and what, if any, progress Rob had made in finding a wealthy bride. He couldn't very well tell his father he'd found the right girl but she had no intention of marrying. The earl had been pleased that Rob hadn't

put up any fuss about finding an American bride. Indeed, Rob had been happy to do it, thinking it would please his father. But the earl, plainly, wasn't pleased at the moment.

But MacDougall had clearly given him permission to pursue Anna. Tomorrow he would see him and make it official.

Rob awakened early as usual the next morning, dressed quickly, and came downstairs to find the maids still dusting the first-floor rooms. He straightened his lapels, took a deep breath, and knocked on the library door.

"Come in."

MacDougall didn't look surprised to see him but chuckled and waved him to a leather chair near his desk.

"Sit down, Mr. Radclyfe. It's early for ye, isn't it?"

"No, sir. At home I'm up before dawn, as a regular thing. The early bird gets the worm, and all that."

"Good lad. And what can I be doin' for ye this fine morning?"

"I'm here to ask for your official permission to marry Miss MacDougall."

MacDougall pursed his lips, leaned back in his chair, and laced his fingers together, never taking his gaze off Rob. "Granted."

Rob exhaled and his shoulders relaxed. "Thank you, sir."

"Don't be thankin' me until she agrees. Ye've got a wee bit o' work ahead of ye, to persuade the lassie you love her."

MacDougall opened a drawer and extracted a sheaf of papers. "Here's the marriage contract you'll be signing, if she'll have ye. Take all the time ye need. I'll be back in a bit."

Rob moved to a chair closer to the small fire burning cheerily in the grate. Most of the legal verbiage of the marriage contract seemed to be straightforward. Anna's dowry would be deposited into the Bank of England the day after the marriage.

Then the last paragraph caught his eye. "The bride, Anna MacDougall, shall stay in the United States after the wedding, until the time of her father's death, and after that, as long as she desires. The decision to live in England with her husband shall be made by the bride alone. Any coercion by the groom, or the groom's family, shall result in the annulment of the contract and the immediate return of the bride's dowry. The money inherited from her father's estate shall be wholly hers and under her control."

Rob gasped. Surely this must be a joke. He threw the papers down as Philip Mac-Dougall returned to the study. The older man gave Rob a sharp glance. "I see ye've reached the last page of the contract."

"I have indeed." Rob shook his head. "You can't be serious, Mr. MacDougall. This would make a stuffed bird laugh."

MacDougall smiled. "But I am. Completely serious."

"This is impossible. I must return to England with my bride."

"Her dowry can go. But you and Anna must remain."

"My father will not agree to this."

MacDougall shrugged. "Then there is nothing more to discuss."

Rob rubbed a hand through his hair, trying to think. What had he gotten himself into? He sank into a chair and caught movement outside the library window. Miss Mac-Dougall cavorted outside with a wolfhound puppy, teasing him with a streamer on a

stick. She hadn't yet put her hair up for the day, and the curly mass of waves and ringlets streamed to her waist, turned to fire and gold by the morning sun.

MacDougall followed his gaze. "As you know, she doesn't particularly care to be married. So if ye canna agree to the stipulations in the contract, it might be best to return to New York."

Rob snorted, his gaze still fixed on Anna. "And find another heiress to wed."

MacDougall nodded. "Aye. Unless ye're up to the challenge."

Rob pressed his lips together, trying to remain calm. "My father will never agree to this."

"Then I'm sorry. For I believe ye're the man for her, laddie."

Rob turned away from the window then. "Why?"

MacDougall gave him a shrewd look. "She needs a gentle hand tempered by strength. One that won't crush her spirit. And kindness."

Rob sighed. "I don't want anyone else."

"I know." MacDougall smiled. "An open book, ye are. But I'm glad of it."

Then his smile disappeared, and he sank onto the sofa, gasping and clutching his chest. Rob rushed to his side. "What can I do?"

MacDougall fumbled inside his frock coat. "Pills...in here," he gasped as he clutched his chest and groaned. Rob quickly found the small brown bottle labeled "Nitroglycerin." He uncorked the bottle and shook out a tiny yellow tablet. "Here, sir."

MacDougall groaned again. "Un–under. . .tongue," he gasped. Quickly Rob took hold of his chin and wormed the pill under MacDougall's tongue. Then he ran to the bellpull and jerked it hard. Returning to MacDougall, Rob loosened the man's cravat and unbuttoned the top of his shirt, praying desperately under his breath. MacDougall had broken out in a clammy sweat, and his lips were blue. Rob grabbed the pill bottle and crammed another tablet under MacDougall's tongue.

Mortimer appeared then and blanched when he saw MacDougall's state.

"Send for the village physician immediately," said Rob.

But MacDougall gripped his arm. "No...wait." He swallowed. "It's easing." His body uncurled and his breathing normalized. His face lost its ghastly pallor. Rob whipped out his handkerchief and mopped MacDougall's forehead.

Mortimer addressed Rob. "What would you have me do, sir?"

MacDougall gave an infinitesimal shake of his head at Rob.

Rob shook his head. "Nothing, Mortimer. Not a word to the other servants. Close the doors."

"Yes, sir."

The butler withdrew. MacDougall smiled faintly. "Ye read my mind."

"No need to upset Miss MacDougall?"

MacDougall nodded.

"Does she know?"

"I've tried to prepare her. But no child wants to consider the prospect of their parent's death. They think it's morbid to speak of it, ye ken. But sometimes there's things that need to be said."

MacDougall put his feet up on the couch and stretched out, crossing his arms on his chest and closing his eyes. "She took it verra hard when her mother died suddenly. My death will cause her great pain." He opened one eye and stared hard at Rob. "That's why she's going to be needin' ye, lad."

Chapter 7

A nna had a few precious hours to herself, as Mr. Radclyfe, the countess, and the baron had taken the horses out and wouldn't be back until late afternoon. She didn't know what to make of Mr. Radclyfe anymore. When he had first arrived, she'd expected an onslaught of wheedling speech as he pressed his suit and strove to assure her he possessed the fine qualities that made him a worthy match for her and her millions. But so far he hadn't fit any of her expectations. Certainly not after shucking his evening clothes and diving into cold dark water to fix the waterwheel. Baron DeVille would have done no such thing. She contrasted the image of the dapper and vain blond baron with the man who returned to the house soaking wet. Underneath his frock coat, a glimpse of his broad chest and shoulders had sent a shiver through her.

And then his declaration in the garden. She had tried hard not to think about it, about his need to love the woman he married. But she hadn't been successful, and her heart quivered every time she remembered Mr. Radclyfe's handsome, intent face.

She needed something to distract her, so she popped into the library and found her father sorting through papers on his desk.

"Papa, I've asked Mortimer to serve tea in the garden. I thought you might enjoy that."

"Aye, lassie, I would."

They walked arm in arm to the tea table under the old blooming crabapple. When her father had finished his tea, he set his cup down. "Now then, I've somethin' to say."

"Yes, Papa?"

"I want to see you married proper before I die."

Anna took a deep breath and held her tongue.

"I need to know you're settled, lassie."

She nodded.

"And I've chosen the man for ye."

Oh no. "Papa—"

He held his hands up. "Let me finish, Anna." He smiled, and she saw wrinkles engraved on his dear face she'd never noticed before. "I've thought and prayed hard on it. Ye must trust me now."

Anna pressed her lips together as her heart jumped in her chest.

"Robert Radclyfe is intelligent, steady, and loves God. I believe you would come to care for him. As he cares for you."

"How can you know he cares for me? You've known him for ten days."

Her father cocked his head to one side. "I'm a verra good judge of character, lassie.

Don't forget—I've dealt with all sorts of men in my business dealings. And Robert Radclyfe is genuine."

Anna paced in front of her father, her agitated skirts sending a flurry of rose petals into the air. Two weeks ago she would have absolutely refused, but now she didn't know what she felt. "You know he only wants my dowry. And my inheritance." But even as she said this, she secretly hoped it wasn't true.

"And he shall have it. But he also wants you, Anna. I am verra sure."

She sank to her knees in front of her father. "I want to please you, Papa. I do. But—" She shook her head as the face of Stuart Maxwell Gordon rose up. Could she take the risk again?

"He'll be a good match for your headstrong ways, lassie. The anchor to your spirit. And there's one more thing."

"Yes?"

"I have a stipulation. He's not to take you back to England. The dowry can go, but you must remain here. And he with you, if he truly cares for you. Until such a time in the future, after I'm gone, and then only if you wish to go."

Then she would never find herself in a position like Nora. Would that be enough?

"Come here, lassie." She took his hand and sat down, pressing her cheek against his shoulder. "Ye'll be a wealthy woman in your own right. It will be your decision to follow him to England. Your choice."

"He won't agree, Papa. Every American heiress who's married an English lord has gone to live in England. Jennie Jerome, Mary Leiter, Consuelo Vanderbilt."

"Aye." He smiled. "It will have to be for love."

Robert Radclyfe would never agree to such an outlandish stipulation. Or would he? She sniffed. "Then we will see, won't we, Papa?"

"Och, lassie," he said with a smile, "that we will."

Now Anna had a hard time resisting Rob's infectious smile, despite Nora's dark looks behind his back. She'd awakened the last few mornings with a sense of expectation. The four were picnicking near the north cliff overlook, with Winnie sitting chaperone for Anna a short distance away. While Nora and the baron had a lively conversation regarding the merits of singing birds, Anna leaned toward Mr. Radclyfe.

"Did you enjoy your fishing trip with my father?"

"We had a grand time," he said.

"Where did he take you?"

"About an hour from here, deep in the forest."

Anna sat up straighter. "Indeed. Can you describe it to me?"

"To use your father's own words: 'It's a verra bonnie place.' A woodland pool, ringed by tottering old oaks and carpeted with moss."

"The fairy glen. Hmmm."

He tipped his head to one side and studied her. "Why? Does it hold some special significance?"

She smiled faintly. "It was our own private place no one else knew of," she said, "when I was growing up. I used to hunt for fairies under the acorn caps, and once I thought I saw one sitting on a cushion of moss. My father had a dragonfly fairy pendant made for

me, to remind me of our fairy glen."

Mr. Radclyfe nodded. "You wore it the night of the Met Ball. I understand why you thought you could find fairies there. It's a precious, magical place. Enchanted."

"Funny you should feel the same way."

"Yes." He started to say something but then stopped.

"Go on," said Anna.

He smiled shyly. "I thought perhaps we could visit it together sometime. With your chaperone, of course," he added hastily.

"Perhaps."

He drew a brown paper parcel from his pocket. "I went into the village yesterday to cable my father. I browsed the bookstore and found this for you."

She pulled the brown paper off the parcel and laughed. "*The Monster and Other Stories*, by Stephen Crane," she read aloud.

"It's a different monster than the one in *Frankenstein*," he said. "But I thought you might enjoy it."

"Thank you," she said, touched. "You're rather a different suitor yourself." She smiled at him. "No candy, no flowers—just books about monsters."

"Hmm." He cocked his head. "You're considering me a suitor now? That's a step in the right direction then."

She blushed at the eager look in his eyes, speechless for the moment, when fortunately Mortimer approached, bearing a silver salver.

He stopped before Mr. Radclyfe. "A telegram for you, sir."

Mr. Radclyfe stood and walked a few steps away to rip it open. His dark brows slanted together and his lips pressed in a grim line as he crushed the paper in his fist. Abruptly he stalked toward the cliff path.

"Radclyfe," called DeVille, "where are you going? Is it bad news?"

Mr. Radclyfe shook his head and hastened away.

DeVille shrugged and cut himself a cluster of purple grapes with a pair of tiny scissors. "These are delicious."

"Shouldn't you go after him?" Anna asked.

The baron popped a grape into his mouth. "I think he wants to be alone."

Anna stood, and Nora put a restraining hand on her arm. "Don't, Anna. It's none of your business, is it?"

Nora was correct. But as Mr. Radclyfe read the telegram, she had noted the sure evidence of pain in his face before anger had overtaken him, and though she could barely admit it, she did care.

Anna shook off Nora's hand and hurried after Mr. Radclyfe. His tall figure had already disappeared down the slender gravel path to the outlook, the northernmost part of the estate with a brilliant view of the Catskills and the river below. Before the path widened into the outlook, Anna stopped and motioned Winnie to stay.

He sat on the bench, his forearms resting on his thighs, staring out at the vista, and he didn't turn at her step on the stony gravel. She came around the bench, sat down a few feet from him, and remained quiet. Hawks circled lazily in the air currents high above the river, dotted with ships and sailboats.

"It's odd," said Mr. Radclyfe, turning toward her on the bench.

"What is?" Her pulse quickened under his intent gaze.

He smiled faintly. "How when I'm with you, I've stopped feeling the need to fill the silence."

She nodded. "I know." It was true. "I—" She hesitated. "I feel the same." She swallowed hard. "And I have never felt that way with anyone else but my father."

"That comforts my heart."

"May I ask why you need comfort, Mr. Radclyfe? Did you receive some unwelcome news?"

"Yes." He sighed. "I suppose I should come out and say it. I've asked your father for your hand in marriage. And I think you must know of his stipulation?" He gave her a questioning glance.

"Yes."

"I didn't believe my father would countenance such a demand." He shrugged. "And I was correct. He has ordered me to return immediately to New York. Or he will disinherit me."

Oh no. A sense of loss pierced her, taking her breath away. "What. . .what will you do?"

He crossed his arms over his chest and gazed out at the river. "I don't know. But I must decide soon."

He turned to her and sighed. "What a pair we are. Your father wants you to marry and you don't care to. I must marry to keep my family home from perishing. Society has expectations for each of us."

"I hadn't thought about what it must be like for you." She pictured him as having his choice of heiresses. "But I'd like to ask you a question."

"Ask away."

"*Why* do you want to marry me? Aside from the obvious, I mean."

He didn't seem the least bit surprised or taken aback by her question, but instead shifted his weight and assumed a thoughtful expression. "Perhaps it's that you were the only redhead at the ball in apple-green silk." He smiled.

She steeled herself not to respond to the way his smile lit up his face. "I'm serious, Mr. Radclyfe."

"The freckles," he said, nodding decisively.

"Pardon me?" She couldn't keep the frost out of her voice. Was he being deliberately obtuse?

"Your freckles." He leaned closer and raised his hand as if to touch her face then apparently thought better of it and let his hand drop into his lap. "Now that you've been out in the sun, the most delicate freckles have appeared all over your face."

Anna tightened her lips and stood. "Since you're not interested in a serious discussion, Mr. Radclyfe, I will take my leave."

"Wait." He got to his feet. "Forgive me. I was trying to be charming. I see I should leave that to DeVille." He gestured to the bench. "Please."

She sat down, her back stiff as she perched on the edge of the seat.

He sighed. "Now you look ready to make your escape."

She tossed her head. "I would think you'd welcome a sincere discussion of marriage, since you've made it plain you want to marry me."

"I would."

"Then answer my original question."

"Gladly. I think you're an interesting and unusual young lady."

"There must be other interesting heiresses out there. Girls who actually want to be married."

He smiled. "Oh, there are. To be sure."

Anna's spine stiffened. "So you've considered others?"

"I don't think it's in my own best interests to answer that question."

"Who?"

"Now, now, Miss MacDougall." He held up his hands, pretending to ward her off. "It would exhibit extremely poor breeding if I were to"—he paused delicately—"reveal courting secrets."

"Very well. Then tell me something about your home."

"Gladly." He stretched his legs out and relaxed. "It's a magical place, Donalee. In southeastern England. It was built on a gift of land from King Henry in 1412, for service to the crown. Though crumbling into decay now."

"Do you have siblings?"

"Two younger brothers. One in the British army—Ned. And William, at Oxford, studying for the ministry." He snorted. "My brother Ned should have been born first. He would love to be my father's heir. 'To the manor born,' as they say."

"Is he jealous of you?"

"Oh, very. But we don't see each other often. Father sees to that."

Anna digested this piece of information. How terrible.

"And your mother?"

"An aristocratic lady of noble lineage and very proud of it."

"And your parents—have they a happy marriage?"

"I suppose it depends on the definition of happy. They respect each other. My mother bore my father three sons. But their paths seldom cross now. My mother lives in London, while my father stays on the estate."

Similar to Nora's unhappy situation, closeted away on the moors while her husband amused himself elsewhere. "Perhaps most marriages are destined to be so."

"No!" Mr. Radclyfe sprang to his feet. "I refuse to believe that. And you must not fall prey to that pernicious idea, either, Miss MacDougall. I believe with all my heart it can be different. When I marry"—he fixed her with an intent look that stabbed through her—"though I must marry for money, in the end it must be for love." He clenched his jaw. "I need you to understand that."

Anna's head reeled. Awkwardly, she stood up, avoiding his gaze. "I must go."

"Have I frightened you? You didn't realize I could be so passionate?"

Her eyes widened at his use of that word.

"Tell me," he begged. "Let us at least have honesty, if nothing else." He motioned to the bench. "Please, don't go."

What a queer turn this afternoon had taken. A benign picnic on the lawn had transformed into this, this—what were they doing? But she sat down anyway. New thoughts tumbled through her brain like water surging in a flooded creek.

"What are you thinking?" He leaned toward her. "Tell me."

She inhaled and then breathed out slowly. "This conversation—it isn't appropriate." She paused. "Young women and their suitors don't generally discuss—" She hesitated, groping for words.

"What they want out of a marriage. Is that it?"

She opened and closed her mouth several times then settled for nodding her head.

"I know it isn't conventional. But it's our lives we're speaking of. *Our* lives—which other people are making plans for. Isn't that true?"

She found her voice. "Yes. I haven't considered what it must be like to have to find a rich wife because your father orders it. And expects it."

He nodded.

"However, a man may come and go as he pleases, whereas a young woman must first obey her father and then her husband. Her only business is to marry well. And produce sons."

"And I can see you resent this. But, Miss MacDougal, can't you see I have expectations placed on me?"

"I can. But perhaps you should release them."

He lowered his head and frowned. "It that what you have done? Released your expectations?"

Anna hesitated. "I don't know anymore."

Mr. Radclyfe came and sat next to her. "Your father told me. . .of your difficult experience a year ago."

Anna gasped. "He didn't!"

"He wanted me to know what I was up against. And all I can say is I am so sorry that happened to you." His fingers twitched in his lap. "Miss MacDougall, I know wealth doesn't guarantee happiness."

Anna thought of Nora. "No."

Mr. Radclyfe pressed on. "I've seen it in my own family. Although my family's income is much reduced now, I remember when the estate was fruitful. But my mother was never happy."

"But you have more choices than I."

He shook his head violently. "No, Miss MacDougall!" He scraped a hand over his face and stood, his shoulders sagging. "How can I make you see?" He clenched his fists at his sides, his body shaking with emotion. "The only choice I have is whether or not to love the woman I marry. Now, good afternoon."

Chapter 8

Mr. Radclyfe disappeared into the shrubbery lining the path. Anna got to her feet to run after him, but her heart beat so erratically she felt nauseous. What would she say anyway?

She gathered her skirts in one hand and descended the stairs to the riverbank. The stairs cut from the rock were worn and crumbling, but the handrail her father had installed a few years ago made it safer. As a little girl, she had spent hours here, searching for fossils and arrowheads. Pine trees grew along the bank, bent and stunted by the continual wind along the river. She climbed onto a rock, heedless of her dress. And then she prayed. Bowed her head and acknowledged her heavenly Father as Lord of her life. She didn't know what to do, but He did. She made the conscious decision to trust Him and allow Him to lead her.

Her heart lightened, she hurried to the house, but Mr. Radclyfe had disappeared. She laughed at herself, realizing she was looking for him. How the tables had turned. He wasn't anywhere in the house, either, because she checked the library and the drawing room.

Mortimer stood at the door of the great dining room, as footmen carried out the walnut table in pieces, followed by the heavy upholstered chairs. The Oriental rug had already been rolled up. She'd completely forgotten a ball had been planned for tonight. Two days ago she had reviewed the supper menu with Mrs. Ludley, chosen the dinnerware pattern and the silver service. Perhaps at the ball tonight she could let Mr. Radclyfe know that she wasn't nearly as unwilling as he thought.

Rob dressed for the ball in the requisite white tie and tails. After leaving Miss MacDougall, a very long walk at a rapid pace had dissipated his anger and frustration, and he arrived at the house in time to freshen up and change.

He shouldn't have lost his temper with her. Ungentlemanly, to say the least. Tomorrow he would take his leave and return to the city, although he didn't have the heart for it. Miss MacDougall had his heart.

He glanced in the mirror. Perhaps he should send his regrets. Plead some indisposition. Then he thought of Philip MacDougall. The irascible Scot wouldn't go gently, like a dog with his tail between his legs. The old man would fight for what he wanted. Rob nodded.

So would he.

He received his first shock of the evening when he caught a glimpse of Miss MacDougall. In apple-green silk. She took his breath away all over again. It was difficult not to

stare, even when DeVille jabbed an elbow into his ribs.

"Leave off, Radclyfe—she isn't something to eat," he whispered.

Rob hastily rearranged his face, but not until he caught Philip MacDougall grinning at him.

When the guests had been properly received, Mr. MacDougall opened the dancing with his daughter. At an informal country ball, the ladies did not have cards to fill. As soon as Miss MacDougall and her father finished their dance, several young men immediately besieged her for the next one. Rob decided to keep his distance and see what happened. He asked the countess to dance, and several of the older married ladies.

He'd returned his last dance partner to her husband and paused near the supper table, where two portly dowagers had their heads together.

"I've heard Miss MacDougall was a trifle eccentric, but moss?" Mrs. Vanderfelder tsked under her breath.

Rob's ears perked up, and he glanced at the two matrons.

Mrs. Goulet adjusted the pince-nez on her nose and pursed her plump lips as she stared at the main centerpiece. "Very unorthodox. And whatever is that on the top?"

Intrigued, Rob turned and stepped closer. As a rule he seldom noticed china patterns and floral arrangements, but this was definitely different. No flowers. Just moss. Every glorious shade of emerald the forest had to offer adorned the supper table. White violets were tucked among the moss in the central epergne. And there on the top—

Rob broke into a grin. A beautiful dragonfly fairy, with a slender body of gold and diamonds, glimmering opals on gossamer wings of spun-gold threads, cunningly pointed ears, and a delicately modeled face.

He searched the room for Miss MacDougall and found her, standing alone and watching him. Quickly he made his way to her, not caring that several guests turned to stare after him.

He smiled at her. "So, I'm forgiven for my outburst this afternoon?"

She nodded as the musicians launched into a waltz.

"May I have the honor of a dance?"

"You may."

He took her in his arms, reveling at the feel of her gloved hand in his. He wanted every dance for the rest of his life to be with her.

Anna woke early the next morning, though they had been up very late the night before. It was as if her heart had awakened her, skipping along with merry jumps and hops at the unconscious thought of Mr. Radclyfe.

An oppressive heaviness filled the air, in contrast with her light heart, and thunder rumbled in the distance. But nothing could dampen her spirits. Let it rain all day if it wanted to. She was in love!

A soft knock sounded at her door. Anna went to answer it and found Nora, wrapped in a Japanese dressing gown, with a gloomy look on her face as she entered the bedroom.

Anna repressed a sigh and closed the door. "Nora, I don't want to argue about Mr. Radclyfe. He's not Peter. Rob loves the Lord, wants to do right by whomever he marries, and he's honest."

Nora scowled. "Rob? You're on a first name basis with him now?"

"No. I just. . .think of him that way." Anna pressed her lips together. She didn't want to have to defend the fact that she had fallen in love with Mr. Radclyfe.

"How can you know? Peter was sweet, too. In the beginning." Nora's lips twisted. "And as soon as he had my money, everything changed." She snapped her fingers and Anna jumped. "Like that. I'd give anything to be single again. Like you."

Anna shook her head. "You're wrong about Mr. Radclyfe."

"You need to think longer. And harder." Nora went to stand at the balcony railing, gazing toward the Catskills. Then she turned to face Anna. "I wish I could make you see how difficult it has been. Shunted off to the country. Left alone for weeks. The snobbery of the English, and the way they make me feel as if I'm less than human for being an American. I'm an outsider, never to be allowed into the light. As you will be—when Radclyfe tires of you and your American ways. You will be alone. So alone."

"Nora, I understand you're trying to protect me. But you're wrong. Mr. Radclyfe is not Peter." She lifted her chin. "And when I marry him, I know it won't be the same."

Nora gasped. "Then you've decided?"

"I'm going to tell him today I accept his proposal."

Nora's hand went to her throat, and her body sagged. She dropped into a chair and buried her face in her hands. "Oh no," she said, shaking her head. "No." She lifted a haggard face. "I didn't plan on telling you this. I thought I could persuade you. . ." Her voice drifted off.

"Tell me what?" Anna tried to suppress the waves of panic that rose into her throat.

Nora smiled sadly. "He's not a good man, Anna. In London, there was a young woman. . ." She shook her head. "I. . .there's no easy way to say this. There was a child. He abandoned her and the mother."

Anna choked. "I don't believe it."

"It's true." She sighed. "Brace yourself. There's more."

Anna stumbled to her feet. Black spots glittered at the corners of her vision, and she held her hands up. "No," she said in a strangled voice, "don't say anything else."

"I'm sorry, Anna." Quietly, Nora left the room.

Anna slumped against the wall, sliding down into a heap. The giddy warmness that had embraced her since last night's ball dissipated like a coal plucked from the fire and left to die in a corner.

She felt as if she had turned to ice. "It can't be," she murmured. "Not again." She turned her face to the wall and wept.

Chapter 9

The baron and Mr. Radclyfe were at breakfast when she came down.

"Good morning," said Mr. Radclyfe, rising to his feet. Her heart sank at the eager look in his eyes, and she averted her face to hide her swollen eyes.

She kept her expression neutral and poured herself some tea. Mr. Radclyfe moved to assist her with her chair, and she winced at the familiar scent of bergamot from his linen.

"Yes," said DeVille, "good morning. Quite a jolly time last night."

"Yes," she said, fiddling with the sugar spoon. Through the french doors, black thunderheads towered above the Catskills in the distance. "I'm afraid you may have to change your plans to go riding today. A thunderstorm is coming, and you wouldn't want to be caught out in it."

"Certainly not," said Mr. Radclyfe. "What do you propose we do instead?"

"I've ordered the archery targets set out at the southern edge of the estate. I thought we could shoot."

"You know I love a challenge, Miss MacDougall," said Mr. Radclyfe lightly.

Anna swallowed. She couldn't meet his gaze.

"What is it, Miss MacDougall? Are you not feeling well?"

She pressed her handkerchief to her mouth as the sour taste of bile rose in her throat. "I. . . It's the heat. Please excuse me."

She rose from her chair, and Mr. Radclyfe again jumped to assist her. Nora walked in as Anna hurried out of the room. The urge to run flooded her and she left the house, running as fast as she could, until a stabbing pain in her side stopped her and she sagged against a pine tree, gasping for breath. She had run all the way to the cliff path.

"Miss MacDougal!"

Oh no. Mr. Radclyfe had followed her. She couldn't face him.

"Why won't you speak to me? What's happened?"

Anna shook her head and waved him away, stricken at the beseeching look on his face.

He put his hand on her arm and turned her to face him. "Last night. . ." He searched her face. "You gave me hope. Made me believe you felt something for me."

Tears smarted in her eyes, and he drew closer. "I knew immediately at breakfast something had changed. You've been crying. What's wrong?"

He took her other arm and pulled her toward him, gazing into her face. "Since yesterday, I've dared to hope you could care for me. I want to love the woman I marry with my whole heart. Just as you wonder how you can know if a man loves you for you and not your money. I didn't think it would be possible to reconcile those two things. But it's

happened. I love you. And I want you to be my wife. If you didn't have a penny, I'd still want to marry you."

Anna sat frozen. Fear had reached up and grabbed her heart in its jaws and wouldn't let go.

"What are you afraid of?" His face darkened like the lowering clouds when she didn't answer. "Is it because of him? Stuart?" He spat the name out scornfully, and she gasped.

"I'm not him." He stared down into her face, and she shook her head and turned away.

"Don't do this, Anna." She gasped at the intimate use of her first name. "I know you have feelings for me, and you won't allow yourself—you won't allow *us*—the chance to see if they are real. I'm prepared to give up my inheritance for you. That's how much I love you. I've never met such a stubborn fool!"

He turned and stalked away toward the cliff staircase as the sky opened up and rain fell in heavy drops. She stood frozen, blind between the rain and the surge of confusion that had enveloped her, and then she realized he'd started down the staircase.

"No," she screamed. "Rob, it's too dangerous!" She ran toward the staircase. "Stop!" she screamed at the top of her voice, but the wind and rain carried her words away, and in the next instant he slipped on the mossy steps and cartwheeled horribly down the stairs until he lay in a limp bundle on the sand below.

The air around her wobbled and spun, and she grabbed the trunk of a tree to steady herself.

"Oh, dear God," she sobbed. "Please, Lord, let him be all right."

She hurried down the stairs, knowing where to put her feet, until she reached the bottom of the staircase. He didn't answer when she called his name, and with great difficulty she managed to turn him over. Blood covered his face from a deep gash over one eyebrow. His right arm lay twisted backward at an awkward angle.

"Rob!" She shook him. "Rob!" She sobbed into his cold neck. "Don't you die on me. I love you, I love you—do you hear me?" She shook him again harder, and when he didn't respond, she tore a strip of cloth off her petticoat to bind his wound. The she ran back up the staircase as fast as she dared and on to the house to summon help.

It took DeVille and three burly footmen to carry Rob up the staircase, after improvising a stretcher and hooking the men to a rope tied to a tree for safety. Anna waited as the rain slackened, wringing her hands, tears streaming down her face.

He was still unconscious when they reached the top, his face pale and still.

Her father sent for a physician, and Rob's valet hastily undressed him in one of the guest bedrooms off the solarium. They covered him in hot blankets. Anna sat on a stool drawn up next to the bed, and held his hand under the blanket.

"You were right," she whispered. "I was too afraid to admit I've fallen in love with you." She squeezed his cold fingers. There was no response, but a pulse beat slowly in his neck, and his breathing seemed regular. "Please wake up, Rob."

The doctor arrived to examine him while she waited in the solarium with her father, Nora, and the baron. The revolving clock in the solarium chimed nine, its cheerful tinkling notes at odds with the somber group waiting there. Her father stood apart, resting his forearms on a pedestal, his face hidden in his hands. Anna knew he was praying. But she couldn't sit still and paced the mosaic tile floor instead. *Dear God, let him live. Let him live.* She pressed her fist to her mouth and bit down until the pain made her gasp. *How*

could I have been so blind?

DeVille gave her a faint encouraging smile as the minutes ticked by. Nora sat in a corner, her face unreadable, while the servants hovered, waiting for instructions.

When the door hadn't opened by ten, Anna retreated to the back veranda and sank into a chair. The rain had stopped, and the fresh scent of pine resin lingered in the air.

Her father came and laid a hand on her shoulder. "All will be well, lassie. Have no fear."

She choked back a sob. "Papa, he's willing to give up his inheritance for me."

"I thought he might."

"Why, Papa?"

"Because that's the only way ye could know he loved ye for yourself." He withdrew into the solarium.

"Dearest Lord Jesus, You've answered my prayer." She wiped her eyes. "Now I pray You let him live so I can tell him."

A sense of peace and well-being washed over her. She felt her heart beating and heard the sound of her breath filling her lungs, and knew the presence of the Lord surrounded her.

A shout came from the solarium, and her father rushed onto the veranda. "He's awake, lassie."

She searched his haggard face, afraid to ask. Her father smiled broadly. "He's going to be fine, lassie. A broken arm, some broken ribs, and a nasty gash is all."

Her father helped her to her feet, and she ran to the bedroom. Rob's arm had been neatly splinted, and a white bandage circled his forehead. His eyes were open, fixed on her, and she dropped to the side of the bed, laid her face on his chest, and wept.

His good arm came up and embraced her tightly. "Shhh. All is well."

She raised her tear-stained face. "You were right. I am a stubborn fool." She hiccuped. "I do love you. I was afraid, I realize now."

He laughed and then winced. "I'd have fallen down the staircase two weeks ago if I'd known it would have helped." His expression sobered. "What were you afraid of, darling?"

"Someone told me something terrible about you. About your character. But underneath I knew it couldn't be true. And when I saw you lying broken on the sand, I thought I'd never have the chance to tell you I loved you."

Nora made a choked sound behind them. "I'm so sorry, Anna. Please forgive me," she wailed and fled the room.

Papa looked at her. "What did she say, Anna?"

Anna swallowed. "That Mr. Radclyfe had. . .had a child with a woman in London, and abandoned her."

"What?" Rob tried to sit up then sank down again with a groan.

"Lie still, laddie." Her father shook his head. "I could have put your doubts to rest, Anna. I had Mr. Radclyfe thoroughly checked out before I gave my consent for him to court you."

Rob blinked. "Indeed." He smiled ruefully. "I should have known, Mr. MacDougall. You don't do anything by half."

"Nora lied to me." Anna frowned, trying to understand.

"Either she wanted to save you from her own fate or she couldn't stand the thought that you might be happy with Mr. Radclyfe." Her father smiled grimly. "You'll have to

speak with her, lassie."

"I will. And I will forgive her." She smiled at Mr. Radclyfe. "But I'm busy at the moment."

Her father smiled broadly at the two of them. "I'm going to leave for a bit. I've something to take care of."

When he left the room, Rob squeezed her hand and beamed at her. "Despite several broken bones and a devil of a headache, I'm perfectly happy."

Anna nodded. "My heart is so full it might burst."

"So you're going to say yes when I ask you to marry me?" He smiled tenderly.

"Ask me and find out."

His eyes widened. "I can't very well get down on my knees. But, Miss Anna Mac-Dougall, will you do me the honor of becoming my wife?"

"Yes," she said, tears coming again, happy this time. "Yes!"

Renee Yancy is an archaeology nut who's been writing historical fiction since 2004 and has visited Ireland, Scotland, and England in her quest for historical accuracy.

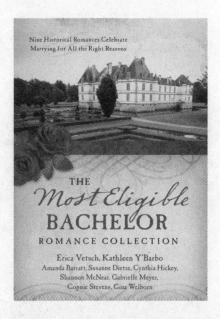